BLACK DOVE *'Budgie'*

Black Dove: Emma, disenchanted with her life in London, buys and renovates an old inn along the Cornish coast which she soon discovers is haunted, and still harbours secrets from its legendary, smuggling past. One day, while wandering along the beach, she meets the enigmatic artist Anton who is fleeing from his own strange mystery, and the sinister predictions that his paintings reveal. Emma pursues her perfect romance until Anton's turbulent past catches up with him.

The River Tale: Isobel, an artist, finds the perfect idyll, living on a houseboat on the canal at Little Venice, with her musician boyfriend Rick, but soon discovers a serpent lurking in her romantic paradise.

Castle of Dreams: Claire meets the stunningly attractive photographer Mike who whisks her off on a dream holiday to a romantic castle in Ireland, only to discover he is hiding a dark secret.

Dark Goddess: Laura a TV executive, seeking inspiration, goes to Glastonbury to ignite her muse, but finds herself unearthing a deep mystery.

Black Dove

A collection of stories

Black Dove
The River Tale
Castle of Dreams
Dark Goddess

Bridgette Cassese

Grey Raven

Copyright © Bridgette Cassese 2007
First published in 2007 by Grey Raven
Barn Cottage, Tregiffian Farm, Sennen, Penzance
Cornwall TR19 7BE

Cover Photo by Mike Newman / Ocean-Image.co.uk

www.amolibros.co.uk/greyraven

The right of Bridgette Cassese to be identified as the author of the work has been asserted herein in accordance with the Copyright, Designs and Patents Act 1988.

All rights reserved. This book is sold subject to the condition that it shall not, by way of trade or otherwise, be lent, resold, hired out or otherwise circulated without the publisher's prior consent in any form of binding or cover other than that in which it is published and without a similar condition including this condition being imposed on the subsequent purchaser.

All of the characters in this book are fictitious and any resemblance to actual people, living or dead, is purely imaginary.

British Library Cataloguing in Publication Data
A catalogue record for this book is available from the British Library.

ISBN 978-0-9550399-0-4

Typeset by Amolibros, Milverton, Somerset
This book production has been managed by Amolibros
Printed and bound by T J International Ltd, Padstow, Cornwall, UK

Dedicated to
Justin, Richard and my parents, Ian and Tristran.

Bridgette Cassese comes from Bromley in Kent. She attended Beckenham Convent, Orpington College and studied Social Anthropology and Psychology at Sussex and London Universities. She enjoys psychology – humanistic, Jungian and Rogerian –, art, computers, body surfing, music, and lives in a converted barn at the top of a cliff at Sennen, Cornwall. She has a son called Justin.

Contents

Black Dove

    Part One   3

    Part Two   167

The River Tale   283

Castle of Dreams   385

The Dark Goddess   465

Many thanks to Richard Shiells, without whose input and support the book could not have been finished.

Thanks to everyone who helped: my tutors at UEA, Sussex University, where I did most of my research, Tony Montcrieffe (tutor) and Valerie Sneath.

Black Dove

Part One

Emma, The Water Nymph

Emma gazed in the mirror, a man with dark gypsy eyes was staring back at her. His face was appearing, then fading in the glass, like a mirage. She watched amazed, as his reflection melted into thin air. Was someone standing behind her? She turned round, but the room was empty, she could see no one there.

West End—London—Emma

Emma looked around the room for a familiar face. She was late, thinking of the huge pile of wedding invitations she had to send out. She spotted John, huddled around a screen, listening to Graham Wilkington-Cox, creative director. Emma eased into a seat next to him. Sarah, accounts director, handed her the schedule. Someone passed her some water, she took a cup and filled it to the brim.

'The Evans water account goes ahead today,' said Graham, giving them his full-on professional stare. 'We begin shooting at noon tomorrow, is that okay with everyone?'

They nodded.

'Emma, have you finished the storyboard yet?'

'Yes, I've completed first copy,' Emma said, lifting it up for everyone to see. 'My idea is to highlight the health and fitness angle: Cascades of fresh water wash away tiredness, put the sparkle back into your life.' She lifted up the board, pointing to the photograph of some surfers gliding down an avalanche of a wave, and to one of some jolly sailors swigging back mineral water. The pitch line: 'Drink Evans water—refresh, refocus, revitalise!'

On a computer screen, a surfer shot across the wave, his eyes sparkling with health.

'Yes, it's a brilliant idea, I really like the location,' said Graham, giving the account the go-ahead. Emma sat down and sipped at her water.

Sarah walked over and handed her a set of photographs.

'I saw your photographs in the *Daily Column* last week,' she whispered, a small smile fleetingly crossing her face. 'Congratulations on your engagement to Toby.'

'Thanks, I can hardly believe it,' said Emma looking up at her, eyes sparkling with happiness. She showed Sarah the ring.

'Very elegant and stylish,' said Sarah. 'It suits you. He has good taste. He is quite a good catch, I heard he has just landed a partnership in one of the most cutting-edge agencies in the city.'

'Graham told me they've just started up a new branch.'

'He behaved a bit wildly before he met you. I am so glad that you are the one he's settling down with.'

Emma beamed a huge smile, her blue eyes dancing with delight.

'Yes, so am I,' she said ecstatically, flicking back her mane of freshly shampooed hair. 'We spend most evenings at home now, snuggled up on the sofa, doing our work together or watching old movies.'

'Sounds idyllic. When's the big day?' asked Sarah, trying to hide her doubts.

'In a month's time,' said Emma looking around her. 'I'm walking on air until then.'

Sarah smiled with a dangerous glint in her eye. Emma needed to be. When that man actually made it to the altar, she would give her next month's pay cheque to charity. She liked Emma a lot, and wondered what a truly nice person was doing with that rogue. Emma was a kind and refreshingly honest person, a pleasant change from the predatory women he'd usually become entangled with. Call me sceptical, thought Sarah cynically, but does a leopard ever change its spots? Sarah pointed to the photograph Emma was holding.

'Gosh, what beautiful scenery! I wish I were there now, surfing on a sun-drenched beach surrounded by all those beautiful, tanned, fit bodies. I don't think I can bear another summer here, choking on car exhaust fumes!'

Emma laughed. 'Yes, it's my dream to move there one day.'

'Going anywhere special for your honeymoon?'

'We've rented a secluded villa in the Caribbean,' said Emma, smiling, radiance oozing from every pore. 'Toby's going to teach me how to windsurf. I can't wait.'

'Sounds wonderful, have you got the brief?'

'I've made some copies,' said Emma shuffling the papers; she stopped as she came to a photograph of a Cornish sea galleon, being tossed around on a stormy sea.

'Gosh, look at this one,' she said, pointing it out to Sarah, 'a gory shipwreck, quite awful. Cornwall has such a dark history.'

Sarah grimaced at the men's faces contorted in agony as they were swept helplessly onto the rocks—it was grim. 'Yes, a lot of places in the West Country do have a very dark history,' she agreed, 'especially Jamaica Inn and the First and Last Inn, they're well known for their smugglers and nefarious deeds. They do have quite a turbulent past.'

'I agree, just like this picture.'

'How awful, the smugglers are drowning,' said Sarah, shooting it another cursory glance. 'Who would want to put this on their wall?'

'Um, not the image we want to project, too scary. I don't think we'll use it,' said Emma quickly, pushing it back inside an envelope and pulling a face. 'It's too gloomy. A ship of drowning men, honestly, it won't exactly inspire our audience, will it? It might give them nightmares. Who sent it?'

'One of the researchers, I suppose. You did ask for pictures of Cornwall.'

'Yes, so I did, but couldn't they have sent us happy sailors, not demented ones?' snapped Emma irritably. 'We are supposed to be inspiring our audience, not depressing them.' She opened her briefcase and took out a romantic picture of a woman harpist, serenading some sailors, on the rocks. 'Let's use this one instead. It's so much more dreamy,' she smiled. She quickly filed away the rest of the photographs, hoping to get away early.

'That's so beautiful, you are such a romantic, Emma,' laughed Sarah, adding it to the others in her file.

'I like to think so,' said Emma shyly.

Sarah studied the picture, hovering for a moment, about to say something.

'Is there anything else?' asked Emma.

'No, no,' Sarah shook her head, 'of course not, I just wanted to say, I hope you will both be very happy.'

'I have never felt so deliriously happy,' admitted Emma, beaming with pleasure, pushing a stray hair back from her face. 'Are you coming to the reception? I'm sending out the invitations this week.'

'Wild horses wouldn't keep me away,' Sarah said cryptically, snapping her file shut. 'Well that's it for today. I'll see you all tomorrow.'

Sarah walked back into the office. Emma closed her briefcase and sat up straight, ready to bolt like a deer. She glanced at her watch, shifting restlessly.

'Some final items before you go, so don't rush off yet," said Graham, handing round the shooting schedule. 'Find enclosed your pack, and some free theatre tickets, for Bram Stoker's *Dracula* playing tonight at the South Bank National theatre if any of you want to go.' He shook the tickets: 'Plus, I have two complimentary bookings for the new Thai restaurant that's just opened along Tottenham Court road. Anyone interested?'

'Sounds like fun,' said Emma, taking two—she had a passion for anything darkly romantic. She'd surprise Toby tonight, they could start with a Thai meal, then perhaps go on to the theatre later. She had told him she was staying in, to relax for tomorrow's shoot, but the idea of a walk along the Thames, followed by a Thai supper, was just too tempting to miss. She smiled happily to herself, excited; she had been engaged a month today, they could celebrate. The wedding was booked for a month's time, and she was counting the days eagerly. Life was so hectic, what with planning the wedding to the last detail, and being creative in a demanding job, she'd hardly had time to think. Still, it was the most important day of her life. She felt herself drift off into a daydream—visualising herself standing next to Toby, as he put on the ring, her heart lurching in happiness. After the wedding they would have a quiet weekend, nothing lavish, at a small hotel tucked away in the wilds of Scotland—followed by a day of celebrations, a circus and jousting tournament, at a Celtic Castle. Afterwards they would fly off to the perfect honeymoon, for two weeks sailing and windsurfing in the sun-drenched Caribbean. Emma hugged herself, ecstatically joyful, brimming with excitement. She could hardly wait. They'd bought a flat in Bloomsbury, her dream. She glowed with happiness, especially at the thought of paying Toby a surprise visit tonight. She loved to dance with him, go to the newest nightclub, or discover a new restaurant together. After work, he always took her to Groucho's, or Teatros, then on to a play at the theatre. Life flowed like an idyllic dream, edged with a silver glow. Punting last weekend had been such wonderful fun. Toby had fed her strawberries and champagne, and they'd gone for a surprise picnic on the riverbank. Each moment they spent together was so special. Her spirits soared in anticipation; she felt restless, wanting it to happen soon. She raced outside and glanced up at his studio. Good, the lights were still on, she observed, clutching the tickets tightly. She pulled her jacket around her and sprinted across the road.

Revelations

Toby was working late, immersed in his latest project. But the play didn't start until nine. She bounded up the narrow stairs and pushed against the studio door. It was locked, a 'do not enter' light blazing across the dark hallway; Toby must be in the darkroom developing some prints. The inner door was shut too. How strange she thought, he never usually locked that door, must be a very important client. Lucky he was still there. She typed in the code and released the inner lock. She stopped suddenly, her heartbeat uneasy, as she listened—she could hear strange, heavy breathing inside. What an odd sound? Was someone ill? She stood still for a moment, then went inside. She jumped back in shock, nearly collapsing at the sight that met her eyes. Her mouth gaped open as she stood there helplessly, hit by an excruciating stab in the stomach. Toby was naked, lying under a woman, dressed in a tight topless PVC dress, fondling her breasts. Emma stared at them in horror, then white-hot anger hit her in waves.

'What the hell are you doing with that woman?' she cried, the colour draining from her cheeks.

'Emma? Is that you?'

'Get off him, you bitch,' she screamed, throwing a file at them. Her heart leapt into her mouth, and her blood ran cold as ice. A wave of nausea gripped her.

Toby pushed the woman off, stunned and stared at her sheepishly. 'Oh Emma,' he muttered meekly, 'I wasn't expecting to see you tonight.'

'So I see,' she snapped furiously, holding onto a desk to steady herself, about to keel over. Gripped by a sudden surge of anger, boiling with rage, she hurled his priceless Nikon camera across the floor. It shattered into tiny pieces above his head. The woman threw on her jacket and ran out of the studio. Emma stared at Toby; his face was crumpled with embarrassment. She threw another box of files at him, so that they split open on his head. He buried his head in his hands and ducked behind a desk.

'Look, I am so sorry,' he stuttered. 'Oh god, what have I done?'

'You selfish, lying bastard,' Emma cried, running over and slapping him sharply around the face. 'So is this what you do when I work late? How could you do this to me?'

Shocked, he backed away, his face flushed, his eyes filled with tears.

'Shit, Emma, look,' he stuttered. 'It was stupid thing to do, and it meant nothing. I've never done it before.'

She tugged at the ring on her finger, but it was stuck.

'You must think I am such a fool. Why?'

Toby crushed, looked pleadingly at Emma, lost for words. 'Emma, I am so sorry,' he said putting his head in his hands. 'Let me at least try and explain.'

'Forget it, there's nothing to say.'

'Please don't go, wait, please. I do love you. It was just a silly mistake, things just got out of control. She came in for a photograph session, took off all her clothes, then started doing some erotic poses and pulled me onto the desk. My animal instincts took over, it just got out of hand,' he said clasping his hands to his head, his voice quivering with shock.

'You're pathetic! Don't you have any self-control? Are you so immature? You are so wrong if you think I could ever forgive this!' she spat, devastated. 'It's insane. I'm glad I found out what you're really like before we got married. How could you throw it all away?'

'But it's you I love,' he pleaded. 'It was just sex.'

'What do you mean?…It was only sex! We're supposed to be getting married. You are a first-class fool.'

Emma on the verge of hysterics, went over to the latest photographs, packed ready for an important client, and tore them into shreds. She stood shaking, her soul torn in two.

'That's it, final, we're finished. Toby, you just killed what we had stone dead,' she spat, tipping the contents of the stationary tray over his desk, then turned to go. Toby winced, and ran after her muttering apologies. He pulled on his shirt, tripping up on the stairs. Emma shot him a dark look and bombarded him with a tirade of verbal abuse, showering him with film reels. Her face burned with rage, her body shook, she clutched her hand to her chest, breathless with a heavy searing pain. She felt another burst of fury—the shiny bollard outside was too much of a temptation. Standing next to the expensive glass exterior that lined the agency, she swung it through the window. Cascades of glass sprayed all over the pavement. The window shattered into millions of shards. Toby stared at her in disbelief, then chased her across the street. She jumped into a taxi, and sped along Tottenham Court Road to her flat in Bloomsbury. She stumbled into her flat, close to hysteria, slammed the door and cried her heart out, before cutting up all wedding invitations and Toby's suit. She couldn't bear to stay there, so took the car and drove as fast as she could, away from the city into the night.

Her hands shook as she gripped the steering wheel, her knuckles turned white, her heart thumped, she felt sick and betrayed, her face was burning. She looked around the desolate motorway feeling the pain grip her in waves. Her eyes blurred with tears, she moved the car slowly, her mind in turmoil. She felt slithers of pain cut through her like the broken glass she'd left behind. She pulled off onto the hard shoulder, cars honking loudly. Her romantic dream had turned into a nightmare and she had to get away, far from there. She sat parked at the edge of the motorway, not sure which way to go, letting it all sink in. In too much of a state to drive on, she stayed where she was, listening to a sad song on the radio, before resuming her journey, coming off at the next exit, circling the roundabout, and entering the motorway on the other side to drive home.

She walked into the silent darkness and slumped down on the sofa, her body crumpled up in a heap, as if someone had just punched her. Anger and shock hit her in waves, shards of jagged glass tore at her heart. She fumbled awkwardly, trying to open a bottle of wine, unable to focus through her tears. Everything was washing over her, she was sinking in quicksand, drowning in a sea of despair, as waves of pain washed over her. She gulped the wine quickly, waiting for oblivion to hit her, then fell back onto the sofa, and cried her heart out. Her life was in ruins, her hopes and dreams gone, vanished in a second. There was nothing left but the distant shadows of what could have been hovering over her like a ghost from the past, covering the cold numbness of an empty broken heart.

An awakening

In the morning, Toby still hadn't returned. Emma changed the locks, bundled up the rest of his clothes and sent them to his office by courier. She threw the sparkling new wedding invitations in the bin and wept; eventually, she found the will to empty her briefcase. She could barely see through the tears until she picked up a photograph of the 'Evans' surfers gliding down the wave in Cornwall and studied it. She sighed with relief: a spark of sun shone through the dark clouds as she hatched a plan. It was crazy, but perhaps she could drive there now. Why not? Escape from this nightmare, leave the rat race behind, and start again. She felt a sudden surge of optimism, a glimmer of hope. So her world was shattered, but it wasn't the end, there was still a lot of life to see, wonderful things she could still do, the planet was hers to explore. Wearily she thought that maybe it had happened for the best, and that she was destined to find another path. As one door closed another always opened.

Exhausted, she called in sick, and started making plans; she couldn't face the sympathetic looks, the shock and disbelief on the faces of her colleagues. She switched on the television and let the sound drift over her, falling into a deep sleep. She began dreaming, falling down an endless tunnel into a cold, lonely night. Someone's arms caught her. She looked up to see her spiritual guide watching over her, his vibrant eyes smiling as he led her along a river into a tranquil garden full of beautiful flowers. Then, suddenly, she was standing on a sandy beach. In the distance was the vague outline of a man with dark hair, standing by the waves. He saw her and beckoned her over, holding out his hand. She caught it, her pain melting like thawing ice as he pulled her into his arms. Gently, he kissed her... . She woke up with a jolt, disappointed the dream wasn't real. She sighed and stared grimly out of the window at the dark, rainy day that had descended over the city. Her mood hung heavy with despair and she wished she hadn't woken up—the dream had made her feel so warm and happy, yet now she had to face the bitter desolation of reality, swamping her like an icy cold tide. Grey storm clouds swirled around the dull damp buildings outside, a heavy mist hanging in the air as she walked into the empty bedroom and shuddered. Never had she felt so desperately alone. She tried to shut out the memories of all the times she and Toby had made love in their bedroom, and knew she couldn't stay there; she had to move on. The pain wrenched through her like a knife. She cried again, the humiliation was too much to bear. She cried so hard, she thought she would never stop.

☦

A few weeks later, she sold her flat, selling it at a profit, and handed over her unfinished work to her colleagues. They would survive without her. She drifted into a half-sleep, images of the last few weeks racing around her head. Giving up her career hadn't been easy, but it had been the only way.

She dragged herself back to work and told Graham she was leaving; he had stared at her in surprise, and offered her a huge pay rise to stay. But it was too late, the dream had fizzled and died, along with her creative streak. She felt numb, struggling painfully through the last weeks, putting on a brave face, all enthusiasm squeezed out of her like a sucked lemon, with only the dream of moving to Cornwall keeping her sane. Fate had forced her hand.

Three months later—Return to Sennen

Emma drove into the cove right in the middle of a heat wave, and swore as a sudden blast of heat hit her, and almost choked her. She hadn't expected Sennen to be quite so hot, even in mid-August. It was wonderful to be back, she thought hazily, staring out blissfully at the horizon, looking at the beach arching around the rocks to the Atlantic Ocean. It was almost as warm as the Mediterranean, and getting hotter, she mused. The beach was filling with people setting up wind-breakers, and swimmers were bobbing and surfing on the waves. The sudden soar in temperature had taken her by surprise. It had rained heavily in London for the last few weeks, and she wasn't used to such intense heat. She wiped her forehead with a wet tissue—still, it was a lot better than being in the city, and the drizzling rain, she mused, pulling on the handbrake. Somehow, she always managed to get a better suntan in the West Country than in the Cote D'Azure, where the sun was stronger. Cornwall always gave her a lasting tan. She pushed her sunglasses up into her hair, and carefully manoeuvred her car into in a small space, on stony ground in the middle of the small fishing village in which she found herself. Her mood lifted at the sight of the long, white beaches, and she wound down the window, gripped with the sudden urge to dive off a rock into the crystal clear azure sea.

'Is this okay?' She turned to Andrea, the hitchhiker sitting next to her, who had travelled with her since Devon. Andrea fidgeted, pulling down her tight mini dress. She flicked back her coppery red curls and nodded.

'How long are you going to stay?' asked Emma.

'Just for the summer. I'd like to work as an artist's model, or even a chambermaid.'

'Sounds great.'

'I've just escaped from a dull secretarial job, I had to come away or I would have gone mad. Last month I passed my holistic therapy exams and want to work here for a while—go with the flow, lead a more spiritual life, with no ties. And you?'

'I'd like to live here,' smiled Emma. 'That is, if I can find somewhere cheap enough to buy.'

'I'm sure you will, there are some good properties around, if you are prepared to put in some work.'

'Keep in touch then,' Emma said, handing her a mobile number.

✢

At last, Emma sighed, she had reached her final destination, the furthest point of west Cornwall, beautiful Sennen Cove, next to Land's End. Her dream come true. Emma leaned back against the seat massaging her throbbing temples; she wiped some suntan oil lightly over her skin and tied back her hair. She smiled, relieved to be out of the traffic; the roads had been jammed since Exeter, her car had overheated all the way. If it hadn't been for the zany company of Andrea, the hitchhiker, she would have gone mad. She pushed back the seat and took in a deep breath, and slipped off her shoes. She pondered on how nice it was to be away from London, the overcrowded hot dingy streets. The city was over three hundred miles away, another place, a different lifetime. She sighed a huge sigh of relief, relieved to be away from it all.

She would never go back to so many bad memories—Toby had destroyed any chance of her ever again being happy there. What a nightmare it had turned out to be, and why had she been so unlucky as to have fallen in love with such a traitorous man? During her last week, Toby had phoned constantly, begging her to give him another chance, to think twice about giving up her career, but there was no forgetting what had happened, he had destroyed their love. She took her mobile, deleted his number, along with the past. She was glad she had made up her mind, there was no going back this time, the past was over. Toby was history, she was moving on— a sudden glimmer of hope bathed her in light: a new life was calling.

Reflections

Emma sat and mused over the last few weeks: it had been a torment, needing all her strength to get her through. She realised in a flash of clarity that Toby had probably been deceiving her all along, and that all her hopes had been perched on a fragile, empty dream. She was glad she had left the mess behind. As she worked out her notice, Emma had gone into overdrive, working all hours, fighting to purge the demons from her soul, trying to blot out the pain. She saw a glimmer of hope shining through the dark clouds, as a new future beckoned, guiding her to start again. She knew it was now or never, she had to take the plunge, to move on without looking back. Like parachuting off a cliff, freefall, not knowing where she would land, she had taken the challenge, and knew she had to start again, build a new life. Feeling scared, she knew, however, that she would survive and that her steely determination would always get her through. Underneath her gentle nature, she was a born survivor. She felt the tension melt away, her mind relax from the turmoil as she listened to the faint haunting tones of some Celtic music playing on the radio. She let it drift through her head, lifting her spirit. It had a calming effect, soothing her anger, letting her thoughts flow in harmony with the rhythmic roar of the sea.

She sank back, her hands clasped behind her head, glad to have left her work at the studio behind. She had worked like a slave for the past six months, arranging shoots, taking calls from irate clients and training new employees alongside her normal workload. Her career had seemed so rosy, then it had all blown apart, leaving nothing but emptiness, a trail of sadness. Still, now at least she had found a perfect excuse to escape the rat race! She closed the car window, rubbed her stiff neck, amazed that it had been a blessing in disguise, thankful of how lucky she was, knowing things had turned out for the best. After listening to her friends wishing they could leave it all behind for the sun and surf, she had found the courage to do it. She sighed happily at how different her life was going to be.

Emma parked the car and stood poised at the cliff-edge above the beach, lured by the cool, inviting sea. She watched the silver streaks of light shimmer on the ocean, the frothy waves ripple onto the sand under the bluest sky she had ever seen, glowing with a peaceful, happy vibe. For a moment, spellbound, she watched the foamy waves drift over the rocks, and swirl in the rock-pools, before racing along the shore. Her pain began to thaw like melting ice. Enthralled, she gazed at the horizon, seeing a single small boat sail past. A sense of freedom surged in her. She walked up to the top of the enchanting Sennen Cove, and looked down onto the sparkling turquoise sea lapping on the white sand. Two miles of pale sand curled around a choppy aquamarine sea stretched out before her, to infinity—just like a picture postcard; her heart surged in delight. The tide was rushing in, throwing foamy waves over the rocks.

Emma made a dash down the dunes, to the beach, and dived, letting the salty water lap against her skin. She floated and bobbed on the waves, feeling the cool sea rush over her face and the waves ripple over her shoulders. Swimming in it was pure heaven, freeing her body after such a tiring journey. She swished and splashed round like a mermaid, floating on her back, letting the waves lift her along, bobbing along on the current. Lazily, she did a slow crawl out to the island. She sat sunbathing lazily on the rocks, dipping her feet in the rock-pools, the rays beating down on her face as some greedy gulls circled overhead. How wonderful it was to be back! To be free again! Free of deadlines, routines and confinement. The only person she had to answer to was herself. The sky was so dazzlingly blue it made her draw in her breath, as the hot sun streamed onto her face. She laid her towel out on some rocks and lay back in the sizzling heat, using the opportunity to reflect on the last few months. She could see her mistakes with clarity now, her soul was at ease. She was glad she had made the sudden break.

Now, in Sennen, on the verge of discovering a new dream, she was filled with light and hope, felt almost human again. Her spirit refreshed, she climbed up the hill and sipped a bottle of lemonade. Her sense of elation grew as she forgot her worries and tuned into the simple pleasures of life—the birds singing and the gentle sound of the waves crashing on the shore, making her spirit soar. Her once dulled senses, from working long hours in the city, came alive at the sight of Sennen twinkling in the bay, sending her into ecstasy.

The new dream was coming true: she cried with relief, finally sure that as one door closes, another always opens. She slugged back the cold lemonade in huge thirsty gulps and let the cool stream trickle down her throat as she began tucking into a hot Cornish pasty. She smiled happily as the clouds of depression lifted from her mind. The Cornish countryside was healing her, it was so exhilarating, and always gave her a huge appetite. She opened an umbrella and sat in its shade. The warm climate soothed her jagged nerves. She thought of her colleagues struggling at their desks in London, and smiled to herself—at last, she thought cheerfully, she was free as a bird.

She squinted against the bright midday sun, and made her way slowly over the ridge. Some people were hiking up the dunes, pitching tents. She followed them, her gaze lingering on the sand, then ran down the hill, climbed past the empty lifeguard's hut and sat on a dune to read. Carefully, she unfolded a copy of the city newspaper. City dwellers were stuck in long queues in London, fanning themselves with their papers, in long traffic jams, trying to squeeze out of the town's sweltering heat. London was in the middle of a heat-wave. Surprised, she spotted a photograph of Toby coming out of a restaurant with a tall willowy blonde. She slammed down the paper angrily. That just about did it! He would never change, he was a philanderer by nature, and she had got out just in time. How could she have been such a fool? Everyone had known what a reputation he had—that is, everyone except her.

Returning to the car, she took out her bag, and walked over to the surfers' flats in the cove. The flats were part of the Olde Success Inn, a seventeenth-century smugglers' haunt. She put on some sunglasses, walked up to the holiday flat, and checked in. As she took the key out of her bag and unlocked the door to her room she saw it was a small chintzy cupboard space with the loveliest view. She climbed over the bed, levered open the tiny window and breathed in the sea air. Drawing in her breath at the spectacular view, she only hoped the property she was viewing next week was half as good. Sweltering heat rose over the rocks in a hazy pale mist. Her eyes squinted up at the lush green fields stretching away to the top of the hill, leading to some mystical Celtic out huts and arches. The haunting atmosphere intoxicated her. She wished a knight on horseback would ride through the arch, and carry her off to his gothic castle. She walked outside and looked up the hill, letting her fantasies fly, loving the idea of a knight awakening her, and she began conjuring up enthralling visions of the past. The rolling hills and Celtic arches emanated a magical air, a haunting memory of where King Arthur and his knights had once ridden. A chough flew past, and she recalled the myth, that, as King Arthur died, his spirit was said to pass into the bird, possessed of a mystical spirit. She could just imagine the romantic sultry maidens weeping by the black rocks, praying for their knights to return. The scenery fired her imagination—this was a land of myth and mystery, with fairy tales and dark, shadowy gothic arches and lairs. Her mind soared into a whirl of fantasies.

Keen to take the path alongside the beach, she wiped the perspiration from her face, drained a can of orange juice and rummaged in her bag for her hairbrush. She swept her hair from her forehead, tied it into a ponytail and undid the top of her shirt, then put on some khaki shorts, and slipped on her new leather sandals. She added a hint of lipstick, threw her bag and camera over her shoulder, and headed for the beach. Being in a wide-open space made her feel quite heady. She jumped down a sand dune onto the beach, gripped by a childish excitement, not knowing what was ahead of her. At last, she was happy, and at last, she was free!

That night she dreamed of the dark-haired man, a shadowy figure, walking along the beach, and for the first time in months, she slept like a log.

The Cove

The next day Emma walked for miles along the cliffs. Cornwall had lost none of its charm, it was a sunny idyll, steeped in myth and mystery. She jogged along to the beach, turning into the store to buy some paints—her creative urge had sprung to life again, her muse was awakened. She would get her ideas down on canvas as soon as they flowed into her, and try to become a passable artist while she was there. She was feeling inspired again and took some photographs to paint later. She climbed up onto the terrace garden at the Olde Success to take a few shots of the bay. Keen surfers skimmed over the waves, dolphins and sea lions bobbed playfully in the foam. She ran over to the edge, clicking furiously, thrilled to be in a place of such outstanding natural beauty and gazed down onto a long stretch of pale yellow beach glistening under the hot summer sun. She planned to swim every day in the cool blue ocean. She captured the sparkling sea, glittering under the sun, with one click of her camera, then sat back and let the sun soak into her body and heal her wounds, the light filter into her soul and ignite her spirit. She took in the view of the sparkling pool of sea curled deep into the curve of the sandy coastline. Huge waves rolled into the bay.

Suddenly, she was filled with an intoxicating euphoria, and knew there was something she had to do. She hired a surfboard, ran across the beach with it tucked under her arm, and leapt onto a wave. She whizzed across the wave; she could still surf like an expert, and had not forgotten a thing. As she caught the peak of the wave, it gripped her and propelled her, fast along the swell, rushing her to the shore, like a speeding bullet. She loved the feeling of gliding across the waves at a high speed and held her breath in ecstasy, flying along. She waded back, and waited with the other surfers for the large waves. As they came, she rode each one fast, each one more of a challenge than the last. How she loved to surf! She found it invigorating and one of the best sports ever! Good for releasing pent-up energy, and it always empowered her. She stopped for a drink at the Olde Success Inn and took in the view. She sipped at her drink thoughtfully, tucking heartily into a seafood platter, how delicious! The food was even better than she had remembered, and her appetite had returned. The locals broke into a raucous rendition of nautical shanty sea-songs. Happily she soaked up the atmosphere, tingling with delight, living her new dream, soaring into paradise. Relaxed, she gazed out from the roof terrace as far as she could see, across the choppy sea, hypnotised by the gentle rhythm of the waves.

She jumped into the car, undid her jacket and threw it on the back seat, then scanned the estate agent's card for the time of her appointment. Good, it wasn't until next week. After such a long and tortuous journey, she didn't relish the idea of meeting the agents too soon. She would spend the time unwinding, basking lazily in the sun. She would find a house, close to Sennen and Gwenver beaches, where she had always been happy, and had spent many enjoyable summers as a child. As she manoeuvred round the corner she looked back at the secluded cove; a few stray surfers were still struggling in the waves, the beach was glistening under the summer sun. Going there had been a good idea—she had found the ideal place to escape to, her utopia.

Later, captivated, she sat in her room gazing at the glistening pink sunset, her eyes closing as she sank into a deep, restful sleep.

Memories

The next day, sitting in a café by the beach sipping coffee, she opened her diary and a photograph of her ex-fiancé fell out. It still hurt her to see it so she quickly tore it into tiny shreds. Toby had gone a mile too far this time, having an affair with a model from the studio, one who had been only too quick to offer him her charms. Emma sat licking her wounds, nursing her shattered pride. She cringed every time she thought of how badly he had humiliated her, sure she'd never get over it. Betrayed a month before their wedding day! How could he have been so foolish to have thrown it all away for a mere fling? The memory of that awful day recurred and stung her like a poisoned arrow, seeping into her thoughts like a bad film.

She read the letter again slowly, the one he'd sent when she refused to see him again, Toby begging her to forgive him, to give him another chance. Carefully she filed it away, wondering where he was, then changed her mind, took it out and tore it up. She hoped she would never see him again. The hazy memories filled her thoughts, why should she care? He may have broken her dreams, but not her spirit.

Broken dreams and reminiscences

Her mind flashed back to their engagement party, a lavish flower-strewn event, celebrating her engagement to one of the top photographers in London. Photographed outside Kettner's restaurant by a celebrity magazine, sipping champagne in the back of a limousine, showered in rose petals. She had been living an illusion, a lie, she reflected, living under a dark cloud ready to burst—a fairy-tale dream, turned into a nightmare. She had built up all the trappings of success, a brilliant job, a good-looking fiancé, only to see her world crumble, and her plans turn to dust. She had been a success, flying high, then suddenly it had all gone so horribly wrong. Her blood ran cold at the memory. She could never forget Toby's betrayal, how she'd stood there with her illusions shattered. Her happiness clung to an elusive ideal, evaporating in seconds, a wish never to be granted. The expensive ring still glistened on her finger, like a poisoned dagger, reminding her of Toby's treachery. Months before, everyone had told her what a good catch he was, that they were a perfect match, and she had not seen through the illusion. It had started with an old-fashioned courtship, seeing each at the weekends, so as not to interfere with their careers, working late most nights, a civilised, genteel romance, but, in retrospect, perhaps lacking a wild, hot passion. Her thoughts suddenly jolted into sharp focus: so the bubble had burst, and it was time to leave London, her job, and find real happiness. She had tried, really tried to keep it all together, but her life had lost its allure, her existence its meaning. She and Toby had grown apart before they even began. Her happiness had suddenly turned to despair, she had been consumed by raw pain stabbing at her heart. Devastated, she tried to carry on, knowing she would have to change her plans.

She recalled that terrible day, how she had walked into her studio to overhear her colleagues gossiping about Toby's affair, and had turned and fled, unable to face them, feeling a total fool. Humiliated, she had packed up her things and went home.

All her illusions fell away, and she was faced with cold reality, the desolation of being alone staring her in the face. Her life had been the fruition of an incredible dream, now it was slipping away. What could she do now? She had to take stock of her life. Did she still want to be meeting her friends after work, for dinner in Soho, in ten years time? Living a 'singles' life forever? Her job, which she had once enjoyed, was tiring, her creativity had dried up. Stifled and depressed, she could no longer find any satisfaction in doing the simplest of things—she was just struggling to carry on. She thought long and hard about her future, and change was calling. What was the alternative? Her dreams had died, she felt just like a fading star. She sighed at the thought of facing life alone and, worse, the thought of failing in her job because she couldn't focus any more and her confidence had gone. Better to get out while she was still on top, to fight against the heavy clouds threatening to consume her, sapping her strength. Angrily, she threw everything out of the wardrobe, sold her designer dresses, and packed up her suitcase. There was no reason to stay; she would get away from the memories, for if she stayed she would surely never forget. She tossed her bikini and snorkel gear into a bag with renewed determination, realising she had to fight for her survival, or let the pain push her under, and she was stronger than that. She had ridden on the crest of a wave, eating daily at the best restaurants, with photographs of herself splashed all over the media magazines, now it was time to leave the media circus, before it left her. Living on a shoestring would not be easy; she would have to work hard, use her creativity to start afresh. Besides, she couldn't afford the mortgage on their Bloomsbury flat on her own. She would miss living on a high, riding the crest of a wave of success, being charged with adrenalin, her pulse quickening at the start of each new project, her ideas reaping all the top awards, being a minor celebrity in the advertising world. The heady allure of the limelight and free champagne, and living on a cloud—those days were gone.

It had all been an empty broken dream, ready to burn out. Now she had to search for something real, a life with meaning, a more fulfilling existence. She had loved living in the fast lane, enjoying long holidays abroad, long business lunches that she worked off in the gym. Still in her mid-thirties, she had to take a different direction. She had worked hard to become one of the most respected copywriters in her field. Given the most obscure concepts, she had been able to come up with new and innovative ideas to please even the most difficult clients. There were other careers where she could use her creative mind, she reasoned, so she would take a new path. She felt drained, and hoped to find a more fulfilling existence. Could she give it all up? And not look back? There was still time to start again, or maybe she was having an early-life crisis? As the dream turned sour, her creativity had gone. How could she face them all now? She couldn't struggle on, she had tried to stay in London, really tried. But things were never the same. The ideas stopped flowing, she couldn't generate the copy, her heart was no longer there.

After weeks of soul-searching, she couldn't think of a good enough reason to stay. She struggled at work, the humiliation of what Toby had done echoing through every conversation she had. Tired from the strain of trying to avoid the subject, she patched herself up and lived with a strained dignity. The Friday parties were a chore, trying to avoid Toby. Mingling with the same faces, acting bravely, drinking too much, or taking too much cocaine in an attempt to blot out the pain, putting on a brave face while inside she was falling apart. Heartbroken, and unravelling, she struggled on for a month, any inspiration gone. Lacking her usual zest and vigour, a heavy thud dragged at her heart. A crisis was looming over her. After work, she walked through the grimy West End streets, pulling her expensive cashmere coat around her, her spirit empty and cold, unable to face the grubby London streets. The West End had turned into a tawdry, grey mass of pale, lonely faces. The glittery veneer faded into dust. She walked alone through the dirty, slimy streets, avoiding the sad faces, feeling lonely and empty.

Then a face sadder than hers caught her attention, she threw some money to a tramp lying in a doorway, pain etched around his eyes. How had he got there? What was his story? 'Many thanks, my dear,' he said, in his educated accent, and held out his wrinkled hand. Who was he? An ex-public schoolboy, a city banker perhaps or a top financial director, who had lost his dream, and had his hopes shattered? What had happened to him to bring him there? His marriage had broken up? Maybe he had turned to alcohol to ease the pain, and soon found he couldn't make it into work every day, living in a state of oblivion where nothing could touch him, where he could no longer feel pain. The slide downhill was fast and easy, once you hit rock bottom, there's no crawling back. She stood there in shock, if she didn't get her act together, she could go the same way. He looked up at her with the haunted gaze of the abandoned, the dispossessed, still holding out his scrawny hand. She took out a bank note and gave it to him. He smiled, and touched her with the loneliness in his eyes, making the tears well up in her own. 'My wife left me, nothing left to live for,' he whispered hoarsely, then stared back impassively at the empty space in front of him, his eyes dead from long having given up hope.

She gulped back the tears. At that moment she saw how transitory life was, illusory. It was up to her to make sure she would never let it all go. How easy it was to lose it all, all hope, to become like this, to give up. She wrapped her jacket around her, feeling the icy bite of a cold wind, knowing that in a split second she could lose it all. She had to keep above things, keep buoyant, change her plans, survive. She shivered; if she didn't make the right choice, here and now, it could be her lying there, desperate and alone. Life could fall apart so easily, if she lost the will to carry on. She couldn't afford to indulge her pain any more. She looked around her, filled with new hope, a new impetus. Nothing was safe in this world or secure. Dreams shattered so easily. She didn't want to go on the slide downhill. Her world was crashing down; she was drinking far too much, trying to escape, and cringed at where it could all lead. Later, she pulled herself together and sat quietly thinking, then threw all the empty wine bottles in the bin and flushed out the line of cocaine, given to her by a work colleague, into the sink. She wasn't going to go that way. The city that had once lured her with its glittering friendly restaurants and clubs now looked cold and unfriendly. She felt swamped by the sheer oppression of it all. She picked up a local paper, a local reporter had got hold of the story, and had a field day. There was nowhere to hide. She gazed out of her window at the dark, bleak, sullen buildings forming a half-circle under her office and felt stifled, claustrophobic, static, her life had ground to a halt. The oppressiveness of London overwhelmed her. The buildings glistened like morgues with dirt, so dingy and grey. She felt numb—a flash of insight told her she would never be happy there again. Somehow, she knew she just had to forget the past, and move on.

Changes

As she got ready to leave London, Emma looked out of her window: people hurried past, locked in a soulless, alienated existence. She picked up the photographs of the surfers gliding down the waves at Sennen, and felt her spirit lift, giving her a glimmer of hope. Perhaps she could go there now, escape to the beach? It was a sign to follow her dream! She could even buy a house there. Give up the city, the late nights and smog, and live an ecologically-friendly life growing organic vegetables by the sea? Perhaps buy a horse, some land, and relocate to Sennen? Life had become pointless, she could easily leave it all behind; she would miss her friends, but they could visit. There had to be a new purpose to her life, she smiled, and this seemed the perfect solution. She had been aware of a growing void in her life for a long time and had taken up yoga, tai chi and meditation, to calm the existential pain. It had worked for a while, but she had lost her zest and creative flair. Sadness and dissatisfaction took root, flaring up as a gnawing discontent, until she felt more and more alienated, with an odd feeling that she was in the wrong place, where she no longer belonged. Gripped by an adventurous impulse, she decided to break free and go on an adventure—there was nothing better than travelling to cure a broken heart. Her creativity soared as the chains of conformity and routine fell away from her. She would buy a haven where her friends could come and stay. She'd take a job as a lifeguard on the beach, or even as a waitress—any job to tide her over, as she worked out her new direction. Her life was changing direction and she wasn't sure which way she was going, but she knew she had to start again, away from the past and its bleak memories. Optimistic, she finished the last details on her last advertising accounts, handed them in and felt a surge of renewed hope flow through her. She had awakened her adventurous spirit, and it was spurring her on. She threw her folders in the bin, cleared out her desk and locked her office door for the last time. It was time to go, time to move on. Back home, she switched on the TV, a documentary about homeless children in the Philippines flashed up on the screen. She shuddered as their desperate faces stared sadly at the cameras, their eyes blank, devoid of any hope as they clawed at the bars of their foul bare cage. In that moment she realised how lucky she was, so very lucky to be alive.

Sennen

Sitting in the beach café, Emma felt a sudden sense of exhilaration at being away from London, and the past. She had been in Sennen for a week, exorcising her ghosts as she felt the memories grow distant, and fade. She felt optimistic, ready to start again. As people crowded into the café, she watched them order their Cornish pasties, their healthy bodies fit and gleaming, their long, tanned arms clutching their surfboards. The sun shone brightly and the light shimmered on the silvery blue sea. She smiled, filled with hope, and liked the idea of becoming one of the surfing crowd—it had a romantic ring to it. She signed up for a few refresher courses, hoping to take on an interesting challenge and meet some new people. Her hard work had paid off, she could easily afford a house here now. She picked up her mobile phone, to ring the local estate agents to reconfirm her appointment for the following week. As she looked up she saw a man placing leaflets on her table. His long dark hair blew over his face and his blue eyes squinted against the sun. She looked up at him: his denim shirt was open, and she felt a surge of lust, her heart leaping into her mouth as his arm brushed against hers.

'Would you like one?' he said, handing her a leaflet. 'It's for an exhibition we are holding next month, we're recruiting new students for our next arts group.'

'Yes, thanks, I'll take one.' He was incredibly good-looking, like a sensitive poet with warm blue eyes, long dark hair and a strong chiselled jaw.

'Perhaps you would like come to our group? I'll leave you a brochure if you're interested.'

She took one and scanned the cover quickly, it was adorned with beautiful pictures of romantic women, long flowing hair fanning over their shoulders, basking by a waterfall, their hands trailing through the water, one of them holding a crimson rose.

'Yes, I'd like that,' she said, giving him her warmest smile. 'I like the picture on the cover.'

'Yes, it's one of my favourites too. It's from a painting inspired by Oscar Wilde's *Rose and a Nightingale*, the pursuit of elegant beauty and true love.'

'A lovely idea,' she said wistfully. 'I adore the romantic artists and writers.'

'You could join us, you might enjoy our Wednesday group. I teach a class in the town. It's called "Art and the Romantic", we copy the style of Waterhouse, Leighton, Rossetti, Millais and Burne Jones, and create art along the lines of the Pre-Raphaelites. You could come along next week if you like, we meet every Wednesday at four,' he said, watching her closely. 'We're always looking for new members.'

'Yes, I'd like that,' she nodded. 'Might be fun.'

'My number is on the back, give me a call any time,' he said.

'Thanks, I will.'

She opened the flyer and studied it intently; for a moment he hovered over her, then, sensing her distraction, he walked away. A few minutes later he returned.

'May I join you for a quick coffee?' he asked.

'Yes, of course.'

She smiled, thinking he was one of the most attractive men she had ever met, with the most incredible, sultry eyes. There was something vaguely familiar about him, she was sure she had met him before, but she couldn't recall where, perhaps it had been the beach café or in the sea. She shrugged and stared straight at him and felt a bolt of electricity shoot right through her and a surge of excitement at the thought of seeing him again. He was good looking in a bohemian way, with high, artistic cheekbones, long hair and beautiful expressive eyes, edged with long black lashes. His dark brooding presence made her quiver with excitement, captivating her. He looked just like a romantic artist poet, with long strands of black hair snaking over his collar, a fit svelte body tucked into torn, faded, black jeans. He looked around him, his expression alert and intelligent. His eyes shone with excitement and wonder, as he gazed at her longingly, his deep blue eyes emitting the most beautiful powerful aura she had ever seen. His intense, edgy sadness veiled a warmth and immediately she felt a connection with him. He exuded elegance, like a deer, tall, refined and yet rugged at the same time. His body was deeply tanned and lean. She sensed in him something powerful, poetic, inviting and dangerous.

He flipped open his camera.

'Would you mind if I take a few photographs of you? You have the type of face I'd like to use in my paintings. I would like to use you as a model. Perhaps you could come to my studio one day and I could paint you?'

'Yes of course, I'd love to sit for you,' agreed Emma enthusiastically, thinking how much she would enjoy being an artist's muse. Her eyes lit up with pleasure as she spoke, happily discussing art knowledgably and enthusiastically. His eyes hovered over her with desire—he was so attractive that she nearly spilt her coffee. An instant chemistry sparked between them.

He steadied his camera and took a few photographs of her, smiling at her with such a smouldering, sexy smile that Emma felt herself blushing slightly and turned away; it was as though he could see right inside her soul and knew all her secrets. Usually she handled herself with sophistication and poise, now she felt like an awkward schoolgirl. 'Now, don't be coy,' he said softly, directing the camera at her, still smiling. 'That's perfect. You have an a amazing light in your eyes.'

She shifted around to give him her profile and threw her head back, her mane of long blonde hair tumbling down her back and making her look quite ravishing. She pulled her dress slightly over her long tanned thighs. It had the desired effect. Well, if he wanted a confident woman, she would be one. They chatted for a while. She noticed he seemed slightly on edge, haunted. His eyes darted restlessly over the tables for a few minutes, then he smiled.

'Sorry, I had a bit of a late night, I've been setting up my work for an exhibition, it's nice to come here and relax, I can think more clearly.'

'Yes, I can forget my worries here too.'

'Are you from London?' he asked.

'Yes, you?'

'The next cove. Sussex originally.'

He looked up, something had caught his attention. Quickly he gulped back his coffee. Distracted, he grabbed the leaflets and got up. His eyes narrowed. He fiddled with a strange ring on his finger, a black gem.

'Look, I'm sorry, I must go, one of my students is waving at me to get back, give me a call if you are interested. I'd like to see you again.' He dashed off, and ran across the beach over to the woman.

Emma watched him arguing with a dark-haired woman, next to the sea; she was shaking her head, lifting her arms in protest. They were arguing furiously. He threw his hands up in the air and moodily strode off in the other direction. The woman chased after him, flung her arms round his neck and kissed him. Emma's heart sank: damn, he was with someone, she thought disappointed, her dream man was taken. Still, she thought smiling, she wasn't sure she wanted to get involved again so soon, not yet.

The surfing tournament was starting. Emma turned her seat round to watch some surfers skim over the waves, their light feet guiding the boards over some high swells, thundering towards the shore. A man's voice broke through the tannoy, the competition had started. The next set of surfers rode the swell, dipping and skimming through the waves, gliding onto the beach. One of the surfers, a tall blonde man, rode the next wave at a breathtaking speed. He slid down the wave like descending a ski slope, a huge avalanche of a wave rising behind him. She smiled, how nice he looked! He zigzagged the board over the wave, then swerved it onto the sand. He rode the next wave to the edge, in perfect balance, up to the seashore. The tournament master shouted through the tannoy.

'Maximum points to surfer, ten. You've broken this season's record with the highest score of twenty clear points.'

She clapped in admiration. Perhaps she was ready for a holiday romance, after all. Well, perhaps a fling, nothing serious. There were some nice men here, and things were looking up. Thoughts of Toby were fading fast. She grabbed her board and leapt on the waves at the beach, speeding along the fast turbulent waves, then ran back onto the beach, rubbed herself down and sunbathed between the rocks. She would show them she could surf just as well as a man. She was riding on the crest of a wave, feeling rapturous and back in control.

New beginnings

Emma strolled along the beach, glad that Toby had gone. She loved her newly acquired luxury of being able to do whatever she wanted, whenever she pleased. She had no one to answer to but herself, and sighed in euphoric bliss at her newfound freedom. She was having so much fun, chatting with the other swimmers and female surfers. Without ties, she was free as a bird. She flicked through the newspaper and spotted Toby, outside a club with the 'fetish' model he had used for an advert, the one whose lethal charms he had been unable to resist. Hadn't taken him much time to get over things, and it was more than just a fling, she thought bitterly. Still, his betrayal had shown what a rogue he really was, and now she was heading toward a better life. She tasted freedom, discovering a peace of mind that had eluded her for so long. To her surprise, she found she enjoyed living alone. She recoiled at what would have happened if she had stayed with Toby. They would have stagnated in suburbia, while he had a series of affairs and left her alone with the children, trapped at home. She shuddered at the near escape and realised how lucky she was to have avoided a messy divorce and traumatised kids. Now she thought excitedly, she could do exactly as she wanted, take any path she chose and the euphoria of being free flooded her veins. She skipped down the path feeling so happy, she felt as though she could fly.

She threw the paper with Toby's picture in the bin and walked briskly across the beach into a new beginning; her demons were gone, her zest for life had returned. She leapt effortlessly over the slippery rocks, her legs springing lightly, gradually losing their stiffness from sitting at a desk all day. The past slipped away with the wind as it blew through her hair. She climbed up onto a rock, gazed out to sea, and looked out to infinity; she took some deep breaths, gulping in the warm salty air. She looked up at the orange-pink sun, it was larger and hotter than she had seen in London. A huge wave tore into the cove, rushing over her feet, propelling sandy water around her ankles. She leapt onto a dry piece of sand as the water rushed in and swirled around the rocks. Seagulls dived into the waves, emerging with their beaks full of small fish, swooping over the small fishing boats lined up against the quay. Greedy gulls bombarded the shore, searching for scraps. Emma dipped her hand into a rock pool, and tried to catch a small crab, but quickly it darted through her fingers. A shimmering seahorse expelled hundreds of tiny babies into the water. It was heavenly! Foamy sea spray showered over her face. She licked it off, thinking how glad she was to be back, the freedom sparked her muse, and her creativity, her wonder for life, had returned. The view of the village had changed, a new hotel and guesthouse had sprung up along the sea front, with a new 'Beach café', art gallery, and a new-age vegetarian restaurant. A new surfing centre was built into a gothic church, crowding with surfers. Down on the beach, people scurried about like ants, women strolled along the beach in bikinis, their bodies slim and athletic.

Her mind flashed back to her first visit there with her parents, when the cove had been a quiet fishing village, with only the local fisherman for company. Later, voted one of the best beaches in England, a magnificent stretch of white surfing beach, it was the place to go. She watched a female surfer skim elegantly over a wave, her long hair billowing out behind her as she tunnelled through a high wave. Emma smiled: it was mostly men who dared to tackle the high sea—six-foot blonde, tanned Australians with perfect bodies. Now she observed happily, more women had taken up the sport. They were easily as good as men. She loved to surf, and it was her favourite hobby. She watched as the blazing orange-pink sun sank behind the horizon and happiness welled up inside her. Pale wispy clouds drifted across the sky. Her dream had come true, she had found her spiritual home, a place that inspired her and where she felt she truly belonged.

Catching a wave

A week later, Andrea, the hitchhiker, joined her for a swim. They jumped over the waves, splashing each other, shrieking like schoolgirls, chasing each other over the dunes.

'It's great to be here,' said Andrea, lying back on the sand.

'Yes, I wish I'd come sooner,' admitted Emma, turning over, rubbing suntan oil over her arms. 'I can't believe I stuck it out, travelling on the tube every day, for years. If I had known how good it was, I would have left years ago.'

'Are you feeling better now?'

'Yes, I've managed to get things in perspective. I can see more clearly. This is the life I should have led all along.'

'I came here to find an amazing man,' admitted Andrea, eyeing up the surfers wading out of the sea. 'They look so pale and washed out in the city, so dull.' She struggled out of her t-shirt, revealing a skimpy bikini.

Emma smiled wistfully. 'Yes, the surfers do have bodies to die for.'

'I've never seen so many fit men in one place,' Andrea admitted, jumping up, adopting her Amazonian poise. 'Gosh, look at him,' she said, pointing to a bronzed surfer sauntering by with his surfboard. 'I'd love a holiday romance.' She threw her red hair back, pouting furiously, and began doing a belly dance. Emma laughed and turned on the CD player. Some heavy rock, Robert Plant and Led Zeppelin blurted out loud.

A whistle blew, the race was starting; the zap cats started racing across the waves in a figure of eight, tearing across the waves. A DJ set up a sounds system, music was blaring out, the Bodyrockers— 'I like the way you move'. A beach party was in full swing at the café.

'I've come here to have wonderful sex,' Andrea confessed, almost falling out of her bikini top, her hips swaying and twitching in time to the music. 'I'm really in the mood.'

'For me it's more a spiritual awakening, a time for healing,' sighed Emma.

'Don't worry, you will soon get back into the swing of things,' said Andrea, throwing a towel at her, 'and learn to have fun again. You will find someone else in no time.'

'I don't think I want to go through that again. You're incorrigible!'

'Footloose and free,' Andrea insisted, jumping over a wave. 'That way you don't get hurt.'

'Race you to the rocks,' laughed Emma. She sped past the solitary blonde surfer clutching his board, and gave him a huge grin. He grinned back. Soon he was joined by a pack of gorgeous, blonde bronzed men strutting across the sand, who leapt into the water racing each other over the waves. The lifeguard leapt on his quad bike and sped off across the beach. Andrea leapt into the waves and dived into the blue ocean. The surfers stopped to whistle at her, so she jumped up and gave them a dazzling smile. Emma raced past Andrea at a fast crawl. The surfers sped across the waves after them.

'Come on, boys, show us how it's done,' Andrea shouted, throwing off her bikini top. 'I love to feel the water on my skin.'

The surfers tore past her, riding across the waves.

Andrea watched them in admiration, and flirted with them.

The blonde surfer swerved back and grabbed Andrea and pushed her onto his surfboard; he steered her out to sea, she fell off giggling into the waves, her arms clinging to him as she kissed him, then she fell off backwards. The surfer sped off on a wave and swerved it back to the shore.

'You are a wild one, safety in numbers, I guess,' said Emma, licking the salt off her lips. Her face was cold, her wet hair stuck to her skin like seaweed. They were treading water, in a calm patch of sea.

'Suits me fine, I have no illusions.'

'But don't you think romantic dreams are important? Too much reality, well you know what T S Elliot said about that. I can't bear it either, life has to be romantic, lived through a rosy glow, or it's unbearable.'

'Dreams have a habit of crashing down to earth, making you feel disillusioned, it's best to be grounded in the real world. You are such a dreamer, Emma, with such high ideals and expectations—how can you not expect to be disappointed? Illusions are only dreams to be broken.'

'I suppose so. But is it too much to expect someone to be faithful? Race you!' Emma splashed Andrea with water, as they rode the waves back to the shore.

'I'd say monogamy is an ideal dream. It's not always a reality and in some cultures it doesn't even exist.'

'But I think it is the only decent way to live,' protested Emma, 'to find true love and stay true and devoted.'

'Well I hope your dream comes true.'

Emma raced past Andrea, beating her by minutes.

'Okay, you win, drinks are on you tonight,' laughed Andrea, splashing her. Emma feeling playful like a child, doggy paddling in the water, started a water fight. The surfer came back, carried Andrea off on his back; she fell off, shrieking, and they fell on the sand, their limbs entwined.

As Emma sat down, the zap cat championship heat was warming up; the heavy rock music blared out, the sea spray mingled with the hot summer sun. They lay back watching the small yachts bobbing and bouncing over the waves, the zap cats racing round a sea circuit, bouncing over the waves. People were clapping, and rushing into the sea as the race stopped, to cool off, some were surfing, others were dancing. Emma and Andrea sat sipping cocktails watching the sunset glow and the sea grow calm. Slightly burnt, they headed up to the beach café for the party, to listen to a night of rock violins and raucous Celtic music. A barbecue was starting on the beach and people were setting up tents, deep among the dunes. They rambled on to the rock concert, to watch the firework display. Life was near to perfect, mused Emma, watching the band play some raucous riffs to the backdrop of a wild crashing ocean and the most incredible orange sunset she had ever seen sinking behind the rock formations. Beautiful beaches, amazing surf, perfect scenery, rock concerts and excellent food. What more could anyone ask for, she thought wistfully? They partied and danced till dawn, to the sounds drifting over the sea. Andrea disappeared with the gorgeous surfer, tumbling back into the tent in the early hours, a half-empty bottle of wine in her hand. Emma told her off like an enraged parent. They both collapsed giggling in the dunes.

'What do you think you are doing?' said Emma, shocked. 'You don't even know him!'

'Live each day as if it were your last,' advised Andrea. 'How could I resist such a scrumptious body? He's pure heaven.'

Emma raised her eyes upwards and warned, 'Oh come on, Andrea, it will be your last if you're not careful.'

'Sex is good for you,' protested Andrea, winding a sari around her tanned, sylphlike body. 'My diploma in holistic therapy taught me how well it clears our stress and tension, releases the endorphins. It's my favourite form of exercise.'

Emma shrugged and laughed. 'What can I say? You are mad, Andrea!'

In the morning, as they made their way back to Emma's holiday flat, Emma peered back over her shoulder, struck by the wide expanse of wild beauty. Her life was changing, she didn't know who she was becoming, but it was someone new. She liked this new feeling of being free and independent. Life was timeless; no more routines or schedules to tie her down, she could do as she wished, swim every day, and spend hours lazily soaking up the sun, followed by blissfully perfect meals and sipping cold wine at the local inn. She would live every moment indulging her desires, at least for the summer, then she would have to start up another project with the idea of making money again. Now, she would pamper herself, let her true spirit emerge and discover her real self, shed all her baggage.

She sighed happily, glad to have met someone as wild as Andrea, who made her feel adventurous and carefree again. They were having so much fun, giggling and acting irresponsibly, just like two adolescent schoolgirls. Emma picked up a handful of sand and let it run through her fingers, cool tiny fragments of stone piled onto a small mound in front of her, like the infinity of time—reminding her that every moment was precious, not to be wasted. Life was to be lived to the full! For the first time in months, she was starting to enjoy life again.

Inspired

Emma ran across the sun-drenched beach, a gentle breeze blowing in her hair, her skin glowing and tingling in the sun. She smiled and ran with joy, glad to be free! Her dream had come true. She felt her feet sink into the sand and the sea run over her toes, she climbed onto a rock and made a clean dive in the sea, and came up covered in seaweed, then dived down again and swam along the coastline, a fast crawl, then backstroke, bobbing up and down on the waves, floating on her back. She was so excited, knowing that soon she would have her own house, her own refuge from the world, and her own beach; life was just perfect again. The waves swirled around her and lifted her along on the current. The hot sun's rays burned onto her face. She swam out for miles, by the rocks, feeling the energy flow into her. Buoyant and light, she drifted along with the waves, going with the flow. She couldn't remember feeling this good for a long time, letting her life go with the flow. Emma climbed back up the dunes, took a jump into the sand, then strode across the hills for a picnic. Ambling past the stream, forking through small cottages scattered deep among the rock-filled, grassy valley, she found a sheltered dune. Sun-warmed rock pools sparkled under the hot near-tropical sun. Tents were going up on the hills, campers were setting up picnics behind wind-breakers. Surfers struggled into wet suits, and raced each other across the dunes, leaping into the sea to catch the highest waves of the day. Emma set out a pale blue tablecloth and munched on a baguette oozing with brie and ham, and began picking at grapes, reflecting that life suddenly seemed much brighter. She could think now, with a new clarity. She glanced out past the lighthouse, where small boats were speeding along the horizon, sailing past the Scilly Isles. She recalled the strange tale of Lyonesse, the island that once joined Cornwall and the Scillies to Brittany, until a huge tidal wave had pushed the village under the sea, so that its remain were submerged, like Atlantis. The turbulent Atlantic Ocean waves had risen to split them into two separate lands. It was such a magical, mystical place, the most inspiring place on earth and it was such a wonderful day, such an exciting place to start a new life! She started chatting to some locals, her city persona slipping away. She walked briskly back to her room to make a quick call to Melanie, her sister, an employment law barrister, to tell her about her plan.

They had a few polite exchanges about the weather, then chatted about the journey. Her manner growing a little frosty, Melanie said, 'Darling, how can you give up that lovely apartment in town, those gorgeous restaurants and boutiques, and go and live in the wilds? Where on earth will you buy your clothes?'

Emma sighed, exasperated: 'Does it matter? I'll just wear a bikini and sarong.'

'Well, if you insist on spending all your time lazing on the beach, aren't you a bit old to become a surfer hippy?'

'I can't think of anything I'd rather be,' retorted Emma. 'I just want to be free.'

'So does everybody,' sighed Mel. 'We'd all love to give it all up, and run to the beach, but some of us have responsibilities.'

'Oh come on, Melanie, chill out,' said Emma, irritated. 'You could easily do the same, you just don't want to.'

'I wouldn't give up a good legal career, just to be a beach bum,' Melanie snorted scornfully. 'No one is really free, and there is no such thing as "free will". We all have responsibilities. Don't forget, it can be great fun there in the summer, but cold in the winter and it's miles back to London, so it can be pretty lonely.'

'Well there's nothing worse than being surrounded by lots of people and feeling lonely,' retorted Emma. 'And worse if you can't trust them. Here, I have the chance to start again, make some new friends.'

'It's not that easy,' sighed Melanie, her tone softening. 'Look, what you are doing, it's really courageous, living your dream, and if anyone can make a go of it, I'm sure you will, but please be careful.'

'I'll be fine, Mel, it's only Cornwall, not Outer Mongolia, I don't think I'll die in a storm, or perish in the desert.'

Melanie laughed. 'Bye, sis, take care.'

Later, to relax, Emma took the Scillonian ship to the Isle of Tresco, to sketch the wildlife. Puffins and birds, sea lions and dolphins circled the blue lagoons. After a sumptuous meal at the New Inn, Emma took her sketchpad and sat on a rock and made some sketches of the scenery, adding small verses of poetry to the drawings. She wandered along the rugged coastline past some yellow gorse bush, the bright cornflower-blue sky laden with seabirds. She stopped as she found an unusual flower, a wild orchid, when she saw something slither off a rock, and its tail swish behind it as it dived back into the sea, long red hair trailing out behind it. What was that? It must be a mermaid! She gasped in surprise, watching the red hair swish around in the waves, the long limbs flailing under the water. She looked closer and laughed as she realised it was some feathering seaweed caught up on a long water stem. She saw a flicker of a tail swish out of the sea, it circled round, then stuck its nose out of the water, it was a dolphin! The dolphin, sensing her presence, leapt out of the sea and, in a perfect arc, dived back into the waves. Emma smiled at such a wonderful sight, her spirit soaring.

Later, when she got back, she noticed the room was icy cold. There was a strange vibe around.

Emma climbed the hill, feeling happy, as high as a kite, her spirit soaring in a state of euphoria. How could she still be sad with such incredible scenery around her? Sennen was such a beautiful place, with nice happy people around. She felt a warm tingle rush over her body. She sat on a rock to meditate, pleasure rippling through her pores, as she felt her soul elevate. She chanted a mantra, reaching a state of transcendence, a peak experience, floating in perfect synchronicity with the universe. Her mind and body relaxed to the sound of the gentle rush of the sea, waves of delight washed over her, her head was light and her spirit danced. Her thoughts flowed effortlessly in harmony with nature, and as the stress slowly melted, she felt as light as a feather. How different from how she had felt in London, always balancing on a fraught jagged edge, rushing from one meeting to another, pushing deadlines.

Back on the beach, she wandered past the lifeguard's hut; he was sitting with a pair of binoculars looking out to sea. Suddenly he stood up, grabbed his surfboard, tore along the beach, dived into the turbulent waves and pulled in a floundering surfer. Quite a sex god, brave knight of the sea, she thought, wishing she had been the drowning surfer. What a thrill to have a beautiful hunk push his mouth over hers. The idea made her tingle with excitement. She found men attractive again, a good sign. She churned over in her mind what to do next, perhaps take a part-time job? Do freelance work for her agency? Or start her own business? She was self-motivated and creative, and enjoyed the thought of embarking on a new adventure. Her mind started buzzing with ideas again. She felt the muse bite, perhaps she would start a gallery, a new-age awareness group for reiki healing, or an art gallery shop? She pondered the ideas with growing enthusiasm, a new stream of ideas flowing fast, as she reeled with creative thoughts. Then, the perfect idea came to her. She would start a wine bar, an arts club, where painters could come and paint, research other artists, read about art, and learn how to paint. To finance this she would carry on with her freelance work, start an arts centre, combine all her ideas, and rebuild her life all over again. There was a lot to work out but she sighed with pleasure, pleased with herself that she was on the ascent.

Reflections

Emma climbed over the slippery rocks, gazing out over the shimmering, silver-blue glistening bay. The sight took her breath away, the choppy waves curling around the bright, white-yellow sand, the turquoise sea glittering all the way to the horizon. The view was empowering, and gave her a spiritual high. She felt confident, high, strong like an eagle ready to fly, to soar high above the waves. She leapt on a rock, in the throes of a peak experience. The image of a sun-drenched beach used so often to associate a product with pleasurable thoughts was hers now for real. She felt as though she was flying—a goddess, rescued from the demons of the deep, awakening to a happy sun-filled world. She strolled across the beach; the sea was choppy and rough—how she loved it there, so wild and unspoilt, where she could feel her true nature emerge, the beauty around her light her soul. Blissfully, she dashed down the dunes to the sea for a quick dip.

She tied her shirt up around her waist, the tide was coming in so fast. She loved the sea, it sparkled like a lagoon and it was warm today. Sand tapered up to the cliffs, reaching up to the stone huts dotted along the horizon. She took a clean dive off the rocks and swam for hours through the warm sun-drenched rock pools. Drying herself off, she made her way along the coastal path, climbing the hot stone steps one by one, feeling the strains of history echo around her as she made her way up to the old church. She felt the coldness of the wet stone cool under her feet against the haziness of the hot sun. A beam of pure white light pierced the tall gothic windows. She climbed up and sat in the alcove watching the bay. Islands of light shimmered on the crystal turquoise sea. Her timing had been perfect, it was the best time to arrive in Sennen, she reflected, at the height of the summer season. Suddenly, she recalled the day when her mother had first taken her there.

Emma licked the salt from her lips and gazed up at the empty blue sky. Memories came flooding back—of jumping down the hot sand dunes, and diving in the high waves and swimming through the rock pools in the rocky sea. She remembered the many summers she had spent there, riding across Lands End with her father, a sporty figure who insisted she join him for a brisk run every morning. They would meet up for a punishing run of at least two miles every morning while her mother sat sunbathing on the beach. A little too delicate for exploring wild terrains, or swimming in the rough sea, she preferred to sit behind the windbreaker, rubbing suntan oil over her body, reading women's magazines. After their morning swim, Emma and her sister would devour Cornish pasties and bottles of Scrumpy, trying not to get them filled with sand. Being expert swimmers, they would soon rush back into the sea, surf on the waves, then explore the rocks and caves for the rest of the afternoon. Emma, an artistic type, and sensitive rebel at her convent school, would spend her days painting at the top of the hill while her sister, a tomboy, played basketball or tennis with the surfers below. They organised wild beach parties at the beach café—the memories were fresh in her mind—spending the nights dancing to rock music, or listening to the local bands. Her first stolen kiss was with a boy she had taken off to the hills for a day. She'd loved every minute of camping on the beach, basking in the sun, or sitting in the beach café watching the surfers jump on their surfboards and ride the waves. Wandering back through the cove, she realised how much she had loved being there! Recalling the memories made her feel warm and secure, of happy times as a teenager.

Almost on cue, she saw a silver lining around the dark cloud, a rainbow rising on the dark horizon pointing to a new life, as though a spiritual entity was guiding her. Feeling on top of the world, so agile and buoyant, she leapt over the rocks, recapturing the happy atmosphere of the past. She was like a bird, ready to fly. She loved the freedom of being in open space, glad not to be queuing at a crowded supermarket off the Tottenham Court Road or being crushed in the tube. The sun dipped behind the clouds, then poked through a cloud, throwing hot rays across the beach. Emma stretched out like a cat, feeling better than she had for a long time, her heart and spirit glowing under the sun's healing rays. She was feeling calmer now, getting things in perspective, reflecting on the past year, gaining insight into her inner feelings, finding out who she really was and getting in touch with her needs. She scanned the area with her binoculars. The beach café was crowding with swimmers. Surfers were balancing their surfboards against the tables, chatting about the currents, their tall tanned bodies bronzed and oiled, glistening with suntan lotion. They sat down next to some pale artists drinking tea. Sea spray splashed over the balcony, throwing frothy blue waves over the wall. A ball landed next to her; she kicked it over to a group of teenagers sitting on the sand. Elated, gripped by a childish excitement, she ran across the beach whooping and throwing the ball back and forwards feeling seventeen again. Nothing had ever captured her imagination, released her playful inner child, quite so dramatically as the cove. No wonder artists came there in their hordes, hoping to be inspired. Life is an art, she thought, seeing nature's palette of colours swirl around her. It was as though she was standing in a beautiful painting of earthy shades and hues. A flock of seagulls swooped overhead, two white butterflies laced and circled each other, playing over the pollen of some solitary flowers swaying gently in the sun.

'The sun is shining, the birds are singing,' she trilled, glancing at the estate agent's photographs, as an idea came to her. The Inn had a studio with a spectacular view that dipped down to Gwenver beach, reputed to be one of the best views in the country. She would turn it into an art studio, rent it to artists, to help with an income. She laughed to herself; Andrea would certainly approve, it had a view over one of the best surfing beaches, where Andrea would spend her days with her eyes glued to the local talent. Emma would turn the Inn into studio-come-gallery, where she could display the work of local artists.

'It's so good to be alive,' she sang out loud. She ran past the golden beaches and dramatic cliffs spreading out in front of her, breathless at the sight of the Cornish countryside—its enthralling magical coves, wild moorland hills awaking in her a sense of mystery. She had backpacked around the world, through some of the world's most beautiful domains, but nothing quite held the same allure as Cornwall. She had spent so many happy days there as a child. What was it her sister had told her? Freedom was a state of mind, we were either imprisoned by our thoughts or liberated by them. Such a magical place! The gentle rhythm of the sea calmed her while the sun's rays sparked her with energy. She watched the galloping waves crash on the shore, the cycle of the moon and the sun had begun. Her head whirling, she felt a peak experience ignite her soul, as she touched the heavens in bliss.

The Inn—secret dreams

It was peaceful, and relaxing, yet Emma longed for an adventure, for something exciting to happen. She wondered if she could adjust to a quiet country life, as it would be even more deserted in the winter. Perhaps her sister was right, she did need a challenge and a busy social life. She put any doubts aside: this was the place she truly loved and where she belonged. Excited, she thought about the Inn, which she was viewing today. She ambled up the rocky terrain back to the cliff top where she had walked as a child. The view from the top of the path was incredible, miles of rocky terrain and open shores. She took out a towel; maybe she would sunbathe for a while, while the sun was hot. Soon she lay sprawled out on the sand. A slight breeze scattered sand over her towel. She took a photograph of the Inn from her bag, wiped the sand off, and looked at it more closely—it had an air of mystery. Spacious, quiet, set high in the cliffs, it stood on the coastline, a three-bedroom inn overlooking the beach with spectacular views—it was a dream, with a small side studio overlooking the beach. She glanced at her bank details quickly and smiled, satisfied that her accounts were in order. Perhaps she could persuade them to accept a slightly lower offer, then she could use the rest to renovate the property. A spark of excitement flowed through her as she envisaged the new project she could start. There was her new destiny, an inn she could turn into an arts centre. She smiled, pleased at her new plan, then gathered up her things and made her way over to the beach café.

If all went according to plan, she would soon be a very happy woman. She ordered a coffee, and sat reading the details of the sixteenth-century inn, learning, with some excitement, that it had been used by pirates as a hideaway for smuggling contraband into the cove. She wondered why it was still empty, surprised it hadn't been snapped up. In such a beautiful location with so much potential, why had it been vacant for almost a year? Why was a property like that still on the market? Some artists had squatted there, and it was obviously in need of some repair, but she would enjoy restoring it to its former glory. She hoped that no one had put in an offer yet. It was just what she was looking for, within her budget, and reduced for a quick sale. The sparkle returned to her eyes as she ran down the sandy path onto the beach. She spent the morning on the beach, booked into Sennen surf school for a few advanced surfing lessons, then, feeling more confident, jumped on the surfboard and paddled it out to sea, floating over the waves, all her anger and worries slipping away like melting ice. The sea crashed over her feet as she stood up on the board and swerved neatly over a wave.

Emma threw her bag over her shoulder and headed for the inn, where she was due to meet the estate agent at two. She walked quickly over the hot scorched earth, feeling the heat burn through her sandals onto the soles of her feet, her toes sinking slowly into the soft sand. Emma made her way through the fields, along the coastline, by the sea and held her breath at the stunning beauty in front of her. She scanned her surroundings with growing interest, a smile lighting up her face—her creative spark was pushing her in the right direction. The scenery around her was so inspiring that it gave her a natural high. Small wild ponies frolicked in the fields, butterflies flittered into the bushes, and sailing boats drifted by. Unfolding a map, she quickly traced the route to the inn. It was one mile north, and gave her an opportunity to enjoy the views along the way. Her skin tingled with excitement as she rambled along the rugged coastline, map in hand, her cares slipping away. Her long blonde hair, usually worn tied up in a neat bun for work, blew across her shoulders and she felt the sun burn her cheeks.

She made her way over the cliffs, through the purple heath bushes, treading softly on the mossy grass, jumping over the rocky terrain. Intoxicated by the balm of the sea air, she recalled the words of a poem by Emerson:

'A mocking thrush, a wild rose,' and she added, 'the crashing of the sea. Salve my worst wounds.' A calm spread over her, her spirit rose, and the only sound to invade her thoughts was the gentle roar of the sea. She walked past the cliffs to the other side of the hills, climbing carefully over the rocks. The wind blew more forcefully so she pulled her jacket around her and headed along the coastline.

Halfway up, she stopped as she caught a glimpse of the inn, on the peak of the hill. Its solitude surprised her, for it stood there alone, at the top of a cliff, nestling amongst rugged beauty. It overlooked the sea. It looked as good as it had in the photograph, and had its own field and path to the beach. The name 'Black Dove' rung softly in her ears, so easily conjuring up images of dark shadowy secrets. No wonder it had been used as a pirate haunt, as it was so close to the sea. The guidebook described it as a smuggler's rendezvous, once used for hiding contraband. The sound of the sea crashing on the rocks below made civilisation seem far away and an odd eeriness hung over the bay. She felt strangely detached from the world. Time was suddenly suspended, giving a surreal edge to reality. She stood for a moment, taking in the scene around her. Strange—she felt as if she had been there before, and that there was something remarkably familiar about the place. Then she remembered the night after Toby's betrayal, when she had dreamed of the inn, and now she recognised the area. She had been there before, it was the place in her dreams. How strange! She had seen into her future. That convinced her even more that this was her destiny, and that she was doing the right thing. The inn was enchanting, even better than in the photograph. For a second she stood looking at the inn, perched at the top of the cliffs: it was a fairy-tale gothic inn, its air mysterious. It had been empty for a while and Emma thought it an ideal location, either for a haunted house, or for a tormented dark character like Heathcliffe to inhabit. Was it haunted, she wondered? She walked along the narrow coastal path taking her to the inn, and it seemed to be beckoning her.

As she moved closer, the air of mystery grew stronger. Making her way carefully along the narrow path, she followed the signs pointing to the inn. She walked in the middle so as not to fall over the edge. Her mind filled with images of pirates sailing into the cove, hiding contraband in the caves. She was lost in a dream, losing all sense of time. Suddenly the path under her started to crumble. She grabbed onto a twig and fell back onto a grassy bank, sighing with relief. A few more seconds and she would have fallen straight into the sea, over the cliffs onto the black rocks below. She fought to catch her breath: her heart was beating fast, like a bird caught inside her chest. She'd never had such a fright! She closed her eyes, adrenalin pumping through her veins, and she couldn't stop shaking. Could this be a portent? Slowly she climbed back onto the cliff path. She was determined to carry on, and just had to buy it: nothing would put her off now, nor get in the way of her dream. Gentle rain splattered over the hills, yet the hot sun broke through the clouds. A rainbow arched over the hills, edged with a silver glow and she took this as a good omen. She peered over to the beach at some surfers riding the waves daringly on the high tide.

She drew in her breath as the inn came into view; it looked quite derelict and lonely. Anyone chasing smugglers in the dark would have fallen straight over the cliff onto the jagged rocks below. Had men swung from the gallows pole outside? Or had they been thrown into the cellar under the bar, never to be seen again? Her sense of intrigue grew. All the mythical stories she had heard seemed to be coming alive and she could feel the presence of the people who had once lived there, making the inn look all the more spooky.

Gothic arches hung over the doors. Pretty rose petals were carved into the wood. Were there bats nesting in the roof? She came to the door; there was a small plaque above, an image of a skull on a ship, with a black dove flying overhead. A vestige from its torrid past? Emma wondered if it had been empty for a long time and detected a ghostly air. She raced up to the windows and peered in, but for a small glimmer of light throwing its tiny beam, it was dusty and dark inside. Taking a key out of the envelope, she opened the door, and let herself in. It was magnificent, with a huge, long room and arched tall windows providing stunning views of the sea. What had once been a bar nestled in the corner. She couldn't help feeling that it looked vaguely like the inside of a chapel.

Captivated, Emma set off to explore, thinking of the poets and artists who had stayed there, and stepped across the stone floor into its various rooms. She looked around her: it was amazing, spacious, with dancing beams of light penetrating the long gothic windows. Silver light streaked through the large gothic arches, giving them a heavenly glow. Heavy wooden beams lined the ceilings. She felt the history rise from the walls around her and from the flagstones under her feet. Chunky oak tables and chairs stood on the uneven stone floor. All the rooms led off to a huge room in the middle. It was spacious and airy. She walked around, jumping as she thought she felt a cold hand brush past her. She turned round in surprise, but could see no one there; it must have been a cold blast of air. Gothic sconces stood in the four corners of the room. The interior had been designed to stir the imagination, and she felt electrified by being in a place with so much history. The sun sparkled outside in a rainbow of colours, throwing a ray of light across the room. The rooms, despite their oldness, glowed with a sunny vibrancy.

Gripped with curiosity, she wandered through the low-ceilinged oak-panelled rooms, past the small alcoves where the pirates had sat, touching the carved wooden beams, letting her fantasies fly. She stroked the ornate tulip glasses hanging by their long slender stems overshadowing the half-circular mahogany bar, next to the elegant red-brick wall fireplace stacked with logs ready for the winter. She watched the heavy velvet drapes swirl in the light breeze over the long arched windows. Enchanted by her surroundings, she twirled round, pleased to have the inn to herself. How she would love to own it!

She walked back out onto the path. It was perfect for her, she loved it, and it felt like her ideal home.

Once outside, she looked for the estate agent—still no sign of him, perhaps she had missed him? She decided to wait just a little bit longer. Re-entering, she wandered through the rooms, touching the low oak beams. Who had lived there, she wondered, noticing some dust drift across the room? The place hadn't been cleaned in months. She ran her finger along the dusty fireplace, seeing it needed some spring-cleaning. It smelt musty and damp. There was an ornate spiral staircase, leading to three bedrooms upstairs, one large and two small. At the top of the staircase, stood a tall arched stained-glass window. Ivy leaves covered one stained-glass window, blue alternating with light green, through which she had an uninterrupted view of the sea. She could hear crickets chirruping in the long grass and the crashing of the sea on the glistening rocks: it was the perfect haven to give her the solitude she craved, and she knew she would be happy there.

Curious, she discovered some of the furniture had been left behind by the previous owner, a four-poster bed and some church pews, with intricate carvings of strangely formed winged demons. The estate agent hadn't shown up but it already felt like it were hers, as though she had been guided there, and that it had been designed especially for her. She just had to buy it.

She walked into a small circular garden, laden with the perfume of many flowers—roses, white jasmine, honeysuckle—and a heavy musk hung in the air. It was a strange garden, with a strange atmosphere, the scent of roses wafted under her nostrils. She felt quite dizzy, and looked down to see the garden was filled with black roses, covered in prickly thorns, concealed behind the deadly nightshade. Growing around the studio were white lilies, foxgloves and white poppies. So many deadly flowers! It was a poison garden, emanating a dark mysterious air, with a strange musky odour. She half expected to see bats fly from out of the roof. It had a wicked aura—something dark had happened there, she could feel it. Suddenly a cold wind blew around her. She saw the window of the studio glisten, half-hidden behind some weeds. She slipped past the dip that concealed the tunnels leading to the beach, and pushed back the weeds hanging over the door. She walked inside, finding it strangely tranquil, and a gentle energy swirled round her. She looked up at her reflection in the window, when suddenly, a beautiful woman's face, with long golden hair, appeared, her sad face shimmering in the glass. Emma jumped back in surprise, blinking as she saw the beautiful eyes of a woman staring back at her. Then, she blinked again, and saw her own reflection. Who on earth was that? She stood still, shocked, looking around her. Was there someone wandering inside the inn? Was it haunted? Or perhaps some people were squatting there? She had to confess that she felt a mystical otherworldly feel about it. Had dark misdeeds been committed in the tunnels? She pushed all worrying thoughts from her mind—the pane of glass was clear, it must have been her own distorted reflection. She had stumbled into a Garden of Eden, but, somewhere, lurking amongst the foliage, she was sure there was a serpent. A dark cloud hovered in this musky utopia, where the innocent had fallen from grace and been thrown into the infernal dark fire of the abyss. Who was the beautiful woman, who had appeared in the windowpane?

A raven perched on the gate, swivelling its eyes toward Emma. It gave her such a fright, she jumped back. She walked quickly past, stepping onto the stone baroque courtyard lined with gargoyles—they seemed to be staring back at her. Brushing aside some foliage, she found the entrance to the tunnels, running beneath the inn, once used as an escape route by pirates. She walked straight over to the entrance: it had a gloomy air, and led to the beach, where pirates had been brutally killed as they left their ships. Immediately, she felt surrounded by a distinctly icy and unfriendly aura, as though an evil presence lurked in the underground caves, and she felt a cold wind swirl round her. What dark secrets lay hidden there? She pushed hard on the heavy wooden door—it wouldn't budge, was locked and bolted with rusty locks. She peeked through the keyhole—she could just about see a dark tunnel with a speck of light at the end. A cold icy breeze blew around her. She shivered despite the burning hot sun, then went back inside and closed the door.

Was the studio haunted? Had they been happier living in the past century? Did the inn hold tales of magical mystery or of debauchery and piracy? She'd had enough of civilisation and its discontents, and welcomed a more peaceful retreat in the wilds. Now she had found a haven of tranquillity, but it also concealed a dark mystery. Throwing her pack over the chair, Emma poured some water from a flask. The day was stifling and getting hotter. The inn had a friendly aura, like stepping into the past, into a different era. Perhaps it had once been a mystical kingdom, inhabited by dark knights of the sea. Parts of it, the studio and especially around the tunnels, had a strange atmosphere. Had it been a paradise? Or had it been a living hell in those dark days? She would love to have been there, but she would bring her own aura to the place, and transform it into her own heaven. She would love to be able to travel back in time and hear their dark tales. Had rugged pirates spent hours planning how to hijack a heavily laden ship that had suffered the misfortune of sailing within their shores? What sort of people had stayed there? Highwaymen and other dark-hearted rogues? The inn still vibrated with the dark characters who had passed through—yet it felt quite tranquil and serene. She dipped into the old oak bookshelves and took out a book and read its title, *Haunted Houses of Cornwall*, thinking it suited the ambience of the room. This part of Cornwall was reckoned to be the most haunted part of England. She flicked through the local guidebook, turning the pages slowly. There was a short passage about two brothers coming to a watery end and details of the inn's murky past. Suddenly, everything outside became still, she could hear no sound, neither waves nor birds. Then she heard someone tapping gently on the stairs and ran out into the hallway, but there was no one there; only sand blew against the windows. A grey mist swirled around the spiral staircase; as the mist cleared Emma saw the shimmering outline of a woman walk up to the door, then it faded away. All of a sudden, the room went quiet, and a black cloud hung in the air, a strong gust of wind blew papers across the room, scattering them over the floor. Emma closed the window, but the wind was strong and it wouldn't close. Suddenly she felt an eerie sensation creep over her neck and, looking up, she saw clouds of white dust drifting up the stairs. Wondering what it was, she stood and peered more closely at it, watching the dust take on the shape of a face hovering in the air. She jumped back, freezing in shock, as it swirled around the room, a cloud of white specks. It disappeared up the stairs, and she watched as it moved slowly past her face. She shivered, what the hell was going on? She pulled herself together quickly: there must be a rational explanation. A strong wind must have disturbed some debris. Satisfied, she walked back into the small shady room. It was grey and misty outside, some dark clouds were gathering ominously in the sky. A cold chill ran through her, as if she had stepped into a patch of ice. Dark shadows shimmered over the walls. It had suddenly turned quite eerie. The sky was misty grey, the sea a dark sludgy green. She looked out of the corner of her eye and saw a cloud of dust shaped like a face swirling across the landing, she couldn't quite make out the rest of it, something like a billowing cloak disappearing into the wall. The curtains blew in the wind, and the shutters slammed hard. She jumped, her skin crawling with fear. What on earth was it? Maybe it was just the wind, she thought, trying to be rational. No, she was sure it was a ghost. She ran outside. Where was the estate agent? Suddenly, she was interrupted by the loud, insistent, shrill ring of her mobile phone. It was Andrea. She sighed and answered it, her mood pensive.

'Hi, how's it going?'

'Guess what? I think I have just seen a ghost,' said Emma, breathlessly.

'Are you sure? When? How exciting,' said Andrea, livening up at once.

'No, I'm not sure,' laughed Emma, 'It might only be my overactive imagination, but I thought I saw a face, a shadowy figure disappear into the wall.'

'A face?'

'Yes, drifting through the studio.'

Emma told her about the ghost.

'Well it could have been, but are you sure it wasn't just a reflection? I see faces in the clouds sometimes.'

'No, I am sure it was a spirit,' insisted Emma.

'The only spirits I ever encounter are in the local bar,' joked Andrea.

'It's probably just me,' said Emma. 'I am not used to old empty buildings. It could have just been a reflection of a bird outside.' She described what she had seen.

'Sounds like it might have just been the dust spiralling around, it does make funny shapes sometimes,' said Andrea. 'Or sometimes when we fall into a half-sleep, a doze, especially in the heat, we see figures around us, a kind of lucid dreaming.'

'Yes it could be that.'

'How are things otherwise?'

'Well, it's all so perfect, except for the ghosts!'

'Do you actually believe in them?'

'Oh I don't know…' Emma paused. 'It's like looking at the clouds when they swirl into faces. We see what we expect to see, if something strange happens, our perception doesn't always register events correctly. If I do sleep heavily, it does feel as though my dreams are real.'

'The power of your imagination is infinite, and you are excited,' laughed Andrea, 'so you could be reading things into what you see, along with the heat.'

'I suppose so'

'Guess what, I've some good news, I've just met a dishy artist in St Ives, called Ramone, he's French,' said Andrea breathlessly. 'He belongs to the artists' colony at St Ives, he wants me to pose naked for him.'

'Sounds like you are having fun,' said Emma brightly. 'Shall we meet in the pub, say at eight?'

'Okay.'

'If you can find out anything about the Black Dove Inn, please dig it out. I really would like to buy it.'

'Okay, see you at eight, bye.'

Emma sat back, puzzled and mystified at what she had just seen. Strange shadowy figures inhabited the inn. How strange. Was it all in her imagination? Or could there be a strange dark mystery lurking here? The place was riddled with secrets. Still she didn't really care, it was the most fascinating place she had ever seen and, if it was haunted, well, she could always do it up and sell it. She went upstairs to the bedroom and stood admiring her body in the mirror. Her hair had lightened several shades to a light streaky blonde and her stomach was flat. She looked better than if she'd spent weeks on a sunbed or at the gym. As she walked back into the lounge, Emma heard a car door slam and rushed to the porch to see if the agent had arrived. No one was there. She walked back into the room, but, for some inexplicable reason, it felt different. She stared at the four-poster bed, she was sure the carved wooden faces moved.

The inn suddenly turned icy cold and there was a strange heaviness in the room; a door slammed and the wardrobe flew open. A cat bared its teeth, and jumped out through the window.

A white light glowed in the corner, and was getting brighter.

Emma heard a soft tapping coming from the stairs; she froze as she saw a woman dressed in a long black dress appear, walk over to the four-poster bed, where she sat for a few seconds, then shimmer back across the floor. She turned and smiled at Emma, then vanished. The house seemed to tingle with a vibrant energy, as if it were alive. A woman's face was shimmering in the glass staring at her.

A sound, the soft echo of footsteps, tapped on the stairs. Emma spun round, her heart almost stopping. A swirling mist floated into the room, then faded away. Emma felt the hairs bristle all over her neck. The house was alive! She ran into the hallway—the swirl of dust was moving. She was gripped by an indescribable panic, and froze. Was her mind playing tricks on her? The cloud of dust swirled past her face, out of the door. She could hear the gentle moans of a woman, coming from upstairs, drowning out the sound of the sea, then it stopped. The room became deathly silent and momentarily she felt herself transported to another world. Then the air cleared, the lightness of summer returned. The musty smell vanished. Was the place haunted?

She rushed outside and looked up the path that led that to the beach where the pirates had once been. She saw a woman disappear into the distance. There was a mystery there, she was sure. She walked outside and went into to the studio. She began to clean the old sink in the corner, when she looked up at the cracked windowpane and saw a woman's smiling face shimmering in the glass, then, after a few seconds, it vanished.

She jumped back, and threw the towel in the sink, then someone knocked on the door. It was a woman looking for directions to a campsite. Emma fell back and laughed—it must have been the woman's reflection in the mirror, as she walked past.

She heard the birds sing, and her senses danced with joy again. A plane flew over, casting a shadow over the inn, making it vibrate. Some paints crashed down, but she turned round and saw her own reflection shimmering in the glass. Paint was dripping over the mirror, but she could see the distorted image of the woman walking by the studio, carrying a surfboard. That must have been her 'ghost' she thought, relieved. The vibrations from the noisy engine had dislodged the dust and made the room shudder and knocked over the paint. There it was, another simple explanation! There were no ghosts, just a series of coincidences. The scenic tour flight-path went right over the inn and had disturbed the dust: it was still flying around and there was a strange reflection from the plane as it flew overhead, its shadow looking like a person moving along the wall. She laughed and breathed a sigh of relief.

She tried to ring the estate agent but still there was no answer. She turned on the radio and relief flooded through her as she listened to the comforting, monosyllabic voice of the newsreader. A surfer had been stranded out at sea. Prize-winning turnips had been stolen. The banality of it all made her feel so sane. She felt almost normal again, so was there a ghost? Or maybe just a lot of wind and stormy weather? Her imagination had run away with itself. Should she buy a house with so much mystery? She jumped as the phone rang. It was Andrea asking to meet her straightaway. She grabbed her jacket and ran to the pub.

'I found something interesting at the library, a story about a ghost in the cove, and pirates from a sunken ship,' Andrea said as they ordered drinks.

'Yes, go on.'

'Well, a French aristocrat called Antoine used to live there, at the inn, and dabbled in the black arts. He lived with a beautiful woman artist called Letitia and they made friends with a woman smuggler called Annie Treeve.'

'Yes, go on.'

'Well it seems the area does seem to have a bit of a dark history. Antoine was a rather magical, mystical character; myth says he was in league with the devil and conjured up a storm, which sunk a famous count's ship. But the truth was they were all running a smuggling ring, and Annie fell out with Dionysus Williams, the owner of the First and Last Inn at Lands End. She turned Queen's evidence against him and she was drowned at Sennen Beach for her betrayal, and now haunts the place.'

'Is the Black Dove Inn haunted?'

'There's no actual mention of that, but it does appear in the "places with an interesting past" guidebook. It seems that Antoine had been in league with Annie and all the other smugglers, but somehow they were always betraying each other or falling out.'

'Tell me more, it sounds fascinating.'

'Well, Antoine was good friends with the "Count", another pirate, who had originally been of high birth but "took to the seas for adventure, and whose heart was dark and murderous as the night". For a while the two were great friends, enjoying their nefarious deeds and studies in the occult. Then one day Antoine accused the Count of going too far, and said he was evil. Later, he informed the coastguard of the Count's intended piracy during the next run. Anyway the coastguard turned the warning lights off in the lighthouse and the Count's ship was wrecked and all his men killed. His ghost is said to haunt the bay as he seeks revenge.'

'How awful!'

'Annie Treeve was a smuggler from the First and Last at Lands End who used to visit the Black Dove to buy and sell contraband, and to see her aristocratic friends, who shared her interest in the occult. Antoine, who gave up his estate in France to pursue a bohemian lifestyle with the beautiful artist Letitia Faulkner, held séances there and they met frequently to practise the occult. Antoine was in love with Letitia, a beautiful and gifted artist, but they were unhappy as she was unable to give him a son, and he became prone to rages and drinking to excess. Anyway she too died under mysterious circumstances and some people have reported seeing Letitia's ghost there too.'

'Wow,' whistled Emma, 'it sounds as though the place is teeming with ghosts! I thought as much, it has a strange vibe. I do sense that something odd has happened there,' she said, wondering if it might have been Letitia's reflection she'd seen in the windowpane. Then she decided she had just seen the visitor's reflection distorted in the glass.

'Thanks, Andy, and I really appreciate it. Please look and see what else you can find.'

'Doesn't it put you off?'

'No, not at all, nearly every house in Cornwall is supposedly haunted by a ghost.'

'Well, good luck and here's to the spirits,' laughed Andrea, and they raised their glasses. 'If you find out it really is haunted, will you still buy it?' inquired Andrea, intrigued.

'Yes, I'll give it a chance, if just the studio is haunted, it won't affect me too much.' She shrugged. 'What harm can a few ghosts actually do?'

'None, I guess.'

Back at the inn, Emma stepped into an alcove. How wonderful it was to have such splendid views of the Atlantic Ocean. Where sharks drifted in and out of the bay. She closed her eyes, lulled by the rhythm of the sea. So! She had walked right into a mystery! How thrilling, but she wasn't sure whether there was a ghost or not, the place was so atmospheric. Andrea's discoveries, rather than deterring her, only spurred her adventurous spirit. Like so many of the old buildings in Cornwall, it had a ghostly history. Emma's spine tingled with a mixture of fear and excitement as she watched the curtains move. What was that? She held her breath as a cat jumped onto the floor. Laughing, she opened the window and let it out. She would just have to stop thinking so much about ghosts!

Grabbing her surfboard, Emma ran down the path, leapt over

the rocks, and headed for the beach. It was a warm bright day, the sea lapped gently on the shore. A few choppy waves crashed in the sea and Emma rushed in. She soared, exhilarated at the rush of being carried on the surfboard and propelled fast on the wave. Surfing lifted her spirits and made her forget her worries. Then, as the sea became calmer, she put her board up against a rock and went for a swim. Carefully, she dived off the rocks into the calm waves, deep down to the bottom of the sea, coming up tangled in seaweed. The sea was quite cold. Afterwards, she walked along the cliff top to dry off. Climbing past the lifeguard's hut, she remembered she had to put in an offer for the property, that day, if she wanted it. She leapt across the dunes, jumping and splashing through the small pools in the rocks, the wind rippling through her hair. She took a pasty from her bag and ate it ravenously. She had made up her mind. The inn, despite its strange history was perfect for her, it was time to start living her dream.

Jeremy

'Okay, I'll take it,' she said, ringing the estate agent, 'subject to the surveyor's report.' She sat back, knowing she had made the right decision. Haunted or not, she had to have it. She wasn't afraid of a ghost! That is, if one actually existed. It had such a wonderful vibe—with its panoramic views over the cove it was the kind of property she had always dreamed of owning. She could not pass up the chance; she would never be offered such a brilliant house again, overlooking her favourite beach. The previous owners had left quickly a year ago, mysteriously. It had been standing empty since then, so the sale would go through without a hitch. A strange noise caught her attention. She turned and saw an tall attractive blonde man standing at the door.

'Hi—sorry to bother you,' he said, startling her. 'I'm looking for Emma.'

'That's me, and you are—?' Emma asked, startled. His hair was bleached almost white by the sun, and windswept, his face was bronzed and attractive. He wore a miniature silver surfboard around his neck. She stared at him. He stood in the doorway, leaning on the post, tall and athletic, covered in a deep tan.

'Jeremy,' he replied, moving into the archway, a smile slowly spreading across his face. She saw the outline of his strong supple thighs rippling through his incredibly tight worn blue jeans; his shirt was undone so that she could see his chest hair, and she fought back a surge of lust. He grinned. His blonde hair hung over his collar. He tucked away his mobile phone. Looking at him closely, she saw it was the championship surfer!

'From the agents…sorry I'm late, there was a lot of traffic. I do apologise,' he said. 'I was called away so suddenly, I couldn't get through to you.'

'That's okay, it's given me some time to look around it myself, and I've just rung your office to put in an offer.'

'That's great. I'm afraid something important cropped up at the last minute. I've just come back from a surfing tournament in Newquay. Please accept this as a peace offering,' he said. Grinning boyishly, he handed her a rose plucked from the garden, a black rose. Emma shot him a wary look, he was devilishly charming, but, boy, what a physique!

'Okay, I forgive you, I suppose that's a good enough excuse,' she laughed.

Jeremy laughed too. 'I surfed through to the finals and we won the tournament.'

'Congratulations, sounds like you had fun,' she said smiling at him.

'Perhaps you would like to join me at the local restaurant tonight, all being well, we can sign the contract and I promise I'll make it up to you. We can celebrate if you like.'

She looked up at him surprised. 'Okay, why not.'

'I'll see you at seven then,' he said grinning, walking backwards into the hall. His blue eyes crinkled with warmth as he talked, his expression was open and friendly. He looked around the room, making some notes.

'Oh, here's the surveyor's report,' he said, 'I nearly forgot.'

She scanned it quickly. There were no major problems. She watched him as he hovered by the door, unable to tear his gaze from the amazing power of her eyes. He turned suddenly, bumping his head on the low beam.

'Are you staying in the cove, by the way?' he asked her.

'Well since it is empty, I would like to stay tonight, to see if it has the right vibes,' she said, opening her eyes innocently. 'Besides it would save me the hotel bill.'

'Well, I won't tell anyone. I should think it would be all right since your offer is bound to be accepted. I'm pretty sure the owners won't mind,' he said. Stepping backwards, he banged his head on the low beam, almost losing his balance.

'Be careful!' She laughed, throwing back her hair, enjoying the effect she was having on him. 'The ceilings are low—we're in the land of the pixies and elves!'

Dreams

Later, in the restaurant, Jeremy was the perfect host, obviously growing to like her more by the minute. He found her inspiring. He had met many women on the beach, but she was special. Maybe she was a dancer, he mused, absorbed by her healthy spring-like steps. She sat down, crossing her legs. Her misty blue eyes stared directly into his. They reflected an air of mystery. Perhaps he could get to know her better. Her long blonde hair rippled down to her waist in waves, she looked just like a goddess. She jolted upright like a pert schoolteacher, took the pen out of her mouth and scribbled something on a pad.

'Shall we eat first?' Jeremy said, and handed Emma the menu. 'Is seafood okay?'

'Sounds fine to me.'

'Look how amazing it is out there tonight,' said Jeremy, pointing at the sparkling array of lights shimmering in the harbour. 'Look at that, a perfect sunset!' A pink orange sunset blazed in the sky, and the lights of the boats twinkled brightly, making it look like a fairyland.

'Yes, it's incredible,' Emma nodded, absorbed by the scene.

Jeremy watched as Emma curled the tip of her tongue over the curve of her melon and took a delicate small bite.

'Well, here's to the new owner of the Black Dove Inn,' he said, raising his glass. 'Would you like to sign the papers now?'

'Then it's mine?' asked Emma, dreamily pushing the empty plate away.

'Then it's yours. Completion should take a few weeks.'

Jeremy quickly signed all the papers, and handed them over to her.

Emma sat hypnotised by the sound of the waves, overjoyed that, at last, her dream had come true. She put all thoughts of ghosts and hauntings out of her mind. What did she care? Nearly every property here had a mysterious past. She just had to view it with common sense, not from the tides of her imagination. It is so magical here, she thought, slowly sipping her wine. What was it about the place that made her feel so dreamy and romantic?

'Emma,' Jeremy waved a form at her, 'as much as I hate to interrupt your daydream, we must get down to business.'

Emma blinked, giving him all her attention. She stared into his eyes; they were bright blue, his face was tanned and his hair was bleached white from the sun. He was attractive, athletic and with a powerful body, just what she needed.

'I'll just get my pen and sign it,' she murmured. 'Does this include the four-poster bed?'

'Yes, all of the contents,' he said, handing her details of the inn. 'The previous owners left suddenly.'

'Oh, why?' Emma asked, growing slightly suspicious, wondering if she should mention her strange experience there.

'Because they were called back to a job up—' he said, coughing awkwardly. 'In Yorkshire I think.'

Taking the pen, she signed the contract.

'Right,' he said, shuffling some forms, 'that's it, it's yours bar a few legalities and some money. You can move in straightaway if you like. I won't tell anyone.'

She dipped a prawn into the sauce and put it in her mouth. 'Yes,' she said grinning, 'I think I might stay there tonight.'

'I thought you might.' He grinned cheekily, raising an eyebrow. 'People have squatted there in the past, so it is good to have it occupied. I do think you'll like living here. It's just right for you, overlooking the beach and quite a bit cheaper than any of the other properties in the Cove,' he added.

'I know, it's an absolute dream. Is there anything wrong with it?'

'No, not as far as I know the reports all say it is sound. Here's something that you might find interesting,' he said quickly, handing her a guidebook. 'Am I right, you worked for an advertising agency?'

She nodded. 'Did, on the advertising copywriting side. I happened to come up with a popular idea and it took off.'

'Are you well known?'

'I suppose so, in certain circles. I don't think many people know who I really am. Just my advert.'

'Well you are a creative artist, so you're in good company,' he said, pointing to some pictures in the guidebook. 'Lots of famous writers and artists have lived here, D H Lawrence wrote here, hundreds of famous artists have stayed in the place, Daphne Du Maurier wrote many novels here too. Have you ever been to Jamaica Inn?'

'Yes, on the way down, it was quite eerie.'

'It has an interesting history, and like many of the places in this part of the world it is haunted and was a haven for smugglers. Apart from its reputation for smuggling and pirates, the place has attracted some of the best artists in the country. You should feel very inspired— you might want to visit the Tate at St Ives, the Eden project or the artists' shops and colonies, or the places of natural beauty like Kynance, Chapel Porth and Lamorna. You'll find a lot to do. I think you'll find it a very interesting and stimulating area. There's a lot to interest you. It's a unique place, many artists, musicians, poets, writers and visionaries have lived here and it's full of mythological heritage—and many legends. In the nineteenth century it became a meeting place for artists, especially St Ives, a bit like artist gatherings in France. It seems to grab hold of people; some become totally obsessed by the place.' He handed her a leaflet of the area and she read:

> 'In this day and age where the mystical is seen as dead, the cove serves to re-enchant the world and those who visit it, to re-awaken and enliven the spirit, to caress the soul with its mystery—it is for romantics and the young at heart and those who wish to be inspired. Some of the buildings here are even said to be haunted.'

'Yes,' she said, 'I am definitely a romantic, and it is the most inspiring place I have ever visited. I am so lucky.'

'You are, especially to have bought the inn for such a good price, property is rising fast and people are moving here in hordes.'

'Tell me more about the inn,' asked Emma, picking at some fruit, growing excited. 'What is its history? I'd like to know more about it. It has a fascinating atmosphere.'

'Well, there is a bit of a story,' he confessed, running his hands through his hair. 'But I am not sure of all of the details,' he said, evasively.

'Tell me what you know,' she insisted. 'I have heard all about Annie.'

'Annie Treeve, as you know, was a smuggler in the cove. She lived at the Land's End Inn and her two pirate friends, the notorious Jack brothers, owned the Black Dove. At the time, the cove was used as a haven for smuggling contraband. It was quite a notorious place with a dark history. One day, Annie turned Queen's evidence and betrayed Dionysus Williams, who owned the First and Last; he was caught smuggling contraband at Lands End; later, she was drowned on the beach. Well the new smuggling operation was taken over by the owners of the Black Dove. Pirates used the tunnels below the inn to smuggle gold from the cove at the dead of night. It would land by ship on the shore, be taken to the inn via the mazes of passages running underneath. Later, they rented it to an aristocrat with dark tastes, a man called Antoine, and his friend known as the "Count" a practitioner of the dark arts. He named it "Black Dove" because a dove often used to appear while the pirates were landing, as a good luck symbol, to lead the men safely to the shore. Antoine, the Frenchman bought the inn; he was a bit of an artist, philosopher and romantic who loved to paint the wildlife, but had a bit of a dark side. He loved danger and the wild seas. Some pretty lawless characters used to hang out there.'

Emma's face lit up with interest. 'Yes, I have heard so much about it. Tell me the details. Go on.'

'The inn grew even more dangerous, pirates competing for a venue where contraband could be landed; the pirates would wink at the barman as the money was exchanged for goods. Soon it became one of the most important smuggling places in the west. The pirates chose the inn as it was an ideal hiding place, it has a sheer drop running alongside it that stopped anyone chasing after them. They would just fall and smash on the black rocks below.'

Emma's remembered her visit to the inn, and how the edge had nearly crumbled under her, and nodded. So it did have a dark secret! The place was brimming with pirate ghosts and nefarious tales of a deadly past.

'Yes, tell me more.'

'It was the perfect hideout, with secret tunnels running straight onto the beach. The pirates could just land and take their gains to the inn undercover. For years they evaded capture, but the locals complained, and wanted the pirates brought to justice. One night, as a heavy load was due, after his argument with the Count, Antoine tipped the coastguard off about a pirate raid. He switched off the warning light in the lighthouse and the brothers' ship was washed onto the rocks and wrecked. All the crew were drowned. Aboard the ship had been the evil man, the Count, reputed to indulge in dark practices, the myth goes he put a curse on the cove and he still haunts the bay. Antoine would sometimes flash the lights to let the pirates sail in safely, this time he let the Count sink.'

'How interesting. What a lurid past it has! I can almost feel its dark mystery seeping through the walls!' exclaimed Emma, listening intently. 'Does the inn have a ghost? I think I might have seen one.'

'Of course there isn't a ghost,' Jeremy snapped irritably, waving his hands in the air. 'Ghosts don't exist, at least as far as I know. All the buildings here have a dark history. This area is the most haunted in England, or so they say. I think it is just to attract the tourists. A few people say they have felt Annie's presence at the First and Last Inn, and others report a few sightings at the Black Dove. But I think it is all just a myth that has been passed down by the artists who have stayed there, to add mystery and intrigue to the place.'

Emma nodded, intrigued by the local history.

'Each place has a tale or myth to tell. It does have quite a friendly aura, although there have been some sightings reported in the bay. Last summer some tourists reported a strange figure roaming along the road at night. A few years ago a coastguard saw the old pirate ship sailing into the bay and then drowned at sea, others have seen strange figures wandering along the road outside. But it's all just folklore and legend, it has been empty for a year so I suppose it has fired up people's imaginations. My guess is it's just the local children dressing up and playing ghosts there. Is that what you saw? Some kids messing around?'

'No, I have a feeling it was something more than that,' said Emma, shaking her head, deciding not to mention the 'ghost'.

'Probably just someone trying to frighten you,' Jeremy insisted, sensing her worry, trying to reassure her.

Emma blinked, unsure what to believe. 'What? Like an eccentric neighbour poking around?'

'Possibly, but listen, there is more to the story,' he admitted. 'The brothers' ship was wrecked, torn in half, their bodies washed up on the shore. The Count, who died with them, is said to sail a ghostly spectral ship into the bay on stormy nights, and disaster is said to strike those who see it. They call it the "Count's revenge". He returns to take revenge for each one of his men killed. His "ghost" has sworn vengeance on those who have betrayed him.'

'I think I have seen it,' said Emma, sitting up sharply and paying attention.

'Don't be ridiculous, it's just your over-fertile imagination,' he scoffed. 'Of course you can't have seen it, it's just a myth.'

Emma shot him a dubious look. 'But there is always an element of truth in myths,' she insisted. She was about to say more, but stopped, Jeremy was unsympathetic, and his arrogance annoyed her. But she shrugged it aside; she was tired and keen to move on with the sale. So the inn *did* have a dark history, and, what's more, it fascinated her. She had always loved to listen to stories about ghosts and spirits and always wanted to visit a haunted house. Now she actually owned one. She just had to know all its dastardly details.

'I am sure that there is a ghost haunting the inn,' she said.

'And I assure you there is not,' said Jeremy, looking at her in surprise, waving his hands dismissively. 'Don't take it too seriously. I'm shocked that an intelligent woman like you could believe in such drivel. Do you think I would be trying to sell you the property if it was haunted? Surely you don't believe in ghosts and all that mythical nonsense?' he asked, pulling a face.

'I do actually, I believe there is an afterlife, a spirit world,' she insisted. 'But even if there was a ghost, it would not put me off buying it, so don't worry about your commission. Nothing will put me off living my dream, and if there is a ghost, then it's all the better, as it will make life so much more interesting,' she said scathingly, smiling sweetly at him, and wiping her lips with a serviette.

'The wind does shake the building as it is so high on the hill,' he admitted, 'but I've always found it has a very good vibe.'

'Don't worry, I won't back out, I have made up my mind that it is my dream home. Where else would I get something so cheap with such incredible views and bordering one of the best beaches in England?'

'I agree, you'd find it hard. I'm sure you will be happy there,' he said, admiring her determination. 'You are the right sort of person for the place, you seem to have a natural affinity with it already. I had hoped an artist or writer might buy it, who would appreciate its aesthetic qualities. Don't worry, if you need anything at all, I will come and sort it out. It's quite safe there. I almost bought it myself, but…' he stopped and said slowly, '…I have too many other things in the pipeline at the moment.'

He shifted in his seat uncomfortably, and poured her another glass of wine. He smiled nervously, wondering if he had said too much, then relaxed and started laughing.

'They are great storytellers here, especially after a few pints.'

Emma stared at Jeremy frostily. 'There is a strange story surrounding the cove though,' she insisted, the tension rising in her. 'I have seen a shadowy figure on the beach. Could it be a ghost?'

He smiled at her affectionately. 'I doubt it very much, it's probably just the priest who wanders over the beach at night, he wears a long black cloak and looks a bit eerie. But yes, there once was a serious conflict between pirates on Sennen Beach, and it became quite notorious for a while.'

She laughed, relieved. 'Oh gosh, yes, of course, that must be who it is. My imagination is in overdrive.'

They both laughed.

'Let's not talk about it any more,' he said, raising his glass. 'Shall we just relax and enjoy the wine? Why don't I order another bottle? And you can tell me about yourself.'

'Okay, if you're paying?'

'Of course.'

He called the waiter over; swiftly he uncorked a bottle of Champagne.

She told him about Toby, the job and her career and life move.

'Sounds like you had a bad time,' he said. 'I hope you will find the happiness you are seeking here.'

'I am sure I will, it's everything I ever dreamed,' she admitted, swirling the wine thoughtfully around her glass, 'and I have a lot of ideas, the inn has enormous potential.'

'Well, here's to your new home and its resident ghosts,' he laughed, pouring her another glass. 'Perhaps you will join me for lunch some time?' suggested Jeremy. 'Then perhaps we could go surfing? Say in two weeks, when I return from London?'

'Yes, okay, I'd like that. How did you know I like to surf?' asked Emma, surprised.

'Because I have seen you most mornings.'

'Oh where? At Sennen?'

'Yes, I am a lifeguard at the cove,' he admitted. 'I usually work there at weekends.'

'Ah, that's where I saw you.'

She laughed and made a mental note to go to the library, do some research, and write a story to send back to the agency. Graham had rung and asked her to do some freelance work, and she had jumped at the chance, glad to be able to generate some extra cash. They liked her quirky ideas and she could even add to their database of artists in the UK. She would search the internet for more details about the inn. Its dark history fascinated her. She'd meet up with Andrea later, to see what else she had found.

Emma played idly with her napkin. 'The more of these stories I hear, the more intrigued I've become,' she said, her passion in the subject growing. 'I can write about it, and send the story to my agency. They publish a travel book each year and compile a big dictionary of artists, so it will give me an interesting hobby while I am here.'

'Good idea. But don't you have enough to do already?'

'No, I need an intellectual interest too.'

'Have you ever been to the Minack Theatre at Porthcurno?'

'No, I'd love to go, I've heard it is very romantic! The rock theatre was designed by Rowena Cade.' She spoke dreamily. 'How lovely to have one's own theatre.'

'It is. Quite an incredible place, a theatre carved in the rocks. I'd like to take you there one evening if you are free. *King Lear* is on next month.'

'I'd like that.'

'See that light over there, that's the lighthouse where the sailors were wrecked.'

Emma turned her chair round to look at the lighthouse twinkling in the distance. Like the Knight's sword at Lands End, the lighthouse was next to a stone that protruded from the sea, a veritable Excalibur's sword rising from a stone shaped like a knight. Emma felt gripped by the Celtic atmosphere. She stared outside, some cars were leaving, their lights blazing across the rocks.

'It has turned very cold,' she said shivering, pulling her jacket over her shoulders.

'Yes, the days are sweltering here, but we have cold, windy nights. When the wind blows across the bay, it does sound quite eerie, especially to those who are not used to…'

A mysterious expression covered his face, he stopped and poured her another coffee.

'…The Cornish weather,' he added, quickly putting the signed contract into his briefcase. 'We'll go over any details when I get back and I officially get to take you out.'

'Okay' she said shooting him a look that told him, if he did, it would be on her terms.

'I'll meet you at the lifeguard's hut, then, at two, two weeks on Saturday,' he said, his eyes narrowing against some headlights flooding the car park.

He stared at her strangely, there was something unfathomable about his gaze, thought Emma. Was he hiding something?

Outside, the brightness of the moon shone on the rocks making the night seem sinister. Dark, spindly shadows danced across the sandy path. Bats circled overhead. Strange noises echoed in the night air. Jeremy looked at Emma, suddenly serious, his eyes lit with a flicker of concern.

'Shall I drive you home?—these winding lanes can be quite dangerous in the dark.'

'No, I'll be fine,' insisted Emma.

Emma turned on the ignition and sped back quickly through the dark narrow lanes to the inn. She could see a light on in the distance. That was strange, she didn't think she had left a light on.

Suddenly she looked up and saw a man's face appear in the car mirror. A gypsy face! The chilling eyes stared right through her with an icy glare. She swerved to the other side of the road, narrowly missing the car ahead. She gripped the steering wheel, fighting to bring the car back under control.

'What was that?' she cried, pulling over into a farm gateway to catch her breath.

Who was trying to frighten her, and why?

The Haunting

Two weeks later the contracts were signed and sealed. The sale had been quick. Taking what few belongings she had, Emma moved in. Ghost or no ghost, the inn was hers now. Emma gazed out of the window dreamily, feeling like she was walking on air. Her wonderful dream had come true. She sat watching from her bed, gazing at the clouds gathering on the horizon, swirling into patterns like faces. She sighed with satisfaction, then crawled back under the duvet, and nestled into the pillow, reluctant to leave her warm, snug bed. She felt elated and excited, her dream had come true, life was so exquisitely wonderful, perfect. She listened to the haunting ethereal tones of Kate Bush sing on the stereo—'the wind is whistling' and 'the waves are coming in'—the music fitted in so well with her new location, her home. She lay back letting the beautiful instruments lift and inspire her. The contract lay signed beside her in the drawer; she had put it in a folder, brimming with a sense of satisfaction at having so successfully completed her affairs on her own. She was flooded with happiness. She had made the first step towards being independent and free. Melanie phoned and could not stop praising her, telling her how capable she was, and how marvellous that she was succeeding so well, without a man. Emma knew she did not need a man, or anyone else to help her achieve her dreams, she could do it all by herself.

Since meeting Jeremy, though, she had to admit she had made a nice friend, and was glad of his companionship. She thought of Jeremy's blue eyes and strong warm face, stirring her into a thrill of delight. She smiled at the thought of meeting him at the weekend. The memory of him had eclipsed the brooding artist, he had almost faded from her mind; as he was with someone, it wasn't a road she wanted to travel.

Later, she climbed up into the attic and started clearing the rubbish left behind by the previous owners. As she scrambled amongst the debris, she found a painting. She picked it up and wiped off the dust. The picture was of a man, very dark and swarthy, good-looking, with a scar on his right cheek. A gypsy aristocrat, and he looked just like the artist she'd met at the café. His eyes shone brightly in the painting. She stood the painting up, and eyed it critically. Yes, there were definitely similarities to him; they had the same eyes, he too was windswept, and wild-looking. Perhaps he was his ancestor; she felt a shiver of desire, but pushed it from her mind. He had a slightly austere, aristocratic air, with a wild untamed streak, his hair was long and black, his eyes full of dark promise, his body sensual, his eyes glistened dangerously, like a gypsy—a man concealing a dark past, who would take you to a magical world, to the heights of passion, then hell and back. As she put the painting down, his eyes seemed to follow her across the room.

She felt a sudden wave of interest, he certainly was nice! She would place the painting in the hallway. He made her feel strangely excited, stirring in her a deep, dark desire, and a feeling she could not quite define. The idea of sailing the seas with such a wild-hearted man made her draw in her breath, to be his lover—it was far too rousing a notion to entertain. Then, she remembered she had arranged to meet Andrea for lunch, and quickly drove over to St Ives.

It was a beautiful morning as she drove along the empty coastal road, empty of traffic for once. At the height of summer it was often difficult to find a road that wasn't jammed with tourists; today she glided through as though heading for a greater destiny. She parked the car outside the pub. As she walked through the door, Andrea rushed over and hugged her.

'I'm so glad you could come, this is Ramone,' she said, introducing him. Standing in front of her was a blonde man, towering over her by nearly a foot, with the palest blue eyes she had ever seen. He took her hand in his; she shook it thinking how strong his grip was. He swished his blonde hair back over his shoulder and lit a French cigarette.

'Hi Emma, at last I meet the gorgeous Emma!' he said in a thick French accent, blowing out a puff of smoke. Emma stepped back, trying not to cough, noticing his beautiful hair. He looked like he was straight out of a shampoo ad, perfect shiny blonde hair swishing round his shoulders, streaky blonde from the sun, flowing over his deeply tanned body. His face looked fragile, ethereal, with the most feminine gaze, but on a strong chest and a surfer's body. He stood with one of his muscular legs wrapped around Andrea, who was bursting out of her low cut t-shirt dress. She rested her hands into the top of his jeans and fiddled with his hair. Clearly they couldn't keep their hands off each other.

'Ah Emma. So pleased to meet you, I hear you have just moved into the cove? Are you happy there?'

'Yes, it's my dream, what I have always wanted.'

'What would you like?' he asked, heading for the bar.

'To your new home,' Andrea said excitedly, raising her glass of tequila. 'What's it like?'

'Perfect, I think I have found the ideal place to settle in. But there is a small problem; I saw a strange shape drift up the stairs, at first I thought it was just dust swirling, but when I looked closer, it seemed to have a face. I think I might have seen a ghost.'

'Oh,' said Ramone, handing her a glass of wine. 'Perhaps zee headless horseman rides there or the pirates rise from the deep.'

They laughed.

'Oh come on, Emma! Surely you don't believe in ghosts!' he snorted.

'I did tell you,' said Andrea, 'it was probably the light; dust does swirl into funny shapes at times, and I thought you discovered the mystery, that it was the lady surfer who takes a short cut past the studio every day? Though I do believe in ghosts,' she admitted. 'Of course there must be other spiritual energies, death isn't necessarily the end.'

'But I might have had other sightings too. While I was at the studio, I was sure I saw a woman's face appear in the glass.'

'What did the estate agent say?'

Emma recalled the story of the inn. 'Well, he thinks it was the reflections from outside and some children playing, but I feel there must be another explanation.'

'I doubt whether it was a real ghost,' said Ramone.

'Yes, I suppose it's unlikely. Who cares, today I want to have fun! I am so happy to have found the house of my dreams,' said Emma brightly, in a jolly mood, draining her glass. 'I think I'll have another, I want to celebrate.'

Ramone took her glass and queued at the bar.

'What else have you found out?' she asked Andrea, burning with curiosity.

'Just that the eccentric aristocrat, Antoine, who had a bit of a penchant for women, used to live there,' said Andrea. 'He was a wild-hearted, dilettante artist, poet and seducer of women. He had an interest in the occult and held séances there, so it could be that a part of him remains, or at least the energy he evoked.'

'Hmm,' said Emma, stroking her hair. 'I discovered a painting of him in the attic.'

'Yes, he did have a powerful presence. I also found out that he was a friend of the famous Count, the one who was drowned in the shipwreck, but that they had an argument before the Count was killed. They shared an interest in the occult, and often experimented there. I am not putting you off, am I?'

'No, not at all. Sounds interesting. Jeremy has already filled me in on some of the details.'

'One thing that is a bit of a mystery, is that Letitia the artist, with whom Antoine was reputedly madly in love, came to a mysterious end. I get a feeling she was murdered.'

'Oh?'

'I am not exactly sure what happened, it just says she was found dead in mysterious circumstances. There is some dark mystery about the place, I am sure.'

Emma clasped her hand to her mouth in surprise. 'Yes that's exactly how I feel.'

'Annie Treeve, the smuggler, used to frighten people away with stories of witchcraft and threatened to put evil spells on anyone who tried to go to the inn, she let everyone think the inn was haunted so that they could continue their smuggling operation undisturbed. She scared everyone away from finding the true purpose of the activities at the inn, that it was used for contraband. Some say if a person grew suspicious, she would flirt with the man, get him drunk and push him straight over the cliffs onto the rocks below, never to be seen again. She would sing to them, and they would blindly follow her. Just like a siren. The pirates paid her to frighten away any intruders who might discover where they were hiding the gold—by making the people think a strange woman roamed there, it kept everyone away. For a while it worked well, then it seems, people told tales on each other.'

'Thanks, I'll have to read more about it.'

'What else do you think you saw?' asked Andrea.

'Just the woman's face a few times, and I have heard the odd strange sounds. Maybe it's just the wind, it does sound scary when the wind howls through the building, but it's a very happy place and does have a very spiritual vibe.'

'Yes,' agreed Andrea. 'There are some strange mystical energies there, it is probably not a ghost, just residue from past vibrations, it's quite a spiritual place.'

'You don't really believe in all that?' asked Emma scornfully. 'Isn't it just superstition?'

'Of course I do, there is much of value hidden from our normal conscious thoughts, the occult, phenomena other than the rational. You just have to open your mind to receive it,' said Andrea seriously.

'So it could have been a ghost I saw?'

'Maybe, but it is unlikely. More likely to be old energies hanging around, don't worry, once you are there for a while, your own energy will bring it back to life, all the old vibes will fade away.'

'I hope so,' said Emma, sipping her drink thoughtfully.

'Come on, girls,' said Ramone, returning with the drinks. 'It's summer, time for fun, let's talk about the beach, the sun, making love, the surf, not so heavy, please.'

At that moment, the wind blew the door open and a man walked in; he looked around him, then strode over to join a woman sitting in the corner. Emma's heart skipped a beat, and she felt her pulse quicken as she recognised him, it was the man from the beach café. The beautiful artist, Anton. She drew in her breath quickly and her heart lurched into her mouth. She noticed he was even more good-looking than when she had first seen him, dressed in black jeans and white shirt. His long, dark hair framed his face, making him look deep and brooding, his tallness made him look elegant as he strode across the room. He seemed so powerful, like a god. Never had she seen anyone look so gorgeous, his eyes were large and blue, yet his face finely, perfectly chiselled, like a sensitive poet, a Renaissance man. He stood elegantly at the bar, his gaze glimmering intensely like the man in the painting, his eyes flickering with the same wild intensity.

She felt a sudden flash of desire and a strange intuitive feeling that one day they would be more than friends. Their eyes met, she jumped. He smiled.

'Look over there, he's a friend of Ramone's,' Andrea whispered, watching Emma closely. 'Shall I introduce you to him?'

'No, he's gorgeous, but I think he's with someone.'

'Quick, he's coming over.'

'Hello,' said Anton softly.

Emma nearly dropped her glass and gave him her most bewitching smile. Why did he have such an alarming effect on her? Their eyes locked and a spark of attraction flowed between them.

'It's nice to see you, Emma,' he said, his eyes sparkling with a potent force.

'Hi,' she murmured, stuck like a rabbit in the headlights, unable to draw herself away from his gaze. Awkwardly she put down her glass.

'You didn't come to the group, perhaps you will turn up some time? I hope you haven't forgotten my offer, to sit for us, you would make a wonderful muse.'

'Yes, yes of course. I am so sorry,' she stammered, caught in his glare. 'I'm really busy at the moment. I have just moved house. I promise I will come soon,' she said, wondering if he really liked her.

'Well just in case you have forgotten, here is my number again,' he said, giving her a friendly smile. 'I thought you might have lost it.'

'I think I might have done,' she admitted, blushing furiously.

His soft blue eyes crinkled at the sides as he spoke.

'Don't worry, we have only just started, and it's a class for beginners. You'll feel quite confident there, there's no pressure.'

She sat staring up at him, quite breathless, lost for words, hoping he didn't notice that she was starting to breathe quickly. At that moment a woman walked over to them; she tossed back her hair and shot Emma a withering glance, her eyes glinting dangerously. She stood next to Anton, sulking, clinging onto his arm possessively. Emma looked up at her and smiled. The woman grimaced and flashed her eyes vengefully at Emma. Then she stamped her foot in annoyance, as though she was going to throw a tantrum, and threw her black crinkly hair over her shoulder in an manner of defiance.

Seething with jealousy, she dug her fingers sharply into his arm: 'Are we going?'

He turned to Emma and gave her a disarming smile.

'Ouch, sorry, but I have to go,' he said. 'Duty calls.'

'Goodbye then.'

'Not goodbye, au revoir. I hope we meet again soon,' he said ignoring the woman shifting restlessly at his side. She began fidgeting, and was looking even more murderous. She dug her long, black nails so hard into his arm that he pulled away, then she shot Emma a look of pure malice.

'Anton, we are late,' she snapped irritably, 'or have you forgotten, that we are supposed to be meeting friends?'

'I do apologise, I must go,' he said, turning quickly to Emma. 'I have a meeting that had slipped my mind.' He pulled his arm away from the woman, then turned and walked away.

The dark-haired woman was left standing there, and, biting her lip, she slammed down her glass and stormed after him.

Strange, thought Emma dryly, some people were just made for each other. For a second she felt a strong bond with him, as though he was already her soul mate—wasn't it a pity he was with that annoying woman? Was she his girlfriend? There was something strange and unsettling about her.

'Do you plan to settle in Cornwall for good?' asked Andrea, interrupting her reverie. Emma turned round, her body still tingling with excitement. She felt a surge of desire, a soaring spirit, she could hardly focus on anything, her thoughts were so totally dominated by Anton.

'Pardon?'

'Emma, come back to earth, you are in such a dream today, I just wanted to know if you are planning to stay in Cornwall or rent out the inn for part of the year.'

'Oh yes,' she replied slightly distracted. 'I want to stay for the rest of my life if I can, it's the most beautiful place on earth, where I have always dreamt of living.'

'I know the feeling, I love it here too,' admitted Andrea.

Emma felt a guilty pang as she remembered Jeremy. He was such a nice guy, body toned like a god, a face to turn the heads of most women. But there was something strangely compelling about the dark-haired man; he evoked in her a powerful feeling she had never known before, as if he was *the one*. She had never seen such a good-looking man, exactly the type of man she had always fantasised about but didn't actually think existed. Now she had met her perfect man—the man she had been waiting for, she could see it in his eyes. She'd felt a magic spark between them, each time she had seen him, as though he charged her with a strong chemistry. There was a strong connection between him and the inn in some mysterious way, she could sense it. He looked just the man in the painting. Still, maybe he just had to remain her fantasy, for the dark-haired woman would not give him up easily.

'How about you? Are you going to stay in Cornwall?' she asked Andrea.

'We're going to France tomorrow, for a whole month.'

'Brilliant. I've got some good news too, I've just met a nice man.'

'Who?'

'An estate agent from Mousehole.'

'Oh God! How dull!' Andrea smirked disapprovingly.

'I think you need some more wine, no, something stronger, roll a joint, baby,' Andrea ordered Ramone.

'No, seriously, he's fun, and a champion surfer. I really enjoy his company.'

'Then why do you go all gauche, like a lovesick teenager when Anton speaks to you?'

'Who?' said Emma, innocently.

Ramone produced a joint and took a long drag. He passed it to Emma.

'No thanks, I'm fine.'

'Anton—you seem smitten with him! You prefer the estate agent! How dull can you get.'

'He's a surfer too,' protested Emma.

'That's okay then,' said Ramone. 'He sounds fine.'

'He's just doing a temp job,' said Emma, 'and he's quite dishy—with a body like Adonis, the most amazing legs and the sexiest blue eyes you've ever seen. A champion surfer.'

'But is he creative enough for you?' asked Andrea, looking serious. 'You need a sensitive, artistic type of man, Emma. Does he understand your spiritual needs?'

'We have a good enough time. Oh come on, I just want to enjoy life for a while, nothing serious, I want to be with someone who is fun and kind. He's a nice guy,' said Emma in Jeremy's defence. 'I just want someone to go to the beach with, and explore the countryside.'

'Then why does that man seem to have such a strange effect on you?' asked Andrea, mystified, pointing at Anton who was still arguing with the woman outside. 'I've never seen such a powerful connection.'

'What do you mean?'

'Well it's obvious he likes you—' She pointed: 'The sex god with the incredible eyes. When he walked over you practically jumped off the seat. You've acted like a gauche teenager both times you've seen him. He's more your type, a brooding poet artist.'

'And a lot of trouble, besides I hardly know him. I only met him at the beach once a few weeks ago,' said Emma. 'Anyway, he's not free.'

Her eyes followed the man as he walked away; slowly he turned the corner, and was gone.

'I need someone a little more predictable,' she said. 'I've had enough shocks and excitement to last a lifetime.'

'It's so obvious he's interested in you. I saw the way you looked at each other, there's a real chemistry, you are destined to be lovers one day, even if it's only a brief fling.'

Emma laughed and put down her glass, almost choking.

'Don't be so ridiculous, your imagination is in overdrive. I already have someone. Anyway, he's with someone already.'

Andrea smiled: 'I sense though, not for much longer. He's like a dog straining at the leash, he can't get away from her quickly enough, and she's just hanging on. That's not a problem. I feel if you like him, he will be there for you.'

'Well it's none of my business,' said Emma. 'I just want to join his art class, and I do like Jeremy. He's such a good sport.'

'No, it's not just my imagination, I have a strong psychic feeling about him, one day you will be lovers, I can tell.' She took some cards out of a silk scarf from her bag and shuffled them.

'Okay, let's see what the cards say, see if I am right.'

She spread the tarot cards out in a Celtic cross formation on the table.

'Uh huh, yes, there it is, it says so here, you are destined to meet a man dark in both looks and nature, a creative man, a scholar. I told you.'

'It's wrong!' insisted Emma. 'You can't believe what a few cards tell you. Jeremy is perfect, sexy strong and virile and just my type. I think you are just trying to make things go the way you want to.'

'We shall see,' said Andrea, drawing a scarf over her face like a gypsy.

'The cards never lie. And he's more your type, creative, free, I can just feel the chemistry sizzling between you when he is around, you are meant to be together, he will help you in your work and forge your success. One day it will happen, I promise you. You cannot fight your destiny.'

Ramone and Emma started laughing. Gently he eased between them, poured out three glasses of wine, handed them round, then kissed Andrea's neck and scowled:

'I can't believe you are still discussing ghosts, the paranormal,' he said dismissively. 'At this time of year when the sun is hot, we should talk about the surf, the sea and love,' he said, his French accent thickening 'Let's talk about romance. Let me show you real magic,' he whispered.

'No, we are fortune telling,' snapped Andrea, 'so please don't disturb us.'

'Come to me and sit on my lap, my beautiful fortune teller,' he said, 'I want to kiss you.'

Andrea raised her eyes to the ceiling, then fell back gracefully into his arms, as Ramone buried his face in her chest. Emma sipped her drink thoughtfully, and watched the dark man usher the arguing woman into a car outside.

Who was he really, she wondered? She glanced at his card: it read 'Art-waves Group'—Anton, with his number.

She turned it over, there was a small image of one of his landscapes—he was clearly an unusually good artist with a clear perception, and a photographic, unique and precise way of capturing scenery. She hoped she would see him again and secretly wished that they might meet again soon. Was Andrea's intuition right?— That one day they would become more than friends? The idea filled her with a strange sensation, like having butterflies in her stomach. She felt a tinge of excitement, like she was falling in love. No one had ever sparked off that feeling of yearning and excitement in her before. Her life would not be complete until she had caught him, that is, if he ever became free, and Andrea was quite convinced he soon would be. She sighed, she couldn't stop thinking about Anton, he was becoming quite an obsession.

Shadows

Back at the Black Dove, the builders had finished decorating the lounge, and turned it into an inviting art gallery chill-out area. Emma sighed, satisfied; they had done a good job and turned it into her dream. It had a gentle air with arches and small pebbled streams, large gothic windows and a small conservatory where she could spend the evenings watching the sea. It was perfect. Beautiful romantic paintings and prints lined the gallery area leading to an extension that included some of the original features of the bar, the old antique mirror, fitting the new theme—of romantic elegance. A *trompe d'oeil* mural of angels and nymphs delicately shimmered on one wall, with white squashy sofas, huge delicate plants, and gothic stained glass windows adding a magical air. The bathroom was painted in soft pastel shades, with water nymphs rising from the sea. Emma climbed into the conservatory, tripping over some priceless items of furniture left there that she planned to add to the bar. She spotted an old mirror with the most beautiful carvings at the edge, hidden among the furniture. She hung it in the lounge, thinking it fitted the 'romantic' theme of the room perfectly. She scratched the dirt with her fingernail to reveal a beautiful carved border of delicate flowers and foliage, and swirling goddesses etched in the wood, and, mysteriously, a skull. She studied her reflection for a moment in the mirror. She stroked it, fascinated, when she saw, staring back at her, a dark-haired stranger, his blue eyes gazing hypnotically into hers. His face kept appearing and disappearing in the glass like a mirage. She watched as his face faded, then reappeared, his gaze filling her with excitement and fear. She shivered, watching the strange dark hypnotic eyes follow her every move. Was there someone standing behind her? She turned around, but there was no one there. It looked just like the gypsy aristocrat from the painting! She drew in her breath, watching the mirror—his eyes were still gazing at her. She felt a sliver of fear run over her spine, as she slipped down onto the seat, trying to fight against being drawn under his spell. She could feel him touching her. Gently, he kissed her lips, his gypsy face soft with desire, pressing his lips softly on hers. Then he vanished into thin air.

Who could he be? 'Come back!' she cried. Was she dreaming or had she just seen a ghost? Perhaps she had fallen asleep for a few minutes—she must have had a strange dream. She shook her head in disbelief. She ran into the bedroom searching for him but could not find him. Was it a joke, being played by one of the builders? She went back upstairs and after a few seconds the room turned icy cold. Emma looked around her anxiously, and sat down on the bed; suddenly she was aware of someone bouncing on the bed next to her, the hairs on the back of her neck stood up. The motion stopped, walking out of the mist she saw a dark shadow slither across the wall, then float outside. What the hell was that? She had to get a grip on herself. The inn was stirring her most primitive fears and fantasies. She shivered, despite the fact it was quite a warm day, wondering who on earth her strange visitor was.

Mysteries

Thunder cracked in the heavy grey sky, heavy clouds hovered overhead and rain lashed against the windows like bullets. The sea was choppy and turbulent, turning a slushy grey-green and the sky was dark and stormy. Emma sat inside wrapped in a blanket, sheltering from the wind; it was too wet to go out. The builders had left a note to say they had gone for the day, rained off. The wind howled and whistled around the cove like a banshee. Sand whipped across the beach like a tornado. The waves had come in as far as the beach café. Emma looked out onto the threatening sky, and over the grey unsettled sea. She was mystified and confused. Whose face had she seen? Despite watching the mirror, it hadn't reappeared. Then rational thought took over, it must have been someone walking past outside again, she decided, covering the mirror with a cloth. She went into the kitchen, dug around for a mug, and made a cup of blueberry tea. She took out a pad from her bag, and began sketching the new interior, planning where the furniture would go. In a few strokes she found herself sketching the mystery man's face. Her hands froze. His features were alive, she was sure she saw his eyes move. She dropped the pad—the picture was alive! She stopped, wondering who it was—who was haunting her and why, or was it just the weather making her feel uneasy? There was a strange mystery about the place. Why? Was it just her imagination or was someone playing tricks on her?

She chanted a mantra, feeling calmer. She picked up an art book from the table and flicked through it. There was something strangely familiar about the pictures, as if she had seen them all before. She peered at one of a maiden, with long flowing hair, riding with a knight on horseback, and held it against the wall. Peering closely, the knight reminded her of her mystery visitor, his chiselled gaunt, haunted face and dark penetrating eyes awakening a strange fascination in her. She felt dizzy and euphoric, then it stopped. For some reason she could not get his image out of her mind. She was seeing him everywhere. She held it next to the sketch she had just drawn, and saw the strong likeness. The memories of the man's strange presence lingered around her. She shrugged. What were the secrets of the cove? She wondered, her head thrown back defiantly. She would not let them scare her. She would have to go to the library, find out about the previous owners.

Later, she fell back in the chair, with a glass of wine, and kicked off her shoes.

'Total luxury,' she said out loud, as she began sorting out her papers from her briefcase. She could not let a mere storm scare her away!

What was it Andrea had told her about Cornwall? That it was full of ghosts and ghouls, mischievous Celtic spirits, and she may have actually seen one! The thought filled her with an impetuous curiosity. Sitting there, watching the sunset, a sense of foreboding swept over her. Had she gone quite mad, thinking she had seen a ghost? There must be a logical explanation. Or did it mean that the inn was inhabited by echoes of the past? A reflection from a builder's overall hung outside, flapping in the rain. She laughed; well that explained her moving shape. But what about the mysterious kiss? She looked up and saw something move out of the corner of her eye. Emma watched as a dark, thin shadow darted across the room. She blinked and it had gone. Then she saw shining in the darkness, two beautiful, deep blue, slanted eyes staring at her. She jumped up out of the chair, raced to the kitchen, and gulped down some more wine quickly. She gulped several glasses more and shook herself in disbelief. What on earth was that? There really was a strange presence lurking at the inn! Whatever the mystery, she was determined to find out what it was! Who, or what, was haunting her new home?

Surfing—Jeremy

The next weekend Emma headed for the beach where Jeremy worked as a lifeguard. She caught him riding a wave to the edge of the sand.

'Hi,' he called out to her, as his surfboard shot over the sand. 'Come on in, come for a swim!' He walked over, grabbed the surfboard under his arm, his chest glistening in the sun. His wetsuit hung around his waist; he pulled it off and she saw he wore no underpants underneath. She felt a shiver of lust. 'Okay, just let me get changed,' Emma said, throwing her towel out of the bag.

'How are things? Did you enjoy your first few weeks at the Black Dove?' he asked.

'Yes, it's everything I've ever dreamed of,' said Emma, stripping off to her swimsuit.

'I missed you,' he said, kissing her.

'Do you like the area?'

'Yes, I wake up to an incredible view of the sea every morning, it's absolutely perfect.'

'Glad to have a satisfied customer,' he winked. 'No problems?'

'Well now that you have mentioned it, I think I may have seen a ghost.'

'Oh come on, Emma. I mean real problems. I didn't take you as a woman given to such flights of fantasy. There must be a rational explanation.'

'No, I don't think there is. Are you sure the inn isn't haunted?' she asked.

'Well, not from what I heard from the previous owners, they lived there for a few years quite peacefully and never mentioned anything.'

'I know I did see something.'

'What exactly?'

'It looked like a face, a woman's face, a strange reflection.'

'No, it was probably someone wandering outside,' shrugged Jeremy, then he added scornfully, 'There is no such thing as a ghost. It's probably just kids playing tricks, I told you not to worry.'

'Yes,' she said lightly, deciding not to tell him about the face in the mirror. He brushed the sand off her shoulders, then slipped his arm around her.

'Any more complaints?' he asked jovially, as they waded into the sea, and jumped over the waves.

'One or two,' she joked.

'Here, have a surf,' he urged, offering her a board.

'No, I think I'll just swim for a while,' she said, jumping over a wave.

'All right, I'll race you,' he said, jumping onto the surfboard, and paddling far out to sea. Emma bodysurfed into a wave and followed him, circling him like a dolphin. Jeremy raced past laughing, his strong arms splicing through the waves. She swam faster, keeping up with him. He dived underneath her, grabbed her legs playfully and lifted her above the waves. Then, he threw her into a large breaker just about to roll over them. He jumped back on the surfboard.

She emerged from under the sea, diving up swiftly with the ease of a mermaid, and tipped him off the surfboard, pushing his head under the waves. Then she climbed on herself and caught the tip of the wave. She jumped off and swam along the coastline, the two of them wrestling playfully until he broke free and dived into a huge breaker. Laughing, she swam away, quivering like a mermaid, slithering through the waves.

'You can't catch me,' she teased. Grabbing the surfboard, she paddled off and glided down the next wave perfectly, balancing the wave to the shore.

'You're a good swimmer. I am impressed,' he enthused.

She glided over another wave with ease, riding the surf like she was floating over ice.

He sighed in admiration.

'You can surf well too.'

'It's not just a male sport,' she said sharply.

Bobbing in the waves, they stopped and watched the most incredible sight; two dolphins leapt into the air and dived in a perfect arc, back into the sea.

'Oh what a wonderful thing to see,' gasped Emma in the throes of happiness, having a wonderful time.

Jeremy chased her and pulled her down onto the dunes. She felt her body entangle with his, filling her with warmth as she lay back on the sand feeling his wet, warm embrace. They crawled inside the lifeguard's hut, and he took her in his arms and kissed her urgently. As he lay on top of her, she gasped in anticipation. Feeling the gentle rhythm of his body push against her, she felt his wet body sink into hers, along with a long-passionate kiss.

Emma and Jeremy explored the local beaches and coves, taking photographs, travelling to various museums, art galleries and haunted castles, and looking at paintings from the local galleries. Three weeks went by, and they picnicked at the lifeguards' hut on the beach and slept under the stars, while the builders made their final touches to her home. One balmy night, they drove to the Minack Theatre and sat picnicking amongst the open rocks, listening to the mad rantings of King Lear, insane from betrayal, more sinned against than sinning. His vanity had been his downfall. It struck a chord—like some of the men she had known, she thought fleetingly. She noticed a change in Jeremy's usual carefree mood; he had grown increasingly restless throughout the play.

'Look,' Jeremy said, 'I might have to go back to London. Will you come back with me?'

Emma shook her head, dismayed.

'No, I can't. I have just moved here, and this is my dream and I can't give it up,' she said wistfully, 'and I am not ready to make a commitment or try anything serious yet, I just want to have fun. No promises, no ties.'

'Okay,' he said, disappointment covering his face. 'I thought perhaps we could move in together, go back to London, stay here in the summer and you could always rent out the inn.'

'It's too soon,' said Emma shaking her head. 'I love it here and I want to be free, to find what I really need, develop my own life. I need to find my own way.'

Jeremy's expression became glum; he looked down at the sand, downhearted.

'Well, have it your way,' he sighed wearily, looking resigned.

'Look let's keep it as it is,' Emma pleaded, 'I am having so much fun.'

Three weeks later at the Lobster Pot restaurant, Jeremy sat at their usual table looking despondent.

'Emma, I'm so sorry, I have some bad news,' he said, shaking his head.

'I'm being sent back to London tonight, to be relocated. It's been a great summer but there's no work here for me now. I have to go back. Please, will you come with me?'

'No I am sorry, Jeremy, I can't. Surely you understand?' she asked, taking his hand.

'I am so sorry, I will miss you,' he said, kissing her face tenderly. 'So this is goodbye for a while?'

She nodded, trying to look cheerful.

'Yes, it has to be this way. Just look upon this as a lovely holiday romance,' she joked, already missing him, but she was not prepared to give up her dream.

'I'll phone every week,' he promised. 'You know how things are. I'll make it back whenever I can,' he said, lifting her chin and gently kissing her lips. 'Are you sure you won't come with me? You could work there again.'

'No, I have started my new life here and there's no way I could ever go back,' she insisted.

'Okay, I'll be back soon, I promise,' he said, taking her for a last walk along the harbour. Emma stared at him, tears welling in her eyes—she closed them to stop the tears. Why did she always lose her heart so easily? She was fond of Jeremy, he was great fun, but living her dream was more important than anything else, she mustn't let anyone get in the way.

'I'll write to you every week,' Jeremy promised, jumping into his old battered car. Emma giggled and waved, wondering if he would make it back to London.

The next day Emma drew a caricature of Jeremy as a pirate with a parrot on his shoulder and e-mailed it to him.

'Settling in, it's brilliant here, like being in another world.'

Sennen—new dreams

Emma woke up to a faint scratching at her window. She loved being so close to the sea, waking up every morning to the rays of sunlight shimmering on the clear blue ocean. A twig from the solitary tree outside was tapping against the window. She looked out—a large black ship was sailing by the cove. She watched it drift past. Seagulls were circling the ship's mast, flying toward the dusky sky burning pink and orange. Strange, it must be a tanker from abroad. She noticed that it was pulling down its mast. How had it got there? Her thoughts were suddenly interrupted by the shrill ring of the phone. It was Jeremy calling. She listened reluctantly in a half trance while Jeremy apologised, he could not make it back for a while.

'Emma, I am so sorry, I can't come back for a while. Something has come up, I do miss you, but right now I just can't make any promises at the moment.'

'Yes, I understand,' she said, realising things had come to an end.

'Unless you want to come here? The offer's still on?'

'No, I am certain, I have to stay.'

'There is something I have to tell you, I have a son and while I was away he was quite ill. He needs me around for a while. I really care for you a lot but I have to stay in London. Can we just be friends for a while? See how it goes?'

'Well, you seem to have already made that decision,' she said tersely, trying to bite back the anger rising in her.

'Good luck, Emma, I know you'll be happy.'

She slammed down the phone. How dare he do this to her? She felt uneasy; was it just a simple holiday fling, nothing more? Yet, it wasn't his fault, and he had asked her to go with him, but she couldn't bring herself to make that sacrifice. She decided it was for the best, and wasn't ready to start a new relationship just yet. She let the petals from the roses he had sent slip though her fingers, they felt cool against her hot palm. Obviously he had only sent them to put her in a good mood before he dropped the bombshell. Cheerfully, she put the flowers in a vase. As she did one scratched her finger and the blood dripped onto the floor.

'I feel quite happy being free again,' she told Melanie on the phone.

'Win some, lose some,' said Mel philosophically.

She didn't need a man, she had everything she needed right there. She was strong, independent, and free. The artist with the dark swarthy looks crept back into her thoughts, and she could not get his face out of her mind. She tried to fight the urge, then began searching everywhere for the number of his art group. Where had she put it? She'd give him a ring, but his card had gone. Suddenly she felt compelled to get in touch with him. She wandered back through the house, wondering what to do, realising there wasn't a lot to do in a small fishing village at night; perhaps she could join his class, as a friend. She sat down, strangely subdued, alone in a strange place where she knew few people. But she was an optimist and saw every situation as a positive challenge. If only she could find the card, she might make friends at the art class. She felt her sense of excitement slip away, and listened to a Tori Amos CD, the gentle strains about love making her feel better. She loved to play her music when she felt sad, Tori knew about pain and love. Her dark eerie voice dipped and rose in dark mysterious tones as a strange melancholy mood overtook her.

Emma lay back, moved by the lyrics, when she saw her new paints stacked on the table, enticing her to create life. Deciding not to waste any more time, she took the water colours out of their wrapper and dabbed them on the palette. If she was going to join an art class, she had to develop a talent, or at least know the basics; besides painting made her feel better and always lifted her mood. She made a rough sketch of the bay that wasn't too bad, a little amateurish, but passable for a first attempt. Carefully, she applied a wash, then with a thin brush, painted in swift light brushstrokes, put in the boats bobbing on the horizon. The overall effect was not too bad. The haunting notes filtered through the room gripping her with their sadness, awakening and inspiring her at once. Time passed quickly, and her thoughts gained clarity. Whenever she wrote or painted, her thoughts fell into place and the answers to complicated problems always came to her. Everything had a beginning and an end, love and loss were simply part of the cycle of life. She could see everything much more clearly now, as though the clutter had been removed from her soul and the focus of her true path lay ahead.

Feeling more content, pleased that she was working her troubles out for herself, she found she possessed a newfound wisdom. Jeremy had been a necessary step toward her own development, to lift her from the habits of past. In a way he had served his purpose, the relationship lacked the spiritual depth she needed, but it had been fun. Now she would prepare herself for a new adventure. Emma snuggled up in her warm bed to read about the romantics—Mary Shelley, Polidari, Byron, gothic outsiders, decadents who embraced the darker side of life, who ventured from one experience to another, pushing boundaries as far as they would go. In one scene Byron walked in, standing foppishly still, in elegant gothic clothes, and began reading a love poem, arrogantly dismissing the wanton affections of a beautiful female servant who sat at his feet peeling an orange. She asked him if she could be of service to him, and he asked her to bend over so that he could use her as a footstool. Resting one leg on her back, he recited his work, his pale, arrogant moonlit face was partially obscured by his pale blonde hair. She laughed, thinking how ridiculous they were, such parodies of human nature, dreamers, just like her?

Then a thought struck her, was her artist friend a little like them? Rather avant-garde? Or perhaps he followed the same gothic romantic philosophy. An outsider? He did have some strange friends, she noticed, like the vamp woman, and there was an unusual air about him. She tried to piece it all together, maybe the gypsy man was his ancestor, they seemed to form a group of very unusual people, just like the gothic poets. Whatever her thoughts, she knew somewhere in the back of her mind, that he was her destiny, a road she had to travel. She put the book down, unable to concentrate and opened the window to let in some air. A dark fog was rising over the hills. She shivered slightly, thinking of Jeremy's stories about the ghost ship, then laughed. There were no ghosts here, she thought defiantly. Just lingering ghosts from her past. Still she felt uneasy and tried to focus her mind on decorating, and her next step. As she closed her eyes, she didn't see the glistening eyes watching her from the darkness.

A Visitor

Sultry, stormy air hung in the bay, a loud wind whistled across the sea. A storm blew in the distance. Dark clouds hovered over the waves, swirling over the beach, under a blue mist and eerie grey fog. The lighthouse lights flickered across the grey sea. The beach had turned ghostly and bleak, with black rocks glistening like daggers. It reminded Emma of a scene from a Shakespearian play and she half expected Hamlet's ghost to appear at any second. Dense fog rose over the turrets of the inn. As darkness fell, heavy rain began to lash at the windows.

Why was it so gloomy today? Emma sighed, thinking how dull it was. A heavy thick fog swirled over the bay. It made everything seem quite atmospheric out there, like a horror film. Then, as she sat up, she saw a cloud of smoke shimmer and disappear into the wall, like an opaque grey cloud. She blinked: surely shadows can't pass through walls? It must have been a shadow from outside. Irritably, she put down her book and paced restlessly in the kitchen feeling like a caged animal. She stretched out, annoyed that she could see nothing but grey sky for miles. It was too cold to go out and she felt claustrophobic in the heavy electric storm. She sighed; the weather was depressing with only the twinkling pub lights breaking the tedious blanket of fog that was descending on the bay. Still, it would take a while to start a new life, and make things happen. Perhaps she would ask the artist for details about his group. She rummaged around for the leaflet, but gave up the search, it was nowhere to be found. She was driving into town tomorrow so she'd get another one.

It was so very quiet. Not even the laughter from the tourists on the beach at night broke the silence, only the sound of the waves crashing in the distance. A strange tapping on the window made her look up. It sounded like someone was trying to get in. Emma got up and looked outside, she could see nothing but a storm rising in the sky. The atmosphere was electric. Suddenly, a flash of lightning lit up the sky, followed by a heavy crack of thunder. The rain pelted down. She thought she saw something, a silhouette slither past the window. A tall thin shadowy figure moved past her, then it vanished. She jumped back, there was a crash, a bird flew into the window, shattering the pane.

Outside on the ground she found a black dove. She jumped back, startled. It had broken its wings. How strange, could it be an omen? She picked up the dead dove lying under the window, and threw it on the bonfire.

Just an accident she thought, dismissing the incident. She must not let her imagination run away with itself. Ravens flocked under the roof, staring at her with their black menacing eyes. She felt a chill run over her spine. Huge black crows huddled in a circle as though hatching an evil plan. In the light streaming from windows she thought she saw something move—looking past the dunes, she could just about make out a shape. She rushed over to see what it was, almost slipping in the rain. She saw rustling and pulled out a young boy crouching under a bush.

'So you are the one playing tricks on me!' she cried scornfully. 'What are you doing here at this time of night?'

'I am so sorry,' he stuttered apologetically. 'It's raining so I thought I would shelter here until it stopped.'

'But what are you doing so far up the cliffs?' she asked.

'We always play pirates in the tunnels. It's much scarier at night. I didn't know you had moved in.'

'Were you pretending to be a ghost?'

'Yes, I was, we did try and spook you a few times, when you were around,' he admitted.

'Well I'd appreciate it if you took your games somewhere else,' she said gently. 'There is a lookout hut on the beach, why don't you hide in there?'

'Okay, we will,' he said running like the wind back to the beach. Emma returned to the house, laughing. So that was her ghost! It was just kids having some fun, just as Jeremy had said! Her heart sank—so that was the mystery, she was being spooked by some children. She gave a sigh of dismay, that's all it was. Her dream lover was just a fantasy.

She turned on the radio, thankful to hear the broadcaster talking, it gave a focus for her thoughts. She had to get a grip and stop being so neurotic. After hearing Jeremy's tales, she had become obsessed with the idea of ghosts and the supernatural.

The next day, she took a long walk, deciding to forget the cove and its mysteries, all disturbing her too much. She dropped in on her neighbours, some local hippies staying in a caravan, in a field behind the inn. They drank chamomile tea and played backgammon.

'Are there any ghosts, here in the bay?' Emma asked Kasha.

'No, no one has ever mentioned one to me. Plenty at the First and Last Inn though.'

'What about at the Black Dove?'

'A few people have held séances there, and there was some talk about the inn being "darkened by deed" in the past, but it all seems to have cleared away. No one I know has actually seen anything there. It belonged to some business people who never really fitted in, and who only stayed here occasionally, and now to you. There has been some subsidence, and loose floorboards. It must have needed quite a bit of work.'

'Yes, it looks a dream now,' said Emma, her eyes widening in delight.

She recalled Andrea's words, just to reassure herself: energies often lingered in a house, but the new owner would be able to put that right by bringing a new energy.

'Yes, that's right, people have been known to move into a house with a sad or malevolent presence, but within a time to have replaced it with the warmth of their own vibrations,' said Kasha. 'It doesn't matter what has been there in the past, it's what is there now that matters.'

Assured, Emma nodded. 'Yes, I suppose so.'

At that moment Jerome, Kasha's husband walked in and placed some vegetables on the table. They sat drinking mulberry wine while he played the guitar.

'There is a story though,' said Kasha, her eyes narrowing over a candle flame, 'that on one night of the year the inn turns fleetingly back to how it once was, and the ghosts of the past return, that all the smugglers can be seen sitting round the table—. But it is just a myth,' she shrugged, 'all the places around here have them.'

Maybe the mystery had been solved. The 'ghost' was just the kids playing around as Jeremy had suggested, or had she walked straight into a supernatural mystery? She was intrigued and forced herself to think logically. If there was a ghost, it would reappear; if not, then it was likely to be her imagination, or the boy. She would just have to wait and see. The thought of a dark romantic knight trying to seduce her at night, while she slept, whipped up her darkest fantasies. Climbing into bed early, she hoped to dream about him again, longing for his soft embrace, but instead she slept soundly.

The next morning she went to the library to investigate. When she got home she searched the internet, then took the book that she had taken from the library and scanned it for any clues. She flicked through the pages carefully, stopping as she came across a photograph of a dark, swarthy figure; it was just like the man in the painting. Quickly, she read all she could about him, absorbing every word. He was an aristocratic pirate of noble birth, who stayed at the inn, a painter and a poet. He was listed in a dictionary of early artists, there were his works listed—dark rocks in the medium of oil on board, arches and empty towers. Her heart leapt into her mouth as she turned the pages. Yes, that was him! He actually did exist. She opened another internet page, there was a short article about him on the Cornish myths page. He was a genius, with a dark past and had been an occultist who dabbled in the dark arts. His paintings reflected the eeriness of his subject. She sighed with relief, so he wasn't just a figment of her imagination. He had once existed and lived at the inn. She found out all she could about him— there was no mistaking those huge vibrant blue eyes or haughty gaze. Alongside the article was a small picture of a man with long dark hair, incredibly handsome, bohemian, with eyes that could be both chilling and warm. Yes that was definitely him, he even looked like the artist she had met at the café. Baffled, she knew she was falling a little in love with him. Was he a ghost? Did he still haunt the inn? Had he been unable to leave this world and move onto the next? Why else would he appear in the mirror, and in her dreams? She felt drawn to the artist too. She wanted to find out found more about her mystery visitor, and, to her amusement, found he was becoming her obsession.

She stopped as she came to a brief paragraph about the famous pirate ship that was wrecked in the bay. Then, at the corner of the page she saw printed under a picture of this rugged amazingly attractive man, his name: Antoine. Excited, she scribbled notes for the agency magazine, and artists' database, then put them down so that she could explore further, trying to find a clue to help uncover the mystery. She read on quickly, the man had come from France, he had worked in Kynance, where he owned a studio. She decided to go there and take a look.

Dark Mysteries

Emma took the twisting path down to Kynance Cove. Once a smugglers' bay, now due to its strong, lethal currents it had become more of an adventurers' challenge, as the only path was a torturous and dangerous climb down some steep cliffs. Carefully, she made her way down the steep rocks. On the beach she could still see the shadows of the old ships that had sailed into the cove and had been wrecked on the treacherous rocks. Today the sea was too choppy for most people to swim in, and it was high tide. Its reputation of being one of the most haunted and dangerous beaches in the West Country was well earned, with a jagged rocky landscape, pure heaven for climbers. A strong swimmer, Emma loved to dive there; she handled the currents well, and the beachside café, up on the hill, had stupendous views. To her surprise, she found some rock tunnels, covered in seaweed, that led from the cliffs to the beach. She climbed slowly down onto the beach holding the camera tightly against her chest, carefully clambering down the steep jagged rocks. It was at times like this she felt glad to have some climbing experience. Only the most agile and fit could scramble up and down these steep paths easily. She jumped down from the last rock onto an empty beach bathed in summer sunshine. It was quiet, miles away from civilisation. She ran straight into the sea, and began kicking at the waves and frolicking in the foam.

Some playful dolphins swam into the bay, flicked their tails above the waves, leapt into the air in a perfect arc, then dived a slippery dive, back into the sea. Grey seals bobbed on the water, their puppy faces looking inquisitively around them. She walked up to the cliffs covered in dark twisted gnarled branches that had been dead for years. She found the house where Antoine had once had a studio, and found it had been turned into a beach café. She walked over to the huge rock standing in the middle of the adjoining beach, next to the caves.

A shadow moved over the rocks: seaweed was blowing over the beach. Suddenly, her attention was caught by a ship's loud horn. A huge black ship was gliding into the bay. Emma slipped over the rocks to get a closer look. It was enormous, like a Spanish galleon, flying the pirate skull and crossbones from its stern. Emma gasped, surprised to see such a large ship sail into the bay. Its mast stretched high, swaying into the sky, its decks shimmered with a drab ghostly air. It slid back, and plunged through the waves back out to sea, sailing off as silently as it had come, then disappeared into thin air. Emma watched, fascinated, almost falling off a rock in shock. Was it the ghost ship? She shivered with a mixture of excitement and fear. Aiming her camera, she clicked frantically hoping to catch it as it sank below the horizon. Clouds drifted over the sun, the beach felt colder, the place suddenly seemed unfriendly and remote. It had become dark. She turned to go back, unsure, feeling something was about to happen, when she slipped behind a rock. She felt her ankle wrench and stopped to tie her scarf tightly around it. The sea had become choppy and wild, tearing across the beach. She steeled herself against the wind as the sun sank behind the rocks, leaving the beach cold, shadowy and dark. As she looked out to sea, a strange black mist was swirling over the bay, coming closer.

Emma turned and saw a tall figure walking towards her, a man swathed in a long black cloak. He stared at her, moving closer. She stepped back, squinting, trying to make out the figure, but couldn't see him clearly. As he came closer, she caught a quick glimpse of his face, and stepped back. Surprised, she saw he looked just like Antoine. He pulled a hood over his head and walked across the beach. She turned to run, panic rising in her, but her ankle gave way. A stab of pain shot through her, and she fell. Who was he? She blinked and the man had gone. Suddenly there was flash of lightning and he re-appeared from behind a rock, moving in a gloomy stupor toward the caves. Grabbing her camera, she photographed him. Intrigued, she followed the man to see where he went. Limping, she eased herself through a gap in the rock past a waterfall tumbling into a black cave. Dark dank and cold, she shivered. It was dark and musty inside, covered in orange lichen. Suddenly, she was struck by a streak of silver blue light, imploding from the cave wall. It burned her. Silver threads spun around her, bright stars shot across the cave, lights flashed around her. A heavy web of fisherman's rope fell on her head, capturing her in its threads. She twisted and turned, trying to get out, but her ankle caught in the rope and she fell back, trapped. She heard footsteps, and a cold claw gripped at her heart as she saw two eyes staring at her out of the darkness. Frozen with fear, she struggled to get free of the twisting rope, aware of a fork of white lightning outside the cave. Rain started seeping in through a crack in the cave.

The cave was suddenly awash with a white light; the rope snapped, she broke free and ran. Rocks flew across the cave, scattering bats out of the shadows, one got caught in her hair. Letting out an earth-shattering scream, she lost her balance and slid down a slippery slope, landing in the middle of an old fire, under some strange symbols carved on the walls.

She stumbled over the jagged rocks, easing herself into another part of the cave, and found herself in a dim corner where orange embers glowed in the remains of a fire. Someone had been there. Decayed remains of rotting bones were strewn around the floor. She held her breath, scared to make a noise as she listened: the feint footsteps were coming closer. Was the man still following her? She poked the remains of the fire but soon the last flame flickered and died. An eerie silence filled the cave. She stood, filled with a paralysing dread. He was getting closer. Seawater dripped onto the rocks, a splash echoed through the cave. Drip, drip, the sound grew ominously loud. The footsteps stopped; her heart pounded so loud she thought that she would faint. She turned and came face to face with a tall ravaged man, his dark beautiful eyes set in dark hollows. She screamed and tried to run, but he caught her. She had seen those eyes before, in the mirror, at the inn. First giving a bloodcurdling yell, then whimpering, she struggled to get away, terrified of what he was going to do to her. His gaze softened and he wrapped his cloak around her. His strong arms held her gently and she struggled against the weight on her chest. His embrace grew heavier, he was crushing her. She tried to run, but his grip was stronger.

Then she looked up into his eyes, and turned to liquid—it was the man in the painting! She pushed off the hood he was wearing, no longer afraid, and saw his beautiful eyes staring right into her. He smiled a devastatingly charming smile, she felt herself weaken. Too tired to fight, she collapsed exhausted into his arms, and felt his wet salty kiss on her lips. She felt his hands move skilfully over her body as he kissed her. She sank back, feeling his caresses, arching to his fingers, succumbing to his touch, letting the saltiness of his lips cover hers, surprised at herself for wanting him so badly. His eyes burned wickedly into her soul. Then his face started to fade.

So, it was an illusion! Horrified, as if falling into an abyss, she saw his face slowly turn to ash, his warm smile turn to a chilling cold glare, his eyes glow and his remains fall to the ground. She whimpered and climbed back through the tunnel, tearing at the slimy walls, tried to pull herself up a rock, but, losing her grip, fell down the slippery slope. Her hands reached out to a rock ledge, but a wet slimy hand touched her face. Terrified, she fell back among the bones scattered round the fire. She crawled back up, struggling along the wet slimy cave tunnel toward the spark of light in the distance, her fingers tingling with fright and numb with cold. She shouted out 'help', but her voice drifted off as a fading echo, no one could hear. Trapped in the blackness, she was alone. Panic began to rise in her as she stumbled through the caves, her fingers bleeding, scraping along the slimy damp walls, trying to find her way back out of the cave, jumping in sheer terror as wet seaweed brushed past her. She ran toward a slit of light streaming from a rock, following the light to a small ledge leading to outside. She climbed up and eased herself along the narrow ledge, her heart pounding as she pushed through a tiny tunnel, and stumbled out onto the beach flooded in daylight. She sat on a rock, her heart almost stopping, her body flooding with relief, as she struggled to catch her breath. In the distance she could see the strange ship sinking behind the waves. A portent? Of what? An impending disaster? The storm raged like a whirlwind in the bay, the tide blocked off the footpath. How could she get out? She clutched her jacket closer to her and climbed over a rock, shivering with fear. What would happen next? She held fast onto a rock as a hurricane ripped across the beach, and hoped she had the strength to make it back. As she did so, she saw a dark cloud racing toward the cave.

Lucky escape

The rain had stopped. A rainbow arched across the sky, its shimmering misty colours fading into the hills, and the beach turned sunny and bright again. The tide was out, making the path visible. Emma smiled, relieved to hear the laughter of people climbing onto the beach. She shook slightly—had it all been a nightmare? Was it just all in her imagination? Everything seemed normal again; warm sunlight lit her face, taking the chill out of her soul. It was impossible to remember everything that had happened. She wondered if it *had actually* happened; perhaps she had been so scared that she had imagined it all, or she'd bumped into a lonely tramp sheltering in the caves. Children ran laughing onto the beach, kicking sand at each other. She lowered herself from the rocks into one of the huge waves rolling into the bay and let the cool sea flow over her, cooling her swollen ankle, bringing her back to her senses. The physical effort of swimming drove the demons from her, as she fearlessly spliced the waves.

She took a taxi back, stopped for a drink at the First and Last Inn, and arrived home late. Stumbling in through the front door, she felt pleasantly tired, and, climbing the stairs, she fell onto the bed with some magazines and began nursing her ankle. It was only sprained slightly, but it had already swollen badly. She quickly read Jeremy's letter, telling her how sorry he was to have left so suddenly, then lay back thinking. She got up and scrambled through the drawers for the leaflet but it was nowhere to be found, she'd get the number of the gallery from Ramone. She lay back again, the echoes of the man's touch still lingering over her body, and she knew she wanted him. He had eyes like Anton—their eyes were the same eyes. She couldn't stop thinking about the man who was haunting her dreams. Her body ached for his touch. Was it Anton? Or Antoine, the French aristocrat who had once lived at the inn? Or were they the same person? She turned over and let out a long dreamy sigh. She was spending too much time indulging her fantasies, obsessed by her dream lover. She lifted up a magazine and the artist's card dropped out, with the name of a gallery at the top. That was a sign, she decided! She would go there tomorrow, find out about the class, and who he was. Maybe he worked there, or maybe he just advertised through the gallery? She had to focus her mind on something. Why did he keep appearing in her dreams? Was he haunting her? Was it his face she kept seeing in the mirror? Had the kiss been real? She could not get the image of his face or his voice out of her mind, and the memory filled her with an intense longing.

Her eyes were getting heavy. Sleepily she tucked herself into bed and looked up through the attic window to see a rich sunset swirling overhead, clouds weaving through the pale sky and spreading over the silvery-orange horizon. She watched the sun sink behind the horizon as her eyes closed. Her mind wandered aimlessly into a trance, the sea crashing gently on the rocks, lulling her into a tranquil sleep. Slowly she drifted off. She woke suddenly, her sleep disturbed by a noise coming from downstairs. She tiptoed down the stairs and saw a light burning. She went to switch it off, but saw an inside light was blazing too, and she could hear voices.

Tentatively, she opened the door to the lounge, and walked into a shimmering pool of light—a group of people were gathered there, sitting bathed in a silvery glow. Shimmering opaque shapes were sloping around the room. Emma blinked, surely they could not be real? She held her breath and focused: she could see a clear outline of bodies, the shapes of men, rogues of the sea, the pirates hunched over a map, their dark eyes glistening with murder. She felt her skin prickle, fighting her fear, but her fascination overcame her doubts and she was filled with curiosity. She could just make out the shadowy figures: one was Antoine hunched over a map, plotting, accompanied by a strikingly beautiful woman, in a gown, who was kissing him, and sitting next to them was the woman in a long black dress. She was sure it was the ghost of Annie Treeve, the woman smuggler, certain it was a ghost she had seen wandering through the inn. Some very strange music began playing, then they started to fade. Suddenly there was blood everywhere, people were screaming, the scene swirled around like a mist, evaporating into thin air.

Waking with a start, Emma felt someone kissing her, his lips on her lips. She lay back limply, savouring the exquisite kiss. Gently he released her from his grasp and lay beside her, stroking her face, rubbing her breast and she felt herself lift up to him, wanting him. She opened her eyes and jumped back, surprised. It was him! The man in the picture! Antoine! Then suddenly, he vanished. She woke up with a jolt. Slowly, her eyes began to focus. She fumbled around the bed, but he had gone. Was it a lucid dream, or was she imagining things? Had she really gone downstairs? Did he really kiss her? Or had she been dreaming? Was he real? Or just a figment of her imagination? She looked round for traces of him. Turning over, she found some dark strands of hair on the pillow—so he really had been there, her mystery visitor was real! She felt her body tingle from his gentle butterfly touch. Was her over-active imagination conjuring up imaginary lovers?

The next morning, she dressed hurriedly, and rushed over to the gallery, her ankle still paining her, but it was closed: the owner had gone away. She read with sadness a note pinned at the top of the door: it said the gallery was re-opening next week, under new management. Her heart sunk in disappointment, Anton had gone, moved on and she would probably never see him again.

Black Dove—opening night

Emma stood and looked round her, the arts centre-come-gallery-wine-bar was almost finished, it looked perfect, far more elegant than she had dreamed it could be. She had created just the right atmosphere, a cross between an artist's den and romantic arched alcove, with romantic pictures scattered over the walls, the women with sylph-like ethereal gazes staring down from the wall. It had little streams running through the rooms with tanks filled with hundreds of brightly coloured tropical fish. Through the arches were small rooms where people could paint, and, in the main enclosure, a bar where they could socialise. She planned to hold many magical, mystical parties there and decided to hold one straightaway. She had created a mystical atmosphere that made the room look intriguing. Her final step was to buy some paintings from the local artists and hang them along the wall. The builders were making finishing touches, putting up shelves, painting the arched alcoves and adding the final touches of paint. Pre-Raphaelite prints adorned the walls, and exotic plants, computers and workspaces lined the corridors: it had the air of a relaxing elegant lounge and art gallery. She would throw an opening party, invite everyone she knew. Perhaps Anton would turn up; wherever he was, he was bound to hear about it, and might do so. She added some scented candles, put on some soft new-age music, added some silky fabrics and did some final polishing as haunting sounds wafted through the room. Her dream was complete, now she had to launch her ideas.

That weekend, at the opening party, the first guests trickled in slowly, Emma hoped that Anton would be among the artists flocking to the venue, would be among her guests, but there was no sign of him. She walked over to a group of surfers talking to Ramone and Andrea. It was still early, plenty of time for him to show up.

'Man, did you see those waves yesterday? I was really stoked, flew across them so fast thought I'd take off. My feet were flying,' said Gordon 'Lightfoot' Jones, this season's prize surfer. Another group of surfers joined them, gesticulating with their hands to show the movement of the waves. They all laughed. Emma, crestfallen, handed round complimentary glasses of wine. Ramone took her to one side and spread some white powder across a small mirror.

'Here, have some of this, you look like you need cheering up,' he offered. 'What's wrong?'

'Oh it's just that I thought Anton might turn up,' she said.

'Well,' ordered Ramone, looking slightly concerned, a dark shadow flickering on his face, 'forget the man, enjoy yourself.'

Emma hesitated, then thought why not, what the hell, it was her party and she was free to do as she pleased. Besides she needed to lift her spirits. Carefully, she curled up a bank note and inhaled the white powder. Immediately a buzzing energy surged through her, and she no longer cared about Anton or anyone, and felt so confident that nothing phased her any more. She rushed round, chatting to the guests, transforming into the perfect hostess. The room seemed lighter, glistening and gleaming with fairy lights and a magical glow. Hordes of surfers, still in their wetsuits, piled in, slapping each other heartily, opening their beers. A group of artists and local residents, were talking animatedly about this year's exhibitions, Emma quickly made a quick note to hold at least one exhibition a month, featuring a local artist—when she got a moment she would set up their details on a database. Then more guests arrived, showering Emma with compliments and flowers and gathered in the chill-out rooms, enthusing about the decor. Emma's heart sank with disappointment, noticing Anton wasn't among them. Well, all was lost, she thought sadly, growing subdued, swirling her drink thoughtfully around the glass. So he had sold the gallery and moved on, and she would never see him again, that's just the way it was. She sighed deeply and threw back another drink. Reluctantly she went back to mingle with her guests, wondering whether she would ever see him again. She sat quietly, he could have at least turned up for her opening night, everyone else knew about the party, and some of his friends were there, but no one seemed to know where he was. Where was he? Had he gone away for good? Was he finally lost to her? What was he really like? Sadly she realised as she turned off the light, that, now, she would never know.

Anton – the Edge
A month later – Start of an idyll

Anton watched Emma walk past—she was shopping in the village. She swirled her beautiful long blonde hair around her tanned shoulders, and strode across the pavement like a goddess; she looked radiant, her face fresh, just like an angel. Her tight white cotton dress fitted her figure well and her body was tanned. Such a perfect example of woman, and his new muse, he thought admiringly. Her body swayed, teasing him. Her face was so serene, like a dreamy sea nymph. 'My beautiful goddess,' he whispered, 'soon you will be mine.' She stood looking in a shop window, unaware he was watching her from behind the desk at the gallery. She was in her mid-thirties, and astonishingly beautiful. On the few occasions he had spoken to her, she had possessed an air of mystery, as though she were an angel coming into his life. He observed her every move, hoping soon he would get to know her. Quickly he made several sketches of her, and was interweaving her into his work and creating paintings around her. She was his water nymph. Now that he had bought the new gallery, he would invite her to come and sit for him. He had spent the last few weeks in London, finalising business and couldn't wait to get back, realising how much he had missed her. Since meeting her at the beach, he had thought of no one else. Dutifully he had tried to work things out with Angel, but things weren't the same after he had lost his heart to Emma. He could no longer fight his true feelings, which were growing more powerful each day. He sat preparing his astrological chart for the day. Yes, there it was—the sign that told him she was about to enter his world. He smiled, pleased with himself. His plan was working. Soon, she would be his, the woman of his dreams. He yearned to paint her from real life, capture the light in her unusual sapphire-blue eyes, splashed with dots of violet, her long pale blonde hair rippling over her like a sea nymph. He stole glances at her, photographing her and painting her, his imagination spurred by her beauty, his yearning growing deeper with each passing day. He was using her as his new model, and used no others, memorising every fine detail of her face and perfect body, studying how she moved, how she walked and smiled. She would come to him soon, according to the tarot cards. He just had to wait for destiny to unfold. Meanwhile he painted her slender body onto the canvas, each stroke applied with tender loving care.

He was falling in love with her, imagining himself to be a knight come to rescue his maiden, and so creating a scene for his latest painting. Her pretty face dominated his thoughts; he had tried not to let his heart rule his head, but he wanted her and could not let her slip by, out of his life. He would catch her and make her into his star. Each time he saw Emma, he discovered a new aspect to her—the way she flicked back her hair, the way her eyes widened in surprise—and he recorded each revelation in painstaking detail. His paintings often predicted the future, one showed Emma lying in the woods cradling him—it all looked very promising.

The tarot reading predicted that he would soon find a woman who loved him in the purest way, that she would remain devoted, loyal and true. Anton hoped it was Emma, for she filled his heart with love and light. Her presence gave him life and fired him with the spark he needed to create brilliant work, her soul shone with the light that led him away from the darkness and the pain, taking him out into the sunlight. She was about to enter his life. He looked admiringly at her sylph-like body, converted to a figure on canvas. The oppression of the narcotic heaviness lifted as he felt her lightness fill him with hope. He felt high-spirited, alive again. His desires were awakened. He wanted their meeting to occur naturally. He had lived in the darkness, without light for so long. Secretly he was glad that Angel had left, she had become tiresome, clinging to him like a leech. She had wanted only the darkness and dragged him down too. Her cloying suffocation had made him lose the desire to paint, and his freedom. Still, the image of her face sprang into his mind. There are some flames that never fully burn out, that smoulder on for an eternity, but their flame had finally withered. He realised painfully that he had lost any desire he once had for her. She had destroyed their love through her obsessions. He took the photographs of her out of their frames and tore them up; everything had to be right and pure before he started with Emma. No baggage, no memories from the past, to spoil, pollute or confuse things.

Anton spent the rest of the day weaving Emma's elegant face onto his canvas. He mixed the paints, cobalt blue and lilac, then brushed the strokes swiftly over the canvas, adding the silvery lights to her hair. Emma as the water-nymph, playing in the sea, as a goddess of the sea, a serene mermaid flicking her long mermaid's tail, and as a siren, singing a song for the sailors sailing by. It was his way of expressing his love for her, now that he had found his dream woman, he felt content painting her image for hours. He portrayed her as a tempting maiden being carried off by a knight, himself, on horseback, to the gothic castle, where he lived as a dark swarthy knight. A siren, or a temptress who lured men deep into the underworld, and down into the abyss of Persephone's lair. She made the perfect muse for his new collection, and her look adapted well to his varied female roles. He based his new collection around her—'Woman as goddess. Mythical maiden—women's mysteries.'

Her enigmatic presence charged him with a psychic vision he'd never known before, and lifted him to a pure transcendence. Inspired, he worked for hours, engrossed, absorbed by her beauty, knowing he could go on forever. Once the creative fire hit him, he could not stop. Each stroke was applied with care, each curve perfectly drawn, every picture elegant and conveying intense feeling and provoking thought. Emma was his inspiration, firing his new ideas. He worked quickly, trying to capture all his ideas before they slipped away. He entwined her face into drawings, recording her beauty in painstaking detail. Emma fired his creative spark, bringing his artistic talent back to life. Once someone or something became too familiar, or lost its edge, it no longer inspired him. Wonder filled him with new ideas, ignited a fresh vision, and it helped to live on the edge. He drew in the gentle curve of her eye, as she stood quietly in a tranquil garden, collecting flowers, under a waterfall. He stood back pleased, it was a good likeness; her blue eyes sparkled with a vibrant energy, reflecting a hazy light. She gazed down gently at the water, her arms holding a basket brimming with lilac summer flowers.

He felt the energy flow through him, as he painted with renewed vigour, and was feeling inspired again! How glad he was to paint again, his talent flowing stronger than before. The light fell on the canvas, and the random shapes began to take form. The break-up with Angel had left him exhausted, he had lost all interest in his work, lost touch with his creativity. For a month, he could not face the canvas or lift a paintbrush.

Since he had started watching Emma, his creativity had reawakened, his artistic spark now flowing ceaselessly. He counted the days until he would see her again, convinced that destiny had brought them together. Angel had been his dark goddess, inspiring his darker paintings, a vampire who drained him emotionally. Emma was a breath of fresh air, a fresh, fragrant maiden, life-giving, like embracing a new spring. The newness of exploring and discovering a new model always roused him; he loved to discover a woman's mysterious allure, uncover her secrets, discover her every facet. He gathered his notes on the archetypes: temptress, siren, maiden and goddess, and made some quick sketches of each one. Emma was a chapter of his life he was soon to discover. Away from Angel's clutches, he was free again. Kali was her goddess name, suited to her destructive nature. Sex had been for her liberation, now he wanted sex as an expression of love. The many shades of love—devotion, longing, passion, innocence, desire, addiction, obsession, idealisation: how many had he known? His lovers, his models were many. He had loved them all, but none made him so happy as Emma, she was the one for him. Had his muses filled him with all of these? Carefully he finished the curve of Emma's face, and shaded in the shadow under her cheek.

His work done, he consulted his book of shadows. He lit a candle and began his incantation for 'Drawing down the Moon and Sun' ritual—for evoking the female goddess of light, to channel energy and light into him, to give him psychic power. He imagined himself standing under streams of moonlight, bathing in the serene, tranquil rays of the goddess. The goddess appeared before him, bathed in shimmering light, filling him with power. He visualised Emma in his mind, wandering through the garden, happily picking flowers, smiling her perfect smile. She was a goddess in every sense of the word, and he her servant. He recalled the laws of courtly love, to have an intense longing for a lady. Act with patience. The pain of his unrequited love made him restless, he had to prove his affection for her, his unwavering devotion first.

His energy flowed back with a powerful force, he felt stronger than ever before, empowered, his psychic vision had returned. He concentrated deeply for a moment, and could see Emma lying on the bed, her long hair rippling over the pillow. He saw her quite as clearly as if he were in the room with her. He sighed with satisfaction. Was she aware of someone watching her? He wanted her so badly! He kissed her and wanted to take her. Touching her gently, he knew she could feel him kissing her! He must stop! Let events take their natural course. Also he didn't want to frighten her, she might not understand.

He mixed tyrian purple and gentian violet, dabbing them onto the canvas, with some hues of orange mixed with ochre and tempera for a glossy skin tone. He added a few brushstrokes to her cheeks, then painted the folds in the lilac silk dress. He added some tempera as a gloss, to create a natural sheen. In the gentle scene, Emma stood, picking some flowers by the waterfall. Her long hair cascaded over her shoulders, spilling onto the lilac silk dress. Soft lilac to deep purple hues glistened in her robe. She was an ethereal maiden, basking in the rays of the sun, a nymph full of moonlit mysteries. He added the soft blues hues of the sky. He wasn't interested in the mean petty things of life, he liked the darkness, his own power, and a woman who made a good muse. He lived as a free spirit, away from rules, beyond moral boundaries, seeking only knowledge, beauty, art and truth in its purest form. He loved Emma; she attracted him with her elegance and youthful spirit and the fact that she was an artist too, a writer.

Angel was a Circe who had torn his mind and body apart, fuelled the dark side of him. For a while he had adored her decadence and chaos, but it had enslaved him. Angel! But she hovered over him like a dark cloud, quivering with a dark twisted mind, and her strange love, and, despite his protestations that he was no longer in love with her, she refused to go. The day after he had told her they were finished, he went away, and strange things had started to happen to him. She used witchcraft against him, draining his energy, sucking his soul into her dark abyss. For a while, he'd been tormented by terrible dreams as she led him along the dark corridors of Hell, then, suddenly, she stopped. Now all he wanted was peace. He lit the candle, and, using his creative visualisation, could see Emma lying alone on her bed, her long hair rippling over her breasts and he felt a twinge of desire. He imagined again what it would be like to make love to her. No, he would wait, he didn't want to spoil things, let it happen naturally. He picked up the paintbrushes and began to paint in the delicate curve of her eyes.

Suddenly, in a fit of anger he threw down the paintbrushes, aware of a strange presence in the room. Were they still following him? He was no longer one of them: why couldn't they leave him alone? How could he finally push them out of his life? Moodily, he went over to the window, knocking over the table, scattering brushes over the floor, and made a gesture in the air. He pulled back the blinds, anxiously watching the dim light shine on the wet rocks below. Their jagged edges glistened menacingly under the moonlight, sharp like daggers, glittering silver knives. He stepped back and listened, as a tall thin shadow slithered across them. Who was watching him? Was Angel still following him? He would not give in, he was much stronger than her. Since leaving her, strange things had started to happen. Anton walked over to the painting of her, and stared hard at it. Her dark eyes appeared to gaze down at him mockingly, her dark lips parted, her eyes flashed with a malevolent glare. He could have sworn that she blinked. He felt himself weaken, falling dizzily under her spell; then he summoned all his strength, took a knife to it, and started to tear into the canvas, slashing it to pieces. He jumped back; a stream of red paint ran down her cheek, was it blood? Fear and revulsion hit him at once. Angel's face was bleeding, her eyes full of pain. Perhaps he should burn the paintings he'd done of her, but he couldn't bring himself to destroy his own art and they were an integral part of his theme. Yet if he kept them, she would always have a hold over him. Reluctantly, he took a blowlamp and held it against Angel's face on the canvas: the flame shot out and burned the colours, until her face shrivelled and the paint ran into a blur. The colours merged into a trail of sludgy greeny-grey and dripped down the canvas, mingling with the red blood oozing from her lips. Sickened, he wondered, how he could he do this to his own work, was he becoming unhinged?

He pulled back the blinds and peered outside. His heart thumped, a dark shadow crept over the rocks; he let go of the blinds, and it looked like they were getting closer. A cold grey mist rose over the turbulent sea. His haunted eyes darted from the side of the beach to the rocks: they shone anxiously, he squinted, and saw a silhouette of a man standing alone on the beach. A strange compulsion dragged his gaze back to his paintings of Angel stacked in the corner, they were a mass of grey sludge. He thought he heard a whimper of pain. Were they coming for him? He looked up at his latest painting, of the boats moored in the bay, the study of Newlyn Harbour: suddenly the peaceful scene was replaced by one of carnage—the figures started to move, their faces screwed up in a tortured expression, their laughing faces now grim, stern, waxen stares. In the painting gone was the serene calm sea; instead, turbulent waves tore over the breakwater, a man was drowning. Anton stood transfixed, unable to believe what he was seeing. He felt his blood freeze. The terrible predictions had returned. Perspiration dripped down over his face. No, surely it could not be them? The picture was moving. They were haunting him, trying to send him out of his mind. He recoiled in horror, squirming in fear, crawling from the wreckage of a broken dream. His face contorted in agony—he thought he had escaped them, now they were back, seeking revenge. He had destroyed Angel's paintings and all traces of the coven: now they sought their revenge. Distraught, he put his head in his hands, drowning in a sea of darkness, caught up in a web of fear. He had crossed the line, there was no turning back. How could he escape them, where could he run to now?

Destinies changing
The gallery—chance meetings

Emma changed into a long dress ready to visit the gallery. She unwrapped the photographs from the chemist and tore the cover off hastily and sighed. How exasperating! She hadn't caught the dark shadowy figure she had seen at Kynance on camera. All the shots were blank. Annoyed, she threw them away. Perhaps it had all been in her imagination. She rushed outside; she wanted to catch the gallery before it closed for lunch. She drove to the cove and parked by the sea. Walking past the bay, she saw a tall thin figure perched on the edge of the rocks, ready to jump. She gasped in fright, hardly daring to look, suddenly it faded into a cloud of dust. She stood transfixed, unable to move. What the hell was that? A mirage? She wiped her forehead, perhaps it was a hallucination brought on by the shimmering heat. Gulls flocked in a circle overhead, and began squawking like vultures. She fought to gather her composure and picked some wild flowers, breathing in the lemon scent. They cleared her head, making her feel better. The heat was becoming so intense that she headed straight for the shade. She was so jumpy. Why were so many strange things happening around her?

She stopped at the gallery, captivated by a beautiful picture, called *Goddess of Dreams—Savage Garden*. It stood alone in the window, displayed on a huge canvas. She wondered briefly whether she had time to go in, but the painting was enchanting and seemed to lure her. Emma, taking a closer look, caught her breath sharply; she had never seen such a wonderful painting. The perfectly formed contours on the woman's face made it look as real as a photograph, the woman's eyes shimmered like a sparkling blue ocean, her gaze wise and knowing, like a true goddess, her long burnished hair hung in curls around her shoulders and flowed over her silk dress. It looked so perfect, each brushstroke applied so precisely that the artist had made her look stunningly real. Emma had thought it looked like a real photograph. The ethereal woman sat posed in a magical garden, weaving a tapestry, her hair entwined with delicate purple flowers, next to another nymph smelling a rose. Such a romantic painting, sighed Emma longingly. She just had to buy it. Going inside the gallery to get a closer look, she touched the painting and as she did, a strange thing started to happen. The tranquil scene suddenly changed to one of darkness and chaos, the blue skies turned black, a dark threatening storm raged across the sky, the flowers shrivelled and died. The sea raged and the storm howled, the woman's face aged rapidly, becoming withered and shrunken, her hair streaked with grey. Her ashen face disintegrated before Emma's eyes. Her hollow sunken eyes burned full of terror, her soul was being torn apart. She banged at the painting, mouthing some words, pleading to Emma, trying to escape. Emma, stood in disbelief, touching the soft pliable canvas; the woman was crying, tearing at the foliage.

She ran out of the gallery, shocked at what she had seen. After a few gulps of fresh air, she steadied herself and walked back in again. The woman was back in the painting, the picture was normal again, serene, filled with a pastoral scene of enchantment and bliss. She blinked, had she imagined that too? Soothing new age music filled the room, relaxing her frazzled nerves. What was happening? Was her mind playing tricks on her? How could a painting just spring to life? It was irrational. The coolness of the gallery made her feel calmer, she felt herself drawn back into reality with a jolt; gradually her anxiety subsided as she began browsing around the beautiful pictures in the gallery, the combination of the music and tranquil scenes filling her with a soothing calm. Quickly, she became absorbed by the beautiful images of landscapes and romantic ethereal women on display. Women with long flowing hair sat posed on rocks, playing the harp, nymphs sirens and goddesses in the throes of creative dreams.

She spotted water-colours and oils from several local artists, Paul Williams, Sarah Vivien, Ithell Colquhoun, Robert Lenkiewicz and Jane Ducker—elegant swirling sunsets, landscapes and seashores, turbulent moody seas crashing on the shores, dazzling landscapes filled with clear bright lights and vibrant colours, beautiful voluptuous women caught in the throes of sensual ecstasy. Then her gaze wandered round the room and fell on an artist displaying medieval fantasy, handsome knights wooing princesses with long flowing locks, wild horses galloping into the sea. She particularly liked one she thought reflected the mystical atmosphere of the cove. Then, feeling impulsive, she decided to buy the one in the window, the *Goddess, of Dreams*. As she made her way over to the desk, she felt a man's presence. She turned round to see the profile of a tall man with long hair, and a mysterious demeanour. It was Anton! She jumped back in surprise, her heart skipping a beat and fluttering violently. It was like she had been shot, and a surge of adrenalin ripped through her. It was the artist, the man she had dreamed of meeting again and who haunted her dreams, her nights. So he was back! The sight of him sent shivers down her spine and filled her stomach with butterflies. She stepped back, noticing he looked even more attractive than ever and felt overcome with lust. Her mouth felt dry and she was afraid he could hear her heart thumping loudly. Her pulse speeded up, and she thought she might faint. A confident woman who could steer board meetings with ease, she was surprised to find herself suddenly tongue-tied and acting gauchely.

'Hello,' he said, absorbed, then he glanced up and immediately recognised her. 'Hi Emma, how wonderful to see you! I wondered if I was ever going to see you again.' He walked round from the other side of the counter, took her in his arms and kissed her.

She looked up at him, surprised, her pulse quickening at the sight of him, desire rising in her like a tempest.

'How lovely to see you,' he said, his eyes lighting with pleasure. 'I hoped we would meet again soon.'

'Hi, it's wonderful to see you too,' she said, outwardly calm. 'I thought you had sold the gallery,' she questioned, surprised to find him still there.

'No, I used to work here, but now I have bought it. I own two galleries now, a small one in Porthcurno too. What can I do for you?'

'I came in to buy that painting. Could I take that one?' she said, pointing to one in the window.

'Of course. I'll just get it for you.'

He opened the window and climbed in, his long black hair spread over his shoulders, like a fan. His face was handsome and tanned like a gypsy. He had a strong masculine jaw and slender features combined with sculpted cheekbones, and reminded her of the artist she had seen in the painting, the French aristocrat. He turned round and she gasped at the similarity.

'This one?' he asked. His legs were bent under him, his dark blue smouldering, almond-shaped eyes piercing right through her; there was a quizzical, mystical expression as though he knew all about her, and knew her deepest secrets. He leapt back from the window like a panther, lean and agile, giving him an enigmatic air. He wore long, black leather boots and he moved swiftly and elegantly, with the agility of a deer; for a second, his eyes glinted dangerously, his hair flopped over his face. Emma, intrigued, imagined him holding her, her gypsy pirate. She coughed, slightly embarrassed. Despite his initial effusive display of affection, he now seemed cool and detached, his elegant, professional persona taking over.

'Oh wonderful, it's just what I am looking for,' she said, as he handed it to her.

'Yes, it's one of my favourites,' he admitted.

'Is it the same as the other one in the window?'

'That is a multi-media screen. You have the original painting, oil on canvas. Yes, I made an interactive film based on the painting, it's displayed on a large plasma computer screen, that's what you saw.'

'Ah, so that's why it changes,' said Emma, suddenly aware of her folly.

She laughed, relieved that she hadn't been imagining things.

She stared at him thinking how beautiful he was, especially for a man. His beautiful feminine eyes, framed by long lashes, stared straight at her. He glanced deep into her eyes and wove a spell over her with one passing glance. She smiled back, curious to find out who he really was, watching his every move intently as he flicked through the pages of the catalogue for the details. Despite herself, she began making comparisons. He possessed a wild, impulsive streak, in contrast to Jeremy's down-to-earth air and rugged physique. He was urbane yet naturally wild, he moved deftly, had a perfect, slender physique; his expression exuded a strange sense of gallantry, she could imagine him in the days of courtly love wooing the maidens. He reminded her of a wild, wandering gypsy, but with a touch of elegance. His dark eyes shone out of the darkness enigmatically. She imagined him in a swordfight, his shirt undone to his waist, or riding across the moors, or as a knight in an Arthurian romance.

'Tell me, what have you been doing, my lovely Emma?'

'I've been moving, then decorating. I am sorry I didn't make it to the class, I have been so busy,' she apologised.

'Don't worry, at least you are here now. We run other classes. I am so glad you came to see me.'

'Me too. It's nice to see you again too,' she said cautiously, not wanting to seem too eager. 'You mentioned that I might like to view the work of the local artists, when we met at the café. Perhaps I can spend some time looking at them now?' she asked.

He nodded.

'Why of course, yes. I'd love to show you. I'm just compiling a dictionary of all the local artists, I'll show you their work as I take you around. Are you coming to our art group? There's one next week. You can view the rest of our work.'

'I promise I will try and make it soon. I'm glad we bumped into each other, I wanted to ask you all about the class.'

He brought back a brochure and handed it to her.

'Come to the studio next week. You have missed the first group, but we have another one starting soon. I can show you what we've done, what to expect.'

'I'll be there. Could you give me some lessons? I know a little about water colours, I'm just a beginner really.'

'I'll be more than happy to show you. Our Wednesday class for beginners starts in October so you will feel no pressure. Perhaps you'd like to come to that?'

'Yes, that sounds perfect,' she nodded enthusiastically.

'Shall I take that?' he said pointing to the painting.

Emma passed it to him, slightly confused. 'Yes,' she stammered, caught in his gaze.

He went to the back of the shop and removed the label, brought the painting to the pay desk, and wrapped it. His gothic shirt was unbuttoned at the top. He looked so achingly sexy, like a wild graceful animal about to pounce, his dark, hungry gaze full of promise. A flame of desire shot through her as she watched him. Her beautiful, cultured, intellectual gypsy. She noticed how elegantly he moved. He had looked so scruffily handsome at the beach, but here, as gallery manager, he looked like another person, elegant and stylish.

'Do you like my painting?' he asked, giving her a friendly smile.

'Yes, the *Savage Garden—Goddess of Dreams*. What an interesting title,' she said.

'That's because the painting shows two sides, dark and light,' he explained. 'To some it depicts a serene view of idyllic pastoral bliss, to others, it reveals a more menacing side. What you see is the perspectives, dark and light. Contrasts. Depending on the perception of your own soul. It is painted to be deliberately ambiguous.' He turned the computer on, flicked a mouse and the painting changed. 'What you saw was an interactive multi-media version of the painting you have just bought—one click and it changes scene.'

'That's an unusual idea.'

His eyes lingered over her. He smiled.

'I like to think so. I paint living ideas, not just static scenes. I see art as dynamic, a process that evolves. I like to bring my ideas to life, make them real, give them that extra dimension. I like to see both sides,' he said.

He led her over to another computer, a huge Apple Mac standing in the corner of the room.

'Look, I'll show you how it is done,' he explained as the screen flickered to life. 'My main area of interest is painting in any medium, although I use mostly oils and water colours, and some silk screens but I also create interactive art web sites and moving art.'

Women stepped out of the paintings and swirled all over the screen, they began dancing, maidens flirting, temptresses swirling seductively and sirens luring men onto the rocks with their sweet song; maidens ran barefoot through the grass, twirling their pale ribbons, their silk dresses around their knees, dancing in the sunlight. They ran over the sand, frolicked by the sea, or ran through a buttercup-filled meadow. Emma sighed, gazing at the most beautiful pictures she had ever seen. He pressed a button and the scene changed to one of maidens sitting by a brook, then a maiden turned into a witch. 'I create short films of famous paintings,' he said.

'That's quite clever,' she said, impressed.

'I'll show you how to do it one day,' he offered. 'You can make a film for the café.'

She laughed. 'I'd love to.' She watched the film, fascinated as the pictures dissolved and changed. So that's how it was done. She smiled to herself, so relieved she wasn't going mad. He clicked on the mouse and the images started moving round the screen. The picture changed to one of maidens dancing in a garden.

'We could start our own café society.'

'Yes, I'd like to join forces,' he agreed.

'Perhaps you could help me. I need someone to help, a partner,' she said. 'I want to run art groups and sessions, that's why I bought the inn. I want to start a cutting-edge arts group here, and start painting and offer still life classes. Perhaps you could teach one or two?'

'Well, I'll be pleased to help you in any way that I can.'

'Thanks, I appreciate your time.'

'Well I do have a busy schedule,' he admitted. 'I work every waking second, and have quite a few classes this year, but I can fit you in on Wednesdays. I am working on the project I've just shown you, creating three-dimensional, moving art, bringing paintings alive. I take one painting and develop it into a short film. I hope you like it, it's my own concept and I've just received a commission to complete a whole series based on romanticism. I do some illustrating too.' He clicked the mouse and up came the original *Birth of Venus* by Botticelli; slowly Venus stepped out of her shell, her long hair flowing out behind her; Zephyr flew through the sky.

'Gosh, that is wonderful,' gasped Emma, her eyes fixed on the swirling images.

'The Americans love the idea,' he said changing the scene. 'I make the original paintings come alive, give them an extra dimension, it's caught on well in London too. Here, I tend to sell more landscapes, but some big companies have commissioned me to develop this idea for them. Paintings of Cornwall, or anywhere, that with a switch,' he said, flicking his wrist, demonstrating the action, 'will start to move.' He switched to a seascape, then surfers appeared gliding down a wave. 'That's why you were confused, the Garden of Dreams, where the tranquillity of Eden changes to a scene of Hell, desolation and darkness, I am sorry it upset you.'

'No, it's a good idea,' said Emma, crossing her arms, intrigued. Glad it was a moving film, not a hallucination!

'Dark realism,' he said; 'one moment serene and pleasant, the next turned to chaotic turmoil.'

She smiled and felt his arm brush against hers, and turning to face him she felt herself being drawn into his gaze. He kissed her, she could smell his male smell and her mind spun into overdrive at the thought of him touching her, his hand caressing her face. She shook herself for being so wanton. Feeling her face redden, quickly she got up and went over to the stand, grabbed a book entitled *The Goddess* and scanned it quickly, flicking nervously through the pages.

'Can I take one of these too?' she said, trying to distract him.

'Yes, this is a popular one with my students, a brilliant book, about female empowerment. It shows you how to reach a higher stage of consciousness and find your goddess within, how to reach your inner potential and enhance your spirit. Come to my class and as well as teaching you how to paint, we also run a course for art philosophy and techniques for transcendence, evoking the muse, then you can make a study of the goddess.'

'Yes, an all-round approach, I like that.'

'We use a range of styles, from figurative to abstraction, I prefer naturalist. I will you teach you the different techniques, how to bring your art alive. We can start with principles of painting and drawing and as you develop your chosen topic and skills, we can advance to more sophisticated works. You could use the *Goddess* as your main theme. The book will help you grow spiritually. Have you heard the saying by William Blake? "If the doors of perception are cleansed everything would appear to man as it is, infinite." Finding your inner "goddess" will give you clarity, wisdom, vision and enlightenment. You will start to see everything quite differently, with a growing power. Only those with pure hearts and minds and enough courage and vision can perceive through their goddess self. I think you are such a woman, a true and very beautiful *goddess*,' he said softly winding a stray strand of her hair round his fingers.

'Thanks.'

'I am so glad we met again,' he added, taking her hand and kissing it.

'I have thought of you often,' she whispered. 'Do you ever think of me?'

'All the time,' he admitted, softly stroking her face.

She felt a tingling sensation well up in her, then something seemed to draw her attention away; she looked up at the wall, and saw a painting of the vampish woman with raven black hair and flashing eyes staring down at them. A sharp pain stabbed in her neck. Angel's eyes were ablaze with demonic fury. For a second, Emma felt as if the woman was alive and could almost feel her presence.

'That's a painting called the *Dark Goddess,*' he said warily, 'a terrible beauty, Queen of death and destruction, like Lilith, a slayer of men. The goddess can be destructive as well as creative. Her darkness reflects her unfathomable mystery, her fiery depth of passion and her cold cruelty. When we evoke the Dark Goddess, we bring out our dark side, our shadow, we are psychic, and abound with creative and sexual energy. She transforms, destroys to bring about change.'

'Do you still see Angel?' asked Emma, not wanting to become entangled in a confusing situation or make waves.

'No, that was over a long time ago,' he insisted. 'Things didn't exactly work out. She still poses for me occasionally.'

Emma's looked around her, pleased that there were no other signs of a woman's presence in the gallery. She stared back at him warily: well, the woman was no longer around, there didn't seem to be any obstacles, so it was worth a try. Her emotions rose and fell like a roller coaster. She stared deeply into his hypnotic eyes, and was mesmerised. She felt drugged, intoxicated, filled with an exquisite feeling. Her body tingled, her legs turned to jelly, but she didn't want to go too fast.

'Perhaps I can have my first lesson now?' she asked him.

'I'd be delighted,' he said.

He got up and walked over to the other side of the room, and turned round some paintings, talking about the themes and made a few notes on a board. She watched his every move, the artistic way he wrote. Everything about him fascinated her, she felt breathless around him. He had a dangerous side, an edge that made him all the more attractive. She felt a surge of lust grip her. She swore she would not let him get away this time. Would they be lovers? Were Andrea's tarot cards always right?

'Shall I wrap the book for you too?' he asked, seeming slightly detached. For a few seconds, he grew distant, as though he barely knew her. Her heart sank. Perhaps he wasn't that interested in her after all, just hoping to get her to join his class—it had just been all her dream. Then, as he walked past her, his dark eyes sparkled with a potent energy and his smile made her heart leap and her body melt. His eyes sparkled with potency as he searched beneath the counter for sheets of paper. His long, elegant fingers folded the paper quickly, in swift elegant movements. To see him face to face, the fantasy lover from her dreams, made her soar to Heaven.

She handed him another painting, their fingers touched, their eyes met, a flame of desire lit in her. She felt struck by a bolt of electricity.

'I am the artist—Anton,' he said, his eyes flickering with curiosity. 'Would you like me to sign it?'

'Yes, thanks.'

He scribbled his name hastily on the back with the pen. Emma stood like a deer frozen in the power of his gaze, her pulse quickening as he stood next to her. She listened as he talked about art, his voice had a strange edgy quality. She felt like she was watching a film in slow motion.

'When did you move here?' she finally managed to ask.

'Five years ago, I was from Sussex originally,' he replied, walking to the back of the shop. 'But the landscapes are breathtaking, so is the sunset at Land's End, and there is so much to paint here, I felt a bit uninspired, now I have more than enough material to inspire me. I love painting the changing seasons, as the landscape changes colour. And you? What inspired you to come here?'

'I used to come here for holidays and then I moved here in August. I've just bought a new house. I came because I wanted to start a creative project, connected to the arts and saw this as my chance.'

'Yes, it was a very special day, when we first met,' he admitted. 'Do you like the romantic artists, Waterhouse and Rossetti?' he asked, showing her some pictures.

'Yes, it's my favourite era. I really like Waterhouse and Burne Jones,' she said slowly, as though waking from a trance.

'I have a copied Waterhouse,' he told her. 'As you can see, many of our paintings try to capture the Pre-Raphaelite mood.'

Emma looked at the romantic paintings, they were as good as

the originals. 'I like that one,' she said, pointing to one of a woman with long, flowing hair riding a unicorn.

'Then you shall have it. If you like romance, you have come to the right place. We specialise in romance and some medieval fantasy too,' he said.

'Great.'

'Please will you stay for a while? I don't want you to go yet.'

'Yes of course.'

She watched him carry the paintings to put by the door.

'Will you come to my exhibition, it's in two weeks time?' he asked. 'I'd like to see you again.'

'Yes, I'd like that.'

'Emma,' he said, kissing her passionately, 'I have wanted you for so long.'

Her body surged with a longing, shuddering with an intensity she had never known before. He let her go, she looked at his eyes glowing with love.

'Here are the details,' he said, handing her a leaflet entitled 'Mysteries of Woman: Goddess, temptress, siren, water nymph, and maiden'—women drawn in black and white, delicate sketches of them clinging to rocks, portrayed as angels, sea nymphs, mermaids, goddesses, nymphs frolicking in the waves, and sirens bobbing on the waves like mermaids, and of course the dark side of woman, the dark goddess enthroned, her eyes glittering demonically.

'Yes, it sounds fascinating, I'd love to come.' said Emma. 'What exactly are archetypes?' she asked, reading the literature.

'They are symbolic elements of the soul, the deeper side of a woman's psyche, her more spiritual side. For instance, the local librarian is a lady whose conventional role could be described as a local conservative woman who likes playing tennis, goes to work everyday, organises various charities and runs the local flower-arranging group, but she has hidden depths: she loves the sea, sailing and underwater photography. We may say she has an archetype of a "water goddess", she loves poetry and rhythm, and these reflect her hidden depths, her more soulful experience. Jennifer, her assistant, fits the maiden archetype. She is honourable, idealistic, pure in thought, finds enjoyment in very girlish things, whereas Angel is a dark goddess, scheming, enjoys a dark power and the lure of the occult path. They liberate women to access different parts of themselves, away from their conventional roles. The liberation of women through art is central to many of my paintings' themes, and many of the romantic artists, particularly the Pre-Raphaelites, enhanced women through their depictions of them.'

'What archetype am I?'

'A sea goddess, a water nymph and a maiden. So many. You live by the sea, and come to land occasionally, captivating those around you with your special charisma and magic. You possess many attributes of the goddess—strength, courage and intelligence. Your dreamy manner means that you come from another world.'

Emma sighed a wistful sigh and turned the leaflet upside down—it changed from a row of flowers to a row of skulls. 'Gosh what's this? How exciting, it's very original and changes perspective, just like Escher,' murmured Emma, delighted.

'Yes, it shows the dualities of nature, polarities, like the dark and light, the animus and anima. It comes from a collection I did this summer, of the dark and light sides of women. Maidens, pure enlightened, or shrouded in dark gothic mystery. I include the darker side of the psyche, as well as the light spiritual side or what Jung calls our "shadow" he said, pointing at the pictures. 'To be creative you need to study the darkness as well as the light.'

'Like yin and yang.'

'Yes, that's right. Take a postcard of it, I've got one here,' he said, taking one off the stand.

They strolled around the gallery. Anton put on a black jacket that swirled as he moved. He began adjusting the cuffs of his shirt, so that they hung out of the jacket.

'The exhibition will start at eight,' he said. 'Please be there.'

'I'll be there.'

'Let me kiss you again,' he said.

She leaned toward him, he gently pressed his lips to hers, she almost fainted with desire.

'Don't let's lose each other this time, I want you so badly, Emma.'

'I want you too.'

'Stay for a while longer, then I'll drive you home.'

'No, it's all right. I'm parked in the car park, I walked to the studio.'

'Okay, then stay and see my surprise, before you go; there's something I'd like to show you.'

He led her to the back of the shop, through to a huge studio with paintings displayed on stands and on the walls. There were hundreds of paintings scattered everywhere.

He went to a group of paintings, draped with a silk cloth.

'You are a combination of goddess and a youthful maiden,' he said, pulling a cover off a canvas to reveal a sketch of a woman. Her gaze was open, her face serene; she wore a gentle flowing robe, her hair rippled around her shoulders. Emma looked closely and recognised her own face at once. She clasped her hand to her mouth in surprise.

'Aphrodite or Venus,' he said. 'Goddess of love, or you could even be Amphitrite—sea goddess.'

'She looks just like me,' said Emma surprised.

'It is you.'

'It *is me*. How did you do that?' she said, surprised. 'I have never posed for you?'

'Emma, the goddess,' he said. 'I used the image from the photograph I took of you the day I met you at the beach. I captured your essence well. I love to paint you. You have a magic that translates to my themes well.'

'Gosh it's wonderful,' she said, looking down at the swirls and strokes blended on the canvas. Waves of love swept over her, taking her breath away. 'It's so lovely. So wonderful.'

'I'd like you to be my model.'

'I'd love that. Yes!' she said, her eyes sparkling with rapturous delight.

She examined the painting carefully, he had captured her inner beauty and light, her face glowed with happiness. Her eyes shone with laughter. In the picture her hair tumbled down over her shoulders in curls, her silk dress blew in the wind, the sunlight caught her hair as she danced in a meadow, a happy carefree maiden.

'I love it, it is so beautiful,' she said, her eyes misting over.

'You are so beautiful,' he said his eyes sparkling with a happiness, 'worthy of such gifts and beauty endowed upon the goddess.'

He touched her long, flowing hair, cascading to her waist. He ran his delicate fingers through the soft curls, and stood back.

'You combine so many women, the goddess, the maiden, even the siren. You have such a pretty face and perfect profile, a siren risen from the sea, a mermaid. A goddess filled with divine light. You have ethereal qualities, important for a romantic model and a feminine chameleon quality that allows you to adapt to any role,' he said admiringly. 'Your innocence and openness gives you a freshness, conveying your wonder for life, a fluid nature. I have been lucky to find you. My mutable Pisces nymph, who loves playing in the sea with the dolphins.'

He drew a quick sketch and handed it to her. Emma laughed—it was a caricature of a mermaid, with a tail! He had captured her expression exactly. He went to the paintings, and pulled out one of a wood nymph sitting in bracken amongst deer grazing in the background.

'Well, I have to go now,' she said softly.

'It's a pleasure,' he said, walking to her car. 'I want to see you every day, get to know you.'

The next few days she went to the gallery shop, and they would sit discussing art and life over lunch. Once she looked up and saw a sketch of a woman's face, she thought she recognised her.

The woman's face was gentle, her blue-grey eyes shimmered under cascades of gold-auburn hair. Emma thought she had seen her before.

'She is so beautiful, who is she?'

'That's Letitia, my great uncle's love and muse.'

Emma studied the gentle face, it puzzled her, she looked the same as the woman she had seen in the glass.

'Were any of your ancestors famous artists?' she asked suddenly reminded of Antoine, the artist poet. They looked so alike. A dark look crossed Anton's face and he turned away.

'My great-great uncle, also an artist, was quite strange, mad in fact. Here are the paintings from the local artists,' he said, ushering her into the back of the gallery, evading her question. 'I think you'll like these,' he said. He took her round the rest of the gallery. Suddenly he stopped at one of a woman with a wild gaze and long, rippling red hair flowing over her breasts, her thighs open to reveal a red thatch of pubic hair. A wanton smile on her face. Emma gasped in surprise and would have recognised that mane of red, unruly hair anywhere.

'Oh, I recognise her, that's Andrea. What a beautiful pose.'

Anton laughed: 'Yes, it's one of Ramone's, we sell quite a lot of his work.'

'He adds a touch of humour too.'

'They are taken from the love and mythology theme,' he added softly.

Emma smiled to herself, knowingly.

'He has a gift,' she observed, glad to see that Andrea was clearly getting on very well with him. 'I wanted to speak to you the first day when I saw you at the pub, but you were with Angel.'

'Yes,' he said, a dark shadow falling over his face. 'That's all over now.'

'Do you believe in love, real love?' she asked him. He looked pensive for a moment, then replied thoughtfully.

'Love can be a fleeting emotion, fragile and impermanent, often elusive, it can vanish in an instant, but yes, I do believe in it, and know it holds more power than anything else on this earth. Love inspires us more then any other emotion,' he said, softly. 'How about you? Do you believe in love?'

'Yes, I never give up hope of finding true companionship. I am a typical Pisces,' she admitted. 'We live for the perfect love, it is my dream.' She noticed a mystical quality about him and felt a spiritual bond was already forming between them. She wondered if he was the one, she felt easy in his company, as though she had known him for a long time. Perhaps he was the one she had been waiting for, the right one.

'Art reveals the inner soul,' he said. 'It is not for those who are afraid to see, and there is no illusion. Love cannot be faked.'

'No, it lights up the soul, nothing else can make us feel so complete.'

'The mystery of woman and love is explored best by artists and writers, who with their extra vision can see into the depths of the soul,' he whispered. 'They see the hidden secrets of woman and of love. Of course they can see the darkness in a woman's soul too, if she has some, but that just makes her more enigmatic, more of a mystery—a challenge who must be conquered and is alight with the shimmering darkness of an untamed soul, burning with intensity. The goddess, Venus, the siren, the maiden, the huntress Diana. Women are so alluring, enchanting, seductive, and so mysterious. Don't you agree? There are so many sides to woman, and to love. Love can be cruel or kind, it is like the sea and has the power to create or destroy, but it is always powerful.'

Before she had time to answer, he asked, 'You will be there? I'd like you to come.'

'Yes, of course.'

'Shall I exhibit this one?' he said, lifting up the one of Angel. 'I'm not sure whether to.'

'It might frighten people away,' Emma said truthfully. 'She has very powerful, disturbing eyes.'

'Yes, she has a withering, wild and feral stare. It gives a good contrast to the spiritual goodness of the Goddess theme. You must not be afraid to see the darkness, as well as the light.'

Emma looked at it critically, then she added, 'I suppose it shows another side to woman.'

'Yes, that's how I see it.'

'I'll put it with the others,' he said, slipping it in with the paintings. He strode across to the end of the gallery then stopped and turned back to look at her. Suddenly he was next to her again, as though he had appeared out of thin air.

'How did you do that?' she asked.

'Just a little trick I learned. I studied Tai chi and other eastern arts, I move fast.' He laughed.

'Come with me to the moonlight,' he said, 'and ride with me to the gates of dawn.' His powerful sensuality was drawing her deep into his hypnotic gaze.

'I'll follow you anywhere,' she promised and kissed him.

The intensity of his glance made her shiver with desire, she ached for him. He pulled her close, and swept her tightly into his arms. He kissed her for a long time.

'Yes, oh yes. Anton, I want you,' she whispered, falling under his spell, devouring him, feeling his heat against hers, leaving her breathless.

'I will take you on a journey, to another world,' he whispered. He looked up. 'Some people are wandering in, maybe I should close the gallery.'

'No, it's okay, we'll meet again soon.'

'See you at the exhibition. When it's all over, I shall take you to lunch.'

The next few days, on the phone, they discussed art, philosophy and the meanings of life. She went back to the gallery and bought another painting.

'Do you enjoy being an artist?' she asked him.

'Certainly,' he said looking around him. 'The reason I paint is to transcend ordinary life; art brings liberation, and it frees the spirit. It is the most important gift a human has, that of vision and creative talent. I try to teach my students this philosophy, to enhance their awareness, their vision, to heighten their appreciation of the beauty around them, and to educate their mind and spirit. To help them grow spiritually, intellectually and emotionally, to reach peak experiences to be there with the gods, to experience ecstasy, help them to reach their potential and make full use of what the environment has to offer. I would rather be dead than live the tedious kind of life that most people are content with, conforming to a sad, restricted reality. They are only half alive, their senses and natural gifts dulled by conformity. The opiates of existence. They have lost all vision and what is really important for the development of their real selves. They become dead, spiritless automatons who can barely function, who lose their vision, appreciation of beauty, enchantment and wonder, and experience blandness. Hell on Earth. Banality. I try to transcend that state by the study of beauty, elevation of the self. Come to my studio and I will show you what I mean.'

Her instincts held her back; despite the attraction, she didn't want to jump in at the deep end so said, 'Maybe.'

His eyes stared wildly at her, sending out signals that were making her crazy. There was a sense of wild remoteness about him. She was lost in an instant. His eyes burned hungrily into her with a ferocious intensity. A dark, dreamy mistiness overcame her, flooding her with a strange lightness as though a mysterious force was engulfing her, as unfathomable as the sea. She tried but couldn't fight it. Her emotions were rising and falling like the waves, she was powerless to them. Waves of love swept over her as she was ignited by his touch. He held her head and kissed her passionately again, awakening a wondrous magic in her soul. She considered her sudden loss of senses over a man she had just met, and who seemed to be exercising an incredible power over her, to be foolish. Yet she could not stop herself, he had her under his spell. He captivated her with his exciting philosophies and ideas, his mystical, artistic and intellectual traits, and was one of the most interesting, intelligent and sexual men she had ever met. There was vibrant light in his incredibly beautiful eyes that made her quiver with desire. She needed to be a little wary; after all, artists were not the most reliable of men and often had many lovers. Was it wise to jump into something unknown, so soon?

He smiled at her warmly, and her doubts began to fade; she wanted him so badly, she no longer cared. She liked his different sides, the elegant gallery owner, the intellectual and the wild rugged surfer. He was a bit of a chameleon too. She felt him slide against her, her body melt like liquid, then he stopped.

'Look, I hope you don't mind,' he said, 'but I must paint you again soon. Will you like to pose for me?'

'Yes, I'd like that.'

'See you at the exhibition next weekend then. We can talk about it then.'

'Okay.'

She followed him out of the gallery in high spirits.

'Do you live near here too?' she asked.

'Along the cliff edge, at the artists' colony. Shall I come back with you?'

Emma nodded, his voice became an echo; she stopped suddenly, thinking she saw a black figure wandering past. Was it the man she had seen at Kynance? There was a familiar edge about him, and he looked just like Anton. She felt a strange eeriness flow over her. What was it about this place? It had such a mysterious air. What was happening? She turned round and the shadowy figure had gone. Was someone following her? Ever since she had arrived at the cove, her life was brimming with strange mysteries.

'Will you be at the beach party tonight?' she asked him as they drove back to the inn.

'Yes, I might go, if we are not too busy,' he said, dropping her at her doorstep. 'I'll walk back,' he said, 'it's good exercise.'

'Take my bicycle,' she offered.

He planted a kiss gently on her cheek, then pulled her into his arms and kissed her passionately. He leapt on the bike, raced down the road, waving.

Back at the gallery, Anton began mounting the last of the paintings for the exhibition. He chose the one of Emma for central display, hoping it would be a nice surprise for her. He was happy with the way it was progressing: they just met from time to time. He put the one of Angel next to her, a contrast of dark and light females, then thought better of it and put it to one side. He picked up the local paper to read the latest reviews of his work.

'Mysterious, shadowy echoes of the past mingled with rays of sunshine and light,' said one review. 'Contrasts of darkness and light blended with spiritual philosophies.'

Pleased, he turned his back on the studio and turned off the light. As he closed the door, a dark shape slithered across the floor. A rancid smell drifted up the stairs, like rotting flesh. A hollow laugh echoed from somewhere in the distance. Later, Anton drifted off into an uneasy sleep, unaware of the stranger standing alone in the shadows, his bright eyes blazing intensely in the darkness.

A Party

Emma squeezed into her tightest black jeans, and pulled on a skimpy jumper; it was perfect for the beach party. Her figure looked pretty good. She had toned up nicely since walking and swimming every day and had a lovely even tan. As she reached the beach, Andrea and Ramone dashed over and plied her with local cider, then disappeared into the sunset. Behind the lifeguard's hut she spotted Anton going into a tent, he was alone.

She followed him inside, blasted by the sounds of heavy rock. He was lying down, on a lilo, gazing up at the moon. Wordlessly, he looked up and smiled as she crept over to him. His chest was naked, his slim thighs squeezed into tight jeans. He was unkempt, like a laid-back surfer, rugged and covered in sand, quite unlike when he worked at the gallery. 'Hi Emma,' he said.

Her heart skipped a beat; he looked just as beautiful, but wilder, and his eyes were shining with dark shadowy secrets. Tonight he was all wild, rugged surfer again, not so much the urbane intellectual. She felt a surge of hot desire rip through her. In a second, he pulled her on top of him. She felt his tongue probe deep into her mouth as their legs tangled together. Then slowly, she undid his jeans and kissed his stomach. He kissed her hungrily, but suddenly his mood changed. He stopped and zipped up his jeans, then held her in his arms and kissed her again.

'I don't want to rush things, Emma,' he whispered. 'This is special. Let's wait for a while. I just want to hold you. I want it to be magical. Let's go for a ride. I must show you the sunset.'

Emma nodded, her heart bursting with love.

They rode over the cliffs, on horses borrowed from Anton's friend. Together they cantered past the orange blazing sunset, over the sand, past the gentle waves of the crystal sea up to the hills, the breeze rippling through Emma's hair. They stopped at the top of a large dune. A grey hue of misty evening light was covering the landscape. They tethered the horses by the lifeguard's hut and slipped into the grass on the dune and sat watching the moonshine on the dark sea. Later they lay, arms and legs entwined, as he kissed her face softly, and stroked her cheek. The last of the orange sunset was fading in the distance and the moon rose ominously in the sky. A white silvery ball mottled with blue blazed above them.

She looked at him intently, noticing there was something strange about him tonight. He looked different in the half moonlight. Like the aristocrat gypsy! The man she had seen in the mirror! Antoine, just like the man whose reflection she had seen at the inn! Anton wrapped her in his arms, and she felt all sense of time slip away as they kissed, watching the dark clouds drift across the inky black, velvety sky.

'I came here to see you tonight,' he confessed. 'Look at the stars! They seem quite bright. You can see all of the universe, quite clearly.'

Emma lifted her head and gazed up at the sparkling sky. Anton cupped her face in his hands and gently kissed her lips. 'I have been searching for you, Emma,' he whispered, 'for so long. I am so glad that we can be together at last.' The moon shone brightly behind them. 'Don't ever leave me again.'

'I promise I never will,' she said, feeling his heart beat against hers, not quite understanding what he meant. But still she didn't care. They went outside and sat listening to the roar of the sea, watching the flickering lights of the lighthouse twinkling in the distance.

She woke up when the sun was rising, and looked over to the ruffled bed next to her, where was Anton?

Anton had gone.

The exhibition

It was a balmy night, blustery and humid, the wind scattered sand everywhere. Dusty leaves blew across the path. Emma stepped lightly over them. The sand caught in her hair and clothes. She tried to shake it off, ducking under the awning into the doorway of the exhibition. An evening browsing around a gallery was just what she needed. She stopped and gazed steadily at the poster on display, 'Mysteries of woman, art and romance': it featured a picture of a goddess, with an austere and elegant profile. Her heart beat with excitement. She walked down the corridor surrounded by hoards of people, chatting away. She flicked through the brochure 'The Goddess, and the romantic mystery of woman'—and was stunned at the refined beauty in all the paintings: bright vibrant colours splashed over serene pastoral scenes, pastel ethereal shades combined with vibrant colours draped over women with long tresses, their eyes flickering under silver moons. Women frolicking in streams, running through fields, galloping across the plains on wild horses, or basking happily in the sun, shaded under swaying trees. Anton, true to his word, had kept to the style of the pre-Raphaelites, and other romantics painters, fusing beauty with nature, and had depicted the women as true goddesses.

She glanced quickly around the exhibition hall to see Anton's work shimmering in the centre, closely resembling their style, his elegant peaceful women sitting in repose. Ethereal, genteel maidens, with long flowing hair, silk dresses gathered around their slim ankles, gazes gently skimming over the shimmering water. He had captured their expressions with precision and given them a magical, spiritual air. Some pictures conveyed spiritual ecstasy, others the pain and agony of abandonment—all human emotions were there. Evocative, spellbinding themes. Maidens captured blissfully roaming through rural pastures, or swimming in turbulent seas. The enchanting ecstatic smiles of the goddess, lighting up the spiritual within them, love and light dancing in their eyes, an inner glow. Paintings that portrayed inner secrets of beauty and wisdom. Each picture told a story of romance, love, elegance, or of moral dilemmas, and some were living with the gods.

Emma wondered where Anton had got to. Where was he? He should have been here half an hour ago? And why had he left so suddenly after the beach party? She hadn't seen him since.

She wandered into the main hall, and was nearly knocked over a by a pack of unruly students rushing through the corridor.

'Hey, look where you're going,' she scolded.

Emma composed herself, walked back to the main exhibits, and browsed through the paintings. A vast array of shimmering vibrant paintings were mounted in front of her, and lined the walls. She came to the next section, 'The Nude' and gasped at their beauty and elegance; delicate paintings were framed all along the walls, drawn with the precision of real photographs. Women, with long flowing hair entwined with flowers, reclined under foliage, their naked bodies curled against a backdrop of fields and trees. She stopped as she came to *Lilith* by John Collier, a beautiful woman circled by a snake. The next mounted painting was of a beautiful woman, her eyes lowered in ecstasy, in a demure pose, partially covered in pale peach silk, hair plaited with lilac flowers, emerging from a chrysalis, changing into a butterfly. It looked like her, and Emma smiled, surprised: Anton had used her face for quite a few of his pictures. Next she came to a woman with waves of flaming corn-coloured hair cascading over her quivering shoulders, wrapping her hair around her as she stepped out of a shell. Maidens were dressed in veils of thin silk, their breasts thinly veiled under the opaque silk. Maidens dancing in gay abandon under the sun, among butterflies and firebirds, whirling as free spirits of the night. Emma walked past the paintings, her eyes fixed, each one as captivating as the next. Women throwing their hair back, their eyes full of ecstasy, in the throes of love, transported into transcendence, caressing their own bodies, fusing with nature, charged with a female sexuality and spirituality, women empowered as the Goddess. Gentle maidens singing, among the delicate flower petals, and spinning under spiralling tendrils and foliage. Their silk dresses swirled out around them like fans, like a Sufi dervish. The fragility of human nature and form, tender emotions, love of the ethereal, the mystical, glowed before her, brought to life so that she felt they were real. Magical fairy woman depicted with wings and a demure loving magical gaze and a magic touch.

Next, she came to pictures of knights and maidens, myth and magic, with themes of courtly love and *gentillesse*, refined, elegant women pledging their lives to their noble knight. Emma walked straight over to a vivid depiction of a blonde woman called *The Goddess Venus*, a beauty bathed in swirling colours on a canvas, with streaks of sun lighting her flowing hair and a smile of wonder flickering on her face. The woman wore a smile of pure bliss, her eyes shone with light, in a state of ecstasy. Surprised, Emma recognised herself!

The exhibition room was getting crowded. People were filing in to see the pictures. Emma walked deeper into the gallery, where the paintings became more surreal and slightly darker. Here were paintings of women as uninhibited, free, in abandonment, no longer virginal, true, devoted maidens but dark temptresses and predatory vixens, dangerous women possessed by demons with a dark shadow. Swirling, dancing, tantalising and captivating. Art of dualities, of dark and light, abandonment and dark power, a potent fantasy, with several pictures of the femme fatale. The darker side of woman and her psyche. One appeared on a starry night, shrouded in a white gown, lost in the ecstasy of her passion. Others sat on a moonlit hill, their shadows dancing in the night, weaving through the magic stones, casting their spells.

Emma took a leaflet, then stopped in surprise as she came to a painting of a woman crouching on her knees like a lioness, her head thrown back, sensual and wild, ready to pounce, her mane of wild red, coppery hair falling over her body—part woman, part mythical creature, a goddess. It was Andrea. Her legs were spayed open, her body scantily clad in a silken cloth, her fingers were tentatively stroking between her legs, a look of ecstasy on her face. Emma gasped in surprise and wondered who had painted it and what thoughts had crossed her mind as she posed. She wandered back into the main hall, looked around for Anton; there was still no sign of him. She bought a postcard and wandered back into the hallway. The rest of the paintings were displayed in an avalanche of colours neatly woven into vivid scenes of nature.

She nearly jumped back in shock as she saw another one of Andrea, in Ramone's section—naked but for some strategically placed leaves, her wide green eyes stared vibrantly, like a she-wolf, her red hair tumbling over her breasts. Like a pre-Raphaelite model with her red coppery curls thrown back, springing to her waist, she was a wild wanton woman with a ravenous appetite for life and love. Emma peered closely at her face, feeling a twinge of excitement. The paintings glowed with a sexual frisson. Next to her were pictures of women who practised the highest virtues, maidens, of gentle poetic temperament and sobriety alongside scheming predatory vamps and vixens. She stood enchanted, maybe there were more of her too. She looked at the rest of Ramone's collection, women with voluptuous figures, with ample breasts and heavy thighs. In another part of the gallery was a woman as a mystery sun goddess, weaving potent spells. Woman: as magical goddess, endowed with special powers and gifts. Next to Ramone's paintings were more of Anton's exhibits. Delicately romantic females posed next to Ramone's Rubenesque, raunchy women. Anton's women were genteel, ethereal, virginal, chaste, high-bred maidens who glowed with a ghostly air, were women worthy of courtly love and brimming with high virtue. His intricate strokes had brought them alive; she half expected the characters to move. She stood back to get a better view of the pictures. They possessed a certain power, the women's expressions delicate yet intense. The ideal woman seen as a cross between the goddess and playful nymph.

Emma's attention was suddenly caught by a large picture of a stunning blonde maiden riding a unicorn; on closer inspection she saw it bore a strong likeness to her. She smiled, touched. Like some of the others, he had painted this one without her knowing. Who were all the other women? She wondered. Were all his models his lovers as well as his muse? Had they all been his lovers at one time? She felt a sudden stab of jealousy, and fiercely protective of her role as his muse. Hating the idea of his being intimate with another woman, she quickly moved on. A little further along the corridor was a woman with an angelic face who sat posed under swirling skies to a background of verdant green, sloping fields. So painstakingly drawn, the detail made her draw in her breath. Another rode a wild stallion, galloping across a field, his flowing mane rippling in the wind. Next she came to a group of maidens, bathing in a river, their long hair flowing over their breasts. Then she stopped suddenly, drawing in her breath at the incredible scene in front of her. The maidens were so beautiful that she felt her spirit soar. She looked again at the painting entitled *Lovely maid in the sunlight*—it was another one using her image.

As she walked into the 'dark nights' section, she felt the air grow colder, the images were dark and shadowy, mysterious. Suddenly, she sensed someone staring at her. Feeling strange, her senses caught in a whirl, she felt heat burn into her neck, as if pricked by a pin. She looked up and saw the gaze of Angel: she felt the colour drain from her face, such was the air of malevolence coming from the painting—it was Angel as the 'Dark Goddess', her dark eyes staring down at Emma, blazing with fury, her gaze burning with a dark hypnotic power. Emma recognised that dark demonic stare from the day in the pub and shivered. Angel was dressed in a black, flowing dress with a dark veil over her face, eyes shining through the veil like a demoness. 'Dark dreams, of the enchantress'—powerful, magnetic eyes glowing with a malevolent energy burned into her like lasers. Emma felt hot and took off her jacket; the temperature of the room seemed to soar. Here was Angel as a devil woman, of exceptional beauty, with dark hair rippling over her shoulders, contrasting with her lightly tanned skin and slanting, wicked green eyes. Bats and dark nymphs were circling her. Her black gypsy hair flew around her like a raven witch, her gaze burned with a dark satanic power. A moody femme fatal, a seductress, dark and dangerous, swathed in black velvet. Like the living dead.

Emma shivered. Something about the painting made her feel uneasy, and she felt very dizzy. She had to move from the woman's eyes that bore into her soul. Angel was clearly her rival. She walked over to a collection of small paintings, with dark disturbing themes and had to look away, they were strange and unsettling, and made her feel uncomfortable. She turned and looked back at the one of Angel, her eyes seemed to be following her, piercing right through her.

Uneasily, Emma wandered back to the main exhibition area: what had happened to Anton? He was supposed to have been there an hour ago. She fiddled with her guidebook, nervous and excited at the thought of seeing him. She wondered if coming was a good idea and she turned to leave, but a strange force seemed to pull her back. Artists were so unpredictable and already she was aware that Anton could be moody. He was quite different to anyone she had ever met, a law unto himself, changeable, mystical, elusive, otherworldly, a genius and true poet. Then, she spotted him out of the corner of her eye, talking to a crowd, and her body turned to jelly. The local press were swarming around him, clicking furiously. He waved, and she waved back, feeling the familiar flood of longing and lust. She could not resist him, he was the one, the one she had dreamed of meeting, the man she had always hoped to find. For a second she wondered if he was right for her. Then she thought recklessly, who cares? He was her destiny: however dark and dangerous the path, she just had to go there. Her instincts told her to be careful, but her sense of adventure said stay. She wondered if she was just being attracted to her usual type, alpha males who exuded sexual confidence and attracted other women to them, like bees around honey—the fatal destiny she always chose, and that always left her burned. She felt a stab of anxiety, and wondered did she really want to go through that again? But her instincts told her Anton, although a complex soul, had a caring and kind nature and didn't waste his time on a woman unless it was true love; so there was a chance of something really special and wonderful developing between them, and their special chemistry took her breath away. She needed a more caring sensitive type, who was devoted to her. In Anton she detected elements of both; he was everything she was looking for in a partner, a lover. She embraced his restless bohemian spirit, a clever and talented mercurial mind. In many ways he was like her—creative and seeking, and he fulfilled her romantic desires as well as their ambition of working towards their shared dream. She decided to give it a try; besides, the mere sight of him whipped her up into a frenzy of desire.

Abandoning his admirers, he rushed over to her, seized her and kissed her passionately. The cameras were following him, so he pulled her into a quite alcove.

'I thought you weren't coming! Oh, Emma, I am so glad to see you.'

'Me too. I was in the upstairs hall.' Her worries slipped away like melting ice. What did she have to lose? She gazed longingly at him, she was single, free and was already in love, and sensed this one might work out. He took off his sunglasses and kissed her, yet his expression was dark and brooding. She felt herself turn to liquid as he pushed her up against the wall, forcing her to look into those incredible eyes that held secrets of the universe, and of love. He squeezed her body tightly against his: the paintings and people all faded into the distance as she melted into his arms.

'I am so glad that you could come. Where were you? I was waiting for you in the hallway.'

'We must have missed each other, I've been here for an hour.'

'What would you like to drink?' he asked, looking round for a waiter. 'I'll see if I can find one.'

'A glass of wine,' said Emma, gazing up at him.

'I thought I had lost you, I couldn't see you.'

'Sorry, I got lost,' she admitted. 'I was just wandering around, it's a wonderful, amazing exhibition.'

'Yes, everyone is enjoying it so far.'

'I'll just be a few minutes.'

He turned back, disappearing into the crowd. Emma smiled to herself, she wanted the best things in life, and guessed Anton would make the perfect lover. She was a dreamer, and he fitted into her dream very well. Apart from the romantic side, she needed an arts expert and teacher to help with her new business and he fitted that role to perfection. He was everything—lover, partner and business partner in one. Or perhaps his tastes were a little too avant-garde, even for her? She wondered how different a relationship with him would be from anybody else she had ever known—certainly unconventional, with nights of unbridled passion, combined with intellectual enlightenment and transcendence. Like her, he was passionately pursuing a dream. A typical artist. Then suddenly she felt a dark presence hover behind her, as though someone's eyes were burning into her. She felt dizzy and disorientated, turning round just as she thought she saw Angel disappearing into the crowd. Emma shocked, looked around for Anton. Walking back into the crowd, everything seemed to swirl around her, and faces were everywhere. She was confused, where was he? If there was a strange secret, a mystery surrounding him, she wanted to know what it was. He could be so elusive at times. She stopped as she saw him talking to a reporter. They were standing by a painting and Anton glanced over his shoulder at her and smiled. He walked over and shrugged.

'I am sorry, people keep coming over and asking me questions. It's chaotic,' he sighed, handing her the wine.

'Yes, there are a lot of people here,' she remarked, looking round her. Queues of people were filing in.

'Yes I didn't expect so many. Ah, there's Simon, I think he wants to talk to me,' said Anton, being dragged back into the crowd.

Emma took the glass of wine, gulped it down quickly, then took another. She wandered into to the centre of the room, swished the wine around her glass, looking at the paintings critically, when someone touched her on her shoulder. She jumped. Anton stood behind her smiling; he radiated an aura that was so powerful, it almost electrified her.

'I managed to slip away,' he whispered in her ear. 'Do you like that one? Would you like it as a present?'

She felt his panther-like body moving next to hers and her pulse quickened.

He pointed at the picture of Dionysus dining with Bacchus, the god of pleasure, seducing a group of nymphs under the table. 'The pursuit of hedonism is my goal,' he whispered. 'At least in my paintings.'

Emma laughed.

'Yes, it's interesting,' she said, taking in all the detail. 'But I prefer the romantic ones. Women with serene expressions and a mystical air, women swirling, in beautiful flowing dresses, caught in the throes of unrequited love. I am an incurable romantic.'

'Then choose another one. You have excellent taste!'

Emma chose a painting of a woman wandering through a meadow; it caught her eye with its lovely streams of sunlight and shades of silvery light rippling on water. Anton called over an assistant to wrap it for her.

'Why did you leave after the party? I woke up and you weren't there,' she asked.

'I had to get back to the gallery, and it was urgent. Some visitors from abroad,' he said, 'and as we were all sleeping on the beach I didn't want to wake you. I told Andrea. She said you wouldn't mind.'

'No, that's okay,' said Emma, relieved she had done nothing wrong. After all, they had only kissed. As he stood next to her she felt, more than ever, that he was the one.

'Do you like this one too?' he asked, pointing to one of the goddess Venus.

'Venus, the goddess of love,' she said softly. 'Yes, I like this one,' she whispered.

He kissed her ear. 'Then you may have it. Shall we go?'

'You can't leave now.'

'Yes I can. It's my exhibition,' he said sternly, looking at her closely. 'I'll just say I was called away. Oh hell, I don't have to make excuses, I'll just tell them that I am going.'

He strode over to the exhibits and spoke to a colleague; the woman handed him some documents and nodded. Emma watched him closely: he was dressed in tight, black jeans and t-shirt, with long black boots and a black frock jacket. She had to admit the look suited him, like a Left-Bank anarchist, so smoulderingly sexy. He pushed his long hair back with his sunglasses, his presence was sizzling. He slung his bag haphazardly over his shoulder, turned for a flash of a camera, then went back to his conversation. She watched his every move, studying him with fascination for a second—he reminded her of the priests at school, the way he stood, and it brought a flashback to her mind of cloaks swirling around their slim ankles as they glided through the corridors, crucifixes tied to their waists. Their eyes had glittered with a dark intensity—concealing dark secrets and desires, and for whom she'd had a strange fascination. At school, she had been drawn by their deep, dark mystery and thought them seductive. Now, men who wore black excited her. She found them mysterious and erotic. The lure of the darkness, the dark side, fascinated her. Now, Anton was evoking something dark, dangerous and disturbingly erotic in her. She blinked, brought back to earth by the noise of a group of school children.

'Shall we escape now? I want to be alone with you,' he whispered urgently. The gallery was growing more crowded and noisy, cameras were clicking, some new age music wafted through the hall. 'Would you like me to take those home for you?' Anton said, interrupting her thoughts.

She almost melted with desire, and sexual tension. 'Let's go somewhere we can talk.'

'Okay, let's go,' he whispered, 'while the guests are busy, I don't think they will even notice. I have missed you,' he said.

Emma giggled, excited at the idea of doing something impulsive. Together, they made their way to a local pub. He watched her over his glass of wine, his eyes sparkling with intrigue as they ate, intelligent, moving quickly, full of wit and humour, as he told her anecdotes of the art world. She could see that he found life amusing. He looked at her intently, summing her up.

'Where did you disappear to after the beach party?' she asked.

'I had to go, I am sorry, I've been worked off my feet.' Changing the subject he went on: 'Emma is such a romantic name.'

This time his voice was slightly clipped, academic. It was like she was meeting him for the first time. After seeing how famous he was, at the exhibition, for a moment she felt like a student back at university, slightly awkward in front of this sophisticated man, a highly intelligent, creative artist. She could see another side to him from the gentle artist she had spent cosy afternoons for the last few weeks with. Her pulse was racing, she had never been this attracted to a man before. Yet when he relaxed, she sensed a vulnerability in him; when he seemed less sure of himself, he became friendlier.

'What else do you do,' he asked her, 'besides buy paintings and build arts centres?'

'I used to be a copy writer, now I'm trying other things.'

'How interesting, I can see you have talent.'

'What do else do you do,' she asked, 'besides paint and run the gallery?'

'Well, I also teach part time at the university.'

Emma clasped her hand to her mouth in surprise.

'Yes, till now I've always rented the gallery; the original owner moved to Spain, I put in an offer and it was accepted. It is entirely my own business now.'

'Have you always been an artist?' she asked.

'Yes, it is my raison d'être. Tell me more about yourself,' he said, sitting back on the leather chair. 'Come and sit next to me.'

She joined him on the seat. She felt a heady rush of anticipation mixed with growing pangs of love. No one had ever made her feel quite like this before. She looked at him closely, her heart fluttered.

'I'd rather talk more about you today,' she said, daring to uncover his mystery. She could write about him for the agency magazine, and would keep him to his promise to give lectures at the arts centre.

'I missed you, Emma, these last couple of days,' he said, kissing her hand.

'I missed you too. I've read so much about you in the paper, you're quite famous, and have quite a national reputation in the art world. I didn't realise,' she said. 'I want to know more about you. We keep being interrupted.'

'Yes, I've noticed,' he laughed. 'It's nice to be alone at last. Maybe later, we can go somewhere even quieter.'

'Yes, I'd like that. Where did you learn to be such a good artist or were you born with a gift?'

'Well, both: some degree of artistic ability is obviously innate, but I studied art, at the Slade, where I took my PhD. I taught there for a while, as a researcher. While I lived in London I exhibited my work in London, and Sussex, and, through a contact, brought and developed my work here,' he said, swirling the wine thoughtfully in his glass. 'I came here for a working holiday and never went back, it's such an inspiring place to paint.'

'It's the best place in England for an artist to be, with such incredible landscapes,' she agreed.

'We're doing quite well now, the summer tourists snap everything up.'

'Is this your dream?' she asked.

'Yes, coming here was realising my dream. So many of my paintings have been inspired by the landscapes, and from the Celtic myths and the sea; there is so much natural beauty here,' he nodded. 'I love it here—to wake up to a sunrise every morning, and paint the sunset as it fades and falls behind the earth, and throws darkness across the seas. It's such a breathtaking experience. I run along the beach every morning, go surfing and swim every day, it's an idyllic existence. I work all night, and whenever the muse bites me, I am always inspired.'

'Me too, but is that the only reason why you came here? To paint?'

'Yes of course—what do you mean? Isn't that reason enough?' he asked looking at her strangely, moving his feet under the table. 'Yes, I suppose there are other reasons, it is the ideal place for a journey of self-knowledge, to seek transcendence, for self-actualisation. I suppose I am on a quest for a spiritual Nirvana, an awakening,' he admitted. 'Yes, it is my spiritual dream too, not just a good move for my career.'

'I had sensed you might be trying to escape from something,' she said suddenly, not sure why she said it.

'What on earth gave you that idea?' He looked at her sharply, shocked.

'Oh I'm sorry, I don't know. I shouldn't have said that. Perhaps I'm being a little intrusive.'

'Yes, that was a strange thing to say,' he said mystified.

'I feel so free here,' she added.

'Yes, me too, it's the perfect place for writers, poets, and for the arts, and of course for surfing and the sea,' he added, laughing. I love the sea, the way the glistening blue ocean goes on for infinity.'

'I think it is the most beautiful, magical place on earth,' Emma agreed, gazing out wistfully across the bay. 'A fairy tale dream, come true.'

'So you came for inspiration too? Not for personal reasons?' he asked, looking at her questioningly. 'Do you have any family here?'

'No, I came here as a child too. Well, I came here to escape the past and follow a dream. I had to leave the city, it felt so claustrophobic, I was working for an ad agency, but life took a dive when my engagement broke up and my life felt empty. I needed a change of scene and wanted to find a more meaningful spiritual existence—so I sold my flat and bought the inn. I followed an inner desire to find my true destiny, my real self, and the only place I really love is Sennen.'

'My poor darling,' he said kissing her softly.

'Well, I thought I would reinvest somewhere else and start again.'

'A wise move.' He nodded approvingly. 'Buying the Black Dove Inn.'

'Yes, the Black Dove Inn is my dream,' she said glowing with pride. 'Do you know anything about its history?' she asked him.

'The Black Dove's?' he repeated, his face suddenly darkening.

Emma felt uneasy, it was as though a dark cloud suddenly hung in the air.

'Well not really,' he said looking away.

'What's wrong?' she asked, worried.

'Nothing, I just heard that it has a bit of a dark past,' he said, frowning. 'Some pirates lived there. It's quite a strange place.'

'In what way?'

'On nothing really, just some old myths,' he said shifting awkwardly.

'What sort of myths?'

'Oh, nothing at all, it happened so long ago,' he said, growing tense. 'I shouldn't say anything, look it's nothing. I did hear some mysterious rumours, strange energies trapped from the past, that sort of thing, which I am sure is blown out of all proportion.'

'Is it haunted?'

'Oh no, I don't think so,' he said edgily, his face turning pale. 'I didn't mean to alarm you. Let's talk about something else. I'm so sorry. It has a bit of a turbulent history, that's all. Pirates once lived there as they have done in many places in Cornwall, such as at Jamaica Inn, it's nothing unusual. Just my over-active imagination,' he said, a dark shadow crossing his face.

Emma thought he looked so beautiful, late thirties, or even early forties, with an exquisite tan, dark features and alert bright eyes. He had so much energy, he was an expert conversationalist and his mind came up with new ideas at the speed of light. He had a youthful, boyish face, that could look clever and serious at times, but today he was scrambling around for the right words.

'Oh I see, never mind. I just wanted to know.'

'I don't really know much about it,' he said turning away.

'Did you always dream of being an artist?' she asked changing the subject; right now she didn't care if the place was haunted by a whole platoon of ghosts, they were fast fading into the background in Anton's presence. Although it was beginning to concern her that he could be so evasive.

'Yes, for as long as I can remember, I only ever really wanted to paint. My ancestors are painters,' he explained. 'Being creative is the only task that satisfies me,' he admitted. Carefully he undid his shirt, which seemed to be choking him. 'And I always loved to surf,' he added. 'So coming here was my ideal choice. The beaches here are amazing, and it's such a spiritual place. Is that why you came to this cove?' he asked her.

'Yes, for the beach life,' she laughed. 'It gives me a spiritual contentment. Sennen is a very beautiful place, it uplifts the emotions, makes me feel as though I am surrounded by magic, it's my special place.'

'I feel the same way.'

'We have something in common then,' said Emma confidently, putting down her glass. 'But I heard it's not that easy to make a living here. I have always thought being an artist means you have to starve.'

He relaxed and laughed. She watched his face as he spoke; he looked very sexy and unshaven, as though he had done things she could only wonder at. The thought made her sizzle with desire; she drew in her breath sharply, excited at the things he might show her.

'It does sound a bit of a dream, but I manage to scrape by. I teach art as well as paint, I also own the gallery and that does reasonably well too. I feel the energy flow into me when I gaze at the Cornish landscape, it connects me to my higher spirit,' he admitted, delving ravenously into a tray of chicken wings. They ate quickly. There was so much to say, yet a silence fell over them.

'Do you have anyone special?' he asked her after a while, wiping some grease from her cheek and moving a wisp of hair from her face.

She sipped at her drink thoughtfully. 'No, no one. There was someone, until he betrayed me. But I am over him now. He wasn't the person I thought he was and I was upset to be so disillusioned more than anything.'

'I know the feeling,' he muttered.

'You too?'

A dark shadow flickered over his face.

'Yes, I am alone now. Angel, she was a vixen. A dark goddess, a daughter of darkness, her motives toward me were not always pure.'

He darted a quick look at Emma, who was looking sceptical.

'Do you have many models?'

'No, I use models from the university, just one or two at a time.'

He looked down at his food and pushed it away. 'Angel should just have been a friend really.'

'Do you sleep with all your models?'

'I used to, if the mood was right, but now I only want you,' he said truthfully. 'I need to connect with a similar spirit. After a while pure eroticism loses its appeal.'

'Angel couldn't have been that bad.'

'No, seriously, she was into some strange things.'

'Well, I hope she hasn't put a spell on us,' joked Emma.

'I *am* serious,' he said irritably. 'Still that's all in the past,' he added quickly. 'A day hasn't passed when I haven't thought about you, wondering what you are doing,' he confessed. 'You have such a powerful spirit, so radiant, the opposite of Angel! She was needy. She was a genius, her poetry and writing were extremely poignant, bitter and twisted, but immensely perceptive. In most ways she was an amazingly talented woman. As lovers though, we were a mismatch. You glow with an inner beauty, sunshine and light, and have a love of beauty. I spend many hours absorbed by your beauty. She spun confusion around me, a dark suffocating web. You inspire and enchant me with your fresh nature, and wonder for life.'

'Well, I don't know,' she said seriously. 'Maybe it's because I have found fulfilment with my own self, but I can have my dark moods too.'

'You are everything I want in a woman,' he said gazing at her lovingly.

Emma listened intently, glowing with love. She felt him reach out into her soul and light her spirit with his love.

'Women in art and literature are often portrayed in archetypal form, that is a kind of stereotype, but a more romantic one, like in mythology. That is not to say that women act as witches, or sirens literarily, just that women possess deeper, more spiritual qualities represented by mythical roles. Well as a woman you are very special and magical, if there is an ideal archetype, then you are the ideal.'

'Thank you, and you are mine.' A dark Celtic poet with a touch of the gypsy and an astounding intellect, she thought, snuggling into his arms.

He laughed and squeezed her tight.

'I see, a woman may have the gentle charms of the maiden. Or the wisdom and strength of the goddess.'

'Yes that's it.'

'Or the scheming wiles of the dark goddess?'

'Yes, just like Angel,' he admitted gloomily. 'I was lost for a while because of her.'

Seeing the sad expression on his face, Emma dared not to question him any further.

'It sounds so fascinating.'

'Yes, the Pre-Raphaelites always depicted their women as romantic, fairy-tale characters, as sirens, goddesses or temptresses. Women were seen as otherworldly, above ordinary mortals. This added to their mystique and gave them an aura of mystery, so that they became the goddess ideal. Artists always elevate their models to the role of goddess, emphasising their mystical gifts as their muse.'

'Yes, didn't Rossetti turn an ordinary shop girl like Lizzie Siddal into a powerful figure, a sensual goddess?'

'Yes they empowered their models with romantic traits and gifts, turning them into magical, mystical women.'

'Do you use "archetypes" a lot?'

'All artists and writers do, they look at the spirit and the soul, reveal an inner vision.'

'Is your work well known?'

'Yes, it is fairly. I bought the other gallery, in Porthcurno three years ago, and have taken on many brilliant local artists. I get commissions for a lot of romantic paintings now,' he said, pushing the hair off his face and tucking it behind his ear. 'We have a steady flow of work, and now with the internet, our work has reached worldwide, we can hardly keep up with the demand.'

Emma drew in her breath at his elegance of spirit.

He looked straight at Emma his eyes lighting with a gentle soulful charisma. 'I made a study of the mysteries of woman, the archetypes in her soul, uncovered her creative essence and her feminine secrets. Her imagination is limitless, infinite, her gifts are endless.'

'Do all women possess the goddess power?'

'They all have the potential.'

'It's a beautiful gallery. I love to be surrounded by art,' she admitted. 'I'll have to learn all about it—the local artists, who they are and what mediums they use.'

'I can show you,' he offered. 'I display most of the artists from here, Paul Williams and Sarah Vivian, they are my favourite—and Sarah has a pagan edge, which I like. And we've been researching a dictionary, and now have archives of all the older artists like Samuel Birch. I'll give you a copy when it's ready.'

'Thanks, that would really help.'

'Let's go to your home,' he said. 'I want you, Emma. I want you so much.'

Hazy days

Anton followed Emma into the Black Dove Inn and put the paintings down.

'Shall I put them here?' he asked, placing the paintings next to the bar. He turned round and looked about him.

'Over here,' she said, directing him to the lounge.

Emma spun round the room, showing him her ideas and work.

'What a wonderful place,' he said admiringly, 'it has an incredible vibe. It reflects your inner beauty. It could only have been created by someone with an appreciation of exquisite things such as you. William Morris once said, "Only have in your home that which is useful or beautiful." Everything here is chosen with care, I can see that,' he said.

'I am glad you like it,' she said. 'I wanted to create an art centre, a nice environment where my guests can be creative, not like a formal gallery.'

They walked into a room glowing with delicately lit candles on tables nestling under Pre-Raphaelite prints. Anton sighed in awe: *Hylas and the Nymphs* and *La Belle Dame san merci* by John Waterhouse, *Lilith* by Collier, what romantic taste! You must buy some more originals though.'

'Yes, that's why I came to your gallery.'

'I must say, I'm really impressed, and it looks great! We'll starting hanging these here,' he said, finding a space for the new paintings.

'I've just finished decorating it,' confessed Emma. 'I have created a café wine bar where people can sit and observe beautiful art. A gallery can be a bit formal, here people can sit and relax and drink, chat with friends and enjoy the paintings at the same time.'

'A good idea,' he said, looking pensive as though he was hatching a plan. 'Maybe I can exhibit some of my art here too?'

'Yes, I would love to. I hope you can still run a class?' she asked.

'Of course, and we can hold exhibitions here and display some of the best artwork from the students.'

'What a wonderful idea, I am so glad we joined forces. I was wondering where to go from here.'

'You can join our website,' he offered, 'and I'll tell all my clients about you.'

'Thanks,' she said gratefully.

'Shall we celebrate?' he said pulling a bottle of wine out of his jacket. 'To my partner: we could work well here, and you could receive a percentage.'

'Good idea,' she answered. 'The café bar has an art club. I could turn the studio into a proper gallery.' Emma took down two empty glasses, and poured out the wine.

'Perfect, we are looking for new venues, perhaps we could also hold a group here too?'

'Sure.'

'Here's to us, and a successful business union,' he said, holding up his glass.

They clinked glasses, and Emma smiled, hoping they would be a success.

'This painting is beautiful,' he said, pointing to the one of the maiden being carried away by a knight on horseback. 'Waterhouse is one of my favourite artists.'

'Yes, his paintings are so romantic,' she sighed.

'I agree,' he nodded. 'No one else captures the essence of romantic characters as well as he does.'

'The knight reminds me a little of you. He has a Celtic wildness.'

'Yes!' He laughed. 'Why who else! A noble knight, a courtly rover taking the hand of his fair lady, whose virtue he protects, for whose love he has suffered in dark solitude,' he said, taking her hand. 'In that case, I shall follow the highest rules of courtly love to win your heart, and will remain forever your servant,' he joked, bowing. 'I will serve you always.'

She felt a flash of desire as she knew he wanted her too. His shrewd eyes scanned the room, he took her hand in his and kissed it.

'Oh Emma, I want you.'

'I want you too,' she said.

He cupped her face in his hands and kissed her tenderly.

He gazed at her with dark sensual eyes, boring into the deepest part of her soul, unleashing her wild nature. What did he conceal behind those dark orbs? She saw a light glowing in them, as though he had found the secret to existence. She sighed with desire. She wanted to hold him right now. Leaning over, he suddenly licked the salt from her lips with the tip of his tongue. She gave a gasp, feeling her knees weaken. She clasped his hair, and pulled his head down between her breasts. He kissed them, his warm quick breaths covering her body. 'Oh Emma,' he muttered, burying his face in the warmth of her breasts, smelling her exquisite scent. 'I have dreamed of this moment for so long.'

'Me too,' she said, pulling him closer, pushing her dress down; he sucked heavily on her nipples.

'Who are you?' she asked him, wrapping her legs around his back, kissing him passionately, her tongue exploring his mouth, her waterfall of hair swirling around them like a fan, then over her delicate, partly exposed shoulders. She kissed him urgently, wanting him so badly. He swept her into his arms and laid her on the bed, his eyes running over her breasts, and she felt herself helplessly drawn into them. She felt his body sink into hers, and his gentle thrusts push inside her. She gripped him and pulled him close, feeling she herself might explode in ecstasy, kissing him urgently. She became wet and slippery, as he pushed gently, then he thrust more urgently inside her, the two of them moving in a perfect synchronicity. Her body arched and then quivered as she let go, falling into a state of bliss, waves of pleasure rippling through her in deep pleasurable spasms, her whole body filled with ecstasy. Never before had it felt so good. He let out a groan and kissed her face.

'Who are you, Anton?' she asked as they lay panting on the bed. 'My magic man? My weaver of dreams?'

'Anything you want me to be. I am traveller, an artist, your muse, your destiny, your lover. All of these,' he whispered, winding a wisp of her hair around his finger. 'And your spiritual master,' he said softly. He lay back, sprawled on silken cushions on Emma's bed, cushions embroidered with fantastic tales of demons, running his fingers along her cheek. 'I am your magic man. I will turn all your dreams into realities, take you to the places of your wildest dreams, help you realise your dreams, if you want me to. And you are my goddess, to inspire my genius, the essence of my paintings,' he laughed. 'And I shall take you on a journey of the spirit, to the light and to the realms of darkness, if that's what you desire.'

'A big promise, an elaborate dream.' She laughed too, shooting him a wary look. She lay back, stroking his hair. 'I want someone who touches my spirit, who lights my soul with his wonderful secrets, fills me with the gentle echoes of love,' she said smoothing back his hair, 'and you do, Anton.' She kissed him gently on the lips.

'You have touched my spirit too,' he whispered tenderly brushing the hair from her face.

'Take me to your magical world. Teach me to paint like you,' she pleaded.

'I shall,' he promised. 'You have the sensitivity to make a good artist. But first may I paint you?'

She looked up at him, he traced his finger along the line of her cheek bone.

'A perfect profile,' he said, turning her face from side to side. 'And a sweet little nose,' he added, kissing it tenderly. 'Will you pose for me now?'

They walked downstairs, into the new studio gallery room.

'Please sit down on the stool, I just want to make a few sketches.'

She sat perched on the stool, her arms clasped behind her head.

He plaited her hair in a ponytail, and quickly made a few sketches of her in charcoal. He stood over her, drawing his fingers down over her cheek, feeling the contours of her face.

'That's wonderful, stay like that. You have such exquisite cheekbones.' Satisfied, he smoothed her cheek.

She reached up and touched his face. He was part of her puzzle, her destiny. 'What do you mean by the "darkness"?' she asked, curious.

'What I mean is, any good artist, or writer, will have to be aware of all aspects of existence including the darker ones such as the shadow, that means exploring the darker side too. Take Goya, for instance, and Bosch, Van Gogh, all powerful painters who studied the darker side.'

'…And went a bit too far, I would say.'

A dark shadow crossed Anton's face.

'Does everyone have a dark side?'

'Yes to some degree, but you have mostly sweetness. That is the side of you I adore and use for my paintings. I like you just as you are. I don't want to tarnish you with the darkness, that is not your real nature. Oh my dear Emma, I love you so much,' he whispered, taking her hand and leading her to a stool. 'Let me capture your essence, and bring you to life. I love finding out all about you, exploring all your different facets. I already feel I know you deeply, spiritually. It is such a luxury to paint you from life, not just from memory.'

He put up an easel and painted her for hours; at last, she got up and moved around, while Anton slipped off to the cellar for some more wine.

Emma stared at her reflection in the mirror, pleasantly surprised. She looked so radiant, she was glowing, it was as though he had turned on a magical light within her. Her eyes sparkled, and her skin glistened. Anton called out from downstairs, 'Red or white?'

'White,' she called. Suddenly, she caught a glimpse of a tall silhouette moving across the room, an opaque shadowy figure. She sat up straight and blinked: the strange, shimmering figure drifted across the room, it swirled and hovered for a few seconds, then vanished.

'Anton,' she shouted, 'come quickly there's a ghost in the room.'

She had turned pale and sat shivering on the stool.

Anton rushed back from the cellar clutching two bottles of wine and some glasses. 'What's wrong? You saw a ghost?'

'Yes, just now,' she said, suddenly going pale, looking shocked.

Anton rushed outside onto the landing and searched all round him. He opened the cupboards and came back. 'I can't see anything, I'll look downstairs.' He rushed down to the cellar and came back. Looking anxious, he hugged her. 'Are you sure you didn't just see a shadow from outside?'

'No, I am sure it was a ghost, I have seen one before.'

'Don't worry, my darling, it was probably nothing,' he said, looking worried. 'Just some shadows from outside, there are a group of paragliders flying around in the field. It was their shadows that you saw, the image of suspended bodies. Let's finish the wine.'

As they left the room, he looked back over his shoulder: strange glowing eyes were glinting with a strange malevolence in the darkness.

'Oh maybe,' said Emma, relieved, 'that could have been it.'

'Let's call it a day and start again tomorrow,' he said as she snuggled into his arms.

✠

The next day Anton lay back on the bed, watching Emma put on a long, black embroidered Chinese dress, with a slit up the side, and some black stockings. She clipped her hair up with an oriental clasp, creating a sleek elegant look. She loved to dress up, and was really getting into the different roles he asked her to play; now, she was very much the vamp-goddess.

He made some quick sketches, then put the pad down.

'I love that pose, it's so sexy, but that's enough for now. I wanted a few drawings to use for the new painting, I am not sure whether you should be sitting or lying back.'

She lay back, spread out like a lioness at rest, her hands clasped behind her head.

'Like this,' she said, purring like a cat lifting her legs to reveal suspenders and a black g-string.

'Yes, that's amazing, a very erotic pose.'

'Let's not do any more painting today, I just want to make love,' she whispered urgently.

He walked up to her and undid the Chinese dress slowly, he pulled it down gently and the tips of his fingers slid gently over her thighs.

'You are good at being so many women, and I love to make love to them all. I want you, Emma, now,' he said urgently, kissing her passionately. She felt his body go hard against her. He kissed her neck, her eyes, her lips. He ran the tip of his tongue along her stomach, between her thighs. Gently he pulled off her panties, his face nestling between her legs, and flicked his velvety tongue across her clitoris. She arched her back, gripping him harder between her thighs. He moved up, and eased himself inside her, and began thrusting slowly, then stopped, then made several quick thrusts. She felt herself grow heavy with desire, her face buried in his neck as he lifted her into waves of pleasure. She kissed his hair, his face merging with hers in total ecstasy as she screamed out, her body convulsing and quivering with pleasure.

'Oh Emma, my goddess!' he cried, a moan escaping from his throat.

They spent the whole day this way, making love for hours on end, talking, eating simple food, then through the night again, breaking off occasionally to watch the moon or talk.

In the morning, Emma woke up alone. She had never known such passion, this was the man of her dreams, sex had never been like this before, but where was he?

Had she said something wrong? Yesterday had been perfect. She lay back in a daze; well perhaps he was too busy today and didn't want to wake her up, but she found his disappearances slightly unnerving, despite growing used to his elusive nature. In all other ways he was perfect, the lover she had been looking for, who filled her with a passion she had never quite reached before. She lay back, drifting in a tranquil dream.

Suddenly the phone rang, interrupting her reverie. It was Anton. 'I'm in the studio,' he said. 'I'm working all day. I shall see you tonight.'

Emma got up and looked in the mirror, life was blissful and she looked so radiant. She thought about Anton. Carefully she brushed her hair, and smiled to herself

Anton was the most sexy, smouldering, beautiful man she had ever met. He was also the most sizzling and fiercely passionate, but he *was* contained. As they had walked back to her place last night, he had suddenly kissed her with real force and then had bitten her –unusual! But it was a wonderful bite and didn't really hurt. He seemed to have a thing about biting her. He had an inner darkness that was not the usual torment but a pleasurable, contained energy, a driving force. It was as though he was made to make love to women. A sophisticated but poetic man. Each movement and touch was so powerful and expert. When one bite was a little too much, she'd had to pull away. He left, saying he would call. She thought he meant to come back soon but he was like a gipsy and she couldn't pin him down. He said to her, 'I went out with the wrong woman in the past and now I can never go back.' Emma wondered what he'd meant. She noticed how his eyes would become dark, focused, as though he had a pent-up energy coiled up inside him that he dared not release, a smouldering, whirling energy that was too dangerous to control. His gaze filled with a dark brooding intensity. There was a feral streak in him that he kept under control. She could see glimpses of this darker side, like a caged panther waiting for release, prowling in the darkness seeking the light, wanting to be set free, and to find its power in an abandoned, unrestrained run—to be its true self.

He had looked up at her with his blue smouldering eyes and she had been lost, had succumbed to his power, as she felt the fire of his touch. Where would it lead to?

She put the brush down, he was the most exciting man she had ever met and she couldn't wait to see him. An enigma, he always seemed to disappear just as he had aroused her.

Surprises

'Sorry I had to leave, I didn't want to wake you. Come and see me at twelve o clock. I love you, Emma.'

Emma raced over to Porthcurno, past the Minack Theatre to Logan Rock. Her heart pounded in anticipation as she climbed up the cliff to his other studio. The warm memory of his gentle caresses still flicking through her mind She wondered why he always left early, during the night, it seemed an odd thing to do.

'I'm so glad you could make it,' Anton called out from a window, throwing her the key. She climbed up the long spiralling stairs, to his studio. He opened the door, smiling.

'The new paintings of you have turned out well. I am working on them every waking second, and I think I've captured your expression exactly. Come upstairs and look.'

She rushed up the stairs excited. She couldn't wait to see them.

He kissed her and led over to a series of sketches and paintings mounted on several canvases. They stood in the centre of the room, an array of pastel shades and textures shimmering in the light. He had bared the inner secrets of her soul. She was a naked nymph, frolicking in the sea. Emma stood in front of it filled with rapture, enchanted.

'It's just like me!' exclaimed Emma, surprised. 'It's beautiful.'

'Do you like it?'

'Yes, it's lovely,' she said admiringly.

'I have called it *Emma*, the water nymph, a sea gypsy.'

'Why did you leave? I wish we could wake up together.'

'You must understand when the muse bites, I have to work—ideas are like butterflies, and have to be captured in an instant. If not worked on at that moment they fly away.'

'I see,' said Emma, understanding now.

It was the first time she had been to his home and studio, a tall building with huge glass windows.

'Welcome to my home,' he said warmly, and led her through the hallway, his eyes glinting dangerously. He led her past Renoir's *Nymphs Bathing in a Mediterranean Paradise.*

'Do you like it?' he asked her. 'The pursuit of heavenly pleasures. A paradise.'

'Yes, it's quite idyllic,' she said. 'But I prefer the romantic ones.'

'The next one,' he said, pointing to some water nymphs frolicking, 'is of Eros, the Greek god of love.' He gave us the word "erotic". He made people fall in love using a few arrows, playing havoc with people's emotions. Shall we go inside?'

Emma laughed, she did not need the mischievous presence of Eros to enhance her desires, she felt amorous enough already. She looked around the studio; it was spacious, comprising large, arched windows overlooking the sea, with a circular balcony, like a lighthouse. She flicked through the paintings, of various women. She came to one of him with Angel, in an erotic pose, Anton performing oral sex on her. Quickly she pushed it back into the pile and fled into the warm, comforting light of the lounge. Beams of light shone through the huge, arched stained-glass windows. Sunbeams danced across the wall. The sumptuous lounge was filled with exotic plants hanging in the corners, their shoots sprawled across the floor. She found herself wandering through the white-carpeted room, with a lilac chaise-longue tucked behind an ornate Chinese screen, under billowing white curtains. Vases of white lilies filled the room.

'It's incredible!' exclaimed Emma, holding her breath, and going straight to the window. 'What a stunning view.'

'Yes, I like it,' Anton admitted, standing next to her. 'There's so much space, and light, I can be very creative here.'

He pushed open a door, leading to a room lit with soft lights. Piles of huge canvases, and sculptures were heaped in every corner. Tall stained glass arches spiralled up to the ceiling, giving spectacular views, from every angle, of the sea. Romantic paintings adorned the walls. Swirls of colour were splashed all over the heavy canvas, Emma sunk down into a leather sofa.

'I will teach you how to draw. You can paint some pictures for the inn.'

'I'd like that.'

'I will teach you some useful techniques. What would you like to drink?' he asked. 'Wine, or something more exotic?'

'Something more exotic.'

He poured out a glass of green velvety liquid. Emma noticed how elegant his fingers were, how deftly he sliced the lemon and balanced it gently on the edge of the glass. How attractive he was, how refined. He handed her the drink, their fingers touched and she felt an electric current pass between them.

'Thanks, it's so beautiful here, quite breathtaking.'

'I'm glad you like it, it's perfect as a studio, with so much light,' he said. 'It hangs so closely over the sea—at times I feel as though I am flying over the cliffs!'

She listened while he sparked her creative vision with stories of artists, their lives, what inspired them. His knowledge of fine art impressed her too. She did not know the difference between a Monet, a Manet, or a Matisse. His love of fine art, it was his passion, his raison d'être, he explained: 'Art is life.'

She followed him around, dreamily touching the canvases filled with swirling colours of landscapes and beautiful women, all naked. paintings of all styles, of all mediums, were scattered and stacked on easels, or strewn across the floor. She studied their rich oil textures, or their soft flowing watercolour hues, watching Anton from the corner of her eye, knowing he was a chapter in her life she was about to discover.

'Here, try one of these,' he offered, pressing a handful of purple berries into her palm.

'I love to eat different fruits, strawberries, blackberries, when I paint. They inspire me. Purple sits on my tongue, with the sharpness of wild berries, resonates with the tender strains of a harp, in harmony,' he said, poetically.

'Come onto the balcony,' he gestured. 'Look out there. Isn't that the most beautiful view you have ever seen?' he said, pointing to the bay, circling his arm protectively around her.

She nodded, the bay glistened in the sunlight, the sea roared and crashed like wild horses galloping in the bay. The dark rocks were black, drenched in sea spray as the misty grey light fell on the sparkling green seaweed. The sea stretched out for miles to infinity, as far as the eyes could see, almost to the Scilly Isles. A small lighthouse flickered in the distance. Small boats bobbed and floated in the small sandy harbour, and on the horizon. Emma drew in her breath: she was in heaven, and waves of sheer happiness enveloped her. Holding hands, they stood looking at the sunset burning in the sky, a cool breeze hit her as she watched the para-gliders drift past the slivery pink-blue clouds, in the greyish ochre sky. The sky, nature's palette, was filled with every colour and hue.

Part Two

Confessions ~ Descent of darkness

Anton stood over her, his hair flapping in the gentle sea breeze coming through the window. His eyes shone with a potent dark power, like a gypsy. She stared deeply into them. He took her hands in his and kissed her gently. 'I missed you, Emma,' he said, ruffling her hair. His gaze was a chasm of mystery. His influence over her grew as he filled her dreams with the strange myths of the universe. She had strayed into a dream, a mirage, with her knight, taking her to his lair. He stood in front of her, real as any man, yet so mystical.

'Where did you go last night? You didn't wake me,' said Emma, wondering what the mystery was, but she was growing used to his sudden and inexplicable disappearances at any time of night or day. He didn't like to be tied down. Something around her was changing; she could not put her finger on what it was, but there was change in the air. Something odd had flown into their orbit, and a strange aura circled them.

'Oh, I went over to my other studio, I felt too restless to sleep,' he said nonchalantly. 'When the muse bites, I am driven to put my ideas down on canvas. I'm sorry, I didn't mean to be rude. I rushed back to prepare my work for a class and get ready,' he said, his expression vague. 'I didn't want to disturb you. I thought it was better to leave you sleeping.'

'But you've been gone for three days,' she said, 'without a word. I was worried.'

What is he hiding, thought Emma, growing suspicious, as a sliver of anxiety wormed its way into her consciousness; she looked at him worriedly. His eyes glazed over, as though he didn't care to discuss it, this banal detail of life, and he drifted into another world.

'I'm glad I have found you, such a wonderful muse, a spur for my creativity and my work. But I cannot always explain my actions or be tied down to time and place. To be creative, I have to be free,' he explained.

She nodded sympathetically.

'Have you ever heard the quote by William Blake? "He who binds himself to a joy, does the winged life destroy. He who kisses the joy as it flies, lives in eternity's surprise." That elusive quality is necessary for me to create, it gives a sharp, unique edge to my work. If you squash it I cannot reach out, or be creative. I lose my gifts and my spirit dies.'

'I'm sorry,' she said.

She glanced out of the window at some boats bobbing up and down outside.

'That's our boat,' he said pointing to one. 'I bought it for you yesterday. Would you like to come out in it? It's a wonderful experience to go sailing in this part of the bay in the summer.'

'I'd love to.'

'Perhaps you would like to move in and rent out the inn,' he suggested to her.

'No I would love to but I can't. I have so many responsibilities at the inn, and I have to be there. It is my project.'

'I understand and admire your resolve,' he said. 'I have never seen a woman as quite such an equal before.'

'I adore this cove,' she said, suddenly jumping to her feet. It is so quintessentially Cornish.'

'I chose it because of its wildness, it is so inspiring. Here I feel free, to soar like a bird. I have to be free,' he explained, 'to be able to paint, and I live for being creative.'

'What exactly happened between you and Angel?' questioned

Emma. 'I sense some mystery surrounding you both. I don't know why.'

He looked at her uneasily, his eyes narrowed into slits.

'Nothing of consequence,' he said curtly. 'We were together for a while, then we realised that we saw things too differently to make it work. What else do you want to know?'

'Are you running away from something? I just sense some unresolved business. It's just a feeling I have, I suppose. Did you come here to find a refuge, a haven? It seems strange to me that you are not telling me everything, that you keep secrets from me—like when you keep leaving without saying goodbye.'

'Well, I'm so sorry, I thought you would understand,' he snapped. 'I don't work to a timetable. When I feel the need to paint, I just go with it, go with the flow, being an artist is not like a regular job, you know. Please, Emma, let's not get too complicated now, I want to keep things simple and just enjoy your company, I don't want to spoil our wonderful day. You know the story of Pandora's box? She couldn't curb her curiosity, and so let loose all the world's ills. Perhaps you shouldn't follow her example. Don't look too deeply into things, or you will destroy them. Just let go and enjoy the moment and immerse yourself fully in the here and now. There is a saying— "Man cannot discover new oceans unless he has the courage to lose sight of the shores".'

'Humankind, not just man,' corrected Emma. 'We are all capable of intuitive or psychic vision,' she said, defensively. 'It protects us, and I often pick up on things. I trust my own vision, it warns me. Flying too high can blind us to important details.'

'That's very perceptive of you and it's a wonderful gift to have,' he agreed, his eyes narrowing against the light, a deep frown on his face. 'Though, I must admit, it is sometimes to our peril. Certain things are best left alone. Would you really want to know, if something terrible was going to happen?'

'Yes, then perhaps you could avert it.'

'Perhaps not, things happen as and when they do. We can't always change our destiny. Just go with the flow, enjoy life. Look at the beautiful scenery. Doesn't it fill your heart with joy?' he said, changing the subject.

'Yes, of course. But I can sense that you are trying to hide something.'

'Not exactly, but I shall tell you my secret. You see,' he started to say, 'I am psychic, or at least when I paint I am. I can predict future disasters through my paintings. Knowing what is about to happen is terrifying, the future does not always hold what we want.'

Yes, I can see that,' said Emma, surprised, 'that's a wonderful gift to have.'

'No, it's more like a curse at times,' he confessed.

The next second, there was a loud crash and Anton rushed upstairs. He came running down, his head in his hands. 'One of the windows has cracked, there is rain coming in,' he said, alarmed. 'The studio window is loose.'

Anton went upstairs to fix it, while Emma wandered round downstairs in the studio.

Later, he showed her the view from the balcony again, renewed in different weather:

'I've painted this view, so many times,' he said, pointing to the swirl of blue-grey sea under pink misty clouds, rising above the landscape. It went on for miles, shimmering under a silvery pink and grey sunset. A solitary boat sailed along the horizon, in the hazy distance. Emma drew in her breath. The sun shone pink orange through the mist, like a fire in a storm, in a very ethereal pink haze. Emma stared out to sea, then back at Anton.

His eyes were sparkling with excitement: 'I've just finished a new picture of the bay, with me in a rowing boat. Would you like to see it?'

Emma looked at the beautifully painted picture of Anton in the boat.

'How sweet,' she said. 'I can see your features so clearly.'

'Come with me, I'll show you the view from upstairs,' he said softly.

Emma took his hand and followed him up the iron spiral staircase. She leaned out of the window, gazing over the cliff-edge sloping down into the sea. She caught sight of some black jagged rocks glistening in the sea below.

'What are those?' she asked. 'They look very dangerous.'

'Those are the black rocks of doom,' he explained. 'Boats have been wrecked there for centuries, it's quite deceptive. It's clear and tranquil on the surface, but under it are treacherous black rocks, deceptively hidden.'

'Were many pirates killed there?'

'Yes, quite a lot. There is a lighthouse by the rocks now.'

The sun glowed in deep orange and yellow, like a flame. Streaks of silver-blue light shimmered on the tranquil water.

'Wow, it's incredible,' Emma said impressed, moving back from the edge. 'It's so beautiful, it's hard to imagine anything terrible happening there.'

'Well it has,' he said grimly. 'Please would you sit for me again?' he asked, kissing her.

She sat down on an old leather sofa at the end of the room. He picked up a canvas.

'Emma, you have inspired me; for a while I could not paint. I had lost all interest or inclination.' He stood dabbing brushstrokes on a canvas: 'Now, thanks to you, I can paint again. I was so afraid the predictions would return.'

'Well, maybe they never will.'

She sat still as he draped a lilac dress over her and arranged her hair so that it cascaded over her shoulders, and as a finishing touch, applied some dramatic make-up. She looked in the mirror, her blue-lilac eyes were smouldering like those of a dark mystical goddess.

'Oh yes, it's good,' she admitted, pleased.

'To my beautiful goddess-nymph' he said, quickly adding some more brushstrokes. 'I paint you as possessing mystical powers, your gaze transcends that of every other woman in existence. You make an excellent Zena, a goddess of the sea.'

Emma held up a small mirror, her expression had changed, it was sultry, her hair lay around her shoulders in soft ripples over her robe. She looked just like a high priestess, wife of Zeus, or a mermaid, her eyes were glowing with the strange secrets of the ocean. The transformation was incredible. Elated, she arranged the gown so that it draped to the floor and then stood haughtily, with one arm outstretched. Anton placed a laurel on her hair. She enjoyed acting the part, it was like being an actress and it made her feel very free. She felt liberated, pretending to be someone else.

'You look as though you have risen from the sea,' he said in admiration. He folded her in his arms and drew in her scent, kissing her neck. 'Every inch the perfect woman, I only dreamed of finding such a woman, such a lover and muse.'

Outside, Emma caught sight of a black dove flying across the sky. Perhaps it was an omen, she thought, fleetingly. Then she heard a crash: the window had fallen in.

Anton spent several hours installing a new one along with the help of local friends. It was late evening when he sat down and drank some wine with her.

After a while, the drama over, Emma joined Anton in the lounge; he had calmed down.

'What happened exactly?'

'Don't worry, it was nothing serious, the studio window smashed that's all, it's fixed now.'

Drawn deep into his magnetic power, Emma kissed him, falling deeper under his spell. He had a way of kissing her that made her feel so special. He ruffled her hair, kissing her with urgent desire, setting her senses aflame.

'Shall we eat? I have made you a special dinner, of the best fish caught in the bay. You deserve a thank-you dinner.'

'But I haven't done anything,' she protested.

'Yes you have, you have made me very happy,' he whispered, leading her to the dining table. Some music, chords from a Celtic harp, filtered softly through the room. The eerie, haunting notes had a hypnotic effect. She felt a very mystical mood overtake her.

'For my beautiful Emma,' he said, handing her a pretty ring inside a box.

'At first you were my muse, my inspiration. Now, I realise, I am so in love with you.' He slipped the ring on her finger. He poured her some wine. Inscribed was a card bearing the words: 'As with my hand my heart is bound to yours forever, may the sword upon my heart burn deep and true if my love for you should ever waver.'

She kissed his lips.

'That's a beautiful present.'

'And it is yours for eternity,' he said, kissing the ring. 'Emma, my divine goddess.'

She was interrupted by a noise outside; she looked out of the window, there was a commotion on the beach. Men started shouting, climbing over the rocks, she could hear the sound of an engine. They were unloading a boat. A solitary person stood at the edge of the waves, watching. It looked like Angel. Emma quickly shut the curtains and walked back to the table.

She shrugged, she would let nothing upset her tonight. She ran her fingers lightly over the silk tablecloth, watching her ring sparkle. Candles glowed on the table, sylph-like shadows danced on the wall. A faint smell of rosewood drifted across the room. White flowers were strewn everywhere. Her anxieties slipped away as she felt herself soar to bliss. The mood was perfect, she watched Anton eat his meal, and gave him a loving glance. They sat in quiet empathy, savouring the creamy fish, washing it down with mellow wine. He scooped some melon brulée onto a spoon, and fed it to her; it dripped over her chin, he licked it off.

The drama over, Anton led her to the bedroom.

'Are you sure you want to stay with me?' he asked her. 'There's no going back.'

'Yes of course, why? Is there a problem?'

'No, none at all, Emma,' he said, an edginess creeping into his voice. 'It's just that…that I want you so much, I feel so serious about you, I want to know if you feel the same.'

'Yes I do,' she said, feeling reckless, wanting him so badly. Why did he seem so haunted at times? Strangely carefree one moment, angst-ridden the next. He evaded her questions about the inn, or about himself. She had an odd feeling that there was more to find out, secrets that would bind them together.

Suddenly the phone rang; a dark shadow crossed Anton's face as he picked it up. He listened for a second, then, with an agitated expression, slammed it down. He glanced anxiously out of the window. Emma watched a shadowy figure drift past the drive, a woman with long hair.

'Is everything all right?' she asked him.

'Yes, of course,' he said, smiling. 'It's nothing. Just some problems at the beach. It's over now.'

He led her to a four-poster gothic bed, surrounded by billowing white curtains, set under a mural of angels. White scented candles flickered, the room had a delicate heady scent.

'I always have white candles burning,' he said softly. 'They purify the aura.'

She fell back against the silk sheets, letting its luxury envelop her skin. Soft music drowned out the sound of the sea outside. She sighed—to be in the most romantic bedroom she had ever seen. Lilac and white, a spiritual haven, black iron sconces arched over white columns, next to paintings of angels and cherubs. Anton lay back on the bed next to her. He kissed her lips and flicked his tongue gently across her neck, then over her breasts; her nipples rose in anticipation. The gentle rhythm of his fingers rubbed her body, arousing her. His shirt fell open and she noticed a strange emblem around his neck. She faltered for a second. He uttered a few words that she could not understand, that sounded like Latin or an ancient language. Gently he pulled out a small knife and made a small incision in his arm, then in hers and held the two together.

'Now you are my spiritual wife, not just my muse,' he said, kissing her ring, then her neck and shoulders fervently. 'Making love is like food, it can be a gourmet meal, or a quick snack. Today we shall have a banquet, a feast,' he commanded, lifting her dress and gently removing her lacy underwear. He began stroking her thighs, making her body tingle with desire. She arched her back, feeling his hand push between her thighs, his fingers plunging inside her, touching her magic spot. He kissed her lips, her eyes. She writhed in ecstasy, he pushed deeper and deeper. Then he licked his velvety tongue across her clitoris, torturing her.

'Don't come yet. Savour the exquisite feeling, the ecstasy.' He spoke softly.

She was immersed in pure sensuality, her body pulsating with pleasure, gasping in ecstasy.

'Let me light up your body with bliss, and succumb to waves of sexual frenzy. Let your power rise. This is called holding the delight—as a lamp in the storm, hold back for as long as you can,' he whispered, gently stroking her with a feather. 'I want you to wait until you are ready to burst, I want to release the energy of Kundalini, build up your psychic and sexual power. When you reach your peak, you will blend in total harmony with the universe and reach the highest intensity of pleasure you have ever known.'

She wound her legs around his back. He let his silky tongue linger between her thighs, flicking gently over her clitoris. She almost fainted with desire, pulling at his hair, feeling his soft velvety tongue lap her swollen vulva. Then, he lay on top of her, and pushed in gently, gyrating in soft strokes, becoming faster.

A warm glow spread through her, as he pushed deeper and deeper into her, filling her with pure pleasure. Her whole body consumed him as she hovered on the edge of orgasm. A shot of white-hot pleasure pulsed over her, filling her with exquisite bliss. The muscles in his neck stood out, he made several deep thrusts, then stopped as she came even closer to orgasm. He pushed inside her, in fast rhythmic strokes, over the edge to orgasmic bliss. She felt waves of pleasure ripple through her, gripped by the most powerful orgasm she had ever known, engulfing her, swelling her with pleasure. As she let go she felt herself explode.

Her body quivered and shuddered in spasms of the most powerful sensation; she screamed out, shattering the silence of the bay. She melted into Anton's body, merging with him—how she loved him. She kissed his head, he bit her mouth. The veins in his neck stood out as his thrusts became more urgent.

'You are so beautiful,' he moaned, running his fingers through her hair. His body was rising and falling above hers, his touch spread through her like a furnace as he gripped and pulled her hair at the peak of his pleasure. 'Oh yes,' he yelled. She spiralled toward bliss again, throwing back her hair, waves of pure pleasure rippling through her—a long orgasm that seemed to go on forever, her body arched while small spasms led to a shuddering climax. She felt a groan escape from his throat and echo in the night air as he buried his face in her hair and he came inside her.

'That was amazing,' she breathed, feeling him slip out between her legs. The feeling of his kiss on her mouth aroused her again. He knelt between her legs and kissed her. She felt as though she was floating on air.

'It's a simple technique, basic Tantric principles.' He smiled. 'When Kundalini is connected with Shiva, the joy of completeness is achieved. You enter a realm of harmony and deep sensual pleasure. Just holding and connecting enhances the power, the Chakras give you empowerment you have never known before.' He gazed at her: 'How are you feeling?'

'Wonderful,' she whispered dreamily, her body tingling and vibrating with energy.

'It's a clean, healing energy to tap into, it can cure almost anything and rebalances the body to its natural rhythm.'

He was weaving a miraculous web of enchantment over her, in another night of magic passion. She had never felt like this before, or surrendered to a man so totally; their lovemaking was growing more and more intense and powerful. She felt obsessed by erotic desire, she was growing hooked on the pleasure he gave her to the exclusion of everything else. She completely forgot about the wine bar. She leaned back, basking in a deep state of bliss, her mind and body relaxed. Making love to him had been a dream, she let the waves of fulfilment wash over her. He rubbed her neck gently, now she was feeling sleepy.

☩

The next day they talked for hours, their plans flowing in perfect synchronicity.

'Try this,' said Anton early that evening, handing Emma a glass of red wine. 'It's home made.'

She sipped the drink slowly.

'Would you like to see some more of my paintings?' he asked; opening his portfolio, he took out some artwork.

'Did you paint this?' Emma asked, flicking through them, stopping at one of a unicorn galloping along the beach, its white mane flying out in long tendrils.

'Yes,' he said, 'it's based on stories, fables and myths of the "other world". Do you like it?'

'I love all of them,' she said, entranced. 'They are very mystical.' Seconds later she felt the tip of her fingers come alive, and a warmth spread through her body. Her senses were heightened, Anton showed her another one, the colours were very bright.

'Dionysus causes Hell and anarchy among the maidens, as he watches with devilish intent from the shadows,' he said, pointing to the painting of maidens running away from a dark knight. I hope you enjoyed the drink,' he said, noticing her change of mood. 'It contains a potent herb that enhances perception, and fills you with joy. Artists used to drink it to enhance their work.'

'Yes, I do feel quite high,' she admitted, looking glazed. 'The scene looks real, alive, the faces look as though they're moving.'

'The maidens served a dark knight who was powerful, arrogant, clever and seductive, the beauty of the devil is very compelling. Yet it destroyed them, their curiosity for darkness. The maidens became temptresses under his control after he had taken their virginity. Did you know the term Lucifer means bearer of light, not darkness?'

'No, I didn't.'

Suddenly there was a loud knock, and Anton peered outside.

'I have to go to the other studio to work for a while,' he said, suddenly looking defensive. 'I'll drop you off and see you tomorrow at the class.'

Night was darkly drifting through. As Emma stood in the dark hallway, she was suddenly overwhelmed by an atmosphere of mystery and intrigue. Who was the mysterious night visitor? And who was following them?

Art Dreams

Back at the inn, Emma handed out some leaflets to the arts group. The café bar was noisy, filled with surfers, artists and poets of the cove and members of Anton's weekly art class were piling in. Emma closed the door to the lecture room; she was helping him today, delighted to have found a creative role. The local artists piled in and began sampling the avant-garde atmosphere and interesting drinks, absinthe and herbal wines, as well as tippling on the local cider. Computers buzzed and sprung into life and books were being avidly studied; an art class was starting alongside some people lazily browsing through art magazines. Others were buying postcards or wandering through the gallery. Some local artists had rented out the adjoining studio for a week and people browsed round the exhibition. It was a hive of activity, attracting energetic, creative people. The place was pulsing with life, buzzing with conversation, ideas, and a vibrant creative energy. Andrew, a friend of Ramone's, had been installed quickly as manager and head barman. Emma stayed at Anton's so often she needed a manager there. Emma was swept along with mystical feelings of love, and let out a dreamy sigh at the thought of Anton's magic touch. The love he gave her filled her with the deepest bliss she had ever known.

She strolled down the hallway and saw that he had put all her paintings of wood nymphs and water nymphs on display, she felt so happy that her art was light and sunny, reflecting this joyful time. Waves of happiness rippled through her as she placed a picture of him receiving an award on the wall. They had been having mysterious phone calls: suddenly she put together these and Anton's mysterious disappearances and the fact that whenever she answered the phone, it went dead. Her euphoric happiness evaporated and her good mood came crashing down as she twigged it must have been Angel who'd phoned last night. Why was she still hanging around him? Anton walked into the room and started setting up the paints for the weekly class.

'Do you still see Angel?' asked Emma, concerned. 'I have to know.'

'No, not really, she did come over last week to collect her work.'

Emma tilted her head to one side and looked at him blankly. 'Are you sure?'

'Of course I am sure. Please trust me.'

He put an arm around her, assuring her that everything was fine, but Emma, her instincts aroused, could not help feeling that something was wrong and pushed him away. Anton looked at her surprised. 'Oh come on, Emma,' he pleaded.

'I need some fresh air,' she replied, walking towards the door.

The blazing sunshine shone on the secluded empty beach, Emma skipped over the white sand, feeling her toes sink in. She ran over to her favourite rock and sat watching the sea ebb and flow. The waves raced in, gentle foamy waves, splashing on the rocks, and she got lost in their rhythm. Her thoughts began to drift and swirl. When Anton had phoned and asked her to meet him, her heart had surged with hope. Elated, she had gone into town to buy a new dress and some perfume. But, wandering through the artists' lanes, she had seen him talking to the woman, standing in the shadows, the Latin woman with long, shiny, dark hair. She stood and watched them, hidden behind a column. The woman had been gazing at him intently and he had been looking straight at her. The gaze of lovers, she wondered disconcertingly. Was there still something between them? Now slithers of doubt invaded her mind and seeped through her like a cold fog descending on a warm, sunny day. Her serenity was disturbed and a dark cloud hung over her. Why was it always like this? She would find something precious, then it would be snatched away. Was her love life always destined to be so turbulent? Just what had her karma been that it had always to be this way? Slowly she walked home, the warmth of the inn welcoming, and she felt the coldness of loneliness dissolve. She climbed to the roof terrace and ate a chicken salad while watching the sea. For a moment she thought the sea had been the only constant reality in her life, her romantic life had been built on shifting sands.

She went back to his studio.

'Oh Emma,' he said, looking down at her, his expression torn.

Emma's heart surged into her mouth; she felt as though the ground was about to crumble under her.

'We went for a drink and I told her about you. She acted oddly,' said she'd had to see me.'

'Oh,' said Emma, wondering what he was about to say next.

'I know it's over, I just had to be sure,' he admitted, 'and then she kissed me. I didn't return the kiss,' he said. 'She lost a baby last year and had been a bit dependent on me.'

Emma felt her blood run cold.

'But I told her we have to move on, I can't always be there for her—she must lead her own life.'

'And is it over for you?' she asked, her voice starting to shake.

'Yes, of course,' he said.

She could still see the sadness in his eyes. Did she really want to know? Or was it better just to put it all behind them and hope for the best? Move on without a backward glance?

'I have made up my mind,' he said, his chin tightening determinedly. 'I can't go back. I want us to work, Emma.'

'Yes, so do I. But only if your heart is true, listen to your inner voice and heart. Don't deceive yourself or do what you think is right, but follow what your soul desires.'

'Yes, and I know it is you I love, who I want to spend my life with. I am so sure, but sometime bonds are hard to break.'

'Yes, they can be,' she said empathically. 'We are only human and cannot switch off our feelings like a light. Some residue is always left,' she added, watching the sea wash over the twinkling sand. 'Nothingness does not exist, and it is really impossible to achieve.'

'How do you feel about Toby now?'

'Well I don't think we were ever really that close or even soul mates,' she admitted. 'We were a good business match. Oddly enough, I barely think of him, I seem to have erased him altogether. We worked so much when we lived in the city, it wasn't very deep, and we never really got to know each other well.' She sighed: 'And if we had stayed together much longer, I've a feeling we would have found we had little in common. Our break-up happened for a reason, because it wasn't right.'

'I see,' he said. 'Then it was good that you did.'

'There was no other way. Were you and Angel soul mates?'

'I thought we were, when we first got the studio, we seemed to work in synchronicity. She had some good contacts and was an intelligent and cultured woman, good to work with, but there seemed to be a part of her I could never reach. She was a good source of knowledge, interested in goddess empowerment and quite creative and at first brought some inspiration to my work. But then she took a swing in another direction, her tastes became dark and she changed. She became demanding and wanted more of the profits, her moods went out of control. That's why I met her today: she wanted some settlement from last year's profits from the gallery. I felt very alone for a while. Then I met you, fresh and energetic and youthful, and you seemed like a breath of fresh air. I felt a joy and a sense of liberation I had not enjoyed for a long time. Life with her had become static, I felt like nothing new was going to happen. I feel we are more suited, as though life stretches in front of us like an adventure. With her I felt everything had died. You are inspiration and light, brought to bring my acrid desert of love to life. She was trying desperately to fit in with a more sedate lifestyle, and the vibrancy I had liked in her was fading as she embraced her dark ideas—her youthful side seemed to sink and get lost altogether. The magic had gone.'

'So I am just a new form of inspiration? A new muse?'

'No, you are so much more than that,' he said, shaking his head. 'You are the woman who I have always dreamed of meeting, whom I wished I might meet one day. A total love, everything I ever wanted in one woman.'

Emma looked out to the beach over the vast expanse of the Atlantic Ocean; she could see infinity, sea all around. She suddenly felt adrift. Anton caught her face in his hands: 'Stay with me, Emma, I adore you.'

She felt as though he was throwing her a life raft and pulling her in. He kissed her passionately: she fought her inner doubts and sank into his arms as a raven sat perched on the wall, its dark eyes swivelling.

☦

She had to talk to a friend so rushed into St Ives to meet Andrea for lunch.

'Well I'm glad to be honoured to have your presence at last,' joked Andrea. 'I haven't seen you for ages. We only got back last week.'

'I know, I'm so sorry,' said Emma, still breathless. 'The wine bar is taking off well, we made a fortune last weekend, and I am painting and having a wonderful time. Anton has made me his model and muse, there just isn't enough time in the day.'

'But what's wrong? Are you happy?'

'Blissfully, and so totally in love.'

'I told you it would work out okay. Was I right?'

Emma gave Andrea a hug. 'I love you so much, Andrea,' she said.

'Is there a dark cloud hovering over the perfect paradise?' asked Andrea. 'Do I detect a slight problem?'

'Yes, well, sort of, there have been a few strange events, and I can't quite put my finger on it, but it's his ex, Angel—she has turned up at odd times. I've a feeling she's trying to get him back, and I know that he still sees her.'

'Just be strong, she might try and undermine you, but don't let her, and don't worry—you are much stronger than her.'

Emma couldn't quite understand why, despite everything going so well, she had such a sudden sense of foreboding. She gazed outside at the beach, where waves crashed wildly on the shore.

Andrea fished some tarot cards out of her bag and spread them in a fan shape over the table.

'There's nothing in the cards to say he cares for her,' Andrea said reassuringly. 'It definitely says that it's you he loves.'

The muse awakes a spiritual light

Emma sat posing for Anton, against the backdrop of the sea, as a 'water goddess'. Anton's class was gathered round, drawing her. He worked intensely, weaving delicate swirling blues and greys into Emma's dress, his eyes focused dreamily on the canvas, a deep frown on his face, so immersed in his work that he barely noticed her. He gave her just the occasional glance, then went back to his work. She was feeling cold and restless as though she couldn't connect with him, and it frustrated her. While he worked he seemed to disappear, and his mind became so lost in what he was doing, he would transcend and leave the physical world. Hours later, he turned the painting round so that she could see the nymphs dancing playfully in the shimmering mist, under the pale moonlight. *Emma and the Water Gypsies*—her nymph's hair cascaded all around her like ribbons, she reclined on pale silk cushions, with black feathery wings, like an angel, surrounded by angel sea nymphs with blue feathery wings. Emma sighed, what a lovely, magical, fairy tale scene. All her angry thoughts dissolved. Her eyes moved to the next painting; Emma stepping out of a pink shell, her long hair cascading over her shoulders, a white lily in her hand, while some mischievous nymphs watched her from behind a tree. Her long, pink silk dress clung to her, making her look naked. Anton turned the canvas round, to show the students.

'She looks real,' observed one excitedly, 'the maidens are moving!'

Anton laughed: 'It's the metallic paint, it gives them a shimmering effect.'

'How romantic!'

He turned to another classic painting.

'This,' he said, '*The Birth of Venus*, is a classic romantic painting that illustrates woman as the "goddess" of love, the goddess is the highest stage of wisdom and intellect a woman can reach. In Jungian terms, she has reached a stage of transcendence above ordinary mortals. That can be our theme for today. How do we portray women in romantic art? You may use any of the archetypes or fantasy roles, in another of Botticelli's paintings, *Primavera*, woman is seen in many roles; mother, seductress, nymph, you may use goddess, vamp, siren, maiden, lover or mistress. Romantic depictions of women lift them above the banal, the everyday. Choose very carefully your own study of woman—a "dark goddess" on a stormy landscape, wild elements of her soul, a maiden sitting in her garden sewing, visualise the idea in your mental landscape, then start to construct your painting. The goddess is endowed with the most powerful gifts, is pure, yet wise, intellectually gifted and creative. Show these in your painting.' He turned and looked at Emma. 'The goddess exists in all women, and the woman who is able to tap into this archetype is a very special woman.'

The students set up their boards and made some quick sketches.

Anton stopped painting, and turned to his students.

'I want you to try and follow the tradition of the Pre-Raphaelite artists and create paintings that are mystical, beautiful and reflect beauty and nature. Waterhouse combined his fascination for natural detail with a love of the mythical and poetic, he painted wonderful pictures of mermaids, while Edward Burne Jones developed a mystical style based on medieval fantasy. I want to see some evocative ideas emerge, your own vision inspired by the landscape and the romantic artists. As holy, wise, gifted, tragic or pure, your "goddess" can show many traits, but do so with elegance. I want you to be as painstaking in detail as the original artists were.'

Emma sat down with the students, sketching a maiden rising from a perilous sea. She studied the canvas, pleased with the effect.

'Create a story around your subject, examine the theme deeply that tells me all about that person, not just as a one-dimensional object. Try and make certain aspects of your "goddess" come alive. Try and capture the mood. Spin a story around your figure, give it a magic energy that lifts the spirit. Take your ideas from the pre-Raphaelites, Holman Hunt, John Collier and Rossetti,' he said, encouraging them in their work.

'Once, when we respected the natural beauty of the earth, living in tune with nature, we used it as our inspiration. Then commercialisation destroyed this love of beauty. The Pre-Raphaelites formed a movement against this, recapturing the beauty and innocence in art, with dream-like ethereal images and spirituality. They painted pictures to inspire and enthral us, reflecting the higher values of art and love. We must follow their philosophy.'

'Now, we live in confusion blinded by too many rules. Beauty is simplicity, we must return to this, focus on the fragile detail, the purity, not destroy it with everyday banalities. Let the essence shine through and enthral the observer. We have so much information thrown at us. Do you realise that we take in more information in one day than Renaissance man did in his whole lifetime?'

'I can believe that,' said Emma. 'That is the main reason why I moved here,' she said, handing round some pictures, asking the students to name their chosen archetype. She looked at a picture painted by one of the students entitled *Mermaids of the Shores*, a beautiful nymph being chased through kingdoms of the sea.

'We must ignite the creative process and this can be done in several ways,' suggested Anton, writing on the portable board. 'The awakening of our muse will increase our vision, enhance us, make us see things in a different way. Open our minds to appreciate beauty. Try and sit alone, somewhere quiet, in a private place, by the rocks or by the sea, and you will feel a sense of your spirit fly, your curiosity and life force grow, becoming more receptive to ideas and beauty, when our minds are no longer channelled to some specific task, but runs free. The bio-association of two ideas linked together makes a new concept. This is essential for creative work. Brainstorming is useful. Different ways of seeing the everyday, don't be afraid to experiment with your ideas, be imaginative, explore your subject and find your passion.'

'Should the female characters be symbolic or real?' asked a student.

'Both. They are symbolic, embodying ideas beyond the normal perception of the female, but they also include the real traits of woman. Botticelli's *Birth of Venus*, the goddess of love, studies the mythical and magical interpretations of the female, and Waterhouse painted many mystical Arthurian themes, whereas others such as *Persephone* reflect the real emotions and dilemmas of all women. Most works of art are archetypal, even if it is just a reflection, an echo of an echo. Everything has two aspects, what we see in everyday life, what ordinary men see and the ghostly or metaphysical aspect, which only creative individuals see. These transcendent experiences can be reached during a peak or in moments of clairvoyance. This higher form of thinking creates a further dimension to our subject. A work of art must convey something beyond the obvious. Art should convey a deep ocean of secrets, without limits, the infinite possibilities of creativity, and archetypes help with this process. Art brings energies and concepts alive, enhances our vision.'

'They reflect a higher consciousness?' piped up a student.

'Yes, it reveals the qualities of the goddess, symbolically, by abstraction.'

The students sat at their canvases, making a study of the goddess, their heads bowed in concentration, as they sketched busily.

'Now turn your head slightly,' Anton said to Emma, sitting as a goddess, 'I'm almost finished for today.' Compliantly, Emma tilted her head to one side.

Anton made some finishing touches, as Emma rose, as Venus, goddess of love, from the shell, splashing some sunny highlights into her hair.

'See how it shimmers in the sun? It adds that spiritual, ethereal quality.'

The students nodded.

'It's a halo, it makes me look sacred,' observed Emma, delighted.

'Otherworldly,' corrected Anton, packing the equipment away. The students filed out and Emma felt it was the right time to ask Anton about some things that had been on her mind all day.

'The pictures have a ghostly quality,' she said. 'Do you believe in ghosts?'

'Yes, I do.'

'I'm sure I have just seen one at the inn,' she confessed.

'Did you?' he said turning pale, looking worried. 'I doubt that very much, it could have been a passing shadow.'

'No, I am sure this time,' she said. 'Do you doubt me?'

'No of course not, a shadowy figure from the past, echoes of what once was, perhaps it is a trapped energy. A spiritual aura, we all have psychic energy fields, every living being has one. We create psycho-magnetic fields which exist all around us. That's how we give power and essence to life. We become naturally receptive to things, the higher we evolve, and able to see knowledge in a more refined way. You probably just saw an energy.'

'Well that's enough, isn't it?' she insisted, wondering why Anton, usually so opened-minded, refused to believe her. She looked at him bewildered.

'Perhaps you did see a ghost from the inn's murky past,' he said softly. 'You may just have seen the spirit of something on its journey through time. It's nothing to worry about. See that up there,' he said, pulling out from his portfolio a painting of a woman changing into a goddess with wings.

'I won an award for that painting, it is called the *Mysteries of the Soul*, and is of a woman dreaming of her animal archetype. How energies change and re-shape. She is a shape shifter. Energies can change shape, and drift around us all the time.'

'Yes, you might be right, the faces were just reflections, without power. Look at this one, it is of the ship that sank,' she said, studying a painting that she'd pulled out of the cupboard.

'Oh that's strange,' he said, trying to take it from her; she held onto it tightly. 'What's wrong?'

She looked at it more closely, a shipwreck, recognising it as the one Sarah had shown her at the agency. 'I'm sure I have seen it before, at my agency.'

'You could have, it was made into prints,' he said surprised. 'You have such an active imagination, it could have been any galleon.'

'No, I recognise the terror on this man's face. Did you paint it?'

'My Uncle Antoine painted it, the artistic temperament seems to run in our family.'

'Yes, I know I've seen it before, how strange that you should own it.'

'Coincidences happen all the time.'

'I am taking a risk lying down for an artist,' she joked.

Anton looked at her and laughed. 'Well I'm glad you have decided to do so.'

'Promise you won't turn me into a nymph.'

'I promise.'

Emma stepped into the shell, and pulled her pink silk robe around her so that it flowed around her ankles touching the floor. She was posed as Venus, and slipped out of her robe, her pale hair rippling over her naked body. She stood still, feeling light and happy. Anton arranged some flowers in a circle around her hair, and began sketching her. He stared at her with the devoted gaze of a knight in pursuit of his lady fair. The hues of green and grey splashed onto the canvas, took shape as he curved the gentle brushstrokes and moulded her into Venus, goddess of love.

'I've just had one of my papers published in an arts journal,' he said. 'Would you like to see it?'

'Yes I'd love to.'

He handed her the article 'Romantic Females in Art and Mythology'. It included an interpretation of one of her as the lovely maiden in the sunlight. 'Inspired by his new model, he continues to enchant with his ethereal themes.' She smiled proudly, the sunlight catching her hair.

'It's wonderful,' she exclaimed, reading it. 'I am now a famous muse.'

'Yes, and you are a very beautiful one. Have you chosen your special subject yet?'

'Yes, I have chosen the "Water nymph", with intellectual gifts, music and a song, a kind of siren, and a sea goddess too,' she revealed.

'That's a good choice. You have captured my heart,' he said. 'You are an angel. I have loved you, Emma, from the moment we met. I thought I had strayed into a dream. You are all I want in a woman.' He showed her his latest sketch of his muse, a mermaid, riding on a surfboard: they laughed.

'You have worked your spell over me,' she whispered. 'My magic man.'

'Yes, I am a magician, a weaver of dreams and I will love you, Emma, for eternity.'

She dived into his new work, excited; she loved to see the dark side of Anton, his otherworldliness.

'Can I see the paintings in the attic?'

'No,' he said, a dark shadow crossing his face. 'They are not my best work.'

'Oh please?' asked Emma, growing insistent.

'They are too dark, look at these instead,' he said, showing her his new painting of her. Emma had risen from the sea, as a sea nymph, flicking her hair—a mane of silvery hair.

'You suit the romantic paintings, you don't want to see that kind of thing, do you?'

'I love the darkness,' whispered Emma, tantalisingly.

'Okay, you might like this one, on the darker aspect of the soul.' Anton turned to the next picture of Emma, portrayed as a beautiful night spirit, with dark feathery wings. 'The muse's inspiration is brought to us by them, by these divine creatures: they give us word images pictures, ideas. There are dark muses too,' he added.

Suddenly, Emma found herself flying inside the painting, a black cloud hovered menacingly above her. Nymphs on the shore, in black weeds, danced around, as maidens of death.

'Be careful!' their voices cried out. 'Leave here, it is not safe!'

Emma jumped; she heard Anton's voice behind her, calling her: 'Emma, are you all right?'

'Yes, I'm fine.'

'I warned you, an angel should not see such things.'

'But I love it, the black fairies are enchanting.'

'All right, if you insist,' he said, offering her the painting as a gift for the wine bar.

'Oh I can't,' she protested, trying to shake off the heaviness of the heat and the wine.

'Have it for your new home,' he insisted, 'if you like it that much.'

Taking it carefully from him, she noticed he spoke at times like a poet. She felt quite dizzy.

'I put some strong herbs in the wine,' he admitted. 'It's a mystical wine I use for enhancing visions, I use it for painting mystical scenes,' he explained, 'they are harmless.'

She wasn't so sure, for now her head was spinning. She stood still, but the room was spinning round, making her feel giddy. Then it went back to normal. What was she doing drinking hallucinogenic wine in the middle of the afternoon? She didn't really know Anton that well, or where he came from. But who cared? She enjoyed living dangerously, and had a wild unconventional streak, that's why she'd always chosen wild, creative men. She was a woman with a gypsy in her soul too and he was the only man to have ever touched her there. The sun rippled under ever-changing skies, a whiff of acrid grey smoke drifted under her nose. All her senses were springing alive. Swirling around her were the vibrant colours from the paint-box of the Earth. A rainbow rose in the sky, its gentle arc shimmering like a stairway to heaven. Emma sat for hours watching the scenery swirl, so incredibly in awe of the wild beauty of nature.

Later, Emma hung the painting up in the bar. It shimmered with a kind of magical glow, and gave the room a gentle aura. She looked into it, hypnotised by the unicorn galloping across the beach. The painting was moving, like it had come alive! She stepped back, surprised. Was she having a flashback? She sat down aimlessly drifting through another world, the herbs in the wine making her feel quite light-headed. She pulled herself out of the chair and walked slowly to the bottom of the garden, and looked out over the sea. The black rocks had risen, like the rise of Atlantis; she thought she could see Lyonesse, but it had sunk centuries ago, perhaps it was emerging from the deep, an ominous portent. She breathed deeply and felt better. The tide was out, the sea was choppy and wild, turbulent waves raced along the misty shore. She closed her eyes and when she looked up, there was no risen Isle, just a grey patch of mist hovering over the sea. The sand drifted back, leaving the stark black rocks protruding, their jagged edges glistening like daggers. Change was in the air. The wind blew small ripples across the calm sea. She wandered inside the studio, and began sketching the landscape.

Out of the corner of her eye, she watched the reflection of the waves on the window. Suddenly, the mirror began to shimmer: a gentle woman's face appeared from out of the mist, and she was smiling. Emma dropped her pad, surprised. Her shadowy figure passed in front of the sun, and the studio was thrown into darkness. Then she walked outside, and light streamed in again. Emma caught her breath, shivering despite the warmth of the sun's rays, letting the sunbeams dance on her face. There was a mystery there, what was it? Who was the mysterious woman who kept appearing in the glass?

New dreams

Emma put on some music, and began dancing to the gentle tones of the harp, in time with the rhythm, skipping in tune with nature, the chords having a hypnotic effect on her. Her feet skipped lightly over the ground. She had grown used to the 'ghosts' now—she even saw them as friends. She had only seen them from time to time in the studio, and recently the house was clear. They often appeared on dark and stormy days; a strange light would flicker in the window and sometimes she saw faces, but mostly it was quiet.

Tonight she looked up and saw an incredibly attractive man looking in through the glass, and got up to let him in. As she walked closer to the door, he vanished. Intuitively she knew it must be Antoine, returned to find his love Letitia—the doomed lovers. He kept trying to come back—how romantic! It didn't bother her at all; an incurable romantic, she rather liked the idea of having a house with such romantic ghosts!

Pale pink feathery clouds swirled across the bright pink-grey sky. Gold sun rays danced over the shimmering horizon, a single silhouette of a dark fishing boat glided on the calm sea. It had been a hot day and the air felt heavy.

Gradually, as the sun fell in a giant orange ball behind the horizon, the sky darkened. A flash of lightning lit up the sky, then there was a heavy clap of thunder. The inn was shrouded in sea mist, swirling around its gothic turrets, a whirlwind of sand sprayed against the arched windows. A fog horn blasted in the distance. Suddenly, back at the inn, all the lights went off.

Emma crinkled her face at the rising storm, pulled the curtains and went downstairs to get a candle and a bottle of wine. She blinked as she saw out of the corner of her eye something start to move. She looked over as the cellar door, which led down to the tunnels, swung open.

Slowly a door below creaked open and the room flooded with a candescent light.

Annie's dark figure emerged from the tunnel, her eyes glowing with a malevolent energy. She pulled her long, swirling clothes around her and glided slowly across the room. An ethereal shadowy figure, her face was half concealed in the shadows. Emma fought back the fear rising in her and steeled herself—after battling with some of the top executives in the boardroom she refused to let a mere ghost frighten her.

Emma caught a glimpse of the woman's stern expression under her dark lacy veil. Then it softened to a mystical gaze. The woman looked up and smiled at Emma; her black eyes glinting with menace and a strange, dark power. A wicked grin flickered across her face as she disappeared into the wall.

Emma stood back aghast as the swirling wind outside was whipped into a hurricane, and sand blew in through the tunnels. A sandstorm!

A strangled cry ripped through the room, then faded with the wind. The cellar door slammed shut and the lights came back on. Emma rushed downstairs and quickly dialled a number.

'I've just seen a ghost and I am sure it was Annie!' Emma shouted down the phone to Andrea. 'She came out of the tunnel and floated along the hallway. I saw her! Annie was in the cellar!'

'Gosh! How exciting, are you sure it was her?'

'Yes, she looked just like the others had described her, dressed all in black, with a long solemn face and a wicked gaze.'

'Did you see her for very long?'

'Only for a matter of seconds. Do you think she can see me?'

'I am not really sure, spirits exist in another dimension, another time frame. I don't know whether they can see us. She might be aware of you, but is there in another time.'

'It must be her and I thought I saw her the other night when Anton was here.'

'Sounds like it was her! The woman was mad,' sighed Andrea. 'Twisted rationalisations drove her to blackmail Dionysus Williams after she was found stealing the takings from the inn. He asked her and her husband to leave, so for revenge, she turned Queen's evidence against him. And for her betrayal, the local smugglers took her to the beach and drowned her.

'Oh, how grim!'

'Her ghost still haunts the First and Last Inn,' continued Andrea, 'as she used to operate her smuggling ring from under the tunnels there, they connect the beach to the "Black Dove" cellar.'

'So she was probably just passing through her old smuggling route,' laughed Emma.

'Aren't you scared?' asked Andrea puzzled.

'No, I can live with it, she doesn't bother me,' Emma said bravely. 'When anyone comes here to poke around, the spirits get restless and doors slam, and I can feel their presence like a cold wind. The atmosphere seems to change. But mostly they are quiet and when they settle, I don't even know they are there. The hallway above the tunnel is never warm. I don't mind living with them, after all they were here first!'

'The First and Last has so many ghosts— around thirty according to the investigators. I only have three—Annie and the woman and man who keep appearing in the mirrors.'

'Well, at least you never complain that you are lonely,' joked Andrea. 'What did the paranormal investigators say?'

'That the ghosts are really quite harmless, if I can get used to living with them.'

'Can you?'

'Yes, it's not a problem for me. I'm getting quite attached to them.'

'Well,' explained Andrea, 'they are left over from Sennen's dark past, days when Sennen was notorious as a smuggling bay. Everyone was in on it, all the locals from the church downwards. The lighthouse lights would be turned off so that boats would crash on the rocks, and the locals, led by Annie Treeve, would rush down to the beach and pick up all the goods from the wrecks, then smuggle them back through the tunnel to the inns. They did this at Lamorna too, which is why the inn there is called The Wink—where the smugglers would wink at the barman to hide the contraband.'

'So there were no customs and excise around then?' joked Emma.

'Apparently not, The First and Last Inn was full of some really dark characters, and according to the psychic experts, it still is.'

'Why are they still there? After all this time? It was so long ago.'

'Well, there is an explanation,' sighed Andrea. 'If a person suffers a violent or sudden death, before their time to go, they may become trapped between this world and the next, unable to move on towards the light where they should go, so they stay stuck here wandering around in a kind of limbo. Annie died on the beach and her body was carried back to the inn.'

'So I should hire a paranormal psychic and have them moved on?'

'No, not yet. I've got a better idea. Why not use them to pull in the crowds? As a tourist attraction? Start a ghost tour, it'll attract hoards of people with an interest in the supernatural.'

'Yes, that's a good idea, I'll give it a try. But I doubt whether they will put in an appearance just as I'm showing people round.'

They both laughed.

'Only a Master of Wisdom can reach a level receptive enough to communicate with them.'

'What is a Master of Wisdom?' asked Emma mystified.

'A Master of the Wisdom is one who has undergone the fifth initiation. That really means that his consciousness has undergone such an elevation that it now includes the fifth or spiritual kingdom,' explained Andrea. 'He has worked his way from simple human existence to a higher consciousness through meditation. A psychic has the same powers and is usually in touch with a dead relative, who is in the spirit world, on the other side.'

'Where can I find one?'

'I can put you in touch with one if you want.'

'I don't know, maybe I shouldn't disturb them too much. I might stir up something that won't go away. I think let them rest, they can't do much harm.'

'I suppose you're right, they are quite powerless to do anything serious, they are detached from life, except for blowing open a few doors and making their presence felt. They can't hurt you.'

'That's a relief. Ok, bye, see you soon.'

Emma gazed wistfully out of the window: if only she knew all the answers, the universe was such a mystery. A small shoal of fruit bats flew out from under the awnings, their dark silhouettes flapping against a silvery moon.

Well, she thought philosophically, sitting back in the alcove, sipping her green tea, there was no going back, she had no intention of changing her plans now. She would just have to learn to live with her ghosts!

She called in a psychic, who told her it was nothing to worry about. 'They are friendly,' she said; 'we have many hauntings in this area, it is the most haunted part of England, the First and Last Inn has quite a few.' And, reassuringly, 'They won't hurt you if you can live with them, my dear.'

Emma shrugged, she did not mind them at all, in fact they made life more exciting. Everything was turning out so well; she was glad to have met Anton—he ignited her creative spark, spun her raw thoughts into a myriad of potent ideas, made her ideas flow with a higher vision. She had never known such passion before, or such heights of ecstasy. He was her magic man. She felt very creative and special around him, when he awakened her muse, stirring and shaping her ideas. She sat in the garden overlooking the sea, painting the sea-goddess, adding blue hues to lilac, to the swirling shapes of her goddess's dress: her hand could not stop. Her ethereal goddess sat alone by the sea, her enigmatic gaze turned toward the waves. Anton had taught her many things, opening the door to a fascinating world where she could play and develop her own gifts and talents: an intellectual lover, he satisfied her in so many ways. She painted each line with growing confidence as though a higher energy was magically guiding her hand over the canvas, painting with a clarity and perception she was unaware she possessed. The ideas kept coming, and they flowed faster. She felt so inspired and sat painting for several hours. Anton was making all her dreams come true, turning her into a real artist, taking her to Nirvana, igniting her talent so that she was bursting with inspiration. His lectures guided her, made her buzz with ideas. She had found a soul-mate, the man she had always dreamed of loving. He touched her dreams with an extra spark of magic, endowing her with insight, vision, her own genius. She had found in him an excellent teacher, lover and magician, a rare man. She skipped around the room, the secrets of the universe unfolding at her fingertips, golden dreams she could easily grasp. He had unlocked the door to heaven. Later that night, she took her paintings to his studio.

'You have a gift, Emma. I always knew you had a talent for art, it just needed to be awakened.'

She pointed to the picture he was putting up of a tree; he always treated it with sacred respect.

'What's that?' she asked him.

'The tree of life,' he answered.

'It shows the energy of the true will, the innermost spark of life, a secret for those who follow the path. The tree of life represents our progression from earthly ignorance to divine knowledge. We hope to create heaven, here on earth. By stilling the noise of the lower mind, and focusing on higher thoughts, you become receptive to creativity, synchronicity; with intellect and emotion in harmony, you can reach Nirvana. That is what I am teaching you. You may reach ecstasy, live in the throes of peak experiences. But be careful to take the path of light, not one of darkness. Let your spirit guide you to enlightenment and light.'

'Did you venture into the darkness?' she asked, softly.

'Yes, I was lost there for a while, and nearly didn't make it back,' he whispered hoarsely, kissing her. 'I don't want to talk about it now. Hell is no place for an angel.'

Emma sat watching the sea; his words echoed around her head, and she wondered what he had actually meant.

Revelations

Anton took Emma for a spin around the bay. The shore sped by quickly. He steered the boat expertly over the high waves, skimming lightly over the silvery-grey sea. Emma wondered if they were going to make it over a high wave, then the engine stopped and they drifted into a calm patch of sea, and stayed there for a while.

Today, Anton was his usual mysterious self. Would she ever get to know all of him? Emma's heart lurched into her mouth as they sped off again and hit another heavy wave. The boat bounced off, sea-spray splashed onto the boat, over her face. They landed in the curve of a secluded bay and sat down with a picnic. Then they took their boards, and rode the waves for a couple of hours, Anton surfed the waves like an expert, skimming along the peak, in perfect balance, zigzagging to the shore. Emma grabbed her board and rode after him, the wave propelling her along in a huge whoosh, swerving her onto the sand. Later, tired and sunburnt, they climbed happily back into the boat. It had been a perfect day and Emma's heart almost burst with happiness: she looked around her at the incredible landscape—she was seeing life like a child, tinged with wonder, and was very much in love. An impish grin spread across her face. She let her hand hang over the edge of the boat, letting the sea lap over her hand, as Anton steered them back, the boat tossing from side to side, juddering over the breakers. Smiling, Anton fished two mackerel out of the sea.

'Tonight I shall cook them for you, in my favourite sauce,' he promised, throwing them in the boat. He switched on the engine and they sped back to shore. Back at the inn, Emma changed into a tight black dress and pulled on silky black lace stockings. She put on some blood-red lipstick and a hat with a black lacy veil, she was a vamp. He caught her as she was pulling up the stockings.

'Very nice,' he said, admiringly. 'Makes you look incredibly sexy.'

She glimpsed out of the window; it was turning dark, the moon shone in ghostly silver ribbons on the grey rippling sea. She watched the pale shadows dance on the rocks. The stars shone brightly against the velvety sky. A light shone outside, throwing a spiral light across the water. A dark shadow slithered across the rocks. She squinted her eyes but could not see; it looked like a body moving outside. The silence was suddenly broken by the sound of an engine revving on the cobblestone path. The engine stopped, then started again. Horses from the local riding school rode by.

Anton pulled the curtains, his eyes widening in fear. Emma had never seen him afraid before. The sound of hooves grew louder, his face tensed, then relaxed as they faded into the distance. It was dusky and windy outside.

He turned and smiled. 'Just the farmer starting his tractor,' said Anton, relief flooding his face, his voice quivering as he struggled to sound normal. A strange atmosphere hung in the air.

'What is wrong?' she asked.

'Nothing at all.' The wind rushed in, slamming the door shut, papers blew around the room. Suddenly the lounge was filled with a dark and menacing aura, the candles blew out. Emma gasped; there was something moving in the corner, a tall, thin, dark figure drifted across the room. She clutched Anton's arm and stood frozen, watching the shape move, her wide eyes following it as it disappeared up the stairs.

'Did you see that?'

'Yes,' Anton admitted. 'What the hell was it?'

Emma felt it was the time to tell him about the strange events.

'Anton, was Antoine, the man who once lived at the inn, your uncle?'

'Yes, Antoine was my great uncle. A wild heart, a dilettante, he was a pirate for a while, he loved a challenge and liked living dangerously.'

'You look quite a lot like him,' said Emma.

'Perhaps.' Anton paused. 'I do resemble him, in more ways than one. We shared the same creative personality, his gift came with a form of madness, he was a manic depressive, one moment high, producing hoards of beautiful paintings—he had such immense talent—the next minute low, plagued by doubts and insecurities, and unable to function, totally paranoid and prone to mood swings.'

Emma's eyes widened; she was burning with curiosity.

Playfully, Anton put his hands over Emma's eyes. 'Don't let's talk about it now, see no evil, my darling.'

'Be serious,' she ordered, pushing him away. 'I keep dreaming of him, and once I even thought I saw his ghost wandering through the caves at Kynance. Like the tall, shadowy figure we just saw.'

Anton stopped laughing and looked at her disturbed, his eyes narrowing coldly. Suddenly he changed.

'It can't be—you must be mistaken,' he said quietly.

'But we have both seen him.'

'It's not possible,' he insisted, his face dark. 'Focus your mind on something useful, like the paintings you will create. Don't give in to fanciful ideas,' he ordered her curtly.

'But Anton! You just saw the ghost too!'

'I will not discuss this with you, drop the subject or I shall go.'

'Well, go then,' she snapped, and, slamming the door behind her, walked outside.

She had never seen him angry like that before, or cold toward her. He muttered something unintelligible, and stood staring at the sky. She felt the muskiness of his body next to hers, then his anxiety. 'I am sorry,' he said, 'I can't bear to talk about the past. It disturbs me.' His mood changed like quicksilver, his face lost its thunderous edge and, as the sun faded, he relaxed again. Outside a dark cloud hung over them threatening to unleash a storm. Then it vanished, the air was warm and clear again.

As she stepped back inside, she found Anton to be unusually quiet. He looked away, afraid to meet her gaze.

'Look, I didn't mean to snap at you. I am so sorry, Emma, I've had a very hard day,' he apologised, speaking softly. 'I didn't mean to be so rude.'

'That's all right,' she said, 'maybe I shouldn't pry.'

He quickly recovered and became cheerful again, and led her over to the table groaning with the most elegant dishes—salmon en croute, fish baked in lemon sauce and a platter laden with strawberries and champagne. Sparkling among the lilac orchids, was a beautiful necklace, Anton picked it up and fastened it around Emma's neck.

'For you, Emma, just to say how much I love you and to say thank you for all your inspiration,' he said, raising his glass. 'I mustn't take my dark moods out on you.'

Ravenous, they both tucked silently into their meal. She watched him, as she scooped up the fish, her mind in a whirl, still reeling with questions. He was only an artist, or was he? Suddenly she had the distinct feeling that he was hiding something from her—her instincts were nearly always right. She shouldn't delve too deep. Surely an element of mystery was crucial to a relationship and fired the imagination and kept the passion flowing. Anton made her feel so special, intoxicating her with his presence, endowing her with his magic, sharing with her his wonderful gifts, she was lucky to have met such a man. Yet there was a mystery surrounding him too. He was like the sea, kind, sometimes cruel, but always masterful. He set her senses on fire—she was captivated, caught under his spell. Tonight, she could sense that something was troubling him; she had no idea what it was, but knew he would tell her in his own time, so she didn't want to keep pushing for details. She knew she could be demanding, but preferred to live life with a passion. He sparked her creative side with his vibrant energy, his mind flitting from one possibility to another with the speed of light, his free associative mind balancing several ideas with equal fascination, an ability Da Vinci was also endowed with. Often she found it hard to get his attention when he was absorbed in a creative period, wrapped up in a world of his own. Tonight, Emma couldn't help noticing how worried he was. What was preying on his mind? Lately, he had grown so obsessed with the human spirit, the psyche, its dark secrets and shadows, that she could no longer reach him. She caught a fleeting glimpse of his darker side, emerging from the chrysalis of a broken dream, a troubled soul. She knew she had to just ride it out, and support him. His quest for knowledge was ceaseless, but so too was his *angst*. Maybe that was all just part of being an artist, the highs and the lows, she pondered. She spent hours observing his technique, learning and imitating his obsession to detail, his hate of mediocrity and pursuit of perfection, his exacting precision when recording the details on a flower or leaf, or each shadow on a face and she tried to apply the same dedication to her own work. His same obsessive thinking also fired his anxieties, whatever they were. After dinner, they sat in the alcove under the tall gothic window, watching the sea. It was a wild, stormy evening and the wind howled relentlessly. Suddenly, she heard an urgent rattling outside; someone was trying to get in. Anton looked up, startled, his smile fading, a haunted look glazed his eyes. Then the rattling stopped. Anton leapt up, bolting the doors saying, 'Ignore it. I have a surprise for you, Emma.'

'What is it?' she asked, intrigued to see him lay an array of paints on the table.

'Another gift for you,' he said smiling, his happy mood returning. Drawing back a screen, he revealed a picture of Emma, intricately drawn as in a photograph, lying on her bed at the inn, her hair cascading over the pillows.

'I don't remember posing for this one.'

'Oh, I made a few sketches from a photograph,' he said, cryptically.

'It's so realistic, such an incredible likeness! As good as any photograph I have seen, better in some ways—how did you do it? It was painted a long time ago,' she said, examining the date. 'Oh!' She shook her head, surprised. 'You did it before we even met! How did you do that?'

'Ah, that's a trade secret,' he laughed, kissing her. She smiled up at him, it was a beautiful, if somewhat mysterious, present. She glowed happily.

'Come and see me tomorrow, I will give you a lesson that you will enjoy, be at my studio at one,' he ordered. 'Bring these paints and brushes, they are for you too.'

She unwrapped the water-colours, tore off the cover, fingering the tubes of paint and touching the brushes with excitement.

'They are lovely,' she muttered, kissing him, thinking how perfect everything was turning out to be. Yet she still could not quite ignore the doubts circling at the back of her mind. A feeling of apprehension flooded her. What was causing his angst? Was her intuition trying to warn her about something? She had been let down so often, her senses were becoming finely attuned to the betrayals of men.

Surprises

The next day, a blustery, autumn day, Andrea phoned.

'Guess what?' she said.

'What?'

'I think I'm pregnant.'

'Congratulations. Is Ramone pleased?'

'He's ecstatic.'

'I have some good news too, I'm so in love, Anton and I are getting along fine.'

'I know.'

'Well, yes, but…'

'I was right! Told you so, the cards never lie. I'm so glad. You are destined to be together. I really am so happy for you.'

'In a strange way I feel like I have met him before, he is the man of my dreams. Oh, Andrea he is so gorgeous and romantic,' she added, quickly.

'Well I'm glad I was right. The cards were right. Looks like everything's going well for both of us at last, Ramone's delighted.'

'I just hope it turns out well, for all of us,' said Emma, as a sense of foreboding welled up inside her. Things were looking so good, something was bound to go wrong.

Angel

Emma sighed heavily and threw down her drawing, did true happiness ever last? Under every silver lining, there was a black cloud ready to burst. Life came in peaks and troughs, and there were few fairy-book romantic endings. Reality had a terrible habit of messing up her perfect fantasies. The next day, as she walked into Anton's studio, she felt uneasy and sensed something was wrong. Earlier, when he'd phoned, he had sounded edgy—she could sense it—and had tried to cancel her lesson but she had insisted that they met. She could detect a strange vibe in the air. A cloying heavy perfume drifted through the hallway. A stranger was there. She climbed to Anton's studio, and peered in through the window, the room was empty—no one was there. The door had been left ajar. She pushed it open. Anton was standing in front of an easel, painting a beautiful naked gypsy woman, splayed out on some cushions! She looked closely and saw it was Angel! Emma nearly fell backwards; her first instinct was to run, but she grit her teeth, determined to stay. What the hell was she doing there? Emma watched them from behind the door, holding her breath, her chest stabbing with anxiety. Why was Anton painting Angel, half-naked, in the middle of the afternoon?

She shot Anton a furious look, flashing her eyes murderously at him. He turned round and smiled, she had caught him offguard; so that was his secret, she could barely conceal her annoyance. She had no idea that he still used Angel as his model! Why had he failed to mention this to her? She had thought they were enemies, but Angel was there, posing naked for him! How dare she! Why did he try and hide it? Emma fought hard to curb her anger. Then a terrible thought came to her—were they still sleeping together? The girl lay with her long black hair cascading over her pert breasts, entwined with blue flowers, her legs slightly open so that a black thatch of springy pubic hair was visible. She walked in feeling uneasy, reminding herself that he was an artist, that such people did not live by normal rules. It was probably nothing, it was quite normal for an artist to be painting a naked woman, they used live models all the time. She would keep her cool, and find out if he had anything to hide. There was something about the woman, so brazenly poised, that made her feel uneasy. The last few days Anton had been vague, as though something was on his mind.

Forcefully she strode across the floor. Anton looked up, waved at her and smiled, then returned to his painting. Emma smiled at him, inwardly seething. He stood behind a large easel looking so achingly sexy, in old, torn, paint-smeared jeans held up by a black studded belt. His tanned body moved sveltely, like an animal as he applied the paint, his eyes focused hard on the painting. A black scarf was tied around his neck, his long black hair flowed over his bare shoulders; just like a gypsy. They looked alike, their raven black hair shining in the light. Emma felt a stab of jealousy, then she heard some soothing notes of new world gentle tranquil music wafting through the air. The music filled her soul with tranquillity, and her anger began to subside. She walked slowly toward Anton. A strong smell of incense hit her. Conflicting emotions fought inside her as she came closer to him. How dare he do this! Burning with curiosity, she smiled at him. Damn, she wasn't going to let Angel get the better of her.

'Hello Emma,' said Anton, edging out from behind the easel, 'I'm so glad you could make it, I've been expecting you.' Emma felt even more annoyed to see that he was half-naked, and smelled of paint. How dare he be alone with this predatory woman!

Emma kissed him possessively, and shot a look at Angel as if to say, keep off, he's mine!

'I just heard the good news, I spoke to Ramone this morning,' he said.

'Yes, it's wonderful news,' Emma said, gritting her teeth.

'He also said there has been a reporting of strange things happening in the bay.'

'On the beach?' asked Emma, dazed from fighting to keep her feelings under control.

'Yes, people have been spotted sailing in late at night, strange figures have been seen wandering across the beach. There is an air about the place.'

'Smugglers?'

'Yes, possibly, gold, diamonds or drugs. No one is sure.'

Emma noticed something odd about Anton, his eyes were burning with a feral lust, he moved like a wild animal. He was dreamlike, in a hypnotic trance. Why did he look that way? Was it for her, or for the woman lying on the floor? Her instincts were suddenly alerted and she felt like slapping him. Anger rose in waves in her, but she was damned if she was going to let it show. He seemed distant, in another realm, and she could not reach him. He moved slowly, as though in a trance.

'Perhaps you would like to paint Angel too. I'm sure she won't object—this is Angel,' he said, introducing them. 'I am painting her today as a present for her new boyfriend. She came to collect some old paintings I did of her. She represents the vampish, dark side of a woman, her eyes are stunning, don't you think? She embodies the spiritual gypsy, and has a wild untamed character. I am finishing off my portrait of her, for my dark mysteries collection.'

Emma looked away, trying to hide her irritation.

'This is Emma,' said Anton, looking over at Angel.

Angel stirred sleepily, mumbled a cursory hello, and shot Emma a look of pure malice and then lay elegantly back and resumed her pose. She crawled over the rug and took a bite of a sandwich, with the delicate ease of a cat, then sat back, her legs curled underneath her. Her feline gaze mesmerised Emma, who stood staring at her. Angel turned away.

'We have met before,' she said, in a strange voice.

It was nerve-wracking as though everything hung in the balance and could tip either way.

'Take the pencil,' Anton instructed Emma. 'And draw in the outlines of her body like this,' he said, guiding her arm. She looked up at him reticently, doubting her ability to draw anything more than a basic curve.

'You do want to learn, don't you?'

She nodded, fighting a slither of insecurity.

'Start by paying more attention to shadow and light, shading inside a curve,' he advised, taking her pencil and shading in the area on the girl's thigh. You need some lessons in technique,' he added.

Emma took the pencil and began to draw in Angel's huge brown eyes and profile, her eyes fixed on her olive skin. Angel lay back compliantly, her hair cascading over the pillow, her lips parted wantonly, her nipples hard and dark. She suddenly coiled up like a sleek panther, and folded her tanned legs under her. She wore an unfocused expression that turned into a bold stare like a cat, scrutinising its prey. Her eyes pierced right through Emma, her gaze flickering with a strange power, an intensity that spelled trouble. She started wiping herself with a cloth. A mixture of anxiety and excitement made Emma feel strangely and inexplicably sensual, and the strong smell of paint made her feel giddy. She watched Angel's every move, and to her surprise found herself flushing hot with desire. She was coiled up, ready to pounce. Anton's attitude of tormented master made her tingle with a sort of fascination for him, she found him attractive in that role. Angel lay back, her eyes closed, her brazen pose arousing in Emma all sorts of strange fantasies. Was she doing it on purpose? Emma turned away, blushing, suddenly thinking of them all making love.

'Perhaps we can go over the technique,' suggested Anton, handing her some paintbrushes. 'That's quite good for a beginner,' he said, guiding her hand over the canvas. 'Just a little more attention to detail, here,' he said, putting his arms around her. 'Try and draw a series of circles and rectangles, you can build a perspective from that.'

Emma drew an oblong circle for the body, and shaped it to Angel's body. She drew in her breath, shot with desire at his wet perspiring body rubbing against hers.

Anton took the pencil and drew a perfect circle.

She felt his body move against hers, his tight jeans pressing into her back, swaying in a rhythm. He guided her hand over a perfect arc on the canvas. She took the pencil and drew an oblong. It was the best she could do. Impulsively, she lunged her hands over Anton's jeans and felt his thighs, her fingers running over his body as she gave him a passionate kiss. Was the presence of the woman making her act like this?

Anton kissed Emma. The woman coughed awkwardly. 'That's enough for today,' he said, and went into the side room and started to pack his brushes away.

'Who invited you?' Emma asked Angel. 'What are you doing here?'

'I'm a friend of Anton's,' she replied, demurely, gliding across the floor. 'You remember me, don't you?' she said, a hint of hostility in her voice. 'We met at St Ives.'

'I believe I do,' said Emma nonchalantly.

Angel's hair swung over her buttocks like a curtain. Her glistening nipples stood up against her olive skin. Her eyes glistened like a wild gypsy, full of strange lights. There was something powerful and mysterious about her, she stared like a witch. She had a perfect figure that swayed sensually as she walked. She tied a pale chiffon scarf around her hair and put on her dress. The hot room filled with a cool breeze as she climbed on the sofa and opened the window.

'We are friends from our London days. He's using me as his model. We used to go out together. I am sure you saw us together in St

Ives. In fact, we were quite happy, then,' she said, then added bitterly, 'until you came along.'

Emma felt like she had been slapped.

'Well, he told me you were finished, had been for quite a while,' Emma said softly, her usual composure unwavering as she studied her rival's face stonily.

'Did he tell you that? No one understands him like I do,' she spat, her eyes becoming slits. 'You just aren't advanced enough spiritually, and never will be. We do have our problems, but he always comes back to me.'

'I don't think so, not this time.' Emma's tone was curt, her eyes fixed firmly on Angel.

Angel shot her a cold look and was about to say something, then stopped, and simply said, 'Some flames never die.'

Emma, irritated, turned away. She wasn't going to listen to this. For a moment she felt a twinge of embarrassment at having such sexual feelings for a stranger, and especially an enemy, but a strange feeling overtook her in the hot heady atmosphere. Now that it was cooler, a darker mood had descended on them. They viewed each other coldly, as rivals. Emma shot her an angry, wary look, to tell her that there was never a chance of them ever being friends. Angel's eyes widened and glared with a dangerous energy.

Then Emma began to feel slightly dizzy, as though she was going into a trance. She fought against it, using her will, trying to focus on something in the room to stay awake. Her head was giddy. They had been lovers, but was he still attracted to her? Or was it purely professional? Doubt seeped into her mind—there was a serpent in their paradise and she must not let this woman sow the seeds of uncertainty in her or she would win. How dare she intrude on their lives, and try and come between the special love they held for each other? Why was she still hanging around? Everything had been perfect, now a cloud was cast over them, and there was a strange discord.

As though reading her thoughts, Angel spoke softly: 'There are things that he will never tell you,' she said gloating, staring coldly at Emma, 'secrets that only we can share.'

Emma fought the desire to slap her and shuddered. At that moment Anton walked back into the room, and Angel's menacing tone dipped to one of warmth and friendliness, she had become a different person. She laughed a tinkling laugh and suddenly became friendly toward Emma.

'Two-faced bitch,' thought Emma, biting her tongue, fighting to keep her anger under control, thinking how much she hated this woman. She did not trust her one inch.

Anton handed Angel some money and ushered her out. She turned and kissed Anton lingeringly on the lips. Emma felt a stab of jealousy as the woman's dark eyes focused lovingly on him. Angel shot Emma one last defiant look and slammed the door behind her. Emma turned to Anton, hoping to see some sort of clue as to how he felt, but she saw only tiredness. He could be so exasperating. Just as she was feeling so secure, this had to happen. Was it a deliberate ploy to keep her on her toes? She would never know all of him, to try and fathom him out was impossible. But she hated the idea that he was still good friends with this woman.

Back in the sink room, feeling indescribably turned on, she walked over to him. Fuelled by a mixture of lust and anger, and asserting her dominance, she pushed him back against the sink. She sucked Anton's fingers, then undid his jeans and sucked him heavily, he was already erect; then she pushed his fingers inside her own slipperiness, pushing back onto his hands, imagining taking the woman's dusky brown nipples in her mouth as she thought of Anton between the woman's legs. It was as if she was in the room with them. A ménage had always been a fantasy, but she knew better than to make it a reality. She pushed him onto a chair and sat astride him—she was his woman and don't let him forget it; she felt an incredible spasm run through her as she imagined the three of them writhing there together. As she thought of Angel's breasts, her body spasmed with desire, crying out in ecstasy as Anton's hard body pumped harder in her wetness, quivering as a groan of pleasure escaped from his throat.

'Anton,' she asked later, 'why didn't you mention that you are still seeing Angel?'

'Today was the last time,' he said truthfully. 'She arrived to finish a painting. Would I have introduced you to her if I had something to hide?' He grinned boyishly: 'Come on, Emma, you know me better than that, I don't play around.'

'But you seemed to like her being there. So why did you try and put me off?'

'I didn't want a scene, she became quite insistent that I gave her work back to her, and she begged me to paint one last painting of her, I did it as a favour—she has a new boyfriend and wanted to give him a present. And it was a chance for me to finish one of her.'

Emma struggled to hide her scepticism, and did not believe Angel's lie for a moment; she suspected it had been an excuse to try and seduce Anton.

'Do you still find her attractive?'

'Oh Emma, not any more, I only love you.'

'I thought artists were above the failings of flesh,' she said seeing a flicker of excitement in his eyes. 'Immune to physical temptations and desires—rather like doctors.'

'All artists admire the naked body of a woman,' he grinned, 'it's only natural.'

'Would you have slept with her, if I hadn't turned up?' she asked him, not sure if she wanted to hear the answer.

'Absolutely not, would I have invited you?' he asked, a strange glint in his eye. 'She turned up to finish the painting and to collect the money I owed her. Do you think I would jeopardise our relationship for a fling?'

Emma scowled, thinking perhaps she would never know. She made a note to be more watchful of Angel, in future. Angel had tried to hypnotise them, she was sure, with her strange heady power and was trying to control them, to get Anton back. The shock of this revelation reverberated through her; their idyll was perfect, and she sensed Angel would try and do anything, to manipulate the situation if she could. She dared not trust her. She decided to be more wary.

'How long have you known Angel?' asked Emma.

'A few years,' he said, dismissively.

'Were you very in love with her?' she found herself asking, unable to stop.

'No, she was my muse. I thought I loved her once. She means nothing to me now.'

'Are you sure?'

'My relationship with Angel ended a long time ago,' Anton said truthfully, as though reading her mind. 'There really is nothing between us any more. We had very little in common, we were never true soul mates, not like us,' he said, cuddling her.

'Okay,' Emma said nuzzling up to him.

'Do you like my painting of her?'

'Yes, I do. But I don't trust her. She's dangerous, I feel uneasy when she's around,' admitted Emma. 'I think she may be following us.'

'I won't paint her again if it upsets you,' he promised. 'The painting's finished anyway. She's a vampire, drains everyone of life, I don't trust her either.'

Emma smiled, re-assured.

Since meeting him she had encountered so many odd situations. Nothing was as it seemed, she thought darkly.

'Admit it, Emma, you were turned on by her naked body, weren't you? It's only human and it's why you followed me into the sink room.'

Emma blushed. 'Do you want us to all sleep together?' she asked, dreading the answer.

'No, of course not.' He frowned. 'Fantasies should never become reality. Not if you have any sense,' he added, echoing her own thoughts.

Suddenly she found the idea very exciting and felt happy again, the scene had really fired her sexual imagination. Is that what he had planned?

'Do you like her painting?' he asked, pointing to the picture of a dark wench, with a dark heart, and flashing eyes.

'Yes,' she said, but the image sent an emotional shock wave so strong that she had to turn it around.

'It is the last painting I will do of her,' he said.

Emma had to admit that thinking of the girl's naked body had added an exciting dimension to their lovemaking. What on earth had got into her? Had she lost the plot completely and finally gone quite raving mad?

Predictions

Anton was giving a lecture. 'You must recognise the presence of light in your soul. Your soul and the brightness of its being connects you to the rhythm of the universe, tells us that we all have a special destiny here, that behind the façade is true beauty and spiritual delight.'

He felt tired, and went home early to finish a painting.

Anton painted the soft curve of Angel's face, adding the raven black strands of her long flowing hair, then her smooth buttocks. She still stirred some strange feelings in him. He felt a flicker of ambivalence: he had loved her once as his muse, and he always tried to become obsessed with his models, it helped if he fell a little bit in love with them. Yet, their time had run its course and there was nowhere else to go. It had ended and he had no feeling for her, all she did was block his spirituality with her darkness. He had enjoyed that path for a while and he had learned so much from her, but he had taken a different direction, the same one as Emma. He was surprised, when last Sunday on a warm cloudy morning, she had turned up at the studio to collect the money he owed her and her paintings. She had been at her most tantalising, coaxing him to go back with her, but he had refused: their love had died a long time ago. Drained of the energy to fight, in a momentary lapse of reason, he had agreed to paint her one last time. He thought it might distract her attention, make her realise how little he felt for her, but he had made a mistake, and it had upset Emma. He could have said no, but he didn't. Angel had been insistent on staying, obviously she had motives, using the excuse of one last painting as a gift for her new boyfriend. But he had sensed yet another motive, connected with the strange events around him recently. He had felt strange and dizzy, and he passed the day as though in a dream, even after Emma arrived.

Angel had tried to break them up, but luckily Emma had insisted on coming. Or God knows what might have happened, maybe Angel's tanned body would arouse any man—and for a second he felt a fleeting desire—but he was no longer under her spell. He had never really loved her, in the deep way that he did Emma. She had been his muse. He was besotted with Emma and felt a deep spiritual connection with her, they were soul mates and he adored her. Emma was the woman he had been waiting for. Yet he had felt a strange aura around Angel. Usually after he painted her, he had sex with her, but this time there was no desire. His sex life was more satisfying with Emma, and it had a kind of innocence. A sudden gust of wind interrupted his musings. He got up and closed the window. There were other things too, things that puzzled him. Who did Emma keep seeing in the mirror, in the cracked window, at the old studio? The dark place, he thought shivering, his blood running cold, where, on that terrible black night, Letitia had been murdered, by Antoine's dark hand! He put his face in his hands and imagined the dark solitary place where Antoine had committed suicide. Were they still haunting the inn? Would the terrible prediction still come true? Was he placing Emma in danger? That terrible night was hard to erase from his mind, it was stamped indelibly in his memory, and the tortured ghosts of Antoine and Letitia still tormented him, condemned to unrest by their terrible deed. He dare not tell Emma the truth, for she would never trust him again. To live with the fear that he may be driven to commit the same evil as his uncle?

When he thought of the prophecy, that he would lose his mind, and be consumed by the madness that had inflicted his uncle, be led to killing the woman that he loved, the idea filled him with revulsion and horror. He would rather die than hurt Emma. He looked down at the painting he was working on and dropped his brush. Suddenly images flashed through his mind like a film, and he saw Emma in the scene, crying. Fear seeped slowly through his veins: he saw a mist swirl over the canvas, and another scene appear, slowly taking over. He gasped, seeing, to his horror, that the predictions had returned. As he saw the scene gradually take shape, as a summer scene changed to one of death, he saw Emma's limp body lying on the ground. Then he saw her arranged in a coffin, a wreath of red roses around her head, the thorns digging into her skin.

Was this the prediction as told by the Count? Was it going to come true?

He cried, holding his head in his hands. Damn them for bringing darkness into his life—the evil Count Damien Davragne, and his descendent, Angel. He fell back reeling from shock, trying to catch his breath. They had come for revenge; there was only one thing to do. He took a knife, slashed the painting, and threw it out. He sat in the darkness for a long time, tortuous thoughts welling up in his mind. He put his head in his hands, wondering what to do next. What could he do now? They were moving in on him, and he had nowhere to run to; they had caught up with him and this time he was doomed.

Friends

Emma, worried, took over from Andy at the bar. The rain was lashing down in torrents outside, and the café was quiet. Most of the tourists had gone home, only the more serious surfers hung around with a few stray artists and some students. Andrea came in, shook out her umbrella and ordered a bottle of water.

'Gosh that's a first,' said Emma, almost reeling back in surprise.

'Well, we are having a family now,' she said, suddenly a picture of sobriety. Emma hoped her fun-loving friend was not going to change much. Andrea's craziness had kept her sane and she had been the nicest friend anyone could have been.

'Like to join me?' she asked Emma. 'You look like you need a friend.'

She told her all about Angel, and the session.

'I don't think you have anything to worry about, I read the cards every week, and I can't see anything. He does love you.'

'I know she is following us. She is stalking us, and when I caught her posing for him, he did not seem concerned at all. She had engineered the whole thing.'

'Well he didn't take the bait, did he?'

'No. He seemed quite indifferent towards her.'

'That's because she doesn't mean anything to him.'

'Every time I think I have found love, an obstacle seems to get in the way, a problem always arises,' cried Emma. 'I never have an easy time.'

'Do any of us?' asked Andrea, philosophically.

'I don't seem to have much luck with men, they come into my life and just seem to disrupt mine, sometimes I wonder if I am not better just being on my own. Why do they come into my life at all?'

'Because you have something valuable to learn from them. They are part of your destiny. Anton has taught you so much, he is part of your puzzle.'

'But will he stay?'

'Who knows? Life is not static. But I have a strong feeling that you will stay together, and that you are a very good match. We move from one space to another, learning different life lessons. That is the cycle of existence. Some say we move on to the stage of Nirvana when we have mastered true, unselfish love. But yes, I think you will be happy, but he does have a dark secret, and only true love can overcome such a secret.'

'What is it?'

'I don't know, but you will discover it soon. When he is ready to tell you, he will tell you.'

'I am too traditional when it comes to relationships, I believe in devotion, and monogamy. I want the man I love to stay with me forever.'

'You are such an incurable romantic,' laughed Andrea.

'Aren't you too?'

'No, I am a realist, I have no illusions about love. I just enjoy good sex and a friendship for as long as it lasts, nothing lasts forever.'

'I want to live cocooned in cosy domestic bliss. I prefer romance,' said Emma.

'But does Anton?' said Andrea looking away. 'He is a creative genius. Would he be satisfied with one woman, kids running around and dirty nappies? He needs to live on the edge a little, to be creative. You have to understand him, take him as he is and not make too many demands. He is married to his work, every woman is just his muse.'

'I suppose so,' said Emma gloomily 'I will love him always, whatever happens.'

'Cheer up, he loves you, it says so here,' she said, pointing to the tarot cards. 'The cards do say be careful though, there seems to be a dark cloud hovering over you both, and a dark secret from the past will emerge. It may taint your perfect happiness for a while. But with the power of the strength of your love for each other, you will overcome it. Have some faith, he is yours, there is no one else in his heart. There is a dark, scheming, manipulative woman around him, but she is no threat. He loves only you. Be careful, she may try and disrupt your happiness, but, if you are clever, you won't fall into her trap. She is a very jealous woman and has some very dark motives.'

Emma looked out of the window, anxiety creeping over her. Whatever the problem was, she was determined their love would pull them through and that they would win, and stay together for always. She loved Anton more than anyone in the world, and would not lose faith in their love, nor let anyone drive them apart. She would rather die. A glass suddenly shot across the bar, and smashed on the floor. She looked up shocked. What on earth was that?

The Dark Goddess

Emma drifted into a restless sleep. Strange dreams of Anton haunted her.

She woke up in an empty room next to the dark and dusty tunnel, under the inn. The path echoed noisily under black stallions tapping their hooves restlessly on the cobblestones outside. Solemn people dressed in black were dismounting from their horses and walking into the tunnels under the inn. She peered out of the window, a woman dismounted, carrying a posy. Her face was covered in a black wispy veil. Anton stood behind the shadows, his tall dark silhouette slithering along the wall. He stepped back, hiding from them.

The veiled woman tossed Emma a black rose from the posy. Emma caught it and breathed in the aroma, suddenly a snake crawled out of the petals, the stalk turned to ashes leaving a burnt black stamen. A maiden danced in a soft pool of light, swirling, then faded. The woman opened the door, she lifted up her veil; it was Angel! She jabbed Emma with her long taloned hand, her eyes narrowing into dangerous slits. She stood hard eyed, the poisonous snake wrapped around her arm; she threw it at Emma.

'I have come for you,' she whispered in a hoarse voice. She pushed Emma into the dungeon, onto a dark stone slab. Angel handed Emma a skull, black snakes writhed out of it onto the floor. She dropped it. They slithered up Emma's legs, she jumped back as they wormed their way between her thighs. Angel stood with her legs apart like a soldier, her eyes blazing with fury. The ghost of Annie Treeve the smuggler was at her side.

'You have taken something that belongs to me,' she spat. 'I am the Dark Goddess, I have come to take what is mine! I will destroy you, you will burn in Hell, if you do not give Anton back.'

'Never!'

'Anton, my beloved Anton—I am the goddess Kali, destroyer of all women who cross my path, my demonic nature will claw at you and destroy you unless you give Anton back to me. He is mine! I am the creative power that will destroy or renew. I can transform your existence into Hell.'

Emma felt the pain of a thousand swords rip through her. Her mind was filled with crazy images of a woman coming at her with a knife, she felt a torturous knife plunge into her.

'She is crazy,' thought Emma, writhing in pain screaming out with fear, 'completely insane.'

Anton took his sword and beheaded the Count, his head rolled, landing at Emma's feet. She was drifting through a dark tunnel into an abyss.

Emma woke up with a jolt, she was pouring with sweat. She sat up quickly, feeling anxious, and her hands were still shaking. What a terrible dream. She had lost all sense of time, her mind was in a turmoil. Where was Anton? Fragments of light flew around her. She took in some deep breaths, feeling calmer. The dream had made her feel very odd. What did it mean? She ran downstairs, the phone was ringing, it was Melanie. She thought she saw a shadowy figure glide over the stairs. She blinked and it had gone.

'What's up, sis?' said her sister, in a friendly voice.

'Oh nothing, I just had a bad night.' Emma felt relief flood through her at the sound of her sister's voice, she told Mel about Anton.

'Sounds dreamy, but a bit arty though. Whatever happened to Jeremy?'

'He moved on,' Emma said, tersely.

'Well I'd say good riddance. Anton sounds more your type but be careful if he is into strange things.'

'He's a brilliant artist and teacher,' she said loyally, speaking in his defence. 'He's wonderful but a bit wild.'

'Yes, sounds a bit eccentric, look at Van Gogh. Can lose touch with reality, a bit psychotic. I'm just reading a newspaper heading that sums men like him up—it says: "You can trust any man to botch things up, but to achieve a real fiasco, you need an intellectual."'

'Oh Melanie,' laughed Emma, 'don't be so cruel.'

Ever since Melanie had taken a course in psychology, she couldn't stop analysing everyone.

'Slightly introverted, neurotic and intensely sensual?'

'Spot on.'

'What's he like in bed?'

'Beyond my wildest dreams.'

'That makes up for any drawbacks, I guess.'

Emma raced over to see Anton. She kissed him lightly on the cheek as he was sleeping. What was his secret? She gazed lovingly at him, pushing the hair from his face—he was full of surprises. She enjoyed the new experiences he was showing her. He woke up, and stared moodily over at the studio.

'I must do some work,' he said. 'I need some space. I've just had the strangest dream.'

'What about?'

'That we were in Hell, that we were thrown, twisted and burned, into the abyss.'

'Too much Stilton last night maybe,' Emma whispered, cradling him in her arms. 'Is everything all right?'

'Perfect,' he snapped tersely, his face tense. 'I'm sorry. Oh Emma, I feel so awful. Perhaps I should go for a walk and get some fresh air. Look, I'm sorry I didn't tell you that Angel was coming. I've been trying to avoid her. She's up to something, I know. She sees herself as some kind of reincarnation of the dark goddess, with special powers. My ancestor was responsible for killing her ancestor, the shipwrecked count. But there is nothing between us any more, I promise. I found her captivating at first, but then I discovered she's bordering on psychotic. She was into some odd things and I'm not likely ever to get involved with her again. It's the last thing on earth I want. But I do feel weird, as if someone is trying to invade me, psychically attack me.'

'Does she really possess a dark power?' inquired Emma, becoming alert. 'Surely it's all in the mind, I don't believe in that kind of thing.'

'She likes to think she does.'

'Surely she knows she cannot influence us.' Emma got up and paced around the room. 'It's simply suggestion that she uses.'

'No, some people can manipulate the wills of others, if they put their mind to it,' he said, truthfully.

'Only if you let them,' said Emma wisely. 'If you collude in their little game, you will give them power.'

'I suppose so.'

Day turned into night, a raging storm howled outside. Emma pulled the curtains, shutting out the flashes of lightning that lit the darkness, and bolts of thunder cracking in the sky. She dived back into the warm and cosiness inside. Anton paced the floor, agitated. His eyes were red. He looked tired and drawn. She looked at him concerned, what mystery was unfolding before her very eyes?

Anton grew more irritable. His face was etched with worry. He looked drawn and haunted. She tried to jolt him out of his melancholy mood. What had got into him?

'I'll go and work in my studio for a while,' he said. 'Is that okay? Otherwise I will just annoy you.'

'That's a good idea, it might take your mind off things,' Emma snapped, sensing something terrible was going to happen. She tried to push all negative thoughts out of her head. Perhaps they were both just tired from overwork. The electrical storm was making them edgy. She noticed a growing darkness around him, and was sure they were being watched. An odd vibe hung eerily in the air. Silently, he crept from the room and came back carrying a handful of roses.

'I'm sorry, Emma, I didn't mean to take my dark moods out on you.'

'It's okay,' she said. 'Perhaps there's something I can do to help?'

'I don't know, Emma, I just feel very strange, I sense that something awful is about to happen. I'll go up to the studio and paint for a while and try and relax and unwind. Dark moods are part of the creative process, the highs and the lows,' he said, cheerfully.

The storm died, the rain stopped, the humidity deepened. Anton seemed different. There was a darker side that she couldn't quite fathom. Distracted, he picked up his canvas and left. She sighed wearily, then a surge of optimism hit her—for the first time in her life her mind was free from restraint and petty rules, open to new levels of creativity and awareness. She was learning so much from him; her spiritual enlightenment lifted her into a magical universe, inspiring her with a boundless vision and energy. She had discovered a deeper meaning to life, opening her to an awareness she had never known before. Yet a dark angel lurked in this utopia. A dark shadow followed them. Angel? What was Anton's dark secret? She found his mercurial personality confusing at times. One minute he was the gentle, scholarly philosopher, the next a wicked, tormented master. What exactly ate into his soul and filled him with doom? He would not tell her. He spent long periods alone, after which he would emerge, brimming with enthusiasm. He was capable of turning every day into paradise, or hell.

She gazed wistfully out of the window; it was sunny outside, and the sea was calmer, a pale watery sun shone into the room. She lay back thinking she couldn't imagine ever being without him. Yet recently she had felt like she was riding on an emotional roller-coaster. She hated the stifling boredom of conventionality, preferring to live with a touch of wildness, on the edge herself at times, and sometimes, she had to admit, flirting with danger made her feel alive. But this was confusing. She wanted to settle down, start a family. She had met men who were afraid of commitment, she was afraid this might be going the same way. Did love ever work out perfectly in the real world? Was Anton her magic man? Or was he just a dark knight in disguise? He conjured up different fantasies in her like a magician, showing her the highest ecstasies of love, then plunging her into the darkest pit of despair. Did his dark secret stop him from being free to love? She was walking on a tightrope, ready to plummet down into an endless void—such a dangerous thrill but she knew that no one had taken her to such heights or inspired her so much. She enjoyed the thrill of lovemaking, letting her fantasies fly, discovering her boundless sexuality, reaching transcendence and mystical levels of awareness. Yet there was a dark, mysterious, unfathomable quality to Anton, who always evaded questions about his past. What was he hiding? She stood in front of his latest painting: an enchantress bathing among maidens, while knights watched them through the trees, Anton the central character in the print beside it—Hades and the nymphs, his elegant face being caressed by them. She sighed, hoping he would be in a better mood when he came back.

The next day, she walked into the classroom while he was giving a lecture.

'The Celts had a wonderful intuitive understanding of life and of the complexity of the psyche,' he explained. 'They believed in divine gifts and presences and also acknowledged the darkness. In the current day we have become disconnected from our intuitive spirituality, due to civilisation and its discontents, and here in Cornwall we can get back in touch with the power of the earth, and hence our spirituality, through the energy of the earth.'

'When the soul deserts the wisdom of love and desires knowledge, without the love of a subject, life becomes a brittle one without substance. We have to have a balance of both to be truly inspired. Our aim is to bring the energy of a wild magnificent horse under the control of the rider, without using the whip that will kill its spirit, but to coax its essence to life.'

'Hi Emma,' he said, smiling. 'I'll be two seconds.'

They went upstairs for a coffee.

She was starting to veer and daydream from one idea to another. She'd had enough adventures to last a lifetime and felt it was time to put down roots. She opened her easel and started work on her new project—the fairy water nymph dancing by a brook. With each stroke she felt better, propelled to a higher plane. She sighed, satisfied. The creative ideas were flowing freely through her psyche and she felt in control again. She felt alive, empowered. She packed away her things and rushed home to find Anton in a good mood, cooking a meal.

'Without dark, there cannot be light, to be whole there has to be both light and dark, good and evil,' he said, slitting open some fish with a sharp knife. 'The negative shows us the truth. Have you read any Carl Jung?' he asked her.

'Yes, a little. I've read about the soul, the collective unconscious and psychology and alchemy. But I think a lot of it is too complex, too deep.'

'And you don't like going too deep?' he questioned, his eyes furrowing as he stared at her intently. 'Why, what are you afraid of?'

'No, I didn't mean that, just that it all seems to be a little too abstract, irrelevant to everyday life.'

'It depends on what you consider important, trivia can be stimulating, but it is vacuous, it has no pattern. Depth and wisdom pertains to spiritual development, once you have transcended the illusions of the contemporary world, you will become attuned to what is really important.'

She listened intently, it made sense, his theories on the spirit, art and love, the mysteries of the universe. Releasing her inner child, he showed her how to see with renewed wonder, experience the highest form of vision, explore her own natural gifts.

'Listen with the heart of the brave,' he said. 'Reflect on your inner needs and the answers will come to you. Purity of thought and a higher knowledge will steer you toward your right destiny.'

She soaked up every word like a sponge. What was the secret he was too afraid to share with her? She had to know, he needed to be totally honest with her. But she sensed now wasn't the time to ask when his mood was so fragile.

'What about your great-uncle, was he a very spiritual artist?'

'He was filled with illusions, obsessions, not clarity. He became so deeply plunged into the darkness that it distorted his vision, he became psychotic and he saw things that weren't there. He was delusional.'

Towers of darkness

Emma put some flowers in a vase—irritated that Anton only ever wanted to discuss art. He hated emotional scenes, especially when he had work to do, and said that telling people your deepest secrets was not the wisest thing to do. He lived for passion, romance and was inspired by mystery, hating practical realities. He had to let his thoughts flow, his vision be clear, to be creative. He often became so wrapped up in his work that he became unbearable. She felt happiest when they were curled up together on the sofa, watching the clouds drift by over the sea. Why was he so anxious? What dark secret was tormenting him?

'Are you afraid of anything?' she asked.

'Isn't everybody?' he answered.

'You seem distracted today, your mind is elsewhere.'

He looked away, a tense expression crossing his face.

'There are some things that are beyond my control and too terrible to mention,' he admitted to Emma.

She looked up at him puzzled.

'Please stop probing.'

'I am just concerned.'

'Oh Emma,' he confessed, 'I love you and want you to be happy, but there may be some things that I like to keep to myself.'

She looked at him questioningly.

'Will you help me sort out the paintings for the next exhibition?' he asked, changing the subject. 'Do something useful, there are some good ones still in the attic. I've got to set up the new collection this week, it's going to get very busy.'

'I thought you said you didn't want to display them.'

'I've changed my mind.'

Mystified, Emma climbed up into the attic. Something brushed past her; it felt like a cold, clammy hand. She shivered, then got back to her work. She brushed the dust off some old boxes.

She had been in the loft all morning, exploring, until she had found some canvases covered by a silk scarf. She lifted the scarves and underneath were some dark paintings with a strange emblem. One was of Antoine; she stopped as she recognised the symbol as the one she had seen carved on the rocks in the cavern below Kynance cove. What did it mean?

She called out to Anton, 'Do you want me to bring them down?'

'Yes, I must sort through them. Do you like them?'

'I do.'

'They do have a certain dark charm,' he admitted, piling them together, his face ashen as he turned them over. He turned white, as though he had just seen a ghost. 'No maybe not, I must throw them out.'

'What's the matter? Are you all right?' Emma asked.

'Should have got rid of these ages ago,' he said. His face darkened, his hands were trembling.

'Why?' she asked, becoming curious. 'What's the matter with them?'

'Because they are evil,' he insisted moodily. 'I must get rid of them. Do not touch them! We must get rid of them!' A wave of dark fear crossed his face.

She looked closer at them, some fascinating drawings, an intricate row of flowers bordered the edge, surrounded by faces; upside down they were skulls. They were beautiful, but very dark and disturbing. Emma looked at him puzzled, sure he was going quite mad.

'Do you understand what they mean?' Anton asked.

'No, what do they mean?'

'That situations are never what they seem, that what often appears safe, normal, often conceals a darker side. That appearances can be deceptive. They represent the forces of darkness.'

'They are only paintings,' sighed Emma.

'The faces are three-dimensional, they look as though they are moving, they have a life force,' he explained.

'I must have one.'

'No, give them to me, I must destroy them,' he snapped, taking one from her, and throwing it on the fire. 'There's an evil force, a darkness coming from them,' he said, suddenly angry. 'Give them to me.'

'No, please let me keep one. Don't destroy them all.'

'Let me get rid of them, they are evil!' Anton shouted. 'Please do as I say!'

'How can a painting be evil?' she asked, surprised. Just *what* was he so afraid of? She had never seen him like this before.

'I painted them at a bad time in my life, a time that I would rather forget,' he said, taking a canvas, cracking it in half and throwing the broken wood on the fire. 'If I keep them, they will cause terrible things to happen to us, they are cursed. I hate the darkness! I like the gentle, harmonious serene things in life now, but once I had been stupid enough to embrace the darkness,' he said anxiously. 'I was involved in the occult, and the paintings remind me of that time. I don't want to see them again,' he said firmly, climbing back into the attic and throwing more paintings down.

'I should have burned these,' he continued, showing her paintings of ships sinking, tormented faces writhing in the sea. 'After a while, I realised my paintings were becoming psychic, I started to have terrible predictions, like living nightmares.'

'What sort of predictions?'

'Strange dreams, predicting disasters and when I sat in front of the canvas, I would paint them, as though I was overtaken by some strange force that was guiding me. I saw a tanker disaster that sunk in the bay, the suicide of the local headmaster, the drowning of a whole cargo of fishermen who hit turbulent seas. I had seen them because I had asked for the gifts of darkness, asked to see into the future, I was given a curse, seeing everything, including Hell. Those paintings showed me evil. I had opened the gateway to Hell.'

'But why get rid of them? What harm can they do now?'

'They will bring evil into our lives. No, they have to go, they must be destroyed because they hold a deadly curse,' he insisted, throwing them down the stairs onto the rubbish pile. He fixed his stubborn gaze on her, his eyes, red from tiredness, blazing angrily. Emma felt too tired to argue, she hardly knew him when he was like this.

His eyes flickered with anger, his face was hard like granite, and his manner cold. He snatched the pictures from her roughly. She was stunned. A look of contempt flickered across his face, as he threw the paintings into the fire. He poked at the fire, flames licked over the paintings, melting the paint into muddy swirls of grey.

'No, Anton, please don't do that,' she cried. 'Can't you just sell them?'

'No, because they will spread their poison to anyone who owns them.'

He ignored her and closed his eyes; just looking at them made him feel he was sliding over the edge. The more he opposed her, the more she argued. How she hated to see his own art destroyed.

'But they are so unique, so intricate, a set of religious symbols interwoven into a skull.' She spoke wistfully. 'They are so beautiful and mysterious. Can't you just sell them quickly in the gallery instead of destroying them?'

He closed the door softly. He didn't want anyone to hear what he had to say.

'No, I'm sorry, Emma, they have to be destroyed,' he insisted. 'They are evil, they hold a thousand Hells and will bring endless torment to whoever owns them.'

'Don't be so ridiculous! Goya and Bosch created very dark art.'

'And look what happened to them! A lot of artists went mad, like my uncle.'

His face cracked into a smile, then clouded with dismay. He handed her back a painting.

'All right, if you insist, you keep one, but you will be cursed! Look, I am trying to warn you, Emma, that you don't know what you are dealing with. You are being foolish,' he said, scornfully. 'You'll find out yourself, your naiveté can be wearing at times. Just believe me when I say they have some bad associations.' He took one of the best paintings out of the pile and threw the rest across the room.

She looked at him in astonishment. 'They are only paintings, how can they be cursed?'

'Because they are evil. You can have this one as you seem to like them so much,' he said tenderly, the warmth flooding back into his smile, 'but don't blame me for the consequences.'

Emma touched the frame protectively.

'Do you believe in the other world?'

'Yes, I do. I see strange faces at the inn, I'm sure it is haunted.'

Anton's face turned ashen grey. 'What exactly did you see?'

'A woman keeps appearing in the glass, and a man, who looks a lot like you. I saw him in the mirror. I thought perhaps it was Antoine? I have seen the woman's face in the studio window.'

He slumped down on the chair, staring at her in disbelief.

'Do you know who they are?' she asked him. 'Please tell me.'

'There is nothing to tell, it is just your imagination.'

'I know what I saw,' she insisted angrily. 'You are hiding something. What are you afraid to tell me?'

'I don't know what you're talking about, it must have been all in your imagination,' he insisted, brushing the paintings and avoiding her eye. Anton stared out of the window, fiddling nervously with a paintbrush, then he looked down at the floor. 'All right, there might be something there, anything is possible,' he said softly, not wanting to alarm her. 'I can't tell you everything, not yet.'

Mystified, Emma stared at the painting. A dark, malevolent force started oozing from it, an evil aura flowed around the room. A grey smoke drifted from the painting. She dropped the frame, feeling strange and dizzy. She put her hand to her mouth in surprise, then the most awful nausea engulfed her, and she jumped back in revulsion.

'You see!' Anton said, darkly. 'It's evil! What did I tell you?'

She knew better than to argue any further and threw it on the fire with the others. 'How strange.'

Anton's face was haunted, troubled, a muscle in his cheek twitched nervously. A guilty expression crossed his face. He bit his lip.

'I'm sorry, Emma, to have involved you in all of this. I hope I haven't upset you.'

'No. I'm not that fragile. Please tell me what happened at the inn,' she coaxed.

'I trust you, but don't know if I should. Okay, I suppose you have a right to know,' he said quietly. 'I will start at the beginning, maybe you will understand. One day while I was creating a series of web pages for a client, I flicked through scenes of Cornwall and was idly going from place to place: it made me wonder, wouldn't it be useful to travel in seconds, to different places, like on the computer? At a party a few weeks later, I mentioned this to a group of people who said they could travel like that, by astral travel, that is, on the psychic and spiritual plane. You must have heard of people who have had out-of-body experiences, who remain tied by a silver thread to their physical body? Well, I knew then I wanted to try it.'

Emma listened intently, fascinated.

'They showed me how to travel to other realms, and so I joined their group, and they taught me all sorts of occult practices. If I had known it would be so dangerous, I would never have joined.' He stopped and looked down at his palms. 'But it all seemed so innocent and harmless at first; besides, as an artist, I was looking at other forms of consciousness and experience, and I have a great respect for darkness. But this went too far.'

'I learnt to travel on the astral plane, to the future and beyond, to different places, through infinity. Then it got slightly darker, I attended séances, contacted my dead uncle, I found out some terrible things about him. One day, after an argument with his friend the Count, they say that he conjured up a storm and lured the Count and his men onto the rocks, and killed them. The Count, enraged put a terrible curse on all of his descendents, which means me,' he said darkly. 'Oh Emma, I'm so sorry to upset you, it is all a little strange,' he said kissing her hands.

'No, it's fascinating,' she said.

'Well it all went wrong and my uncle who killed him was driven mad, the same fate they said would happen to me, I would be haunted by the Count as his revenge. I suffered for my curiosity and I wish I had never got involved.'

Anton, her sensitive, creative lover, was deeply wounded. Emma scowled, sad to see him so tormented, his beautiful sculpted face worn and strained; she felt tenderness and love well up inside her. His tampering with the darkness had dragged his spirit to its darkest depths, from which only true love could lift him. He had become withdrawn. His mind was clouded by fear and uncertainty, his face plagued by dark shadows, a black aura enveloping him, as he took the journey to confronting his dark secret. She tried to coax him into sharing it. But just as she thought she had won his confidence, and he was on the verge of telling her, he grew defensive and backed away, growing more irritable.

'Well, maybe I will tell you the rest of the story later, but all I remember is that I found myself in a strange twilight world, and things got pretty black. Let's go for a walk,' he said changing the subject, 'I need some air, and to forget about this for a while. I dabbled in some dangerous things and they backfired, I don't want them to plague me for life, that's all you need to know.'

Wisps of hazy sunlight streamed through the windows, and the pink-grey light filtered through the room, streaks of orange cloud filled the pale blue skies—it had turned out to be a beautiful day. The glittering turquoise sea was calm and white foamy waves lapped gently on the shore. Anton led Emma to the cove next to his studio. They took the path along the cliff edge, high above the curious wild landscape, leading down to the sea. Carefully, they stepped over the treacherous black rocks, climbing up onto the grassy dunes. Emma looked out to sea, hypnotised by its strange unfettered power, the wind whipping through her hair. She felt herself being drawn to the edge of the cliffs. As she stood there something touched her and stroked her hair, then it stopped.

'What was that?' she asked, turning round. 'Something just touched me.'

'I didn't see anything, it must have been the wind.'

'Where are we?' she asked, concerned.

'The locals call it "The Edge" as so many ships have been wrecked here and people say it is like standing on the edge of the world. It's a sheer drop into the sea, to the lethal jagged rocks.'

Emma suddenly felt cold, uneasy, as if something terrible was going to happen. There were some strange dark clouds swirling in the sky, it had turned cold.

'Look out,' he said, pulling her back as some rocks came hurtling down and missed them by inches. 'Let's get out of here—that was a bit too close for my liking.' He caught his breath, relaxing and gazing out to sea. 'Look at the wild beauty all around us.' He held out his arms, a rapturous look on his face. 'What an amazing landscape! Why do we worry, when we can have all of this beauty for free?' he asked, gazing at the miles of beach and rocks stretching out in front of them.

'It is so inspiring,' agreed Emma.

'It's perfect, unspoilt by human intervention. We've found paradise on Earth: ask the universe a question, and it will give an answer. It enhances vision, sparks my creativity, takes me to a higher plane. Stay true to your path, strengthen your will, Emma. Feel the power of the earth, in tune with nature and be master of your own destiny. Follow the will of truth and beauty.'

She nodded. Her blissful mood changed to one of horror as he jumped up on the cliff edge and balanced precariously over a sheer drop. Balancing on a narrow rock ledge, he leapt deftly from one ledge to another like a surefooted and confident deer. Emma looked away, afraid to watch.

'This is the only life worth living,' he said, pointing down to the sea from a narrow ledge. He leapt back down onto the path.

'Like Vikings, sailing the turbulent seas!' joked Emma.

'Yes,' he answered, distracted by a boat in the distance.

'I wonder who that is,' he said, looking at the ship.

'It looks like the ghost ship, but I think it's just a tanker,' guessed Emma.

'Oh, I love you, Emma. Before I met you, I lived in a broken dream. You gave me inspiration and the strength to start again. Let's build our lives here, you are the most special woman I have ever met, to me you are the one I have been waiting for. Will you marry me?' he asked.

'Yes, Anton, I will. I will always love you.'

His eyes started to look misty and far away.

'There are some things I have to do first. I will love you forever, but first there's something I must lay to rest. Some demons I have to exorcise, or we could be doomed.'

The sky clouded over; it suddenly turned very grey for an early evening.

'What demons?' asked Emma, worried.

A dark expression covered Anton's face. 'I must rid myself of the past,' he said evasively, walking on quickly ahead. Emma ran after him up the hill. The wind blew wildly behind her, pushing her up the hill—she could barely fight against the lashing wind. She ran up the hill and caught up with him as he was about to disappear behind a sand hill. The worried look on his face had grown deeper, the wind blew his hair, making him look untamed. He parted his lips as though to say something, then stopped and put his arm around her protectively. 'I'm sorry, Emma, I get so worried, it's nothing.'

She pushed him back playfully on the shoulder. They fell back onto the dunes. He kissed her affectionately, holding her in a firm embrace as though she was all that was keeping him from starvation.

'Stay with me, Emma, forever,' he pleaded.

A ship sailed into the bay, and suddenly a strange atmosphere saturated the air. An old, wizened woman stood staring at them from the top of the hill, her face thin and gaunt. She pointed accusingly at Anton. 'Be careful,' she cried in warning. 'You are in danger, dealing with things you cannot control. Dark forces. Leave them alone! Or the prediction will come true. And you, my dear,' she warned, turning to Emma, 'beware of what you are getting into.'

'Who are you?' asked Emma, mystified. 'And how do you know my name?'

She climbed down the dune, and handed Emma a card with a strange set of symbols on it; they looked like something to do with witchcraft, one of them was a pentagram. 'I am a psychic, I see all there is to see.'

Anton's face turned black, his eyes screwed up against the sun. 'Go to Hell,' he shouted back at the woman.

'If you ever need my help, call me, Emma' she said, cryptically.

'Who are you?'

'I'm a clairvoyant, the spirit world has a message for you, it says you are both in danger,' she said, simply. 'I have seen a vision and I have been sent to help you, leave the others alone or you are doomed.'

'What others?' stuttered Emma, curious.

'Come on, Emma, let's leave now,' demanded Anton insistently, striding over. 'This is nonsense.'

'He's waiting for you,' warned the woman. 'They are coming for you,' she said, pointing a finger at Anton. 'Leave them alone, or they will turn their destructive powers against you. Your so-called friends are evil, and they want to harm you. You must be strong to come through from the other side. You are not yet out of the darkness,' she warned Anton.

A bolt of lightning flashed across the sky, followed by a clap of thunder rumbling in the distance, the storm was getting nearer.

'You are mad!' Anton accused the woman, his voice fading into a whisper. He pulled Emma back. A dark expression crossed his troubled face.

'Don't dabble with powers you cannot control,' advised the old woman, turning away.

'Let's go, it's getting cold,' Anton insisted, his face full of fear. He put an arm around Emma.

'What was that all about?' she asked looking round as the woman wandered away.

'Just some crazy, eccentric woman who claims she can see into the future.'

'She knows who we are…what are you hiding from me?'

'Nothing. When the time is right, I shall tell you everything.'

They raced back to the studio. Emma drove them to the inn, with the rain bucketing down. 'What is it, Anton? Why do you look so afraid?' asked Emma.

'I've unleashed the forces of darkness,' he said, defeated, 'and there's no going back.'

The Count

Anton walked into the studio; he lit a fire and burned all the old paintings that he'd made of the Count and Angel. He climbed into the attic and dragged down the rest of the pictures and threw them in the fire too. He cleaned out the attic so there were no dark paintings left.

A few minutes later, he felt the sudden urge to paint. His hand seemed to take on a life of its own, the paintbrush starting to create perfect life-like images. He stood passively, letting the ideas flow through him. He drew a man, struggling in the water, a man who was drowning. He started shaking—it was another prediction! The evil visions had returned! What was going to happen to them? He looked back at the painting, the studio was on fire, his paintings were burning. Angel was screaming, trying to get out of the debris.

Then in a flash, it faded, and he looked at the painting: he was pushing Emma over the cliff. He grabbed his head in torment, if the curse came true, he would harm Emma! His own true love would be killed by his own hand, as in the prophecy. His future was there before him, a living nightmare.

Emma knocked on the window, interrupting his thoughts. Anton turned round quickly and showed her the picture of the drowning man, he seemed tortured.

'What do you mean, Anton, who is still following you?' asked Emma. 'What the hell is going on?'

'It's all a bit of mystery, but this prediction is that I'm going to kill you,' he said, slowly.

'Don't be silly, Anton, it's only a painting. Someone has put these ideas in your head, you must fight them, they are not real.'

'Maybe we shouldn't see each other for a while, there are some dangerous times ahead; I don't want you to be involved,' he said, fighting for breath.

'No, I will stay and never leave your side, whatever happens, we shall face this together,' she insisted.

'Then, it's at your own peril,' he warned.

'I don't scare easily,' said Emma, remembering the battles she had with some of the most difficult executives in advertising—she wasn't going to let a mere dead Count get the better of her, or scare her away.

'When I left the group, Angel and the Count swore that they would never let me go, for a while I was free of them, but now they have come back. He put a curse on me and on my family, they would kill me for my uncle's betrayal. Oh Emma, you must trust me, we need to get away for a while, soon.'

'Yes. It doesn't feel safe here.'

A ship sounded its horn in the distance and crows scattered across the beach as though they had been shot at from the barrel of a gun. Emma saw a black dove fly overhead. She pointed to it.

'Look, the dove, it's an omen.'

Anton narrowed his eyes and squinted up at the sky. 'Yes,' he said, worried. 'Something terrible is going to happen.'

He walked sombrely back to the loft house. Emma was watching him, questions swirling in her head. She stood alone for a few minutes, a flock of crows circling overhead, one dived down and almost collided with her. 'Hey,' she said swishing it away. She ran over to Anton, pulling at his jacket. 'I want to know what is going on,' she insisted. 'I think I have a right to know, after all, some strange things keep happening to me too.'

'Okay, What do you know about the occult, Emma?'

'Nothing really.'

'Well, it's been practised for centuries, and there are many unscrupulous practitioners of the art as well as some very good people who use it. I became involved with the wrong people. I made some stupid mistakes. I experimented for my work, out of curiosity, I followed the dark path, the occult and went too far.'

'Just how far did you dabble in the occult?'

'Too far. I used to teach a course called "Dark side of the soul" to my art group. The dark side fascinated me. Bosch, Goya, and Michelangelo, even the Pre-Raphaelites, depicted the dark side of human nature and I felt it was an important part of art. Rossetti emphasised the brooding darkness when he fell in love with Jane Morris and dug up his poetry from Lizzie Siddal's grave. Well I was drawn into the darkness. Jung calls it the "shadow", it contains our darker, more primitive desires, the *id*, but is also a well of creativity. I became so obsessed with the power of the darkness that it became an addiction. For a while I spiralled deeper and deeper into danger, seeking paranormal phenomena. I joined a group of occultists, who drew me further into the darkness. Unfortunately, after a while, I discovered they used it to gain power to manipulate others, rather than for creative purposes. I had intended to use it for enhancing my work, exploring my imagination. My curiosity overcame my common sense. I thought it was an area worthy of study, as many artists have done in the past. But they used it to control and destroy, to change the destiny of others, which is evil. At that moment I realised what I was getting into and how dangerous it was, I was walking on thin ice, but I couldn't stop.'

'An easy mistake to make,' said Emma sympathetically.

His eyes narrowed. 'I did try to get out, but they stopped me. I threw caution to the wind. A chance arose for a séance, for raising the dead. I was fascinated and only too eager to try, so I said yes. It was an exciting experience—who isn't interested in the idea?' he said, seeing the look of surprise on Emma's face.

'The lure of the darkness was by now compelling, and became an obsession that nearly destroyed me. During that séance, in search of a dark spirit, we unleashed an unpredictable force, a dangerous entity we couldn't control. I had wanted to call up the most evil soul. And to my surprise, we found one.'

Emma looked at him amazed.

'I raised a dangerous twisted soul—the Count answered us,' he said grimly. 'He had gone down with the ship, when my uncle had betrayed him by informing the coastguard. So I had called up a bitter enemy. His men were all killed, so my uncle went mad and did some terrible things. He was haunted, imagining things, believing he was possessed. One day, he became so tormented that, during a paranoid episode, he killed the woman he loved, then himself, and the curse was activated on my family. It was the Count's revenge. Swearing that we were trapped forever in Hell, for betraying him, he told me I would follow the same destiny.'

'Oh how terrible,' gasped Emma, feeling very scared. 'So what will happen to you?' she asked, her eyes glazing over with fear.

'I don't know. It was a long time ago, I consulted a psychic who said they would not be able to harm me if I stayed away from the darkness—the prophecy would be ineffective, but, if I rejoined them, I would activate the curse. Now do you see why I want nothing to do with the occult any more?'

'Yes, I do, but you *are* away from them now.'

'But they are still pursuing me, and if they catch up with me again, I will be doomed. They are trying to send me mad, by using dark forces.'

'Then we must fight back, tell me more about them.'

'Well, apart from all of this, I learned how to astral travel, using the mirror. When I discovered that my friends were going even deeper into darker realms, I began to realise I was making a fatal mistake, but I carried on.'

'They taught you to astral travel?'

'Yes, they taught me to travel through the realm using clairvoyance, using the rituals of the shaman to explore the spirit world. To our horror, we discovered the entity we had called up was too powerful for us to control. "Do as thou wilt shall be the whole of the law" was their philosophy, but I felt uneasy. One night we attempted one of the most dangerous rituals, calling up the demons and dweller of the abyss, and all chaos broke out. After that I became cursed and started painting terrible predictions, until I became too scared to paint any more. That's why I had to destroy my work, because those pictures hold an evil power. And, oh, Emma, I feel that they may be trying to get to you too.'

'How?' she asked, dumfounded.

'When I called up the Count, he was bent on revenge. He said any woman I loved would suffer too, as I am the descendent of the man who betrayed him. He seeks his revenge on me too. Don't get involved, Emma, or they will bring their dark powers into your life as well.'

'I will fight against them with you,' she argued. 'Is there really such a thing as a dark power? I don't believe in it, they can't harm me.'

'Of course it exists. I have no reason to lie to you, what I have told you is true.'

'You were right to destroy the paintings. How can we break your link with them for good?'

'I don't know. It was me who appeared in the mirror, through astral travel. That's how I managed to paint you.'

Emma felt a shiver run over her; she had to admit she was scared at Anton's dark secret, it was worse than she could ever have imagined. His dark secret was unfolding, revealing the maggot-ridden centre of the apple: outside was shiny and bright, inside rotten and dark. She always knew there was more to this than she had imagined. Yet she was still oddly intrigued.

'How could you have been so foolish?' she accused, slithers of icy fear running through her veins. Her head ached and she was annoyed. She wondered why, for someone so clever, at times he had so little common sense, and no sense of danger—he just kept pushing boundaries as far as they would go. She just kept thinking how similar he looked to Antoine, the man in the mirror, and it all started to make sense. The mystery was beginning to fall into place—the haunted inn, the ghost, the shadow, Anton's past, and the mad uncle who still haunted the inn, searching for his dead love: his dark secret was unravelling, so was their idyll, and she shivered. She felt like she was falling off a cliff.

'I don't know, I admit I was a fool, but there is something else. I used astral travel to see you, it was me that kissed you.'

So the 'ghost' was Anton! She looked at him, shocked. He had been haunting her, seducing her! The ghost of his uncle haunted the studio, the tortured Antoine, and his dead lover Letitia: it was they she had seen in the mirror. She suddenly felt out of her depth. What on earth had she got herself into? The place was teeming with ghosts.

'What happened at the inn?' she asked. 'And what was his connection with Annie?'

'Annie used to rent the Black Dove Inn, then when Antoine met Letitia, she moved to The First and Last, a place owned by a landlord called Dionysus Williams. Williams was a smuggler, and Annie, when she found this out, started blackmailing him to let her live there rent-free. He got fed up with her and told her to leave; in retaliation she told the coastguard about the smuggling and he was imprisoned. His men, including the brothers at the inn, took Annie and tied to her to a stake at low tide on Sennen beach; when the water level rose she drowned. It is said that she sends nightmares of drowning and strange dreams to people, and still haunts both inns. She is one of the ghosts, and she built the tunnels under the inn, as part of the large-scale smuggling operation for both the inns.'

'I see. Yes, I also saw a photograph in the library of her with Antoine—he had a fairly lugubrious past too.'

'Yes, it was Antoine, my uncle, he hailed from the landed gentry of France, and moved to Cornwall. I take after him in many ways. He dabbled in the occult too, and was a dark, nefarious rogue. That's why I was drawn to the occult. He lived at the inn for a while, and he practised black magic there; there are many strange stories about him. Once good friends with the Count, Antoine told the coastguard to switch off the fog light as the pirates were coming in, and so sank the ship.'

Suddenly, it all fell into place.

'So the inn really is haunted, it wasn't just my imagination? Or just children playing at the window?'

'Yes,' he finally admitted, 'my uncle and the Count lived there, they are the ghosts that haunt the inn, and their dark deeds haunt it too.'

'So that was your dark secret,' she said, relieved she now knew. 'How was Angel involved?'

'She showed me the dark path. Seduction, sex and magic is a powerful combination.'

Emma suddenly realised why she disliked Angel so much. She *was* a black witch! Emma had always wondered why she had seen such a strange and menacing energy in her eyes. The power of evil and corruption was reflected in the darkness of her soul.

'At first, it seemed to provide the extra dimension I was looking for, the darkness. We need the opposites, the dark and the light, the moon and the sun, the black and the white to be whole. White magic is good and useful. The person needs both the dark shadow and lightness for individuation. But I should never have explored the darkness without a guide. "Don't show me the moon shining brightly, show me a glint on broken glass."'

Emma nodded, he was right. Fear crept into her like slithers of ice, running coldly through her veins. She paced restlessly around the room. What could she do now? She was in too deep and things were spiralling out of control. Anton walked over to the window and glanced out at the clear blue sky.

'Would you like to hear the rest?'

'Yes,' insisted Emma, forcing a smile. 'I want to know what I am up against. If the inn really is haunted, I need to know. I have been followed by a dark figure, and I have seen you in the mirror. I nearly crashed the car, I could have died.'

His eyes narrowed against the light, and he looked tired. 'Yes, that was the count. You're right, the tunnels under the inn are haunted, so is the studio. That's why my uncle and the Count argued. Antoine said the Count went too far. What started as an intellectual interest became an obsession when the Count began to resort to evil occult practices. Antoine was shocked; he drew a firm line when it came to murder. He soon discovered that the Count's actions were becoming sick, ruthless and evil. So he had the Count and his men drowned.

'I am so sorry, Emma. Look, I do trust you enough to tell you what happened, to confide in you. To get in touch with these people, the ghosts that haunt the bay, I experimented too far. I was staying at the inn, as I felt I could reach them easily, and it wasn't long before I made contact with the Count, who wanted me dead too, and tried to kill you to punish me. My uncle was a womaniser and drunkard, but he was also a genius. I called up a spirit far more destructive than I could have ever imagined. After that, strange things happened, two of my friends who had been at the séance died in fatal accidents. I opened myself to a power that tried to use my soul and body for its own will, sucking my life force away—a sick and twisted mind, intent on my destruction, who tried to live through me. One night I woke up to see a horrible creature standing over me, its grotesque face grimacing, his slimy clawed hands touching my face. It was the evil Count from the pirate ship, the evil beast, his eyes sunk into his skull like a cadaver. As he moved towards me, I started to run, but my legs turned to lead. I fell, and he took over my will. I felt his pure evil, foul, devilish aura take possession of me, and send me to Hell. He took over my life, leaving me weak and drained. Empty, living in fear, destroyed, locked in a struggle against evil. I chanted some spells hoping to get rid of him, but he was too powerful, I couldn't destroy his black and twisted soul, and it was taking over mine.'

'What happened next?' asked Emma, almost fainting with shock. 'How did you get away?'

'I tried everything I could think of to get rid of him, but failed. My soul was like a wilderness, empty and bleak. He infested me like a parasite. I was possessed.'

Emma gasped in horror.

'Eventually, my spirit clinging to life, I found a psychic who was an exorcist. He performed a ritual, turning the power of light against him. Letitia's light shone for me, showing me the light, guiding me back and she saved my life. Evil spirits cannot exist in the power of the light, they can dwell only in the shadows of darkness. The Count left us, but he always tried to get back to me. Somehow, a part of his spirit remained in the paintings.' Anton looked tormented, his face ashen as though he had seen the Devil himself.

Emma looked away, too frightened to listen.

'I was suffering from a high fever and was plagued by a series of terrible dreams. I knew that they were not dreams at all, but were real, and that on a spiritual realm I was being possessed. Oh Emma, I think I am still being followed by them.' He sighed wearily. 'They are trying to take me back, take revenge for what my uncle did. They will destroy me and take you too. I'm so sorry to have dragged you into all of this, but I delved too far into the darkness and stirred things up.' He put his head in his hands, shaking his head in dismay. 'Please forgive me, I just don't know what to do.'

'Was Angel part of the coven too?'

'Yes, she was one of them. She found the allure of the dark, dangerous power too enticing to ignore and taught me how to use it by carrying out dark rituals on the pentagram. She was evil, Emma, I had to leave her. Her powers are a lot weaker now. I have broken away from them. My uncle hid a terrible secret and I'm afraid I might follow his path.'

'What? Fulfil the prophecy?' asked Emma.

'I hope and pray not,' he said his eyes turning black. 'It's too terrible a thought to contemplate.'

'If you believe it will happen, then it might happen, but if you dismiss it, it will lose its power,' she advised carefully. 'It only has power if you believe it. Then it may become a self-fulfilling prophecy and could drive you insane. That's how I see it. He told you that to undermine you. To make you suffer.'

Curses

Emma sat at the table, sipping tea, still reeling with shock. She knew nothing of the occult, except for once visiting a clairvoyant and she'd found it interesting. But it sounded a bit like a wild fantasy to her.

'I left the coven,' he continued, looking defiant. 'I refused to experiment any more with dark forces, they tried to stop me, making it clear they would destroy anyone who left them.'

'That's why you came here, to the attic?'

'Yes, for a while I was hidden from their prying eyes. I chose the inn for making contacts with dead spirits. But it was so haunted I had to leave,' he said, his face tightening. 'And I came here.'

Emma drew in her breath sharply, so there *had* been recent hauntings at the inn.

'Men were sometimes killed and left to die there, starving to death in the tunnels, their skeletal frames chained to the walls below the inn. The depraved Count slowly poisoned them, then cut up their bodies and used their remains in a black ritual—observing the bodies writhing in Hell in front of him, enjoying torturing and inflicting pain. Harnessing their spirits through fear. A mirror, which reflected some of the dark deeds, was left on the wall and still holds a strange power. Some say they can see our past and even the future through it. When you first arrived, I watched you through the mirror, longing for your touch. The person you saw in the mirror, the mysterious lover who seduced you at night, was me!'

Emma stared at him in disbelief; she sat down, stunned. She knew why Jeremy had been in such a rush to sell the inn and why it had stood empty for so long. Was it safe? She felt instinctively that it was, that the ghosts could not harm her. Anton's eyes shone with an unnerving force. Emma looked at him in dismay, not wanting to believe that horrible rituals had taken place in her precious home. She looked at the floor, downcast. Suddenly, everything fell into place and she realised with a heavy heart why Jeremy had pushed her into buying it. He had known about the haunting too. Everyone had known but her.

'The curse, could happen to me,' he said softly.

She sat taking it in, her head spinning at the incredulous story.

'What can we do? Surely there is something we can do?'

'Just pray that they don't come back.'

Emma sat feeling that nowhere was safe. She tried to phone her sister, but couldn't reach her. Mel would only insist that she travel back to London. She felt sick and scared, but had to pull herself together, she couldn't let it get the better of her. She would meet the challenge head on and with courage as she always did, nothing had ever scared her and she wasn't going to let it now.

She walked over to the window, filled with a new steely determination, realising she couldn't bear to part with the inn or with Anton. Whatever it took, she would stand by him. She would phone a priest and arranged for him to exorcise the inn. Surely they could overcome any obstacle together, if their love was strong enough? She sat down and devised a plan, wondering why Jeremy had failed to mention the ghost.

'You are the only person who has been able to live there,' Anton said, a hint of admiration creeping into his voice. 'Everyone else has left after a few months. It's because your soul is pure. You won't be attacked by other forces because you have never invoked any. You are quite safe.'

'I hope so. I want to stay there, whatever has happened. Or maybe just rent part of it out and keep the wine bar and live in one of the cottages in the bay.'

'I travelled to you at night to watch you sleeping, your hair cascading over the pillow. I fell in love with you instantly and painted the picture from my visits.'

'Oh,' she cried, putting her hand over her mouth, 'so it was you haunting me?'

'Yes, I'm afraid it was. I was trying to protect you from the Count. Oh Emma, please forgive me,' he begged. 'I didn't want to involve you in all this, but I had no choice.' He took him into her arms. 'I will protect you. You will always be safe,' he whispered, wrapping his fingers in her hair and pulling her towards him kissing her deeply. 'I am the dark stranger,' he confessed, his eyes sparkling. 'The other side is the dark side of me, my shadow.'

'You are my dark stranger,' she said. 'Oh I love you, Anton, whatever you have done.' His words spun webs of confusion around Emma, her head was spinning like a whirlwind. 'So I really did see them, in the window, in the mirror?'

'Yes, so it seems,' he admitted. 'They were my Great Uncle Antoine and his lover Letitia. And once I used my astral body to project me there, and I walked past your door. Listen,' he said softly, twirling a loose strand of her hair around his finger, 'we all have different sides to us, the dark, as well as the light. I didn't actually do anything wrong, I was just naïve. My only mistake was thinking the dark side could work for me and often it can, but this time my guide was evil. Here, look at the pictures in this book,' he said. 'Can you see the similarity? Don't you think my uncle looks a lot like me?'

'Yes,' Emma nodded, holding her breath, disturbed that his dead uncle had been haunting her. 'Yes that's him, the man I saw.'

Anton looked at her gravely. 'Well let's hope he has gone now.'

Emma sighed heavily, she was tired, and she'd had enough surprises for today.

'When I look at the paintings, they seem to move. I am sure the Count is in the paintings, Emma. He became trapped on earth, not dead, nor alive, stuck in the borderline between earth and the spirit world,' he said, his mouth tightening. 'For a while I managed to trick him. Oh Emma, will you help me get rid of them?'

'Yes, of course, but how?'

'I don't know. We must escape them.'

Emma stared at the picture of the man, and a strange feeling rose in her. 'I can feel his presence, but I don't believe they are omnipotent, he must have a weakness.'

'A bad energy from the darkness can only be neutralised and dissolved by a white witch,' he said. 'Perhaps if we find a witch to help us neutralise the evil…'

She stopped listening, and stared out of the window, watching the sylph-like waves rising and falling on the beach, like elegant horses with white flowing manes, galloping across the bay. Somehow, talking about the occult had made him seem even more dangerous, more attractive, even lethal and, to her dismay, she wanted him more than ever. Her lover from the deepest abyss of night, her weaver of dark dreams—he filled her with dark desire and invaded her nights, took her to paradise, but gave her glimpses of hell. Her reticent mood changed to one of excitement, his presence filled her with the creative fire, and dreams of lust. Sometimes, she lost all reason and became obsessed with him, intoxicated by his presence.

'Oh Anton!' Emma laughed, amazed, mystified and confused all at once. She looked him in the eye: 'I knew it was you.'

'Come over to me,' he grinned. He grabbed her playfully, and wound her arms round his neck. Celtic music played in the background, gently he swayed her body against his, slowly he twirled her around the room.

'Do you want to hear another ghost story?'

'Yes, tell me the one about the Count. Who was he?' asked Emma.

'He was a Hungarian aristocrat, with a murky past, who was given his land and title as a reward for hiding refugees during the Civil wars. Later, he became a pirate, drawn to the sea because of its wildness, and he developed a taste for the gold he could seize as a privateer. He was wildly eccentric, some think he suffered from a madness, and had sailed the seas to escape, sinking deeper and deeper into a nefarious lifestyle. He gained a reputation as the most evil man in the world, unscrupulous and black-hearted. Obsessed with the black arts. Some said that, according to romantic myth, he was the servant of the Devil. He began committing diabolical acts, such as hanging the bodies of his crew from the yardarm, for no reason. He was reputed to have been one of the most powerful white magicians to walk this Earth but became evil and greedy in the pursuit of power until that fatal day when he died in the shipwreck. He wanted to push reality to its limits, becoming obsessively greedy; there was no other place to go than to the darkness. He reached the most extreme levels of power and became a very accomplished magician, able to conjure up the most extreme ecstasy, along with the darkest Hell. It was a grave mistake.'

'Now you say, part of his soul still exists in the paintings?'

'Yes, in the darker ones, now do you understand?'

Emma nodded.

'Isn't it wrong to try and make someone fall in love with you, by using black magic?' Emma asked.

'Yes it is, but we happened quite naturally.'

'With a little help from the mirror?'

'Perhaps,' he answered shyly, his eyes glinting. 'But it would have occurred anyway.'

'I am so glad you did,' she whispered, holding him tight.

✝

Emma rushed home and arranged to see the priest, and a psychic the next day. Despite the past exorcism at the inn, she was afraid of what might still be lingering there.

The priest came along immediately and with the help of the psychic laid some divine objects on a table and chanted a few phrases in Latin. After a while he said it was safe and pronounced it clean and ghost free. The psychic went to the studio where she located a 'cold spot'.

'A terrible deed was committed here, but don't worry, the evil has gone, these spirits have only love in their hearts now.'

'There is nothing evil here,' the priest added, holding out his arms, 'no trapped energies, but there is a force that may have passed through here, a man of great evil. But he left a long time ago, and is not attached to this building,' the psychic said, and after chatting for a while, the priest took his holy water and spread it around. When he visited the studio he nodded gravely. 'There are a few friendly spirits here, who will not harm you. Once something terrible did happen here,' he said, blessing the building. 'But I think you will find it is safe now. The darkness has gone.'

Emma thanked them and suddenly the place seemed much lighter.

That night, she had another a terrible nightmare.

She was drowning under the sea, then someone pulled her out of the raging ocean. It was Annie! Then she was riding in a carriage, drawn by four black horses, with black-feathery plumes. The headman turned round, he had no face, his fingers were long slimy claws that gripped the reins painfully. He jumped inside the carriage, she lifted the hood; he had no face, just a dark worm-eaten skull. A dark stranger galloped over, took off his mask, it was Anton. Behind him was a man swathed in darkness, his evil eyes glinting dangerously. It was the Count.

'I'm so glad I have found you, my lady, at long last,' said the Count

laughing wickedly. 'I have waited so long for you, my dear, sweet Emma, I have watched you day after day, from the dark dingy tunnels under the inn. I have spun around you at night when Anton came to you, the one you yearn for. Are you afraid of me, Emma? Come to the other side with me. I shall show you how much more fun it is there.'

He opened the door of her carriage and beckoned her to come out. She stared stonily at him. He grabbed her arm, she fought back, biting him.

'You little minx, you cannot escape me this time.' He pulled his arm away, sharply, still laughing. 'I am long past feeling any pain, in fact I quite enjoy it. I shall show you the powers of the endless night, my dear delectable Emma. Come with me, I want to take your lovely soul for my own. It is so pure, so nice, not like my decayed old one. I have come to collect you. Come with me and see your wildest desires and darkest fantasies.'

Taking a black rose, he pierced her skin with its thorns, and let her blood mingle with his. He drank her blood. She looked away, repelled. The Count leered at her with cruel satisfaction. Emma blinked, she felt herself falling under his power.

'No, no, I cannot live in your world of darkness,' she cried. 'Let me go!'

'Ah, my dear lady you are already there,' sneered the Count, laughing mercilessly, 'in the darkest abyss, with the darkest souls. Come with us!'

'I will never come with you,' she protested.

'I will never let you go, you will both soon be under my power.'

They rode into the mist on a black stallion until they drew up alongside a dark pit. He led her down a shadowy tunnel, into the underworld.

'Welcome to my world of dark pleasures,' taunted the Count, his eyes lighting with malice, his evil lips grinning wide in a haggard face as he led her into his den of darkness.

'Not for the faint-hearted,' he said, grinning at her. Anton was tied to a bench, Emma tried to break free to run to him.

'Try this, for the most exquisite pleasure,' he said, handing her a silver goblet and fixing his eyes on her breasts.

She drank the rest of the liquid. Her head was swimming in total ecstasy, *aflame with sheer bliss, her body and soul covered in rays of golden light, basking in pools of golden pleasure.*

'See, I can give you heaven,' he leered, 'better than anything you can find in real life. The potency of the darkness!'

She tried to fight the Count's evil dream. Anton's shadow faded into the darkness.

She woke up feeling afraid. Surely the Count did not really exist?

Art dreams

Anton walked back to his studio and set up a new painting, to put it in the new exhibition. Emma would like it, and he loved to surprise her. He went back to his painting of Emma, with himself as a knight pursuing her. It was a lovely tranquil pastoral scene, with Anton wooing Emma in the long grass, smelling a bunch of purple flowers as he gently kissed her cheek. He stopped suddenly, needing a thinner brush and went out of the room. When he came back, he noticed that the painting had changed. Gone was the serenity, all hell had broken loose. He looked at it more closely, and clasped his hand over his eyes, as his blood ran cold. The full horror of what he saw took minutes to sink in. The pleasant pastoral scene, of freshly cut grass and meadow flowers, had changed to one of violence, the ground was soaked in blood. He was stabbing Emma with a long sacrificial knife; she lay on the ground, her face deathly white. The colour drained from his face as he clutched his chest, a sharp pain stabbed at him. The dark prophecy was coming true! The evil predictions had returned. His paintings were predicting the future, the death that his uncle had committed, he was going to do the same to his true love, he was going to kill Emma! He gripped his chest and fell onto the floor. He had to get away, destroy his work, he was afraid to paint again. Suddenly out of the corner of his eye, he noticed an evil presence moving through the room. Just then, a withered hand reached out of the darkness and gripped at his throat, and began choking him. His head spun: a strange mood filled him with a wild, crazy, poisonous lust for anger and malice. He was paralysed, his mind drenched in evil. The evil Count had taken control of him. He felt the dark force forge through his veins, he felt like a beast, a tyrant. He was possessed.

Retribution

Emma woke up from a terrible dream: a dark cloud had burst over her and Anton while they were walking on the beach, and they had become entangled in a slimy, black web of giant seaweed. She went downstairs and made some coffee, then walked over to the window and breathed in the fresh air: the sight of the sun shining brought the happiness flowing back into her again.

Emma stood in the doorway of the wine bar, pleased with the final effect. A cat suddenly leapt out in front of her, baring its teeth, then shot out of the window. She looked around the inn. It looked amazing, the art club was filled with ethereal paintings of goddesses and maidens, romantic pictures hung on the back walls and pretty tables nestled among long, trailing plants in the corners. 'Nice touch,' said Emma to herself as she viewed some of her own work hanging on the walls. Among the foliage, in the conservatory, stood Anton's paintings, displayed in the magical garden at the back. Outside the jasmine climbed a trellis and roses were planted in buckets around the patio. She picked up an arts magazine: her story 'Knights of the Sea' about the cove had just been published in a weekly. She placed a copy on the coffee table, thinking how well the room looked now, with squashy white sofas, and a long, thin elegant bar. Quite elegant, and finished to perfection. She loved having such a wonderful creative space to live and work in, with an inspiring view of an ever-changing landscape. At lunchtime, the bar filled with surfers, health food fanatics, tourists and students; some students came to enrol for Anton's art classes and others to use the internet. The romantic theme had worked out well. The light wood blended with the grey stone outside. The gentle autumn breeze blew sand across the garden. The summer had passed, the warm bright autumn shades started to filter through the air, throwing burnished lights across the rooms. She had filled the tunnels with cement and burned anything she had found there. That should clear the ghosts who were trapped there. The wine bar was warm and inviting again, with exactly the right rustic touches. Some rock music throbbed gently in the background. The party would soon be in full swing, and she couldn't wait for the party to start. Students were setting up a small exhibition of Anton's art class's work. She read Jeremy's card wishing her good luck for the future.

Andrea dropped by for a coffee, and Emma told her all about Anton's dilemma.

'Sounds a bit strange, I'd say get out of there, and don't look back. That family seems rather odd and prone to disaster.'

'That's not like you, Andrea, to advise me just to give up? You've always said my relationship with Anton would come out okay.'

'Well perhaps I've just seen sense, some challenges are just too dark, even for me.'

'But I do love him,' protested Emma. 'Shouldn't we try and tackle it together?'

'It's too dangerous: don't get involved with the occult. Dark forces are unpredictable and can easily destroy anyone who comes into contact with them. You don't have the experience to fight them. Ramone says Anton's a good guy, and a brilliant artist, but he is too wild, reckless, into dangerous things.'

'Is that why he seems so moody?'

'Yes, and I see another problem. I can only explain in psychological terms as it lies outside normal experience. He over-identifies with his "anima", which makes him oversensitive, moody and delusional, often receptive to the wrong ideas. Angel over-identified with her "animus", which is why she was so argumentative, and why they couldn't make it work. He has lost touch with reality, getting involved in all this occult nonsense. Basically, what I mean is, he has become so obsessed with the fantasies he uses for his art, that he believes in them and they have overtaken him.'

'Yes, I thought so too, but it is real,' said Emma solemnly. 'But I know I can trust Anton. His curiosity was fired by a purely academic interest; he doesn't actually follow ideas of evil. It's the connections he used to have that are the problem. Somehow, we have to find a way of laying the whole thing to rest and avoiding the people who he knew.'

'I don't know if it's that simple. Maybe the psychic you met on the beach could help you?' suggested Andrea helpfully.

'Yes, sounds a good idea. I've got her card, I'll contact her as soon as I can.'

Emma fiddled nervously with the exhibition cards. Andrea sat back looking radiant and exuberant. Her hair spread like a fan around her shoulders, lush and shiny; her eyes shone brightly. Local artists filed in and began putting up their work. Emma placed a few of her own beside Anton's display. Their styles were different: apart from his gift of bringing a painting to life, his magical, dark and ethereal pictures seemed to capture a spiritual quality; yet hers, in soft pastel colours, wispy and light, full of romantic imagery, complemented Anton's well.

'What time does your exhibition start?' asked Andrea. 'I'll go home and get changed.'

'Eight, you must come to our small party,' said Emma.

She flicked some dust off the shelf, adding some final touches, a few aromatic candles, before the party. A thought came to her: maybe all the problems could be erased by an occultist, if much of it had happened on the metaphysical plane—if one had travelled into the future, perhaps one could erase the past? Still reeling from Anton's confession, she saw now how it all made sense; his dark secret, first too incredulous to believe, had led him to his misfortune and marked his fate. The strange dark deeds he had encountered had changed his destiny, but she loved him enough to weather the storm. She was caught up in a world of intrigue, a maze where there was no clear exit. But she did not give up that easily. She shuffled the invitations thoughtfully, then arranged the paintings, thinking of the best way to display them. She found the one of Angel, wearing nothing but a sneering smile and put it at the back, not wanting to remind Anton of her feline charms. She put instead, in the empty space, one of her own, *The Sea Goddess* in centre display; her own ones would show the full extent to which Anton had developed her talent, and he would be pleased to see how far she had progressed.

Later, as some more guests were arriving, Emma wandered over to Anton. He stood in a corner staring moodily into his drink. She felt a twinge of concern as he looked up at her with a dark scowl on his face. Something about the way he was worried her. She kissed him. There were some important people there tonight and she wanted him to meet them.

'Cheer up,' she said. 'It's your night—what's wrong?'

Anton stared glassy-eyed at Emma; there was something strange about him. She felt frightened of his sudden change of mood.

'No! Nothing's wrong. Please don't panic, Emma.' He backed away from her, as though she had burned him. He looked confused, he ran his hands through his hair edgily. His expression changed to one of dark moody gloom.

'I need some air,' he said, swinging out of the room.

'I'll come with you.'

'No, I don't want to speak to anyone,' he snapped, an unfriendly chill in his voice.

'These have to go on display,' she said, taking some paintings from him.

'Don't touch those!' he snapped. 'I've spent ages putting them in the right order!' He pushed her back, wrenching them free from her grasp. Abruptly he threw them into the corner.

'What's the matter?' asked Emma trying to stop him. 'The Devil seems to have got into you.'

'Perhaps it has. Please go back to your guests,' he said brutally, his eyes red and glazed. He pushed past some people, a cruel arrogance spreading across his face. His voice was cold, rough, hardened. 'Look, there are things you just cannot understand,' he warned. 'Let me go, Emma, I need to be alone. Let me have some space to think. Look, I'm sorry, Emma. I have to get away, it's best for both of us.'

She reeled back in shock, fighting the desire to slap him. She jumped in front of him, blocking his exit. Rudely, he pushed past her and she fell backwards.

'You bastard!' she spat angrily, her eyes widening in disbelief. He stared at her coldly, his face like granite, his eyes glinting like daggers.

'Go back inside, Emma,' he called out, 'to your bourgeois little cocktail party, for your sycophantic artists and dumb surfers. Right now I have more important things to attend to!'

She boiled with anger. He stared back at her with wild, burning eyes, then swirled out of the grounds, his long cloak billowing out behind him.

'Shit! Don't ever come back!' cried Emma, shocked. What had got into him? She ran after him, still shaking. He had gone. Her anxiety deepened as she saw Angel disappearing down the drive. Her heart sank, and everything swam around her as her eyes blurred, her happiness evaporated, her soul crushed. So that was it! He was back with Angel, she might have known that she was involved. Summoning up all her dignity, she returned to her guests, her jubilant mood subsiding as she handed round the wine. She fixed on a smile. Inside her heart was aching and she felt a searing pain in her head. Their faces were swimming in a fog. She ran to the window to see Anton's dark silhouette disappearing up the gravel path. Deflated, she turned back; she had never seen him behave like that before. She sat down, feeling the joy of the evening's success subside, the reality of what had just happened slowly sinking in. Things had just spiralled out of control; it had turned into a nightmare and she didn't know how to stop it. What could she do now? She served some more wine to his guests, putting on a cheerful façade, while wanting to strangle him. She saw out of the corner of her eye that Anton had left his wallet behind, and tried to phone him. There was no reply. She felt a renewed wave of anger sweep over her. How could he do this to her? As she showed the last of the guests out, she breathed a sigh of relief. No one had even noticed he had gone: in every other respect, the evening had been an unprecedented success.

Dark days

She sat for days not seeing anyone, just watching the sea, nursing her wounds. How could he let her down so badly? She felt the familiar pain of betrayal. They had been soul mates, and she had trusted him; this time she had hoped it would work out. She began to feel murderously angry. What's more, he had behaved appallingly at his own exhibition, and walked out on everyone. She looked at the pictures, the one of Angel as a vamp, and kicked it, splitting the canvas in half. Was it something she had said, or was he just losing interest in her? Where was Angel and what part did she play in all of this? Emma was sure she had gone back to London too. Maybe she was the reason that Anton had grown moodier over the last few weeks, withdrawn, reticent whenever she tried to talk to him; perhaps he had decided to go back to her. At first she put his erratic behaviour down to his creative streak, how he hated rules and deadlines, they killed his spark and made his life unbearable, made him feel trapped, then she realised that a deeper issue was troubling him. Her mind flipped back to the night before the exhibition, when he had thrown his paintbrushes down angrily, as they fought and disagreed over which paintings to exhibit.

He had insisted the dark ones were left out, she put them back in, wanting them for the 'dark and light' stand—thinking they represented some of his best work and reflected the more mysterious side of life. He argued that they were awful and too dark, his face had tightened, their easy rapport had gone.

Distraught, she phoned again. There was no reply, it was late, and she put the receiver down, feeling sad and deflated.

Her sadness turning to fury, she took the last painting he had done of her and threw it across the floor; she smiled as it landed among the rubbish. He had run out on her, when she had needed him most, a mortal sin. She knew what to expect from men—however well things started off, sooner or later things went wrong as their dark side emerged. She looked at the twisted branches of a tree outside; it looked like an evil spirit, its long gnarled branches extended like limbs reaching out to catch passers-by. She felt a blackness cover her, throwing her into a despondent mood. She stepped outside into a shallow pool of light, but a bat flew close, almost tangling in her hair. She let out a shriek. She was drowning in a malignant darkness, strange ghostly silhouettes slithered across the beach. For the first time in her life, she felt truly scared. That night she was tormented by nightmares. She woke up, shaking.

Silvery daylight streamed in as she opened her eyes against the watery opaque sun. Lethargically, she went over to the window. Swells of water raged in the distance, taking her away from the blissful indolence still running through her veins. Suddenly she was overwhelmed with torturous images of Anton making love to Angel, and the events of the last few days hit her like a hurricane, throwing her emotions into turmoil. Why had he left her? Was he seeing Angel? She felt pain like a knife tearing at her heart. Is that why he had been acting so strangely? Had he rejected her last night, because he was still in love with Angel? Why was he being so paranoid? She felt jumpy and irritable, refusing to see anyone. Her mind crashed and gave into her fears. She was nearly sick at the thought of them writhing in lust together. Then her mood changed to one of icy fear, paralysing her soul, plunging her into a nightmare. The safe feeling of being cocooned that he'd given her had been replaced by cold desolation and frightening emptiness. She sat down and scribbled some words, she sang the words softly to herself—her sanity was hanging on by a thread, she was thrown to the cold bitter wind. Once again, her dreams had been dashed to dust. When would she ever learn?

Sea of Dreams—Fragile Winds

Sailing into your arms,
Taking it all in my stride,
Holding on fast to my dreams,
Hoping they won't subside.

Flying high on the waves of fragile winds,
Soaring into the skies
A ship at sea,
Living close to the edge,
It comes as no surprise.

Drowning in the swirl
Of your empty sea of dreams.
Trying to find the shore
but there is nothing left,
An empty cold horizon,
I should have known before
Away from this whirl of confusion
Where nothing is as it seems.
Flying high on the winds of fragile dreams…

Flying high on the waves of fragile winds,
Soaring into the sky,
A ship at sea,
Living close to the edge,
You told me only lies

Emma

She put the poem in an envelope, sealed it, then sent a copy to Anton, hoping he might read it one day that is, if he was still around. She suspected that he might be miles away by now. Maybe he'd just had to get away to escape the Count. The thought of him with Angel made a bitterness rise in her throat and almost choke her. She nearly buckled under the heavy searing pain. She wiped the tears away and looked out across the bay, a dark mist swirling over the rocks, a foghorn sounding loudly. It was eerie. She plunged into an unsettling reality from which there was no escape. Unfolding before her was her own personal Hell, the repetition of an irresolvable nightmare. This was a road she had travelled before and one she didn't want to go down again. Slithers of grief tore through her like broken glass. She went to the riding school and hired a black stallion and rode along the beach. She tried to escape her demons by galloping along the waves, trying to purge the pain from her soul. Riding always helped her lose her anger. The wind whipped through her hair as she cantered faster and faster, the sea spray lashed against her skin. She was drenched, riding faster, trying to escape. The tension lifted from her, she felt exhausted. She stopped and caught her breath—in the distance she spotted a figure, it looked like Anton! She rode closer to take a look, yet as she drew nearer it vanished into thin air. The horse reared up in the air and threw her onto the sand. What was happening? She screamed out in frustration. Shivering, angry and disturbed, she wondered what stupid games he was playing, trapped in his own purgatory, acting as if she no longer existed. She felt almost dead inside.

Who can shelter me when I feel so cold inside she thought, wishing he was there with her? She took the ring he had given her and hurled it into the sea. She had planned to spend her life with Anton, now her dreams were broken, her future unsure, everything was confused and ground to dust. The dark brooding intensity of her feelings lifted as she watched the blazing orange sun rise behind the hills. Maybe there was some small glimpse of hope, somewhere.

She jumped into her car and drove at top speed to Anton's Porthcurno studio, swerving recklessly through the narrow lanes. A cold hand gripped her heart. She didn't care about anything any more. Would she see Anton again? Could she forgive him? How could he do that to her? The thought of never seeing him again filled her with a cold empty desolation. How could he erase all the love they had created together with a few careless words? She felt as though she was being sucked into a quicksand, suffocating, losing control. Her anger subsided and she was flooded with sadness. She clutched at the thought that he might have some sort of explanation, that is, if she ever found him. Tears poured down her face. She wiped her face with a tissue. She looked up in the mirror and saw Anton's eyes staring back at her. She swerved and nearly hit a car. What the hell was he doing? She slammed on the brakes, got out of the car and stood by the cliff watching the sea, its white foam drifting onto the beach.

She collapsed on the sand. Tears racked her body, and she felt like giving up. Was there any real purpose to anything? It felt like it was the end. Where was he? Why had he done this to her, spoken to her like that? Surely she had not misjudged him? What had gone so wrong? She walked past the verdant grass borders leading to the loft. Just then, she saw Jeremy leaning against his car—there was no mistaking his bleached hair and healthy physique; he looked paler now, not so much the glamorous surfer. More like a city executive in a suit. He waved, his eyes focusing on her. Her heart sank, if only it had been Anton standing there.

'Oh hi,' she said.

'Congratulations,' came the reply, as he shifted nervously. 'The inn's become quite a success, I see. The locals all say it's the place to go.'

'Yes, it has taken off rather well,' she muttered, slightly distracted. 'Have you seen Anton?'

'The artist?' asked Jeremy, his eyes scanning her in admiration. 'I heard he's returned to London, I thought you two were friends?'

'We were, a bit more than friends.'

Jeremy looked down at the ground. 'Oh I see. You look great, and a tan really suits you. Look, Emma,' he said, taking her hands in his, 'I have really missed you, I have to talk to you, nothing else has been on my mind since I left.'

'I'm in love with Anton,' Emma said, struggling with her words. 'You left to be with your family. Or don't you remember? I was just your holiday fling.'

'It wasn't like that' he said sheepishly, going pale. 'Yes, we had fun together, but it was a lot more. I am in love with you.'

Emma snorted with disbelief. 'I don't think it's love, just brotherly concern.'

'Give me time, please let me explain. I thought that once I was settled I would come back and get you.'

'Before you waste your time, Jeremy, let me make this clear, I am not in love with you and I can never leave my home. In fact I am in love with someone else.'

Jeremy looked down, his face taut with disbelief, then he became animated and talked about his new job, his life in London. Emma hardly heard the rest of the conversation. Had she misjudged Anton? Surely their love had not been so fragile, so easily destroyed? What other explanation was there? Why else would he leave her like this? Without even saying goodbye? Where was he now?

She still burned with anger that he dared to do that to her. *Was he with Angel?* It must be something to do with her. Amiably, she took Jeremy's arm.

'What's the matter, Emma?' enquired Jeremy, pushing her hair from her face. 'Why are you crying?'

'I'm not, and nothing's the matter,' she insisted, biting her tongue, annoyed that he had turned up at a time when she wasn't feeling sociable. She wished he'd go away; then she relaxed, perhaps a friend was what she needed right now.

'Let's go for a drink,' he offered. 'It'll cheer you up, it does get lonely around here after the summer,' he admitted.

'Yes I'd like that,' she said, thinking Jeremy's company was better than none; for a moment she thought of his strong arms wrapped around her and felt a warm glow, but that was the past. He had let her down and she had moved on.

'I'm sorry I left you, Emma, like that,' Jeremy said, interrupting her thoughts. 'I wanted to come back, but I had to see my son.'

'Please, Jeremy, don't bother to explain. You lied to me. That's all I know. You made a quick sale so that you could rush back to London to be with your son. You knew there was something strange going on at the inn. Why couldn't you have just been honest with me, and told me the truth?' she said, accusingly.

He reddened, embarrassed.

'I'm sorry if it appears I didn't tell you everything. But I didn't really believe in all that rubbish myself. I don't believe in ghosts, or the supernatural and I didn't lie about my feelings for you,' he admitted, 'I really was falling in love with you. It wasn't just a fling.'

'Then why did you leave so suddenly?' she asked.

'My son needed me. I came here to get over a relationship, the same way that you did, to escape the problems, and I suppose for a while I forgot about everything else. When James became ill I realised I had responsibilities. Well, what else could I do? I thought you would understand. We could try again.'

Emma softened for a moment then looked at him with resignation.

'No, Jeremy, I can't go back, I want Anton,' she confessed. 'We can't recapture the past. The magic has gone, there is no way to get it back.'

'Okay, that's sad, but let's just be friends for now. How can you trust someone like Anton, that irresponsible dilettante? He spends most of his time in the college bar chatting up his pretty students.'

'Well, it's no longer my affair. I can't trust you either it seems,' she said, dryly. 'At least he is free, whatever his lifestyle. I don't want to come between a family.'

'That's well and truly over,' he insisted.

'Too little, too late!'

'Let's just eat, Emma, if you can stop the accusations. I know I was in the wrong.'

Throughout the meal she fidgeted restlessly, unable to concentrate on what he was saying. Jeremy kissed her fondly goodbye as he got ready to leave, knowing she was lost to him.

'I have a confession to make,' he stumbled. 'I did know why the previous owners had left in such a hurry. It was haunted, it had a strange history of people practising the occult there, I knew the people had left because they thought it was haunted. Once word got around, nobody here wanted to buy it. They're too superstitious here. Someone from London was the ideal purchaser, someone who knew nothing of its past and didn't have any worries about the place. So I thought you were ideal, I knew how much you loved it and how much of a gypsy you had in your soul. I thought if anyone could make a go of it, it was you. You have spirit. I was sure that once a person lived there, it would be okay. I am sorry, I should have warned you. But you seemed so eager and why should I spoil your dream? Please don't become too involved with Anton. He won't make you happy.'

'Well I don't care, and it is none of your business!' She paused. 'I discovered he has a dark secret,' she said, quietly. 'I wish I knew how to help him.'

Jeremy looked at her surprised.

'You mean you know?'

'Well, yes, I do, but I wonder if there is anything else.'

'While I was in London I did some research. I discovered that his uncle was considered one of the best artists of that century, a true genius and writer philosopher, an artist commissioned by the royal family. He knew the Count, with whom he shared many intellectual discussions, but they became enemies. His darker side became obsessed with the occult, and he was convinced it gave him power. Anyway, eventually no one knows if it sent him mad, or if he was mad already but it tipped him over the edge—he started imagining things. He was diagnosed as a manic-depressive; one stormy night he killed the woman artist he lived with during a rage. He accused her of being unfaithful, but she hadn't been at all. She was a beautiful fragile creature without a dishonest bone in her body. During the argument, she fell and banged her head on the window. The coroner said it was an accident, but the uncle could not forgive himself and dug up her grave, he would not let her rest, and kept trying to get her back. He held so many séances there it was said to be teeming with ghosts as he tried desperately to bring her back to him. He killed himself weeks later. While Anton was dabbling with the occult, he made contact with his uncle, who was by now happily reunited with his lover. He asked his uncle to make him psychic, able to see into the future. His wish was granted, and it was predicted during a séance that, one day, Anton, would take the life of his true love, and the cycle would be repeated. That he, Anton, would kill his true love and only be reunited in death.'

Emma looked at him, stunned, so he had known all along the terrible secret that Anton was hiding. 'Yes, I know all about it, Anton told me,' she confessed, 'but I didn't realise that you knew too.'

'Oh I know all about it. Wasn't it ghastly?' he shuddered.

'Do you think it is all true?'

'Anton seems to think it is, he is scared that he might do the same as his uncle, he has been obsessed by the idea, and was afraid to get truly involved. That's why he has left suddenly, he fears he may hurt you.'

'It explains a lot,' she admitted.

'So why do you still want to see him? He's in too deep.'

'I know what I am doing,' said Emma, defiantly. Her eyes widened in annoyance. 'I don't need you to tell me how to live. I don't care. I still love Anton. I don't believe in this stupid curse for one moment and I don't care if it is true.'

'Well, I think you are making a mistake. You should leave him alone, or you'll drag yourself down into his nightmare.'

She went over the last few days she had spent with Anton—had she missed a vital clue? Or had it turned out just to be a doomed tragic romance. Was that all? His dark edge had taken him over, the same as with many creative intellectuals or artists. But he had seemed very normal in every other respect. There was something ennobling about a tragic romance, but she didn't exactly need one. Her heart sank. Jeremy had betrayed her too. There was no one she could really trust apart from her sister, her friends and Andrea. Men always let her down. How was she to know what went on in the deep caverns of Anton's dark mind? What was he doing now? She wished Jeremy would go. She couldn't think straight any more.

'There is a mystery surrounding the Black Dove. And I know it is haunted now,' Emma said. 'Antoine and Letitia died there; Annie died below on the beach, the Count put a curse on the cove, and Anton's family. I think the whole thing has been blown out of perspective by the locals though. Anyway, I brought in a psychic to clear it, and the energy has gone now.'

Jeremy stifled a laugh: 'Surely you don't believe in ghosts, do you, Emma? I thought you had more common sense. It's so ludicrous an idea. Who believes in ghosts these days?'

Emma looked down, her eyes filled with tears. Suddenly everything seemed unreal.

'Well I do,' she said. 'I have seen one, several in fact.'

'Oh come on, Emma,' he laughed in disbelief. 'I suppose when someone gets very upset, it's easy to believe anything. When reason and the dictates of common sense give way to flighty ideas mixed with love, you can become crazy—especially when you meet someone as crazy as Anton, who encourages you to have wild ideas. It's easy to share in his delusion. They say that he is an artistic genius, but slightly manic too, as many artists are; it's necessary for the creative fire. But you know you cannot rely on him, he has just upset you with his bizarre problems.'

'I think you are being narrow minded,' she argued, finding Jeremy's down-to-earth attitude irritating. There was no magic like there was with Anton.

'Are you all right now?'

'I'm fine,' she said.

'I don't think so, Emma,' he said softly, kissing her gently on the cheek. 'Let me assure you,' he insisted, 'I didn't betray you, I just don't believe in ghosts and all that crap, that is why I was happy to sell you the property. Anton was into séances, tried to contact the spirit world and all that rubbish—for his art he says—but I think the man is as mad as a hatter, and it's genetic. Keep away from him, Emma. You need someone you can depend on, not someone who is ruled by creative ideas and his muse. He is selfish, obsessed with art, and himself, and he doesn't live in the real world,' he said, gently. 'You need someone who is stable and secure.'

'But you were not exactly a stable partner,' accused Emma.

'No, I admit that. But I do know the difference between fantasy and reality, which is more than I can say about some people around here!'

'What shall I do?'

'You are involved in things you don't understand. Come back with me.'

'No, that's out of the question. I love it here and I just want to be friends with you.'

'If you insist. Take care—phone me if you need me, and don't let your dreams slip away.'

'I am dancing with fire,' she mused, her heart twisting in loneliness, 'just to get burnt in his flame. Do we always get burned if we get too close to happiness? Have it all snatched away?'

'No, it doesn't have to be like that. If you ever change your mind, come with me. I've just bought a house in Surrey,' he said, handing her his number, his voice fading into the wind.

Emma walked away deep in thought. The rumours about Anton were true: he could have called something up, or it could all be a strange coincidence, a myth blown out of proportion. Her thoughts seemed a lot clearer now. Everyone had become a little hysterical over the story of the pirate ship that had sunk in the cove and gave it more attention than it deserved. That also explained why Anton had seemed so reticent. She had been looking for a mystery and she had found one. She loved excitement and secretly enjoyed the drama. She walked faster; Jeremy had been right, of course real ghosts didn't exist! It had all been her stupid imagination. Castles in the clouds, castles made of sand. She had let her thoughts run out of control and her dreams get the better of her. She had come crashing down to earth with a thud. Anton had been equally as stupid, pursuing dark things, but he was an adult, and it was up to him. She had idealised Anton, thinking his genius streak made him special, but he had proved as unreliable as the rest. She always took flight into fantasy and ignored reality, preferring her dreams to the real world. She had always had misgivings about Anton, but life would be pretty dull without him. She had to follow her intuition more closely, it was easy to get carried away.

She tried to phone Andrea, but there was no answer. Emma went back to the inn and tried to phone Anton, but there was no reply. Somehow, she must get his paintings back to him, at least say goodbye. She would tell him she didn't care about the past, his dark secrets. Perhaps she'd catch him at the studio; maybe he just wasn't answering the phone. Bewildered, she ran across the beach looking for him. Would he leave without saying goodbye to her? Surely their love was deeper than that. What was he doing? Where was he now? Her heart ached; she felt so lost and lonely without him.

The Final Dark Conflict

Anton hurried back to the studio to collect some of his paintings. As he pushed open the door, he sensed that something was wrong; it felt so odd, strange. He looked around and saw his brushes and paintings scattered in pieces around the room, broken all over the floor. He surveyed the damage, his face tightening with anger. Someone had wrecked his studio. It had been destroyed, completely ruined. He picked up a canvas and, dismayed, threw it back on the floor. How could anyone do this to him? He shuddered, then boiled over with anger. Paintings were strewn and broken all over the floor. His antiques were gone, the white carpet and furniture smeared with oil and paint. How could they do this to him?

'Angel!' he swore under his breath, trying to blot out the loud buzzing sound in his head.

'That bitch, bloody Angel!' He sat down, trying to make sense of it all, take it all in. He felt guilty at being so abrupt with Emma, now this had happened. He was losing control, too many things were going wrong. How could he have spoken to her like that? But he knew in his heart, his happiness sinking like lead, that he had to leave here, and Emma. If he stayed, he would only drag her deeper into these things and she didn't deserve that. Worse still, the terrible curse could come true—what had happened to his uncle might happen to him. The prophecy might come true; he had seen it in the painting. He couldn't risk that. He picked up the phone and dialled slowly, ready to apologise, then lost his nerve and replaced it again; it would sound better seeing her in person. He wanted to tell her he loved her so much, but that he had no choice, he had to go, it was best for both of them. He was tainted, she could never find happiness with him. His mind was in a turmoil. What was happening to him? He was manic, out of control like his uncle. Would he lose control completely and commit a terrible act like his uncle had? What did they want from him? He turned round, aware of something evil lurking in the room.

They were back and were trying to destroy him. He strained to listen in the silence, he could hear a strange moaning. It was them! They were after him, hell-bent on revenge. He felt a wave of anger sweep through him, burning with rage that some unthinkable horror was still lurking in his house. His mind churned like a furnace, he was going insane. He had to get out of there. He would kill them if they touched Emma. He didn't trust himself any more.

He collected up the broken bits of paintings, shaking his head in disbelief, reeling with the shock; angry, he kicked the burnt pieces over the ground. How could they destroy his beautiful paintings?

How could anyone do this? He felt sick as he uncovered each one, burnt to ash. What evil person had done this to him? Vandalised some of his most precious life's work? Luckily, all his latest paintings were still intact. A horrible sound filled the air, and as he turned round to see what it was, he was suddenly flung against the wall. A dark force, a noxious black energy hovered in the room. Then, there was a deathly silence—the living dead were here. The room filled with dark shadows, dancing across the wall; figures of death marched past him, their hollow eyes blazing with terror. He looked up at the window and saw the reflections of death, skeletal forms, on the pane. He prised his way around the wall, and stood face to face with the evil force, confronting his deepest fears. They had found him. Like a boat without a rudder, he was whirling through a dark space, being dragged into a vortex of terror.

A mass of black slime slid over the canvas in front of him. The force in the paintings had come alive, and the paintings were moving! His mind spun in fear. He glared at them angrily; the evil was still in the paintings and they were trying to control him! He felt sapped by a malignant poison, as it spread its spores over the room. He had to get away. Slowly, he climbed the stairs. He would hide until it was safe to leave, he had no other choice, and he didn't want to involve Emma in any danger. He had to go, *for her sake*. He closed the door behind him and threw his clothes into a suitcase, his heart beating loudly, his body pumping with adrenaline. There was so little time left; he had to tell her how much he cared for her before he left, that they were soul mates, but he couldn't place her in any more danger. He had to go before it was too late, before there was another tragedy.

Suddenly, the room filled with a dark smoke; he choked, suffocating. He looked up slowly afraid to see. Damien, the evil Count stood in the centre of the room, his devilish smouldering presence coiled like a poisonous snake ready to erupt into a malignant destructive force. He had come to destroy him. Then the image vanished. Was he seeing things? No, he was there, hiding, he sensed it with every fearful bone in his body. He had got rid of all the dark paintings, thrown them away; now they had reappeared in the room. Following him, they had found him. He chanted some spells to rid the room of their evil influence. But nothing worked. He fell back, exhausted, were they haunting him again?

He would have to destroy all the paintings, his lifetime's work, once and for all, piece by piece, until they no longer had any power over him. Anton stood facing the mocking energy in the paintings, the *Angel of Death*. The room froze. He felt cold, drained of life, death and decay seeping into his soul. Then, suddenly, the painting came to life, colours ran and blistered over the canvas, the dark angel flew from the painting spreading its wings and flapping across the room. Black smoke drifted across the ceiling through the darkened shadows. Anton could just about make out a human shape in the rancid smoke. It was the Count!

Anton held his breath, this was real, not an illusion.

The Count's empty eyes shifted restlessly over him, he smirked cruelly. 'Hello my friend,' he said. 'We meet again at last. It is so good to see you.' An evil leer spread over his face, his eyes scanned the room. 'I haven't had the pleasure of your company for such a long time.'

The room darkened into blackness, a few flames shot to the ceiling. Anton touched his face, it was hot, he felt like he was burning in Hell. 'Go away, leave me alone,' he begged.

'You invited me here, it was you who summoned me, remember? You wished to meet a practitioner of darkness, and I obliged. You wanted the power of darkness, and I, in my endless generosity, gave it to you.' He laughed darkly, his gaunt cheekbones tightening as he stoked the flickering flames in the fire. He smirked wickedly. 'Now I have returned to gain the power of life from you as payment for the vision I endowed upon you, out of revenge for your uncle's treachery. I want the dear Emma.'

'Never, never! I will destroy you first. You must take me instead, I will die rather than let you have her,' said Anton. 'I will kill you if you try to go anywhere near her.'

'She is in no danger, only from you,' laughed the Count. 'The terrible prophecy, remember? It may come true soon.'

Anton's face dropped and he looked anxious. 'No, that's just a lie,' he said, shaking his head.

Angel sauntered over to them. She smiled at Anton, gently touching his shoulder.

He pushed her away roughly. 'Leave me alone, you stupid bitch,' he screeched at her. 'Get out of here or I will make you leave!'

'Oh darling, don't be so angry, come back to our little circle, it will be just like old times,' she whispered darkly. 'The dear, sweet Emma will forget you easily. No one will actually miss her. I used to make you feel so happy, the things that I did for you. We can try again. You haven't forgotten our little secret, have you?' She smiled seductively at him. 'Of course not! Give the Count our dear Emma, and we can be happy again.'

'It is over between us and has been for a long time,' he said, pushing her hand away, moving back. 'I am in love with Emma. I will never leave her, and I would never come back to you; it didn't work then, it couldn't now!'

'Oh dear, that's so sickeningly loyal. How could you bear to lose the precious sweet Emma?' she mocked, wrapping her body around his. 'Does she do things to you like I do? Does she know what dark tastes you have? The games you *love* to play?' She pushed his hand onto her breasts.

He pushed her sharply away. 'Get lost, she knows everything. Now leave me alone, I don't want you or any of your weird friends near me, get out of my life for good,' shouted Anton, 'you are manipulative, wicked!'

'Decadent perhaps?' interrupted the Count. 'Beyond good or evil, I am the living dead,' he said, in harsh, bitter tones. 'How could you be so inhospitable to such dear old friends? You were so glad of our company once and I thought we shared similar dark tastes,' he sneered. 'After all, the pursuit of darkness is your aim as it is ours.'

'Not any more,' said Anton, emphatically, 'that was only a stupid phase I went through for my art. I have changed now that I have found someone I really love.'

'Then I pity her,' sneered the Count.

'The prophecy is a lie. You told me that, so that you could control me, not my uncle.'

'Oh dear, how quick of you, I see you have lost none of your powers of perception. My beautiful Emma,' he said, pursing his lips together seductively, 'we have met only once, but I would like to see her again.'

'Leave her alone,' cried Anton, 'get out of here, out of my house and my life. If you ever go near her I shall destroy you. Now take your dark, rotten, stinking old corpse away and do not come near me again.'

'Tut-tut, how uncharitable you are, after all I have done for you. Such an unworthy friend,' sneered the Count, looking over his shoulder. 'I gave you the darkness, I will unleash the forces of darkness on you, if you are no longer of any use to us,' he said, his cruel eyes burning, his hand shaking with fury. 'I was your mentor. Perhaps I shall use Emma's body to return to life? Or shall I take yours? Hmmm, I think I would still prefer to enjoy the pleasures of the flesh as a man.' He grinned, wickedly.

'Why have you come back? I am not interested in you or your dark powers any more.'

'Because I have come to settle the conflict, to tell what really happened to my men, to let the whole world know how your evil great uncle killed and trapped us, fifty of my men and myself, wrecked at sea. It was a historical event, and we have revealed all to a historian, so that it is written, on display, your uncle's betrayal, for all to see. I have come here to right a wrong and let my spirit return.'

Anton grew weaker and almost fainted. He chanted a phrase for psychic defence, to protect himself. He looked away from the Count's black withered face, avoiding those blazing eyes burning deep into him. He stepped back and covered his face; he could not breathe, a heavy weight pressed on his chest, suffocating him. The Count's malevolent energy was drowning him in venom. He fell to the floor, taken over.

Suddenly, the room filled with a gentle voice, and a white light. The Count screeched, and fell, slithering across the floor, stunned. His face was contorting in pain, turning old and ashen, his power dissolving. Angel shifted restlessly in the corner. Her long, black cloak blew around her, a gust of wind blowing her web-like dress. She started to age, lose her good looks, her face withered. Anton pushed her toward the door.

'Get out, take your warped soul out of my life and take that old warlock with you! Go to Hell if you're not there already, and don't come back!'

Roughly he shoved Angel outside. She scowled at him, her face beginning to crack, her beautiful long hair suddenly streaking with grey, her face becoming wrinkled, old and withered. The dark malice in her shone through, showing her true nature. She lifted a clawed hand to his face. 'Anton, don't do this to me,' she begged.

He pushed her away.

'You will not be forgiven for this,' warned the Count, his shadowy figure weakening, watching them from the window. His red eyes wide with anger, he screeched at Anton, 'Hell and damnation to you. We will wreak revenge on those who have betrayed us,' he threatened, pointing a bony hand at him.

'Over my dead body,' argued Anton, at boiling point.

'As you wish, you may have won this time, but I assure you, I shall be back and I will make sure you get what you deserve, Anton, I unleash the forces of Hell on you!'

'You have betrayed us,' screamed Angel, her eyes blazing with fury. Anton watched as they both began to disintegrate into swirling smoke.

There was one last conflict: the dark angel of death from the abyss, the shadow and servant of the Count.

The angel of death flew across the ceiling flapping its wings. It lunged at him, pulling out locks of his hair, its cold, deadly, black claws ripping into his skull. It turned and flew back into the painting.

'Leave me alone, forever!' Anton cried out in desperation, and kicked at it. A black slimy mass fell from the picture and slid across the floor. Anton coughed, the smell was rancid. The room was silent, trails of smoke drifting out over the bay.

'Now I'll destroy every trace of you!'

Anton took an axe, and, using all his strength, swung it against the paintings. It swung back, rebounding and cut deep into his arm. 'Shit!' he swore, trying again. This time, he put his weight behind the blow, shattering them into a thousand pieces.

'Thank God,' he cried, kicking over the carnage. He threw a can of petrol over them, then lit a match.

'I will destroy you once and for all, you fiends!' he cried, lighting the pile. Orange flames shot out, the room filled with a heavy black smoke.

Anton ran to the window, choking for air. It was locked!

A white light flashed. A woman with white hair stood over him. Anton felt her cool hand touch his, healing him. She led him to a room bathed in a white light. The Count faded and withered away in the darkness, melting into a pile of ashes on the ground.

'This has never happened,' promised the woman, 'the past has been erased, the part of it where you made contact with the Count has gone. They are back where they belong, in the dark limbo, dead for a long time. They will not get back again. But you must fight!'

A flash of white-blue light filled the room, then faded away. Anton opened his eyes. There was no sign of the Count or Angel. There was still an entity in the room, in the painting. The evil had still not left, some black rancid smoke still swirled in the room. An evil spirit, one of the Count's followers, still remained.

Stumbling into the blackness, he began fighting against the force with all his strength. The angel of death moved towards him, engulfing him, despite his physical effort, he could not fight it. He felt a heaviness push on his chest. Something was trying to get inside him, take over his soul, his spirit. It grew heavier, he could not breathe. It was spreading its poison into him, ripping out his soul. He fought back, he could not give in, or it would destroy him. He struggled with all his will. It was coiling its evil body around him, piercing him with its claws, injecting him with its poison. He had to think fast, there was little time left.

He clawed his way across to the door, the force was suffocating him; if only he could only get some air. Moving along the wall he smashed a window, then choking, collapsed. Where the hell was Emma, he wondered, as he lost consciousness and spiralled down into the empty blackness?

Redemption

'Anton, are you there?' called Emma. She pushed open the door of the studio, left ajar, aware of a cold bitterness in the air. A strange smell drifted across the room. Emma froze. What was going on? A tension hung in the air. She looked in all the rooms, but no one was there. Going through to the lounge, she noticed there was a terrible stench, a rotting and putrid odour. All she could see were paintings burnt on the floor. Fear clawed its way into her brain. She tried to fight it, trying to focus on Anton. Where was he? What had happened? She had to find him!

She walked over to the middle of the room and started to pick up the remains of the paintings, scattered all over the floor. Twisted black debris fell off, leaving ash in her hands. As she turned them over she saw they were completely destroyed. She examined them one by one, hoping to find a clue. Under them was a strange symbol of a pentagram, drawn in charcoal on the floor. She gently touched a portrait of Anton and Emma, the last one he had worked on, where Anton was portrayed strangling her. She stepped back shocked. What on earth did this mean? Was it another prediction? Where was Anton? Had he gone mad?

She ran over the house, through the studios, calling out for him, but there was no sign of him. She shivered. Fear crept down her neck along her spine. A hollow laugh echoed from behind her. She jumped, and turned round for a moment, so scared she started to panic. She looked around her, but there was nothing; she had to pull herself together. Her first impulse was to run. What exactly was she dealing with? She had never been afraid of anything before. Carefully, she turned over each painting.

Suddenly one of the paintings started moving; it was of the bay outside, and the wind swept the sand across the beach in a sandstorm. Emma jumped back: a black mist was slithering along a shadowy beach. There was something odd about it, the people were moving! The waves were rushing along the beach. The painting was alive! A man was drifting in the water, he was waving to her—struggling in the sea.

Emma froze in shock and horror as she saw it was Anton—he was drowning in the sea! Outside in the bay! Going under the waves. Black smoke swamped the sky, as the sea crashed mercilessly below. Emma raced down to the lifeguard's hut, took the rowing boat from the quay and pushed it out to sea. Rowing past the lighthouse over the rocky waves, she saw Anton struggling in the waves, drowning! She rowed faster, the waves pushed her back, almost turning the boat over. She struggled on. Just as he was about to go down under a massive wave, Emma gave three hard pulls on the oars and drew alongside him, pushing the oar out for him to grasp. He grabbed it and she pulled him back into the boat; then, using all her strength, she rowed them back to the shore.

Anton collapsed on to the sand, shaking violently. He spluttered a few words, but Emma couldn't make out what he was saying. His unkempt hair strewn across his face, his body convulsed, and his eyes rolled manically. Quite suddenly his peaceful smile returned. The evil force had left him. His eyes opened gradually, he looked up slowly at Emma and smiled.

'Thank God, you are still alive!' cried Emma, taking him in her arms.

'They tried to kill me,' he gasped, as he caught his breath.

'Who tried to kill you?'

'The evil entity, the Count!' he spluttered. 'He came to get me. He dragged me through the window, over the cliff into the sea and tried to take possession of my soul.' Anton's hands were trembling violently, his face white and shaking. His skin was deathly pale.

For a moment Emma though he was going to pass out, then he looked up at her and forced a smile:

'I am sorry, Emma, for everything I have done, I am sorry for how I have treated you.'

Emma fell into Anton's arms. He gazed up at her, with love in his eyes.

'Don't worry, it wasn't your fault,' she whispered. 'I'm just glad that you are still alive,' she said, relief flooding through her. Gently she pushed the wet hair back from his forehead.

The old wizened woman stood on the beach, her arms folded. Her hair was white. Anton sat up, he recognised her.

'I have destroyed the evil one at last,' she said to Anton, 'he will not bother you any more. The past has been erased, the prophecy will not come true.'

'You saved me from the Count?' he gulped.

'Yes, with Emma's help. She came to me to see if I could stop him: we had to capture his energy force. We tried destroy his power, turn his evil back on him and Emma used her love to cast the white light around you, to protect you with the help of Letitia, who has always tried to protect you. Angel we couldn't save, there wasn't time.'

'Letitia saved me, after what my uncle did to her?'

'Yes, especially after what he had done. She was your guardian angel and acted out of love as well as a sense of duty. She felt responsible for the dark forces your uncle had called up, that looked set to destroy you too. You had inherited their legacy, of darkness.'

'I can't thank you enough,' said Anton, smiling, his eyes shining brightly again, 'both of you, for all you have done.'

'It isn't quite over yet,' said the woman hugging them, as they turned to watch the flames engulfing the studio. 'There are still some dark energies around, but they will be gone in a few days.'

'My poor studio, it's burning!' groaned Anton, putting his head in his hands.

'The fire brigade is on its way,' said the woman. 'Don't worry, the curse is lifted, you will not make the same mistake as your uncle. The lie you were told, of the prophecy coming true, was a lie invented by your enemies. The Count tried to push you into committing to the same fate as your uncle, he wanted to undermine you. He hoped it would become a self-fulfilling prophecy: that if you believed in the curse, then the idea would slowly drive you insane. That was his revenge, for your ancestor's dark deeds against him. You have lived in fear and are free from the curse. There is no disaster awaiting you, your soul is cleansed. I want you to forget him, and to find the happiness you both deserve.'

'Thank God for that, their prophecy isn't true!' Anton laughed with relief and pulled Emma into his arms.

'Be careful in future. Do not provoke forces you cannot control, or venture into the darkness ever again. Be sure to find people whom you can trust.'

'I will,' swore Anton, still choking.

Emma held onto him tightly. 'Why did they haunt us?' she asked. 'Why did they keep appearing at the inn?'

'Because they died so suddenly, their deaths traumatic, and all associated with betrayal of some kind. They were stuck and couldn't move to the place of light. They wanted revenge, or in Antoine's case, to find peace.'

An unearthly crack thundered through the air, making Emma turn round; the loft was exploding with fire, dancing red flames ripped through the roof. Black smoke poured out of the building, billowing across the sky. A loud bang thundered and ripped through the air as the studio burned furiously. Clouds of black ash rose into the darkness. Exploding fragments of fire shot through the sky, spreading into mushrooms of smoke rising overhead. A loud wail ripped through the air, followed by a tortured cry. Angel had gone inside the building looking for Anton, no one had seen her. Then it stopped. Silence again.

A flash of lightning ripped through the sky, white sparks shot out, melting as they fell to the earth. A few flames lingered, fading in the wind. A peaceful calm returned, ripples flowed across the blue sea. Anton smiled, and his eyes were alive with the energy Emma so loved.

'Thank you for saving me. I'm so relieved that you're safe. I can always build another studio, and all my best work had been moved out to the exhibition site. As long as we are alive, that's all that matters.' He cupped Emma's face in his hands and kissed her passionately. 'I do love you so, Emma,' he said. 'Will you ever forgive me?'

'Yes of course, it wasn't your fault.' She licked his salty lips and felt the warmth flow back into her.

'Oh Emma, will you marry me?'

'Yes, Anton, of course I will,' she nodded, falling into his arms. It was all over, the nightmare was over at last.

When Emma returned to the Black Dove Inn, the air was clear and warm, the ghosts had gone: she ran to the studio and could only see her reflection in the mirrors and the windowpanes shone clear. It felt light and breezy, the musty smell had gone. She stopped. There was, momentarily, the gentle smile of a woman, Letitia, in the pane, her gaze resting lovingly on Emma. Then she kissed Antoine, and they both vanished. She breathed a sigh of relief that their torment was over. The haunting had passed, all the dark demons had gone and the rooms were filled with her laughter and happiness again. Emma smiled happily—Letitia had been a friend, their guardian angel, and at last she had found peace and her true love.

Happy days – a new summer, August

Emma started serving lunch. Anton and Ramone dived into the waves, then ran out of the sea and balanced their surfboards against the table, shaking off the wetness of their rubber suits. They raced back across the sand throwing a Frisbee. Emma smiled, so happy now, watching them leap in the sand, like schoolboys. It was so refreshing to listen to their laughter. Andrea sat down, smiling, with her new baby. Emma smiled to herself, delighted about her own happy secret.

'Come on, everyone,' Emma called, easing herself past a chair, 'food is ready.' Anton ran over laughing at the latest story of the cove. Melanie sat with her barrister boyfriend Gavin under a golf umbrella. He scowled, nibbling at a sandwich nervously as the Frisbee whizzed past his ear, then ducking as it flew past, knocking his perfectly styled hair into chaos.

'Come on, man, chill out,' said Ramone, throwing Anton the Frisbee. Emma caught it as it was about to demolish the trifle and threw it back.

'Oh come on, don't be so cruel,' cried Emma. Anton smiled, their eyes locked. They were safe now that the nightmare was over. A secret, loving smile passed between them, the darkness had gone. Anton gave Emma a hug. After journeying to hell and back, nothing could stop them now. Anton's eyes shone bright again, free from pain and confusion. They were happy and free once more. Life had returned to normal and become all that Emma had dreamed of. Anton, the perfect partner, was loving and attentive and had started painting landscapes of rural countryside, resulting in several lucrative commissions; he never mentioned the occult again. They kept the inn as an arts studio and café, and had moved to a pretty cottage in the dip of the cove by a running brook, with a peaceful happy vibe.

Emma filled the plates with potato salad and handed them out. Anton poured out hot coffees. The sun shone brightly, the turquoise waves moved in gentle ripples, it was clear and peaceful. She thought of the words to the poem she had read that morning:

'Pleasure gives way to pain, and day turns to night, and the darkness descends and covers all things light.'

Shuddering, despite the warm sun, she sighed, surprised at what they had gone through, so glad it was all over. She could barely take in what had happened. But they had come out on top. She must have a charmed life, she thought wryly. At least their love had stood the test of time. It had been a difficult time, but had it ever been easy? This time they had weathered the storm together, instead of letting it drive them apart, and she had found true love, and the passion for life she had always dreamed of. How strange and unpredictable life was! And how wonderful at times! The uncertainty of existence was a mystery.

The sea roared in the distance, a flock of gulls flew across the shimmering blue of the bay past the burning sun. A new day was dawning. Anton kissed Emma softly on the cheek; she turned and smiled, and patted their new baby kicking inside her. Gavin and Melanie sat on the deckchairs, laughing at Ramone struggling out of his wet suit, falling onto the sand, his legs caught in the sleeves. He ducked as Gavin, vengeful, threw the Frisbee back at his head and knocked him over. 'Touché,' said Gavin, grinning triumphantly. Andrea burst into raucous laughter and threw a towel at him. The sun broke through the clouds and warmed the beach. A single black dove flew into the air, joined by another. Together they soared past the setting sun towards a dark cloud, rolling ominously away in the distance. Emma clutched Anton's arm and smiled. Gavin, in a playful mood, threw the towel over Ramone's head, leapt up and took a photograph of them, laughing together, arms linked, standing happily on the dunes.

END

The River Tale

The River Tale

'Woman is the being who projects the greatest shadow, or the greatest light'

Baudelaire

Isobel the Maiden, Felicia the Dark Goddess

The Dark Goddess watches from the darkness,
Her eyes blazing with an hypnotic power,
Luring her victims to the abyss
Leaving only their fragments,
The slithers of their soul,
In the hollow empty void.

For me your love is only pain,
I've opened up my eyes,
And seen in you my lady fair,
The devil in disguise
Tannhauser

Dreams of lightness? Or, of darkness.
What lies beneath the shadowy realms of our soul?
Give me the dreams of the enchantress,
The power of the dark goddess
Are they real? Or just an illusion?

The Canal

Outside, somewhere in the distance, Isobel heard a loud scream. As it faded, she woke up, realising the scream was hers. She turned to Rick, sleeping silently beside her, and breathed a sigh of relief. It had just been a nightmare. Thank god, it hadn't been real. She looked at the bedside clock. It was two a.m. and the canal was deathly quiet; nothing moved or flickered except a solitary light in the keeper's lock. The night was unearthly still. She wandered out on to the deck of the canal boat, and stared up at the sky, breathing in the cool air. The moon shone eerily on the canal, casting strange shimmering shadows across the water. It was a dark night, with few stars. She shivered, recalling the bizarre images, the terrifying dream.

She saw a tall, shadowy figure glide slowly across the water. She blinked and it had gone. What was it? Was something really there? Or was her mind playing tricks on her? She looked out over the water; all she could see was the gentle ripples on the canal. She shivered and wandered back inside. Had it had been more than a dream?

The next morning, Rick jumped up out of bed and stared at his reflection in the mirror. His face was pale, drained, his eyes haunted. He ran his hands through his hair, a look of fear spread across his face. Disturbing images raced around his head. He started to shave, carelessly cutting himself. He sighed in desperation. Last night he had been haunted by some terrifying dreams, and his hands were still shaking. What the hell had got into him?

'The tour starts next month, I almost forgot, I'm rehearsing today,' said Rick, packing away his instruments. 'I had hoped to get a good night's sleep. What was that awful noise on the canal last night?' he asked.

'Just a chug boat going by, carrying some logs,' Isobel replied.

'It sounded like all hell was being let loose.'

'The sky looks so dark,' observed Isobel. Dark storm clouds swirled above in the sky, a blustery wind blew ripples across the canal and the wind shook the trees. 'A storm is coming.'

'Yes it might be, stay inside. I'll be back late,' he said, pecking her quickly on the cheek.

Isobel eased herself out of bed to kiss Rick goodbye. She touched his cold cheek and was gripped by a sense of foreboding. Something wasn't right. Rick turned round—there was a strange, haunted look in his eyes.

Michel—The River

Michel strolled along the canal, wondering whether or not to rent a friend's houseboat at Little Venice, a perfect location for writing, and far enough away from the rat race, a place where he could let his mind wander and be creative, enjoy his solitude. It was a warm spring day and the bank was heaving with primroses. It had everything he was looking for—small bird-inhabited islands twinkling with glistening leaves, with the kind of energy that attracted the artist, the bohemian. Herons and other birds flew by, skimming across the water, drifting down the river. It was his kind of place, a watery utopia in the centre of London, with access to the delights of the city alongside the wildness of the country. Streaks of grey smoke rose from a bonfire, and the faint smell of burning wood wafted under his nostrils, giving the place a rustic air. He was drawn by the city, its cosmopolitan lure, yet needed to be in a quiet haven where he could work. Here, he decided, he could have both. He decided to take the offer of the boat.

It was an ideal place to escape city life, he thought, and give free reign to his muse. The stillness was interrupted only by the steady hum of passing boats, a peaceful haven for artists and writers who shared his need for solitude at times. He rang Andrew, the boat owner, to ask if he could move in straightaway. He said yes, offering Michel the use of the rowing boat attached to the boathouse, for rowing into town. He looked up as some herons flew past. Two bright gypsy boats sailed by, painted in many colours, adorned with buckets of flowers. People were dancing on the deck to music wafting across the water, their vibrant bodies swaying under the tepid sun. They waved, Michel waved back, his attention caught by a smile from one of the dancers—she tossed him a garland of flowers. They seemed like nice people, he thought, perhaps he would stay for a while, away from the demands of the city, the faster pace of life.

The watery sun shone on the soft ripples of the canal, making it warm for the time of year. The river shone silvery bright on the surface, dark and weed-ridden underneath. Boats drifted by. It was a sleepy afternoon. Light streamed brightly through a cloudy haze. A shower of rain, lasting seconds, freshened the sultry air. He felt free sitting close to water. The serenity of the canal filled him with wonder, a kind of euphoria. The natural flow of life lulled him into a rhythm. He could think clearly. He sat picking at some grass, immersed in his thoughts. The water swirled, giving him a feeling of tranquillity. He had driven for the last hour and welcomed a rest. He sat back on the soft grass, feeling the dewy blades sink under him like a soft mattress and squinted against the burning sun. It suited him well now that he had to leave his London flat.

Coming to this oasis was getting as close to Nirvana as anyone could get in the midst of the city. Never before had he felt so at peace. Nice to escape from the noise, crowds of people, traffic, and jarring, impersonal, disembodied voices. He listened to the gentle ripples of water drifting on the canal, the clunking of oars, the wind in the rushes—natural sounds resonating in harmony with his thoughts, not grating against them.

He climbed down onto the houseboat *Heron*, past the small kitchen diner to the bedroom. He threw his suitcase on the bed and stared out of the small porthole looking at the many houseboats lined up along the sides of the canal. He poured a drink, then climbed back up out on to the deck of the boat to get a closer look at the other boats. A grey houseboat stood moored by the willow trees. It fascinated him, it stood imposingly on the canal, dwarfing the other boats, next to a garden filled with stone statues of pale-faced ethereal goddesses.

Intrigued, Michel cycled along the shaded winding path past the riverboats to the large grey houseboat. It stood out among the others, looking quite majestic; he tried to get closer. He jumped off his bike, and peered at it. It was like a mansion compared to the other boats, dwarfing them all with its mock gothic presence, many times the size of his own small boat. At the rear were several strange sculptures scattered in the garden—maidens with heads covered by wreaths of roses and Pre-Raphaelite goddesses with long flowing hair. Stone angels, and ornate water fountains were neatly tucked onto the tiny lawn.

He stood looking at it for a few minutes, intrigued. What sort of people lived there? Was it a famous designer, poet, or maybe an actor? A restaurant boat drifted by, playing music: people were dancing, celebrating, throwing flowers onto the bank. One of them tossed a wreath of roses at his feet. All the other residents were busy, painting or cleaning their decks. The area had an easy calm. The swirling water rippled, shaded by trees, creating a haven of natural tranquillity.

Later, untying the rowing boat from a handy jetty, Michel cast off the rowing boat and headed for town. The cloying heat of the afternoon filled the air as he rowed towards Camden. He reflected sadly on the love he had left behind; he felt marooned, love-locked in an endless situation. Leisurely, he moved towards the bridge, feeling torn, the inertia of the past enveloping him, as droplets of rain began to fall on the oar. He began to consider the emptiness of his future, when a small sunbeam began to break through the clouds throwing rays across the boat.

'What am I going to do?' he asked, putting his head in his hands, wondering how he had found the courage to pull away from Amelia, his fiancée. They had argued that morning, and she had told him it was over. She had met someone else who gave her the security and material possessions she craved. He had shouted at her, told her to go. He had to face up to the fact that he was not ready for a family and knew that her emotional blackmail was frustrating his moves toward a more lucrative career. He rowed on, feeling tired and drained, torn apart. The sun glowed, its rays healing him.

The warmth filtered through the clouds, as the sun rose behind the grey slate buildings. His anger was subsiding as peace flowed through him. Suddenly a rainbow appeared, its vibrant colours arching up through the sky, filling him with hope. With renewed enthusiasm, Michel rowed towards the tunnel, out of the sun into darkness, feeling the splashes of water as they fell on the boat. For a moment he was gripped with pain, then it eased as he saw a light shimmering at the end of the tunnel.

Emerging as the sun began to shine, he stopped when he saw a reflection of the boat rippling on the water—reminding him that life flowed endlessly, like water, not in a set pattern. Life went in cycles, he mused, and he was entering a new one. He had to move on. Optimistically, he rowed away from the past, the memories gradually fading to become a fragment of his imagination. Feeling alive, he began to row faster, as he moved towards a new beginning, a different life. The heavy indecision left him as he realised things were finally over with Amelia; he could never make her happy. There was no going back, he had made up his mind.

Gliding past the bank, he spotted a girl sitting by the grey boat, she was painting. He stopped.

'She is so beautiful,' he sighed wistfully, rowing slower, trying to get a closer look at her. Steering toward the bank, he watched her. She moved elegantly, like a goddess, her long hair cascading over her pale shoulders in soft blonde curls. Her silk dress rustled in the gentle breeze, a sliver of pale sunlight swirling around her, making her angelic. Streaks of light beamed through her hair, the strands catching the silvery light—the whole scene had an ethereal air as though she had just stepped from a painting by Millais. She sat sideways on a stool, a sea nymph risen from the river. He rowed past the mooring and turned round. Glancing up, he saw a dark cloud had begun to fill the sky. The boat suddenly gained speed as he was carried along by the gentle current. As it did so, the woman picked up her sketchpad and walked away, going downstream. Michel let the boat drift on the water for a few minutes, feeling sad, though he fought to stop a dark mood from engulfing him, as he stared over the side of the boat, watching the gentle ripples. He lifted the oars lightly, steering toward the bank, when a shadow fell across the water. He looked up and caught sight of the willowy maiden wandering back into the garden, her gentle beauty enthralling him as he lost control of the oars.

Isobel

Isobel opened the small gate and set up her easel, in her tiny garden on the riverbank, hoping to get some privacy. She often escaped there, trying to avoid Rick's bad moods. His manic highs and lows drove her mad, making him unbearable. When he was composing or preparing for a tour, she had to escape, get out of his way. The open air made her feel better, giving her the space to think. She took in breaths of fresh air, feeling calmer. It was a nice day to be sitting alone, with only the clouds and trees for company, working in gentle harmony with other artists on the canal. A quiet empathy resonated between them. She opened up her easel and perched on a stool, and began painting. Peace and tranquillity flowed through her. Her hair flowed around her bare, lightly tanned shoulders, rippling to her waist in pale wispy curls, her dress billowing in the gentle breeze. The coolness of the wind eased her troubled spirit, setting her thoughts free. Light streamed onto the canvas and shimmered in silver strips on the canal. She felt inspiration flood through her as she held a brush up to the sky, angled it, then started to dab on some paint—purple, rose, titian—in the shape of some wild flowers. Abruptly, she got up, still smarting over the argument she had just had with Rick. Painting helped soothe her mood, drove away the demons, calmed her angst. But today she couldn't concentrate. She needed to unwind. She leapt up and raced along the riverbank, running through the foliage, her hair streaming out behind her, free, unrestrained, her feet skipping lightly across the wet dewy grass. She released her inner child and instantly felt better. The cool air had cleared her head. She stopped suddenly as she saw a good-looking man, tall, athletic, with blonde hair, struggling with some oars. She stifled a laugh, noticing he seemed a bit lost. She giggled, lifting the black weight that had descended on her over the business of Rick's coming tour. She watched the man for a few minutes, letting the diversion take the weight off her mind. Isobel sighed: it had been a long week and was going to be an even longer weekend with the arrival of Felicia and some other guests. She wasn't looking forward to the party; Felicia would no doubt spoil things somehow, darken the day with her wicked presence—she was a constant thorn in the side of her happiness. The idyll she and Rick created had been disrupted by the recent re-forming of his band. She would have to stop suspecting him whenever he toured with Felicia. She had no right to tell him what to do. She had to trust him.

Life had been perfect, her dream—that was until Felicia had come back into their lives and started stirring things up. Her arrival had made her uneasy, and her rival's bright idea of getting Rick's band back together had thrown everything into chaos. Since then, things hadn't been the same. They used to spend their weekends sailing along the canal, stopping off for quiet pub lunches, then heading home and making love for hours. Now it was all pressure of rehearse, play and tour, all instigated by the predatory Felicia. Isobel was wary of her motives, but could not let herself give in to paranoia. Her happiness was evaporating, the peace and contentment had gone, and she felt the easiness giving way to anxiety, made worse by having to be alert to someone else's stirring-up all the time. Felicia spelled trouble, and had shattered their calm idyll. Rick, frustrated, had insisted it was all in her imagination and refused to listen. He could be stubborn and hated the trivial issues of life. Music was his life and his love, almost to the point of obsession, and he could not live without it. If he stopped playing for a while, he would become morose, act as if life wasn't worth living. He needed to create, to play, to feel alive, and he was a brilliant and gifted musician, who could only find fulfilment through the muse. She sighed; if only she did not love him so much, for the life of a musician's girlfriend was not a happy one.

She saw the man struggling with the oars—a boat dweller, new to the canal. He looked nice, perhaps the sort of man she should have chosen, the sort of man her mother would have approved of, who would give her a much easier life. Clean cut, and traditionally handsome. To her dismay she always chose the other type—the dark, brooding, tormented geniuses who tore her apart. Besides, she couldn't live without Rick or his wild edge—she adored him. Last night she'd had another strange dream; it had disturbed her—a strange serpent, rising from the canal; it had wrapped itself around her ankles and slowly suffocated her. Rick had been acting strangely lately. They had both been working too hard, neglecting each other, they needed to go out for a meal and unwind. Or perhaps they could take an early holiday together? But her heart sank; it was impossible with the touring coming up. She went back to her painting, it was the only thing that lifted her spirits and made her feel in control again. Absorbed by the scene around her, she felt her muse awaken, the love of her work flow into her and her spirits rise.

Goddesses

Michel lost control of the oars, as Isobel glided past him, and a smile lit her face. She leapt lightly across the wet grass, a water nymph, her sketchbook in her hand. She was walking along the bank elegantly, briskly, like a ballet dancer, poised. Wearing a pale blue leotard under a silk wrap dress, she tossed back her mane of curly pale hair like a goddess. She was swirling in the mist, rising from the murky water of the underworld toward the light, the mysterious maiden of the deep, a water spirit shrouded by a delicate ripple of water. She looked like one of Hylas's ethereal nymphs emerging from the water, a delicate swirling damsel, gliding across the grass. He watched her dancing barefoot, ecstatically, in a pool of light, filled with a feminine grace: she was totally captivating.

Michel stared at her longingly as she beckoned to him from the bank as he rowed past, struggling with the oars. Elegantly, she waved to him, the brushes in her hand, paint on her face.

'Are you all right?' she asked him.

'Fine, just mastering how to use the oars, I think it must be easy once you get the hang of it.'

'Yes, it's quite simple really, if you get the rhythm right.'

'Have you got a minute?' she asked. 'I wonder if you could help me?'

'I'll try,' he said, steering the boat into the edge of the bank.

'I think you might need some help too,' she giggled, watching him struggle with the oars, grabbing the rope and pulling him in. He climbed out of the boat.

'I haven't see you here before, have you just moved here?'

'Yes,' Michel replied. 'I'm renting a boat, from a friend, I'm not used to rowing.'

'You'll get used to it,' she laughed, 'you have to, it's the only form of transport around here.'

They both laughed.

'I need to dismantle the easel. Perhaps you can help?' she asked.

'Okay, I'll try,' he replied.

He stepped out of the boat and climbed to where she was painting. She got back onto her stool.

'Thank you for your offer to help,' she smiled gratefully, cleaning her brushes.

'Not at all, I was just sailing by.'

She added some final touches, silky white petals to the roses and lilies, and smiled. Her brush flowed with ease and she felt much better. The strange intruder had broken her tense mood. He'd lifted her spirits and made her laugh—something she rarely did with Rick any more, he was too intense.

Michel walked over, pointing to the circle of flowers painted in watercolours.

'That's a very beautiful painting,' he said, admiring her work.

Her porcelain-like hands moved quickly in small precise brushstrokes on the canvas. 'I must pack away,' she laughed, 'once the creative urge hits me, I just can't stop painting.'

'I know the feeling.' He watched her wipe the brushes with a cloth.

'It helps me relax. I'll just put the brushes away,' she said, watching him dismantle the easel. Observing him, amused, she stifled a giggle. He struggled, trying to line up the three legs; one kept shooting out and he had to start again.

'There, that should be okay, I was never any good with these things,' he said, as it collapsed.

Isobel laughed, and pointed toward the large grey houseboat: 'That's mine: during the day I work as an artist on this shared boat,' she explained. Michel nodded, fascinated. The identity of the owner of the grey boat had mystified him: now he had met her and she was all he had expected her to be; a princess, a goddess-water nymph.

'Do you like it here?' she asked. She sat back in a wicker chair and began fanning herself with a pale blue fan.

'Yes, I enjoy the freedom and the space,' he admitted. She could clearly see he was enchanted by her. She did not want to question him further as she thought he looked sad. 'Would you like some tea?'

'Yes, thanks.'

'Come inside our boat. We are a group of artists, who run a business from here,' she said, climbing down into the small cabin. The room was narrow inside and full of paintings. 'Make yourself at home,' she said, offering him a seat. 'This is our studio.'

'I've always wanted to know who lived on the grey boat, it's incredible,' he said looking out over the water.

'Yes, its quite a work of art,' she admitted. 'We bought it from an architect who designed it in his own style. We have lived here for two years. It is very inspiring.'

'I can see,' he said, enviously.

He fingered some sculptures lining the windows. They were mysterious, small figures of women, and they looked like goddesses of all kinds, dark and light, taken from mythology.

'Did you make these?' he asked, fascinated.

'Yes, they are part of a collection called "The Goddess".'

He picked up one and looked at it closely; it was a woman in a long, flowing robe with snakes coming out of her head.

'That's the dark goddess, Lilith, a witch.'

'Who was she?' he asked her, intrigued.

'Adam's first wife, who was demonic in nature.'

'I didn't know he had a second wife.'

'Yes, according to folklore.'

She turned round, her pale hair shone in the light.

Perhaps she was with someone—she'd said 'we'—Michel wondered fleetingly, but didn't like to ask. He sat on the seat toying with some tarot cards laid out on the small table. He overturned a card, it was one of the lovers. The picture, of lovers entwined in the Garden of Eden, their long hair covering their naked bodies with a snake writhing at their feet, made him gasp. He smiled to himself. He told her about his recent break-up with his fiancée, and she listened sympathetically.

'Don't worry,' she assured him, pointing to the tarot cards. 'There is enough love for everyone in the universe. You will find the love you need soon, it says so here.'

He watched Isobel turn back, busy making coffee, weaving her long hair into a plait. It hung down to her waist in soft ripples, now tied up with a black silk scarf. Her almond-shaped sapphire-blue eyes stared at him like a doe caught in headlights, vulnerable yet powerful. He had never seen such beautiful eyes with such power. He saw her breasts point through the fabric of her dress and fought the urge to kiss her, wanting her. She handed him the coffee, her hand brushing against his. He felt a wave of desire and realised how he wanted her. He offered instead to carry things out of the boat, preferring to indulge a chivalrous impulse.

'Come to dinner with us on Saturday,' she offered. 'You can meet the others.'

'Yes, I'd like that—I don't know many people here.' He noticed she wore a ring with a strange emblem on it. He asked her what it was.

'My aunt gave it to me and it has a strange story,' she explained. 'It once belonged to a goddess, who used her dark powers to enforce her will. She misused her power by killing her lover after he was unfaithful. Eventually, she was punished by being reincarnated as a rat.'

'It has a certain charm,' said Michel laughing, looking closely at it. He saw it had the face of a goddess with wild, snaky hair. Drinking the tea, he got up. He saw a painting of a woman sitting by a lake, her long hair flowing over her as she played the harp. Angels danced around her.

'Who is that?' asked Michel.

'Those are the muses, sunbathing with Venus, the goddess of love, basking in the golden rays of divine light; their gifts are the muse, they create musical ability and artistic talent. She inspires others with the endowment of her creative gifts. There are many composers, painters, poets and writers who are touched by the spirit of the creative goddess, her force of light and inspiration, and her muse. But when the goddess enters the underworld, she turns into the dark goddess. She becomes destructive and brings chaos to their idyll.'

'How fascinating,' he said. 'Did you study mythology?'

'Yes I did, as part of my fine art course. Romanticism is my special subject. I love their mystical themes, it's how we all should live, in the throes of creativity, making art and music. I try to live in the higher spiritual realm of existence, transcendence.'

'Thanks for the tea, see you on Saturday then.'

She smiled at him, a flash of desire passed between them.

'Okay.'

Later, alone in her boat, Isobel sat thinking, she was happy to have had made a friend in Michel. She needed an ally. She liked him a lot, nothing sexual, just a nice friend to have. She compared him to Rick, no one stirred her in the way that he did, no man could ever come close. The chemistry between them was like lightning, or had been. Rick was becoming difficult; still that was the mark of a genius, and she knew she couldn't live without him. Being with him was like an addiction; there was a strong bond between them, even after four years of being together. No other man had ever made her feel quite as happy, sexy and inspired and generally wonderful as Rick did. He was a law unto himself, a wild and creative man, and she sometimes had difficulty keeping up with him. Michel was softer, gentler, a confidante. She pulled off the waxy petals from the dark purple roses. How fragile love was. Did Rick really love her? Why couldn't he just be content like she was? Why did he need the constant spark of the creative fire to feel alive?

Michel

That weekend, Michel made his way to Isobel's boat *Lilith*. He was glad at last to be away from the oppression of the city and crushing boredom of suburbia, relieved not to have given in to Amelia's growing demands for a house in Surrey, with demanding children to be groomed at the best public schools—a boring, stifling existence where he would have had to work all hours just to keep all the bills paid. He was glad he had stood his ground, and refused to give up his freedom. A bohemian existence suited him well. The river was an interesting place, vibrating with energy and buzzing with free-spirited people who lived creatively. He walked along to the other end of the canal. In his pocket was a small book, a dictionary of mythology. He had looked up the name 'Lilith'. Lilith was Adam's first wife, but because she wanted to dominate him, God replaced her with

Eve, a more compliant, subservient female. Lilith had been a storm demon, a succubus who seduced men in their sleep and gave birth to hundreds of baby demons afterwards. Michel read it, fascinated. He couldn't wait to meet people who named their boat after a demon. A raging, demonic, nymphomaniac one, at that.

The Party—Angels and Devils

Michel pushed open the huge medieval door of the grey houseboat, and peeked in—it looked quite strange. It was a huge wooden boat four times the size of the other boats on the river. It had a huge deck, and two storeys and one long hallway lounge leading to a galley. Mysterious, ornate rooms were divided from the rear of the houseboat by an iron gothic gate. Black heavy medieval lamps jutted out from the walls, and exotic plants with spidery shoots occupied the floor. He caught a glimpse of a huge gothic bed in a room at one end. It was unique, designed like a film set, elegant and perfect in every way, with huge lilies in the corners. Isobel smiled as she saw him, handing him a plate filled with canapés.

'I'm glad you could make it,' offered Isobel warmly, taking his arm.

'Come and meet the others.' She led him past the white poppies and lilies into the lounge. Large black leather sofas lined the walls, and black candles were flickering in wrought iron, gothic-style holders on the walls. Michel climbed down into the room, observing the other guests, noting that they looked as odd as their surroundings. Several tall people stood talking, dressed in arty clothes.

'Do you like our home?' enquired Isobel.

'Yes, I'm quite impressed.'

Isobel handed him some nibbles.

'Yes, I thought you'd like it, it's quite a special place to live, especially for the artist. A lot of famous people live here—Richard Branson owns the large boat up the river, and the Emannuels used to live by the Island. Lots of famous writers and artists come here to be inspired. Robert Browning composed here, the Island over there is named after him,' she said, pointing to the end of the canal. 'And the restaurants in the village are to die for. Where else could you find such tranquillity in the centre of the city?'

'I agree, I can feel the good vibes already,' said Michel, taking off his jacket and smoothing back his hair.

'Let me introduce you to everyone,' she said.

'This is Rick,' she said, taking him over to meet a tall attractive man with chiselled cheekbones and long black hair. Michel stepped backwards. Rick cut a very imposing figure, dressed all in black, six-foot-four, with dark make-up around his eyes. He had the visage of an intelligent man with a hint of arrogance and Michel found him a touch intimidating. His large eyes stared intensely at him, they were sloped and dark, almond-shaped, beautiful, changing from innocence to wonder, aflame with a mysterious dark power, yet there was a chameleon quality about him, hinting at a mercurial mind. His long hair rippled down his back. He flicked back his hair and gave Michel an engaging smile.

'Hi,' said Rick, walking over and unplugging a guitar from an amplifier. 'We are happy you could make it. How are you enjoying life on the canal?' he asked.

'It's great,' Michel replied.

'Sorry, I'm not dressed for dinner, I've just played a gig,' said Rick.

'Oh don't worry.'

Michel noted that his anarchic appearance concealed an articulate manner. He stood in a long black t-shirt over jeans, tall and foreboding with strangely hypnotic dark eyes. Isobel kissed him, clearly besotted. Rick passed Michel some wine.

'What do you think of civilisation? So-called reality?' Rick asked him, fuelling an already heated intellectual discussion.

'Well, we seem to be a fairly civilised society,' he said, glad to be slightly conservative in his approach to life. 'A decent but crumbling NHS and school system, and a pleasant country to live in. We are not plagued by floods or famine, and this safety allows us to be civilised.'

'Civilisation is a relatively unstable concept and can easily be destroyed,' said Rick scornfully. 'Civilisation is nothing more than a façade, an illusion, even the most advanced societies are only four meals away from anarchy,' Rick said, drinking from a goblet filled to the brim with wine. 'It is an illusion, a constructed false dream.'

'Anarchy is the only true freedom, a real expression of the human spirit, not built on lies to placate the masses into behaving themselves,' said a beautiful dark-haired lady, her dark eyes beaming with a blazing force.

'Yes, capitalism consists of the opiates of existence, celebrity culture, television, false dreams and the desire for more. We should live by our own vision find our own creative path, our own gifts, not be channelled into some meaningless existence to serve the lust of governments,' said Rick, his eyes blazing with a strange potent energy.

'What do you mean by anarchy? I don't like violence,' asked Michel.

'They reject the need for a state of any type, and see decision-making as shared by the people,' said Stuart. 'They are revolutionaries who desire to smash the capitalist state and create a free world without class division and, property and repression. No, it's more about equality, a refusal to live by convention and antiquated patriarchal rules. Freedom is essential to feed, to enhance our true spirit. We only grow by challenging these outdated ideas, by bringing about change, creating new ideas and lifestyles, alternative realities. It is a catalyst for change; if that's the case, we should all be anarchists. I think their aim is commendable.'

'Yes, our "safety" in this life, is a relative and fluctuating concept,' agreed Rick. 'I despise people who follow convention blindly and kill what ignites our natural spark, our creativity. They become afraid to take risks, preferring instead to live an automated existence, an illusion that numbs the soul and spirit. Don't you agree?' he asked, turning to Michel.

'Yes, but we all have to compromise to some extent. That's reality, risks don't always work out as we plan,' answered Michel sensibly. 'And we have to pay the bills. In practice, we do need some structure to govern.'

'You surprise me as a writer,' Rick said, slightly scornfully. 'Isobel said you have come here seeking inspiration.'

'Yes I have, but sometimes I find it useful to have regularity and routine, and some structure,' admitted Michel. 'I know where I am then.'

'Me too!' smiled Isobel contentedly. 'I follow the will of truth and beauty, principles of higher thought and awareness. But I love domesticity too.'

Rick smiled, then shot Michel a scornful look.

'How can you say that? Routine is the enemy to creativity. You lack an adventurous spirit!'

'No I just prefer to be able to predict my future, I have no desire to go where angels fear to tread.'

'I prefer living on the edge, playing with danger, a wild existence, an element of anarchy alongside structure,' said Rick. 'The wildness of a Dionysian existence fires my creativity and ideas. I fire my muse to write original, haunting music. It spurs that burning desire, the mystery, the hunger, the spontaneity that drives the impulse. If I led a normal life I'd die of boredom, I couldn't bear to live a life of imposed routine or mediocrity. Out of the well of creativity springs the synthesis of new ideas, a fire that lights the imaginative powers, and leads us to genius.'

'Surely discipline, hard work and talent too?' argued Michel.

'Yes, but what ignites it? What force generates new ideas? Where does the talent or inspiration come from? It comes from the creative fire, going out on the edge, taking risks. Routine? That's a bit tame, to prefer to live in safety. How dull and boring! I should imagine it's like being dead.'

'It depends,' said Michel, for a moment wishing that Rick would disappear so that Isobel could talk to him alone. He was finding him a trifle overbearing, in contrast to the quiet, gentle charms of Isobel. 'I think the creative process is a mixture of many things, not just ideas,' admitted Michel. 'It requires hard work and dedication for years.'

'To some extent, but real creative flair is rare, a gift. It is reaching out to a higher energy that has no boundaries, a higher source of information. If you can dare to reach it. The fire of inspiration, and original thought comes from the wildness of nature, the light and the darkness, the essence of spirit, the true self unfettered by reality or mediocrity—fired by that which is free,' Rick argued. 'Our true self can reach out and tune into the genius of the universe, into higher thought. Too many rules can blind us to that.'

'Sounds like you prefer to live by the muse,' observed a guest.

'Isobel is my muse, and my life,' Rick admitted, putting his arm around her protectively. 'She inspires most of my work.'

Michel looked at them enviously.

'Sex and death, that raw energy that drives us, the libido,' argued Rick, looking down at Michel with an arrogant sneer, 'not conventional tame thoughts! You have to fly, how can anyone be creative leading a half-baked mediocre existence?'

'Take no notice of him,' laughed Isobel. 'He always tries to shock people into having heated intellectual debates, it's his sport.'

She went to the table to pour drinks for some new arrivals. At that moment Felicia walked back into the room; tall and strikingly beautiful, she looked like a fashion model, but Michel could see her dark looks masked a passionate and rebellious nature. She strode across the room purposefully, poured herself a drink and sat watching them, her eyes flickering with a curious dark intensity.

'What about the mystery of woman?' Michel asked Rick. 'How does she always inspire?'

'Through her creative gifts she projects the greatest shadow or the greatest light,' said Rick, looking slowly around the room, his eyes resting on Isobel for a moment, before his gaze wandered and fell on Felicia. 'They can inspire you with a sacred, inspiring light, or they can tear your soul apart and burn your whole world to ashes,' he said quietly.

'Interesting quotation, whose is it?' asked Michel sensing his distraction.

'Baudelaire. I must go, please excuse me for a moment. I have to talk to someone.'

'What do you think?' Kayla asked Isobel.

'Well, I believe in both, everything has its value, freedom and natural laws, and Karmic law,' said Isobel, 'there is a cause and effect to human behaviour. It cannot be lived by chaos. Both are of value, we have to have creative ideas for newness, but they have to make sense to everybody else too. There has to be a structure, a plan; predictability has its place, otherwise ideas become so confusing and egocentric to the point of not making sense. We try to live by both creativity and structure. We learn how to balance these different aspects of ourselves. We forge our own direction, we reap what we sow, we create our own destiny.'

'What comes around goes around?' said Michel.

'Yes precisely, we cannot always be anarchic, we have to consider our actions against others, and following such nomadic principles would mean that nothing could ever take root and grow, but we do need iconoclastic people to move ideas and shift paradigms along a bit, and change is necessary for growth. Anarchy as a theory is fine, but it doesn't always work in real life. It is healthy to discover fresh ways of looking at things. Find new perspectives as long as they come with a set of principles. We also benefit from the good things we do, but suffer if we are too indulgent, or if our creativity becomes an obsession and blinds us to other areas of our lives. It's all about balance.'

Rick walked over to Felicia; she turned and followed him out onto the balcony. Michel strained to see where they were going, but they were soon covered by the shadows of the trees. He turned back to see Isobel standing next to him looking concerned.

'Have you seen Rick?' she asked him, her face flushed. He

couldn't tell whether she'd had too much wine, or whether she was upset.

'No I haven't, he was here a moment ago,' he said truthfully.

'Oh, the music is about to begin, and the other musicians want to start,' she said, her eyes looking unfocused.

Michel looked over to the musicians who were setting up their instruments, one signalled to Isobel.

'I think they are starting, and I can't see Rick anywhere. Where is he?' she asked, exasperation creeping into her voice.

'It's okay. I'll go and look for him if you like. Don't worry. You look after the guests and mingle.'

'Thanks I'm really grateful,' she said, glad to have an ally.

Michel headed outside, sliding past Isobel as she turned to speak to Stuart. He crept alongside the houseboat by the canal and saw Rick with Felicia, deep in conversation. He was staring down at her, she was gazing up at him. Michel coughed as he approached them, glad to be disturbing this intimate moment.

Rick looked up startled. 'Yes, what is it?'

'Isobel wants to see you inside,' he said, 'the musicians are ready.'

'Okay thanks, I'll be right there,' said Rick, going back inside.

Felicia shot Michel a murderous look and scowled angrily at him, then stormed back into the houseboat, her petulant expression reminding him of a child.

Love was always complex, thought Michel, wondering if anything was going on between Rick and Felicia. Was he playing some sort of double game? Did Isobel know? Wondering at the same time about his own hypocrisy. Oh why on earth could he not stop thinking about her? Didn't Breton say love was a means of creation, a source of revelation? But rarely was it simple—when at first you practise to deceive, oh what a tangled web…he thought wistfully.

Rick walked over to the corner, sat down and screwed his face in concentration as he tuned his guitar.

'What goes around comes around,' muttered Isobel quietly. 'I don't think you need to have an obsession to be creative.'

'I agree,' said Kayla.

Rick picked up his fender guitar and began strumming it loudly, playing some wild heavy rock riffs, then slowing down before evoking some melodic chords. The stunning dark-haired guest walked over and interrupted them.

'I thinks that's absolute nonsense: you can't create brilliant work without obsession and you need anarchy,' she insisted. 'Creativity enhances our vision. To be a good artist, or academic, you need to be obsessed. The spark that ignites our artistic thinking, has a life force of its own. The creative fire is all we need to spur us on, it is beyond and above morality. Try and chain it and you lose the power. True genius cannot thrive alongside too much reality, and it has to be free. Rules just strangle and destroy any real flow. We need anarchistic flow. Rules are the enemy of creativity. We are not at the bloody convent now, Isobel,' she snapped, 'this is the real world.'

'This is Felicia,' said Isobel, exasperated, introducing her to Michel. 'She is the lead singer with Rick's band.'

'Pleased to meet you,' said Michel, his pulse quickening at the sight of her. Tantalising and hypnotising, he quickly summed her up as a right bitch. A stunning beauty hiding a wild heart.

'Hello,' said Felicia, in a dark voice, her eyes flashing dangerously. She stared at Michel with interest, opening her large vibrant, dark eyes wide. He smiled back nervously. Her eyes were dark like a Spanish gypsy, and stared at him with a fierce intensity, her olive skin glowing. Michel felt drawn into the grips of her strong hypnotic power but he pulled back: he wasn't sure it was safe. Rick looked over at them and lowered his eyes, then began playing a gentle instrumental piece. Felicia walked to the centre of the room and glanced possessively at Rick. She was a woman of exceptional beauty, her long raven hair tumbling down her back, contrasting with her olive complexion. Her amber eyes were cat-like, calculating, alive with a dark demonic power.

She walked over to the piano and started playing Vivaldi faultlessly. Everyone listened entranced, surprised to hear that she was such an accomplished musician. As the last notes faded, she got up and tossed back the hem of her purple and black silk dress, to reveal black fishnet stockings and a black lace petticoat. She stood perched on high stiletto heels, her delicate toenails painted black to match her eyes and fingernails. She bowed briefly, and walked over to the window. Caught unawares, she stared back at Michel provocatively like a temptress, her eyes conveying a feline cruelty. He smiled approvingly. Then, in a matter of seconds she changed from graceful, elegant goddess to wild rock performer. She picked up Rick's guitar and strummed a few heavy chords and swished back her hair.

She glared back at Michel, shooting him a look that told him, *you couldn't handle me so don't even try*, her eyes burning into him with an intense gaze, creating a strange aura around him. He suddenly felt quite light-headed and blinked to clear his head. Michel wondered if he'd had too much wine or whether this wild woman was casting a spell over him. There was a strange malevolence to her gaze. She sat watching him, like a black widow spider, spinning him into her own web of darkness, bad news for anyone who got caught in it. Something dark, coiled and predatory lay behind the pretty feline looks. She looked at Rick in a strangely menacing, and disturbingly sexual way. She tossed her long, raven black hair around her shoulder and twisted a strand of hair around her fingers, she was trying to flirt with him! Isobel watched them hopefully, and soon Michel wondered whether he'd been brought there to attract Felicia's attention away from Rick. His heart sunk; he liked Isobel. He busied himself by getting a drink.

Felicia followed him, her laser eyes boring into him, her dark energy glistening beneath a sophisticated veneer. She walked slowly like a panther, sleek, dangerous, ready to pounce on him. There was something wicked, wild and dangerous about her. He could not escape her, she seemed intent on snaring him, playing with him, but not seriously, just to trap him because it was her style and because, he suspected, she wanted to make Rick jealous. She stepped around him, and looked up at him as though assessing the value of a piece of art. She became friendly.

'I hope I haven't shocked you, I study witchcraft, the Dark Goddess,' she said.

'Do you? How fascinating?' he said, gulping down the wine and setting off to get another, but she grabbed him and pulled him back by the arm.

'I live for the source of all life and creativity, the unleashed, untamed forces of our dark passionate self. I suppose I am a witch.'

'That's interesting,' quipped Michel. 'Aren't all women witches?'

She ignored his remark. 'And Isobel tells me you are a writer,' she said enticingly, touching his arm, luring him into her web with her vampish charm.

'Yes, I write, some copywriting, mainly I research academic dictionaries,' he said.

'You haven't been here for long. I hear you are a new friend of Izzy's? Do you like living on the canal?'

'Yes, it's very inspiring,' he said, edging away. 'What do you do?'

'I sing, I am a performer, a musician, rock and classical, and I have an interest in the occult,' she said darkly, her eyes flashing with a bright demonic energy. 'I am the lead singer with Rick's band.'

'I see,' he said, suddenly seeing the connection.

'This is Stuart, Dave, Kayla and Imelda,' interrupted Isobel quickly, handing round a tray of quiche. Michel relaxed, relieved that as he got to know them, they seemed more normal. He backed away from Felicia: the last thing he needed was to get caught in the web of a woman displaying the charms of a black widow spider.

Felicia laughed: 'You'll get to know us all soon, we are quite strange really, but I am sure we'll grow on you. We are all musicians and artists here, who try to live an alternative existence.'

'Sounds wonderful. Do you live on the canal too?' asked Michel.

'No, I live in Highgate, in a converted church,' she replied.

'How quaint,' said Michel.

'I'm so pleased you could meet everyone,' said Isobel, slipping her arm through his. 'Would you like some more wine?'

Michel took it, wondering if it might be devil's blood, and he was about to be the sacrifice. Michel couldn't help seeing how feminine Isobel looked, and his heart lurched. Her hair was pushed back like Alice in Wonderland, an angel, her face vulnerable, and he wanted her so badly. It was as though Cupid's arrow was in the room and set on causing chaos. Her quiet, ethereal elegance contrasted with Felicia's dark, vampish presence. Her glacial, detached poise gave her an unobtainable air. She was so high above him, so out of reach, the woman of the formidable Rick. So he would live forever in the throes of unrequited love! Still, to be a friend was enough. She handed him a canapé, then smiled at him, her small elfin face mellowing into an impish grin, her sapphire-blue eyes opening wide like a child's and he felt his heart ache. She was almost childlike, innocent. Michel felt a pang in his heart. Felicia walked over to him, her predatory dark gypsy eyes burning into him.

'Why don't you two go outside?' Isobel said softly. She exuded an air of quiet confidence, as though she was offering him the lure of a sensual paradise, a rapture, but he knew with Felicia he'd be thrown into the fires of hell. He felt as though a dark web of evil was being spun around him.

'No, I am quite happy to mingle,' Michel said, slithering out of the direction of Felicia's glare.

He badly wanted to talk to Isobel, but every time he turned to her, she pushed him over to Felicia, who would flirt with him, then back off. Felicia made it so obvious, she was only playing with him for her amusement. Soon, he realised, that her only real interest was in Rick.

Party moods

Michel felt awkward, not sure how to act around Felicia, thinking it was better to humour her than to get mixed up in anything deep.

He started to make small talk but she was always one step ahead, and quick to put him down. She glanced at him as though she could see right through him. It was clear that Isobel was trying to pair him off with Felicia. He was reluctant in that: whenever he spoke to her she seemed always to catch him out in some way, exert her superiority, even make him look inferior. He guessed correctly that she played this game with all the men she encountered; it was though she dared not be vulnerable in their presence and always had to be the one in control. He had never met anybody quite like her before, and couldn't summon much enthusiasm for her at all. His desire to go there was about as inviting as attending his own funeral. She was incredibly beautiful, but so wild and tempestuous, he would find her exhausting; he preferred his women soft and feminine. Besides, he found her wild, staring eyes and long, black shiny hair quite alarming. He was suspicious of her charms, whereas he did like Isobel. He went over to the bookcase, noticing there were a lot of books on the occult and some with psychological themes. He turned round to see Felicia standing next to him; she reached up and took a book out of the bookcase and stroked it lovingly. It featured a famous surrealist artist, whom Michel had never heard of, but Felicia scanned the pages, absorbed.

'That's an interesting book,' observed Michel.

'She's a very interesting artist,' murmured Felicia. 'A visionary, an independent spirit, a Surrealist.'

'I haven't heard of her who is she?' he asked, intrigued.

'A woman with immense vision, and a very good artist, and a writer, who studied surrealism, the occult, the Kabbalah and belonged to the Golden Order of the Sacred Dawn. She was a very spiritual woman with some wonderful philosophies.'

'Sounds quite fascinating.'

'Yes, she was, and was even thrown out of the British Surrealist movement for being so pre-occupied with the occult, and often created art that was mystical. She wrote some very interesting articles on art and psychotherapy.'

'Perhaps a little too esoteric for her day.'

'Perhaps it was their loss then,' she said sharply.

'Do you enjoy studying the occult? What exactly do you get out of it?'

'Yes I do,' she said, her eyes shining with a mysterious dark power. 'I study it because as with all knowledge, it helps us grow and empowers us and allows us to understand the world around us. I don't think that logical, rational explanation tells very much, except how to operate within a system. What lies outside is far more enriching and expansive and beautiful, the core of genius.'

'Yes, you are right, but isn't it a bit outdated, the occult and witchcraft?' asked Michel.

'No, not at all, the secrets are eternal, timeless and hold infinite power.'

Isobel looked over and winked at him.

'I like to live in the here and now, in the rational world, with common sense.'

'How tedious and boring!' cried Felicia scornfully, looking up at him disdainfully. 'I prefer theories with depth, people with exciting personalities, filled with labyrinths of creativity and ideas. Beyond the usual boundaries of existence, I like playing with ideas.'

'I like simplicity and good friends I can depend on,' he argued, 'country walks followed by a nice barbecue, or a day spent sailing quietly along the river, an afternoon's cricket to the sound of humming bees.'

'Well, each to his own,' she muttered.

They moved in front of a painting by Leonora Carrington, of a woman with a half-skeleton surrounded by dark gothic imagery. 'I love this artist's work, it conveys such an exciting feeling,' said Felicia, 'of intrigue, of darkness.'

'Yes, it's very striking,' Michel admitted, aware of how little they had in common and how differently she saw things. Like Rick, she liked living on the edge of strange, shadowy worlds. He wasn't interested in a relationship based on lust or desire. Isobel was far more on his wavelength, attuned to gentle, easy conversation based on mutual interests. Felicia could be compelling, but he soon grew weary of her—so impassioned about everything, he found her too edgy and avant-garde.

Her dramatic dark eyes bore into him like lasers, a seductive smile slowly crept across her lips. He felt himself weaken but struggled to preserve his resolve, mustering his dignity as he said in a choked voice, 'I can see that you have many talents—music, philosophy… . You are quite accomplished.'

She fluttered her long eyelashes and swept back her long hair back over her shoulders and stared at him, her eyes unblinking. 'I like to think so,' she said coyly. 'But there is someone else who lights your fire,' she said knowingly, running a sharp nail along his cheek.

'I don't know what you mean,' he said backing away. He shivered. She was a captivating woman who set off a spark in him; she spoke knowledgably on many subjects, but he did not share her obsession with the darkness. She was supremely confident, too unpredictable for him. Her slightly defiant attitude made him think that no one could ever tame her, her wild lioness nature was unconfined, she needed to be free to explore and inhabit her own universe, chase her own dreams. If he was truthful he found her a trifle intimidating. No one would ever tame her, he sighed wearily, least of all him. But he had other fish to fry. Isobel. What could he do? She was involved and clearly in love with Rick, but at least he could be her friend. She seemed to need him, and he was content to play that role, simply to stay in her orbit. Yet everything she said resonated with some experience of his own and he knew if she had been single, he would have considered her to be a true soul mate. Silently he watched her; she was smiling, twirling around the guests, her eyes lit up and her voice animated. She was clearly enjoying herself. Michel slipped behind the kitchen door to observe her and found himself wishing he had met her a long time ago.

Isobel went over and stood next to the dark temptress Felicia. They were complete opposites, he mused: the dark and light princess, dark mystery and purity, night and day, the sacred and the profane; a cool maiden duelling with the fiery dark goddess; a cool, calm English rose competing with the hot-blooded tempestuous Spanish singer, wild and frenzied. Fire and ice. Felicia was a witch, a vamp, ready to erupt at the first provocation—a venomous scorpion with a poisonous tail who would chew you up and spit you out when she'd had enough of you, and your charms no longer pleased her. Once she got her claws deep into you, she would play, cat and mouse; a fatal black-hearted temptress who would never let you go. After a man had tasted her nectar he would never be able to leave. She was potent, deadly and addictive, like the sting of sex and death. An addiction.

Felicia placed a glass in his hand, and curled her long claw-like hands around his. He almost jumped, for her hands were like ice.

'Thought you might like a refill,' she said.

'Do you like it here?' asked Isobel, coming over to them, tossing the salad nervously. Michel wondered what had happened to change her mood, for her usual poise was suddenly shaken.

'Yes, it's very relaxing,' he said. 'Can I help you with this?'

'No, no, I'm fine,' she said quickly. 'I just wanted a chat, it's okay, maybe later. Yes, we like it, we moved here two years ago. I wouldn't want to live anywhere else now.'

'Are you hungry?' she asked. 'The food is vegetarian, I hope that's all right.'

'Yes, that's fine,' he replied.

She handed round some small plates filled with black beans and salad.

Michel noticed a growing edginess in Isobel he had not seen before. There was something strange about Rick too—he couldn't quite define what it was, and it puzzled him. Everyone seemed to have hidden depths. Isobel smiled cheerfully, her normal elegance shining as she handed round food, her svelte body gliding gracefully across the room as she went from guest to guest. Her hair fell over her shoulders in a silky curtain. Feminine and bewildered, she looked quite angelic and sweet. She smiled at Rick; he turned and patted her affectionately on the bottom. Michel felt an uncomfortable emotion he could not quite tie down—like a stabbing pain in his chest. Then it occurred to him: he was ripped apart with jealousy.

Rick strummed a few chords on his acoustic guitar, losing himself in the haunting, melodic notes. Everyone wandered into the room to watch Rick play. His fingers slid up and down the frets fast, over the neck, with precision as he created some elaborate classical notes. They sat back, blown away, mesmerised by the haunting, dark music, as his fingers moved faster over the frets. Then he stopped.

'We are touring next week. This will be my last chance to relax for a while,' he said. 'It's going to be a hectic six months.' Rick put down the guitar and joined them at the table.

'I'm sure it will go well,' said Isobel flustered, pouring more wine. 'Here's to the tour and the success of Andromeda.'

Michel raised his glass and looked around the boat, taking in the strange, gothic-Freudian imagery and occult artefacts. He wondered if the interest in the dark paraphernalia was Rick's. It seemed at odds with Isobel's spiritual aura, her personality. He sensed a strange vibe in the room.

'Where are you playing?' he asked Rick.

'In Brighton, then we go to Europe.'

'What kind of music do you play?'

'Dark, ethereal rock-music, this latest tour is called "Spirits of the Night—the fire burns from the darkness within". It has a certain appeal really, for those with dark tastes,' Rick said, opening his manic eyes wider, their strange hypnotic energy making Michel feel odd. 'I doubt you will have heard of us. But if you'd like to come to one of our gigs, I'll get you some free tickets, you might enjoy it,' he drawled, dragging deeply on a joint.

'Yes, I might do that. I don't have a lot on next weekend,' said Michel, taking the joint from him.

Rick turned to Felicia to ask her about her evening class.

'How did the meeting go?'

'Okay,' said Felicia, fiddling with her hair, parting her dark lips sensually. She fixed her mocking gaze on Michel. She tossed back her long black hair over her shoulder. It shone like a raven's wing.

'It's an amazing course, but I'm not so keen on all the written work,' she said, getting up and wandering round the room, watching everybody like a bird of prey. Then, when she was sure she had everybody's attention, she hitched her long skirt up to her knees, revealing legs covered in black fishnet stockings. Her nails ran along them like swords.

Michel coughed awkwardly, his desire stirring in the presence of this gothic temptress. He turned away; he didn't want to get caught up in her games and he knew she enjoyed playing with people. She certainly was very strange. She moved towards him like a dangerous predatory animal, ready to strike, trapping and destroying her prey.

Only for men with a death wish, he thought moving away quickly. He breathed a sigh of relief, and was glad she wasn't his girlfriend. She was making it quite obvious that she had her sights set on Rick, yet was flirting with him as a kind of decoy, to make Rick jealous, to throw Isobel off the scent. Guessing her true motives, Michel looked away to avoid the petulance in her eyes. She threw her head back defiantly.

Turning to Michel she said, 'I am taking a course in the occult and witchcraft. To learn how to prepare for travel into other realms.'

'Fascinating,' he said dryly. 'And what realms are those?'

She scowled at him. 'The other side, the world of spirits.'

'How interesting,' remarked Paula quickly, 'I'd love to take a course like that, learn how to be psychic. Do you need to have inherited psychic ability to study witchcraft?'

'It helps,' admitted Felicia. 'It tends to run in families like clairvoyance. Mine does have psychic powers, and I've inherited psychic ability,' she confessed. 'My aunt was a medium, but in practice, anyone can learn how to do it.'

'So you can use your powers to manipulate your own destiny?' asked Michel, clicking on to her wavelength—he could see where she was coming from, a woman who liked to control everyone around her.

'Something like that,' she replied, her dark eyes flashed dangerously. He had touched a raw nerve.

'And are you psychic?' he asked her.

'Sometimes,' she admitted.

'You use the occult to influence people to your way of thinking?'

'So what, if I do? I am a Scorpio, we like to explore the dark side of things,' she said, gazing at Rick. 'I will stop at nothing to get what I want.'

'Is the "Goddess" class still running?' Rick asked edgily, changing the subject.

'Yes. We have a lecture on "stability zones" tomorrow.'

'What exactly are "stability zones"?'

'Our own place of safety, the strength of our will,' explained Felicia. 'Where we return to re-balance ourselves after we have travelled into other realms, on the astral plane. We may enter a realm where we encounter an energy that may be harmful.' She paused. 'We need to be able to re-balance our own boundaries.'

'We occasionally need to protect ourselves in life,' declared Isobel, prophetically. 'Psychic protection is a useful tool.'

Michel looked over at Isobel, thinking the conversation was getting too crazy. Psychic attacks! Whatever next? Felicia took a morsel of bread from Rick's plate. Her long black talons scraped the crumbs together in a predatory manner, reminding Michel of a bird of prey. She was piqued, but she played with him anyway. That was her style, her forte.

'Tell me more,' asked Michel, joining in. His face lit up excitedly, thinking how much fun it was humouring her, like toying with a dangerous animal at the zoo, but one false move and he'd be mauled to death. She was entertaining, a serious challenge, he thought, more so than any other woman he had ever met. It was easy to walk into the lion's den, he reflected, but not so easy to walk out again.

'I am interested in the dark goddess, of living in harmony with creation, enhancing my female power,' she said pointedly. 'I belong to a group where we explore the darker side of female psyche, the source of creative vision and awakening psychic energy. It exists at the centre of all of us,' she said, putting her fist to her breastbone.

Michel couldn't help wondering if she belonged to a coven.

'Women should celebrate, empower themselves, find their spirituality and live as if totally free.'

'But I thought they did now,' interrupted Michel. 'Women live as equals to men.'

'No sadly, we still live in a society dominated by male rules, but we can fight against it. The old oppressive ways still dominate us,' she added. 'We must be like Lilith who refused to give in to male domination in a patriarchal society. She destroyed those who got in her way without conscience or remorse.'

'Yes, but that's a bit extreme, isn't it?' uttered Rick.

'No, there's no other way. Destroy in order to renew. We can dance to the goddess, celebrate our darker powers and allow our spirit to roam. Soar empowered into the universe, dancing the dance of freedom, without wings,' she said, moving her hands in a dramatic gesture. 'We can all live freely, away from the lies and restraints of society.'

Rick shot her a wary look.

'Gosh, how exciting!' said Michel, completely absorbed. Whatever his personal feelings, Felicia was at least fun.

'Who exactly is the dark goddess?' he asked.

'She is the wild untamed spirit in all of us,' said Felicia, 'a psychic entity, a potent force of creative energy. She is wild, powerful, creative and free. Some say she is the uncivilised part of woman. Men are scared of her power, her dark deep sensuality, yet are drawn to it. She is woman without rules. She fights for change, renewal through destruction. Sometimes she uses dark forces to get what she wants and has a sexual power few men can resist. They are drawn to the wildness, the wilderness of her nature, she's a will unto herself. She can also cast spells just like me,' she said, her eyes flashing dangerously. Michel could see she was warming to her subject and clearly identified with the goddess.

'When we get in touch with the darker side of our nature, we find the spark of creative power within ourselves and empower our lives.'

'Well, we had better watch out that you do not turn me into a frog,' joked Michel, taking some more bread.

Felicia shot him a disdainful glance: 'And I thought you had the intelligence to take it seriously,' she said, shooting him a withering look.

He smiled back as if placating a child, listening spellbound and amused at once, enjoying her enthusiasm, but not taking her too seriously. He enjoyed teasing her. But he was beginning to feel like the joke was on him.

Rick shot him a dark look.

'Yes it's a good theory,' agreed Isobel, 'the freedom of love and creative power is the driving force in a woman. She has the ultimate gift. Women are more in tune with nature and their souls. They endow others with life, they give birth, they can be whatever they wish. Men have a limited experience and do not often develop their higher intuitive qualities so acutely. Although I must confess that using the darker powers doesn't interest me. I don't believe in manipulation. We should only use our creative power for love and personal empowerment.'

'How wonderful,' said Michel, seeing Felicia's seductive gaze aimed at Rick. He turned away.

'The dark goddess has more power,' argued Felicia.

'Only the power of destruction,' retorted Isobel.

'No, of renewal,' insisted Felicia. 'Of making things as they should be, sometimes we have to destroy in order to renew. To put things right,' she said cryptically.

Michel looked at Isobel then Felicia, thinking both goddesses were compelling, the cool, angelic, maidenly goddess and the dark devious one.

Felicia stared at Michel, her eyes narrowing, weighing him up. There was a dangerous glint in her eye. Was he friend or a foe? He could detect a cruelty in her. Her anger seemed directed at him. Her eyes burned with a barely concealed dark desire, and he felt trapped in their glare. Michel looked uneasy in Felicia's Machiavellian presence. Her friendly camaraderie with him was obviously a decoy to annoy Rick and he was starting to pale under Rick's watchful eye. Felicia flirted playfully with Michel, then looked back at Rick, wanting to see a reaction: to her dismay, all she could see was an expression of indifference on his face. Felicia, seeing her charms were not working, turned back to Michel and put her arm through his. She was clearly using him and had no qualms about upsetting Isobel; she was acting like a real bitch, he decided, as she walked over to the mike stand, now trying to get attention. Michel picked up a guitar, and tried to play a few notes from a song. The whole thing sounded confused and discordant. Disheartened, he put the guitar down.

'I'll give you some lessons if you like,' offered Rick, taking the guitar and expertly running his fingers over the frets, creating a melodic sound.

'Okay, thanks.'

Isobel went over to Rick, and put her arm around him. Michel sat down on the other chair, watching the river. The sun was sinking, a great orange ball. Felicia glared out of the window watching the birds dart in and out of the shadows. A tree hung over the boat, its spiky branches tapping the window.

'I have written a new song, it's called "the Dark Moon Goddess",' said Felicia. Her eyes were shining too brightly. 'Would you all like to hear it?'

They all nodded.

She whispered the lyrics—'I am the Dark Moon Goddess, the

demon witch of Moonlight', in an eerie recitation, the swooping lyrics getting louder and louder as she sang with more power. Her eyes turned as dark as coals, her body swayed, she sang the words softly at first, then louder.

> *She shone so darkly in the fiery night,*
> *Her wicked presence disturbing mortal souls,*
> *Dragging them into darkness from the light,*
> *No earthly desire can capture the Dark Moon Goddess,*
> *Rapt in Tantric self-love casting erotic spells,*
> *Ensnaring men in her dark dreams,*
> *She takes them down to the deepest of Hells,*
> *No earthly desire can capture the Dark Moon Goddess,*
> *As she spins her web of illusion,*
> *She tortures their minds until they scream,*
> *No mercy she gives to her victims in confusion,*
> *Forever imprisoned in her dark dream.*

They clapped.
'Brilliant,' said Rick.
Felicia moved sensually, weaving through the musicians.
'I was hoping you would like it. It's a new song about luring men with dark charms and sex and death really. There has to be darkness. Even Michelangelo, Bosch and other famous artists accepted that. Some schools of philosophy recognise the creation and ultimate destruction of the world. That there are cycles of good and bad, it cannot be any other way. Women know that life goes in creative cycles and that we must first destroy in order to renew. It's more fun in Hell, I should imagine,' she joked.
'I don't know about that,' quipped Michel. 'I am not sure that raging fires would inspire me.'
'I like the idea,' said Rick. 'Shall we try it out, see if it works?'
'Must you rehearse now?' Isobel asked Rick, changing the subject. 'I was hoping we could just relax for a while. It's such a nice evening.'

Isobel walked out from behind the speakers like Venus stepping out from her shell, her hair cascading over her body, draped in a white muslin robe that showed a faint outline of her breasts. A row of dimly lit candles glowed brightly behind her. She seemed angelic. She picked up a violin and played a few haunting sad notes: they drifted across the room, catching everyone with their sadness. Felicia, piqued, started dancing. Suddenly images of a gypsy campfire flashed through their minds, nights of magic and passion. Isobel played the violin so fast, in dizzy riffs with sheer hell-stirring passion. Then she stopped and everyone clapped.

'That was amazing,' said Kayla, totally mesmerised. The other guests looked on, spellbound.

'I'm sure our guests won't mind if we have a quick rehearsal before the tour,' said Felicia.

'Yes, I'd like to hear some more music,' piped up Michel.

Felicia turned back from the window, her eyes glinting dangerously. A dark enigmatic expression covered her face.

'Yes, my powers are at their peak,' she said alluringly, 'the best time to sing, I feel very creative.'

'Okay,' said Rick, plugging in his electric guitar. They moved outside into the garden.

Felicia grabbed the microphone, and began singing seductively to the music, swaying sensually, mouthing the words evocatively. She twirled around the microphone, pulling her dress up over her knees, gyrating, hypnotising to her audience. Her wide and powerful eyes flashed dangerously. Everyone sat spellbound watching her twist and twirl as she danced around Rick. She moved like a demoness with wings of fire. 'I like my ideas to take wings,' she said, 'and fly.' She launched into the first chorus of 'Dark Moon Goddess', Rick was playing some flamenco riffs, which grew darker with each chord. Felicia was spinning an illusory web of intrigue around him, the music adding to her aura of mystery. As performers, they were twin souls.

'Did that sound right?' he turned to Felicia, strumming a set of chords.

'It's perfect,' she said. 'Let's try the next track.'

Felicia waited for Rick to do an intro, then danced around the room, agile as a ballerina, her hair flying out behind her. She threw her head back in abandon. Beads of perspiration dripped over her breasts and she lowered the neckline of her dress. Rick played faster, his haunting notes eerily capturing everyone's attention, hypnotising them as they moved in total synchronicity. Michel drew in his breath, reminded of the poem 'To a Gitana dancing', a poem written for a wild gypsy woman:

You dance, and I know the desire of all flesh, and the pain
Of all longing of body for body you beckon, repel
Retreat, and entice and bewilder, and build up the spell.

A witch of desire, a wild feral gypsy, her dark eyes blazed like lasers—an outstandingly beautiful creature, weaver of feral music and devil sorcery; Paganini's muse, his devil nymph-child. Stuart, one of the other guests, stood up and started playing the violin, creating eerie, haunting notes that swept them all away, playing havoc with their emotions, taking them on a journey from the highest ecstasy to the deepest despair. They were spellbound. Felicia pointed her finger at them, as though conveying a warning. She sang in a voice that rose from the sweetest notes to the darkest depths. Her voice rose in a soft sweet tone, then dipped crazily into a raw-edged rasp. She lifted her skirts and stamped her feet, like a wild gypsy flamenco dancer.

Michel stood with his arms crossed, unable to move, the sight overwhelming him. Felicia swayed like a wild feral woman, making each note more dark and disturbing than the last, flicking back her mane of dark raven black hair like an unruly mare. Her eyes shone brightly with a wild, wicked energy. Isobel's acquiescence had been due to her good grace, but inside Michel could see that she was in turmoil. Felicia danced like a goddess; she knew she had captured the attention of everyone, and enjoyed mesmerising them. They were all her playthings, in her dark dusky court. She swayed rhythmically merging with the music, like a fiery Spanish dancer, uninhibited, sensual. Her long, raven-black hair flew out like a bird's wing as she tapped her feet. Isobel watched from the shadows, her arm around the back of the chair. Rick stopped playing, strangely disturbed by Felicia's dancing; it set off something wild in him. His eyes were glazed, and stared blankly as though he was in a trance. Isobel saw, and looked at him in dismay: nothing could ever break the spell Felicia had over Rick. Not even her. She went over to him and smiled a weak smile.

A strange magnetism, a force, an aura flowed between Felicia and Rick, as her sweet voice dipped and rose in time with his guitar, and began emanating some disturbing sounds. She held Rick's gaze in her hypnotic power, his eyes flickering, unable to draw his gaze away. Then the power was exchanged and he was back in control. He led her performance, like a ring master, and, Michel suspected, off-stage too. Then she flared into life like a vibrant flame. She swirled around Rick, like a rampant she-devil, a Circe who loved tempting him, enchanting him, playing with his emotions, enticing him sexually. While he sat there bemused, his waves of black hair fell over his face, concealing his expression. He put down the acoustic, picked up his electric guitar and tore into a set of chords—crashing, zapping chords, a hot electric vibe, entrancing, enthralling his guests with some heady refrain, tearing and slashing the notes with a vengeance. Felicia took control of the room mesmerising them with her ethereal vocal tones. Her dancing grew wilder, frenzied, reaching a crescendo; Rick's guitar swooped into a new set of chords to reach a shattering climax. She belted out a jagged-edge chorus that flowed into an ethereal haze of gentle lyrics.

Everyone felt lifted and twisted by the roller coaster of her voice. Rick's eyes swivelled to follow her, his attention rapt, his eyes glowing with a sombre energy, clearly spellbound. He dived back to a set of gentle chords, picked quietly on the chords on his guitar while playing a long instrumental piece; intoxicated, spellbound and lifted to another universe, the music became propelled by a magical force, driving him with a will of its own.

'I'll just get some drinks, I have invented some new cocktails,' said Isobel slipping off to the kitchen looking flustered She came back with a tray of various coloured drinks and handed them round.

Felicia placed a garland of black flowers around her hair and swirled faster and faster like a gypsy, a dervish pagan witch circling Rick, in gay abandon; free, her eyes lit with a wild passion.

They all watched her intently, sharing her rapture. Everyone applauded loudly, except Isobel who scowled. She slammed the drinks on the table, and picked up the dirty dishes. Michel followed Isobel into the kitchen.

'I'll help you with that,' offered Michel.

'No, it's okay, just enjoy the music.'

'What do you know about Felicia? Who exactly is she?' asked Michel, making conversation.

'Do you like her?' said Isobel, smiling.

He shook his head, 'No, not in that way but she is fascinating.'

Isobel's face dropped, she smiled to hide her disappointment.

'I was hoping you might find you had mutual interests, a spark between you.'

'No, she's the most unlikely partner for me,' he admitted.

Michel suddenly saw the situation with startling clarity and knew his suspicions were right. He was there as a decoy. Isobel had invited him to pair off with Felicia. Not realising she was with Rick, he had hoped it was because she liked him. Now his hopes were clearly dashed.

'Is that why you asked me here? To pair me off with Felicia?'

'Yes, I'm sorry. I thought perhaps maybe you would like her. She is very beautiful.'

'Not to me,' replied Michel, looking deeply into her eyes.

'Oh,' said Isobel awkwardly. 'Look, I ought to get back to the guests.'

'No, I'm sorry,' he excused himself. 'Too much wine.'

'I hope you are not annoyed,' she whispered, opening her blue eyes; they were wide and innocent, like a child's.

'No,' he smiled, touched. 'I do understand.'

'Well, to answer your question,' she said, staying to do the washing up. 'She is the daughter of a famous artist, and a diplomat. She was expelled from every school she went to in France, has Spanish-Latin ancestry, is a brilliant artist too, but studied music, has the worst rebellious streak I have ever known. Is a living force who always likes to get her own way and a real pain.'

'And what about you, Isobel, what is your background?'

'My family were in medicine,' she said. 'I grew up in Suffolk, then I taught English and art to undergraduates at Sussex University.'

'My sister is a GP,' he said, 'and I studied at Brighton, so we have a bond.' He laughed.

'Looks that way.' She laughed too.

Outside in the main room the music grew softer, Rick started to play slower.

'Let's go inside and listen,' said Isobel, leading him back into the lounge.

'Don't stop, I feel so full of energy, play some more,' Felicia begged Rick, her face glowing with triumph. She took another tequila and slugged it back. 'I'm in a wild, passionate mood!' she exclaimed.

'Time to stop,' said Rick, his eyes glazed, 'or our guests will get tired. They have listened to enough. I'm sure they would like to relax by the river.'

Isobel laughed edgily. She was getting tipsy from too much wine, wisps of her hair had fallen out of her headband, and were cascading around her shoulders making her look a little wild. Michel thought she looked slightly drunk, but even more beautiful. Her bright eyes were glazed and she looked like a lost child. Yet she still moved with perfect ease and grace.

'They do a stage act together,' she started to explain to him.

'Felicia portrays the goddess Freya, dancing for the seasons. A very passionate role.'

'Yes, it was breathtaking,' Michel admitted. He smiled, noticing Isobel's sadness, unable to hide his suspicions about Felicia's and Rick's relationship. A growing tension hung in the room. Isobel snapped at Felicia. Rick, clearly frustrated, and caught in the middle, took Isobel outside, away from the dark, hot-blooded gypsy Felicia—the untamed temptress, destroyer of homes, bringer of chaos and wild, dark desires. Wicked, unpredictable, predatory. A dangerous and malevolent woman. Rick kissed the gentle, cultured Isobel, civilised, of higher, almost courtly values. He caressed the demure Isobel, the angel, and went into the kitchen to finish the washing up. Felicia watched them enviously. Isobel glanced back. For a moment their eyes met. There was pure rivalry between them. Then, Rick put on some soft music and the room was filled with a gentle tempo, the emotional storms conjured up by the evening's performance dispersed and everyone relaxed. Michel turned to Isobel, instantly diffusing the situation.

'When are you driving to Brighton?' Michel asked, changing the subject, eager to know more about Isobel's plans.

'Next Saturday,' said Rick. 'We need some time to set up and rehearse. Perhaps you could drive Isobel down?'

He asked Isobel if she was going.

'Yes, after I have finished my artwork.'

'I can take you next weekend,' offered Michel. 'I'm not busy.'

'Next weekend then, thanks.'

Felicia stared at Michel, about to say something, then stopped, her eyes moved restlessly from Isobel to Rick. Michel was trapped in their glare. He sensed somehow he had thwarted her plans. She looked at Michel, simmering with rage.

Her eyes widened, then she shrugged and looked away. She was so beautiful, but a temptress, with a cold heart, and clearly a woman with no scruples—Circe, Lilith; enigmatic, mysterious and dangerous, these were traits he usually found attractive in women, but on this occasion made him recoil. Her dark, shimmering eyes slanted and narrowed; she looked lethal and moody. Michel shivered: if he went too close, she would tear him apart. She was used to getting whatever she wanted, at any cost. He wasn't in the habit of letting his animal instincts take over—he had done that once before and regretted it. He preferred Isobel's sophisticated elegance, her gentle mystical and mysterious aura, to the predatory energy of Felicia. He felt he could trust Isobel. Felicia, he could see, was a very different story.

He wondered what it would be like to make love to them. He had to admit they were both very powerful women. Felicia was toxic. Isobel, on the other hand, was like the wing of a dove, sensitive, caring and gentle. Being in Felicia's presence was like being devoured by a serpent.

Michel smiled at Isobel. He looked forward to the coming weekend, when he could speak to her alone. He liked her a lot after spending the evening with her, and wanted to get to know her even more. She untied her hair, letting it flow all over her shoulders like a cascading waterfall. He drew in his breath: never before had he seen such a vision of ethereal beauty. Reluctantly he had to admit she would never be his, a pang of unrequited love pierced his heart.

Rick picked up an acoustic guitar and strummed some chords. Isobel poured out some Irish coffee to the gentle strains of classical music. Felicia turned, scowling out of the window. Isobel sat staring into space. The other guests sat in a soporific post-dinner haze, musing on the quality of the whisky. All that could be heard was a glass being put on the table. The swish of oars mingled with the delicate notes. Michel's fading attention was captured by the bright boats sailing by. He looked outside; it was growing dark, there was a heaviness in the air.

'I think there is going to be another storm,' commented Isobel, getting up to pull the curtains. Michel agreed. The air was stifling. A black cloud moved over the boat, obscuring the moon.

'Thank you for coming,' she said.

'See you next weekend, then,' said Michel, thinking how sad she looked.

As Felicia left the room, the black cloud lifted and the moon shone through the grey wispy clouds.

Later that night, Michel reflected on the evening; he felt a growing love for Isobel, despite the fact she was involved with someone else. His instincts were telling him something was about to happen. He turned over the tarot cards Isobel had lent him. It was of the Tower, change, rebirth, then death and finally one of the lovers. He felt sure that something was about to happen, and that one day Isobel would be his. Was she his destiny?

Dark Dreams

Isobel walked back along the canal. Groups of larger boats drifted noiselessly up the river. It was unbearably hot, and she needed to cool off and head for the shade. There was going to be another storm, she was sure. She peered through a bush and saw Felicia talking to Rick; he was picking at a leaf nervously, they were arguing. Felicia glared at him angrily.

Isobel, unable to hear what they were saying, climbed onto the bank to get closer.

Rick shifted restlessly like a caged bird, a worried expression etched across his face: 'But Felicia,' he was saying, 'just listen for a moment,' then his voice trailed off. Isobel strained but could not hear any more; she slipped and, as she fell, she grabbed onto a branch. Rick and Felicia turned round, then went back to their conversation. Isobel crouched in the bushes, peeking through some stray branches and held her breath.

Rick's dark expressionless eyes were heavy and he was tired; he looked torn. His red-rimmed gaze was heavy. He looked like he was living too close to the edge. Maybe Isobel was just imagining things, but her intuition was crying out and it was usually right. Felicia was playing games with him, trying to get him back. Tantalising and seductive, she was spinning her web around him. Isobel looked down at the water, Felicia was rubbing Rick's arm. Isobel nearly fell out of the bush, anger rising in her. How dare she touch him! Shadows moved edgily on the river, there was a strange reflection of the light. Isobel chided herself for seeing motives in every conversation he had with Felicia, annoyed at herself for being so paranoid. Felicia threw Rick a dark look. He scowled, pulling off the edges of a leaf. He fiddled with it, then threw it down and walked away. Isobel could not hear any more, their voices were muffled by the sound of a boat passing by, but clearly they were arguing. She climbed into the bushes to get closer, but still couldn't hear what they were saying. As Felicia turned towards the rustling in the bushes Isobel gently backed into the foliage and then went back to the boat.

Isobel sat down cross-legged and started doing yoga, fighting to keep her anger under control; then she sorted through her paintings to sell to the local gallery. She was particularly fond of the one of *Meadow Flowers*, pleased she had captured the expression on the maidens' faces and rich nuances of colour in the *Summer Fayre* paintings which managed to convey their enchantment. She knew she had their ability to conjure up magic and mysticism in her art, for those who wandered into her domain, entrancing them with her magical talent. Yet at the same time they were saleable, and that really was the point at this stage. She stared wistfully at the clouds, listening to the gentle waves rippling on the canal, but something was wrong, and her heart was heavy.

The next morning, Felicia bounded in.

'Hope you don't mind,' she said curtly, 'I've come to collect my guitar.'

She wore a black t-shirt with the words 'that which nourishes me also destroys me' over black tight jeans, and her long pony tail was tied up high so that it trailed over her shoulders like a horse's mane. Her Amazonian body and large breasts made her look powerful.

'It seems Rick forgot to bring my guitar to rehearsals last night, so I had to leave early, what a bloody waste of time.'

Isobel felt a twinge of annoyance at the thought of Felicia spending so many hours alone with Rick and was about to say something, like 'Find it yourself' but refrained, and, wordlessly, handed her the guitar.

'Thanks. Is something wrong?' asked Felicia. 'You seem a bit edgy today, are you pre-menstrual?'

Isobel wanted to slap her, to say, 'Yes, you're a pain, Felicia, get out of my life,' but stopped. Instead, she took a long look at Felicia and realised she would only win if she kept cool.

'No, it's just that we had a late night. We've been so busy, we hope to have a romantic weekend away soon.'

'Well,' retorted Felicia, a glint in her eye, 'don't keep Rick away for too long, he's got a tour coming up,' she said triumphantly.

'We will do as we please, the band is not his life,' snapped Isobel.

'Well Rick seems to think it is,' said Felicia petulantly.

'And I think it's none of your business,' she said, slamming a plate down on the sink.

Isobel fought to get a grip on herself, she knew she had to keep her cool. She found Felicia's presence unsettling, but she couldn't let it show, or Felicia would enjoy provoking her even more and she refused to rise to the bait. Perpetually troubling, she always wore t-shirts covered with some outrageous attention-seeking caption, last time it said 'bitch, whore, vamp-fuck'. She hated to admit it, but Felicia looked more beautiful than ever with her large eyes, olive skin and the longest legs she had ever seen. And she moved with the grace of a Spanish gypsy. Isobel gritted her teeth, trying to be polite. What was it about Felicia that irritated her so much? Why did she make her want to lose control and rip her hair out? Was it because of the natural rivalry between them? Or that she had once been Rick's lover? Or because she always tried to upstage her. Isobel treated her in turn like a recalcitrant child. Felicia acting rebelliously, lit up a cigarette.

'I'd rather you didn't smoke in here,' said Isobel. 'We've given up. Can you please go out onto the balcony?'

'Rick was smoking too much last night,' Felicia said, puzzled, ignoring the request. 'Far too much, I thought. You're making him happy, aren't you, Isobel?' she asked pointedly.

'We are certainly happy, and if we weren't, it would be none of your bloody business,' snapped Isobel irritably.

'Well, he is my good friend too.'

Slighted, Felicia opened the window to conceal her annoyance. She shot Isobel a dark moody look, fiddled with the cigarette, then, like a gauche teenager, leaned back indifferently against the wall in a manner of sophisticated poise, her eyes swivelling around the room as though she was looking for someone. Her eyes narrowed; she was about to stub the cigarette out under her foot and kick it out onto the balcony when Isobel took it from her mouth and threw it out of the door.

'In future, please do use an ashtray,' demanded Isobel, her eyes blazing. How she wanted to kick her. 'As you can see, Rick is not here and I am very busy.'

'You don't like me, do you?' Felicia asked, sulkily.

'Whatever gave you that idea?' snapped Isobel.

'It's okay, I don't really care what you think, I just wanted to speak to Rick. Let him know I called.'

'And Felicia,' Isobel almost spat, 'don't worry about us all the time, find your own man, get a life.'

Felicia threw back her hair like a horse ready to bolt and stared at Isobel with contempt, then closed her eyes and bit her lip; she was about to say something, then stopped.

'Isobel,' she stated dramatically, 'I nearly forgot. I am so rushed and Rick must have forgotten, can you give this to him?' She handed her some lyric sheets. 'It's the lyrics we worked on together.'

Isobel glanced at them, the words of the song called 'Never can forget your smile' jumped out at her. 'Rick won't be back until late. I suggest you phone in future.'

Isobel took them roughly and was about to say she was going out, when Felicia piped up, 'Okay, I've got to go, just let Rick know that I'll be at rehearsals tonight.'

She slung her bag over her shoulder, picked up her guitar and walked out, slamming the door behind her. The boat rocked. Isobel breathed a sigh of relief, feeling incensed as she thought of Rick and Felicia spending an evening together. How she would love to push her in the canal. Was there still anything between them?

An hour later, Rick strode in with his guitar slung over his shoulder, his hair tied back in a pony-tail. His eyes were red and tired from rehearsing all night. Isobel's heart lurched into her mouth, and her pulse quickened at the sight of him. How badly she wanted to hold him, and make love to him. How badly she wanted him, whatever time of day it was. But her anger overtook her passion after seeing him with Felicia. He looked so gaunt and tired, yet still amazingly attractive and boyish. Anger and doubt flooded her, and so many questions, but, sensing defeat, she just turned round and made a cup of tea. She bit her lip as she tried to stop herself asking him the troubling questions that had burned in her mind all day.

'Is there still anything going on between you and Felicia? Do you still love her?' she asked, afraid of what the answer might be.

'No, of course not,' said Rick, looking up in surprise. 'We were finished a long time ago, there is nothing between us now. Why do you ask?'

'I have had some strange dreams lately, the same one every night, about you with Felicia. Oh Rick, please don't go on a tour with her.'

Rick shot her an angry look, and seemed annoyed. 'For Christ's sake, don't be so ridiculous, Isobel, I have to go on tour with her, I have no choice, it's my work, you must trust me. Felicia is the driving force of the band, she creates our special sound, our image and is a brilliant classical musician as well as a singer. But that's as far as it goes, it's purely professional. She's just someone I work with, the romance part was over a long time ago. She means nothing to me now.'

'But I can't help worrying,' said Isobel, 'that these dreams might be some kind of premonition, a warning.'

'Why do you choose now to bring this up? It's becoming an obsession. Can't you see I am busy rehearsing? I don't want to be bothered with this right now. You say this is all due to a dream? You are worried about a dream? Dreams are just unconscious fears or unfulfilled wishes. If you must go to clairvoyants all the time, what do you expect? They fill your head with strange ideas and paranoia. You must trust me.'

'No it isn't that, they are not to blame,' said Isobel, shaking her head. 'It's just the way Felicia acts around you, like she hasn't let go. She seems to think she has a kind of power over you. What were you talking about on the canal?'

'We were just discussing what time to start rehearsals. None of us can agree about practice times, or make it at the same time,' he said, annoyed.

'You looked as if it was something important.'

'For fuck's sake Isobel, why should I lie to you?' he said, his face tightening angrily. 'Can't I get some peace?'

'Then why do you keep looking at her?' said Isobel, unable to stop herself. 'Like you still have feelings for her. Please stay in tonight.'

'Look, Isobel, you are just imagining things. I don't look at her at all. I haven't slept for the last few days,' he said, irritably. 'Rob and I have worked all hours trying to get the sound check right. I'm getting really fed up with your questions about Felicia, it was over a long time ago. There's nothing between us. I have to go tonight.'

He picked up his guitar and strummed it loudly, Isobel jumped.

'What do I have to do to prove it?'

'I'm sorry,' said Isobel, 'I feel so anxious, it must be my hormones.'

Rick jumped up, and threw his guitar down, trying to control his temper. 'I'm never going to get this bloody band ready in time. Do you have something urgent to say? Because if not I need to go and rehearse.' He slammed down a music sheet, scattering notes all over the floor.

Isobel sat sighing wistfully. She sat under the light of the window, feeling crushed. Why wouldn't Rick just listen, before it was too late? Her thoughts were swirling crazily: what was wrong with her? Her fears were just pushing Rick further away. She shivered, and gazed up as a black cloud drifted past, casting a shadow. Droplets of rain splashed on the window, running in rivers like her tears. She fell back, resigned. Why wouldn't Rick talk to her any more? He was always so busy. She fell into a dream; strange dreams kept her awake, and she had not slept properly for weeks. She knew Felicia was trying to come between them, but Rick couldn't see it, or maybe he could, and liked the idea of the woman pursuing him? He seemed to have lost the connection with herself, and now they kept arguing. The wind was whispering ominously outside. Still annoyed, she put the flowers that Rick had given her in a vase; she pricked her finger, blood ran onto the white silk.

The storm raged across the canal, lightning flashed over the water, lighting up the sky. Wisps of white light forked behind the boat. Isobel felt a strange mood overtake her as she grew more and more uneasy. Watching the storm, a sense of foreboding crept over her. She was scared, but of what? She had nothing tangible to go on; Rick was right, she was acting hysterically. He saw it as madness. She would have to stop voicing her insecurities as it would drive them apart. Last night she had dreamed she had been sailing around the ocean, Rick was tied to some rocks on an island, she could not get to him. As she sailed past, the stormy weather threw her about on the choppy sea. She looked on powerlessly, but could not rescue him, struggling against the currents as a bird lunged into him. Maidens of death danced around him, seducing him, laughing at her. Felicia stood over him, kissing his neck. What was happening to her? Was she losing her mind?

Rick came back in and seemed preoccupied. Was there a part of him that was growing away from her? Was she losing him? A distance was growing between them, a chasm. However much she tried to talk to him, she made him angry with her stupid fears. They had been so close, now he seemed to be irritable and detached. It must just be the rehearsals, he was a driving perfectionist and worked hard to get things right. She could see what Felicia was up to, why couldn't he? Re-forming the band. Was it really the band she wanted? Or Rick?

He left the room with his guitar, his face crumpled in concentration.

Was there a part of him that she didn't really know? Did he keep secrets from her? Did rehearsing at the studio re-awaken the desire they had for each other? The dreams came again, swirling from the depths of her unconscious into her troubled mind, shimmering landscapes that showed Rick walking into a dark tunnel and never coming back. She was sure they were a warning, telling her that something was wrong. Her instincts were always correct. In her dream, she had lost him as he drifted out to sea in a storm. She called out for him, running through a cave, when she reached the end, he had gone.

The next night she dreamed she was swimming through a tunnel into the sea. Ethereal lights hung from the ceiling, beaming light onto gossamer spiders' webs, interwoven with sparkling stars, never had she seen such beauty. As she reached up to touch them, a spider appeared, and began pulling her into its web, devouring her, ripping the flesh from her, eating her alive. The strange imagery in her dreams was becoming more sinister, she was afraid she was going mad. Freudian, dark shadowy figures and silhouettes of Felicia crept into all her dreams. Was Felicia haunting her?

Something odd was happening to their relationship. It was changing. A web of uncertainty was being spun. She turned over the tarot cards, the first one was the Tower, destruction and change, the second was of Death. She knew change was ahead.

'We always need to protect ourselves,' she thought, her intuition crying out a warning, 'but from what?'

Shadows

The next night Rick walked in and handed Isobel a bottle of wine and some flowers; he was in a good mood and full of apologies.

'I am so sorry, darling, I do love you so much,' he said softly. 'I get so bad tempered when I rehearse. I've just been so fed up that no one can get it together—I have to keep asking them to play the same thing over and over again. It drives me mad. We're not making any progress and the tour's any day soon.' Isobel pushed the hair back from his face, and gently kissed his cheek. How she loved him. Carefully, she poured out the wine, and handed him a glass; he took it from her, then cradled her head in his hand. Rick began massaging her body with salts and oils, her body sculpting itself to his loving hands. How she loved him, and so wanted his child, a living part of him. She knew how much Rick needed solitude when he was working. Usually he was the most gentlemanly mild-mannered man she knew. Yet, before a tour, he turned into a demon. The gentle caring Rick was back, and she cradled him in her arms. Gently he rolled her over and made love to her.

'I love you,' he whispered, caressing her face and smothering it with kisses. 'Don't ever forget that.'

'I love you too,' she said, the contentment flowing back into her, her eyes radiating love.

She fell into an easy sleep, dreaming that Rick was making love to her. She felt his warm embrace, his tongue caressing between her thighs, and realised she had never loved anyone like this before.

Then he woke up: 'Remind me, I have to collect Felicia and Rob at ten tomorrow,' he said.

The words brought her euphoric mood crashing down, and she hit the pits of despair once again. 'Oh, go back to sleep, Rick,' she said, dismayed.

Thoughts swirled around her head like a whirlwind. The reality of the tour made her fears erupt like a volcano, her emotions twisted and turned, rising and falling. She was on a roller coaster, swirling through life like a storm, her control gone. Rick lay motionless next to her. She liked him like this, without conflict. Suddenly she was disturbed by the howling wind. The canal looked so eerie. She fought back a choking feeling, turned on the light, picked up a book and started reading, afraid to go back to sleep again.

Felicia

Felicia held the empowering fluid over the flame; she took a deep breath and inhaled its aroma, feeling its strength flow into her.

'Release my spirit and join it to the forces of dark power. Take my blood and ignite my dark goddess, show me the darkness, your divine spirit and join us as one. Feed my power!' incanted Felicia. 'And take me into the night. For eternity and earthly harmony. Damn you, Isobel, get out of Rick's life. Leave us alone. I will get him back, away from you, whatever I have to do.'

Yes, her spells were working! Isobel was in a panic, becoming unsure, and was driving Rick away with her insecurities. Rick hated women who made too many demands. If she made Isobel act strangely, drove her mad, he might give her up. She would mend the broken circle of their love and destroy the circle he had formed with Isobel. She incanted the spell of the winter witch, directing her dark, demonic, psychic power at Isobel, trying to frighten her and bring Rick back to her. She began chanting the spell, evoking the Dark Goddess:

'Give me the power of your endless night, cover me with your raven's wing and the shadowy secrets of the abyss!' she chanted, blowing out the flame, feeling the energy flow into her. Rick had been her love and would be again. Yesterday, she had declared she still loved him, he had said he didn't feel the same, that he loved Isobel. He had made an excuse and left. But soon that would change—with the power of darkness, she would regain his love and banish the hateful Isobel. She had never stopped loving him: she twisted her hands in frustration and pain. He had resisted her charms so far, fuelling her obsession and wrath. But not any more, soon he would be helpless to resist her charms, and would come crawling back to her.

She thought back to the time when she had first encountered the dark goddess, how she'd guided her. She wrote a letter to Rick, to tell him of it, maybe he would read it, and listen.

'At that moment, I beheld the full moon rising from the sea, gleaming with a special brightness. The first watch of night,' she whispered.

'In my isolation that shadowy night, I became aware of the supreme Goddess, the Dark Goddess. Scarcely had I closed my eyes when the divine figure rose from the sea, her hair hung down gradually curling as it spread loosely and flowed gently over her divine neck. What riveted my eyes was her jet-black cloak, her raven hair and her dark eyes. She spoke to me: "You are a goddess, like me, you have fire in your blood and veins." From this moment I was strong, empowered with infinite wisdom of the ages, of the darkness. Felicia the goddess.'

The powers of night would bring him back. Like goddesses of the sea, she would cook up a storm in Isobel's fragile mind and heart, clouds of billowing smoke would be seen, the king of serpents would writhe in Isobel, bring her torment, bring back her love. She would make Isobel suffer, as she had suffered. The poor genteel Isobel would be out of her mind, crying for mercy.

Her thoughts turned to Rick. Anger rose in her that he no longer had any time for her. Things were going to change. Lilith would soon return to her rightful place in Eden, and reign once more. She had to get rid of the good, nice, virtuous Isobel, first, rip her heart to shreds—she was not a faint-hearted woman, but a vixen, a sorceress. She would destroy anyone who got in her way. Lilith was the goddess Felicia admired, a succubus who haunted men's dreams at night, seduced them, sucking their blood, and taking them into her cave. 'Screech owl' was the goddess of rage and abortion, chaos and disorder who left Adam and the Garden of Eden, rather than suffer the indignity of being beneath a man during intercourse, so she copulated with demons, or so the myth went. Rick said she was too demanding, controlling, dominant, like Lilith, but she was just a strong creative woman, too powerful and wilful for many men. She loved and adored her man and would fight to get him back, whatever she had to do, however far she had to go. She smirked wickedly as she chanted his name.

She used the candle to focus her energy, looking into its flame—she could see Isobel if she travelled through the psychic realm. Today she could see Isobel on the boat, cooking. She blew at her; it worked. Isobel shifted uneasily. Felicia laughed—her plan to haunt Isobel was a success, filling her tormentor with power. She attacked Isobel, biting her. Isobel jumped, scratching her arm for midges. At night she filled her with unfaithful images of her lover, so that she would no longer trust him, until she would become insane. Her victim's suspicions would drive her and Rick apart—a self-fulfilling prophecy, and he would run straight back into Felicia's arms.

She looked back into the aura of the candle and saw Isobel wandering alone across the bank. Felicia used her astral power to go there in spirit form. She sat in the room watching her, moving things. Isobel jumped as Felicia brushed past her, aware of something strange happening around her. Felicia began torturing her mind, sending her crazy uncertainties until her victim would be ready to scream for merciful release. Last night, she invaded her dreams, torturing her with disturbing images of Rick and herself making love. Now she would scare her away, make her think they were having an affair, destroy her happiness.

She moved close to Isobel. Isobel jumped, terrified as she felt a cold wet clammy hand touch her. Felicia laughed; Isobel looked around but could not see anyone. Soon Rick would be hers. She laughed mirthlessly at Isobel's look of sheer terror as she ran out of the houseboat.

'I'll haunt you, I'll haunt you, until you are insane, Isobel!' she laughed mercilessly. Her plan had worked, better than she had imagined, yet the best was yet to come. Felicia drew a circle with their names on it: hers—Scorpio, Michel—Libra, Rick—Aries and Isobel—Libra. Yes, she knew what she would do, ready for her pièce de resistance. She stared deeply into the flame, so yes, her spells were working! A look of triumph crossed her face. She could see them walking along the canal.

She waited until she could see Rick walking alone along the canal. Damn, he had his arm around Isobel, but, ah, they were arguing! Felicia smiled triumphantly; her plan was working, she had disturbed Isobel and now she could easily work her magic on him. She sent out an extra-powerful thought wave, making Isobel feel afraid. Isobel looked agitated and started to cry. Rick stormed angrily back onto the boat. Felicia sent more psycho-magnetic thought waves to Isobel, and made her take a trip away from Rick. He had fallen for her story about re-forming the group, it had just been a ploy to get close to Rick again, to work with him so that she could be with him. All she had to do now was ensnare him. That should be easy enough. She blew out the candle. She had all the knowledge and power she needed now. She could handle the situation and wanted to feel the bliss that only he could give her again. She took out the photograph of them together. He had taught her to play music. One day, when they were playing the harp, his arms wrapped around her, he accidentally touched her thigh. She felt a flash of desire at the rhythm of his body moving against hers, in time to the intoxicating notes. She turned and kissed him. He lifted her dress, gently parting her thighs, then undid his jeans and seduced her on the music-room floor. He had been her first lover. In Ancient Greece it was thought that teacher and pupil should be in love with one another. A passionate affair with their tutor was part of their education. That night she had slept with his hair wrapped around her, pierced by the arrows of love.

They had spent every day and night locked in each other's arms, making love to the sound and rhythm of the music, while she learned the art of love from him. They played in different universities and clubs every weekend, with their band, Dark Nights, then, in the early hours, crept back into their four-poster bed, happy and stoned, making love till the early hours of the morning. It was fun, waking up in a different hotel, playing in different towns, doing as they pleased without caring. A non-stop adventure.

He moved away to start a career, teaching music, so they had enough money to settle down. But as they grew apart so she seemed to fade in his mind. One dark and miserable day she received a letter to say he had met someone else, Isobel, an artist at the university. Her life fell apart. She had smashed the guitar he had left with her to pieces, and had sworn revenge on Isobel. Her mind twisted and turned in pain and torment, she had begged and pleaded, but in the end it was hopeless, he told her emphatically, it was the end. He hoped they could still be friends. She had stormed out of his flat, and swore to get him back, whatever she had to do. At night, she would play the delicately haunting chords he had taught her, their sad notes echoing the shadows of their love. She remembered his soft caresses, his embraces as he made love to her, crying for him, wailing like a banshee. Unable to forget him, she thrust the flute inside her, fantasising it was him, pushing it deeper, crying out in orgasm as tears ran over her face. She dreamed of him almost every night, waiting for him, but he did not return.

The happy days turned darker as she wept for him, gloom hovered over her like a black cloud. Growing sadder, she became obsessed with thoughts of getting him back, thoughts that were ever darker. A fury welled up inside her, as she planned revenge. She stayed at home, becoming a recluse, until she was half sick of the shadows of her life. She picked herself up and forced herself to finish her music degree, if only to stop the loneliness that gripped her in its ever-blackening tentacles. She had to fill the void. In the dark hours, she came up with an idea and began implementing a plan. She phoned Rob, he had agreed to re-form the band, and to say it was his idea. She followed Rick as he left his house, fighting the desire to speak to him, watching him from behind the bushes. Her heart lurched into her mouth as she yearned for his touch. She placed her hands between her legs, imagining him inside her, the ecstasy he had given her. She dug the thorns of a rosebush into her thigh, feeling him, the pleasure and pain bringing her to a shuddering climax. But the happiness she felt lasted only a few seconds. She just had to find some way of getting him back.

One day, her prayers were answered. She found she had an unusual talent, a gift of psychic sight. Her aunt, a medium, had died and left her with a substantial inheritance and the power of a witch. She discovered she too was a witch, with the ability to astro-travel, and she had immense power. She had once been helpless to get him back, now it was different. She possessed a power very few people had, but would not use it wisely.

Her pain spiralled out of control, making her more vengeful, wanting to hurt him as much as he had hurt her. He would pay for his betrayal. Her mood was black and angry, she wept with sadness. Whatever she had to do, she would get him back, away from the smug, superior Isobel. They had made a pact in blood, cut their wrists and joined together in a blood rite. He had sworn he would never leave her.

'The phoenix always rises from the ashes,' she said, prophetically, 'and when she does, she regains his love. The Dark Goddess would get him back.'

Twirling round the room, she took a photograph of Isobel and Rick, tore it into pieces, stabbing the picture of her with a knife. She laughed defiantly, stomping, until her feet bled, the dance of the Dark Goddess, her long black hair flowing out over her cobweb dress. She slipped on lacy black gloves and applied dark make-up; it was the persona she liked best, a gothic temptress, a dark angel of the night. She put on some black stockings and a g-string. She prepared to travel to him, on the astral plane, and make love to him like she used to, a succubus.

She started to chant:

'Work like you don't need the money,
Love like you've never been hurt,
Dance like there's nobody watching,
Fuck like you never will again.
And destroy those who get in your way,
Especially in the way of your dreams.
Do as thou wilt shall be the whole of the law.'

She whispered to herself, preparing her ritual. A triumphant smile spreading across her face.

Isobel sat alone in the boat. She shivered, as an icy cold wind blew over her. She was sure something was touching her. Was she going mad? Was she being followed?

Rick

Rick tried with difficulty to concentrate on his music. His mind was out of focus and nothing rhymed today. Tiredness crept over him—from too many late nights rehearsing, he thought wearily—trying to create a new set of chords, and failing. He had lost his creativity, his focus, the thread and he couldn't make anything work. What he had feared happening, losing his creativity, was now consuming him. He was anxiously trying to finish the final touches to his new song 'Angels and Devils', about the different sides of women. A woman's heart was a deep ocean of secrets; he could never quite fathom them out. It had been a mistake agreeing to work with Felicia again. She charged him with an eroticism he could never quite get out of his blood, now she was invading his dreams, and his nights. He was torn apart with lust and she was using her magic on him. He loved Isobel, and did not want to lose her, or spoil things between them. Last night, he had found some time to talk to her, they had wandered along the canal, discussing art, the nature of being, about her day. He could never have done that with Felicia. Their life had been fired by urgency, passion, a volatile match like two opposing magnets sparking each other off, creating amazing music and energy when it was good. Caught in a spiral of destruction, it turned bad. Making love with Isobel was beautiful, gentle and serene, intoxicating, her sensuality unfolding like a delicate flower. But with Felicia, he was ripped apart with desire.

She had given him the most erotic experience he had ever known, her wiles inflaming his desire. For some reason, he had started dreaming about her again. This time, it felt so real, as if she was in the room with him. Surely she couldn't still be exercising sexual power over him? Tormenting him with lust after all this time? Why it was happening he could only guess. Was it because she was trying to win him back? Unconsciously stirring his desires? Even though he loved and desired Isobel? He thought he was over her, over the strange attraction of the darker dreams she offered him, the allure of the wild side of her nature. He was sure he was finished with that kind of love, and didn't want to go down that road again. What did these strange dreams mean?

With Isobel, he experienced a more high-minded courtly, chivalrous feeling towards a woman, and felt perplexed at his sudden, inexplicable change of heart. Felicia did things sexually to him that no other woman could. But surely he had grown out of those kind of sado-masochistic games? Extremes of experience were an addiction. He had once loved Felicia to distraction, but she captivated him with the lure of a sorceress, in the web of her power, destructive, dangerous, impulsive. It hadn't been real. A scheming, tantalising temptress who controlled him, dominated him, kept him addicted to her with deadly charms. Trapped by her sexual allure. Their relationship had been too stormy for him to endure and make a career at the same time. She was too demanding, distracting. He'd had to get away from her wild jealousy, accusations and dark desires, or lose his mind. He could not tolerate her moods that changed with the wind—happy one moment, gentle and loving, dark and destructive the next, wielding power and control over him, sending him on a roller coaster until he was plunged into black chaos. She had refused to give up her desire for the darker arts and will for power. He tried to make her happy, but he could never give her quite enough. He could no longer trust her. She had become strange, cunning, scheming, trying to take all that he had, forcing him away from his friends. Taking over with more control of his life. Isobel by contrast was easy-going, gentle, loving supportive and undemanding. She was fiercely independent, a brilliant artist who understood his passion for music and the muse. He preferred her gentle coaxing to Felicia's stormy demands. Her elegance and undemanding presence left him free to be creative. Felicia swept him away on the destructive tides of madness, while Isobel gently rowed him to the shore.

In those days, Felicia was his muse, she served as a perfect source of inspiration, embracing his darker, more decadent side, awakening his shadow. As he got to know Isobel, his music became lighter, gentler, more melodic, haunting in a different way. He had found happiness on the canal with Isobel, yet recently he felt possessed, as though Felicia was still around him. Was she hypnotising him? Why couldn't he get her out of his head? His love for her had died, but she wouldn't let him forget. She was the devil incarnate, he had to exorcise her from his mind. She had sparked his genius, but stayed in a primitive state of torrid emotion like a child, her desire for compulsive living taking over. She had thrown them into total unreality, as she pursued escape, fantasy, mythos. What had once inspired him now trapped him. She had turned his life into a trap, a nightmare.

One day he met Isobel, an art student in the union bar. She was a breath of fresh air, who gave him back his life. He fell for her sophisticated, ethereal charm and left Felicia a week later. Isobel captivated him with her mystical gaze, the faraway look in her eyes, her sweetness offering him what he needed, healing him, providing a calm haven, soothing him with her refinement and beauty. From that second, he was hooked. Isobel was the opposite of Felicia. Felicia pleaded with him to stay, cutting the blood from her wrist, spurting it in his face. He had escaped, run for miles, slept in the forest so that she could not find him. He had made his way to Isobel's houseboat, and was looking around at Isobel's paintings scattered on the walls, maidens languishing in flowing gowns with cascading hair, frolicking in the waterfalls, when she came in and he kissed her, and fell into a dream from which he hoped never to awake.

Felicia was his dark side, Isobel his light. Day and night, and darkness and light. Isobel inspired him to write. He twisted the amulet of the snake and the moon that Felicia had given him until it left a red mark on his arm. He toyed with it and smiled. The Dark Goddess indeed! A fictional concept that had no real power, or was it? Felicia was actually beginning to believe she was the Dark Goddess and that she possessed special powers.

Yesterday he felt the echoes of the deep passion for Felicia surge in his loins, torturing him with desire. He tried to fight it with all his strength, but it had got inside his head, and somehow she was seducing him from within his own soul. Only she had ever sparked in him that wildness, turned his loins to liquid and stirred him to a sexuality he thought was impossible to achieve. Traces of the erotic desire still burned in his veins. She had danced, flirted, fuelling his satyriasis with her presence. He had tried to ignore her, yet her bewitching aura fascinated him, her dark-edged sensuality igniting the flame he thought was extinguished. Some flames never burn out, some never die. She was dangerous and devouring, still capable of sparking a lethal chemistry in him. He remembered their sex games, becoming more and more adventurous until one day she had chained him to a cross, dominating him, giving him ecstasy, exquisite pain and pleasure, tearing his soul apart—a desire he thought was buried. A mysterious, deep, dark power crept over him, clasping him in its tentacles as he fought the longing for her fatal touch, gripping him with the sting of a serpent. He prayed that she would just leave him alone, so he could forget his desire. He tried another set of chords, but failed, the images of her tortured him. The heady mix of sex and music, her dark mystery had taken him in her power.

She had danced evocatively at the dinner party, capturing him with her graceful movements; he had stopped playing, totally captivated by her power. Had Isobel noticed anything? She was willing him to return, working a spell over him. He tried to focus his mind on Isobel, fighting against his feelings for Felicia with all his will. Logos had finally to overcome Mythos, he had to leave behind his archaic desires. He was strong, no longer captive in her sphere of power. Or was he?

She had become excessively vain until her narcissistic tendencies drove her to new depths of perversion. He was addicted, shot through, begging her for his next fix of ecstatic sex. They had been twins in Hell, he thought dryly, seeing his lethal fairy witch. Did she still have a hold over him? Was she trying to seduce him? Once he had been abducted to the underworld, lost to humankind, rising to find the saving embrace of Isobel's maiden-like innocence, before he finally submerged and drowned in Felicia's dark world. Her dark, dangerous charms had led him to Hell. Only Isobel's purity and her love had saved him. Or did he have the strength to fight her? He read the poem that described Isobel:

> 'She walks in beauty like the night and all that's best of dark and bright, then thought of, when she first gleamed upon my sight, a lovely apparition sent, with something of angelic light.'

He felt a glow of warmth spread through him and chanted her name like a mantra. Perhaps he needed them both to feel whole. He was torn. They fulfilled the different sides of him, the dark and the light. Isobel was his Aphrodite, taking him past conventional realms to the heights of transcendence, to a higher realm of human consciousness, and his highest creative peak. Felicia lured him into the darkness, spinning her web around him, her 'shadow' liberating him, using her dark charms. Both women were necessary for his creative drive. Through them, he found a deeper understanding of the world, and of himself.

They satisfied the dark and light sides of his soul, his synthesis, making him whole. Isobel filled him with a spiritual light, Felicia fed his shadow, left him shaken, screaming and bleeding inside. He would leave the band after this tour, do session work or teaching, no more touring with Felicia. He had found his dream with Isobel and would not let anyone destroy it. Yes, that was it, even if he had to give up music, he wouldn't let Felicia spoil their dream. Isobel was too precious to him, and she was the partner he really needed.

After he met Isobel, his music had changed dramatically. He turned from writing dark songs, chilling, dark, disturbing romantic and shadowy, to lighter ones, becoming more spiritual and serene. He left the music business, hating the touring and constant late nights, and had started teaching guitar lessons at the local college. He hated the Dionysian life of excess. Drugs, death, darkness and dark compulsive sex—the next morning he'd always faced the emptiness and the spiritual wasteland of despair. Isobel, so refreshing, was pantheons away from all that, and just what he had been looking for. The cocaine, parties, living on the edge, had all taken their toll. He stared in the mirror. He looked healthy now, he had lost that ravaged, wasted look. He loved Isobel, her purity, her healing calmness; her beauty inspired and healed him. He was settled and happy, domestic bliss! The sex between them was pure, like flying on the wings of a dove.

Women enshrined many mysteries, he thought, perplexed. He had been dreaming of her often—what was it the Italian artists said? To dream of a woman with long, flowing hair was dreaming of one's own soul—the anima, the creative part of the soul. As this thought hit him he felt inspired; inspiration seemed to flood him as the notes leapt into a life of their own. Isobel awoke his anima, his feminine creative part. A new set of chords were taking shape, it sounded good. It was working.

He would call it 'Angel', for Isobel. For the first time he was really interested in a woman's mind. She was cultured, an excellent conversationalist. They spent hours discussing philosophy and art. He listened intently every night to Isobel's poetry, each syllable rousing him with passion, her sapphire blue-grey eyes widening in excitement as she read to him. Then he would take her in his arms, her body quivering like a bird underneath him, her evocative whisperings evoking in him the most elegant desire. Isobel was the light side of him, the sun in his darkness, elegant and graceful. His nymph of beauty, filled with light and redemption. She demanded nothing but his love. He was free again. The chains had been broken. He felt his soul uplift and fly again.

He wondered if Felicia had put Rob up to the whole thing of getting the band back together, surely she was not that manipulative? But, yes she was. He put down the music, and phoned Isobel to say sorry for being so distracted, for neglecting her. As he replaced the phone, he felt a strange aura overtake him as he was gripped with sexual ecstasy.

His head spun in a dreamlike haze. He could not breathe, he was hot, burning with desire. Felicia was in the room with him, drawing him in to her dark web. He tried to ignore her, but she was stronger. She moved on top of him, her body rocking over his, a deep devouring lust, consuming, burning into him, his mind ripping apart with lust. She was luring him into Hell, feeding his addiction, fuelling his insatiable lust for her. His mind screamed out for more. She was his drug and he needed a fix of her.

'Isobel,' he said speaking through his mobile phone, 'I shall be late tonight, I have so much work to do.' Felicia's lethal touch grasped him, sparked him with that familiar edge. Her lips wrapped round him, sucking him deeper, teasing him, taking him to the edge of ecstasy. He tried to fight it, but spiralled into an erotic hell. His dark dream-weaver was back playing the dark games he so enjoyed.

She mounted him, nibbling him, sending him into rapture, his mind filled with ecstasy, riding him hard as she always did, her fatal touch releasing him. The whip was drawn over him, coming down in swift sharp strokes, sparks exploding, his come shooting deep inside her. She stood over him, his come trickling down her legs, and he licked her warm damp thighs, then kissed her. She sucked it out of his mouth lovingly. Wanting her again, he pushed inside her, trying to fight the exquisite tormenting bliss. She pushed on top of him, lost in a frenzy of wild abandonment. Her hair flew around her head in wild elegance, falling in wisps over her perfect breasts, over the top of her leather basque. She glared like a goddess. Her blood-red lips parted sensually, her eyes closed so that the long lashes swept over her cheeks. Her raven black hair tumbled over her pert brown nipples. He wanted to stay there for eternity, on the brink of ecstasy, spiralling to bliss. He shuddered with pleasure, pulling her head down toward him, moaning. Her tongue was searching deep in his mouth, his body quivering in a frenzy of desire as he felt himself shoot inside her. Then she had gone.

He stared at the wall. What had he done? What was happening to him? Had Felicia been there? Or was it all just a dream? Had he fallen asleep? What would Isobel think? His mind began twisting, burning in torment; he was destroyed, writhing in a pit of Hell. His fantasies were getting stranger, stronger, taking him over. He was ripped apart, losing control. Torn between two women, Rick had succumbed to his feeling for Felicia, and his ambiguity was confusing him, tearing him apart. He hadn't slept, his mind was squirming in torment, and the guilt he felt was crushing his soul so that he couldn't think straight. He had to get away. He was losing his mind.

Daydreams

Isobel took the longboat to Banbury: she needed a day alone, and some time to think, especially after the weird dream she'd had last night—where Felicia had been seducing Rick. She breathed a sigh of relief as the boat drifted up the canal, past the lock, then sailing onto the open river. Rick had been in such a strange mood and now she needed the open air. Last night she dreamed a dark goddess was dancing around a burial ground. Rick was a sacrifice in the underworld. A black eagle came to rest on the cold earth, she laid an egg, and from the egg sprung a demon, a dark and terrible dragon that breathed fire, destroying everything around, then it ate Rick. She chided herself for being scared of a mere dream, when it was nothing. There was a heavy charge in the air that had given rise to a lot of storms recently.

She waved to some people sailing by on a boat, letting her hand fall and trail through the water. Shadows of doubt flickered through her troubled mind. Was Rick still in love with Felicia? What other explanation could she think of for his strange behaviour? Why was he so moody? What was happening to them? Was Felicia trying to get him back? Painful dreams containing images of Rick and Felicia writhing in a state of lust had haunted her last night. No, he said he didn't want her, he had insisted on this many times, but she wasn't so sure. Maybe it was just her imagination: she was just being foolish, she had to stop torturing herself with this paranoia. Yet, she knew differently. She tried to push the thoughts from her mind. Aware that it was just what Felicia had wanted her to think. She would have to be strong, and trust Rick when he told her he was faithful.

Since Felicia had come back into their lives, strange things had started to happen. She was content, happy with Rick, and thought he was too. Now their easy-going relationship had turned into one of distrust. She had lost her security, living a fragile jagged-edged existence, unsure of what was about to happen next, and a menacing force was pushing them apart. She pushed it out of her mind, sat back to enjoy the view, watching the fields speed by. She stopped at a summer fair. She raced over to join the maidens dancing around the maypole, laughing with carefree happiness in the heat of the summer afternoon. Her long hair flew out in long pale curls, her dress swirling around her ankles. All her cares slipped away.

Later, she sat pensively by the river, picking at the yellow flowers glistening in the pale sun. The pollen flew delicately across the water, onto the lilac flowers dancing, swaying in the heat. She lifted her long skirt up and stepped over them, feeling the softness of the grass under her feet. Settling on an oasis of green, she sat watching the butterflies flit aimlessly in the heat feeling like a moth, flitting from place to place, trying to calm the demons in her soul. She threaded some daisies into a garland, then placed it around her hair. The music wafted over from the fair, and she got up to dance, an air nymph in harmony with nature, swaying in the sun, her bare feet tapping lightly on the soft grass—escaping from the real world, time suspended, a million miles away from reality. The sun faded into an orange haze. She swirled among the flowers, with no worries, no cares.

Suddenly, she stopped dancing as she saw a woman in black glide across the bank. It looked like Felicia! She froze. It could not be, and she shook her head in disbelief: she could not have got there so quickly, no one knew she was there. Perhaps it was someone who looked like her. It had shaken her. The unsettled anxious feeling she had whenever Felicia was around suddenly gripped her veins. Was a ghost haunting her? Was someone trying to frighten her? Or was she going out of her mind?

She took a bus into Oxford and sat in the sculpted gardens at the university, sketching the elegant gothic spires. She turned her head. She thought someone had been following her since she had got off the boat and felt something brush past her. A black cloud drifted across the sun, making the spires look black, throwing dark shadows over the gothic building. A few stray bats flapped their scrawny wings under the eaves. A storm was rising behind the ghostly spires. Tourists were being ushered into the building out of the rain. It was early afternoon, yet seemed like night. The sun was sinking behind the grey clouds. She sat alone, sheltering in the grounds.

She felt an icy coldness, a fear creep over her. Something was touching her, a cold fear spreading through her bones, up her spine. She started to run away from the strange, haunting images and sounds that floated around her. Twisted and gnarled trees moved in the wind, their branches moving as though trying to catch her. She ran faster, to the shelter of a derelict church, and hid in the shadows, her hands clasped to her head, drowning out the sounds that haunted her. She felt as though she was going mad. She began to cry, unable to escape the strange, dark malevolence around her. At the foot of the church was a demon sitting amongst fairies. She jumped back, scared, it looked like it was looking at her. Everything was tinged with evil.

'Black death comes shimmering down to eat its victims in the shadow of night,' she thought, remembering the words of a poem. She climbed into an alcove, breathing faster, waiting until the monstrous, dark clouds had passed. The sun peeked out from behind a cloud. The sound of the church bell stopped, the deathly silence bringing the town back to life.

She made for a little street café and crafts market, absorbing the friendliness, feeling safe and secure again. It was bright and sunny. Happy voices echoed through the air as people laughed gaily all around her. She bought some velvet ribbons and drank some herbal tea, smiling, relieved as she chatted to some tourists, instantly forgetting what had happened. Immersed in the bustle, the air of normality, she felt sane again.

As she climbed off the boat back in London, she found Rick practising his guitar. He was picking distractedly at some chords.

'Please don't bother me now, Isobel,' he snapped irritably, his eyes blazing with fury. He got up and walked out to the canal. Isobel followed him. She wanted to put things right before he went away. Why was he so short-tempered with her lately?

'Something's wrong, Rick, we need to talk,' she pleaded, fidgeting with her hair.

'I'm busy, we start the tour tomorrow and I'm tired,' he protested.

'Can't it wait?' His body was hunched over his guitar and his hair fell over his face so that she could not see his expression. She sensed he wasn't really listening. Suddenly, he threw the guitar to one side. 'Can't I get a moment's peace?' he asked.

'What is the matter, Rick? Ever since Felicia came back we just snap at each other.'

'I'm sick of hearing about Felicia and what you may or may not have imagined, this constant bickering is getting on my nerves,' he snapped, angrily. 'I left her for you, isn't that enough?'

'Well if that's the way you see it,' she said, starting to cry. 'Why is she always with us? She's completely invaded our lives! I don't want her here all the time,' she said, slamming her bag on the table.

'It's just your imagination, she's just here because she is part of the band.'

'Don't be so naïve, Rick, she wants you back and is trying to break us up.'

'Nonsense. How can she do that? What can I do about it?' he shouted after her. 'All I want to do is write music.'

'Then do it, go! Both of you can go to Hell!'

'Why waste time worrying about her, Isobel? Do you think I would risk everything we have built for something that didn't work out and never will? She's nothing to me,' shouted Rick after her, a look of indifference on his face.

'She's coming between us and you are letting her, it's you that's doing this to us, no one else!'

Isobel slammed the door with such a force that it rocked the boat. That night, she dreamed Rick was making love to her—it was blissful, his arms entwined around her back, kissing her. Then he turned into a serpent with a skull for a head. Her dreams were becoming more and more strange, and she was haunted by voices that rose through the inky blackness whispering the chant of a demonic she-devil.

A Journey

At the weekend, Michel drove hastily through the winding country lanes with Isobel, towards Brighton. As they passed through the Downs, he looked up in the mirror and saw the sadness in Isobel's eyes. It was a bright, hot sunny day and everywhere around was happy laughter. Isobel sat in subdued silence. Michel sensed her mood was somehow connected with Rick. It must be difficult for her when Rick was on tour, he thought, wondering how he could break the silence. How could he help? He made a few jokes, trying to lighten the mood. She laughed. Then became melancholic.

'I feel settled with Rick, I thought he felt the same way, but just lately I can't be sure. Do you have someone special?'

'No, I don't have any involvements at the moment, footloose and fancy free, that's how I prefer it, my work takes up all my time.'

'I used to be like that,' she laughed. 'Can I ask you something?'

'Yes,' he replied.

'I think I'm pregnant. What do you think Rick will say?'

Michel changed into the wrong gear, and felt the car stall. Shocked, he turned to Isobel.

'I don't honestly know, I don't really know him well enough to know what he feels,' he said with a strange sinking feeling in his stomach, his hopes and dreams dashed to pieces. He saw her subdued mood return. 'I'm sure he'll be delighted,' he said, optimistically. 'Aren't you thrilled?'

'It's all I ever wanted. 'He seems so strange lately, as though he's lost in a world of his own,' she confessed. 'I feel as though we're growing apart, it's just that his mind is taken up with the tour.'

'Yes, I'm sure it's just that,' said Michel, being conciliatory. 'You know what musicians are like, wild gypsies at heart. They don't always make sense when they're writing and composing, they're taken over by their creative fire, the muse bites and becomes their driving force. They're a law unto themselves.'

'I suppose so.'

As they drove past the Downs in the blazing sun, Isobel felt overwhelmed by a sense of foreboding, her intuition warning her that something dangerous was about to happen. She shrugged it off, sinking into a mood of blissful indolence, content that Rick's child was snuggled up inside her and that she would soon be with him. She arranged a shawl around her and slept peacefully for the rest of the journey, lulled by the gentle rhythm of the car. She woke up with a start: a vague, shadowy figure was standing in the mist. It looked like Rick. He turned and waved and they nearly hit him. Isobel screamed. As she looked back, he vanished into thin air. Michel comforted her in his arms, rocking her, and held her close.

'Did you see it?'

'No, I didn't see anything,' he admitted. 'Come on, you must rest, you are over-tired.'

'Was it an apparition?'

'I don't know,' said Michel, disturbed.

They pulled up at the studio a day early, a strange tension hanging in the air. Michel went off to book some rooms for the night. She wandered round the gardens of a lovely house, a mansion, the Grange, used for recording and filming. Isobel was glad that she would soon be seeing Rick, she needed to be close to him. Pushing open the studio door, it was empty. They were most likely to be in the local bar, drowning their senses. Perhaps someone would know where Rick was. She sat for a few moments repairing her make-up in a chair in the conservatory. The sun streamed through the window, the sunbeams dancing across the floor. She felt calm and collected. Her fears and worries dissolved instantly in such beautiful surroundings.

She went over to the water fountain, in the centre of the lawn, and was about to take a drink when, suddenly, a snake coiled around it. She jumped. It frightened her, so she ran into the house. She dashed into the kitchen and fled up the stairs. She heard a muffled sound, like a bird flapping at the top of the building, trapped in the roof. Curious, she climbed the stairs to the attic. She would have to release it. A strange noise echoed from the room ahead. Maybe it was a cat trapped inside, she would have to let it out. She heard it whimpering. Slowly, she opened the door. She jumped back in shock at what she saw. There were two people in the throes of sex, heavily involved in a passionate session. The woman sat on top of the man, straddling him, exuding sexuality and power. Her hair swung over them, hiding his face. Swaying in the rhythm of sex, she eased her legs open wide, then climbed on him, rocking up and down. Her breasts were jigging frantically. They writhed in the shadows, in the throes of ecstasy. Isobel could not make out who they were. The man was groaning in passion.

The woman was dressed in a PVC basque, holding a whip. She thrust on top, her hair flying out, rocking wildly as they let off loud gasps. The man grabbed her hair, pulling her closer, pushing up into her, moaning in ecstasy, reaching a peak of pleasure. Isobel winced when she recognised his voice. Isobel moved closer to make out the figures. The woman threw her hair back. Isobel's blood curdled with fear as she saw who it was. Watching them in horror, it gradually dawned on her. Mortified, she realised it was Rick underneath Felicia. Moving out of the shadows into the light she could see their bodies quite clearly. Shock and anger flooded her. She ran towards the door, not wanting them to see her, and fled down the stairs, with tears streaming down her face. They turned around, aware they had been seen.

'Oh shit, who was that?' asked Rick weakly, swigging back some whisky.

'No one,' said Felicia, grinning triumphantly, climbing off him, his fluid trickling down her legs.

'It must be the door slamming in the wind.'

'Now lie back and enjoy me!' she ordered, lifting her body over his face. 'Before the others arrive.'

He licked between her legs, whimpering in delight as her juices flooded between his lips. Then she strapped on the rubber penis, turned him over and pushed inside him, long hard thrusts as he cried out in ecstasy.

She laughed wickedly, delighted her little plan had worked. Yesterday she had sent an e-mail to Isobel, saying it was from Rick, asking her to come a day early as he was missing her and she had fallen right into her trap.

She threw her black, shimmering hair back and laughed like a she-devil, intent on destruction. Power and control were hers again.

Outside Isobel collapsed in shock, into the car. Tears streamed down her face.

'Let's go,' she said. 'Drive away from here as fast as you can! Get away from here!'

'Where to, what's the matter? What's happened?' asked Michel confused, turning the car round.

'Rick,' she stuttered, afraid to tell him what she had seen. 'Anywhere! I can't stay here. Please get away!' She sobbed, her world was crashing around her. Pain swept over her, overwhelming her.

'Gosh what's wrong, Izzy?' he asked, pulling her into his arms.

Tearfully, she told him what she had seen. Never had she felt so humiliated and betrayed. She hit out at the window. Michel cradled her tighter in his arms. Her heart twisted with pain and loneliness; her sanity hung on by a thread.

'You can't go back there,' he said, feeling it had been inevitable.

But shaking, she phoned Rick from the hotel room; she shouted at him, telling him what she had seen.

He seemed shocked.

'I'm sorry, it wasn't meant to happen,' he confessed. 'It was a mistake. It was nothing, we got just carried away,' he stammered. 'She gave me some pills, I don't know what they were, and we drank some whisky.'

'How could you do this with Felicia? Of all people!' spat Isobel with contempt.

'Look it…was just an accident,' he pleaded.

'How could you! You bastard!' she cried. 'How could you betray me? She was always trying to come between us, that little vixen, whore-faced bitch!' She sobbed, realising that things could never be the same. 'And you fell right into her trap, or should I say web.'

'We had been in the studio and just got a bit drunk and things got out of control,' he admitted. 'Surely, Isobel you can understand these things, don't act so bourgeois. We were just carried away, it means nothing, honestly!'

'But it does,' she cried. 'How could you?' she screamed, feeling doubly betrayed.

'I can't discuss this now, I'm in a recording. Let's talk about it later.'

'No, now! There won't be any later,' she insisted, not letting him fob her off with excuses. 'How could you do this to me, especially now that I am carrying your child?'

'What?'

'I'm pregnant.'

'I thought we had decided this wasn't the time?' he said, shock creeping into his voice. 'We'll talk tonight.'

'Don't bother,' she said, slamming down the phone, realising the line between fantasy and reality had been crossed and they couldn't turn back.

Turning to Michel in the hotel room, she cried, and hit the bed with her fists: 'How could they betray me like this?'

He brushed back her hair from her tear-stained face, and started caressing her neck soothingly, kissing her gently on the cheek. She returned the kiss, grateful that she was not alone. She faltered for a second, then the pain washed over her—torrents of agony. It was so indescribable that any relief from the torture and devastation was welcome. She couldn't go through this alone. Michel took her in his arms, and kissed her breasts, holding her body. She lay back, submitting. His dream was coming true at last. He had wanted her so badly since the first day he had seen her. He felt himself go hard, parted her legs and felt himself sink into her, thrusting against her. She pushed back against him on the bed, pulling at his hair, taking all of him inside her, her legs entwined around his back and as she orgasmed she let out a scream. Then she wrapped her legs around his neck, taking him into the deepest part of her body and soul. In the aftermath, he saw the light on her face and rubbing her cheek, he kissed her softly.

They got up. Isobel washed her face and got dressed, still reeling from shock and despair. Sex had given her a temporary respite from pain, but she felt its ugly tentacles creeping back over her, exposing her to searing pain. She grabbed on the sink to steady herself. She couldn't face seeing Felicia perform for the next hour. In a feckless change of mood she decided to attend the party. Felicia would not keep her away, she thought angrily. Why the hell should *she* stay away? Felicia was the one who had messed up *her* life! Well if it took the rest of her life, she would get her revenge.

Torment

At the party, Isobel walked into the room looking radiant. There was no sign of her tears, or that she had been crying hours before. She stood elegantly in a long, black gown that hugged her slim body tightly, with her hair piled up. Her pregnancy didn't yet show. She turned her head to see if Rick was there. He was standing next to Felicia, being photographed. She stared at them with a cold indifference, Felicia stood stylishly posed, then turned round and began talking animatedly to a photographer who was with Rick. Isobel thought she caught a glimpse of Rick putting his arm around Felicia. She closed her eyes so that she couldn't see them and turned her attention to something else. Rick looked over and saw Isobel and dropped Felicia's arm like a red-hot poker, surprised to see her. Isobel looked back at him murderously. Mingled noises seemed to be coming from every direction, and she felt dizzy; then, suddenly, she heard someone call her name. Felicia came over in a tight black leotard, under a short see-through black lace dress, finished with long black boots, still glowing from the performance, holding tightly onto Rick's arm. She flashed Isobel a triumphant smile, her eyes burning with a wicked malice. Isobel gripped her drink, trying to control herself. Frantically she swished the ice around, wishing she hadn't come.

'Hello Isobel,' Felicia spat, cattily, 'we were not expecting you tonight. How nice to see you! So unexpected!'

Isobel shot her a venomous glance gritting her teeth. What a bitch, she thought, squeezing the glass in her hand, fighting to control her anger.

'So you think you have him now?' Isobel spat back at her. 'Well, good riddance,' she said, throwing her drink over them.

'You cow, Isobel,' snapped Felicia. 'You'll pay for this!'

Rick pulled Isobel away from Felicia.

'I didn't expect you to turn up. Look, I'm so sorry,' Rick stuttered guiltily, taking her hand. 'Shall we talk outside?'

'No, I want to stay here,' Isobel said defiantly, pulling her hand away, struggling against the desire to slap him.

'I promise you, Isobel, it didn't mean anything, it's you that I love,' he pleaded. 'We both got carried away, and it was just a mistake. Felicia says she is sorry. I'm sorry, it won't ever happen again.'

'A weak excuse, too little too late!' she spat back at him. 'I hope you both rot in Hell.'

'It was an accident!'

'How can ending up in bed with someone be an accident? Felicia's idea, I should imagine. But you! How could you be so weak?' she snarled angrily. Knowing that if it had been anyone but her, she would not have minded so much.

'Let's not talk about it now. Are you all right? Did you enjoy the gig?' he inquired.

'As if you care!' she snapped. 'I didn't see it. Do you think I'm just here for the party?'

'Is that wise?' he said, watching her throw back another Tequila and stopping her. 'What about the baby?'

'Since when have you cared so much? If you were that concerned, you wouldn't have fucked that bitch!' she spat accusingly.

Felicia threw them both a wicked glance, that of a cat playing with a mouse, and her dark eyes flashed angrily. She was enjoying having power over Rick again; he had been like putty in her hands. She controlled him like a ringmaster did a horse. Her gaze focused malevolently on Rick. She could not let them get back together, after all she had done to split them up. She'd have to employ more extreme measures. It was time to make her next move.

Isobel shivered, sensing the evil intent in Felicia's gaze: a strange energy, like sparks flying, passed between them. Unable to contain her anger any longer, she walked over to Felicia and slapped her hard on the face.

'Take that, you rotten, stinking, dirty bitch,' screamed Isobel, shaking with rage. 'Betrayal is not something I will tolerate.'

Felicia remained motionless. Her bright eyes glared with victory. 'I am just glad I am not a pious cow like you,' she said, weaving her way back into the crowd.

Felicia danced off around the room, looking back, taunting her, as though weaving a spell, her black dress flying out around her. Isobel finally snapped: she walked over and slapped Felicia sharply across the face again, making her wince. Then in one swift movement, she grabbed a long lock of her rival's cascading hair, and dragged her across the floor, then slapped and kicked her again. The music stopped. Everyone stared. Felicia tried scrambling to her feet but Isobel pushed her down, hitting her again, throwing the dregs of the wine over her. Then she stormed angrily from the room. Felicia sat up laughing, her eyes glowing with the inner fire of Hell. She was malevolence embodied, open, manic, a wild fury.

'Hell hath no fury,' she smiled in Isobel's direction. Her legs were smarting but she was sure as hell not going to show it—after all the trouble she had caused, it had been so worth it.

Isobel ran up the drive, stopping when she saw Rick's car. Taking a flowerpot from the garden she threw it through the window, shattering the glass into a shower of glistening fragments. Rick ran after her.

'What the hell are you doing?' he shouted.

She turned, shooting him a black look. 'What the hell does it look like? Get lost, Rick,' she cried. 'Go to Hell, if you're not there already.'

'Come back, Isobel, we have to talk about the baby.'

'Fuck off!'

More glass showered over the drive. Isobel jumped in the car with Michel and they drove off like the wind.

Later that night, back at the hotel, Isobel dreamed she was falling into an endless abyss, being sucked into a pit of darkness, a misty blackness engulfing her. Images of being devoured by a black feral-like entity, a panther, tormented her. She felt her flesh rip open. Felicia appeared, chanting a strange cry.

'He is mine, he is mine!'

She whipped a branch of thorns against Isobel's stomach. They tore against her, ripping open her flesh, and Isobel watched helplessly as the blood poured down her legs, and let out a cry of agonising pain. She screamed, then woke up and saw the pools of blood. She had lost the baby.

Michel phoned for an ambulance. The next day, Rick walked into the hospital. Isobel swore angrily at him, throwing the flowers he had bought back at him.

'Get out of my life,' she ordered. 'Never come near me again. I hate you, I will never forgive you,' she sobbed, her anger spreading through every pore. Her mind was ripped, and her heart was torn.

'But I have come to apologise,' he stuttered.

'Well, apology *not* accepted. Now just fuck off!'

Rick stormed angrily from the room. Isobel slumped across her bed, and began crying. Her emotions were erupting, screaming and bleeding inside like a knife being twisted inside her. She watched the grey clouds drift by as their love faded and died in the wind.

She listened to the gentle ripple of the canal as her heart broke and her soul ripped into two. She imagined she would die, and, unable to eat or sleep, she withdrew, her world crashed into a bleak, empty void. Her body shook, she sat for hours, looking aimlessly along the canal. The meaning to her life had gone.

Time passed. Isobel woke up, grateful to have survived the pain. The shock gradually subsided, and the sense of despair dissolved. In the wake of Rick's betrayal she passed from anger—fighting the pain that threatened to engulf her—to feeling sad and resigned. The months drifted slowly by. The dark tormenting dreams, which had haunted her night and day, had gone. She dreamed of Rick's face above her, making love, then it would turn to a skeleton, to ash. The pain swirled round her like a cloak of nails. She was fighting for her sanity, on the brink of madness, tormented by the empty cold space next to her in her bed, distraught that Rick was no longer there.

Then a comforting numbness enveloped her, and finally, thankfully, she felt nothing; it was as though she was encapsulated in a soft, feathery cloud. She worked ceaselessly; it always lifted her spirit, taking her from her worries to a safe place, veiling her with the magic of her muse—a safe haven that nothing could penetrate, and where she felt powerful and safe. No longer wanting to be part of the world, she threw herself into her work; on autopilot she gave herself no time to think, just kept busy. She fiddled with the ring Rick had given her, thinking back to the day he gave it to her, immersed in renewed pain and inner torment, as she relived the past. She took it off and threw it into the river. She remembered the day they had purchased their first home, a larger boat, it was all they could afford, he had said, promising she would be happy living on the river with him. She recalled with a smile how he had opened some wine and showered her with kisses, begging her to stay with him forever, then asked her to marry him. The tears coursed down her cheeks as she remembered his touch. She touched herself; crying, she came to an orgasm, thinking of his eyes gazing into hers. Then the numbness took over again, release from those few minutes of feeling alive. Would she always feel this dead?

Images of Rick making love to Felicia swirled in her head, torturing her, the sight of them making love echoing in her mind. She yearned for him, to feel his body next to hers. She was tortured by images of him making love to Felicia, that swirled around her head twisting her soul, tearing open her heart. Where was he now? She felt the pain rip through her, but it wasn't so sharp, it was a storm becoming more and more distant. How could he have fallen victim to Felicia's snake-like charms? How could he have betrayed her so cruelly?—shattering her dreams, destroying their life together, brutally wiping out all they had built, their dreams and hopes of a future together. She still had his acoustic guitar. She fingered the chords and listened to the sad, vibrating sound. He used to play the guitar to her, and she'd sat enthralled by his attention. The images began to fade into distant memories. She had to stop, she would not torture herself, she had to let it go.

Like Persephone, she was cast into the underworld of darkness and pain, unable to see her lover as he really was, trapped in eternal darkness by her illusory love. Blinded by the darkness and the heaviness of her heart, she felt dead. What will she become now, betrayed by the person she loved most?

Gradually the pain began to subside. Michel called and took her along the canal to the craft fayre; she laughed and forgot the past. Each day he called. She spent her days with Michel, sitting on the riverbank, going to the theatre, listening to music. The past began to fade. She started to heal. Rick was living with Felicia in Highgate.

'I will never forgive him,' she told Michel, seeking solace in her art, working harder, trying to forget him, to blot him out of her mind. Michel took her out each day and made her laugh, helped her find her world again. The days grew lighter, Isobel gained strength from the light of the sun, nature, and the awesome beauty of changing seasons. Everything has a life and a death, she thought, philosophically, and life was a series of cycles. She was discovering a new path, finding from somewhere her own inner strength. She enjoyed Michel's easy company and felt as though they had known each other for an eternity, and they became good friends. But it was nothing like what she had felt for Rick.

He asked little of her in return, except her company and enjoyed taking her to places she might find interesting, providing her with pleasant distractions to ease her pain. He was an effortless companion, a comfortable harbour where she could just stay for a while. He took her to art galleries, theatres, restaurants, afternoon tea at snug cafés. Their lovemaking was easy, as between friends. He quietly accepted her sadness, trying to ease it from her with gentle words, happy as long as she was with him. She took flight in his comfort, his refuge, escaping from her endless torment of pain, but nothing could ever recapture the passion that Rick had made her feel.

That night, curled up in the duvet, they listened to the wind howling outside. Michel spoke softly to her.

'It's terribly sad, but there's nothing more sacred than the life of a man or woman unfolding not as it had intended, but not at all. Don't dwell on your unhappiness, as we have such little time here. We have the precious gift of life. Make the most of what you have, not what you yearn for. It is not what we do that we regret, but what we miss.'

She looked at him with shades of growing love, realising pain was part of life, and that she really had lost nothing at all. In the morning she reached up into his arms and gazed at the grey cloudless sky, ready to start again.

Three months later, she received a letter. It read:

Dear Isobel
I need to speak to you. It's urgent. Please meet me if you can.
I'm sorry to impose on your time.
Rick.

The letter was addressed from Highgate. Intrigued, she wondered why he had bothered to contact her after such a long time and her heart sunk in dismay. Why hadn't he just left her alone? How could she ever forgive his betrayal? She forced herself to be rational and threw the letter away—it would be unfair to Michel. Why should he contact her now? The memory of his betrayal re-ignited the flame, but then she remembered his touch and her spirits rose at the prospect of seeing him. She couldn't stop herself being filled with the tormenting image of lust: she had to see him, to know if he had ever cared for her at all.

A week later she set off to Highgate. When she arrived she recoiled in shock at his appearance. He looked gaunt, tired and drawn.

'Do come in,' he said in a whisper. She tried to conceal her shock at his worn expression and grey pallor. He looked strange, he moved slowly, painfully, like a cadaver.

'Are you ill?' Isobel asked.

'No, I just feel drained. I'll explain it all but first, please sit down,' he requested, pointing to a chair.

'What's happened to Felicia?' asked Isobel, amazed at his transformation.

'She's in France,' he answered curtly.

'You seem to be doing well apart from your health,' she observed, noting the expensive furniture and paintings adorning the room.

'I was,' he confessed. Looking at her, he said, 'Now I am in Hell.'

His eyes held a deadness; they stared at her sadly without life, empty and cold. What had happened to change him so drastically?

'What do you mean?' asked Isobel. 'I thought things were working out well for you?' She wanted to hold him tight, make it all right, but she could not let him betray her again.

'They were, but I realise I made a terrible mistake. I misjudged my situation, I need your help or I'll die. I'm fading away, Felicia is killing me by using her black magic against me,' he admitted. 'She has tried to possess me.'

'Why on earth should she do that? And why should I help you? You've got what you deserve,' she said, triumphantly, glad that he had got his comeuppance.

'You are the only one who can help me, who ever really loved me,' he begged.

'Well, don't even ask me. You destroyed our love, or don't you remember? How could you even think I would bother to help you? You have got what you deserve. I can never forgive you, do you think I would come crawling back after what you have done? I would rather die,' she replied callously.

'I am just asking for your help, not your forgiveness, the boat is still half mine.'

'I lost our baby because of you, or have you forgotten?' She got up and started to walk away from him, out of the room.

'Isobel, please come back,' he pleaded, trying to keep the desperation from creeping into in his voice. 'I'm sorry for what happened. Let me at least explain.'

'What is there to say?'

He took her pale hands in his.

'I had lost my own will, and she made me do it. Hypnotised me in some way. Look, I need to stay on the boat, just for a few days. Please, I know that what I did was terrible, but please try and understand. I have to get away from here for a while or I shall die. Half of it is mine, I'm just asking this one favour as a friend.'

Isobel raised her eyes to the ceiling in disbelief.

'How can you even ask me? And don't call me a friend. You are excusing what you did by claiming you acted in that way through diminished responsibility, that you weren't responsible?'

'If you like, I wasn't in my right mind, she had taken me over.'

'Oh Rick, spare me the crazy excuses.'

'I must get away from here,' he repeated, his haunted eyes sunk in hollows, looking at her pleadingly, his voice fading, 'or she will destroy me. You are my only hope.'

'Why should I care what happens to you?'

'Because we cared for each other once.'

Isobel stared callously out of the window. She enjoyed seeing him in pain squirming with remorse. Then suddenly, at the prospect of doing something to destroy Felicia, she agreed.

'Okay, you can stay on the boat, only for a few days, then you must leave.'

'Thanks.'

'Meet me there this afternoon,' she said finally, throwing him the keys, fighting waves of desire as she met his eyes. Their eyes locked for a moment, she felt the familiar shiver of lust. After all he had done to her, surely she couldn't still feel this way?

The boat

A cold winter wind danced in the dead of night over the canal, scattering leaves across the bank. The storm whistled through the trees across the canal. The boat swayed and rocked. The canal was lonely, desolate and windswept. Michel sat reading in the dim light streaming through the window, sensing something unpleasant was about to happen. A grim sense of foreboding enveloped him, he couldn't stop thinking about Isobel. Was she finally lost to him? He turned over the page, gripped with a pain he could hardly bear. He knew what the future held—change and destruction. Michel returned to his lair, licking his wounds, retreating into the shadowy world of romantic withdrawal, reading poetry, writing, taking photographs of the canal, the dark silhouettes of the evening set against the blazing orange sunset. He wished that Isobel would change her mind and stay with him forever. Sometimes he forced himself to go out, see other friends, to have social activity, but he had lost the ability to enjoy life, preferring his own company these days, just musing along the canal or walking over the Sussex downs, anything that did not interrupt his thoughts about Isobel. He wrote reams of poetry about her, and felt happy to just be close to her. Sometimes he wondered if the male ego might be superior, unclouded by so many female emotional issues, the whims of women were so often irrational. But wasn't he too being irrational falling for a woman who was already involved? And worse, who seemed caught up in some sort of ménage. Why did women always disrupt his ideal world?

Outside, it was bleak, empty and cold, like his heart. He threw the book into the corner. It was over, he couldn't deny it any longer, Isobel was lost to him forever.

The River Serpent—confessions

Rick sat rocking in the chair in the lounge of the grey boat, his eyes searched around him nervously. His face was gaunt and torn with worry.

'You'd better tell me what has happened,' Isobel insisted, 'and let me know what this is all about. I want to hear the whole story.'

He looked down at her sadly.

'I don't expect you to understand,' he whispered.

'Try me, start at the beginning.'

Dark shadows danced across the boat, thin branches whipped on the windows. For a moment, Isobel felt a deep sadness, with shades of the love she had once felt for him re-igniting. Fragments of the past returned. She watched Rick's face in the light, the expression in his eyes vulnerable, and she remembered his gaze as they made love. She turned away, fighting the urge to hold or caress him. She still cared for him, but hardened her heart because she knew she could no longer trust him. He had torn her apart, betrayed her badly. She had let him go.

Rick paced across the room, his eyes downcast, looking nervous, haunted, a nerve twitched in his cheek.

'I began to feel ill, inexplicably, I felt tired all the time, drained like I was anaemic, I had various tests and they were all negative. It got worse, I felt as though my will was being sapped, I thought some sun might help. So I went to Spain, thinking the tour had been too demanding, and I needed to rest for a while. I began to feel better. When I returned to Felicia, I relapsed,' he explained. 'After the tour I felt I was disintegrating physically, mentally and spiritually. The doctor said I needed to rest, it could be yuppie flu, due to a demanding lifestyle with little sleep. Everything had started to go wrong. At first I thought it was just tiredness after the travelling. Then I began to suspect it could be Felicia,' he said. 'It was as though she was sucking everything out of me.'

'Go on.'

'She became so intense. I felt as though I was being consumed, devoured by her, my soul was being torn from me, piece by piece. She delved deeper into the black arts, entranced by its strange allure and magic. There was a dark energy surrounding her, an evil aura, until I found it difficult to get near her. My will was being taken,' he said, his expression darkening. 'She used our sexual rituals for some kind of dark power, and left me empty, my will taken. She was using dark forces against me.'

'Why, how?'

'The goal of every witch is control over natural forces, but in her case she wants to control other people. Especially me. Her aim was to seize the infinite energy of the cosmos to use for her own ends. Wielding her power like a sword. A dark witch uses the power not to serve any higher purpose, but solely for her own ends. Felicia uses power over her victims, turning them into her sex slaves to empower her own existence. She wanted complete control over me, taking my will and that of other people. Sex was a means of acquiring occult power. This energy can be passed from one person to the next. Her aim was to take my energy to enhance her own power and will. Rituals enhance a focused will, evoking a different form of consciousness. She identified with a higher power, Kali, the Dark Goddess. She used me as her source, demanding sex day and night, until she left me as an empty shell.'

'I don't want to hear this,' snapped Isobel. 'I wish you would shut up.'

'I'm sorry, but, if you want to know the truth, please listen or you could be in danger. Well, like a fool I followed her even though she was manipulating me. I couldn't fight her, I had become totally ensnared in her power. She was using some kind of hypnosis on me, invading and controlling my will.'

'Are you sure that this wasn't all in your imagination?'

'Yes, I have evidence. One day, I found her performing a ritual,' he recalled, as he put his head in his hands. 'She was cutting up a human head. I buried it, I didn't know what else to do,' he said, shocked at his own confession. She said she had dug it up from a grave, I began to realise how bizarre she really was.

'The neck was cut, and the eyes removed. She'd grave-robbed a man, gone too far, set in motion all kinds of evil. When you set off on a journey like that you are likely to go where you don't want to go. I tried, but I couldn't stop her,' he said.

'From that day on she tried to destroy me, obsessed with gaining dark power without true knowledge of what she was doing. She went further and further into madness and destruction, she doesn't have the discipline to travel into dark realms in safety. She uses it for the wrong reasons, for manipulation, power and control. Like with everything she did, she behaved like a child. She got out of control, dabbling in a very dangerous game, playing with fire. She tried to poison me, she's insane.'

Isobel sat down shocked, unable to speak. Rick's words tore into her like poison darts.

'Are you absolutely sure you are right about this?' she said, disbelief and doubt seeping into her voice. 'It sounds so bizarre, so incredible.'

'Yes, there is no other explanation, and it all seems to fit. How she seduced me to lure me away from you, then destroyed our baby. I tried to leave her, but she wouldn't let me go. I was too ill, she poisoned me to keep me there. I was her prisoner,' he said, bitterly.

'Why did she do this?' Isobel demanded to know, sickened by what she'd heard, her head spinning in disbelief. She felt sick and dizzy, didn't want to listen any more. She was about to suggest Rick see a psychiatrist, when she remembered her own dreams. Rick shifted restlessly in the chair, then walked over to the window. Shakily, he poured a whisky and drank it down at once. Then he poured one for Isobel; she gulped it steadily, feeling numbness creep through her, giving her courage.

'Why should she want to destroy you?'

'For revenge. Power and control,' he reasoned. 'She wants me dead, for leaving her to live with you.'

'But surely she got over that?' Isobel began.

'No, I don't think she ever did. Besides, she needs my psychic energy to fuel her own creative power, and she is dangerous, unbalanced—she thinks she can pay everyone back for any slight injustice that has been done to her. A nun was cruel to her as a child, used to torment her, perhaps that's why she has such a dark side.'

Isobel stared at him, his story was incredulous and he was humiliating her. She felt a stab of jealousy and the stirring of rage.

'Every night I dream about her, she's trying to take my soul!' he cried. 'She's a black witch trying to imprison me. She entrapped me with constant sex,' he admitted, 'and has never really forgiven me for leaving her for you. She wants revenge.'

Isobel looked away, anger surging in her; she felt strangely triumphant at the pain he was suffering. But what could stop her pain?

'If this is true, how can I help?' Isobel asked, suddenly excited.

The possibility of revenge on Felicia made her feel elated. She wanted to destroy her, and didn't care how she did it.

The Dark Goddess lies in wait, coiled like a serpent ready to seize her prey. The wind blew harder and the boat rocked. The windows rattled and the room looked full of strange faces, silhouettes, demons.

'What can we do?' asked Isobel.

'I don't know,' he admitted. 'We have to find someone to help us, because we can't fight her alone. Thanks for trying to help me, Isobel.'

'I'm doing this for our dead child,' she stated, her eyes narrowing with malice. 'Nothing gives me greater satisfaction than the thought of destroying Felicia,' she said in a cold wooden voice. She walked across the room, her high heels clicking noisily on the parquet floor, her tight skirt and suit making her look powerful and authoritative. No longer the gentle compliant maiden, she was a goddess. She began to devise a plan, they had to lure her there, and then attack.

That night grotesque images of Felicia, wearing black, spun around Isobel. She was dressed in black withered weeds. Felicia's evil swirled in her mind, torturing her as they were led into Hell. Felicia danced around a maypole, weaving among maidens of death, devouring her flesh. The maidens of death danced in a circle, their gaunt faces, with cracked smiles, and deathly pale, looking on solemnly at Rick tethered by chains to the rocks, trying to break free. Isobel woke up, she felt the familiarity of Rick's body next to hers and rapturously succumbed to his touch. God she wanted him; she felt him slide into her easily, like he had never been away. His breath grew faster, a surge of love flooded through her as he lifted her body and gently pushed inside her. She felt her body lift in ecstasy, then fell back content. His touch brought her to life again, made her whole. She fell into a restless sleep, dreaming he was making love to her, but when she looked up he was a cadaver, a skeleton, his face had turned to ash. His eyes, still glinting in their sockets like daggers. She was making love to a corpse. She woke up in a panic and tried to wake him. He didn't respond, his expression glazed as if in a trance. He stared at her, unrecognising. He muttered something unintelligible. She watched the dawn break as he lay in her arms and prayed they would be safe. He moved and cradled her in his arms, and rocked her until she slept.

Isobel woke to the howling of the wind ripping through the boat; she turned over, pulled the duvet over her head, and buried herself, wanting to escape the reality of the uncertainty that faced her. Through the dark hours she held on to the thread of hope given to her by her own strength and will. She fought the fear, with the love she still felt for Rick—the father of the child she'd carried. Could they still love each other? After all they had been through?

A deathly scream vibrated through the boat. Isobel rushed to the lounge, where Rick lay on the sofa, shaking and convulsing, consumed by a noxious green smoke. Small rivulets of blood ran down from his neck. His eyes stared emptily at her.

'Rick—what is it?' she cried, shaking him. He was cold, as cold as death. Isobel kept shaking him, trying to wake him, but he was in a trance. He rasped a few words, then his body spasmed violently. His eyes glazed and rolled over, unseeing; they were filled with an evil presence. She looked closely as his eyes opened slowly, then saw he had Felicia's eyes! Her dark slanted eyes stared at Isobel and she heard a maniacal laugh. He was possessed. Isobel screamed, terrified. She felt something move, an energy, a force jumped out of him, she felt its poison tentacles clasp round her neck. The walls were closing around her, she felt a heavy pressure on her chest. She tried to push it away, it clung closer, suffocating her. A loud grotesque wail ripped through the air. Isobel shook Rick frantically and was thrown across the room. Something was moving in the darkness, slithering through the mist. A monstrous serpent writhed across the floor. Behind it, walking toward them, was Felicia. Terrified, Isobel held on to Rick, praying it was an illusion.

Felicia's hair blew around her in black snaky strands, like Medusa's head of snakes. She was a shape shifter, slowly changing into the princess of darkness. The serpent moved towards them, spitting and hissing grotesquely, its tail flaying out. A long tongue lashed from its mouth, spraying them with a venomous green fluid. It disappeared in a flash of smoke. Isobel screamed out loudly, terrified. The snake lunged at Rick, tearing open his flesh, trying to devour him. Its fangs forged bloody wounds, spurting fountains of blood. Blood ran from his neck over torn flesh. Isobel grabbed an oil lamp and threw it at the serpent. It shrieked as flames engulfed its reptilian body, slithering to the other side of the room. Isobel jumped back, fighting her nausea and terror. It slithered away, its body moving more obscenely than ever. Then a voice echoed through the darkness.

'He will never be yours again, Isobel, he's mine now and will be for eternity. I'm sending him to the darkness, where you'll never see him again,' Felicia screamed, her eyes flashing dangerously, alight with destruction. She let out a bitter hollow laugh. 'I have come here to take him back. We have a bond of blood,' she screamed. 'I will not let him go!'

Suddenly she reappeared, dressed in black mourning clothes, moving through the smoke. She climbed onto Rick and began seducing him, riding him as he lay helpless beneath her, unable to resist her power. She rode him harder, a black widow spider devouring its prey. He let out an inhuman gasp, writhing under her, his body lifting in pleasure as several convulsions jolted through him. Isobel, sickened, pulled at the door, but it was locked. She tried again, but the lock was stuck.

A black fog filled the air, dark shadows swirled around like bats seeking their prey. Isobel fell back exhausted. She had little energy left to fight the malignant evil facing her. In desperation, she picked up a book and brought it down over Felicia's head.

'I'll be back,' warned Felicia, backing away. 'You've not won yet, Isobel! My powers are much greater than yours!' she screeched in an unearthly wail, then dissolved into thin air. Isobel looked down at a cloud of dust, stunned, and sat down exhausted, relieved Felicia had gone. The silence returned. Rick was motionless, but still alive. His eyes were closed, but he was still breathing. Isobel leaned over Rick to feel his pulse, it was getting weaker. She bandaged up his wounds tightly. Her mind was in a turmoil. She had to think of a strategy, she could not fight Felicia alone. Rick was in no shape to help. If she didn't act soon, he would die.

She must find someone, but who? Then it came to her, Michel! There was no one else she could turn to.

She ran over to Michel's boat, he was in. He opened the door and looked at her with a hurt expression, but resigned that she was lost to him.

'How are you? I hear you are back with Rick?' he said, sadly.

Isobel, saddened looked away. 'Yes, I'm sorry,' she started.

'Why, Isobel, after all he did to you?'

'I don't know, I really don't know, I can't help it, I'm so drawn to him. Look there isn't much time, you must help me.'

He pressed a finger to her lips.

'No need to explain, I have to let you go. Don't worry, I wish you happiness, but please be careful, you are entering realms you know little about, and you don't know how to protect yourself. He is leading you into danger.'

She shook her head. 'No, this time I know what I am doing, I've a score to settle.'

'Do you still love him, after everything he has done to you?' he asked tentatively, not sure he wanted to hear the answer.

'I don't know, I'm not sure of anything any more,' she admitted.

'You do, I can see it in your eyes.' He kissed her on the cheek.

She kissed him back. For a moment they held onto each other.

'I've come to ask you for help. There is no one else I can ask,' she pleaded.

He gave her the address of an occult expert, a white witch who could fight black spells. 'Good luck Isobel, if ever you need me you know where I am.'

He watched her walk away. Out of his life, forever. He went inside the houseboat, where no one could see him, and let the tears surge down his face.

Dark predictions

The psychic sat before a crystal ball, murmuring as she used her powers to assess the situation, her palms spread out, summoning up spirits. Touching crystals, focusing her energy into her hands, she began speaking softly. Isobel watched her with curiosity.

'Your friend is in serious trouble, you must gain control soon,' she said in sonorous tones. 'The woman in question is your enemy, a black witch with evil powers,' she explained. 'She is using the darker aspects of the occult to get what she wants by manipulating the lives of others. She is evil. White witches are bound by higher principles not to use their gifts in this way. Most witches work in harmony with nature and the Earth. But she's using her power for evil, control and destruction, and she must be stopped. She's destroying your friend. She's draining him of life,' said the psychic, going into a trance. 'I can see him there, lying on your boat, he is dying spiritually and physically. You must free him, or she will destroy his very essence,' she warned.

'But why's she doing this to him?' asked Isobel, distraught. 'I thought she loved him.'

'In a way, she does,' she admitted, 'but wants him back—mostly as revenge. She felt that in some strange way he was the other half of her, she seeks revenge for what he did to her, and wants to take his soul to nourish her "dark goddess". She cannot live without him. She uses his power to make herself stronger, to take every part of him, his gifts too, for her own. She feeds on him like a vampire, and needs his physical elemental energy to move to a higher realm, to the status of goddess of darkness.'

'How?' asked Isobel.

'By seduction, the more souls she collects, the more power she has. She enjoys destroying others.'

'How awful!' shivered Isobel.

'These souls add to her omnipotence as a witch, or so she believes. But she has the blindness of a fool, who does not realise she is playing with fire and that it will eventually turn back on her and destroy her,' predicted the psychic.

'But she can't do this to Rick,' cried Isobel in horror.

'I shall do what I can to help, to rid you of this woman,' offered the psychic, putting away the crystals. 'But there are no guarantees.'

'Please can you save him?' cried Isobel, devastated.

'I have some friends who may be able to help. She takes her power seriously and is quite a strong opponent,' said the psychic, preparing her craft. 'We will try and render the force benign. I can't promise to save your friend, but we shall try. We will try and send the energy back on itself, to destroy her.'

'Thank you,' said Isobel, gratefully.

'Now, follow my instructions and protect yourselves!' she ordered. 'It is vital. Start to prepare yourselves for the events ahead. Your friend is close to death, there's little time left,' she warned.

'What can we do?' asked Isobel.

'Place lavender in the room, watch him at all times, don't leave him. Her plan is almost final,' she warned. 'Protect yourself and your friend with these amulets,' she said, handing her two chains attached to strange symbols.

Back on the boat, Isobel sat waiting apprehensively. A violent storm blew up over the canal, lightning lit up the room. She noticed some dark shadows on Rick's face. He was losing consciousness. His skin was cold, like death. Isobel waited for Felicia with trepidation. She was sure she would show up soon. The storm was raging loudly, intensifying her fear. Suddenly the lights faded, and they were thrown into darkness. She felt an evil force seep into the room, and Felicia suddenly appeared. Isobel watched with dread as she moved out of the shadows. On her face was the gaze of a dark goddess. She held a knife, which glittered lethally, she called up something. The river snake lunged toward Rick, piercing him with its venomous fangs, coiling around him, sucking out his life force, gripping him in its power. Blood spurted out of his wounds, sores stuck on his body like stigmata. He began convulsing, his face contorting in agony. Felicia turned toward Isobel, screaming at her:

'You bitch, Isobel, I shall kill you both. I call up the powers of darkness to destroy you.' A noxious smoke filled the room. Isobel had put the protective amulets around them, so she felt stronger, and Felicia could no longer pierce her psychic shield, but Rick was still suffering. Rick was slumped forward, rasping helplessly, then he fell back, his breathing hardly audible. His lips were deathly pale, his eyes haunted and staring. Isobel thought he was dead, totally consumed by Felicia, who now changed back into human form and straddled him, writhing against his body. Her fangs ripped deeply into his flesh. Barely alive, he let out an agonising wail. He couldn't survive much longer. Isobel grew hysterical. What could she do? They had reached the end. Then, something strange happened. Felicia looked at Isobel's ring, the one her aunt had given her, and fell back whimpering like a wounded dog. Something had weakened her. The psychic appeared before them.

'I have come to assist you,' she said, going into a trance.

Suddenly a loud crack of thunder rocked the boat, and a white light filled the room, a sparkling white energy that consumed Felicia. She screeched as her body was sucked into a bright white tunnel, spinning into a vortex. Sparks flew as she struggled. An earth-shattering wail ripped across the boat as it was tossed turbulently from side to side. The sky grew dark and ominous except for occasional flashes of lightning; the moon was hidden, there was no light, just an unnerving darkness. The sky was inky black, with no stars. Just an unearthly calm like the end of time. Suddenly, there was a bright white flash that lit up the whole dark sky. The sounds of the river returned.

The stench and evil aura dissipated. A feeling of lightness returned to the room. Rick regained consciousness, looking at Isobel in amazement as he awoke from darkness and came into the light. He stood up, his strength returning to full force, then he grabbed Isobel's hand, ran outside and pushed her into the car. He cradled Isobel protectively and kissed her. Jumping in, he locked the doors and drove for the rest of the night.

'I'll never lead you into danger again,' he promised.

Aftermath

A few months later, Michel received a letter from Isobel. It read:

Dear Michel,

We have moved to Spain. Rick has found work as a session musician and we're starting a family, our dream is being realised at last. It's safe here. Perhaps we'll forget the past eventually. Only time will tell. I hope you are happy and that you find true love one day. I'm sorry I was not the one able to give it to you. Thank you for being a good friend. I did care about you, but it is only Rick that I truly love. I wrote this poem, with you in mind, please remember me through it.

Butterflies

Give me the lightness of your being, the delicacy of your soul,
Like a dove, I need to soar above, like a butterfly, I need to brush past your
Translucent light, and feel your touch,
But do not dig your pin in and destroy me, or clip my wings then discard me,
Leaving me to bleed inside,
Let me fly and reach my dreams on the summit of your grace,
The dreams I seek are just a glimpse away,
I need the vision to find my way,
Give me a harbour where I may stay…
So that I can stay…
And find your heart

My affection,

Isobel xxx

Thank you for giving me a safe harbour when I needed one, I will never forget you.

He read it, realising he had only ever been a safe harbour for her, a temporary refuge; she had never really been his. Turning around, he looked to where her boat was moored; sadly, he saw she was gone forever. He thought he saw her gliding across the canal in a white dress, then he blinked and she had gone. He felt her presence as though she were there next to him. Pain ripped through him like a knife, tearing him apart. He read the poem again, wiping the tears from his eyes, then tore up the card and threw it in the river. He shivered as he remembered their laughter, the nights they had spent locked in each other's arms. All he had left was a photograph. Sadness engulfed him. She had fled to Spain with Rick. Well, it was her life to do as she pleased, and they were having a baby. He smiled, happy for her. He recalled her gentle touch, her embrace and reflected how he had loved and lost her. And that no one could replace her.

Then his spirits rose slightly. He knew he would cherish their memories forever. They could never be erased. The pain would fade with time, and it was time to move on. A few days later, a corpse was fished out of the canal, so badly emaciated, no one could be sure of its identity. The description of the body, with long flowing hair, perfectly matched Felicia.

All that remained, found next to the victim, was a single black amulet, known to have been worn by her—a ring with a face of a goddess with wild snakes on her head. Felicia had drowned in the storm: someone had seen someone like her struck by lightning and washed into the canal. No one knew for sure if she had died intentionally, for her mind had been so unhinged, or by accident.

The river swirled past lazily as Michel quietly stepped onto the grey boat. He just had to go to Isobel's house one last time: say goodbye to her in his mind, give it closure. It had been sold and the new owners were due in half an hour. Pushing open the door, he saw it was empty. He looked around him: it looked different, all the furniture had been removed. All traces of Isobel were gone; it was painted white inside. He spotted the ring with the strange emblem of the fated goddess, which Isobel had worn, on the floor. He kissed it and put it in his pocket. Holding it tightly, he walked away from the boat for the last time. The new residents were arriving, coming up the path, they waved and he waved back. He started packing his things into the car.

A raven black-haired rat with staring, evil, vibrant eyes foraged amongst the debris of the rubbish, looking for scraps to eat—Felicia's reincarnation. It hobbled painfully, its coat lank and dirty from the oil of the canal. Another rat bit its neck, fighting for the scraps. All was tranquil and peaceful on the canal. A new cycle had begun.

People were loading furniture onto Isobel's boat. A group of artists were taking a trawl along the river. Michel got into his car, and revved the engine. He hadn't noticed it before, but it was quite oppressive there with tall grey buildings blocking the light. As the engine started, he seemed to spring back into life; he drove through the mist, the chill he'd felt icily seeping in his bones dissolving into warmth as the sky began to clear and the sun began to break through the clouds. He drove south, away from the canal, the city and the dark clouds hovering over Little Venice. He turned on the radio and headed for Sussex, toward the open fields and the sun, saying goodbye to the canal and Isobel, forever.

END

Castle of Dreams

Castle of Dreams

Raphelia—the Dark Angel
Claire—The Enchantress

Dreams

Claire saw Mike Devereux standing in the corner of the wine bar, having a drink, after she had been working late at her television agency in Soho. He stood alone at the bar, his eyes sparkling mysteriously with a dangerous edge that made him seem all the more attractive, with an unleashed energy that few men possessed. He was a tall, elegant man with raven-black hair and granite-grey eyes, and could have been the centrefold pin-up of a magazine, but he had chosen to work on the other side, behind the camera, instead. He stood alone, towering over everyone, six-foot-three, drinking Jack Daniels and smoking a long black cigarette: dark, captivating and dangerous. Tonight he smiled and said hello to her as she walked past. His eyes crinkled with warmth as he spoke. She nearly fainted with lust. A talented photographer, he lived in a large loft apartment in Notting Hill where he exhibited his work and entertained tall, willowy blondes with exotic tastes. So her colleagues told her. Rumours of his love life had been a source of fascination for her friends who labelled him a social butterfly, as he never seemed to stay anywhere with anyone for too long. All the girls in the studio adored him and scrambled to the front of the studio on the days when he brought in his photographs for re-touching or to make a short film. He was a minor media celebrity in the West End, frequently commissioned for his outstanding award-winning, atmospheric photographs and had a reputation for taking out the most glamorous blondes—last week he had been photographed with at least two. Safety in numbers, guessed Claire correctly. Was he *that* terrified of commitment? Tonight, after such a promising start, she might get a chance to speak to him, if she could get close enough. She was sure she could tame a man like that. Her girl-next-door looks often drew the wildest of men, so that they became quite helpless. Men always trusted and confided in her; she was not a femme fatale, but a success in her own right, and a girl who could bring out the gentleman in most males. She wasn't a wild party animal, preferring to stay at home and read romantic novels. She believed in fairness and trust, and didn't play games, but still loved a challenge, particularly tall, dark, brooding men with large expressive eyes. She could be a vamp too, when she needed to be; her long blonde hair reached past her waist and with dark make-up and a slick black dress, she could look intriguing.

She turned and caught a glimpse of Mike. He looked so deliciously sexy and seductive. He was standing in an alcove at the other side of the bar, laughing and joking with some friends from the media, his long legs clad in tight black jeans, his black hair hanging down over his black leather jacket, a priceless Nikon slung over his shoulder. He stopped and glanced across, and said, 'Come over.' He slicked his hair back, and smiled. She stared in his direction, unable to pull her gaze away. He shot her a smouldering glance, then returned to his conversation, and began animatedly discussing his latest ideas with a fellow photographer. He leaned against the bar, a svelte animal ready to pounce, full of untamed energy and sexual charisma. He shook his long black hair loose, and it glistened like a raven's wing. Dressed in black, he looked stylish. His ice-grey eyes scanned her admiringly, as he caught her gaze, his eyes lit with interest. He waved. He was so achingly sexy, feral like a panther. Claire caught her breath trying to read his body language. Sleek, tall and willowy, definitely an alpha male! Putting down her glass, she decided it was now or never. She walked past him, her tight black silk Chinese dress slit at the sides, and threw back her mane of blonde hair. It had the desired effect. He smiled approvingly.

'I wondered when I would finally get to meet you,' he said, his eyes smouldering. She felt like she wanted to drag him into bed that second. 'What would you like to drink?' he asked her.

'Wine, please.'

'Are you from the TV company next door?'

'Yes, I'm freelance.'

'So you are working on the latest Aston Martin advert?'

'Yes, we shot it in Jamaica last year, it was fun.'

They chatted for hours; Claire felt they already had an easy rapport and quite a bit in common.

'I can't stay,' Claire said, 'I have an early start tomorrow, goodbye.'

'Not goodbye, au revoir, I'd like to take you to dinner next week.'

'I'd enjoy that.' She handed him her business card.

'Thanks, I'll be in touch,' he said, smiling.

The next day he walked into her office, clutching a handful of invitations to his latest photographic exhibition at the central gallery and asked her if she'd like to go. She jumped at the chance. She drove back to her flat, and sat down after a busy week, and read about him in *Design News*; he'd won several awards, and had just broken off his engagement to a famous debutante. He might be fun, thought Claire optimistically. Whenever she'd seen him, something seemed to click between them, there was a strong chemistry, and she didn't really care about his reputation, he seemed just right for her. She'd go on a few dates, see where it went from there. She loved a challenge. Men were like kittens, she thought confidently, easily tamed. She was a gentle soul too, who had also won prizes for flower-arranging in her home town of Sevenoaks, in Kent.

Later, he invited her to his studio, Mike handed her a brochure. She opened it, it was full of black and white romantic photographs shot among mysterious backgrounds, and conveying a ghostly, eerie feeling. She turned the pages, glancing at the models posed on rocks, in churches, draped over stones at old cathedrals, posed under stained-glass windows and gothic arches, their dark, heavily made-up eyes full of mystery. She studied the pictures and drew in her breath at their beauty, transfixed by wild beaches, images set among menacing rocks. Intrigued by the romantic, ethereal photographs; beautiful svelte women wandering through old castles, black birds perched on gargoyles, she flicked through some more. Against a backdrop of dark, swirling mists and shadows, which captured dramatically a gothic ambience, she found them haunting, atmospheric, pagan. In the pictures, she saw an incredibly beautiful, ethereal woman wearing a long, black lace dress and pensive smile, with very long black rippling hair, dancing.

'That's last year's exhibition, I made a film of it too. Would you like to see it? The film of the shoot? The video?' asked Mike. 'It looks even more eerie live.'

He pushed the video into the recorder and blurred images shot onto the screen. It shot into sharp focus: a woman was walking through a field, weaving around Celtic crosses, then she began dancing a strange dance on the rocks, her hair blowing wildly in the wind. She had fine patrician features, and slanted, powerfully hypnotic eyes. She was professional, thought Claire, noticing her cat-like almond-shaped eyes reflected an incredible magnetism; they were the eyes of a goddess, a gothic beauty. She danced sensually, like a ballet dancer, her limbs moving with effortless grace. Swirling and twirling above the sea, she leapt down to the edge of the cliffs—it made compelling viewing. Her cat-like body moved rhythmically and in tune with the scenery around her. Watching the scene come to life was even more captivating. He stopped the video. 'I filmed it at the Minack Theatre,' he said slowly, 'a theatre set in rocks, when I was in the West Country.'

'It's so enchanting,' admitted Claire.

'This is the *mis-en-scène*,' he pointed out; 'it identifies my work, I made if for a photographic exhibition. I am a fashion photographer,' he explained, 'and we like to use many different backdrops to create the right atmosphere for the clothes.'

'What's that exactly?' asked Claire, interested.

'*Mis-en-scène* is an essential, defining shot that identifies the feel a film has. The atmosphere of a horror film can be a gothic castle, a bat or a moody, jagged landscape, creating a feel of discord and unrest. Dark music provides the rest. The Celtic backdrop and wildness is my *mis-en-scène*,' he explained. 'And she had the dark, sultry looks and vampish quality that fitted into my genre well. It shows a scene that is romantic, wild and turbulent. It says everything about it visually, that it is haunting, and identifies the work as mine, a kind of signature.'

He stopped the video at a shot of the woman languishing in a graveyard. The woman lay on a tomb, her body spread out, her face toward the sky, her eyes closed. Her fingers gripped the sides of the tomb, the wind was blowing through her hair and her web-like lacy clothes as she crawled slowly over the stone. She had a predatory, yet ethereal air and was a truly gothic princess. A wreath of tiny black roses perched precariously on her head. The sea crashed mercilessly in the distance, and her fine profile was turned to the rocks.

'Who is she?' Claire asked Mike.

'Raphelia? Just one of my models,' he said dismissively, looking away.

'She is so beautiful, ravishing, enchanting. Exotic.'

'Yes I agree, but you are far more beautiful, Claire,' he said, his eyes softening, 'quite a different type of woman altogether.'

'In what way?' asked Claire, curious.

'You are so sleek, clean and wholesome—with your huge bright eyes, you just glow with health and energy,' he joked. 'No, I'm serious, you still have a touch of innocence about you, a maiden, as though your soul is still pure.'

'I don't know about that, anyway, who is she? I've seen her all over town!' laughed Claire.

'Raffy, she's wicked, dark and dangerous, full of darkness,' he said warily, with a wry smile. 'Her innocence went a long time ago.'

'Which type of woman do you prefer?' asked Claire.

'You, of course! Women like her burn brightly, then fade away and when the wickedness no longer lights their spark, their dark souls, they just wither away, lose their allure, fade into the background. She's just one of many brilliant models. We worked together for a while until she turned into a very demanding pain in the neck.'

'I see, is she famous? I am sure I have seen her picture all over town and in some magazines.'

'Yes they used her for the latest vodka advert—the one that says "find your wilder side". I have worked with her quite a lot,' he said, waving his hand dismissively. 'She is one of many, I tend to have regulars that I use all the time. I like to get to know the women I work with, their moods, build a rapport.'

As he took out the print, a dark shadow crossed his face. He turned back to Claire, and smiled. Claire sensed there was much more to their relationship, but did not like to ask.

'Would you like to keep it?' he offered.

'Thanks, so I am the girl next door,' she sighed. 'I don't possess any deep, dark mystery, or exotic beauty?'

'Of course you do,' he laughed. 'You are very beautiful, in a fresh way, the type of girl men marry and have beautiful children with, the other kind of passion soon fades out. She's too predatory. What use is that to anyone except a panther or a lion? I prefer my women to be soft and loving, like kittens,' he said, smiling. 'Not scheming vamps.'

Claire studied the picture, her eyes fixed on the woman's face: she glared like an untamed vamp, wild, dark and mysterious. She put the award-winning photograph back in the frame. She would hang it on the wall of her flat, she'd always been an admirer of his work. He handed her an invitation, a glossy photo. She accepted it at once. He jumped off the desk and invited her to see his collection before the exhibition and offered her a personal tour of his studio, to get a glimpse and the choice of buying the best photographs.

'I'd like you to come,' he said. 'We'll have a few drinks, and I'll let you see my work.'

'Of course, I'll be there.'

Claire felt elated. She couldn't believe the man of her dreams was asking her out. That night, he walked over to her and she caught her breath; he was dressed all in black with a camera slung around his neck.

'Sorry I didn't have time to go home,' he said. 'I had to work late, right up to the last minute.' She smiled, accepted his apologies and gazed at him lovingly. He took her to a new organic restaurant, then to an avant-garde cinema, where they saw a controversial Japanese film, which they discussed for hours afterwards. Things were looking very promising, thought Claire excited, then she remembered the woman in the photograph and for some inexplicable reason a chill ran over her spine. It was almost as though she was there in the room, looking over them.

'She has quite an unusual beauty, very exotic and catlike,' observed Claire, thinking predatory, but not wishing to be rude.

The next day at his studio, she saw the woman's face was everywhere, plastered all over the studio, all over billboard adverts, drinks, her dark temptress eyes staring down at the pedestrians, the mortals of her court, and she the queen, her eyes glistening with dark delights. Mike had used her for a lot of his collections, she noticed. She saw her image emblazoned on the front of *Photographer Monthly* and read that she was modelling for another photographer with whom she was having a torrid affair. Mike picked up the magazine and turned pale, a dark expression covering his face, his cheeks tight, making him look gaunt. He became cool and detached, a stranger. For a moment he looked angry and about to lose his temper, then he mellowed and smiled.

'She's no one special really,' he said. 'Her soul is black, she's evil, her beauty's only skin deep. I'm glad she's gone to someone else. I couldn't bear her tantrums any more.'

His eyes narrowed like a hunter, his features hardened. He took out the picture of Raphelia standing behind a Celtic cross with a raven flying by in the distance, her hair flying outwards, up in the air.

'There, that one can go on display. Do you like the effect?'

'How do you do that?' asked Claire. 'Make her hair fly out like that?'

'By placing a fan heater in front of her. Simple when you know how, it's amazing what special effects can do. Yes, I remember that one, it was taken in France,' he said softly.

She thought she saw tears in his eyes. She put down the prints. 'Was she someone very special?' she asked.

'Not particularly, just an old friend,' he replied, evasively.

'Let's talk about you instead,' he shrugged. 'She's the past. I told you she's not that important. I'd rather talk about you.'

'No, please, tell me more,' begged Claire, 'it's such a beautiful photograph that I have to know more. I feel I almost know her.'

Claire could not help noticing the reticence in his voice as he spoke. Yet she was eager to know all about him.

'Well, if you insist. I met her while I was shooting a series of photographs in Ireland, seven years ago. She came up to me on the beach and started talking to me in a heavy French accent. I met her while she was on holiday, trying to trace her ancestors.' His eyes misted over. 'I thought she looked very unusual, with such large slanting eyes, that she might be good to photograph. So when she came to London, I took her on my books and helped her launch a fairly successful career, which suited us both. We were friends for a while,' he said, a dark tone creeping into his voice.

Claire looked at him questioningly.

'Well, lovers,' he admitted, 'then it all fell apart. It was nothing but a doomed romance. She was looking for a career, I thought she had potential, so I took Raphelia on as my model, but she had a strange temperament, and became difficult to work with,' he admitted, his eyes becoming misty and detached. 'But when we did get the final effect, she was better than anyone else I'd ever used, she could adapt to any style with ease. We developed a brilliant rapport and she suited my genre perfectly. She knew what I wanted without my asking, it was as though she was completely in tune with my ideas. As a team we were very successful for a while, but as time went on she became more and more demanding, erratic and unreliable, until I discovered she was using too much cocaine and was taking other lovers.'

Claire started to feel uneasy and wished she hadn't asked.

'Oh, poor you,' she said, feeling slightly jealous.

'So I stopped using her for a while. She'd become far too much of a liability, acting more and more spoilt, staying out all night, screeching at me if I tried to curb her freedom. Her personality became more and more volatile, she threw tantrums at the slightest problem. The drugs didn't help. She started staying out late, making unreasonable demands. I found out there were two other lovers. She had several suitors, and would have seduced the entire Scots platoon if she'd had the chance, and treated sex as a kind of sport, as cursory as a handshake, with which she used to exercise power over her victims. Whereas, when I make love, I prefer it to be something special,' he said, glancing softly at her. 'We argued all the time, about everything.'

His eyes focused on the pictures he was shuffling rapidly, filling with a misty sadness.

'So I dropped her, asked her to clean up her act or leave. She said she had never loved anyone the way she loved me, but couldn't be tied down, it killed her creative spark. She just had to have a challenge, and she begged me to take her back,' he said, his voice quivered with emotion. 'I couldn't give her what she wanted, there was no point in carrying on. Reluctantly I tried, but the same thing happened over again. So I threw her out.' He laughed. 'She tried to claw her way back for a while,' he said bitterly, 'but soon moved in with someone else. That's all in the past now. I'm lucky to have met someone as pretty as you.'

'She suits the atmosphere of the picture well, there's something haunting and sad about her,' observed Claire, 'she's like a doomed dark princess.' Holding the picture up to the light, she could see a lot of detail and fine work had gone into it.

'Yes, she does have a powerful presence, a special aura, a darkness that I haven't seen in any other model,' he admitted, his voice lowering, his tone conveying disquiet. 'But an ominous one! How about some lunch?' he suggested, quickly changing the subject. 'I don't want to talk about the past, it's irrelevant. Let's not talk about her. I am sure you are just as fascinating. In fact, I find you even more so. You're more human, approachable. You still have inner beauty and innocence. You're like an angel,' he observed, ushering her out to the car. 'Let's go now, our table is waiting.'

'Good idea,' agreed Claire, glad to drop the subject. Really, it was not her business to pry. But she couldn't get the woman's face out of her mind. Her face was plastered all over Mike's studio, and all over the billboards in the street, that latest vodka advert, for 'reach into the dark side of your soul'. At first she had been fascinated to meet the man who had created the photographs and to hear the model's story, but now she started to feel an uncomfortable pang of jealousy, and a momentary worry that Mike might still be in love with her, but, being an optimist she quickly brushed it aside. If he loved Raphelia he would still be with her, the relationship had obviously ended a long time ago.

In the restaurant, she felt her spirits soar as Mike listened attentively to the details of her life, of her family, her friends, when she graduated from St Martin's School of Art. Enthusiastically she told him how she had just managed to buy her first flat in Russell Square and how much she loved working in television. Just when she thought she had said too much, he smiled and poured her wine and asked her some more questions, responding enthusiastically to all of them. Focusing only on her, he seemed totally immersed in her, smiling and nodding in all the right places, genuinely interested in everything she was saying. When they got to the end of the second bottle of wine, although they were just getting to know each other, she felt like she had known him for a long time.

The next day he turned up at the agency holding some flowers, saying she took his breath away and consulted her over designs for his new brochure. For the next week they worked late every night, engrossed on his project for the coming exhibition, re-touching the finished shots until they shimmered with glossy perfection. On the last day of the shoot he took her to dinner again. Set among candles was the most attractive dish of lobster stuffed with lemon crème fraiche and prawns. On the table was a book of his latest work, with some stunning photographs. She was flattered to have so much attention from a man she'd always admired. She touched the cover and read inside.

'To my angel, Claire, love Mike.' An amiable camaraderie quickly developed between them. He gazed at her with love over dinner, his eyes never straying from her, but smouldering with lust. She was aware of a bond growing between them, the mutual attraction was really sizzling. She wondered why he didn't try and kiss her. Perhaps they were becoming more than just 'friends'. She could hardly control herself as his thigh rubbed against her and she felt his animal energy pulse like a lion next to her. He took her hand, arousing in her such a strong fiery passion that she gulped her wine back in seconds. He brought with him a small box. Inside was a lovely Celtic ring, with a black gem stone set in the middle, he picked it carefully out and slid it onto her finger.

'A friendship ring,' he explained. 'I hope we can always be this close.'

'Yes, it's lovely,' she said, seeing it sparkle on her finger. 'Thank you.'

Leaving the restaurant, they jumped into a taxi, and he dropped her off at her flat. He held her, then kissed her passionately, but said he was getting up early and declined coffee, and walked away with a sadness in his eyes. She stood in her kitchen stunned, surely he was supposed to have seduced her? He was perfect in every way, but had made no move to sleep with her. She stood there mystified. The atmosphere in the restaurant had been electric, but something seemed to distract him at the last minute. Still, she admired his good manners and the way he treated her with so much respect, and hoped he might lose his steely self-control soon.

Moods and bleak landscapes

Claire had been seeing Mike for almost a month, but she wondered why he'd never made a serious pass at her. He had kissed her, but never tried anything more, and she was baffled as to why. They'd known each other for an acceptable time, yet he'd never even once tried to seduce her. She, on the other hand, was burning with desire, but did not want to put him off by coming on too strong. What were the normal urges of a passionate man? Was he seeing someone else? Doubts started to smoulder in her mind, and she decided she had to move things along—after all, he seemed to enjoy her company and nobody was forcing him to see her. Maybe he just didn't want to rush things. The next night he kissed her deeply, passionately, almost angrily; she could feel he was burning with desire, but something was holding him back. Just as she felt they were about to embrace, his mind shot suddenly elsewhere, and he curtly said goodnight. His eyes were misty, full of torture and sadness. He saw the look of dismay on her face, and walked back and kissed her. He swept her off her feet and kissed her long and hard.

'Claire, I'm sorry,' he said, 'please be patient. I've a lot on my mind. The exhibition. You know how it is.'

The next few evenings followed the same pattern. He'd take her for a meal, they'd have enormous fun, and get on like a house on fire, the mood would seem perfect, then at the last moment it all seemed to fade, the mood was lost. At the end of the evening he'd plant a furtive kiss on her cheek as though afraid of taking it further. She was baffled. Men, in her experience, usually had to be fought off after a few dates, yet he was the most reluctant suitor she had ever known. One night, he gave her a deep kiss that seemed to grow more urgent and seemed to signal the start of something exciting, but she was wrong, or at least had read the signals incorrectly. He kissed her, pulling her hair and his eyes burned darkly, like a huge passion was erupting that had been harnessed in him. Then he stopped, on the edge of passion, afraid to let himself go. He seemed starved for affection, yet reluctant to make her his lover. The next night he pushed against her body, inflamed with lust, and gasped with some relief at holding and caressing her. But still he didn't ask her home. He apologised to her. She liked a man to treat her with respect but this was getting ridiculous, she had to know there was passion between them.

'I haven't slept with you, because I want to get to know you first, I want this to be a journey of discovery of a perfect fairy-tale love, not just a passionate fling. I don't want another relationship based on lust,' he said softly. 'I want it to get it right this time, for this to be special. I've just broken off an engagement,' he explained. 'To a debutante, you may have read about it in the paper, we weren't suited. I want to take things slowly, I don't want to scare you away, Claire,' he said, looking down at his hands. 'I don't want to rush things, I want to be sure you're the one.'

'There's no pressure,' said Claire, 'let's just enjoy each other's company and see where it goes.' She was secretly thinking it would be fine if it just turned out to be an affair. 'Do I really have to be "the one", why can't we just have fun, see where it goes?'

He looked at her seriously. 'Yes, but as I think you may be the one, I don't want to spoil it. If I'd wanted a quick fling with a bimbo, then I would have chosen one. One day I shall inherit a considerable fortune,' he said tersely. 'I don't want to make a mistake or have another empty affair,' he insisted. 'You're such a special woman, that I want this to work, I want something real. My other relationship was based on fantasy,' he said his eyes taking on a glazed, faraway look. 'I don't have any more time to waste.'

Claire didn't like the sound of things, and she shied away from the idea of having to 'measure up' for a specific role in a relationship; it didn't sound natural and spontaneous. She would rather let things take their natural course and, besides, if there wasn't a strong sexual attraction, no spark, then there was no real basis for love. She wondered if she was doing the right thing, then she decided she didn't have a lot to lose and would give it some more time.

Mike looked at her as if he was reading her thoughts. Then trying to hide his guilt, he became the easy-going Mike again. 'Look, I'm sorry. I didn't mean to say that, there's no pressure. Of course you're right, we must take it day by day.'

She'd had serious reservations when she'd heard he was one of the wildest, sexiest men in the city, but now he was driving her insane with his reticence. The rumours of him being a sex-driven playboy were turning out not to be true. Why was he playing so hard to get? What was going on?

His engagement to blonde society hostess Jemima Wilkins-Smyth, a debutante beauty, had been fast and whirlwind, and then broken off within weeks. She had been his partner in a sailing and yachting competition, but left in tears, accusing him of behaving unacceptably, drinking too much and disappearing for days. She returned home, shocked and confused, after their engagement holiday, and swore she would never speak to him again. She checked into a clinic with depression to get over it. Everyone felt sorry for her, said she was a bit too highly strung and elegant for the wild Mike, who had behaved a little too unpredictably for her. She couldn't quite handle the lifestyle. Some said she found out some strange things about him, his past, but she was soon hushed up. Claire assumed he was taking some time getting over her and she didn't want to push things, so she decided to let time take its course. Besides, they had a nice easy relationship, and her friendship with him was doing her career so much good and she had met some influential people. If it developed, fine, if not then she had found a friend. But she couldn't help feeling intrigued by his mysterious dark side, she was already feeling the pangs of love. What was his dark secret? Yet Claire was feeling a little dismayed at his lack of passion for her. Surely if he found her that irresistible, he could not prevent himself from ravishing her? It wasn't as though she hadn't tried, and she wasn't sure she wanted a sensible relationship; it all sounded a bit conservative! She wanted his red hot-blooded passion, and knew he was capable of hot-blooded sex. She wanted to unleash his passion, make him explode into ecstasy.

Sometimes he would sink into black moods when his dark side took over, and his eyes became the eyes of a cold, ruthless predator. She detected a man who had been hurt, and wouldn't easily allow himself to be hurt again. At other times he was sensitive, caring for her every need, and looked at her with the most gentle, beautiful eyes she had ever seen, kind, warm and sensitive. One night, when he went back to her flat, they kissed and she was ready. Taking things in hand, she made a serious pass at him, lunging her hands into his jeans, and rubbing him, hoping he couldn't resist; after all, she was a very sexy woman who knew how to use her wiles. She had a plan, and it rarely failed.

'I want you now,' she whispered, slipping off her dress to reveal a basque and black fishnet stockings.

'Wow Claire, that looks amazing.'

She smiled triumphantly, glad his libido had not been jaded by seeing scores of sexy, naked models.

It worked. He led her into her bedroom and tore off her clothes. Then he kissed her quite roughly, passionately. She sat over him, using her female wiles.

'You are beautiful,' he said, starting to make love to her. She pulled him on top of her, and wrapped her thighs around him, feeling the exquisite pleasure of him sink inside her. But while they were making love, his eyes became dark and wild, his manner detached. Despite her misgivings, she felt herself lifted quickly to ecstasy, Mike pushing inside her as she felt the most delightful bliss envelope her. He looked away and let out a satisfied groan as he came. Then he smiled at her and said, 'That was lovely,' but she couldn't ignore the faraway look in his eyes. He fell back and put his arm over his head, as though protecting himself. She could hear his heavy breathing, his release, but he did not touch her heart, his mind was not open to her. It had been better than she had expected or could have ever imagined, and she clutched the blankets and couldn't help smiling. She held onto him tightly, wanting him again. He was so warm and tender. Then his mood changed to camaraderie.

'I really enjoyed that,' she said, stroking his face, 'it was wonderful.'

'So did I,' he said, 'it was special.'

He kissed her face softly, but without the echoes of an urgent, deep love—something was holding him back, as though his mind was elsewhere. He covered his face with his arm. She felt a bit confused, knowing the kiss didn't come from his heart. So why was he with her? She had to give it time. He *was* fond of her. It was as though he had two very different sides to him, a dismal and a sunny side, a Jekyll and Hyde, roles he used to conceal a labyrinth of deep complex emotions, that rose like the winds of joy then crashed around him like tides of destruction. What had happened to make him like that, so unsure? Was he afraid of getting hurt, or did his heart still belong to someone else so that he was not free, chained to the past. They made love every day, but she felt he held back. They rarely ventured out of bed, until Claire relieved, saw at last that he was becoming a lot more relaxed and receptive toward her.

'I am going on location soon,' he said a week later, pouring some wine. 'I have to get some new material for my latest collection of photographs. I have to produce at least two exhibitions a year to stay on top of things.'

Claire's exuberance deflated, realising she might not see him for a while.

'I am going to Ireland, perhaps on to Thailand,' he continued, 'home first. I have decided to use the backdrop of Irish castles for my next assignment. I'm taking photographs for a book on Celtic mythology and history. I hope to cover a number of countries,' he added, 'capturing scenes for their local myths and legends.'

She sipped the wine slowly, barely looking at him in case he saw the tears welling up in her eyes. His photography was considered some of the best in London, originals signed by him were sought after amongst the most elite circles. His black and white photographs were so moody, haunting and atmospheric, that they pulled in the awards. He captured the essence of a place using the emotions and moods of his models and the shots had a startling and exacting clarity.

'Sounds interesting,' she replied, morosely. 'How long will you be gone?'

'A month or two, maybe three, even six, for as long as it takes,' he admitted.

Well, he obviously has no intention of seeing me as other than a friend, she decided, her heart sinking, feeling crestfallen. It was obviously just a fling. He was going away, and she hid under the blankets, sad that she might never see him again. All her hopes suddenly burst like a balloon.

'Well, I wondered if you'd like to come with me,' he said, seeing the disappointment in her eyes. 'I would love you to come. You are very special to me and I think I'm falling in love with you,' he said earnestly.

Claire felt her heart flutter, she was falling in love too.

'If you've any holiday due to you, I could put you on my payroll. I think you'd like it there. You can come officially, as my PA. You are a good graphic designer and could help me with some of the design issues, and unofficially as my girlfriend. At the weekends you can sit and sunbathe all day while I work, then in the evening you can sit on the balcony drinking the best wine and eating the best food. I shall pamper you, I promise.'

Overjoyed, her misgivings fell away like melting ice. She felt like dancing and replied at once, 'Yes, I'd love to come.'

'Claire, I *am* falling in love with you.'

Claire looked at him over her glass, relieved he felt the same. She put her drink on the side, put her arms around him and dragged him on top of her. She kissed him passionately and they made love.

'That settles it then, the Celtic look inspires me, I want to get some shots of the stones, behind the rising sunsets, that sort of thing and I may use you as a model there too. I could arrange you as an angel or goddess posing on the Celtic altars, or perhaps you are a pure maiden.' He laughed enthusiastically. 'You possess many talents, and that's what I like about you, you are amazingly versatile and fresh. I think we'll work together very well. In fact you do have some excellent muse qualities about you.'

'It sounds wonderful, I've about a month's holiday due to me.'

'So that's our plan then, I'll book a plane for early next month. My ancestors were French, they inherited a lot of property in Ireland. It's a mystical and spiritual haven with a history of myths and legends, of mystical power and mystery that is unequalled by anywhere else. That's why I want to use it for the "myths and legends" project—there are more myths there than anywhere else in the world! The Irish are great fantasists! Its landscape fits in very well with my contrasts, of darkness and light, and dark mystery. So it'll give me an opportunity to combine it with my latest work. It's full of wonderful old ruins, with treacherous shores and mystical tales. You'll love it, and there are some good beaches there, and a good sailing club in Kinsale and Bantry Bay and we have the regatta every summer,' he added enthusiastically. 'And some spectacular restaurants and cafés.'

'It sounds delightful,' she said, her heart soaring.

'Well let's make a start on the new catalogue,' he said. 'I'm studying contrasts, civilisation with wildness, dark and light, the misty and the tame and the wild.'

'Sounds fascinating,' she purred.

'Here,' he said, showing her a storyboard, 'are some pictures, with some new ideas. Here is Aphrodite by the sea, her red hair rippling and flowing in the wind.' Claire edged her seat round so that she could see them, and they were very beautiful.

'She represents a wild woman in nature. A goddess with a streak of cunning, a demon-witch. Here is one of a Celtic sea goddess,' he said, turning over a page to see a beautiful, dark woman, in a wild rocky terrain. I am using myths of Ireland as my theme, and photographing scenes that fit the myths.

Claire looked and saw another of Raphelia posing in Mike's studio. She was dressed all in red and gold, exotic and mysterious.

'And this last one is of a woman who represents purity.' He showed her one of a woman dressed in a white dress with long, flowing white hair running through a field of red poppies. 'I will use different women to represent my themes, and for the myths they represent. They can be smart and artistic, wild, bohemian or tame and little-girl-lost or little-girl-next-door, the different sides of women. I can encompass a lot within this. I may even photograph you,' he said, 'you have a very pretty youthful face. Okay—you will be my assistant, we can combine business with pleasure! I hope we can get to know each other better while we are there, away from all these interruptions,' he added, filling up her glass to the brim.

'Yes, I'd love to go,' she said happily, her eyes dancing with delight.

'Are you excited?' he asked, grinning boyishly.

'It sounds a dream,' Claire admitted, floating on air. 'If all women have elements of a type of goddess, then what am I?' she suddenly asked.

'You have elements of all of them, basically you are a nice, wholesome girl, a maiden, but you can look quite seductive and vampish too with your hair tied up, wearing the right slinky black dress, I've noticed. I'd say you have a creative flair and that means you have many female traits and characteristics, you're seductive and enticing. Maidenly and youthful is how I would describe you, but you do have a touch of the virgin about you, you are essentially sweet and beguiling, very pretty and natural, fresh and healthy when your hair is just brushed and when you wear one of those fluffy jumpers and glasses you look quite girlish. Like a *Top of the Pops* dancer.'

'Not quite,' said Claire stiffly. 'Pop's not my kind of music, I prefer heavy rock.'

'That's something we have in common then. Shall we go and see a band tomorrow?'

'I'd love to.'

'I've been planning to take a holiday for a while, with you there it will be so much fun. I need a break too, I think I'm becoming a workaholic,' he said, smiling.

'I've been working twenty-four hours a day lately too.'

'One more question, do you like children?'

'Yes, I love them,' she said. 'Why, do you have any?'

'No,' he laughed. 'Not yet, but I would love to, one day, and was wondering if you felt the same way.'

She sighed with relief that he intended it to be more than just a working holiday. She stared dreamily at him over the wine, what was he hinting at? That they may start a family together one day? Her heart almost burst with happiness. 'I'd love to have children, at least two,' she said.

'That's perfect. Start packing, then and I'll pick you up at five on Sunday.'

'What sort of clothes shall I bring?'

'All types, sexy bikinis for the beach, tough shoes for walking and hiking and a sarong to go around an evening dress or bikini in the day. Oh and some sensual evening wear for when I wine and dine you.'

'Sounds good fun. I think I will enjoy it very much.'

'You will, I promise you, the scenery is marvellous,' he said. 'It's quite a fascinating place. I will make your stay as wonderful as I can. The best holiday you've ever had! It's a perfect place to go sailing, there's a regatta every summer. Lots of water sports and swimming, everything you can think of.'

'I'm sure I will love it,' she replied, smiling, knowing it was going to be heaven with Mike by her side.

'First we shall have the publicity party, next weekend, and go straight after that.'

'That's perfect. Where will we stay?' she asked. 'In a hotel?'

'No, at my parents' castle in Cork, it overlooks the sea. They have a lot of room, and my mother lives in mainland Europe, my father is dead,' he replied. 'So the castle will be empty. It's near to Kinsale, so there's a good yachting club.'

She drew in her breath, excited and impressed at once. He was taking her to a castle, every girl's dream. He lived in a fairy-tale romance, life was turning out to be every girl's dream, a real fairy tale. She could barely hide her excitement.

'Does it have a four-poster bed?' she asked.

'Yes, three, two in the West wing and one in the East wing, you'll love it there. 'It's incredibly beautiful,' he continued, 'the castle overlooks the ocean, with rocks that plunge straight into the sea. It has several hundred acres of land too, and an amazing history. It once had a deer park and train station, some descendents of the English Royal family often stayed there. There are several themed rooms, the Chinese room, and a nautical room. We've several horses you can ride, or you can take out one of our yachts if you'd prefer.'

'Wow, that sounds incredible!'

'We're descended from the French aristocracy and the English. It is a very old building steeped in history.'

'Is it haunted?' asked Claire.

'No, he answered curtly, 'whatever makes you think that?'

She looked away, feeling stupid, it was the first time she had seen him angry over anything.

'Not all old buildings are haunted,' he said curtly.

'Well,' she said, swishing the wine around her glass, her poise intact, 'these places often are.'

His mood changed rapidly, a shadow fell over his dark features, so he looked menacing. 'It is most definitely not. No ghosts,' he said, in hushed tones. 'So don't worry, you will be quite safe,' he said, edgily, anger creeping into his voice. 'There's no dark and dismal past at the castle,' he said, a little too loudly. 'Don't you think I'm capable of looking after you?' he snapped. 'You may be the future mother of my children,' he said irritably, then stopped. 'I mean, sorry,

I'm going too fast. I wouldn't expose you to such a danger, even if there was one. You're far too precious to me.'

'Well, I didn't mean to suggest that you couldn't look after me,' she said. It's just that it sounds quite fascinating…' Her voice trailed off.

'Don't worry,' he said interrupting her, taking her hand, 'I'll take care of you. I may have a wild reputation, but I am quite amiable underneath.'

He smiled, his eyes crinkling at the corners. Claire thought it was a genuine smile, and that he was being honest. She'd studied a course in body language for her work and found it useful to analyse everyday situations. After the meal, they went home and made love for hours.

Claire felt flattered that he seemed already to have a special role for her. Almost at once his calm, friendly manner had returned. He laughed and became the old Mike again. His haughty manner had gone. But Claire still felt a chill inside, a wariness she couldn't define. He could become a different person, cold, unfriendly and wild at the drop of a hat. The dark mood evaporated and they laughed together again. What was he hiding, thought Claire? He would seem so kind and loving, then suddenly edgy and strange. They drank the rest of the wine, and began making plans for the working holiday. Mike stayed in a good mood, as the old Mike again. They were now close, passionate lovers: they had spent the last three months seeing each other every night, lunching every Friday, writing schedules and storyboards, designing the new cover.

Yet Claire still sensed he was holding something back. The next night, as promised, they went to see a band—everyone knew him and he had a backstage pass. At the concert a woman walked past them, threw her hair back and disappeared into the crowd—her face was familiar. Claire felt a prickle on her neck. Who was that? Another one of his many admirers?

A Party

A week before the holiday, Mike held a publicity party to promote his exhibition of photographs, called '*Myths and Legends—darkness and light themes*', to promote his latest collection. He invited everyone in the advertising, fashion and design world, and all the celebrities, top models and music rock-band personalities and media turned up. A lavish affair, it was set to be one of the most cutting-edge parties held that summer. Excited, Claire swished around in her most exotic clothes. She intended to look her best, an ideal opportunity for networking, making new connections, and seeing Mike. Her heart surged at the thought of their holiday, eating candlelit dinners next to the sea, spending time on romantic beaches. She tried to curb her excitement, and had hardly slept since he had invited her—she knew that in such a romantic atmosphere, she could not fail to stir his desire. He did desire her, she could see love in his eyes, yet something was troubling him. Still, they were so in love and she was getting a free holiday, all expenses paid, in the beautiful west country of Eire. Was she not lucky? She loved every minute of her life; after all, it wasn't every day she was invited out to spend a holiday in a castle with one of the best-looking photographers in London? She hugged herself, hardly able to believe it was really happening to her. She was sure that, after a week away, pushed together in an old castle, he might propose and they might even start a wonderful family of delightful little children, who looked just like Mike. With no one else around, he'd have all the time in the world to woo her.

She turned sideways, pleased with her appearance. Her long silky extensions curled down to her ankles, being a mermaid suited her. A temptress of the ocean! Realising this would fit well into the theme of the party, she chose a slinky silver dress, that made her look like she had scales, and emphasised the curviness of her figure and clung to her almost indecently—a silver fishy siren, risen from the dark depths of the sea, a slithery mermaid. She wove her long blonde hair with a translucent silk thread and added a few long tie-in gold and silver extensions that trailed her hair down to her ankles, enhancing her ethereal 'mermaid' appearance. That was perfect: now she looked like a true maiden, she thought, satisfied. She added some blue kohl, making her eyes look huge, bold and dramatic, mysterious and sultry, like a mermaid of the deep.

She liked the effect, and threw a blue wispy shawl over her dress, adding some silver stilettos and tights, then called Justin and Rory, her flat-mates, to let them know she was ready.

'Wow,' they whistled, 'you look stunning,' unable to believe it was her. Then as she was about to leave, the phone rang. It was Jemima Wilkins-Smyth, the debutante who had dated Mike.

'Be careful,' she whispered, her voice cracking. 'I heard that you are seeing Mike. Be careful, don't trust him,' she warned. 'Things are not as they seem. He has a dark secret; when I found out about it, he said I was being hysterical and sent me to the clinic. He told the doctor that I'd an alcohol problem, tried to shut me up, and I did drink a lot of champagne, but after what I had found out, it's no wonder...' Her voice trailed off. The phone suddenly went dead. Sour grapes, thought Claire, nonchalantly, her buoyant nature crushing any creeping doubts, her optimism always making things look brighter. The woman was just a jealous ex trying to stir up trouble, just because she wanted him back. She didn't give it another thought.

Claire peered over at his work, elegantly displayed on stands at the back of the room. People were snapping up catalogues and already he had received quite a few lucrative commissions. The photographs were beautiful, displayed in elegant floral wood-carved fames or with simple black silk borders. She had been on cloud nine all day and walked confidently into the hall of a top London, West End hotel. It was elegantly decorated, with champagne and canapés lining the room. She covered her ears from the loud pounding music blasting out of the speakers. Claire looked round the room for Mike—she had arranged to meet him at the party. Where was he? She caught a glimpse of herself in the glass, and was pleased. She looked good, her abundant mane of silvery hair flowed out like a mermaid goddess. She had to admit she looked pretty stunning. She couldn't see him, so she took a few brochures off the side and started browsing through them.

Claire looked all around her, but she still couldn't spot Mike. A wave of panic washed over her, then relief as she saw him talking to another photographer on the other side of the room. She waved and he beckoned her over; she began to feel quite bubbly and burst into giggles as the champagne fizzed up her nose. Justin and Rory came over, throwing back tequilas, already looking worse for wear and greedily tucking into the canapés.

Everyone arrived in fancy dress, eyes sparkling and wearing expressions of delight; the party, fancy dress, was now in full swing, with splashes of bright colour dancing and rippling over the walls in time to the throbbing music. Mike had hired one of the best nightclub DJs in town to arrange the night, with dancers, acrobats and fire-eaters and a circus and side-shows and robotic performers. Harlequin-suited dancers performed wild acrobatics over the floor and ballet dancers twirled and danced like demons. A strobe light flashed over the dance floor; some dancers dressed in black and white got onto the stage and were gyrating to the heavy atmospheric music, and the room vibrated. A fresh flood of party guests swooped into the room and began dancing energetically. Waiters and waitresses dressed in PVC outfits scurried around on roller skates, filling guests' glasses and lighting their cigarettes. The decor reflected eerily against a huge haunting landscape; a *trompe d'oeil* covered the back wall, where Celtic goddesses swirled underneath tall romantic figures, naked, or covered only with the scantiest clothes, an abundance of plants and tall white columns providing the backdrop, suiting the dark, Celtic themes. A projected image of *Miranda and the Waves* lit up one wall. It was the major event of the year and guests dressed as goddesses, vamps, pirates, witches and mermaids swirled around the room.

Claire walked into a cool, empty room with large beds and cushions strewn all over the place. A stream, cascading with cool blue water, flowed over green pebbles, exuding a feeling of tranquillity. This was a chill-out room and had been set up with beds and hookah pipe, and comfy ethnic sofas lining the walls to give an 'eastern' feel. She took a strawberry daiquiri and sipped at it delicately. A long table spread with canapés lined the wall, champagne and crystallised water and ice art stood in buckets. She looked around, delighted. The 'chill-out room' was a calm space momentarily to escape the heavy rock beat pounding from the party. Mike waved, beckoning her over. He was dressed as a count, with black make-up around his eyes making him look even more seductive, with long, pointy fangs. He flashed a wicked grin, and swirled his cloak around him, laughing maniacally. Claire had never seen him look so attractive, thinking how well the look suited him. She drew in her breath sharply. She ran over and flung her arms around him. He ruffled her hair affectionately.

'Hello, my darling, you are my incredibly beautiful and seductive mermaid, lady of the deep,' he enthused, kissing her bare shoulder. 'You look so wonderful tonight.'

She leaned forward as he made some adjustments to her costume. For a moment she felt incredibly beautiful, as though she was the only woman in the room, and he was the only man. The prince of darkness was devouring his siren. She nearly fainted with bliss as he swept her into his arms and kissed her longingly. Cameras clicked as the paparazzi snapped away. Then her heart missed a beat as she saw walking up to him, her rival, the ravishing model, Raphelia. In real life, close up, the sultry, sulky model, looked even more beautiful than ever. Her face was a perfect icon of dark beauty, a chiselled goddess with grey, flashing eyes that were so huge and magnetic, they made her feel quite heady. She looked at Emma, and scowled like a cat, her eyes aflame with equal measures of anger and passion, then gripped Mike's arm possessively.

'Oh Mike,' she whispered to him, so that Claire could hear, 'we need a rehearsal.'

'There isn't time,' he said. 'Just improvise. God, you've done it hundreds of time before.'

'I wanted a quick word,' she said impatiently, stamping her foot.

'Look I'm busy,' he snapped. 'Talk to me later,' and he put his arm around Claire.

If looks could kill I would have been shot a hundred times, thought Claire seeing Raphelia's venomous stare.

The woman tossed back her raven-black hair defiantly. Their eyes met, her eyes narrowing as she surveyed Claire, quickly assessing her as a rival. She shot her a look of pure malice and turned back to Mike. If she'd had claws, she would have got them out. She towered at over six foot. Willowy and elegant, her lashes were so long they swept over her face, a long cigarette in a holder in her hand. She flicked it disdainfully. Claire stared at her, fascinated, never had she seen such an elegant woman. Her cascading hair, dressed for the party with long extensions, reached down to her thighs like a gothic Rapunzel, woven with black feathers and white flowers, lace and black ribbons. She had come as a dark fairy-tale princess, in a red and white dress, the bad witch in Snow White or Cinderella. Claire, confident she looked equally beautiful, was not phased by her, but heads turned as she walked around. She had to admit she was truly stunning. She stood elegantly, a little like a cross between a pre-Raphaelite temptress, a vamp and a dark princess. Her eyes flashed wildly and brightly. She wore a dramatic red lipstick that made her look very sensual. She surveyed the people in the room with a kind of detached arrogance, sneering at the lesser mortals than herself who were lucky enough to have the honour of her presence. Her huge, flashing eyes, slanted like a cat, glistened with a vibrant, untamed, wicked energy. For a second Claire thought she saw a fleeting resemblance to Mike in those unusual dark eyes. All photographers created an identifiable look in their favourite models. She looked like a cat, ready to pounce. The guests stared at her in admiration. Claire gulped down her drink quickly and waved to Justin and Rory. Mike spoke quietly to Claire, who snapped out of her dreamy mode and listened to him as he pointed to the backdrop of Hylas and the nymphs on the wall. They were doing a sound check.

'Do you like that painting?' he asked.

'Yes, it's lovely, sea nymphs. Men being lured to their doom, where they go blissfully to their destruction.'

'Yes,' he sighed heavily, 'don't we all?'

Suddenly, the lights went out. Raphelia walked onto the centre of the stage and threw off her cloak, revealing black lace stockings and a tight PVC and lacy basque. Stepping up elegantly onto the stage, in high stiletto heels and a black feather boa, she walked down the catwalk gracefully, dancing as the 'darkness' themed music began. She was a vamp of the night, a wicked temptress, her eyes shining full of sorcery and dark delights. Strutting with perfect ease along the catwalk, she threw black roses into the audience as the party began and the stills of Mike's exhibition flashed up on the screen behind her. Raphelia went through her fashion sequence, then stepped down, and whispered something to Mike who glided off in another direction, then wandered back to Claire's side and started paying her compliments.

'You look wonderful, Claire,' he commented, taking her hands. 'Enchanting as ever. I didn't realise you could look as amazing as that, I love your hair, I shall include you in my next book,' he said, snapping. 'In fact, as well as PA you might be my next model.'

'Thank you,' said Claire, throwing her head back and laughing.

She looked round to see Raphelia shooting her a murderous stare. Knowing she was observed, the model turned round quickly and pretended to be fixing her make-up.

'Was that the model you use in your photographs?' Claire asked, feeling strange and unsettled by the icy stare. She shivered as though she was getting a cold.

'Yes, that's Raphelia,' he answered, raising his eyebrows in mock irritation. 'Are you all right?'

'I am so glad to have met her, although she seems a little icy.'

'A little,' he laughed loudly, 'is an understatement. She is one of the most difficult women I have ever met. She works as a model to pay the bills, but is actually a good photographer too, when she applies herself. But of course, she prefers quick money, endless parties and free cocaine and champagne, to the work it takes to make a real career out of anything. She has an "I want it now" approach to life,' he said critically.

A lady of many talents, thought Claire dryly, wondering exactly what their relationship was now. Something told her they were more than just friends, and that someone wasn't letting go. Claire felt too foolish to ask any more questions, so she bit her lip, her jealousy subsiding, chiding herself for being so obvious, so gauche, it really didn't do to gush. Raphelia was just a model, he must photograph thousands of women. She had to act a little more cool.

Perhaps their relationship was quite innocent, after all. He was a photographer and she couldn't get jealous just because he spoke to a beautiful woman who happened to be his ex-girlfriend. She would have to trust him or go insane! She must not show signs of possessiveness, especially not this early in their relationship.

'The show is about to start,' he said. 'Mingle with the others, I hope you enjoy it,' he said, taking a microphone as the lights faded and the dark, haunting rock music pounded eerily over the catwalk. Smoke gushed out of the machines at the sides of the stage.

'Our party tonight has a theme of myths and legends of the world, and guides us through extremes, to all terrains, deserts, rivers, raging waterfalls, my studies of dark and light, with scenes of wild shores, tempestuous turbulent seas, locations that evoke and stir the deepest parts of our psyche, our soul and our emotional dark "shadow" and our higher spiritual nature,' announced Mike.

'Sounds very interesting,' enthused Claire.

'And thanks to my incredible models who add their own touch of magic to the scenery.'

Everyone applauded and clapped. The lights went down and the stage area filled with smoke.

Mike wandered back into the crowd and the show started. The

room went quiet, everyone took their seats, haunting music pounded through the air. The show began with a dark, eerie sound, black smoke swirled across the catwalk, several women dressed as nymphs, doing ballet poses, and dressed in lacy ethereal clothes, dancing provocatively across the stage, doing the splits, their wild manes of haired trailing over the ground. The atmosphere was dark and menacing, filled with tones of ominous excitement and teasing sensuality. Applause filtered through the room as Raphelia, in a black sexy basque, gyrated elegantly over the catwalk. A goddess among the nymphs. Confidently, she swept past the others, pushing them to one side. They dispersed quickly, like cubs submitting to the lioness. Smoke belched over her; she walked gracefully out of the fog along a Celtic backdrop, gliding into the scene and the pounding music. Within seconds, she changed to a maiden walking through Celtic fields. She performed a mixture of ballet and wild movements of sensual abandon and delicate beauty, Claire was immediately reminded of the Ballet Rambert, her favourite dance troupe, with their touch of the exotic. She spun a web of intrigue around the audience, her eyes glistening with darkness, an ethereal dancer. The rest of the ballet troupe danced around her on the stage, an erotic, elegant display of beautiful bodies tumbling over each other in time to the music.

Very clever, observed Claire, wondering whether Raphelia had come purely to see Mike. They looked alike, almost identical in their dress. But, judging from the chemistry that sizzled between them, they appeared to be a lot more than friends. Both had the same raven-black hair and beautiful almond-shaped grey eyes. Raphelia gazed at Mike longingly with a magnetism that was dark and menacing, controlling. She turned and shot Claire a look of total malice, then, quickly, seeing Mike was looking at her, changed it to a sweet smile. Then she turned to face the public, lapping up the attention, allowing the crowd to see her in her full glory, towering over the room full of ordinary mortals with her majestic air—her willing subjects honoured to have a slice of her time. She threw them some flowers. Claire stared back, asserting her role as Mike's assistant and girlfriend. She wasn't going to be phased by her, at least not in public.

'You go on too,' whispered Mike. 'You look brilliant.'

'I can't go out there,' said Claire, terrified. Before she could utter another word, Mike pushed her on stage. She strode across the catwalk, her expression glowing with a fiery confidence, her silvery hair thrown back, strutting like a goddess. Claire sensed the role was perfect for her, she was a natural at it and grinned and strutted like a real model. Elated, she strutted across the stage, hands on hip and swished her hair around her face. The crowd cheered. She jumped down as Mike took her hand, and led her down off stage while Raphelia went back on. Her eyes were blazing with fury, how dare Claire steal her thunder! The bitch. She shot Claire a withering glance, stamped her heel and carried on.

Raphelia pursed her lip provocatively and threw her head back dramatically, the vamp who liked to play games with people. She tapped her foot and gave everyone her most seductive, withering gaze. She looked down at Claire with her laser beam eyes, sending out signals of danger. She was playing cat and mouse and was not to be upstaged. She shook out her long black hair, adding to her mystique, her black talons enhancing her predatory air of dark mystery; and strode back over the catwalk, eyeing Claire, her competition, striding like a goddess witch.

How can I possibly compete with her, wondered Claire? Well, I shall try, she thought determinedly. We are very different types of women, she is dark, lean, sensual like a panther whilst I am blonde, petite and studious. I am just as good, even a bit younger and healthier looking, she thought smugly. Will Mike ever be as besotted by me? I'm sure he already is, she told herself, refusing to let this woman undermine her.

Claire decided she was quite happy to be herself and had no desire to be like Raphelia. Raphelia began gyrating and dancing seductively, opening her legs wide, moving suggestively. There was something too edgy about her, dark and manipulative, seeking control.

Seeking power over men through sexuality and seduction gave her a lethal edge. Claire preferred the more romantic side of falling in love. If Raphelia represented the dark side of woman, Claire thought secretly, then she was glad to be different. Still, she was quite overwhelmed with her incredible, magnetic beauty and her wild, hypnotising eyes. Claire watched her intently, fascinated. The model stood at the centre of the stage looking slightly tormented, her eyes glazed over, and she looked like she was going to slip. Mike, sensing it was all about to go wrong, jumped on the stage and steered Raphelia away, taking her backstage for a glass of water. She rushed to the toilet, did another line of coke, then walked confidently back onto the catwalk. Her vibrancy returned; she glared like a demonic princess down at the crowd, her glance unwavering, her confidence flowing as she danced slowly under the images.

After her initial fascination, Claire noticed Raphelia was clearly troubled. She glared at Claire. Claire glared back, sensing it was a warning.

'If looks could kill,' thought Claire, shielding herself mentally from the icy gaze, wondering if she was still in love with Mike. The music stopped, the finale was about to start. Mike had promised a surprise. Raphelia caught Mike's eye and shot him a smouldering look of pure lust. Then, when he refused to acknowledge her, she started to throw a tantrum. Mike, trying hard to placate her, led her off toward the back of the stage. Claire watched them as they climbed back onto the catwalk, his black hair glistening like a raven. Elegantly they both walked down the catwalk. Claire thought Mike was going to make another announcement but to her surprise, he looked as though he was about to dance. Raphelia stood in front of him, as if he were part of her act. Some gothic Spanish music started, and they started circling each other, like Spanish dancers, before abandoning themselves in a frenetic dance. Their bodies poised and arched in passionate defiance. The tension was sizzling. The air was so electric, Claire thought they might whip up a storm. They danced an erotic version of the flamenco, their eyes blazing with undisguised lust. Then Raphelia threw back her head, Mike caught her, and she fell backwards. For a moment their eyes locked, then Raphelia spun away, pointed her heels, threw her cloak over her shoulders and stormed off backstage. Everyone cheered loudly, Claire was excited and fascinated by this surprise dance. The display ended, everyone started to dance.

Why had he asked her to go on holiday with him, Claire suddenly wondered, feeling a sudden pang of jealousy? There was still an incredible passion between them, though, she reasoned, if Mike still had designs on Raphelia, surely he would still be with her? It had just been an act, but she could not be entirely sure. Or perhaps he just wanted her company. How exactly did Raphelia fit into things? Obviously she still had a thing about him, but Mike did not feel the same. Or did he? Was he in some way still in love with her? Did she still love him?

Claire stepped back calmly with dignity and an air of elegant sophistication, and that told Raphelia she was equal to her in every way. She did not fear her, and would never submit to her. Claire held herself erect; she would stay cool, refusing to be intimidated by her, at least not in public! And besides, she could see that the drugs had taken their toll, making the woman look quite manic, running faster to stay in the same place. The evening was drawing to a close, photographers were snapping away, the party had been a resounding success. Claire chatted to many of the media figures walking around, and did some networking. Mike had disappeared. Cocktails were served, in all colours, vibrant blue, or red, with names like 'death', 'poison' and 'lust'. Dancing the night away, she was having a wonderful time.

As the music stopped, Claire made her way to the cloakroom to collect her jacket, when she saw Mike laughing with Raphelia behind the stage. Claire disliked the way she was looking at him, as though they shared some dark secret. Raphelia sat on a stool while he photographed her, legs astride, displaying suspenders under thigh-length boots. She twisted her hair around her fingers, pursed her lips, and opened her mouth as if to say something then stopped. She was pouting provocatively. He was laughing and stood in front of her, reloading the camera.

He took shots of her from all angles, then slid underneath her, while she moved into various poses; her long legs fully open over him, she gazed down at him seductively. Laughing, she lowered her body onto his face. Embarrassed, he pushed her off. Claire peeked closer through the curtains—Raphelia's face was buried in Mike's waist. As Mike took an upward shot of her body, she swung her leg round him; for a second their eyes were locked and an amazing chemistry sizzled between them. She laughed and taunted him playfully, winding her legs around him. He knelt down to take more shots, looking up at her.

'Great, hold it just like that, yes, I like it,' he said. 'Spread your hair out a bit, a wild woman look!' He turned on the fan, so that it blew her hair out in waves and ripples.

Smiling wickedly, she pushed her body over his. A look of ecstasy crossed her face. Mike smiled, thinking it was part of the act. She closed her legs around him, gyrating over him in her skimpiest of g-strings. Suddenly she pushed it to one side, rubbed her body on his, and thrust his fingers between her legs. Gently, with some embarrassment, he disentangled himself and pushed her away.

'Come on, Raphelia you know we can't, it's over,' he said, sharply. Claire could just hear what he was saying. He looked up, blushing as he saw Claire watching them.

'Oh hi, Claire,' he said, looking slightly dishevelled. 'I have just finished, got to do a few more shots for the brochure.'

Quickly he jumped up back onto his feet, holding out his arms to Claire. 'Claire darling, I've missed you. Did you like the party?'

'I loved it, it was such a wonderful night.' Claire, mystified, had been watching the whole scene from behind the curtains, and did her best to stifle her shock. 'What's going on with Raphelia?' she asked him.

'Don't worry, some of my models get carried away when I

photograph them, it gets them in the mood, it is only play, not real. Don't worry,' he assured Claire. 'I am not interested in that alley cat.'

Raphelia adjusted her basque, and stroked her breasts and came out to the hallway where Claire and Mike were standing.

'My breasts are very pert tonight. Don't you think they looked good on stage, darling?'

Mike reddened and said, 'Wonderful.' He turned to Claire and said, 'She's just had a breast enlargement to help with her career, and can't stop showing them to everyone.' He laughed.

'Oh, come on, Mike, you've seen it all before,' laughed Raphelia, crossing her legs coquettishly. She undid her basque and let her magnificent breasts fall out, they were curvy, perfectly formed. Claire, slightly embarrassed, looked away. Raphelia was obviously doing it for Mike's benefit. Unperturbed, he smiled at her, and got back behind the camera. He took a shot of her, standing next to Claire. Claire thought she might have been imagining things, but had the zip on his trousers been undone? She shook her head, it must be her imagination, surely even Raphelia was not that brazen? She was used to playful models in the TV world—they all behaved like that, trying to seduce the photographer. It was just their way of getting attention, creating the right mood, she didn't feel too threatened by Raphelia's attitude. She shifted restlessly, wanting to leave. Mike shot her a sympathetic look and started packing his equipment away. He must have seen many women in similar poses, in various stages of undress, flirting for the camera, reasoned Claire. It was just part of the job; at the next session they would be flirting with another photographer, and it *was* necessary, to enhance the sexual chemistry of the shots. But, she shivered, she was sure she saw a real chemistry pass between them. A menacing, predatory look crossed Raphelia's face. She moved close to Mike and pushed her full breasts against him, her eyes devouring him greedily as though she was about to eat him. He edged away, irritated.

'Are you ready to go now, Claire?' asked Mike, unruffled. 'I'll be with you in a second, I'll just take a few extra shots, I hope you enjoyed the evening.'

'Yes, thanks, I really have,' she said, relaxing; all models acted like divas, it was part of their charm.

'So this is Raphelia, I didn't get a chance to introduce you two properly,' he said, introducing her. 'She's an old friend. Meet Claire.'

Raphelia smiled sweetly, then shot Claire a venomous look, her dark eyes narrowing into lethal slants. She threw a towel on the chair in front of her as though it were a declaration of war.

'Clear that up, will you?' she ordered Mike. 'I spilt a whole bottle of coke, and haven't time to stick around.'

'Forever your unwilling slave,' he joked. 'Makes a change from sticking coke up your nose. Do it yourself, I'm busy.'

'Nice to meet you officially, Claire,' Raphelia said, her cold eyes fixed on Claire. She spoke in a cold sophisticated manner and was the connoisseur of sarcastic wit. 'Well, no time to waste, I really must change into something more conservative, just like you English prefer. Nice fashion show, but don't the English have the most appalling taste, so basic, prosaic? I feel quite indecent next to you, dressed like this.' Quickly, she pushed her breasts back inside the basque.

'You are indecent, Raff, put your clothes on.'

She laughed cattily. 'It's good to meet you,' she said, insincerely, twiddling with her hair.

What a bitch! Claire felt the bristles rise on her neck, how she would love to slap her.

'Pleasure's all mine,' said Claire sweetly, forcing herself to act civilised.

'I must go, so nice to have seen you,' she said, kissing Mike on the cheek, a dangerous glint flickering in her eyes. Claire thought she saw him breathe in quickly as her hand slipped a little too low around his waist. She dismissed him arrogantly: her attention-seeking wasn't working, the femme fatale was losing her touch, failing to arouse Mike in the way she once had. Once she only had to click her fingers and he was her servant and sycophant, now he would just humour her. Had she lost her power and control over him? Her power came from controlling lesser mortals, how dare they disobey! Claire observed that Raphelia's power came from controlling men; if Mike didn't play along with her, then she became quite powerless. It was a game played by lots of photographers with their models, where the woman would flirt and cajole and have her ego boosted by the photographer who naturally wanted her to look her best and ooze with confidence and sexual power; it boosted his prowess too. Claire made a point of avoiding her, she was spoiling for a fight. She was clearly trouble and intent on trying to stir things up. Claire wondered if Mike had kissed her as her hair looked ruffled, her lip-gloss smudged.

Raphelia adjusted her basque, and tossed a silk shawl around her shoulders, looking mysteriously triumphant, as though she had disarmed Mike and was once again back in control. Her hair tumbled down her back in wild, tousled curls. She glowed from the success of the evening. Or was it a sexual afterglow, thought Claire, growing suspicious? The basque was tight, her pert buttocks poked through the g-string, her long legs shimmered in black fishnets. Claire could not help but admire her. Without any trace of embarrassment, Raphelia stepped out of the g-string, and stood naked in front of them, her tanned and athletic body sleek like a gazelle. Claire had to admit she looked breathtaking. Mike coughed awkwardly.

Later, Claire couldn't help asking the question that was burning inside her.

'Do you still see Raphelia at all?' she asked him later, as he drove her home.

'No, of course not, that finished ages ago. She does like to flirt though, please forgive her behaviour, she can act like a spoilt brat, always trying to be the centre of attention, addicted to the limelight.'

'Do you still find her attractive?'

'Only in a professional way,' he said, shaking his head. 'I'm not at all interested in having a relationship with her any more, but she does try to seduce everyone. She can be very trying,' he stressed. Claire decided to take him at his word, he was usually honest.

'We were a couple once, but it has been over for a long time,' he added. 'There is no way that we could have made it together. Professionally or otherwise.'

'Why not?' asked Claire. 'She is a good model.'

'She's just too demanding for any one man to deal with. A wild, lethal Scorpio,' he said, imaginatively, 'too tempestuous and unpredictable for me. There's nothing there now,' he confessed, as though reading her thoughts. Then a dark frown crossed his face. 'It just wasn't meant to be,' he said, darkly. 'She destroyed everything between us. Oh, just forget her! I'm relieved she's gone. I'm so glad to have met a nice girl like you. I need someone like you, who is truthful and honest. An angel.'

Boring and safe he means, thought Claire unsure, convinced he still cared for Raphelia but he just couldn't handle her.

'Look, Mike, are you sure it's over? I don't want to come between anyone,' she admitted, thinking perhaps she had stumbled into someone else's life and drama. She didn't want someone with baggage, and women had been crawling out of the woodwork ever since she had met him.

'What more do I need to say?' he assured her. 'It's been over for a long time.' For the first time his control seemed to be slipping, he ran his hands through his hair, looking anxious, and slightly sheepish. The sad, faraway look returned to his eyes. 'How can I prove it to you? You are the one I want, if I wanted someone else I would be with them,' he said irritably.

'Well if that is the case, if you're sure,' she answered sweetly.

'I'm sure. It's all okay, it's well and truly over between us,' he insisted. 'I only want to be with you, and that's the truth.'

He switched on the radio and his mood became buoyant.

'Let's just have fun,' he said jovially, singing along with the music as they sped off in his Porsche. 'What star sign are you?' he asked, quickly changing the subject.

'Gemini,' she replied.

'A lot less trouble than Scorpios,' he laughed, 'always changeable, flitting from person to person, thing to thing.'

Claire laughed. 'Not me. And you?' she asked Mike.

'A mixture of many things with Venus in Scorpio, the moon in Libra, so I'm a refined gentleman, with a dark passionate nature.' He laughed. 'Don't trust me too much,' he jibed, pulling her by her hair and kissing her passionately.

'I won't,' she replied, kissing him back—many a true word was spoken in jest. She wanted him more than ever. This time he did not stop at a kiss. He tore off her dress and sucked her breasts hungrily. Sometimes, even though he was a gentleman, he reminded her of a starving, wild animal. She touched his body and he was aroused.

'Would you like me to take you home?' he asked, laughing. As they opened the door he tore her clothes off, threw her on the bed, bent her over and pushed inside her, making love to her until she reached the peak of ecstasy. He seemed insatiable and took her over and over again. He had become a wild and hungry lover, rampant as they had non-stop sex. She held him in her arms, feeling his flesh warm against hers all night long, basking in sleepy, post-coital bliss, waking up occasionally to make love again and again. At least soon we'll be hundreds of miles away from Raphelia, she thought happily, free and content at last. That night after the party, his lovemaking had been wonderful, it was everything she expected it to be and more. The day was perfect and breathtaking in every detail—except the strange tormented look on his face she'd had a glimpse of in the morning. A slither of doubt entered her mind, but she tried to push it out, the thought was too terrible to bear. Why had he had such a voracious sexual appetite last night? Had it been anything to do with him seeing Raphelia?

Castle of dreams

A week later they landed in Southern Ireland. Claire's fears evaporated as they sped through the lanes of the Irish countryside and all her worries melted away. Now that they were alone she felt safe, there was no stopping them pursuing their dream. Thank god they were away from the echoes of his past and the awful Raphelia. As the car swung around the corner, she drew in her breath at how incredibly beautiful the landscape was: it was stunning, breathtaking, an incredibly wild terrain mixed with a mystical air, green fields soaked in Celtic charm, captivating in a kind of mysterious, untamed way. A bit like Mike in some ways—full of mystery and lure, with a dark compelling side, a side that could also be cruel and unpredictable. They turned into a small village, consisting of one shop, one pub and a post office. Driving a few miles further on, the castle came into view. It had tall spires and turrets reaching into the endless blue sky and overlooked the glittering sea. Its dark-curtained windows were elegantly framed by high gothic stone arches. Grey stone walls surrounded the building. She couldn't wait to explore all of it. It had the most incredible view over the sea, water lapping gently on the sea wall. There were rocks and cliffs and miles of green fields stretching out behind the building and miles of crashing sea in front. They had arrived, tired after a long journey, glad to have spent more time to get to know each other and she was completely at ease in his company. All thoughts of Raphelia gradually drifted away and vanished. Mike was the perfect travelling companion and did everything to put her at ease. They chatted for the entire journey, about everything, and by the end of it, she felt she knew him well. They sat laughing, arms wrapped around each other, like any other couple.

I hope we get on well here, she thought, without the distractions of work and the London nightlife. We'll be thrown very much into each other's company. He'd seemed happy on the plane, drinking beer and laughing. Twisted black trees stood in the grounds of the castle. It had an air of dark mystery. In the distance she could see the waves lashing on the shore, the caves and small beaches nestling in the bay.

He smiled. 'Welcome, Claire, this is your home too. I'll take you to your room, there's no one here except the cook and the maid. So just ring them if you need anything. They're off at the weekend. I thought you'd prefer it if we had the place to ourselves, we can take turns cooking. It might be fun,' he added, cuddling her. They drank lots of wine and giggled, then ran outside doing headstands and cartwheels on the lawn, watched the sun set over the shimmering sea. Later they fell into bed laughing, filled with exuberance.

The next few days were spent entertaining socialites and dancing till dawn. Mike got lost and for a few hours Claire searched the castle trying to find him. Hours later he turned up, having been with friends with whom he had sat talking about old times, drinking. She laughed but inwardly felt slightly annoyed that he had left her for so long.

The next morning, Mike's eyes had a faraway look, and his mind was elsewhere. She kissed him, keen to rouse him but he rolled over and went back to sleep. Claire, keen to explore, went for an early walk along the cliffs; she peered over them, it was a sheer drop. The scenery was breath-taking. The castle was set in large grounds, surrounded by fields with wild horses galloping through the mist, with a large garden filled with purple rhododendrons. It overlooked the sea and she knew she couldn't wait to dive off the rocks and swim every day. She would take a swim around the bay, dive off the speedboat—it made her think she might really be turning into a mermaid—then make lunch. Twinkling lights flickered from the lighthouse, by the edge of the cliff. She looked round, thinking how lucky she was and how much she would enjoy the experience. She had never seen such wild beauty. The cliffs below were breathtaking, with cruel black rocks, the scenery the most incredible she had ever seen.

When she got back Mike was waiting: 'I'll show you to your room,' he said.

'Aren't we still sharing one?' she asked, surprised.

'Yes, of course,' he said, 'but you need a room of your own to change in, and have privacy when you need it, for your own space.' He insisted: 'Also it's a good cover, the maids know we aren't married, and it is a Catholic country, and we don't want to give the local padre a heart attack.' His tone was jocular. She was slightly perturbed at Mike's sudden change of mood and coldness, as though he was suddenly the master of the house and not her lover.

Her new room was decorated in a Chinese theme, adorned with beautiful tapestries and furniture, and overlooked the sea.

'When you are ready for dinner, just come down to the dining room. The meal is served at seven every evening,' explained Mike. His voice had changed; he sounded austere and cold, detached.

His new haughty persona disturbed Claire, he seemed to have changed into a haughty aristocrat, suddenly a different person. His mood was more sombre, not like the friendly, happy-go-lucky Mike she'd known in London and on the first day here. She dismissed it all as being the result of the new surroundings. Or perhaps this was the way he had always been, until he had left for London? Or was he really like his father? She shivered uncomfortably at the thought.

'Are all the rooms like this?' she asked, determined she would have fun.

'No, each one has a different theme. There are twenty-two bedrooms,' he said, warmly. 'The place is full of Chinese art.'

She looked around her, at the Chinese art and vases, and decided that she loved it. The evening meal was romantic; Mike plied her with fruit, wine and mints, and his undivided attention. Claire felt relaxed and happy in his company, not intimidated as she thought she might be. His coldness had gone. He was back to the old Mike, carefree and happy. The dark hungry look had left his eyes, his cool manner had melted into one of concern. He charmingly recalled the details of his family history. They were descended from minor aristocracy from Europe, who had moved to Eire. His father had been austere and authoritarian, which is why he had moved here, away from high society. He could be a cruel and sadistic man who beat his horses, and had many women in his life. Mike had feared and disliked him until he died.

Later, they talked more as they walked along the steep cliffs. Mike *did have* a touch of the Jekyll and Hyde about him, one minute a kind, friendly, attentive lover, the archetypal nice guy, the next a cool ice man, detached, cruel and dominating. Suddenly, Claire had insight into who he really was. The cold haughty side came from his father, and was not Mike's personality at all.

'Claire, I'm so glad I have met you,' he said, kissing her gently. 'You make me feel so happy. Stay with me here forever, we will live in paradise,' he begged, softly. Pulling out of a bag a solitary rose, he placed it in her hand. It was a black rose and looked most unusual. 'Please, will you marry me?'

'Yes, of course I will. Oh I love you so much,' said Claire, her body tingling with excitement, soaring to heaven.

'The black rose is an Irish icon, and is what a knight gave to his lady fair before he was dragged away into battle,' he explained. 'It symbolises devotion and everlasting love.'

She felt a surge of bliss as his lips brushed her face. She kissed him rapturously, overwhelmed by the passion she felt, pulling his dark hair, wanting him badly, urgently. The flames he stirred in her never died. On the beach they started to make love again, on the sand, shielded by the rocks, her head in a whirl. She watched his grey eyes crinkle as he pushed inside her, planting butterfly kisses over her face, kissing her breasts. It was even better than their first time, and as she lay back feeling the tide ripple around her ankles, she cried out in ecstasy. As he came, she saw a shadow cross his face as he silently mouthed some words that Claire couldn't understand. Then he stopped. He looked sad, but Claire couldn't be sure. The tormented gaze returned to his face. That night he tossed in bed restlessly. Claire wondered what could be wrong, and she began to feel uneasy.

Dreams

Later that night, Claire awoke with a jolt, as she heard a wailing sound coming from below. She got up and peered over the balcony, a person in a long cloak was trailing though the grounds. She saw the strange battered face of an old woman looking up at her. She pointed a craggy finger at Claire, then turned away and ran into the bushes. Then a strange, grey shadowy figure drifting through the grounds caught her attention. Claire couldn't be sure but it looked like a ghost; suddenly she heard the most inhuman yell, and a strange fluorescent light flashed as something darted across the courtyard, running into the rubbish and tipping over some watering cans. Heart-rending screams followed, then a shriek followed by deathly silence in the night air. Frightened, she woke Mike.

He laughed. 'It's just the wild cats chasing each other across the yard,' he said, softly touching her hair, 'when they're mating they cause merry chaos, and the figure was probably one of the locals who sometimes cut across the grounds. The wail was simply the mating call of one the wild cats that lives outside the castle, in the hope of being thrown scraps from the kitchen.' He kissed Claire on the forehead and comforted her until she went back to sleep.

Mike awoke looking shadowed and beautiful. She ran his fingers over his chest, his chest hair arousing her. She felt safe as he put a protective arm around her. The next few days were spent making love, they rarely ventured out of bed: just listened to music, finished sketches, ate rich food and sipped chilled wine from the cellar. He pushed the hair back from her face and kissed her over and over again. She felt a surge of excitement each time he touched her or moved against her. He would take her, until she cried out in ecstasy, making love until she fell back content, in his arms. She told him about the woman that she had seen.

'It's probably just the old lady who lives in the house on the cove,' he explained, trying to placate her. 'She's a baroness, slightly eccentric. She's harmless though, just forgets things and wanders around aimlessly at times. Some nights the wild cats and foxes wake her up and she wanders around the village. Others say her mansion is haunted. She drives a Porsche in the daytime and is quite formidable,' he laughed. 'Don't worry, my darling,' he said, cradling her in his arms. 'You are safe with me.'

They spent the days going out in a sailing boat or yachting with the villagers, the evenings drinking in the pub, listening to the haunting melodic tones of the local music or dining at the best restaurants. Sometimes there was a day's work shooting photographs and designing the brochures for the next exhibition. On sunny days, they took picnics to the beach, swam off the rocks, dived into the deep blue sea. It was perfect. An idyll, a dream.

At night, Claire noticed the castle took on an inexplicable and mysterious air, as though it had a darker, more menacing quality. In the daytime it was a bright and friendly castle, nestled in the cove under a watery sun shining over a bright blue sea. In the evening it was transformed entirely—the dark grey sea lashed at the black rocks, like a dark palace where knights had slain their enemies in battle. Claire loved exploring all the different parts. Dotted around the castle were statues of knights slaying dragons, elaborate coats of arms and books and manuscripts illustrated with elegant pictures, battle scenes painstakingly captured in bright watercolours, intricately painted with detailed floral borders. Mike told her that his ancestors had ridden with the king and the stories were recorded in a set of valuable manuscripts. In the evening, she would read and a deathly quiet air would fill the bay, bats flew overhead and there was a feeling of intrigue and mystery.

She found in the old library some books covered with beautiful, intricate illustrations edged with silver thread, the tattered pages of the Bible and an old copy of Chaucer. They gave her an idea for Mike's next catalogue; she would present the catalogue as a medieval document, with paintings and illustrations set around the side, with some old gothic text.

'You're so clever, darling,' said Mike, clearly pleased.

On the landing was a tall stained glass window, Corpus Christi healing the leper, and the redemption of the sinful. It was spectacular, fragments of coloured lights filtering over the landing, like strands of a rainbow.

The next day a dark mist rose over the bay. Claire looked out, it was so grey and uninviting, with a bleakness in the air; the austere hallway beckoned like an empty tomb.

Yet over the next few months she found she had never been so happy, Mike was the perfect partner and she soon felt that this was where she truly belonged.

Three months later

Claire took another two months' leave and they stayed on at the castle; it was turning out to be a dream summer, with scorching temperatures and calm tides. They went swimming in the magic rock-pools every day, rowing into the caves around the bays, drenched by the sun. She realised now that she never wanted to go back to London and the dirty city traffic. But inside the castle was always cold. Claire noticed that some of the paintings on the wall looked quite menacing in the dim light. Their chalky white faces were cold and unfriendly, staring at her with a malicious intent, their black penetrating eyes burning with a strange evil power. She noticed an odd atmosphere in the hallway—it was damp, but now seemed almost icy. One night she felt as though she was not alone, as though someone was following her. She climbed onto the balcony looking over the castle grounds, the height making her feel slightly dizzy. As she leaned over, she suddenly felt something push her from behind. Disorientated and frightened, she pulled back from the edge just in time. Had something tried to push her over? No, she thought rationally—it was just the wind.

That night, Mike returned from riding in a pensive mood. He seemed restless, discontent, as though ghosts from the past were haunting him, disturbing him. His dark moods were apparent, he was working through his demons, and today they were out in full force. She didn't like to ask him what was wrong. If he needed to tell her, he would in his own time. She wouldn't press the issue. Perhaps coming back to the castle had stirred up some unpleasant memories. He refused to enter the room with the four-poster bed in the east wing and told her not to go there. Maybe it evoked a family memory that he didn't wish to confront, or murky shadows from the past still lurked there. In the morning, she asked him again about the night visitor to the grounds.

'It must be the old baroness who lives by the sea,' he explained. 'She's a bit eccentric and likes to wander around in the night for some reason. Or it could have been one of the locals taking a short cut to the sea after a night of drinking at the pub, it stays open all night sometimes. Tourists often come and walk around at odd hours.'

She smiled, dismissing the incident on the balcony from her mind. They spent the next few weeks exploring the coves and tea houses, eating fresh fish and corigeen, wandering through the idyllic Celtic countryside, taking photographs, jumping in the sea, diving in the waves, laughing like children playing together. They drove up the winding roads along the coastal path to the old inns and ate seafood, washed down with Guinness—heavenly, thought Claire. They spent each day roaming the scenic cliffs, rowing out to sea, walking across the moors, visiting the country pubs and making love on the endless beaches, on the white sand. Her mind was taking in and relishing all these new experiences. She was right about getting away; things were perfect now, away from the confusion of London. They had found themselves and were content, happily basking in each other's easy company and love. It had been a perfect summer.

Dark clouds

The summer was fading away, the idyll of the last few months was giving way to a chillier atmosphere. Then, one cold stormy night, the phone rang. Claire thought she heard Mike arguing, shouting at someone; she tried to listen. When he came back he looked ill; his face was white, gaunt as though he had seen a ghost. He seemed harassed. The next day Claire went swimming, but when she came back she noticed a growing moodiness in Mike. The easy summer had evaporated into an edgy autumn. The carefree mood had become tense.

'I have to go into town,' he said abruptly. A dark shadow fell across his face. 'It's the work I left at the printers, the photos are ready. There's been a problem, the printer is going on holiday and unless I collect them I won't get them for weeks. It's positively archaic here,' he said raising his eyes to the ceiling. 'We may have to fly back to London, if I can't sort this out.'

'Okay.' She kissed him.

'I also have to meet some friends in town,' he explained. 'I promised I'd go for a drink with them later. I can leave it if you'd prefer.'

'No, you must go,' insisted Claire. 'I'm happy to be here on my own. There's lots to do.'

'Good girl,' he said, kissing her forehead. 'It might go on very late and there will be many whiskies drunk, no doubt, so don't wait up. I might stay over. You can come if you want to, but I think you'll be more comfortable here.' He kissed her, lovingly.

'Yes, I'll read and go to bed early,' she said, hugging him contentedly.

The next morning, she woke up feeling happy, stretching out like a cat. Her life was almost perfect in every way. She turned over and realised that Mike was not there. He'd stayed out all night. Her euphoria turned to dismay, then she remembered that he'd said he would stay over at Declan's, rather than drink and drive. Had he tried to phone? She had gone to sleep after he had left and slept right through. He must have had too much to drink and decided not to risk driving back and so stayed with a friend. She climbed up onto the balcony to see if she could see him. It was nearly eleven and he still wasn't back. She climbed up onto the balcony, peered over the wall when, suddenly she felt very dizzy, something moved up behind her, and started trying to push her over, force her over the balcony. The struggle went on for minutes, then stopped as she heard a car pull up in the drive. It loosened its grip and she fell backwards. She ran inside, but could see no one. The strange force had vanished. She heard someone walking around in the drawing room. She turned and saw Mike stride through the door, his face an unshaven mess, his eyes bleary. He staggered into the hallway.

'Where have you been?' asked Claire concerned. 'Are you all right?'

'Sorry I am so late. I was delayed in town. We drank so much, I stayed at Declan's,' he explained, seeing the door of the East Wing bedroom open. 'I told you not to go in there.'

'Why not?' asked Claire. 'Why didn't you phone?'

'I did try,' he said earnestly, 'but it was engaged.'

'I didn't use the phone all evening,' she said, truthfully.

'Then it must be the locals keeping the lines tied up,' he said, wearily.

He looked unkempt and walked slowly into the hall in a half-trance. He was in a black mood and didn't want to talk, the blackest mood she had ever seen. He smiled demonically, his eyes glazed and manic. For a second she felt afraid. Then he softened, smiling at her, his haggard expression breaking into one of concern.

'I'm so sorry, Claire, I really am sorry. I didn't mean to drink so much last night. I couldn't drive home, I feel like death.'

'You look it,' she said. 'Don't worry, go to bed now and sleep it off.'

Still apologising, he staggered towards the stairs. Claire wondered if anything was wrong—he looked ill, totally wrecked. It was as though he had become a totally different person overnight. But it was a small thing, everything else was perfect. Still, she would have appreciated a call. But men often were unpredictable and acted like immature boys at times. She decided to let it go. She didn't want to make waves, and spoil the happy mood.

'Now if you don't mind I must go to sleep. I haven't even the energy to muck out the stables. Perhaps you could do it,' he said abruptly, swiping the crop over the banisters in an angry gesture, then stormed upstairs.

His behaviour was strange and for a moment she caught glimpses of his father.

That night, Mike slept restlessly, tossing and turning and had developed a fever. She wiped his brow with a damp cloth, then he fell asleep. As he turned over, Claire saw some jagged scratch marks, bleeding on his back. A cat let out a bloodcurdling wail somewhere in the grounds. She let out a scream. Claire jumped up at once, shaking Mike awake, she asked him about the scratches.

'I fell into a bush,' he murmured. 'Off the horse, I'm quite an experienced rider, but yesterday Sally was so temperamental that I couldn't handle her. I'm so sorry, darling,' he drawled, putting out an arm and patting her. Then he looked at Claire, sat up and groaned, clutching his head, confused.

'Oh God, you are still here…' he muttered, barely audibly.

He was cool and detached like a stranger, as though for a second he didn't recognise her and had been speaking to someone else. He stared at her indifferently. She shivered at his coldness. Then he smiled a radiant smile.

'It's all right, darling, just an awful, crushing hangover.'

'What do you mean? Am I still here?' she asked, feeling nervous.

'Oh did I say that? No, you must be mistaken,' he said, appearing contrite and loving again. 'Look I shall make it up to you, take you to the best restaurant today. Put on your best dress and cheer up!'

Dark secrets

She dressed quickly and they spent a wonderful day sailing and visiting all the olde-world tourist shops, Mike was unbelievably attentive and responsive to her every need, plying her with flowers and gifts. When they arrived home, she had a rosy glow; it had been a wonderful day.

The next day, she had totally forgotten the incident and the holiday got quickly back into an amiable, easy rhythm. They laughed and went riding and drank the local beer, went sailing and diving off the rocks. Taking the rowing boat out, they rowed to a secluded bay where they ate a cheese and duck picnic. She started some sketches for the latest storyboard of Mike's book. The stories were inserted into the catalogue. She rang her company and took on some freelance work; it kept her mind in tune. It was a perfect existence, swimming every day and eating wonderful food, sampling the best wines, rowing or sailing on Mike's yacht.

That afternoon, she bought a copy of the *Book of Kells* and used the idea of adding an illustrative floral edge to the catalogue, giving it a romantic feel. Later, Mike was so apologetic and romantic, he couldn't do enough to please her, giving her flowers, taking her on a scenic flight across the bay, ending the day with a champagne supper.

'Please tell me the secret of the East Wing. Is it haunted?' asked Claire. 'Has something terrible happened there?'

'I'll tell you about it one day. I don't want to scare you.'

'I can take it,' she said, expecting to hear a ghostly story.

'Okay, if you insist. A long time ago, before I was born, my father had a feud with another nobleman of the town. They argued, one day Father returned from shooting pheasant, carrying his gun. The nobleman stood in the room and confronted him. Enraged that he had come onto our property, he struggled with the man and accidentally shot him dead. The dark deed was committed in the bedroom of the East Wing where my father used to sleep. It was hushed up: he had a lot of Masonic connections that included the police and my father was shipped quietly to France for a while. He took a mistress there and when he returned, I was born, but my father became a wanderer and spent most of his time in France. Since then, some guests have reported seeing a ghost; the castle soon became known as being haunted by the nobleman's spirit. But there's another reason. I used to take Raphelia there. She always insisted we go there when we stayed. She loved the idea of a haunted room as she practised the occult.'

Claire shrank back, stunned—that was why the place was so threatening, there was a ghost, but worse still, it had the vibes of another woman. Raphelia had been there holding séances and calling up entities which were trapped in the castle. This stream of ideas evoked a lot of dark fantasies in Claire. She had realised that part of the castle could be haunted, and suddenly the place seemed menacing. Had a ghost tried to push her off the balcony? That night, she woke up feeling frightened. Something brushed against her and scratched her with long talons, it pulled at her hair. She jumped with a start, drenched in perspiration. What was that? It was hot, so she went onto the balcony to get some air. A cat leapt off the balcony, baring its teeth. It flew at her; she pushed it over the balcony. She gasped, then watched the sea, sanity flowing back into her thoughts. She felt calmer, the coolness of the bay healing her. She listened to the roaring sea, breathing in the fresh salty air. She glimpsed a shadowy figure, running out of the grounds of the castle. Shivering, she climbed up onto the ledge to get a closer look. Suddenly, as though from nowhere, the wild black cat flew at Claire and began attacking her ferociously, nearly knocking her over the castle wall. She struggled to free herself as it clung to her with enormous strength, tearing at her. It spat at her, scratching her badly. She fell back inside the balcony away from the edge. It shrieked ferociously, then leapt over the wall, leaving deep cuts on her hands. Terrified, she ran inside. Mike took her to the hospital straight away. He seemed to have lost much of his easy exuberance and was concerned, kissing her. He began apologising over and over again, admitting to having been in an unreasonable mood and swore it wouldn't happen again.

'I'm so sorry, I love you, baby, so much,' he murmured, trying to calm her, holding her tight and rocking her like a baby.

The next few weeks were perfect, then one day Mike looked at her intently:

'Are you pregnant?' he asked hopefully.

'I don't know,' she said truthfully, 'I might be,' for her period was late. Mike, delighted, was immediately attentive again, showering her with gifts and an expensive meal. She couldn't help thinking he seemed strangely guilty for what had happened. He explained there were many wild cats living by the castle. His mother unfortunately had encouraged them; they lived by their feral instincts, roaming wild. The next day, he took a gun and shot the wild cat. It lay whimpering, its eyes looking soulfully at Claire. Its expression, as it lay dying, was sad, looking pleadingly at her and for its few final seconds, she felt a deep empathy with it.

Mike asked Claire to move in permanently, and announced to everyone that they were engaged, promising that when they returned to London, they would get married. Claire accepted at once, ignoring the fragment of doubt—was her intuition trying to tell her something? That night he gave her a ring, a beautiful emerald stone set in Celtic silver. He then excused himself, saying he was required back in town for one of his meetings, but if she wanted him to miss it he would. Claire feeling so elated, didn't object to him going. He jumped in the car and drove off. She saw he had left his wallet behind, chasing after him, she saw it held all his credit cards. He had gone. She looked inside, trying to find out where he'd gone. She thought perhaps she should take it to him. Was he meeting Declan for a drink? She would take it to over to him.

She went for a walk along the cliffs as it was a beautiful evening, and sat watching the blazing sunset. The sun was setting on the horizon in an orange sunburst glow, the warm hues swirling in the distance. When suddenly, a cool wind started to blow, it grew stronger and she found herself being blown perilously close to the edge of the cliff. Ever more forceful, it was pushing her towards the precipice, and desperately she clung on to a bush until the wind subsided. Using all her strength she pulled herself up, looking at the sheer drop below. Shaking, she realised she had almost been pushed over the cliff by some unknown force. On the verge of hysterics, she went off to try and find Mike.

A Black Ritual

Claire rang the hotel bar where Mike said he had gone. A puzzled receptionist said there had been no Mike Devereux at the hotel all evening and that they didn't know a Declan O'Brian. Claire began to grow suspicious. Her mind fleetingly recalled the nightly, mysterious phone calls and the times when the phone went dead when she answered. Often she thought she'd heard him speaking in the middle of the night. Her imagination began to run wild. She began fantasising all sorts of things, worried that there was something he wasn't telling her. Something strange was going on, all the signs were there, but she refused to see them. Surely the doubt in the deepest, dark part of her soul was unfounded? She shuddered, wondering if Mike kept secrets from her. Was it anything to do with Raphelia? Surely his recent disappearances were not connected to her in any way, thought Claire worried, growing concerned? Yesterday she had seen a photograph of her on the media pages, dancing with her latest beau. Anyway, she was keen to stay in London, and hated the countryside or anywhere without a nightlife. Finding herself in the throes of a mystery, Claire decided to find out what was going on.

Tentatively, she flicked through the contents of his wallet, her only clue. Amongst the credit cards she found a scribbled note that read: 'East wing—in the Old Rectory, Bantry at eight', and gave today's date. She sighed with relief. He must have gone there to photograph the old ruin as a backdrop. She smiled satisfied. They probably went for a drink in the bar first. But he needed his wallet, she realised, so she decided to take it to him. He had taken the Porsche—there was no public transport for at least thirty miles.

She took the old car from the garage and sped fast through the winding lanes to the town where she asked for directions to the Old Rectory. She went on deeper through twisting country lanes, but couldn't find it, until eventually, in the deepest part of an old cove she parked and saw the Old Rectory, set back amongst the black cliffs, an old building overhung with black foliage, so that the entrance was concealed. It was set in semi-derelict grounds with bats flying menacingly around the debris. The rectory was covered in green moss, with gargoyles staring out above the drive. Their eyes glowed with a malignant power. A bat flew past, narrowly missing her face. She shrieked with surprise as she made her way to the crumbling East Wing. Perhaps he has friends there, she thought, seeing a glow of light in the distance. Good, they were still there—the place really would make a spooky backdrop for the new brochure.

She was just going to drop off the wallet, put it through the door, when suddenly she felt compelled to look inside. Instead of knocking, she pushed her way through the overgrown bushes, crept around the back and looked through a leaded window into a room. She froze in shock and horror at the sight in front of her.

In a shabby derelict room stood a group of people wearing hoods, their arms raised high, one of them wearing a strange mask. The room was covered in candles; it looked like some kind of ritual was taking place. Claire moved closer to get a better look. They swayed and chanted as though in a deep trance in a language that sounded like Latin. Then, recoiling with horror, she saw Mike, kneeling in front of an altar, stripped naked. On the altar in front of him lay a woman with a wreath of flowers around her head. Claire stifled a shriek of terror. Mike, who was in a trance, walked over to the woman, his eyes closed, and knelt before her. He kissed her on her forehead, face, and breasts, then drank from a chalice while the woman cut a small wound in his arm. He handed her the cup, and she let his blood drip into it, before drinking his blood. She lay back, her legs under her, as he knelt between her legs and kissed her. The woman threw back her head in ecstasy, pulling Mike's head tighter between her thighs, then screamed and arched her back in bliss. Claire turned away, shocked and dismayed, sick to the stomach, fighting to stay upright so as not to faint. Swaying dizzily, she grabbed the branch of a tree and took in some deep breaths. She couldn't believe what she was seeing, she had walked right into a nightmare!

Perhaps in a second she would wake up from a bad dream, safe and secure in Mike's arms. But the cold realisation of fear crept through her, invading her bones, sending an icy chill through her body and soul. The reality of what was happening gradually dawned on her: this was not a dream, it was real. Horror descended on her like a black, poisonous cloud, permeating her every pore like a cancerous, malignant evil. She fell to the ground as something gripped her throat and she fought for her breath. She began to shake violently, then as she fell caught a glimpse of the continuing ritual, her worst fears confirmed. Through the cracked window, she could see Mike. He lay on top of the woman, kissing her breasts in an impassioned frenzy. Mike climbed on top of the woman and thrust rhythmically inside her, groans of pleasure escaping his throat. The woman twitched in ecstasy beneath him. Mike's eyes were completely glazed over. The chanting grew louder, reaching a manic, hypnotic pitch, the their faces contorting as they reached a crescendo. Moving closer, Claire saw with absolute horror that the woman was Raphelia. Naked women formed a circle around them and began a strange pagan ritual of kissing each other's breasts. A man dressed in a long white robe held a cup over them from which they both drank. Devastated, Claire stumbled to the car, a heaviness pounding in her chest, her head buzzing with pain. A cold feeling, like a sharp knife, pierced her chest. She started choking, someone was trying to kill her. She fell to the ground, unable to move any further and blacked out.

Hours later, she woke up and crawled out through the trees, her face and hands cut and numb. She started tearing at the bushes, clearing a path, staying under the windows for fear that someone might see her. Devastated, she realised Mike had lied to her—he was still seeing Raphelia, and, worse still, he was caught up in her witchcraft rituals. She looked into the room, and no longer recognised it; it was now peaceful and tranquil, with no sign of any occultists. Puzzled, she looked around the front—a family were sitting inside, in a warm, well furnished room; it was no longer an old ruin and was now inhabited.

Back at the castle, Claire shook uncontrollably and was feeling very ill and cold. She put on several jumpers, trying to get warm, but the icy chill gripped her. Still reeling from the shock, she poured a whisky, desperately trying to erase the events of the past hours from her mind. Had the whole thing been just a trick of her imagination? Or a terrible nightmare? She found herself suddenly spiralling into an inescapable nightmare, a web of darkness. She knew nothing of the occult and shuddered with fear. She wished and prayed it had been a dream. For a few hours, her mind was numb, reeling in shock and denial; she couldn't accept what had happened or even think at all. Should she phone the police? But, whatever Mike had done, she couldn't do that to him. She had no other choice but to leave, so went upstairs and packed her things, hoping she would never see Mike again. Her head ached and she felt sick, but there was nothing more she could do. His betrayal had been so final, so bizarre. And it occurred to her that perhaps that was what Jemima Wilkins-Smyth had tried to warn her about—she'd known what he got up to and it had almost sent her insane.

Suddenly it all fell into place and she could see the situation clearly. She felt a wave of nausea grip her—God, she was pregnant! What could she do now? Mike had been deceiving her all along. He hadn't finished his affair with Raphelia, and Jemima had been trying to warn her. Why did he involve other women if he still wanted and loved Raphelia? Wouldn't it just be simpler if he'd just stayed with her, instead of making her life so complicated and weaving webs of intrigue and deceiving other women. There was something strange about all this, a mystery that didn't make sense and that she couldn't work it out. In a panic, she tried to phone Justin; he wasn't there so she left a message on his answering machine.

'Justin. Please help, I'm stranded.' She gave the number, and the address. It was still early; she would have to wait until midday to leave, as there were no trains until then, but she would need to go while it was light so that she could see the roads. Right now she was drunk, as she had thrown back several glasses of whisky already. Exhausted, she fell into a deep sleep on the bed.

When she woke up, it was daylight, and she saw she had missed breakfast. Cook had not woken her. Her head spun and she felt groggy, as though she had been hit on the head with a hammer. For a second she felt flooded with warmth and contentment; here she was with her boyfriend in an idyllic, secluded part of Ireland, then slowly the full horror of what had happened the night before was restored to her. A chill descended on her. Sadness and anger hit her in equal measures—she was devastated. She had been used, as a decoy, for some reason. Mike was still in love with Raphelia, for that she had seen with her own eyes. So why had he brought her here? Her mind reeled in confusion. Mike could and would not give up Raphelia. Perhaps it was a matter of inheritance, or his family wanted him to find a wife, and Raphelia was too wild and uncontrollable for anyone's tastes. Then the truth hit her. She had been brought in as a brood mare. The truth ripped through her like a knife, and the pain was excruciating. Mike had never really loved her, he had just needed an acceptable wife to bear him a child. He was always talking about them having children, it seemed to eclipse everything else. He couldn't be with the woman he really loved, so he had brought Claire in as a substitute. Anger and rage boiled in her—how dare he do this to her! Yet he couldn't give up the passion he shared with Raphelia, and no one could satisfy him like Raphelia. And she could never give him what her antagonist clearly could.

Steadily, she packed her things and began to make her way downstairs, tears streaming down her face. As she walked down into the hallway, she saw Mike walk in. She knelt behind the stairs, afraid he would see her, feeling a mixture of fear and loathing run through her veins.

'It's only me,' he called out. 'Darling, I'm back.'

Claire shrunk back behind the stairwell, her heart beating like a trapped bird in her chest.

'Where are you?' he called out.

She darted across the landing.

'Where are you going? What's the matter?' he asked sleepily, as she tried to slip past him across the hallway. 'Come on, Claire, kiss me, what's wrong?'

She recoiled, afraid to look at him, but she forced herself. He gave her that same easy smile that had filled her with lust. Then, remembering what she had seen, fear began to surge in her veins, the adrenaline pumping through her. She was very afraid. She continued to stare into his eyes, but there was no sign of his betrayal, no hint of the evening's debauchery. He looked back at her lovingly, as though nothing had happened, and held out his arms. It still felt perfect, comfortable, secure. She had to fight back, not let him lull her into a false sense of security. He was using her, and she must not give in. For a split second she thought she must have been dreaming, maybe she'd had sunstroke or had a hallucination and imagined the whole thing. His seductive eyes, with their fatal glint, bored right through her and she felt herself weaken. She wanted to hug him, love him and make everything all right, and sane again.

Then something inside her snapped as she thought of the images of him writhing on the altar with Raphelia. Surely she wasn't just imagining things? She could never forgive him. If she stayed, it would be a tangled web of deceit and lies, for he could never give up his affair with Raphelia. She steeled herself against his lies; however much she wanted to believe them, she could now see him for what he really was—a sad pathetic man who would not let go, addicted to Raphelia's dark charms and sexual lure.

'Where were you last night?' she asked, trying to hide the shock from her voice.

'I went to stay with some old friends from university,' he lied. 'Then stayed at Declan's. I didn't want to drive. I thought you would be pleased, I know you don't like me drinking and driving, and Declan is quite harmless.'

For a second she almost believed him, *how* she wanted to believe him.

'Let me kiss my darling, how is the baby? I'm sure you're pregnant,' he said, smiling.

She smiled sadly, then immediately began to recall the painful memories of last night, feeling fear, revulsion and hatred rise up at the sight of him. 'Keep away from me, don't touch me!' she spat venomously.

Angrily, she picked up one of the priceless Chinese vases and threw it at him. He ducked, but it hit him. Then she took his riding crop and lashed it over his face; blood trickled down his face.

'Claire! What's the matter?' he asked, touching his face. 'Have you gone mad?'

'That's for last night, for lying to me!'

'What the hell do you mean?'

'You were with Raphelia, you lying, stinking bastard. I saw you both at the rectory. You are an evil, sick, twisted man.'

The colour drained from Mike's face. 'You saw what exactly?'

Claire described what she had seen; there was no explanation he could ever give that could make it right.

The blood seeped from the wound, trickling over his cheeks. He held a towel against it.

'Look, Claire,' he stuttered, 'it will never happen again. I was drunk, I don't even remember how I got there. I was in the pub with Declan when she came over, I was hardly expecting to see her there. She bought me a drink and said she was visiting some friends she had made over here, then everything became a bit of a blur.'

She sneered at him with contempt. 'So, being drunk to the stage of oblivion, you had sex with her in a pagan rite you didn't want to tell me about. Oh that just happens every day, does it?' she screamed, sarcasm in her voice. She told him what she had seen, that she no longer trusted him. She was afraid, terrified. Having witnessed a pagan rite, she didn't know what he would do to her. After all, he would want to keep it secret. She could be in danger. He might do something unpleasant to her. She made an excuse of a headache. She had to go and would call him from London. She would get out of there as quickly as possible. She spoke to him frostily.

'What're you talking about? I went out with old friends for a drink last night! And then I behaved stupidly, but a pagan rite, that wasn't me. You must be mistaken. You can't leave me, not with our baby.'

'Oh yes I can, and I will!' she said.

He grabbed her arm: 'Look, Claire, stay and I will give you half of everything.'

Claire looked at him sadly, wondering if he really was going insane and didn't know what he was doing. Perhaps he had a split personality, and had no idea what he was doing most of the time. Perhaps he suffered blackouts. How could he keep lying to her? Was he deranged? She knew everything now.

'I have to go, my mother is unwell, I have to return to London,' she said, pulling away, keeping control in her voice, making an excuse, hoping her emotions would not betray her. Using all her self-control, she struggled to keep up the facade. 'I'm so sorry. It's been a dream. You'll have to find somebody else.'

'But we can talk, I'm sorry, look, let me explain.'

'No,' she decided. 'I saw you last night with Raphelia. There's no doubt in my mind. We cannot go back, it's over.'

'But I've explained, I was with friends in town, speak to them if you don't believe me. Raphelia just turned up.'

Then something inside her snapped. She felt so angry, used; lunging forward, she hit him and scratched his face. He grabbed her wrists, shocked.

'What's the matter, are you ill?' cried Mike. 'It's not true, someone has tricked you,' he cried. His grey eyes glared at her coldly. They were like granite. Grabbing her arms he pulled her to him. 'Please don't go, Claire, you are all I have left! You are going to be my wife. You are carrying my child!'

'Get yourself another brood mare,' she snapped, slapping him sharply.

'Why did you follow me?' he said angrily. 'I don't like being spied on.'

'You left your wallet behind, the hotel had never heard of you, I saw a note asking you to meet someone at the rectory, so I drove there thinking you needed your credit cards or cash and witnessed it all.' Her voice was shaking as she spoke. 'I saw you involved in a black mass, the strange figures swaying around you. You and Raphelia were in the midst of it all.'

His face drained of all colour, he turned as white a ghost. For once he seemed utterly speechless.

'How could you!' Claire screamed. 'I saw you making love to Raphelia, in some sort of awful ritual. How could you betray me like this?' she sobbed. 'Why did you do this to me?'

He stood up and gripped her arms so tightly she nearly fell back. 'It wasn't me! How dare you question me? What right do you think you have to follow me?'

'I was only trying to help,' she protested, lifting her palms.

He let go of her, his expression darkening. 'You've no right to follow me and spy on me,' he spat angrily, pushing her onto the sofa, his mood changing rapidly, becoming demonic. 'What did you see? Tell me!' he ordered, shaking her.

Claire kicked him hard in the groin.

Now his face was grey, ashen, and his cheeks gaunt. Her Mike had gone; this wild, insane creature was a stranger, yet his beauty was even more in evidence, he looked like a knight, his long hair flowing over his shoulders. He was angry, and his eyes glinted dangerously. For the first time she felt frightened of him, and backed away.

'What exactly did you see?' he asked, sounding dangerous.

'I saw you and Raphelia writhing together,' she sobbed, 'on some sort of altar. Now will you admit what you have done?'

His face turned ashen grey; he grabbed her by the wrists.

'If you tell anyone, I shall kill you!' he swore vehemently.

'Why did you ask me here, if you still want to seduce her?' she cried.

'Because I wanted you,' he said simply.

Suddenly she felt her heart sink as she began to unravel his lies.

'You saw her the first week we were here? It was Raphelia who phoned, wasn't it?' she demanded to know. 'You couldn't leave her for even a few months? And you were making love to me all the time! How could you? You were fucking us both!'

'That wasn't meant to happen,' he protested. 'I was drunk, then I remembered the note. I didn't have any idea who it was from. I thought it was about a photo-shoot and I had to collect some proofs. The photographer I met at the bar, I had never seen before. I drank some wine, it was drugged, I blacked out and woke up in a strange place. I felt tired but strange and suddenly I was making love to her. It was all so bizarre, like a dream. She's just an old girlfriend, who won't give up, these things happen,' he said dryly, 'but I didn't know she would go this far, you know how seductive she can be! She used her wiles to seduce me and I feel so weak that it worked, and I couldn't resist her charms. The drug was a potent drug, I felt warm all over, I didn't know what I was doing.'

'So you're still in love with her?'

'No, I didn't say that, she's tried to get me back, but I'd never go back to her. She's impossible.'

'But you slept with her a few times? After you split up?'

'Of course, it takes a while to get over someone, some flames never die, but not once I'd met you. You can sound so bloody provincial, so conservative at times,' he spat. 'Yes, I suppose I did succumb to her charms a few times, but that was long before we met. The flame never really died. She's a very sensual woman who knows how to inflame a man's desire but I knew it couldn't work,' he said, his eyes filling with tears. 'But perhaps it was a ploy to win me back.'

'Well it obviously meant something to her,' stated Claire. 'Is she the reason your engagement broke up? And to keep her quiet, you had Jemima hospitalised?'

'No, she was unstable anyway,' he said airily. 'I take it I'm allowed a past. You don't own my soul.'

'No, but Raphelia apparently does!' said Claire vehemently. 'I saw you both writhing on the altar, this isn't just an affair,' she snapped, 'but something far deeper and darker than you are telling me, she's your obsession. You can't give her up, you're a sad pathetic man who cannot break away! And you let her ruin everything you try to create. Now she's come between us.'

He looked at her wearily. 'Perhaps you are right, but, Claire, there are some things you just don't understand.' He fell to the ground, his face contorting with pain, his eyes downcast and heavy. 'Oh God, have you put something in my food? I have the most awful stomach cramps.'

'No, I wouldn't do that,' she said, shocked, 'but maybe someone else has; it must be the drugs they have used on you.'

'If I told you the truth, you wouldn't believe it, it's a hell that none of us can escape from.'

'She used the group to control you, she can't love, she just wants power. If she cannot have you, she stops anyone else from having you, keeping you harnessed to her with her sexual favours and in strange sexual rites.'

'I'm sorry,' he said, softening for a moment. 'I didn't mean for that to happen anymore, I can't escape them.'

'Escape who?' she asked.

'The group, the dark Knights of Kuldar, they helped my father escape and I owed them something. They follow a mythological philosophy in France, a cult that Raphelia belongs to, and who once stayed at the village. They were relatives of Raphelia, descendents of French Knights of the King, who had once used the occult to save their land and their king. Originally, I think they were from some Masonic order. When my father was about to be arrested for murder, her relatives saved him and hid him. They had built up a force that was supposedly impenetrable. Soon they all rose to the highest positions in the land, a secret society and coven. They became artists and musicians with higher aims in mind than fighting, with the acquisition of philosophy and knowledge. But still had a will to power. Raphelia's family inherited their dark power. The younger ones branched off into the occult, leading more natural lives and philosophies, and called themselves the bacchantes, but still had the acquisition of power as their one aim. I tried to get away, but they had a powerful hold over me. I told you that I met her at the beach in the bay, and she introduced me to them as they were holding a secret rite. They were dark temple poets. Some of my relatives were descended from that part of France too. In one of the ancient rites of the goddess cults, a sacrifice was made of a man who represented the closure of the old year. And this was said to increase fertility in the land and in the maidens.

'Raphelia and I were joined in a goddess ceremony a long time ago, in a kind of marriage. After this our souls were made inseparable, so that we could never be parted. That my soul would always return to her, wherever we were. For eternity. Our souls could never be separated, the bond never severed, even in death. She became an expert in the black arts, and used it to manipulate her own ends, and for dark control. Some covens only do good with white magic using love, but she embraced the darkness and fear.'

'Why can't you escape them?' Claire demanded to know. 'Why don't you just give her up? Why did Raphelia protect your father? Because she loved you so much?'

'Because he is her father too, and she was my wife,' admitted Mike. 'My father always had many affairs, but he was discreet and had lovers in France. She was the result.'

Claire put her hand to her mouth in horror. 'Raphelia is your sister?'

'Yes, half-sister. We were married in a black ceremony, and our souls are bound together; she has sworn that she'll never let me go. She's the dark side of me, and you are the light. You are both very different women,' he admitted. 'Well we didn't discover we were half-brother and -sister for a long time. She was following me, she is too strong.'

'Then why ask me here?' asked Claire. 'And is that why Jemima tried to warn me?'

'Unfortunately Jemima found out—I had to let her go. But you are having my child—I will protect you to the end. I'm in a real relationship with you, you are quite different to Raphelia. She was an illusion, an obsession that can never be. Only we have a chance of a real life together, something fulfilling and real. With her, I found only madness and confusion. I've photographed you both, the dark and the light. I wanted someone I could trust. Someone I could build a real relationship with. A healthy relationship.'

'You sick bastard!' spat Claire, hitting him again. 'I'm only here to bear you children!'

'Don't be stupid!' he said. 'I wanted a wife too.'

'But you already have one. Are you insane?'

He looked at her edgily.

'Yes, I suppose I do have a wife. She isn't my real wife, for a number of reasons she never will be, it was a pagan ceremony, not a legal one. So I guess last night was her attempt to renew it.'

'But she's still your wife in spirit,' argued Claire.

'No, not now and she never will be. I realised my life would never be happy with her, it would never work, and we couldn't have children. I actually began to dislike her after the three years of being in love, or what I had thought was love.'

'But you just went back, to relive the passion.'

'Maybe.'

She started to run off up the stairs.

'I hate you,' she shouted, 'you are beneath contempt.'

'Come here, you stupid bitch,' he said, slapping her face. 'I do care about you. I no longer feel I want to be part of her life any more.' He sighed wearily. 'I want to start a new life with you.'

'Then why are you still sleeping with her then?' accused Claire.

'I don't know,' he admitted, 'it was a mistake.'

'Did she captivate you? What was so special about her? What did she give that you couldn't ever give up?'

He sat down and put his head in his hands. 'It was something I could never define, and had never found with anyone else, a kind of mystical ecstasy, that empowered me, someone who really knew me. But I've found love with you too. With you I feel gentle, I want to protect you, make love to you in a caring way, with her it was like a strange, forbidden ecstasy. Something taboo, dangerous, on the edge that filled me with such a wild fire, it ripped my body and soul apart. She was a wild demonic vixen, who lived for seduction. She was my muse, she inspired a lot of my work. But I do love you, Claire, in a different way. Our love is real.'

Claire hung her head in sadness, he'd told her all she needed to know. It was over, there was no going back. He'd betrayed her. She could not forgive him. She listened to the rest with a heavy heart— it was pointless and always had been. Raphelia was too special to him, his goddess, and she was just a mortal, with whom he planned to have a domestic family life, but not the sensual pleasures. That remained, and always would remain, Raphelia's domain.

'What about these strange people you meet? The occultists?'

'I have to feed my soul, I cannot live without what they give me, I need them,' he attempted to explain. 'They give me the power I need. They showed me the path to get what I wanted. Fame, success, influence. To be able to control other people's minds, to get them to do what I want, to never be refused. They showed me the future, what I could do, who to know, who to avoid. Who to exploit. An ultimate survival mechanism.'

'But why? You could have got it all with your talent alone. It's wrong to manipulate forces for evil or gain and to change events for our purposes. It comes back on you. Why ask for more?'

'Because I want it all. The kind of empowerment that the order had, immortality, vision. I don't want to die.'

'Where was I supposed to fit in?' she asked, shaking, feeling sick.

'We make a brilliant team. You're everything I want in a wife, intelligent, beautiful. It's a good union,' he explained. 'My wife. To give me the spiritual love I need, you are the light on the dark side of my soul,' he admitted. 'And you will have given me the perfect child. Raphelia could not have children,' he added sadly. 'We had no future together.'

'So I was just a convenience!'

'No, not at all. More like a dream, you would have benefited too. I can give you everything your heart desires. Surely you can see how wealthy and happy you would have been. You'd have been richer beyond your wildest dreams and would never have had to work again if you didn't want to. You would've lived the life others only dream about, the life of an aristocrat. And all you would have to do is bear me two healthy children, who would be adored. Is that such a bad thing? What is wrong with that? You would've had everything. Do you prefer to keep your morals and live in mediocrity for the rest of your life? Or be with me and lead a dream existence?'

'But what about love and fidelity, that's all I want. I gave you my undivided love,' argued Claire, 'and that's all I really ever wanted in return. You've sold your soul to the darkness.'

'How naïve you are, Claire, I hope your principles feed you well in life.'

'No, that's not the way I want it. I want true love, not a compromise. Now let me go, I am leaving,' she said, pushing him aside and storming down the stairs.

'But Claire, I can give you everything, please stay,' he begged.

He chased her down the stairs, held her by the arms, but Claire pushed him roughly away.

'Let's talk, we can work something out,' he pleaded.

'And what about Raphelia, you would have to keep her too? On the side?'

'Love and passion eventually die,' he said, wisely. 'Friendship is more important along with a gentle love and mean a lot more than torrid sex. Okay, so what if Raphelia had been my occasional mistress? Would that have mattered if you had been so well protected and cared for, and likewise your children? I'm not saying I would have strayed, but would it really have mattered that much? You would inherit so much, you would be a lucky woman, who could live as she chose.'

'You are a bitter, sick and twisted man,' she said. 'I can't be bought. You can keep your strange, sick ideas. When I meet someone I want that person to love only me,' said Claire. 'I want it to be pure, this is already too tarnished, it is corrupt, totally ruined! You wanted her for the dark side of things, and would have alternated between us both. While I provided the heir for your family? You only brought me here so that I could give you a child.'

'And why do you find that so awful?' asked Mike, trying to hide the surprise in his voice. 'What sort of life could I give you? Only everything you ever wanted and desired! You would live a privileged life, a dream. You would make perfect children, and yes, that did attract me, but I like you too. Anyway many societies are polygamous, it might have worked. In many cultures, women actually prefer that way of life. You take life too seriously—men have had mistresses for centuries.'

That was the final straw, and she couldn't take any more. Lifting her heel. Claire kicked him firmly in the groin. The room was spinning round, Claire sat down, weak from exhaustion.

'Oh God, was that necessary, Claire?' he said clutching at his stomach, his face grimacing in pain.

'I know you still love her.'

'She no longer holds any happiness for me,' he admitted. 'She was an obsession I found hard to break. That's all.'

'Shut up, I've heard enough.'

Claire put her hands over her head, to stop his words ringing in her ears. She shot through the hallway, aware of something pulling at her. Exhausted, she collapsed on the stairs. She had heard enough, his words were fading into the distance, she felt sick, about to pass out. She could feel something strange pushing against her, she struggled, then let go—she was falling down the stairs.

Dark secrets—Dance macabre

When she woke up, Claire found herself alone in a strange room—empty, with a small, darkened window. She assumed she was still in the haunted East Wing. She shivered, what was happening? The wind blew icily cold outside, there was a feeling of anticipation hanging in the air. As it grew darker, someone unlocked the door and walked into the room. Raphelia stood in front of her, mocking her, her eyes flashing malevolently. Claire watched her, astonished.

'So you found out about our little secret, did you? You're more intelligent than the others,' she sneered, 'and have more spirit. I like that. Well, I hope you are satisfied. Still, I suppose it's nice to get to know you at last, the bearer of Mike's children.' She laughed wickedly. 'He always chooses such nice girls, but listen—he can't give me up, or lose what I can give him. I am his addiction, he needs me like he needs air. When he goes away, he always comes back to me. Do you understand?'

'So you were behind this?' said Claire, amazed.

'Yes, I like to think so,' she admitted. 'But I must be careful. Mike said not to hurt the baby, after all that's why he brought you here.'

'You're really sick!' Claire said, with condescension.

'I like to think so,' Raphelia replied.

'Why do you do this to people? What is wrong with you?'

'He needs a child, or he could lose the estate. He could lose it all if he doesn't produce an heir, then it goes to the order. His father was very strict about his ancestral line staying pure. Don't think he wants you because he loves you,' she said cruelly. 'You are just a convenience and always were.'

'He always brings me his new friends to play with eventually,' she purred, stroking Claire's face with her long talons. 'But not all of them are as a good a surrogate as you. I must confess he seems to like you a lot more than he has the others. But he'll tire of you very soon and will come back to me. He always comes back to me, and, once the child has been born, he'll send you back to England.'

'I wouldn't be so sure about that!' retorted Claire, terrified.

'Don't fool yourself. Why should you be any different? He only chose you to give him an heir,' snapped Raphelia.

Like a gypsy dancer, Raphelia began to circle Claire, still tied to the chair, her feral eyes flashing malevolently. She swished her long hair over Claire's face, then laughed. Claire wriggled her hands, but couldn't move; she sat wondering how she would escape.

'That's why when the other little distraction found out, she went totally mad and Mike had her checked into a clinic. Mike stopped me from killing her, but didn't want the story to get out, said it would arouse too much suspicion, but, if she disappeared, had a breakdown, her word would not be quite so credible. Just the neurotic rantings of a disturbed woman. You are not very different to the others he's brought here. You can be dealt with in a similar way. Mike always gets bored with his new women after a while, and always returns to me—no one can satisfy him like I do.' Her eyes flashed dangerously. 'He will never leave me, it'll take a will stronger than mine and there are none who are equal to me, with the power I have. You can't fight me, my power is stronger than yours will ever be,' she gloated. 'So don't even try to delude yourself that he ever really loved you. You were just a nice girl to give him a child, he would have left you soon enough. You mean nothing to him.'

Claire cringed in pain, shutting out Raphelia's voice, not believing a word.

Raphelia put on some music and started to dance. She stretched her elegant arms out, and twirled round the room. 'I so love to dance, don't you?' she said, her body gyrating, as she flowed across the floor like a ballerina, her body twisting and turning elegantly. He lacy dress flowed out behind her. 'I trained in ballet,' she said and touched her breast, then touched Claire's cheek. 'I have so much passion,' she whispered, 'so much life! I need to express myself through dance, through my art.'

'You're no threat, you don't have the first idea,' Claire said, tauntingly. 'You're just a sad pathetic psycho, a mad woman who cannot let go!'

'No, no, you have it so wrong. He finds you a novelty, but this won't last long, soon he will tire of you and seek his old ways, and come back to me. He needs us both. And I have the power he needs. What can you give him?'

'I can give him love, and you can only use control. I want to leave here now!' Claire demanded.

'Oh, you sad thing, I pity you. Love, love, what is love? Such an illusion! We have bonds beyond mortal love. I am the goddess, and you are the sacrificial maiden.' She laughed wickedly. 'The real power lies within a deep sensuality and our kindred spirits. You can't give him the special powers I can. I am a witch, and my power is infinite. He is one of us, not a mere dull mortal. I can't let you go now. I don't know how much you saw. You may tell someone, so I can't trust you. I may have to kill you,' she taunted Claire wickedly. 'You will make a good sacrifice to our master. Each year I want to offer a maiden to our goddess, and Mike usually finds one only too willing to come here.'

'Mike won't allow that, what if you get caught?'

'Mike does whatever I say, he let's me decide.'

'Then he's misguided as well as psychotic,' spat Claire, struggling to pull the ropes off her wrists.

'What can we do to pass the time until then? Play chess? Or Russian roulette?' said Raphelia, thoughtfully. 'I can give you one of Mike's prize guns. Do you enjoy being frightened?' she asked, scratching a long talon over Claire's cheek, drawing blood. Claire recoiled in horror.

'I shall show you things you would rather not see,' she threatened. 'I will make your mind scream, until you say you will give him up. Shall we play that game?'

Claire looked away, the woman was clearly sick. 'But if you really love Mike, why don't you both just stay together?' asked Claire puzzled. 'Why do you involve other people in this charade? Why not just get married and have children yourself, or adopt them if you cannot have them?'

'The bloodline has to be pure with a female selected for suitability, or else the will is null and void.'

'Then why not adopt or have children some other way?'

'Because his father and my father were the same person,' she said, her eyes full of sorrow. 'And what's worse, he was a shady French aristocrat with insanity in his blood. During the time when Mike's father had been a general at a military school in France, he took my mother as his mistress, then after the murder we tried to help him and hid him in our home. Some time later, when I tried to trace my ancestors, Mike and I discovered he was the father to us both, and we knew we had to part. My lover, the man perfect for me, is my half-brother. I wanted his children so badly, but they would be insane, we were doomed.'

'What does Mike think about all of this?' asked Claire, shocked.

'At first it didn't seem to matter,' she admitted. 'He said as long as I didn't get pregnant, it was okay. Then our father conveniently died, and we discovered he had put a clause in his will, stating that unless Mike had at least one child and gave me up, he would inherit absolutely nothing. The arguments started. He said he would choose a suitable woman to give him children, but that he would return to me, promising he would always love me. I couldn't accept this, and it tore me in two. When I discovered I couldn't have borne him a child anyway, I was infertile, he became more and more obsessed with having a child, and the strain, after discovering our origins, blew us apart. I nearly went insane with jealousy thinking of him with another woman and I swore to destroy my rivals. So, confused, I slept around. As I watched him find other women, I tried to win him back.'

She wrung her hands, tears welled up in her eyes. 'I had to destroy any shred of happiness he built with anyone else. It was only a matter of time until he found someone else that he really did love, and then I would lose him forever. I was tormented, insane with jealousy and pain. Fate had been unkind enough to me, it would not take him away as well.'

Claire looked at her sympathetically, then said, 'So you try to destroy the life of anyone he gets close to.'

'Yes! If I can't have him, no one else will!' she cried, her eyes glazed over in pain, her expression tortured and manic; she thrashed around the room like a mad woman, throwing back her hair, her eyes blazing.

Claire backed as far into the chair as she could. Her nerve was slithering away. Raphelia was becoming more and more deranged and was crazy enough to kill her, she had to escape somehow.

Confrontations

'Am I the only woman in your life?' Raphelia screamed, as Mike came into the room. 'Tell me, tell me,' she screamed.

'Yes, I worship you, my goddess, but you are my sister,' he said, his face contorting in pain.

Claire screamed in terror, as she felt Raphelia's nails dig sharply into her shoulders, then pull at her hair. She struggled and managed to turn round and began kicking her, trying to break from Raphelia's clamping hold. The rope tore at her skin as she pulled; she kept struggling, feeling tired, but the knot was too far out of her grasp. Summoning up all her strength, she had loosened the rope so that her hands slipped through. She leapt up and roughly pushed Raphelia over backwards.

Raphelia sprung up and slapped her hard.

'Go back to your hovel, you little bitch,' she said, slapping her across the face. 'I will destroy you, like I have destroyed the others if you try to take him away from me!' she screamed, her black talons clawing at Claire's face with a vengeance.

'No one else will ever have his love as I do. There is another sweetheart buried in the basement, under cement. She thought she could fight me too! He will never leave me, he always comes back to me!'

She tied Claire to the chair. 'You won't escape again. Stop struggling, little bitch,' she said, in a heavy French accent. 'Keep still or I shall slap you again. Would you like to hear more?' she asked. 'Some more horrors?' Her mocking laugh rang through the air, screeching like a hellcat. 'What terrifies you most? What scares you most, Claire, I would love to know,' she said, raking her nails across Claire's cheek. 'Shall I show you some of the evil things I've done? You are close to death, Claire. Do you know what happens when you die?'

'No, do tell me, I am sure you are the expert,' sighed Claire.

'You will go to purgatory, where your soul is cleansed, then you are reborn and reincarnated in a new body. You will only stay a short while in purgatory, being cleansed of your sins, then if you are lucky, go to Heaven ready for reincarnation. A clean pure spirit. I shall stay in purgatory for eternity, I shall never pass to Heaven. My spirit is as dark as night. Those who have committed very dark acts never pass into the light again, but stay trapped in the darkness of their own sins, for eternity. Inescapable repetition.'

They are all insane here, Raphelia is mad, thought Claire, her consciousness fading fast. Claire tried to pull herself up, but felt so weak, she fainted. She felt herself propelled into a pit of blackness. She heard a loud sound, it sounded like police car siren, then there was nothing.

When she awoke she was in hospital, her friends Justin and Rory were standing at her bedside.

'Where am I?' she asked. 'How did I get here?'

'You're back in London. You tried to phone me, I came to get you, you were in a state,' Justin began to explain.

'You sounded drunk, but stayed awake long enough to give me the details of where you were and garbled something about a black mass. You were really delirious, I thought you were ill or had really lost it. You said you were with Mike and his old girlfriend and they were keeping you there, she was a witch or something. We thought you had either had too much potteen or were in serious trouble, so I caught a plane and travelled to the castle. I found Mike delirious on the stairs, then found you in a room with a strange woman who had gone mad.'

Slowly and painfully, Claire began to remember the events of the last few days. She shuddered as the memories come flooding back, the nightmare unfolding before her eyes. The baby, miraculously, had survived.

'Oh, thank you, Justin, you have saved my life,' she cried, hugging him with relief. 'I might have been killed if you had not come and saved me.'

'Ah, what are friends for?' he laughed. 'I am glad you are back in one piece.'

Claire lay confined to bed in shock for weeks, under sedation, gradually forgetting the pain, rebuilding her life. With the support of Justin, a caring and loyal friend, she felt her will to live return, and a glimpse of her life and the future broke through the blackness. She worked on a new project, and planned to work freelance from home for the TV company. Her world had been shattered, but she would get over it. She would enjoy bringing up the baby and would employ a part-time nanny to help her so that she could go to work for a few days a week. She sat in a haze, shocked, unable to believe what she had been through. Mike tried to phone, but she refused to speak to him. A few weeks later, while eating breakfast with Justin she stopped as she saw a newspaper heading; a chill ran through her, a bullet of icy-cold fear shot over her spine. She stared in disbelief at the two people on the front page, recognising them instantly—Mike's good-looking face, and Raphelia's slanted eyes. Claire's eyes widened in horror as she slowly read the caption;

'Fatal accident in Eire on major road—Model and famous photographer killed in car accident.' It was Mike and Raphelia! They were both dead! They'd had a bitter conflict, while heading back for London and she had tried to stop him. Mike had been leaving, returning to find Claire. Raphelia had jumped in the car to take him to the airport, and they sped along the motorway arguing. Witnesses said she'd steered the car into oncoming traffic, drove into the wrong lane. A passing coach had crashed into the car, decapitated them both, killed them instantly. Claire scanned the rest of the story, tears welling up in her eyes. 'Oh Mike,' she cried, thinking of the nights she had spent in his arms, and their baby. She had loved him so dearly. The nightmare was over, so was her dream.

'You won, Raphelia,' said Claire, bitter chills running over her. 'You got him in the end.' Shivers of pain ran over her spine and hot tears poured down her face. The nurse came in and gave her a sedative.

'Now, you must rest,' she insisted, pulling the curtains. 'In your condition, you must not get upset.'

As Claire slid into a hazy dream, a narcotic stupor, her last thoughts were of Mike. Her body ached for him.

'You have him now, Raphelia. You got what you wanted too. Mike is yours for eternity, Raphelia, forever. No one can ever take him away from you now, you are joined in death. You could not bear the thought of anyone else having him, and you killed him rather than let him walk away.' Claire wondered what drove someone to commit such an act of extreme passion. It was chilling.

'Your powerful friends, Mike, they couldn't save you in the end, could they?' she said. She thought of him making love to her, the memory of his face still fresh in her mind and pain wrenched through her like a knife. The drug started to take effect and she became numb, no longer caring, just feeling the sweet release of the tranquillising drug flow over her, killing her pain.

'You could never let her go, could you, Mike? You loved her too much. So you both died, to have your tainted love.' At that moment she looked up, hearing a high-pitched laugh fading in the wind.

The calm after the storm

A year later Claire received a letter from Mike's solicitor, making their daughter Charlotte the sole beneficiary of his will and fortune, the entire Ireland estate, including the old castle. The new inhabitants would replace its terrible darkness with joy and happiness, he hoped, and he wished them success there. In the file was a note, it read:

> 'If you ever read this Claire, and I am departed, I apologise for the pain and upset that I caused you. I was a lost case, beyond redemption, but it was my intention to make you happy. I hope you find the happiness in the castle one day that forever eluded us…yours. Mike.'

Two years later

Claire sat with Charlotte, helping her with her colouring books, their cries of joy and laughter echoing through the castle, eclipsing the once terrible sounds of pain and torment. The rooms were filled with happiness now, thought Claire as she looked up at the paintings on the wall, at Mike's austere ancestors, and saw that as they looked down, they were smiling.

END

The Dark Goddess

The Dark Goddess

Laura, the Goddess, Adrianna the sylph, night spirit

> 'Where love reigns, there is no will to power, and where will to power is paramount, love is lacking. The one is but the shadow of the other.'
>
> *Jung*

Inspiration—the Muse

Laura tore up the invitation to the dating agency party she found on the bedside cabinet and, after staring at it disdainfully, folded it into a paper plane and swooped it over to the bin. Yet another soirée for singles dating, she sighed wearily, for meeting endless dull men who were only interested in a quick affair. She would at least expect a holiday in the wilds of Tuscany next time! She rolled over, snuggling deeper into the duvet, reluctant to leave her warm cosy bed. Last night at the cinema, the film had been enjoyable, the meal afterwards perfect, but now she felt a sluggish inertia and wanted to spend the day hibernating, doing absolutely nothing, having a 'duvet' day. She felt a veil of apathy flow over her, a distinct lack of interest in the new day and wanted nothing more than to take refuge in her own thoughts. She pulled herself out of bed and made a cup of camomile tea. She went into the hallway and checked the post. Still no letter from Zenta, the TV company. They were obviously tight on budgets at the moment and things were not going any better at the studio either. She was well past deadlines and the new funds for their next project had been delayed indefinitely. She sighed in frustration. Why were they taking so long to get back to her? She often wondered why on earth she had ever got into television in the first place—such an unpredictable business. She had reached an impasse, everything seemed to have dried up, ground to a halt and she felt tired.

The media life and its uncertainties drove her mad and she often wondered where the next cheque was coming from. The stress and hard work had fuelled her angst and were giving her a migraine. She threw back some aspirin and turned on the computer and sat in front of a blank screen. Life at the moment was unsettled, unpredictable, hardly the wonderful dream that she had envisaged at her age, her late thirties—with a cottage in the country and a few kids running around freshly cut lawns, munching salmon sandwiches. She had gone into television full of optimism, seeing her ideas swell to the pinnacle of success, screened to the nation, giving her a high that nothing else could equal. When she made her first documentary, she became so hooked on the idea of her work that she lived for her ideas and nothing else. To her surprise, she found she had created a tangible asset as her second and third brought in more awards, and she rose to the top. She loved the highs and lows, peaks and troughs, the challenge of taking an idea and turning it into a dream, the publicity and acclaim—so much so that she put most of her personal life on hold. She flipped open her web page, and eyed her credits; it always boosted her confidence and encouraged her to have faith in her new projects. She had been a star, shining in the glittering sky, gliding on the crest of a silver wave on a shimmering golden carpet. Her life became a whirlwind of brilliant ideas, crystallising into elegant artistic projects. Along the way she had turned down the proposals of two brilliant men: work was her first love, and she found herself immersed in her ideas, too busy to give anyone a morsel of her time, finding the prospect of domesticity too mundane to bear.

But now she felt empty. She loved to live on the edge, to feel the creative fire burning high in her, spurring her to the next documentary, into the universe and magic of the media. Normal life, as far as she could see, was tedious, conformity too cold, flat and uninviting. Now work had slowed down and the ideas were not coming so fast, she felt fuzzy and unfocused. What if it all fell apart, and she could find no more budgets to be creative? Or to bring her ideas into life? Her world would fall apart, dry up like an arid desert. She had sent the new scripts to the TV company, outlining her new 'concept', but had had no feedback, and what if all the funds dried up suddenly? She started to think about her personal life, and with a sharp focus all at once saw how empty her home life actually was. Apart from her work, there was nothing. There were big setbacks in filming now, and funding was becoming harder to get, and the possibility of new projects scarce. What would she have left when it all came to an end? Work had filled every hour but now, with time to reflect, she wondered why she had neglected other areas of her life. Hurriedly, she started to put everything away, realising how one-dimensional her life actually was. She had concentrated on her work to the exclusion of everything else. She had ignored every other aspect of her life, and suddenly slithers of fear vibrated through her as she wondered what would happen when her TV career dried up, and she was left with what? No children or husband? Absolutely nothing. A great big void. She brushed the thoughts nervously aside: she was on the new project, carving out her next masterpiece. It was always cathartic, clearing out her office just before a new project.

    She continued reflecting. Now, her creativity had dipped, no new ideas; her mind couldn't get back into the groove and she couldn't think of anything new. She watched her ideas take shape on the screen, realising she had two projects to finish, a final shoot to meet, and still had no feedback on her new ideas. This next documentary was to be the one where she would be in total control. Often she worked for other producers or TV companies on shared ideas, but this next one was to be her baby and hopefully her best effort yet. But where was the fire she always felt for a project that would literally lift her off the ground and propel her toward her next award? Her energy levels seemed sadly depleted at the moment. The thought of her next project not coming off filled her with depression. She lived for the spark of new ideas and thrived on the challenge of her work, finding a stimulating new project to flood her with creative fire and inspire her, but just lately they seemed to have burned low along with the lack of funds. Who was it, the famous psychologist who said that creativity declined with age as a more conservative attitude takes over? As the libido wanes, the reality principle becomes more focused?

She hoped it wasn't happening to her. Not just yet. She couldn't give up her dreams until she felt she had fulfilled all her ambitions, she still had personal mountains to climb.

Recently though, she had a growing feeling that something was missing in her life; she loved her work but craved something more. To fill the void she sought solace in her spirituality, and each summer attended retreats in rural France, or Italy. Last year she had stayed at a Buddhist monastery and chanted her way to bliss. 'Ohm Yo ho Renghe ko.' It made her feel refreshed for a while and gave her a new perspective on life, but she had a longing to start a family. To fill in the 'resting' times, the delay waiting for the next job to start meant she taught media studies at the local college when she wasn't filming. She had to earn the extra money somehow and enjoyed teaching the kids, but her true passion was seeing the birth and shaping of her ideas. She loved her work and, when she was at her creative peak, was one of the best. Her media colleagues knew this and valued her contribution to the industry. She reached above the shelf, and took down her award brushing the dust off. She eyed it lovingly, it was the one she had won for her 'dietary theories and health' documentary. She knew she could never give up the media life, even when it became an endless hard slog.

She put all her files in order and made a new ring file for the next project. It always excited her, this stage. She could not give up now, she had to hold out hope. Later, when she saw her work screened, it made the hard slog and waiting and worrying all worthwhile. She always felt a new creative idea ready to burst forth and develop, a wave of inspiration creeping over her, until it became a force of its own, and the ideas came through her with little effort from herself—as though some higher, divine entity was working through her, sending her the information. The ideas would flow like a river, waiting to be turned into something tangible. Until they swelled into a tour de force, resulting in an even better project than before. Sowing a seed of genius wasn't easy and, after the initial excitement, she found it quite hard work; creativity was ten per cent inspiration, and ninety per cent perspiration. She worked such long hours it drained her but when it took off, she just took off and flew. Nothing else made her feel so elated, supreme. The recognition she craved made her feel high as a kite. But recently she'd felt burned out, tired and lacking in inspiration. And at times like this, she saw the down side. Nothing was happening and she lost her nerve. Maybe she should have trained as a therapist or accountant, or started her own medical practice, by now holding down a steady reliable job with a regular income; at least in medicine people could always be relied upon to become ill. Maybe she shouldn't have chosen the business in the first place and taken a more secure, reliable route or a mundane job. But she knew that she liked nothing better than receiving the acclaim and rewards for her work and craved the terrific buzz it gave her.

Despite having some wonderful lovers and engagements, her addiction to work always turned men off, for it always provided a greater allure than any of her suitors could provide. Now, as she saw all her friends having their first child and moving into the country with their families, she was aware she did not even have a stable relationship. She'd had a number of exciting affairs, with beautiful men, but men soon became bored of playing second place, being ignored most of the time as she pursued the thrill of her projects. She glanced in the mirror: well, apart from looking tired she was still beautiful with long, naturally blonde hair and young girl looks, even though she was late thirties; a small nose and features, and a good figure. But time was running out and her biological clock was ticking away. Maybe she should have studied medicine like her brother, become a doctor in the Midlands, but she knew the creative life was all she dreamed of. Her other brother was a film director too, in politics, but he had a ruthless streak and they rarely spoke.

Feeling flat and in need of some inspiration, she threw everything into a suitcase and fled to the West Country where she spent the days walking over the hills and drinking spring water from the tor. One day, while standing on the graves of King Arthur and Guinevere, she felt a strange feeling flood her and lift her, like fizzing white sparks of light. She felt renewed, pulsating with a vibrant energy. A new idea suddenly came into her head. Quickly she grabbed a pen and scribbled some notes, hoping to get it all down before it dissipated and slid into oblivion; suddenly all her ideas fell into place and seemed to fit together as the loose disparate ideas seemed to take form and structure and connect together. She dug her heels into the mud and came across a hard metal cup. She dug deeper and pulled it out; it was a chalice. She wondered if it was worth anything and quickly put it into her bag—she would have to get it valued. Suddenly a storm rose in the sky, and it started to rain. She rushed back to her hotel, sat down and wrote for hours. Her creative spark, the silver sparks of fire had returned.

When she returned to London, she felt renewed and her ideas were flowing again. She recalled the images she had visualised while standing on the graves of Arthur and his beloved. Now, rejuvenated, she felt ready to start a new project, to begin the whole process again. This time the creative fire flooded her veins. She looked up gratefully at the silver chalice; it had been half buried in the mud. She toyed with the small silver coin she had found in the chalice and hung it around her neck. Perhaps it would bring her luck.

She had enjoyed her holiday; it had loosened her creative block and had really done the trick. Always, after completing a project, she had to get away, or a frightening emptiness and inertia would engulf her. Then she struggled to think of a new idea to get her thoughts flowing again. She would flee into the wilds to meditate for a while. People called her a workaholic, and it was true, she was totally addicted to her career, and thought of little else. If she didn't have her work she was sure she would fall apart. When resting, she spent most of her time feeling depressed, then she would return, to a cycle of frantic activity and the process would start again and bring her alive. The highs and lows of the media drove her almost demented, and there were times when she found out who her true friends, and enemies, were. But mostly it gave her a sense of purpose. She scanned the photographs quickly. Yes, there were some good ones, detailed enough to use in the next programme. Inspired, she decided her next documentary would be about 'Natural Health—Therapies, Alternative Medicine and Personal Growth'. The idea had a ring to it, but without the money coming in, she couldn't forge ahead. She felt gripped by frustration and anxiety. What if the funds had dried up? The thought was too much to bear. She had been musing on the idea for a while, and her recent break in Somerset had stimulated some new ideas and given impetus to her thoughts. Her reverie began to take over, until some new images started drifting through her head, a seed of an idea swelling to life—she could almost see it, a normal woman, with an ordinary dull job, morphing into the Dark Goddess, and drinking the herbal remedy, and suddenly becoming empowered, strong and fired with creativity and original life; the secretary who became inspired, her dry, arid, conforming life awakening her to one of ripeness and spiritual awareness. The earth Mother-goddess. She let her mind flow and conjured up some new shots. A new series entitled 'Natural health, Empowerment of Women'. She might even use Glastonbury as the location. It inspired all things creative, medieval and mystical. Or perhaps shoot it in some dark medieval city, focusing on a goddess drawn on the papyrus by an ancient order of monks, showing the statue of an ancient goddess transfixed in cement, towering over them, then swinging back to a shot of a woman in the street. Her imagination soared into overdrive, conjuring up all kinds of new images and connections. She was feeling creative, powerful again. The idea of archetypes, of psychic empowerment had really excited her. Particularly one of them, the Dark Goddess, bringer of change, destruction, destroy the old in order to renew the strength of creative fire. She felt her own creativity return and tear through her veins, as she wrote frantically, trying to get all her ideas down. The creative process was what she lived and died for, and it gave her a high like nothing else could.

She turned on the stereo, listened to the magical, new age music and let her mind wander free as the haunting chords filled the room. She danced slowly, twirling around the room.

She looked at the photographs of her trek up onto Glastonbury Tor. It had given her the kind of holiday she needed, a spiritual retreat, quiet, restful in a small village, surrounded by verdant rolling hills, made even more interesting by visits to the fascinating local shops where she found much more to fire her imagination—magical caves filled with swords and other medieval paraphernalia alongside romantic paintings. She had spent the entire holiday walking over the hills, brimming with a kind of ecstasy, skipping gaily through the fields, with a sense of wonder, gripped in an awakening, absorbed by the natural beauty of things. Immersed in a spiritual cloud of happiness. She hadn't felt this free for years and was surprised to find such a wonderful experience, how being alone with nature helped her see life with a new clarity. She had ambled through the valleys, to the top of the Tor, had drunk from the natural springs, ate saffron cake, and rambled across the blustery fields, the wind whipping through her hair, feeling the fresh rain shower her face. Later, she had sat listening to guitars being played in the open courtyard of the pub. So inspiring. She walked down to the mysterious abbey, where she found, curving into the small labyrinthine caves, a café filled with a mysterious aura, alight with a spiritual energy and resonating with friendly voices. She followed the voices to an underground café and later had left to drink a silken, mineral liquid from the outside spring, which according to legend, held properties for 'goddess' empowerment and wisdom, as well as good physical health! It had been an ideal place to chill out, to relax. She had spent the last week cantering across the fields on a black stallion, happy and free, elevated to a harmonious bliss.

Now though, it was time to get back to work. The place had filled her with a mystical inspiration. As she flicked through the photographs, she still felt the reverberations of the magic ripple through her and the old excitement return. She nearly jumped in the air with joy; she had found her mystical and spiritual paradise, a place where she could unleash the true nature of her spirit—to go when she felt at her wits' end, and renew herself, to leave behind the fast pace of London, the anonymity, the bustle, the futile relationships, and find herself. Despite leading a busy life, she often felt empty, as though a part of her was crying out to be fulfilled. Occasionally, fragments of loneliness would creep into her soul at night, sending chills through her body. The room would fill with a silent darkness, scary shadows would dance on the walls. She would feel as though her life was empty; all that existed were the shadows on the wall. Last night she had listened to the silence and wondered if she really did exist without the constant roll of the cameras on an adrenaline-charged shoot. An old teddy bear, was her only 'cuddle'—apart from Graham the cameraman. They had known each other for ten years, and he had become more like a friend; she wasn't sure that she was in love with him any more, just enjoyed his company. She had even dated other men, but the spark wasn't there. She took one of the herbal remedies she had bought in the shop at Glastonbury, off the shelf, a natural relaxant, and tipped the liquid to her lips, hoping it would bring back some of the positive feelings she had experienced at the Tor.

She had very few hugs these days, except from her lighting cameraman; he would come to visit, they would have rampant sex, argue, then he would fly off again! She preferred it that way—she didn't want any really heavy ties. He kept asking her to move in with him, but somehow she wanted her own space and freedom, and couldn't take the final step out of the singletons. She was fond of him, but he was more like a business partner, not Mister Right. She gazed out of her window in her flat at Holland Park, wishing she was back in Somerset, back at the fishbowl again; she sighed, resigned. She wished she didn't have to live in London. Still, it was close to the West End, and only a train ride to Hampstead. Today, she would jog across the heath, then lunch at The Spaniards. She phoned Tanya, a colleague, suddenly feeling buoyant and strong—none of those seeping insecurities were around for a change, and she was feeling excited and positive at the thought of her new goals. She took a moment to reflect on her life: London wasn't so bad. She had a relatively good social life—lunching at Kettners or Smarties every day, then off with her trendy London friends to Sussex or Oxford at the weekend, or off to the country or Henley for the regatta, followed by jaunts to Greece, Tuscany or Spain.

She lunched at a restaurant in Portobello Road with Tanya, and then bought clothes by Elizabeth Emmanuel, spellbound by their delicate, gothic web-like form that fitted her ethereal frame so well.

She attended women's creative writing and art groups every week, to keep up with her work. Although she often wished she had someone to share her life with, she had to stay focused—men had a habit of breaking your heart. Her life was an endless round of social activity and passion for work, anything to hide her crippling inadequacies and insecurities. Then she'd be ready to start again the next weekend. Yet, the lack of true fulfilment got to her at times. Of all the people she knew, she didn't really feel that close to anyone.

She spent the next few weeks completing the filming and taking jaunts into the country.

Her therapist had advised her to take up meditation, and she had, finding it useful for positive thinking, and she'd taken up a hobby to fill the void—sailing—to calm her existential angst. She threw herself into everything from existentialist therapy to co-counselling, but could not think of a suitable hobby near to home.

Collecting empty wine bottles perhaps? She had enough to do with her work—that was her passion, her obsession. What she needed was something real, or her life would continue to lack real meaning. Her work satisfied her, but her personal life was lacking. She would meditate at night to knit back together the fragmented threads of herself after a day's toil. Eventually she decided to take up walking, which led her to thinking about the Glastonbury holiday.

She took a train to Kent and rambled through the quiet gentility of Knole Park, her thoughts drifting to Vita Sackville-West as her poetry filled her mind. She looked at the country with renewed wonder, even deep joy, from seeing deer in the park. They had fed from her hand trustingly, filling her with more happiness than she had known in a long time. One of them came over to her, and nuzzled his wet nose into her hand. Had Vita ever experienced such joy here? The deer stood still, its eyes piercing her.

Their eyes met, and she felt herself empathising totally with him, as though for a second she could see life through his eyes, filled with a surge of warmth and freedom, connected to something important and far greater than she had ever known. She suddenly saw everything in sharp focus, and her world suddenly illuminated with revelations; she knew she was on the wrong path, bored with the endless parties and all the dinners she had attended in the last few years. She told her counsellor about it, she had said it was a real self-actualising experience, flooded with insight and a divine energy. 'What crap,' she had muttered once, as he'd gone on and on about spending days immersed in nature, having peak experiences, 'self-actualisation'—why did they always dress it up in psychological terms, she wondered, when the term 'extreme happiness' would do? Now she could see what he meant. Why did they have to label it 'peak experiences' or 'transpersonal growth', why did they not recognise the simple achievement of being happy and fulfilled? Nature seemed to offer her the tranquillity she craved. It was real. Maybe that was it! She did not have enough love in her life or connectedness with others, real connections.

She threw the new script on the floor and let her mind wander over a few ideas as she relaxed. She picked up the silver chalice and cleaned it, thinking back to the lovely days she'd had when she had found it; it was so beautiful, and it glistened and gleamed and sparkled with a strange energy. As she touched it she felt something move around her, an invisible energy, as though she had dislodged something. She thought she saw a face in the chalice, like in a mirror, a woman with dark, flowing hair. How strange! She began to feel sleepy. She grabbed the chalice and filled it with water, then drank it. It was a warm and balmy night and she was beginning to feel sleepy.

She drifted off, wondering what tomorrow would bring. What would happen next week? Who cared? For once, her mind switched off easily, and her thoughts drifted calmly into a sea of tranquillity. The day was dark, shadowy and misty. Her head switched off from chasing new ideas. A strange dream drifted around in her head. Suddenly she felt a tremor of foreboding slither through her veins: something was about to happen that would change her life forever and she had no idea what it was.

The Dark Goddess

Deep in the forest, the Dark Goddess rose from the ashes; her cry could be heard from the deepest abyss all over the land.

'I will rise!' she warned. 'I will return!' she cried, as a fork of lightning tore across the sky.

Crows flocked from the trees, the raven awaited her…she walked into the light.

She was free again, and had escaped the bondage of purgatory.

Someone had awakened her, another spirit. It had disturbed her and given her life again. She felt the strange vibrations of the woman who had disturbed the chalice and freed her. She saw her, a successful attractive woman who felt lonely, and then she felt the force of life flow through her. She felt its presence flood her with life, liberate her from the endless night that had trapped her for so long. She rose from the darkness, to the light on the earth that had once enveloped her for so long. She had been granted another existence. She was no longer one of the dispossessed, a lost soul. Adrianna gazed into the water and saw her reflection. She was human again. She also saw the image of a woman, the one who would help her, and the sadness in her eyes. She was lonely despite her success. Perhaps she would help her. As she had helped her before.

She had to be cunning, wise, with the heart and courage of a lioness, to carry out her plan. All she had were her few old friends who could help her. Then there were those she could contact in the spirit world. Her life was desolate, empty; she had to rebuild the fragments of her life again. Who would empower her when the time was right? She would take her magic and empower all that she desired. In her deity, as the Dark Goddess, she had the ability to appear to mortal men and women, as one of great beauty, to entice them. A seductress. Her chosen one would be totally spellbound, with a fatal attraction, as the outcome was often the death of the chosen one. She wove her long hair around her. She rose from the leaves, where they had left her dead, three years ago, her body hidden from all light.

Wisps of clouds moved over the sun, spinning patterns across the sky. A blackness began to descend on the hill. Swirling mists fell over the Tor. The Dark Goddess has to destroy in order to renew.

Laura woke up with a start as a heavy parcel landed on the floor. Nervously, she rushed to the hallway, tore open the package and sighed with relief as she read the scripts; she been given the budget for the new documentary. She whooped a cry of joy, the adrenaline surging through her. She was prepared, excited and ready to go. She had just completed the last shot of the last programme she had slaved on. She called her team together, made a few calls; she must get the crew together, ready for the next documentary. She danced around the room filled with bliss. She rang Zenta, the TV company; yes they had a huge budget. If she was careful she could shoot and edit it all within six months. She was on top form, determined to make this project her biggest hit!

Laura opened a bottle of sparkling wine, flipped off the cork and celebrated, thinking she would do it all differently this time. She poured a glass and sipped it thoughtfully—this time she must be more organised, get fit and healthy, give up drinking, and organise a schedule for everyone to know what they should be doing and when. Take a course in time management and optimise her efficiency. She sat considering her next project thoughtfully—how she would set the documentary up, creating the starting sequence to have maximum impact; she was soon making copious notes. Quivering with excitement, she wiped the chalice and poured some wine into it. After all, if it had been important enough for some pagan ritual, it was good enough for her to drink her best Chablis from. She snorted a line of coke too; it gave her an extra lift. She didn't use it a lot, just occasionally, at special times, and then made her way to the bar where she had arranged to meet the crew. Confidently, she ordered an orange juice, feeling a buzz, and looked over to see Graham, her cameraman, sauntering over. She could see he was hung over. His face pallid, his eyes were concealed under some dark glasses and his hair was unkempt. As his tall frame stood next to her, towering over her, she felt a surge of lust. They were still lovers occasionally. Right now, she felt like a quick fling, and he was a powerful man in bed—she had nothing else going on so why not? Being celibate did not suit her: she loved romance, the excitement of going on a date followed by luxurious hours spent making love. The singleton life made her feel depressed, nothing like falling in love to bring back the spark in her life again. He was her co-worker, ideas generator and brainstorm partner. They had got together and broken up more times than she cared to remember; after the last split, a year ago, she had decided to find someone else more reliable, as he often worked abroad on war stories, but there was still some passion. Now they were thrown back together, who knew where it would take her? And often when they had worked together before, the whole affair started up again. She found his slight sleaziness, slicked-back hair and black leather quite sensual tonight. The smell of the leather drifted into her nostrils—it turned her on, making her feel wild and reckless.

'So we have the new budget?' he asked, sipping from his glass. His eyes were half closed, his slightly jaded expression lighting up as she told him the good news.

'Yes, and we've got more than I expected this time—even allowing for expenses, this time they were more than generous.'

'Well done, my beautiful one,' he said, lifting her chin and planting a kiss on her lips.

They moved onto a large sofa in the bar. He stared at her through the dark shades before throwing them to one side; his expression was world-weary from too many late nights, but his lived-in look excited her. She curled up to him instinctively, for she loved being cuddled after being a tough, professional woman all day. Her persona slipped, she felt herself melt, her femininity take over: she could be herself with him. He made her feel safe, protected her. She nuzzled comfortably into his arms.

'I'm impressed,' he said, leaning over her, pouring out some wine. You are my dream goddess, such a genius.'

'Yes, I'm relieved,' she admitted.

'Let's finish this at home,' he suggested, grabbing the bottle. 'We can talk there.'

They were barely inside his studio flat, when she tore off his jeans, and lay back on the futon. She took off her knickers, letting him flick his tongue across her clitoris the way she loved. She felt herself relax into his body. She felt him enter her. He pushed in several hard thrusts. How she needed that, to be full, to let go. Flooded with relief, she came almost instantly, feeling every inch of him thrusting inside her.

There was a brief moment of tenderness, and then it was back to work and sharing creative ideas. She hated to be trapped in sentimental diversions; they wasted time when she could be doing creative work. He understood her, her need for freedom. Maybe he would want children too? Like the comfortable old friends they were, they sat up, consumed some more wine, snorted another line of coke, and began making plans. They had a deep understanding, and worked in perfect synchronicity, knowing each other's ways, as best friends. She could be free with him sexually, expressing her true nature, dirty sometimes, romantic at others, completely at ease with each other, climbing up his tall frame, he held her across his hips, she could be so naughty. The play released the tension in her.

'Oh tie me up, baby,' he would say jokingly. 'Not down.'

She loved it when he kissed her neck all over. And he made her laugh. Sometimes he tied her to the bed, and licked her all over. Other times he gently draped a whip over her, but never anything too extreme. Just gentle fantasies.

'These are my ideas,' she said, handing him the script. 'Take a look at them, tell me what you think.'

'Okay,' he said, 'shoot them to me,' opening another bottle of wine.

'No, read them now, Graham, get the feel, don't let me do all the work.'

'Oh baby, let's spend the day in bed.'

'Let's not, let's get into this now,' she insisted.

'Okay,' he sighed, and glanced at the new script.

She told him about the Natural Therapy Centres she had visited, of the holistic therapists she had met, the reflexologists, how they treated the whole person, not just a collection of symptoms. Her new angle was enhancing the spiritual 'self' as well as the physical. Her plan was to use different facets of women for the film, with goddess, maiden, nymph, siren, to illustrate spiritual empowerment, and nature; to include how natural creative energy is used to empower women's lives. All the answers were there, she just had to utilise them. She looked at the wine and coke guiltily.

'Okay, let's be clean,' he insisted, 'no point on doing a documentary on health if we are stoned half the time.'

'That's the spirit,' she said playfully.

Perhaps now it was time to start living a healthier existence and practise what she preached, but Hell, just one last time, she thought, draining the last drop in the bottle. She had worked hard for the last year, weekends too, so maybe she would just party for a few days. Besides, drinking wine in the evening helped her to relax. They turned off the light and sunk into bed after running through some ideas. They made love, until they were exhausted. Graham drained the last drop of wine from the chalice and rolled over. 'What's this?' he asked. 'It feels hot one minute, then it turns cold.'

'Just a chalice I found on a grave,' she whispered, her eyes lighting wickedly, 'for human sacrifice, where blood was drunk.'

He dropped it and gulped.

'Oh come on, Laura, do you have to be so gory?' he asked, lying back as she tickled his stomach.

He placed it on the table, shining like a torch in the moonlight, glowing red, then silver. It was twilight, shadowy dark and the wind blew and the room was cold. Suddenly a white light flashed across the sky, and outside was an eerie scream, as though the darkness had been disturbed. Laura stared into the darkness. Graham slept beside her and was snoring gently, but she felt a strange presence swirl around the room. What was that? She really had to stop drinking so much.

The Goddess stared out across the bleak landscape into the sunset. It blazed orange and red, like blazing flames streaking across the sky. A serpent writhed through the blades of grass over her feet. She turned to face the storm, the wind whipping around her face. She was tired and hungry, her face was battered by the relentless rain. Fighting the elements, she ran through the forest, drawing her withered weeds around her tightly. The storm raged ceaselessly. Her long, raven hair flapped at her waist. She weaved through the trees, her shadow changing into a black cat. Its feline grace ran sleekly through the foliage. Then she found shelter, a small hut where she could settle for the night. Her wild feral eyes gazed out over the mountains, up into the dark sky. She could see little but the twinkling stars, circled by fragments of light. She would follow their path, and they would guide her. She lay down and curled into a ball and let night begin.

✝

Laura picked up the latest copy of *Creative Design* and scanned it quickly for ideas. She found an article on the 'occult' and absorbed everything about it.

'What is shape shifting?' asked Laura.

'Where a life form changes to another form, like an animal changing to a human or when a person changes their spiritual energy,' Graham explained. He had an interest in astrology, and loved to talk about the esoteric.

'I don't believe that happens—do you?' asked Laura, shaking her head.

'Well, in some cultures, I believe it does,' he said. 'Shamanic priests can take on any living energy and change form, existing in a state between the living and the dead—the higher and Earth worlds. They can travel through time. They are able to do this via a trance. They transform into other entities, as a kind of self-protective camouflage.'

'That has given me an idea,' said Laura. 'Like in the change through ectoplasm. I can show a person changing into a panther, et cetera, by morphing. From one human to another, I can change the shape of, say, an office worker, into a maiden. Give the person many dimensions.'

'Good idea.'

'Well I wish I could shape shift,' joked Laura, 'and I would become the head of Zenta television. They've got one hell of a collective brain for ideas.'

Graham laughed. 'Your brain is fine enough for me. Let's do some bi-sociation,' he said, 'get some ideas flowing.'

'Okay, start with the word—goddess.'

Graham furrowed his brow and started thinking of the associative words: 'Okay, power, strength, other worldly vision, connection to the gods.'

'Any more?'

'Wings, long black boots, long hair.'

'Oh, come on,' said Laura, throwing a pen at him. 'Don't just lapse into stereotypes.'

'Superior advances, strength and wisdom, Myths and legends. Particular attributes such as super strength or the goddess of love who holds all the divine secrets of that specific power.'

'What do you think of the goddess theme?'

'It's great, tell me more, it all sounds so fascinating,' he said. 'Especially the dark goddess bit. Is she very sexy?'

Laura pulled a face and threw a cushion at him. 'You are incorrigible.'

'Well, tell me more about it, what's the main thread of the documentary?'

'Natural health, but there's also a section on archetypes that gives added interest. A touch of Jungian analysis with Rogerian psychology and interpretation as well as some mysticism, and I'll include some therapies. I thought we could also include healing and worship of the elements, wicca and spiritual health too, they are all valid, and fairy power.'

'And devil worship too?'

'Don't be stupid.'

'What's an archetype?'

'Archetypes are symbols, subconscious elements of our own soul with their own energy and a life force, like the goddess—she has wisdom, power and strength beyond the everyday reaching into a higher consciousness of the divine and mystical. They are images from the primordial bank of energy, it enthrals and empowers, and lifts the idea the person is trying to express into the realm of the ever-enduring. It becomes an icon of power, representation. It goes from being a singular act, into the destiny of mankind, and evokes in us beneficial forces that have enabled us to be granted the power of superior beings when we need it. A kind of blueprint for a set of characteristics.'

'Like the hero, redeemer, the dark prince.'

'Yes, that kind of thing.'

'Icons of power in mythology?'

'Yes, and in literature, and we can all tap into that universal higher power to enhance ourselves. Women especially can tap into the regenerative power of the goddess. It is the base of all genius, just finding the right frequency as though with a radio wave, to some extent.'

'Come here,' he said, pulling her back onto the sofa. 'I want to hold you again. My goddess.'

'Oh, yes please,' said Laura, her eyes closing in ecstasy.

The next day Laura sketched some basic ideas for the storyboard. She made rough sketches of figures walking over the hill across the summit, down into the valley, changing from 'everyday' people—office secretary and nurse—then exploding with power through their creativity, and becoming goddesses with extra dimensions and gifts. Giving a sense of 'time' to the shot, her mis-en scène showed a misty silhouette of a woman turning to reveal her many sides. And then added the captions: bring out the goddess in you with natural herbal remedies and treatments: how to reach your potential, become more creative, and awaken your goddess.' She started on the voice overlay.

'Herbal remedies, used throughout time, have helped women to develop their many creative and intellectual talents. Women have many sides, and to discover them leads to a more enriched life,' she said. She was going to make a documentary around spiritual healing, empowerment and the goddess, how to help women reach their potential. She would study a different therapy each episode, spiritual healing via chakras, reflexology, Indian Head massage and body massage, culminating with a programme on the goddess, the mystical archetypes of women, and dreams. The pinnacle of potential.

'I think we have enough material,' she said to Graham, flicking through the storyboard, giving out a sigh of satisfaction, 'and a good intro.'

'You can say that again,' said Graham. 'Sounds good to me.'

'The spiritual, the Earth, emotion, intellect, we don't explore nearly enough of ourselves. This way we encourage women to enhance all parts of themselves and each week of the series we can concentrate on a different therapy and approach, like awaken your goddess with meditation, and then give an outline of herbal remedies, then look at cognitive therapy and intellectual enhancement. Like the idea?'

'Love it! Have we finished the schedule yet?'

'Yes, it's all here,' smiled Laura, pulling out reams of paper. 'We start next week.'

'Well, that's a good time,' he said. 'I'll go to the studio and set everything up.'

'It's a good concept,' she stressed, angling the paper for him to see—a tall goddess stood on the peak of the tor, her hair swirling around her in long, snaking tendrils, followed by the siren, the vamp, the enchantress and the maiden all standing on the peak of the hill, in a circle, representing different herbs and their effects such as strength, virility, energy, creative aura and wisdom.

'That should do it,' she said, throwing the storyboard to one side and putting her feet up. 'I feel tired, my creative surge is over for the day.'

'See you next week then,' said Graham, going off to get the crew.

Laura walked back into the kitchen. She looked curiously at the small bottle she had bought in Glastonbury—the remedy with 'potent' written across it, from the Ye Olde Gothic Shop—and drank the foul-tasting powder. She needed a tonic. She swallowed it after mixing it in the chalice, suddenly aware she was performing a kind of ritual. The drink took a few minutes to take effect, then she felt the energy rip through her, light up her soul. She felt elated, powerful, like a goddess. After a few seconds she was filled with bliss, total ecstasy, as she felt as though she was floating in a sun-soaked sea, lined with golden rays. The room was bathed in a bright white light, engulfing her in tranquillity. She hovered on a plane of bliss. She floated downwards in a whirlpool of water, and music flowed around her. She floated to the ceiling then down again, listening to the distant sound of beautiful singing, with a harpsichord. Waterfalls cascaded gently around her, a healing energy filled her with light. A spirit had awakened in her. Then she woke up.

'Wow,' she cried, 'that was amazing.' She sighed; she'd never known anything like it before. It was a white powder, speckled with grey, and very little was written on the label except 'to empower with the energy and vision of the goddess'. She decided she might give some to Graham.

She wondered what the chalice had been used for. A pagan blood-drinking rite? No, a Christian one, she thought wryly. It had obviously been used for a religious ceremony. Such a chalice could only be found by those with strong spiritual powers she mused, recalling the story told to her by the locals. Well, that certainly made her feel good; she smiled. She began to feel spellbound, light-headed, as she drank again slowly from the cup. Immediately she felt as though she was surrounded by a magical presence. She felt light, and was floating. She had evoked a spiritual energy.

She put the bottle back on the shelf, next to her scroll; she would just be natural from now on—after all, a natural high was the best high and any other kind had too much of a payback and ripped apart the body's own natural chemistry. She would just meditate and work. She only chanted occasionally now; meditation had added to her spiritual purpose. Surprised at her lightness, Laura felt happier than she had for a long time. She stared pensively out of the window, the relentless drive and the striving for power mellowed into a quiet contentment. She succumbed to the waves of ecstasy flooding over her, and she was fully awake and aware.

She jumped on a bus and sped out of the town into the tree-lined coppices. She sat alone in the park surrounded by tranquil scenes. She no longer needed an orgasm to send her to sleep. She was happy in essence and in complete harmony with nature and the elements around her. The trees gave her all she wanted. The air and the space filled her with joy. She had lost the craving for consumption and control. She was just experiencing the sheer joy of being and its simplicity. She was liberated, free.

She had a flicker of concern that her angst had gone! Yet her creativity had spurred her on, and she didn't need to be on 'edge' any more! This was a much nicer state of being, derived from whatever she had taken in the chalice. She was becoming a different person.

She started to type up the itinerary for next week's shooting—the scenes, scripts and dialogue were all ready. She felt the surge of energy fill her again and her enthusiasm grow as the new project was underway, and the new film was about to begin.

Adrianna

A Fallen Angel—Liberation

The Goddess knelt at the altar, her cloak blowing around her as she took the chalice and tipped it to her lips. She drank the warm blood of her sacrifice, of the animal lying beside her with its throat cut. She drank slowly, mourning her dead child as she drank the blood. The patriarchal forces had tried to control her and had destroyed it. When the time was right, she would seek her revenge. Once again she was strong; she would soon speak to the spirit world and her spiritual advisor and guide, Norcha. She had hovered between life and death, now the balance had tipped her back into life to live again. In her unconscious world she had seen many strange things—spirits and entities, the world of the dead—now she found herself propelled back to life, free again.

She would use the elements of the earth to regain her power. Her cold, grey eyes glittered dangerously as she sensed the power flowing through her. She ran faster and faster until she took the form of the black lynx and ran through the forest, devouring the miles. The grey static horizon sped past; it burned a glowing red, like the anger that consumed her.

She would fight her way back into life, out of exile. And she would find the person who had done this to her. She rose from the ashes, more powerful than ever, a woman wounded, who lived again and who would fight for her spiritual liberation. She would join the other spirits one day, but now she had a mission to fulfil. All that was decayed and dead came to life. She was lifted by the creative force surging through her. Her life force. She sat by the waterfall, and her maidens appeared, dancing and singing, to give her courage, and lead the way.

The goddess climbed to the peak of the tor. Awoken after a year in exile, hanging on the brink of life and death, the borderline of existence, she found her life force, her creative power return. Her primordial urge. She had empowerment, energy, and life. She looked at her body: it was the same as it always was, a healthy human form. She ran unrestrained, free. She made her way to the city.

She found herself in London, wandering past the cafés in Soho. She walked into a side road. Passive icons of civilisation scurried past her like directionless blind rats. Their pale grey faces reflecting an empty soulless existence—automatons. She caught a tube out of the city. As she stepped out of the station, beautiful ethereal music seemed to lure her away, capture her attention with its enchanting chords. Hypnotised, she followed the gentle strains until she turned into a building full of people dressed all in black, like her. They understood her, her pain and need for silence. Wordlessly they smiled and made her feel welcome. She sensed she belonged there—a spiritual home where she could stay for a while, where she knew she would be safe. Their vibrancy made her feel alive; a tall man with a beautiful face walked over and touched her, and she felt her pain thaw, lessen. It was as though they knew her, and she them: wordlessly they conveyed their welcome.

Then she saw him. He was tall with long, black hair, with eyes light grey like hers, burning into her like coals. His raven hair hung down to his waist. He was beautiful for a man. Who was he? One of her brethren? He stood watching her, smiling, his eyes full of the beauty of the universe; his manner was gentle, and he moved gracefully.

She felt a shiver of desire. He stared at her. She knew instinctively he was hers, she circled him. Her gentle mystical, but at times predatory, gaze entranced him.

His beauty astounded her; he moved gracefully to the bar, to buy a drink. Hypnotically he walked towards her: they knew each other, from before, in the deepest part of their souls. He was her destiny come to shape her, breathe her back to life. She approved of him, he was worthy of her and fired her creativity. He could be her muse. She sipped the liquid he gave to her; she did not need such earthly things—their weak controlling useless compounds. She had access to higher dreams, forms of consciousness than they would ever find—with visions they were afraid of: the Truth.

Endless visions, and nightmares that would drive ordinary mortals insane. She was a weaver of dreams, a fatal enchantress, taking her victims as they rode a wave of pleasure. They would show her the world she craved, the shimmering world of magic and mystery on the silver edge beyond banality and grotesque mediocrity.

'Have some of this instead,' she offered him, handing him the drink filled with the magic powder. He took it from her willingly. He threw his head back as he drank every drop. His long mane of black hair flowed around his shoulders and back like a rippling raven's wing. She was sparked with an instant desire. She watched his eyes open in surprise, his black painted nails curling around the glass, noble and feminine.

'Together we shall travel into the dark realms, to the abyss,' he promised, curling his long black talons around her hand.

She looked up at him drawn by his ethereal beauty, breathless for him, how she loved him! He lit the flame of her love with his gentle gaze. 'So you know about me?' she whispered. He was psychic and could see into her soul.

His eyes narrowed as he drank more, his long hair cascading around him like a beautiful fan, his eyes filled with wisdom, misting over as she burned into him with her dark energy. He was in her power.

'Yes, I will come,' he said softly.

She belonged with these people; she could never go back to the world that had driven her to her demise. She was in the other world, the kind, grey world of the spirits, who flew between the earth and night, who kept her safe and coloured her dreams with happiness.

'Who are you?' he inquired, gazing at her, his eyes lighting with fire, and interest. He kept a pet raven, sitting on his hand.

'The Dark Goddess, of eternal night,' she replied. 'The darker part of my soul needs the air that you breath. I shall illuminate your darkest fantasies of heaven, but there are those that deserve my hell. So I will fill you with ecstasy, then torture their minds until they scream.' Her eyes darkened and she looked around her furtively.

'I know,' he replied. 'I know why you have come here, and I will help you. I accept your terms; I will follow and serve you.'

She stared at him; she had chosen the right one and the time was right. If he could love her, she would be cured. His dark grey eyes spun webs of desire around her as the shadows fell, and she took him into her soul. Together they began to dance the wingless dance of night.

Suddenly, they were transported to a room lined with crystalline caves filled with ravens and crows, where she lay down on the altar, offering him her body. He kissed her breasts. With a grace and swiftness, he lay above her, and delicately entered her, his movements like that of a dove, flying, fluttering above her. She felt the jolt as her power merged with his as they spiralled toward bliss. It seemed like an eternity while they stayed at the height of their pleasure, his beautiful face above hers, filling her with the beauty she craved. They flew from peak to peak. Together they moved, swaying, gyrating faster. Then, in abandon, they floated into the light, merging into the souls of each other.

They danced and sang together in elegant beauty, away from the darkness. She looked up at Kiran, into his gentle eyes and then at the raven, her guide…liberating her from the doomed dark years, to the ecstatic celebration of freedom. Life was soundlessly flowing and ebbing in her, in waves. Their creative dance of power and passion carried on for many days. They stayed in the cave for a time, his face above hers, looking down with love and tenderness. He planted gentle kisses over her face until she was whole again. They rode on two black stallions across the fields. He reminded her of the raven, free, with blue-black hair and dark piercing eyes. Yet, she knew she would have to make a sacrifice for her life force. She hesitated for a moment; she did not want to kill one of such beauty. Instead she would take the raven. Sadly, it would have to die so that she could live. It had been so long. She cut its throat, as it closed its eyes, then killed it. The blood ran over his neck. The ritual was complete, so she drank its blood. She would not return to the dark. She had sacrificed the raven. It was her survival…

Kiran would serve her, watch out for her. She needed someone she could trust, who could look above the soulless city, the dehumanised elements, and guide her. As she walked across the plains, she crept through the acridity of the cities. He watched from the spires of the desolate cathedrals.

As she stroked the beautiful black bird, the dead raven, another flew out of the cave. No one would ever clip his wings, or hers. She lived again—free as a bird, like the ravens. Kiran's love had given her life. Now she would find those who had tried to destroy her, the evil patriarchs who had turned her to the underworld. And destroy them. She would find the right people around her, the mere mortals who would welcome her. Those she could trust. She would bring them to justice, when all creatures would share life in peace.

She had been liberated, and honoured the others in their darkest pledge. For years she had not known life, but now she had the gift. She was trapped by vengeance, but also by love. Now she had the power, she made her way to those who had called her and was once again with them. Later, she would bring them back to join her, for eternity. The dark goddesses sang, their sweet voices raising the most serene notes, and without hesitation transformed themselves into black ravens and flew down to the sun-scorched earth. They flew over the emerald sea, surprised to see their own reflections dancing on the water. The warm light of the golden crow shone over them. They swirled delightfully, then sank into the fresh green grass. Leisurely, they skimmed over the dark mountains and came to rest on the hillside, covered with moss as fine as silk. When the first bird touched the ground, she folded her wings and returned to her goddess form.

Laura sat looking out of the window, watching the grey mist swirl heavily across the sky and over the rooftops. She completed the plans and scripts for the documentary and tucked them into her brown leather briefcase ready to take to the studio. Shooting was starting today. She was unusually calm and in control, professional. Gone were her destructive urges, as though someone had taken all the negativity from her. She felt serene. When Graham phoned offering to take her for a drink, she declined. She offered to cook him a meal instead. The first day went well, organising people to play the characters, auditions, with sound checks, and rehearsals. Things were taking shape and the structure of the documentary was already forming, not just in her mind but taking on a life force of its own. Graham arrived in a white polo neck sweater, having dispensed with the black leather jacket, shades and wrecked look. He looked almost civilised. A different person. She wasn't sure she liked this sanitised look; she loved him rough and ready, not even taking off his leather jacket, sliding down his tattered jeans as he embraced her. This gentlemanly demeanour really threw her and it didn't really turn her on. If there were thoughts of settling down, respectability, forget it! She liked living on the edge, it sparked her creativity. Suburbia was not for her. He took an apple, gently biting into it.

'You know I am so in love with you, Laura,' he admitted, and smiled.

She smiled back affectionately, wondering what he was going to say next. She looked on him more as a friend, and a lover, but as usual the idea of commitment suddenly made her feel afraid, left her cold. He looked crestfallen, then brightened when she said she was pleased, that she was fond of him too. He had part of her, even if he could never have all of her. She admired him; he was immensely clever, studying medicine before moving into the media. And he was a great source of inspiration on all her projects. But why couldn't he just stay her exciting, dark lover? Could she ever settle down?

'Have you ever thought about getting married, settling down?' he asked her, as though reading her thoughts.

Her heart soared; she had guessed this was coming, and didn't quite know how to deal with it.

'I don't know. I live for my work, yet I'd like a baby. We could start one after the film is finished but it all seems such a dream, I haven't finished with my work yet, there still seems to be a burning desire to make a mark on the world. I don't know if I could give it all up now.'

'I want to spend the rest of my life with you,' he said.

'Oh Graham, I love you too, but marriage? Oh please don't spoil it, it sounds like a death sentence, we are a good team, don't let it all fade into mediocrity.'

'But I care for you, Laura, and we've been like this for years, and it's time to move it somewhere else. To make a commitment. You are so addicted to your work, Laura, look at life from another angle for a while.'

She looked at him carefully for a moment, thinking how much she loved his company, and loved him, but she just wanted them to enjoy their freedom for a little while longer, explore life together, have fun. Have another successful project. She wasn't sure she was ready for baby groups and nappies just yet. Her fear of becoming an old maid had vanished along with the new budget and film and she felt the old surge of excitement that suddenly made a family seem quite dreary. It was only when she hadn't any work, and she lost the high that gave life a shiny glow, that she would plunge to the depths of despair and feel she wanted one. She couldn't give up the highs her career gave her but when it all came crashing down, that was another story. Right now she was on a high. Work was her fix.

'And I care for you, but my work is my love, you know that,' she explained. 'It's my passion, my raison d'être. I can't give it up, Graham, while I can still get a budget. I will work night and day. I like it like this. We are free, life's fun, we can do anything we want. Children mean routine, no room for creativity. Here's to the next documentary,' she said, raising her glass.

'We are getting older,' he sighed wearily, 'and that was fun in our twenties, but if we don't move fast we are going to miss the boat. I want us to have children while we are still young, and can enjoy them. Beside our careers will be over soon, it's not so easy when younger more talented people with new ideas will be taking the focus. You know how short the media life is.'

'I'm casting tomorrow,' Laura snapped irritably. 'I'm busy and I want an early night. I will never give up, I shall always be the best. But here's to you. I love you too and you are invaluable to me. I couldn't do this without you, but can we delay suburban bliss for a little while longer?'

'Anything you say,' he said, emptying his glass.

'And Graham, please wear your black leather when you come to see me! Please don't come dressed as though we are going to a cricket match.'

'Don't you think your desire for juvenile sex is a little immature, Laura? Don't you want tenderness and love any more?'

'Yes, but I depend on you to fuel my creative fire. You are my muse,' she admitted playfully.

He was a producer too, and she liked him to look exciting, dangerous, as though she had just met him in a dark, seedy bar. With slicked-back hair, and an edgy dark expression. His power turned her own and fuelled her ideas; if he became too conformist and tame, the spark would die, and she couldn't bear the thought of losing it all now. She was a Scorpio, and loved the savage, untamed side of life. She felt drawn to his loyalty. Besides she wanted him. She changed into white suspenders and danced around him. He loved her white lingerie. Then she spread her legs either side of him and pretended to ride him. She kissed him on the neck.

'Okay have it your way! Oh Laura,' he said with relief, 'I really want you,' realising how she held his existence in her hand. What power, she had over him, knowing she could crush him with one blow if she wished. She devoured him sexually, but did she love him? How free were those who did not love? How free were those who did not need love? To be free from love was to be free indeed.

She rocked over him, teasing him, fondling him; she loved sex with him, he made her feel like a woman. She liked it when he dominated her, and called her a naughty girl, and smacked her playfully. She enjoyed having him under her, in every way—he made her feel more than a woman, a goddess. She entwined her legs around his back. She unzipped him. He was so hard. She climbed on top of him, gyrating as he gasped, completely in her power, she observed, as she rode him, feeling her dark sensuality unfold. She rocked gently on top, feeling him rub her to bliss, filling her completely. They moved in a crescendo, climaxing a few seconds apart. She jumped off him, sleepy from the endorphins flooding through her, lying in his arms. Satisfied, she fell asleep.

The following day, she woke up as the sun poured in. She was late. She jumped up and quickly made her way to the studio.

Laura shuffled the papers behind her desk, pleased that everything was going to plan and they could begin shooting. She hoped to carry on filming over the next few weeks. She thought about Graham's proposal, perhaps settling down with him would not be so bad after all. They shared a lot in common, and anyone who she got serious about would have to share her interest in the media. Perhaps the answer was right there under her nose after all. Yes, they would get married and have a child, in a year's time when the documentary was finished.

Everyone stopped working and there was a hush as a beautiful wild-looking woman suddenly walked onto the set. She tossed her raven black hair back and stepped onto the stage.

Carefully, her eyes glowing with a strange power, she looked around at everyone.

'I want a job,' she said, simply. 'I need a job. I wondered if you have anything here?'

'Okay, we'll see what we can find; come to the casting session at ten and we'll find you a part,' said Laura, thinking she looked just perfect to play any role.

'Do you have an agent?' asked Laura.

'No, I just found my way here. I read one of the free magazines, it said you were holding auditions. I need a job,' she said in dark, sultry tones, undoing her long cloak.

Laura smiled at her, noticing her long, gothic, lacy clothes, with a tight black velvet basque underneath. She looked perfect for the role of a sylph night siren.

'Well, I think I might have the ideal part for you,' Laura said, flicking through her notes. 'Come and fill in these forms. Would you like to be a vamp or a goddess?' asked Laura assessing her, pulling an antique black lace dress out of the props box. 'I think you're ideal for the documentary we have planned, we need lots of extras, and I think you'll fit in well somewhere.'

'Maybe I could be one of the women in the background,' she said, reading the storyboard, 'one of the nymphs.'

'You look more like a goddess,' Laura said, thinking her air of purity and elegance would suit the role well. She oozed sheer elegance and had the face of an angel. A slightly dark angel or dark goddess. Perhaps a night or moon Goddess?

'Yes, all right,' Adrianna said softly, her soft raven curls tumbling over her cheeks and shoulders.

'Great, that's it, your hired. Rehearsals start today, you can have the part,' said Laura. 'You look fine, I could not have made a better choice myself. I'd like to capture you on film first,' she requested. 'Please step up onto the stage.'

Adrianna stepped up gracefully, easing herself onto the stage, lifting her long skirt to reveal a silk petticoat, and short, pointed, pixie boots. She threw back her hair, revealing a beautifully sculpted face, small rosebud lips and almond-shaped blue-grey eyes that turned grey in the light. Her hair was the longest Laura had ever seen, cascading down her back in soft raven black curls. Laura grabbed the camera.

'I must take a few shots,' she said speedily. 'You look absolutely amazing like that, like a maiden rising from the river.' She angled the camera, trying to capture the elegant pose. She handed Adrianna a few lines to recite, listening closely. The woman had a soft but assertive voice, and excellent pronunciation. She really turned the script into her own, and added a spark to it. She stood at the top of the stage and focused her eyes in that wonderful panther-like stare she had. Adrianna removed her shawl, which had been covering the lacy dress, leaving a black velvet and lace basque, intertwined with silver thread. She took a deep breath, and recited the words in a sing-song voice, reminding Laura of a princess: she had an air of mystery, mixed with a feral wildness and a pout that gave her an air of petulance, as though she had just come out of a fairy tale. She had a compelling gaze, large hypnotic eyes, Laura noticed, staring at her, fascinated. She strode forward elegantly; her hands outstretched as she recited a few lines for the audition.

'She watched, squinting her eyes in the darkness and the swirling of smoke flooded over the stage, it took her breath away to see such glimpses of the darkness.'

'Excellent,' said Laura. 'Okay, I'll give you a try, you know how to capture the mood, and everyone's attention.'

Her dark blue-grey eyes stared vibrantly at Laura. Laura was totally captivated, she was so beautiful, never had she seen such amazing eyes. One minute they were dangerously wicked and alive, holding her in her hypnotic power, then, as she mellowed, innocent and childlike with a soft misty gaze. Her glacial, ethereal poise melted as she spoke. She smiled at Laura impishly.

Laura could not resist her and turned the camera straight on her.

At the sight of the television camera, Adrianna's expression turned to granite, then softened again. Her eyes changed from dark blue to grey. A mystical aura flowed around her. She spoke softly as she lay back on the chaise-longue, her raven blue-black hair cascading in soft curls to one side, sweeping onto the floor. She lifted her skirt, revealing lace stockings. Laura had never seen such a picture of feminine beauty. A spiritual, mystical goddess of the highest order, observed Laura in reverence, the peak of woman power. She combined elements of innocence and purity with immense personal power, gently controlling it like the tides of the sea—power capable of turning moods and the rhythm of gentle tides or tempestuous unbridled cruelty. Her long thin pale hands pushed her velvet skirt up over stockings, her nails ran quickly over her thighs. She wore a small g-string underneath. Even Laura had to admit she was ravishing, and put a wreath of purple flowers in her hair.

Laura watched as Adrianna posed perfectly for the shots. She knew how to act in front of a camera. She was almost professional. She flirted coquettishly, her eyes wide, sexy, playful, then enchanting. A chameleon type nature, she easily became anything Laura ordered her to be. Laura felt totally drawn to her and wondered if she was perhaps too sensible to have a crush on another woman, but she was so intrigued. The woman, seeming to sense this, turned her wicked eyes on Laura, glowing with an energy that could not quite be defined.

Yes, thought Laura, still filming. She had the right image and spiritual energy, so versatile and would represent the 'Goddess of nature and life', of beauty and serenity, in the film. She shot a few stills of her naked, but with her hair flowing around her; then wearing a small black body suit, representing the delicacy of the wild herbs that cured and abated ailments of the nervous system. The central body, the spiritual centre. The soul. Perhaps she could film her chakra, which glowed an unusually bright white. Her breasts were pert, her body lithe like a cat. Graham watched moodily from the shadows. That night she told him all about Adrianna, how much of a find she was, how the ideal woman for the star role of the whole documentary had just walked into the studio off the street.

'What about us?' asked Graham. 'So you don't want me to make a decent woman of you?'

'No, I think I prefer to keep it indecent,' she joked.

He looked crestfallen. 'Well, I want children,' he said.

'Time's getting on. I am not getting any younger. So the answer is yes!'

'Oh I shall make you happy.' His face lit with happiness.

'Let's just concentrate on our work and talk about it after the project.'

'Yes,' whooped Graham, and picked up Laura and swirled her around the room.

The next day she went over her lines with Adrianna. Adrianna watched Laura closely. Yes, the eyes were the same; she felt a flicker of recognition.

'Are you ready for the shoot tomorrow?' asked Laura. 'I would like you to play the goddess.'

'Yes,' she replied, slightly dazed, the eyes brought back the fear…

Over the next few months, filming went on at full speed, some extras joined the team and there were no major dramas to hold things up. A few, though, mysteriously disappeared into thin air. Laura, furious, decided extras could not be relied on these days. Adrianna proved invaluable and hardworking as an actress, working both day and night. She spoke little to anyone, except to a few of the cameramen. It matched her own behaviour. Laura felt a slither of unease but dismissed it, she had too much work to do. Adrianna sat watching Graham. Yes, he could be like a big teddy bear, and protective of all the women on the set. He had reverted back to the dark brooding mafia look. He walked about restlessly, he had been offered a post to work abroad for a while. He would do it and come back and marry Laura. Laura was really confusing him, but he'd wait until she was ready, until she had burned out all her ideas and perhaps was ready to start a family and the normal things in life.

Adrianna watched Graham from the shadows. She seemed particularly drawn to him and liked his darkness, his wildness. Perhaps they could be more than friends, it would suit the first part of her plan well, Adrianna considered, needing occasionally to turn the problems of another dark, tortured soul to her advantage. His masculinity attracted her, and besides she had a score to settle. Wasn't Laura the sister of David Garton? Well, then that made her an instant enemy she thought, her eyes blazing with anger. One day, after a particularly arduous session, when Laura had been extra demanding, shouting and getting flustered, she went off early to have a few days in a health clinic, leaving Adrianna alone with Graham at the studio. Adrianna saw this as being her chance; she wanted him, she needed some comfort from another human being and sensed his loneliness—and any sister of David Garton should pay for that man's betrayal. She took him into the back of the studio, and used her energy to hypnotise him, her fingers undoing his clothing, then she kissed him, wanting him. She needed his power. In one swift gentle movement, she stepped over him, raised her dress and felt his power surge into her, and his seed spill into her. She soared into bliss, her soul renewed. She felt his power pulse through her body, stimulating her spiritual power.

Laura chose that moment to walk in. Adrianna rose at once.

'It's is not what you think,' Adrianna said.

Laura stared at them in total disbelief.

'Then what the hell is it?' She was completely livid, murderous anger surged through her, then pain, she threw a hot kettle at them, scalding them both.

'I am sorry, Laura,' she cried. 'I wasn't aware that you were serious.'

'You disgusting bitch. I will not fire you,' she spat at Adrianna venomously. 'I need you for the part and I've written you into all the scenes. To get rid of you would cost me too much, but understand this, after this documentary, you will never work again. You have done a good job and I am making money from you, but once the set is finished you're out, and don't expect any more help from me, ever,' she swore, her eyes blazing with anger.

'And as for you—' she turned to Graham. 'You really are sick. All this talk of marriage and children and five minutes later you are seducing someone else.'

'But I don't know what happened,' he stuttered, 'what came over me.'

She turned to Adrianna: 'You came to me without an equity card, and I helped you, and this is how you repay me. As far as I am concerned after this you are dead, you stinking bitch. You are finished in this business!' she cried.

'I'm sorry,' said Adrianna, putting on her dress. 'I really didn't know. I though you just worked together. I never saw you together as a couple.'

'What about me?' said Graham. 'Laura, you have strung me along for years, I'm just here to keep you warm. You have never cared about how I felt. You just used me for your own amusement and as a prop. Good old Graham. But you would just forget me and see someone else when it suited you. Then you would come back to me if that didn't work out! You are not entirely innocent.'

'You never seemed to mind. Go to hell! Judas!' Laura screeched.

'You are making a mistake,' said Adrianna, piping up mysteriously. 'We have a lesson to learn from this. I am sorry I was angry with you, but it is not your fault. I broke up with your brother, three years ago. I was angry and upset. I am sorry. You can have my powers too, Laura, you deserve them, but first you must make a journey into your soul, to find your dark goddess before you are deemed worthy to find your true creative power,' she said. 'You will gain creative energy and rise from the darkness, as I have done and through the pain, then you will reign in triumph.'

Laura stared incredulously at them. 'What are you talking about, and who wants your feminine new age so-called powers? Go get fucked, you stupid bitch, alley cat, whore. You are full of bullshit,' she spat. 'What my brother does is nothing to do with me. I had thought better of you!' She slammed the door behind her. She had seen and heard enough. Nothing made any sense any more.

Laura stopped shooting for the day, told Graham to leave and phoned the agency and asked them to send another cameraman, then instantly regretted it as Graham was one of the best and knew what she liked. And she spent hours wasting time trying to get the replacement, she felt it had all fallen apart and she couldn't do anything right.

She phoned Graham and caught him just as was he leaving for America.

'Look, please come back, I need you for the shoot,' begged Laura, 'but you can forget the marriage.'

'I'm leaving the country to work abroad. It's the way I want it,' he insisted. 'I'm fed up with everything here, time to move on.'

'But you are my best cameraman and producer,' cried Laura, starting to panic. 'What shall I do without you?'

'Find someone else to mess around then,' he said angrily.

'Go to hell!' spat Laura, still furious, slamming down the phone.

Pacing the flat, she felt a sudden panic at the thought of him not being around. Who else did she have to turn to? Now she was really on her own. Oh, why had it turned out like this? She had depended on him for so many things, her work, her projects; he had been the thread that held everything together, and she had just taken him for granted. She raced around to his flat, ready to ask him to come back. She didn't have many friends, she had neglected almost everyone for her career. He had stood by her through thick and thin, but she had just laughed at his marriage proposal. He answered the door, and stood looking down at her, his face etched with anxiety.

'Can I come in?' she almost whispered.

'I'm catching the ten o clock plane, make it quick.' His eyes no longer held love, just a cold indifference. She had already lost him.

'Don't go,' she pleaded. 'Not yet—please at least wait until the film is over.'

'But it's over between us, isn't it? You can never forgive me?' he asked.

'No, I can never forgive you,' she said, her eyes filling with tears, 'but you can't walk out on the film.'

'Is that all you want me for, the film? I can't stay any more, I've tried and tried, it's over, after all these years, we are not going anywhere,' he confessed, raising his hands. 'I wait and you promise, then the next job comes along and you push me to the background. You never really did want to get married. You have been stringing me along for years.'

'You had talked me round,' she admitted, 'but now can't we just be business partners?'

'No, it's all turned out to be a disaster, there's no going back. It's all destroyed.'

'Okay then, if that's it. What if the film fails?'

'It won't. There is nowhere to go. I want to move on. Now if you don't mind, I have a plane to catch.' He went back inside, grabbed his suitcase, then walked past her to the waiting limousine outside and she watched it speed off. As it turned the corner, she sobbed uncontrollably, falling onto the ground, her nails digging into the dirt.

The Goddess laughed. How wonderful it was to see others suffer as she once had. She had won the first round. Laura was the sister of the one who had betrayed her. One by one she would take them all down and destroy them as they had destroyed her—her career, her life, her baby—and give back the pain they had given her; she had been left for dead, hovering in the dark world between life and death by the ones she had foolishly loved, and who had betrayed her. The ones who had helped destroy her.

Now the first part of her plan was complete. Nothing could stop her from finishing the rest of it. The ones who had left her for dead, empty and alone, on that terrible night at the party. Laura had been there on that fatal night. She had been working on a project with David. But she had also given her, Adrianna, her freedom.

Laura sat crying hysterically. How could Graham do this to her? Sleep with someone else? She had done it in the past and he had forgiven her, but now this time he had gone too far and it was all over. How could she have fallen for someone so hard despite the precautions she had taken not to get too involved? She couldn't work, sleep or eat. The pain ripped through her like a knife. She had tried hard to avoid this. The documentary was almost finished, but she didn't really care about it any more. She looked at some stills of Adrianna, noticing the strange aura around her, threw them across the floor. She emptied another bottle of wine and sat staring into space, stunned.

A shadow moved in the corner. It must be her imagination, she thought sadly. Then it moved again. It looked like a 'Goddess', with long flowing hair. She looked away dreamily as she felt the fleeting touch of a gentle woman and fell into a dreamless sleep.

Laura worked all day and night, trying to forget Graham. Every little thing seemed to stir up a memory and just as she thought she was over him, something would remind her of him and renew her pain. Work focused her mind and took her thoughts away from the torture of thinking of him with Adrianna. Torturing her mind. She could not eat or sleep. She did not want to see either of them again. Somehow she dragged herself back to the studio to finish the film, some sad, pathetic glory that was.

Who did she have to help her now? After all, the only person she could ever trust had let her down. Now she felt betrayed by the person she had most trusted. She was in Hell. Then she remembered she still had some empowering powder wrapped in the plastic bag in the chalice. She took it. Its warm tranquillising effect spread through her, and she lay back, basking in its numbing euphoria. She no longer cared about anything. Nothing could touch her. The darkness in her soul had taken over. A dark energy began to seep into her soul.

Adrianna sat outside a noisy bar in Soho. She smiled to herself, then was flooded with remorse. How could she have done that to the poor woman who had only tried to help her? She realised she had gone too far this time, stepped over the line. She had to refocus, be reminded of her real mission, and just seek revenge for those who had actually harmed her. She knew where to find him: she had made many useful contacts and now knew where she would find the one who had tried to kill her, and who had killed her unborn child. The night still burned in her brain, now that she remembered what had happened to her. She had gone to her fiancé's party, and told him about the baby. His expression had turned black and he'd told her their engagement was off, he had met someone else, a woman whose father was head of the corporation. She threatened to tell her about the baby, and he had turned and pushed her over the balcony, then left her for dead; she hovered in a coma for nearly a year and lost the baby.

She would now destroy his dreams as he had destroyed hers. The raven settled beside her. It reminded her of Kiran. Following her plan, she would find him, she would complete her mission. Calculatingly, she began to make plans. She was an expert in mind manipulation, and had the power to control, hypnotise or disarm the strongest minds. That's what she had learned as she lay hovering between the worlds in the spirit world: it had given her another vision. She walked into the dark church, where tall gothic windows towered high into the sky. A raven flew past, obscuring her view of the moon, telling her the time was near. They had found him, the evil one.

She began the pagan ritual of a blood sacrifice, as she needed more power.

She pulled out the address of her enemy, glad he still lived near by. She laughed as she watched his photograph burn. She did not fear him or his evil henchmen. She would bring her soldiers of freedom and kill his pervasive forces. The time of conflict was near. The wilderness, the blackness in her soul, beckoned her. Laura would know where to find him.

Laura sat back waiting for the warmth of the powder to take effect, when unexpectedly it had the opposite effect. She felt something strange, dark and bizarre burn in her. She felt the lust for Graham surge through her, tormenting her, a million times its intensity. She had to get some air. She was choking. She walked slowly, like the dead, but she needed a drink. A man dressed in black leather jeans stood drinking at the bar she went to. They walked into an alley, she lifted her dress and they had sex, then she walked away. She was embracing her dark side. The dark goddess of her own soul was taking over. She was hurt, angry, yet her creative surge had returned. She felt empowered with a force she could use for both destruction and creation. She wanted to destroy all around her. She worked like a demon day and night, the relentless energy, never fading, to purge her soul of the pain.

One night, Adrianna came and spoke to her, to try and quell the hatred between them and she tried to comfort Laura. Despite what she had done, she had grown to care for Laura. But Laura resisted and only spoke to her, when necessary, on a professional level. Yet she had managed to find out where David Garton, who was now head of regional TV was. 'My brother was wrong,' she admitted, 'but it is not my business. We hardly ever see each other.'

'Laura, I will bring Graham back to you if you want,' offered Adrianna. 'I'm so sorry.'

'No, it's over,' admitted Laura sadly. 'It was heading that way anyway.'

Adrianna looked down at her guiltily then gratefully. She couldn't confide in her; she had to go ahead with her plan. Torn with guilt and regret, she wondered how she could actually help her. How she could repay her for the terrible betrayal of her she had carried out.

The first part of her plan was complete. Nothing could stop her now.

Slowly, Adrianna made her way to the remains of the church to begin her ritual in preparation for her attack. Her powers were at their peak, now was the time to act—to destroy the repressive powers of those who had taken her freedom and destroyed her. She chanted: her energy was so strong now, not like it had been then. Her mind drifted back to the time when she first knew him. She was an actress, with a promising career ahead of her. Then she met him at a party while he was with his group. They had promised her a great deal in return for her allegiance. She had joined him willingly, a ruthlessly ambitious man in a quest for power, a man who had once been an arms dealer.

One day, she was dancing with her lover, on the balcony. The sun went down as the party had ended. Many people, some famous, were leaving. It was the twilight hours when she told him that she was pregnant, that she loved him and was delighted to be having his child. His expression had grown dark and menacing as he had walked toward her and pushed her over the balcony. She could still see the evil in his eyes as he had tried to remove her very existence and leave her for dead. She had died for a while, physically and spiritually. But it had not been her time. Somehow her spirit had survived and pulled her through, but she had existed in the half world, not dead, nor alive.

She had been rescued by the spirit world, not dead, in limbo between death and life, and was given another chance by someone whose elemental energy was strong, and now she lived again. Then someone had taken the chalice, left alone above the magical grave and evoked her life force, forced her spiritual energy back into the real world so that she lived again. Her mind flashed quickly forward to the present. Could she stop the evil of the man who had tried to destroy her, left her for dead after pushing her over the balcony to kill their unborn child? She opened her briefcase and pulled out all the details she'd managed to find about him. She had carried out her research to the last detail, finding out where he now lived and everything about him she needed to know. With help from her psychic friends, she discovered his whereabouts and looked him up on the internet. There he was, smiling, engaged in all manner of political activities, and still the head of television. She had discovered his plan to kill his rival. He had been driven by corruption, laundered money, blackmail, and gained his information from the high circles he moved in. He had reached a position of considerable power. And was moving in high circles, in government. He was about to make a move to a very influential position. She had appeared at the right time: in time to bring down his empire, and everyone in it. Now she would find and destroy him, as he had their child.

She would destroy the patriarchs that manipulated a society that controlled women, those who had taught her to become one of the dispossessed. A lost soul with the wild, untamed energy that threatened their male-dominated order even more…that intimidated their leaders. With a power they could not fight. She was ostracised. But she could never be controlled. She was a free spirit who no one could capture and chain or destroy, she would stay as free as a bird, her power was too great. She knew how to channel her energy, direct it at her opponents.

She walked up the drive of the manor house where David Garton, head of regional television, lived. Politician, criminal, murderer and millionaire. Corrupt, decadent and beyond redemption and regrettably, Laura's brother. Slowly she changed into a long cloak, to throw off any security. Her raven led her, then as she approached the porch, she put on a red wig so that no one would recognise her. She knocked at the door of the dark mansion. She saw his slick, gaunt face framed by expensive sunglasses, shimmering behind the door. Luckily he did not recognise her. She was invited in. Delighted, she smiled a wicked smile to herself, glad her plan was working. Her eyes danced with impious delight. Her first impulse was to kill him, as he had left her for dead. But she decided to play games with him first, expose his plots that used the internet for contacts throughout the world. Expose him first, then torture him. She walked determinedly towards him.

'Can I help you?' he asked her.

'Yes, I am wondering if you can take these scripts, I was going to call a courier, but there was a wait. I thought it might be quicker to deliver them myself.'

'Thanks, come in, I'm so grateful. Saves me having to go out again.'

He showed her around; she took in every details of the building, plotting her attack, her bitter-sweet revenge. She would take it slowly, she did not want to arouse his suspicions too quickly. The bitter memories came flooding back, as she used all her strength trying to stay focused on the moment. She bit back the tears welling up in her eyes. She grimaced and quelled the pain that threatened to engulf her, then smiled sweetly.

'Don't I know you from somewhere?' He turned to her, smiling.

'Maybe,' she said mysteriously; the sky was turning black.

'Perhaps you would like to come into my studio. You do really remind me of someone I once knew,' he said. 'It's quite uncanny.' Her coma had been mentioned in the papers, and that she would never recover; everyone thought she was dead. 'It's suddenly turned quite cold,' he said, looking puzzled, as though something he could not quite fathom was going on.

'Inexplicably so,' she agreed, turning to give him a seductive gaze. He gave her a similar gaze back. This is going to be easy, she thought, a tingle of fear shooting up her spine, disguising her hatred. 'Not yet,' something inside her whispered, 'not yet. Wait until the time is right.'

She recoiled from him as he took the tapes from her, the thought of touching him filling her with nausea. She choked back the desire to vomit, to claw his face to shreds. Fighting her darkest wish, she struggled to keep the anger out of her voice, as he asked if she would like a drink.

'I had hoped you would ask,' she replied.

Once inside, he poured her some wine. She looked deep into his eyes and saw a flicker of recognition, though he could not be sure.

'What a beautiful girl,' he said. 'Come and sit next to me. You are quite gorgeous for a television researcher, if you don't mind my saying so. Remind me of a beautiful woman I once knew. I hope you don't mind my saying that.'

'I don't mind at all,' she said, digging her nails into her leg.

She wandered over to him, her face dark. She pulled open the slit of her dress revealing her thigh. His reaction was as predicted: his eyes widened with lust. She wanted to make him uncertain of everything, doubtful of who he was. She lifted her dress higher, to reveal her panties. As he looked up, her laser eyes burned deep into his soul, and were hypnotising him, making his mind scream with the tortures and torments of deepest Hell. He tried to cover his eyes, to protect himself, but she was too strong, everything was swimming all around him. He felt pain like white-hot knives tear through his head. She stood over him, pretending to kiss him, the kiss of death, and shone her dark power on him. He lay on the floor, covering his eyes, for they burned as though they were on fire. She clasped some handcuffs on him so that he could not move. 'Well I have got you at last,' she said, triumph reverberating in her voice.

He winced and tried to move.

'But I thought you loved playing games. You always used to,' she whispered, malice creeping into her voice. 'Now where's your sporting spirit? You used to be such a risk taker.'

'Who the hell are you? A ghost? Why are you doing this to me? Please stop. Who the hell are you?' he screamed helplessly.

She told him who she was.

'I thought it could be you, but I thought you were dead?'

'Not quite, although that had been your intention, wasn't it?' she said, kicking him in the neck and in the face with her heel. 'But you did try, when I told you I was having your baby, you became terrified your rich and well connected friends who had invested millions in your company might find out, and you pushed me over the balcony to get rid of me. Then when I was in a coma you hoped I'd die. You thought I had vanished from this earth forever,' she added bitterly. 'Until Laura came along and dislodged the chalice that was pledged to me by a powerful goddess from the past. Who saw my plight, the injustice, and took me out of purgatory back into life.' She made him crawl along the floor. He begged her for forgiveness, for her mercy. She kicked him across the floor, leaving him to crawl after her.

'Now for my finale. Crawl, you evil bastard,' she spat at him, 'that's all you deserve. See how you like it!'

She dragged him to the dark room, chained him to the cellar wall, leaving him that way for days, barely sane, haunted by a million tortures as she fed him a poison that sent him insane. She stayed in the luxury mansion above, watching his soul and spirit fade away, as hers once had. Mental and physical torture, how long could he endure it? Every time he winced, she bloated with pleasure and vengeful satisfaction. She left him locked in the basement, torturing his starving, emaciated frame until he was so weak, he could barely move. He sat shivering with fear. His sanity was hanging on by a thread. She ran upstairs and anonymously sent details of his crimes to everyone on the internet, friends over the whole world. They would think one of his political group had dealt with him, no one would associate him with her.

Growing tired of torturing him, she stopped the images of Hell, and began playing 'seductress' one last time, as her finale to him. She filled him with images of burning lust. She opened her dress, writhing in front of him, softly touching her breasts.

'Go on, baby, don't you want to feel them? Didn't you like kissing them so much? If I remember correctly, you could not stop touching them,' she taunted. He reached up to her, his fingers lightly brushing her breasts, his haunted face sad, lightening at the thought of her change in mood, looking up at her in hope, sad and pathetic, his lust fading. It was the last time he would see her fatal beauty. Who was the victim now? He reached up to touch her nipples, then she slapped him and cut his face. He fell back, then lunged toward her. She wrapped her legs around him, then used a knife to make a slight wound in his chest. She watched his blood run over the white marble floor—what a pretty pattern it made. Rivulets of blood running in small, forked streams over the expensive Italian designer tiles. He was left a twittering wreck.

Suddenly she was covered in a bright light that flashed, engulfing her in complete ecstasy. She was free. She sat chanting the words, 'The vibrancy of your soul sends me to the depths of despair as I watch you destroy the remains of your love. The bleakness of my existence takes on life as I gradually drain your body of its last drop of blood, and watch you quivering heart destroyed as you once destroyed mine.'

She ran without stopping, barefoot to the shelter of the countryside, to a small empty cottage by the edge of the forest. She washed her hands, washing off the scent of him in the calm flow of the river…

Adrianna thought of Laura; she weaved a spell and brought back Graham for one night to her as an incubus, in her dream the seed was planted. Laura would have her child by Graham and she would be redeemed.

David emerged a few weeks later, a changed and compassionate man.

Months later…

'Don't be afraid of your dark side,' Adrianna wrote to Laura later in her letter.

The documentary was finished, and it was received well by the public and critics alike.

'Thank you for helping me; I gained several new contracts as a result of the documentary, it taught me a lot. You sometimes have to destroy to re-new. In your last letter you said you experienced darkness, this will pass. Out of your shadow comes creativity and energy for new life and creative freedom. You have to kill the past to begin the future anew. You will find the light again. Even in your darkest moments, the light soothes and heals the soul. Don't imprison your beauty, strength and wisdom behind a wrathful mask. Every crisis is a challenge and catalyst for change, for renewal. We must keep the wheel of life constantly turning. Do not tie yourself down with the bonds of anger. It will weaken and diminish your soul. Empower yourself with wisdom and knowledge. We take strength from the universe, our dark domain, to empower us. You want to change the world, you are a goddess and your creative energy helps you create films for those whose who are hurt in some way, to help them find their way back. The Dark Goddess always destroys in order to renew.

'I am sad,' she added, crying softly.

'Passionate love relentlessly twists a chord in my heart, and spreads deep mist in my eyes. I found the one I love, but lost him, through my own carelessness and my overriding desire for revenge. When we met there was no place for love in my heart, just destruction and revenge. Now, I know I want peace for eternity if you will forgive me for my betrayal. Until we meet again.

'My best wishes, Adrianna.

'PS. I am so sorry to hear about Graham, and I am deeply ashamed of what I did to you both, but my heart was full of darkness, and destiny sometimes sends us the strangest of challenges. I did not mean to hurt you. I wanted him to hurt as they had hurt me. But I am so sorry, the anger has gone from me now.'

She did not tell Laura the whole truth; no one could ever know the truth—about the loss of her child. It was her dark secret she would carry to her final days. She was grateful and loved Laura for setting her free; she could never see her again, but would always help her, she would always be her spirit guiding her to the light.

Laura pushed the letter to one side and wondered why she had written; Graham had gone, and there was nothing left but his memory. She screwed up the letter and placed it in the chalice. She had hated Adrianna for so long, too long, despising nothing more than a woman who betrayed another woman. She felt herself writing back to her, although she felt sick and giddy, her and Graham's baby was due next month; it was strange the way things often turned out. She wondered about her, deciding Adrianna was quite mad.

She whispered to herself, 'Yes, I am happy now, my life has changed dramatically, but it is now as it should be. I live now in a reality, not a dream, and have taken up spiritual healing, and to forgive is essential for my life experience. The spirit world says all things happen for a reason. One set of events is often sparked off by one simple action, and we set in motion a whole different path and destiny. You were a catalyst for me, to change things for the better. We have both suffered betrayal, but we grow stronger when we survive such a challenge.'

She couldn't go back, Laura thought wistfully, throwing the letter away. Men, it was understood, were often weak, and couldn't help but fall for the pleasures of the flesh, but women should know better than to betray each other, and should stick together. They had been such a successful team, so it hadn't been all bad. Adrianna had proved one of the best actresses she had ever worked with, their finding each other had resulted in a strange and mystifying union. And, Laura thought ruefully, a lot of souls reaching a point of no return. Their lives had run in parallel for a time, then faded into the distance, but for that one special moment when their destinies met, a spark was created that led to a change in both their lives. There were just shadowy memories fading into the past. The documentary had been a resounding success, the reviews gave it a good write-up and a new series had run from it. Everyone had benefited. Laura had enrolled at the local college and was studying holistic therapies, motivated not by the desire for self-acclaim, but an appreciation of her work and its benefits for others. She had found strength through adversity. They had been two women united on a journey, a period of self-discovery, where they had lessons to learn, to find purpose in their lives. After Graham had left, and Adrianna had betrayed her, she spent her time picking up the fragmented pieces and putting it all together again—creating a reality this time, not just another escape route. They had parallel lives, that touched at one crucial point, and found a common aim, to find happiness and fulfilment. Laura strove to find her peace, realising how precarious our lives were and that everything could be changed by a millisecond of chance.

Eventually, after moving to the green fields of Somerset, having given birth to a beautiful baby girl, she smiled happily; they were Graham's eyes, she was sure. She had found what she was looking for, and it had all been so simple and fulfilling when it came. How much pleasure the simple things in life had brought her, for now she could realise her dream.

Laura bought a small house in a village, a cottage facing open fields with gothic arched windows and a sloping lawn and she found a nice man—a local chemist who played golf and tennis in the afternoons. Together they went to smart dinner parties and even to church occasionally. One way of life was as good as another, thought

Laura philosophically, and they had a young son. Graham had been killed in a war zone while filming. She had cried for him. But now she had found true contentment and happiness as she watched as her small son and daughter played together in the garden. A kind of hazy peace drifted over her. How simple it all seemed now, as everything seemed to fall into place and the memories of the past faded into oblivion. She began to see just how important just living in the present was. At last, she felt she was where she belonged. She had no more mountains to climb, no more palaces to build, no more conquests to make. She had reached her summit and was happy with the view, with the simple things in life. Calm and tranquil, she could enjoy the beauty of the fields, the lakes and the miles of open space needing little else to stir her thoughts. She had found her nirvana. She worked on a few children's programmes; she had found the serenity she had sought and the chill had left her soul.

Her imagination, still fertile, planned many projects, but this time they were children's projects. How dark her life had once been, she reflected, but that darkness had driven her creative hunger for acceptance and recognition, had saved her and resulted in good work.

She wandered out to the garden where her son was playing with his friends; he threw a bucket of water all over her, and she started to laugh.

Night was darkly drifting through.

Adrianna stood in the archway of the church, at last at peace. She had purged her soul of its demons, of the darkness that had followed her so long; she had killed her dark shadow and had smashed his evil empire to pieces. Now she was back where she belonged. Destroyed the one who had destroyed her. Laura had written back to her, and they'd arranged to meet up for the sake of the film, then go their separate ways. Adrianna was now an actress; Laura had propelled her to fame. She'd thrown herself at Laura's feet sobbing, 'Forgive me.' Laura had pushed her away and fled.

A white light flashed through the chapel and lit up the pews, in the dark gothic windows was a shimmering shape; it moved slowly toward her and touched her gently. She was filled with a white, tingling light that lifted the heaviness from her soul; she felt an incredible lightness wash over her and her heart was light and like a child's again. Innocence, laughter and happiness filled her dark and empty soul. She was re-born, and would start life again, but before she left there were some things she had to finish. Her demons were gone. She walked back into the gothic church, Kiran by her side, and the Raven perched on her hand. He stood before her and smiled, and gave her a look that told her he had forgiven her. She looked back at him lovingly. All the bitterness had left her, the dark goddess side of her had slipped away, her creativity surged and pushed her towards the light. Kiran kissed her passionately, he was her dark knight, her redemption.

'I can tell you this…' Adrianna wrote to herself, thinking of what she would write to Laura, but would never send. 'I used the darkness to destroy and the light powers to liberate my soul, but now I am at peace, no one shall ever control my spirit. I am free again, I have fought through the darkness and emerged triumphant and shall always be. I wish you luck and happiness, though the darkness that binds us, and has shaped our destinies irrevocably, means that we cannot be happy together just yet—the way life has interweaved our destines stands us apart for now. Although I mean this when I say that there is not a person on this earth that has more of my respect and love than you have.' She cried out in joy, her arms outspread as she breathed in the wonderful night air. Two black ravens swooped overhead and flew toward the wind. 'As the shadows of night descend upon us,' she added, 'we are protected by the powers of light, and that is where we will end this journey.'

The Twilight

Autumn

The two women, Laura and Adrianna, sat silently on the veranda, gazing out, content, over the green pastures, occasionally exchanging pleasant conversation. Adrianna had brought the award down from London. Laura fingered it but she didn't really care. They were happy, empowered now, easily forgetting past quarrels and the conflict that had once risen between them. No longer lost souls, outsiders, they wandered free, their eyes alight with bliss, picking the flowers, absorbing the gentle rays of the sun; they had found their nirvana. Both the dark and light had given them light and only the light fed their souls. For the darkness had saved them; without it there is no light, no life. They were whole now, the redemption of lost souls a gift. Laura sighed; since she had acquired the power of the goddess, nothing could touch her now. Their eyes stared wisely out into the distance, as they knew better than anyone that without darkness there cannot be light. In the end, we are as one. The circle of destiny turns, and we begin another cycle of existence. The wheel keeps on turning. A fleeting second, when two impossible dreams are united for a brief second, then they naturally flow apart to whatever distant shore beckons them.

Laura waved goodbye to Adrianna, and watched her drive off into the distance for the last time. She was moving abroad, to Italy, to live in the sun and work in commercials.

'Mummy, can you read this to me?' a small voice called out from the bottom of the stairs.

Laura turned and laughed: 'Look at you, oh look, you have crumbs all over your face! Let me give you a hot bath first, then we'll read the story together.'

'Okay, Mummy.'

'Who was that?' asked the child, joined by her brother.

'Just an old friend of Mummy's, came to say goodbye,' said Laura as a dark shadow passed over the sun and the wings of night flew past the silver moon, back into the swirls of the black clouds and gathering darkness.

END